DANGEROUS
DREAMS

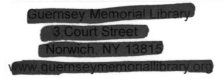

ACKNOWLEDGEMENTS

It's done; and I thank the Lord of all for providing me, to whatever degree, the inspiration to conceive *Dangerous Dreams* and the perseverance to complete it. Next, I thank my most brutally honest and articulate critic—my wife Alida—for her persistent candor and patience over the entire course of the adventure. I also thank my family for politely suffering occasional neglect at the hands of *Dangerous Dreams*.

On the technical side, I thank my incredibly diligent and thorough editor, Irene Chambers, for her gentle instillment of long-forgotten and never-known rules of grammar; and Peter O'Connor, my cover designer, for his uncanny ability to convert written thoughts into an intriguing and enticing graphic vision. In addition, I thank my friend Ed Cobleigh for sharing the lessons he learned while publishing his first two novels. And finally, I owe my grateful thanks to my test readers for their candid constructive criticism—Vic Andrews, Carol Buffington, Rita Hess, Saundra Hill, Jean Petersen, Josh Rhynard, Bob Varnum, Brendan Ward, and Nick Yanniello.

PREFACE

On several occasions in my adult life, I have experienced dreams so real in form, texture, content, and structure that I awoke believing I had actually participated in a true American historical event: the battle of the Alamo. I vividly recalled the dream plot, events, and feelings of closeness I shared with the other Alamo defenders—some famous, but most unknown to me in life. I spoke with them, laughed with them, feared with them, and ultimately died with them. Even today I remember them, and the battle, in the same way I remember my friends and battles in the Vietnam War. Although my dream experiences were in the first person, I never saw my face or heard my name; but I later discovered that two men who shared a common last name with a branch of my family died in the battle. Could I have participated in the battle of the Alamo, across the span of time, through the eyes, mind, and heart of an ancestor? Could others do the same?

My experiences prompted me to present the saga of the Lost Colony of Roanoke through the lens of a series of vivid, sensory, movie-like dreams by a young woman in the present. Because I'd always wondered why and how my own dreams happened, I delved into dream science to determine if any learned people thought such dreams were possible, and if so, how. I found that the sum of mankind's <u>proven</u> knowledge of dreams is, in my opinion, miniscule. But I also found that, with a little extrapolation, I could fashion a theoretical explanation for my dreams from existing dream theory. Thus, *Dangerous Dreams*, with parallel stories in the past and present, was born.

Mike Rhynard

June 2016

FOREWORD

I, Allie O'Shay, was 22 when Father Time clanged us into the third millennium. I remember that time—not because of the new century, but because that's when my dreams began, and I first discovered their wonder, their burden . . . and their danger. And if I'd known then what lay ahead, I would never have slept again.

HISTORICAL PROLOGUE

The New World
1590

The two English landing boats glided ashore in the timid bloom of morning's first light. Eighteen men, faces and clothes heavy with sweat, stowed their oars, wiped their dripping brows. A man with gray, shoulder-length hair, a short, pointed beard, and a broad-brimmed hat leaped from the first boat, studied the wall of trees that stood like an impregnable rampart before him. He slowly, hesitantly cupped his hands around his mouth. "Hello! Hello! 'Tis I. I've returned! Are you here? Hello! Hello!" Streams of sweat trickled down his cheeks through his beard, soaking the white shirt tucked loosely into the blousy pants that covered his tights from his waist to the tops of his thigh-length boots. A few others wore similar clothes, but most were soldiers who wore metal helmets and chest armor, held long, bulky muskets, and carried swords at their waists. All scanned the tree line with anxious eyes, waited for a reply.

Each second of silence begot more frightened glances, more nervous shuffling of feet on the boats. A sudden, loud splash at the left side of the second boat aimed seventeen weapons and pairs of eyes at a soldier who had leaped overboard to relieve himself into the water with a long, satisfied sigh. Three others instantly did the same, while the remaining fourteen climbed into the water, pulled the boats ashore with a loud clamor of armor and weapons that drew an angry scowl from the leader. "Come, men, be at the ready." He drew his sword, stepped briskly across the narrow shore to the forest wall and an overgrown trail, hacking at the branches and briars that guarded its entrance. The men drew swords, lifted muskets, followed warily behind.

Thirty yards in, the leader suddenly stopped, pointed at three bare-foot human prints in the sand, and quickly wiped at the droplets of sweat streaming from his mustache into his beard. He waited for the men to look at the prints, then abruptly turned, resumed his march. The men glanced hesitantly at one another, then again trailed after him with dithering eyes and soft, uneasy whispers.

A half minute later, a soldier in the middle of the line said, "Sir, look at this." The leader stopped, turned, walked briskly back to the soldier, as others gathered around him. The man pointed at three, four-inch-high letters carved into the trunk of a large tree: *CRO*. "Sir, what does it mean?"

The leader's eyes misted, disappointment swept his face; but seconds later, his eyes sparkled briefly, a hint of a smile creased his lips; he nodded slowly. "It means they're not here. They've gone to an island down the coast, and . . . and because there's no cross beside the letters, they did *not* leave in distress. They're safe." He took a long, thoughtful breath, wrinkled his brow into a puzzled look that immediately deepened to concern. "When I returned to England three years ago, I told them to carve a cross next to their destination if they left in distress." But, he wondered, why would they go *there*? He studied the letters, sniffled twice, processed a thought, then turned and resumed his march. "Step along men. We're nearly there."

Moments later, he halted, expressionless, lips parted; scanned left-to-right, right-to-left, then back again, as if he couldn't comprehend what lay before him. The company of men spilled into the clearing at his sides. No one spoke. There inside a palisade of ten-foot-high logs, gates agape, lay the remains of forty or so small grass-mat cottages—disas-sembled, laid flat on the ground, and overgrown by vines and brambles. Walking briskly to the closest gate, the leader leaned forward, studied a word carved into one of the posts.

One of the soldiers asked, "What is it, Sir?"

" 'Tis the name of the island they went to. So let us survey what remains here and be on our way to them, forthwith. You four men over there"—he pointed at a cluster of soldiers—"set up a perimeter guard around us. There may be Savages about." The four hurried out the largest gate, surrounded the fifty-foot clearing that encircled the log enclosure. The remaining men then scurried around inside and outside the palisades, searching the remains of the cottages and the grounds, probing the thick undergrowth beyond the clearing.

An hour's effort yielded several pigs of lead, a few bags of iron sacker-shot, four small cannon, and a few heavy tools and implements. They also discovered a number of open personal trunks sitting along-side the holes in which they had once been buried. The leader stepped to the trunks; a disgusted look suddenly distorted his face. "My God. Two of these are mine. Look here." He plucked a sketchbook from one of the trunks, flipped through the pages. "These are my writings and drawings. Fie! Look how they've been despoiled—the Savages' work. They've taken everything they valued and left the rest to rot in this wretched weather." He shook his head, glanced around the grounds to survey what they'd found. He fingered his beard with his right hand, contemplated their findings. Why did they leave so many necessar-ies—trunks of personal belongings, cannon, shot—and never return for them? Perchance . . . perchance they left quickly, intended to re-turn . . . but were unable. But why did they leave and not return? And why did they completely dismantle the cottages? Perchance . . .

He turned to a soldier at his elbow. "Sergeant, collect your men. There's no more to be done here; let us be away." Impulsively glancing at the patch of darkening sky above the clearing, he noticed the lofty treetops swaying in the risen wind and thought how they looked like death's gnarled fingers warning him away from the place. A sudden chill raced from his head to his shoulders, then down his back. "To the boats, men. Quickly! This storm's caught us by surprise. Leave the trunks. If the sky looks this angry at the ship, the captain will certainly put out to sea to weather the storm—with us or without us. We'll have to pull hard to reach them in time." He stepped onto the pathway to the shore. "We'll return for the trunks and go to the other island to find our people after the storm, perhaps on the morrow. Now quickly, men! To the boats!"

After the short jog to the shore, they stepped hesitantly from the relative calm of the forest into a bludgeoning gale, which caused them to bend sharply into the wind to advance. At the shore, they quickly pushed the boats into the water, scrambled frantically aboard, and pulled on their oars with the desperate strength that only fear instills. The rain started—a light sprinkle at first, then a pummeling downpour that, with the wind and anguished water, tossed the boats like tiny sticks in a churning cauldron. The leader yelled, "Pull hard, men! Pull!" He clutched the prow of his boat. "Stay close! Pull, pull!"

CHAPTER 1

Three Years Earlier

Hugh Tayler sat on the ground, used a short stick to scratch a crude image of a person in the sand. The figure wore a dress. He tried to keep his eyes on his work, but every few seconds his gaze drifted back to a petite young woman who sat ten yards away in the fog that enveloped him and the other forty or so people, many of them soldiers, waiting uneasily on the narrow shore. The girl listened intently to her father, Thomas Colman, and his friend, George Howe. Howe's son, also George, a young man of seventeen, sat with them, staring at Tayler's girl with admiring brown eyes, oblivious to the presence of other souls on the shore.

Tayler was more discreet than the lad, but even a blind man could see God's finest work in Emily Colman's face and, with little imagination, in what lay concealed beneath her bulky red skirt and blue shirt. And when she occasionally glanced at him and smiled, his brain flushed, sent a warm glow sweeping through his body like a hot summer wind. No woman in England—and there had been many—had affected him that way, and he had no idea how to react. What was it that aroused him? Maybe the stunning visage of her blue eyes, long dark hair, full lips, rosy complexion, and beguiling smile; or perhaps the subtle, sensuous bounce of her step; or the way her every movement celebrated life. Probably the entire persona, he decided, but whatever it was, all of it accented her piercing eyes—eyes that at once melted his confidence, seemed to read his soul. He'd noticed she had the same effect on others, especially young Howe, who couldn't take his eyes off her; and yes, whatever it was, it made women envious and men want to do what men do.

He glanced at Emily again, wished young Howe, who was two years too young for her, would look elsewhere. Tayler had spoken with her several times on the ship from England, but never for long, and never in a manner that could develop the relationship he envisioned for the two of them. Her father had always been present, so he'd kept things on a formal level, which frustrated him immensely though her father believed him to be a man of means and substance, which would work in his favor in time. With 119 passengers, ship's crew, small herds of goats and pigs, and a few chickens, milling around the deck or crammed into the hold, it was difficult to have a real conversation with anyone. The damned goats—Lord, how he hated their smell—reminded him of his unhappy youth. Even pigs were better, and if the goats all fell overboard or died quickly at the colony, he'd be a happy man. One day when no one was watching, he'd come close to throwing one overboard to feed the sharks that always trailed the vessel, but at the last second had thought better of it.

He thought the fog had a spooky, foreboding feel to it, like the moors in southern England. He'd learned about those moors as a youth when he and a friend had wandered into their sinister grasp. Terrified of the evil he felt around him, he'd panicked; abandoned the younger lad; run blindly, aimlessly, erratically; saved himself. At the lad's funeral, he'd lied to the parents, telling them he'd searched for their son for hours. Though he'd detested his actions, his cowardice had stuck with him like dried sap on a hairy arm ever since; but with the exception of a few people in England who only suspected the truth, it was *his* secret. Now, as he observed the uneasy eyes of those around him, most staring fearfully at the west side of the clearing where a murky, ghostlike wall of trees marked the edge of the decidedly intimidating forest, he realized he was not alone in his assessment of the fog. And the few who dared speak whispered so softly he couldn't hear them, though seated but a few feet away.

As Tayler ventured yet another glance at Emily, the sound of snapping branches ripped through the breathless fog like a musket shot, sent hands reaching for weapons, people to their feet; they huddled close together, faced the sound. As eerie as an apparition, four soldiers lunged from the mist, wearing ridged metal helmets and chest armor, swords at their sides, and muskets held diagonally across their chests. After halting and bending over to catch their breath, they stepped to an anxious but dignified-looking man with slightly gray, shoulder-length hair and a short, pointed beard. He wore a white, collared shirt and a tight-fitting gray jacket that constrained his modest paunch and matched his blousy pants, which covered the territory between his waist and thighs. Tall leather boots rose above his knees, and his left hand held a round-brimmed hat with a tall, circular crown. With an air of importance, he glanced around the group of colonists, then walked deeper into the fog to the edge of the forest, stopped, faced the four soldiers who'd followed him. Though barely visible to the people who watched from the clearing, he beckoned to a dark-skinned man, with black, shoulder-length hair, sitting with the civilians. "Manteo." Manteo had the brown skin, dark eyes, and high cheekbones of a Savage but wore English clothing, which he meticulously brushed off as he rose, approached the important man, who immediately turned to one of the soldiers, whispered, "Pray tell, Lieutenant Waters, what did you find? Were they there?"

Waters, a handsome, green-eyed, astute-looking young man with a sturdy build and fair hair, hesitated, looked dubiously at his men, then spoke haltingly between rapid breaths. "Nay, Governor White . . . they were not." White raised an index finger to his lips, looked at the people to make sure no one heard, then nodded at Waters to continue. Barely audible, Waters breathed his words. "We found but one; and . . . and . . . Sir, he was dead, long dead, in fact—nothing left but bones and armor . . . and a few strips of rotten flesh. Eight Savage arrows lay with his bones, and the skull was crushed into too many pieces to count, so . . . "

"Could you identify him? I have the names." White bit his lower lip, squinted his eyes into a hard, expectant look. He'd feared something like this. A year was too long to leave so small a contingent in this place, this swirling nest of angry Savages. He assumed a despondent, defeated look and stared at the ground, as if expecting to find solace, perhaps even answers.

"No, Sir."

"And no sign of the others?"

All four shook their heads.

"What of the structures, and the palisades?"

"Cottages standing, Sir, but palisades mostly burned to the ground. They'll be of little use to us . . . at least not until we do some major repair work and a lot of new construction."

White looked away, surveyed the people again. They'd congregated in small groups, spoke in hushed tones, while occasionally glancing his way. *Already it begins. They're waiting for me to tell them what we've found, what we'll do next. What can I tell them? What must I tell them? Why did I persuade Raleigh to make me Governor? I'm no leader, only an artist. A fool I was . . . thought I could do better than Lane, right the wrongs . . . No, Raleigh was the fool . . . for believing me. Yes, 'twas Raleigh's fault.*

"Sir!" Lieutenant Waters touched White's shoulder. White flinched then looked blankly, silently at him, seemed unaware of his presence. "Sir, what would you have us do?"

White heard nothing; his spacey stare saw only the desperate churning of his own mind. Then, as if waking from a dream, he shook his head, motioned the soldiers and Manteo closer—so close they could feel each other's breath. "You must keep this dead man to yourselves. If the people discover what the Savages have done, they'll panic." He looked into each man's eyes. "I need not tell you what that would mean. Lieutenant Waters, how far is the dead man from the village?"

"At least 200 yards. And the spot is well concealed by shrubs and trees. We found him only by accident. Sir, there may be others we didn't find."

White looked into the forest; his mind swirled desperately for a course of action. Finally he said, "Go back to the site; bury the man and the arrows deep. Conceal the grave so none will discover it. I will speak to the people and tell them the fifteen soldiers have gone elsewhere or perchance been rescued by a passing ship. Again, you men must keep your silence on this. As you know, six of our women are wives or fiancées of these men, come to meet them. It will not go well if they think them dead. There's nothing more unsettling than a weeping, shrieking woman. So off with you now. We'll follow shortly. Be quick with your task."

Waters nodded. "Come, men." The four turned, lifted their muskets, and trotted back into the forest.

As White and Manteo stepped toward the people, Emily Colman whispered to young George Howe, "Well, George, it looks as if we're about to know our fate." George smiled, savored the rush he always felt when she looked at or spoke to him.

As White raised his hands for silence, he wondered how he could explain the unexplainable, deceive those he was obliged to lead and protect? Like trusting children, eyes full of hope, they gathered around, six of them desperate to hear their loved ones were but a short walk away. "Friends, I have news. As you know, an English military colony, of which I was a member, inhabited this island from 1585 to 1586 under command of a soldier named Lane. And as many of you also know, shortly after the army contingent abandoned the island about a year ago, fifteen soldiers were left here by a passing English ship to hold the colony for Her Majesty. Retrieving these men was the sole purpose of our landing here. Unfortunately, our scouts searched the village for these men but were unable to find them. The village is long deserted."

Several women collapsed into tearful moans, their hands hiding their faces. White raised his voice; people glanced at one another, shadows of fear in their eyes. "I've dispatched the scouts to another part of the island to continue the search, and I'm most confident we'll find them or . . . or learn where they've gone. I do not believe them to be in danger." As the lie slid off his lips, his heart began to thump like an execution drum a second before the headsman's axe falls.

"Your Honor," said a plain-looking woman, choking on stifled sobs, "I came here to be with my husband. I *must* find him. Pray, tell me how?" She began to wail, covered her face with her hands, and spun away from him.

"We'll find them, Madame. I promise—"

"Governor White," said a plump, unkempt man, "as we disembarked, the ship's pilot told his seamen not to return us to the ship. Why? *This* is not our destination. What does he intend for us to do here? We were to settle in the Chesapeake, where you and Sir Walter Raleigh promised us each 500 acres . . . not here."

"I do not know why, Sir, but I shall—"

"How do we know," a finely dressed man said, "that the Savages didn't murder those men and hide the bodies?"

Sweat poured off White's brow. "We . . . we *don't* know . . . but . . . but I'm certain the men are—"

"When will those who remain on the ship join us?" the unkempt man asked. "And what of our possessions? We've little food, no shelter, the day is late." Grumbling spread like flames through a haystack.

"I . . . I don't know . . . I must return to the ship on the morrow and consult with Fernandez, understand his intent, persuade him." Why did the bastard do this? We can't survive here; he knows it, willfully condemns us. White slowed his racing mind, nurtured a maturing thought. Perchance he's been bribed. . . . Yes, yes. Raleigh has enemies, and perhaps they . . . no, whatever the reason, we *cannot* remain here, must go on to Chesapeake, only sixteen leagues, an easy day's sail. But where are the missing men? If only my love were alive, she'd know what to do. Damn Fernandez! "On the morrow, I shall talk to the pilot. . . . I must also confer with my Assistants when all are ashore. We will—"

"And what of us this night?" the richly dressed man said. "Certainly, there are Savages here. Are they friendly?"

That was the question White least wanted to hear. Pondering his response, he pulled on the tip of his mustache, glanced furtively at

Manteo. "Yes, Master Cotsmur, there may indeed be Savages here, but as to their bearing toward us, I am ignorant." He again glanced at Manteo, felt the sharp, searing burn of guilt from his second lie scorch his soul. He looked at Cotsmur. "However, it would be most prudent of us to be watchful for their presence." Griping ceased, apprehensive eyes immediately watched the forest. "And as for food, we've enough for the night, and there's abundant water. Our scouts inform me that many cottages from the earlier settlement remain intact, so we should make for the village without delay, gather firewood, collect water, post guards, prepare for the night. Now, maintain your weapons at the ready, and be watchful." He turned, stepped briskly into the forest.

The colonists stood like statues, seemingly undecided what to do. Hugh Tayler moved first, picked up his bag, and with a noticeable limp, trailed after White. Thomas and Emily Colman, then the Howes, followed close behind. "Come, friends," said Tayler. "Let us be away with the Governor. We've little daylight left, and we dare not stay here."

Thomas Colman whispered to his daughter, "Tayler's a natural leader, Em, don't you agree? See how the people follow him. 'Tis excellent fortune that he seems interested in you, and I hope you'll return that interest . . . with due propriety, of course." He smiled a weak, mousy smile. Regardless of his intentions, most everything he said to his daughter came out wrong, invariably hit her confrontationally, and ignited her fiery spirit, with a prompt, snippy response the result. No, he'd never had his wife's gift of easy, unprovocative communication with Emily, and this shortcoming both aggravated and wounded him. He knew it frustrated her, as well, but, though it was an ever-present irritant—one they'd learned to live with, and almost expect—both recognized it had little bearing on their deep love and commitment to one another and their family.

Emily's look was at first one of bored hopelessness, but it quickly became one of tenuously controlled anger, punctuated by the burning, venomous glare of her blue eyes. "I shall, Father. And yes, he *does* seem a leader, and witty, and a true gentleman, but don't you think it a bit extraordinary for a father to expect his adult daughter to discuss such matters with him?" It was a statement, not a question, and she didn't wait for a reply. "However, since you've already breeched my privacy, yes, I *am* attracted to him; and, Father, you don't have to explain the proper dispensing of propriety to me. Mother taught me well."

Colman sighed, then said, "I've no doubt." He knew he'd already crossed her boundary, decided not to retreat. "I also note that young Master Howe has—"

Young George, wearing an uncertain, almost frightened look, positioned himself on the other side of Emily, unwittingly quashed her imminent eruption. As they entered the tunnel of trees that entombed the pathway, they kept a slow, deliberate pace, avoided anything that would make a sound, and tried to brush aside the clinging briars and underbrush that had overgrown it. No one spoke; jittery eyes searched the forest, the dense shroud of fog that enveloped them like a stifling, gray cocoon.

A woman coughed. Those near her stopped, glared.

George whispered something, but Emily didn't hear. Her mind was on the wisp of a shadow she'd seen in her periphery near a large tree about twenty feet to the left of the trail. She stopped, fixed her eyes on the tree. George stopped, followed her gaze to the tree. She whispered, "I saw something by that tree, George . . . a shadow . . . a moving shadow . . . I think. But I see nothing now. Perhaps something's hiding there . . . so hard to see in this fog, the dark shadows . . . perhaps an animal . . . perhaps a Savage. Shall we look?"

"I think not. What if it *is* a Savage?"

"Then let's get some soldiers to do it." Emily looked ahead and behind for a soldier; none were close. "Come, George. Let's move on. I'm probably seeing things."

Sixty feet behind Emily, a soldier saw another wispy shadow, this time to the right of the trail. He stopped, raised his musket, pointed it at a thick bush. Two soldiers behind him stopped, did the same. After ten seconds, he said, "Nothing there," but his eyes and musket remained fixed on the spot for another twenty seconds. He slowly lowered his musket, proceeded down the trail. "Come lads, let's be along."

Shortly after the last Englishman had passed, two Savages crept silently onto the trail, nocked arrows in their bows, then followed them cautiously down the pathway.

A minute later, John White stopped. Before him, in a fog-draped clearing, stood a small, lifeless village of grass-mat cottages surrounded by the charred remains of log palisades. Like a squadron of ghosts, the fog meandered silently through the cottages, as if asserting its right of ownership, warning intruders away. As others trickled into the clearing, White took a step toward the village, listened, watched, took another step, listened again.

The coughing woman coughed again; no one looked.

How eerie it is, White thought, how different from the last time, with Lane and the soldiers. Oh, the wrongs done here, how they hang in the air, like the smoke of battle. How can we survive? So much wrong . . .

A man shouted, "I see the house I want," dashed forward to claim it. The others hesitated, then, as if in a foot race, charged ahead, darted from cottage to cottage like bees searching for nectar, laying claim, depositing belongings.

"Stop! Stop!" yelled White. "There are more people to come. We cannot . . ."

Two men standing in front of a cottage began shoving one another. " 'Tis mine," one said.

"Nay, 'tis mine," said the other. "I claimed it first. You can't—"

The chesty crackle of a discharging matchlock rippled through the heavy evening air.

***

In the summer of year 2000, Allie O'Shay awoke with a start, breathed a long sigh as she stared at the ceiling fan's spinning shadow above her, wondered why it looked like an oblong disc. She felt its cool breath glide softly over her face and body, rubbed her eyes, then consciously voided her mind. Her tangled, shoulder-length hair was lighter than brown but darker than blonde, and her half-open eyes begged for sleep. Was that a dream? Weird one, if it was . . . I wasn't even in it . . . but it was *real. Very* real. She took a deep breath, rolled over, then hugged her pillow, squirmed into the inviting softness of the mattress. A feeling of well-being slowly flowed through her body as she drifted back toward the world of sleep. Suddenly, she lifted her head from the pillow, opened her eyes. Who were those people . . . way back in time . . . colonial times . . . strange . . . why . . .

* * *

"But, Sir," said the young soldier, " *'Twas* a Savage. Even with the fog and shadows, I saw him . . . right over there." He pointed at the tree line. "He was creeping toward me, I'm sure, Your Honor."

Jumpy boy, thought White. But the plausibility of the lad's story crept relentlessly into his mind like a hungry weasel crawling cautiously into a rabbit hole, drew him back to Lane's expedition—encounters with Savages, their stealth, their courage. He nodded. "Forsooth, young man. I believe you. I know these people." He looked at Lieutenant Waters, who stood beside him. "Lieutenant, these Savages are crafty, different from any foe you've seen anywhere else. They know how to hide and use the terrain to approach unseen . . . until it's too late. I'm no soldier, but I'll tell you, you must *never* fire too soon because you probably won't get a second shot. Wait until you have a clear, certain target, one you can't miss. A Savage can shoot fifteen arrows in the minute it takes you to reload and prime that matchlock musket, and we don't have enough men for volley fire. So be certain of a kill before you pull a trigger. You must teach this to your men, Lieutenant. Oh, I also suggest you place an archer or two, and perhaps a pikeman, in every contingent to diversify and balance your lethality." My God, he thought with an invisible shudder, how desperately ill prepared we are. He imagined the starving, terrified colonists cowering behind the burning palisades, hundreds of screaming Savages shooting arrows into them, people crying, shouting, dying, blood all around; then the end: survivors bludgeoned to death by stone clubs, dismembered, brains and body parts scattered on the ground, women raped, taken captive to be wed and bred to uncivilized Savages. A wave of nausea rose to his throat. But if . . . *if* I can persuade Fernandez to take us north . . . then . . .

"Yes, Sir," said Waters.

"Very well, Lieutenant. Before it's completely dark, we must collect firewood and water. See to it then post a guard of at least six men around the inside of what remains of the palisades . . . and ensure they have a clear field of view and fire."

"But, Sir. My men aren't laborers. They're soldiers. The colonists can—"

"Lieutenant Waters," White looked sternly into his eyes, "I'm not sending unseasoned colonists into harm's way. Not this night. You and your men are armed and trained for this." He leaned his head closer to the Lieutenant's. "You know what's happened here, the dead soldier, the arrows. But these people know nothing, and they're dangerously unprepared for this situation. You must—"

"Sir, I protest."

"Those are my orders, Lieutenant. Carry them out. You must do your duty."

Waters stared uncertainly, reluctantly into White's eyes for a long moment, knew he'd gone too far. Damned civilians. No business giving orders to men of arms. They'll make a mess of it. Naïve fool . . . yet, my orders are to protect the colony . . . and the governor *is* the colony. "Yes, Sir."

He turned, spoke to his two sergeants who stood twenty feet away watching the exchange. "Myllet, Smith, take four men each. Myllet, your group will gather enough firewood to get us through the night. 'Tis warm, and there's little to cook, so we only need enough to provide light. Smith, take your men and some buckets. Bring enough water to get us to sunrise. There's a stream over there." He pointed to other side of the village. "The one we saw earlier." His voice faded to a whisper. "Near where we buried the dead man. Be wary. I believe there *are* Savages about . . . and, men, 'tis not I who directs you to do manual labor for civilians. The governor believes the circumstances warrant it. And we must obey him. So move out quickly."

As the grousing soldiers left the village, Emily Colman and her father had already started gathering firewood from around the cottage they and the Howes were sharing. The elder George Howe used his eating knife to scrape fog-dampened bark from a pile of dead sticks, then laid them one at a time in the shape of a cone next to a pile of fuzzy, dry tinder from the inside edge of several large pieces of bark.

Young George said, "Father, I have my tinder box. Do you want it?"

"Nay, Son. This dry bark will work. Save the good tinder for a wet day." With a rapid scraping motion, Howe repeatedly chipped his knife across the piece of flint in his left hand, generated a stream of sparks that shot into the tinder, soon produced a glowing ember. He picked up the tinder ball, blew it gently into a flame, then laid it on the ground, placed the cone of kindling on top. "Wood gatherers, prithee deliver some larger wood to grow this flame. Looks like the fog will be with us all night, and we may need its warmth."

Emily and her father laid several larger pieces of wood on the fire. Colman said, "That should hold us until the soldiers return."

Emily sat down beside the fire, pulled a few chunks of hardtack from her tote bag. "Here, Father. We haven't much left, but with fortune, we'll soon have fresh fish and meat to eat. So why not celebrate our first night in the New World with a feast of foul-smelling hardtack? Come, Master Howe . . . both of you join us." She smiled as she handed a piece to each man. "Father, did you bring any beer?"

"Here." Young George sat down beside Emily, handed her a goatskin of warm beer, which she promptly took a swig of and passed back.

"Quite satisfying. Thank you, George."

George took a long pull, passed it to his father, who, with Thomas Colman, had seated himself beside them. The elder George Howe took the beer, passed a canteen of water to Colman. "Thomas, you'd best have some of this, too. And pass it around, if you will. We'd do well to acquire a strong taste for it, for the beer will soon be gone."

Emily pushed herself back another five feet from the fire, wiped a wide bead of sweat from her brow with her sleeve. She slid her hand into her apron pocket, removed a black locket and held it to her cheek, then stared at the flickering tongues of fire, let her senses pull her mind inward to thoughts of her mother. Yes, Mother, we're finally here, after three long months. We're here . . . but *here* isn't where it's supposed to be. 'Tis where two *previous* expeditions were, where murder was done, where the Savages hate us more than death itself, where we can't survive. How do I know? Because Manteo, the Savage who befriended me on the ship told me. He's from an island near here and was taken to England by an earlier expedition and educated. Yes, I *am* afraid . . . but I won't show it. I shall be brave, face what comes . . . as you would. I miss you so . . . young brother John, as well. I long for the day you join us, pray we're alive when you do. She squeezed her locket, saw her mother's gentle, smiling face in the blue and yellow flames. Oh, forgot to tell you: my good friend Elyoner, the governor's daughter, will have her baby soon; and, though it's against custom for an unwed woman to be present, I'm to be there and help. She's four years older than I, but we've grown quite close . . . and she's told me—

"Emily, did you hear me?" Young George, who'd also pushed back from the fire, waved his hand up and down in front of her face.

Emily blinked. "George . . . no . . . I'm sorry, I did not . . . was thinking of my mother and brother . . . how far away."

George lowered his gaze to the ground. "*My* mother's been gone nearly three years . . . but I still miss her as if she'd died yesterday." He snorted. "You know, Emily, I've never mentioned that to anyone . . . until now . . . to you."

She touched his cheek. "Forgive me, George, I've worsened your pain."

"No, Em. 'Tis *always* with me." He closed his eyes, smiled as if savoring the soft warmth of her touch.

"Well, I'm still sorry, for I know how you feel." Her eyes saddened. "We lost my first brother to the Bloody Flux two years ago . . . twelve, he was."

He looked up at her, his slight smile still on his face. "Truly, we're having difficulty finding something un-painful to—"

"Good evening, Mistress Colman." Hugh Tayler sat his lean but solid frame down on the other side of Emily. He had curly, dark, shoulder-length hair that framed a clean-shaven face with hawkish features, and the firelight lent a sparkle to his dark brown eyes as he smiled a deep smile at Emily.

"Good evening, Master Tayler. Do you know my friend, George Howe?"

"Why, yes. We met on the ship." He nodded at George, who gave a slight nod in reply, then promptly returned his gaze to the ground, started drawing in the dirt with his finger.

Emily said, "Master Tayler, do you always make such a sudden entrance?"

Her directness unbalanced him. "Actually, no . . . I . . . I don't. My apologies, Mistress." She goes to the point, he thought, forthright and confident for her years.

" 'Tis George who warrants the apology." She smiled, nodded at George, then back at Tayler, waited for him to speak.

Tayler was astounded that at eight years her senior, he felt like a gawky school boy when she spoke to him, felt her eyes melt his self-assurance like butter in a hot summer sun. "Indeed! My apologies, Master Howe."

George nodded once but held his silence, continued doodling on the ground.

"Are you hungry, Master Tayler?" Emily held out the bag of hardtack.

"Why, no. But thank you. I merely wanted to see how you fared this day. A long day it was." He shifted his gaze to Emily's father and the elder Howe, who had just looked his way. He stood, said, "Good evening, good sirs. How fare you this night?"

George Howe said, "Very well, given the conditions." Howe was on the portly side of fit and, when standing, had to lean slightly forward to see his toes. His head was bald, and he looked like a plump monk as he rose and extended his hand to Tayler. "And you, Master Tayler?"

Colman, who at six-one was the tallest man in the colony, did likewise. "Good evening, Master—"

Governor White and Manteo approached the group. "Gentlemen, I'll have a word with you, if you please."

Tayler nodded, said, "Governor, as you know, I heard your announcements a short while ago; so, with your leave . . . ?" He again nodded at White, then at Howe and Colman, looked at Emily. *My God, she's stunning.* "Adieu, Mistress. Until tomorrow." As Emily started to stand up, he stepped closer, extended his hand to assist her. He'd never touched her before, and when she accepted his invitation, the pleasing warmth of her hand spread through his mind and body like a drink of good brandy on a chilly day.

"Adieu, Master Tayler." She curtsied, watched him turn slowly, walk away, then glance back as he stepped into the darkness.

White said, "The men have returned. We've a good supply of firewood and enough water to get us through the night. Still, I ask you to exercise restraint with both so all may share. Others will join us in the morning, and we'll have to determine a proper assignment of dwellings and gather more supplies."

Colman said, "But what of the Chesapeake?"

White paused. "I shall return to the ship on the pinnace in the morning when it delivers the next group, and I shall confront Fernandez about our plight here, inform him that since I'm the designated captain of the ship, and he's but the pilot, his action is tantamount to mutiny. Trust me, friends. I *will* convince him to take us to Chesapeake. But meanwhile—"

"And the Savages?" asked Howe.

"We've guards posted around the perimeter. We'll be safe enough for this night." An uncomfortable twinge nibbled its way through his insides, made him wish he was in England, sitting by a warm fire, painting watercolors of his memories of earlier expeditions; not here, lying to people, trying to salvage an impossibly dangerous situation.

Emily said, "Sir, what of the dead man the soldiers found this afternoon? Do you think the Savages killed him in retribution for Lane's atrocities?"

The firelight flickered on White's suddenly blanched face. "How do you know of that, Mistress Colman? Who told you such things?" Anger then confusion flared on his face.

Emily started to glance at Manteo, but a jab of caution held her eyes on White. *Why did you ask that, stupid girl?*

White's complexion grew redder; his look hardened; his nostrils, barely visible above his mustache, flared and collapsed with each breath. He glared at Emily, waited for her reply.

Emily held her silence, cringed, knew she'd hear of her blunder from her father. She met White's glare with a defensively bland, respectful look.

The three men watched in disbelief as White leaned his head close to hers, whispered in a hissing tone, audible only to Emily, "Mistress, tell no one of this!"

* * *

Across the narrow strip of water that separated the colonists from the main, a fifty-foot by thirty-foot, bark-covered lodge housed a small fire that cast dancing light on the faces of the twenty Savages who surrounded it in council. Most had clean-shaven heads, but for a narrow strip of two-inch-high, straight, vertical hair down the center; feathers and other objects adorned some of the heads. All were bare-chested, bare-legged and wore loincloths.

One Savage looked different. The right side of his head was clean-shaven while the left was full-haired and long, pulled together and tied just above the left shoulder. Three narrow, striped feathers hung from the tie and down his back. He had an angry, fierce look and stared into the fire as the spokesman said, ". . . and our scouts have told us that another group of white men from across the big water has come. They carry the big sticks that make thunder, and Sees-the-Enemy felt the stone from one of these sticks fly by his ear like a bee. More of these people are on the big canoe floating beyond the narrow banks, on the big water." He paused, momentarily looked at the ground then back at the warriors. "They have brought women this time, so I think they plan to stay. We must decide what to do about them."

The fierce-looking Savage with three feathers wasn't listening. He was thinking about his wife and two sons. He'd mourned their loss for over a year before remarrying, had chosen another woman of his tribe, one whose husband, a close friend of his, had died in battle against the mountain tribes.

The spokesman said, "We all remember what happened the last time they came: the killing, the sickness, the destruction." He paused, looked at each man in turn. "It *must* not happen again. We cannot *allow* *it* to happen again. These are a crude, ruthless people without honor, and I have heard your wisdom on how we should deal with them. I have heard some say we must avoid them and perhaps move our village. Others counsel that we should attack them a few at a time until they become afraid and go away. And still others say we should rub them all out now before more come and they grow too strong." His gaze again drifted from man to man; he nodded, studied each pair of eyes. When he had completed the circle, he said, "This is a grave matter, and I will think on it. But before I do,"—he nodded at the fierce-looking man— "I wish to hear the mind of Kills-Like-the-Panther, great warrior and principal counselor to Wahunsunacock, leader of our powerful allies to the north.

The Panther severed his thoughts of the past, stood, took a deep breath then looked at the spokesman. In the same language but with a slight accent, he said, "I was with my wife and sons, trading with the Chowanoc, on the day the white men attacked and killed many of their people. My wife and both sons died that day after I was shot down by one of the big sticks that make thunder. I watched helplessly as three of them used my wife before killing her. I also saw many people in nearby villages die from the sickness the white men brought upon us. Great leader, I cannot tell you and your people what to do, for hate clouds my mind and does not allow me to see clearly what is best for *your* people. But for myself, I will fight and kill these intruders until they . . . or I . . . lie dead."

* * *

Allie awoke with a long, wide-mouthed yawn, followed by a deep sigh. She then stared at the ceiling fan with a tight-lipped, meditative look. When she sat up, she dangled her legs over the side of the bed, scratched the back of her neck, then looked at the window across the room while leaning her head to the right like a dog trying to understand something. Strange dream. She stood, walked to the bathroom, and drank a cup of water. Wonder what it was about . . . who the people were . . . where they were . . . why I wasn't in it . . . and . . . and why the hell I dreamed it in the first place. As a doctoral candidate in psychology, Allie questioned things of the mind, challenged their reality, and probed their origins to explore the murky world of the brain, the conscious, the subconscious, the unconscious; and, she concluded, her dream had been richly packed with substance for such investigations.

She studied herself in the mirror. You're a bitch, O'Shay! A good-looking bitch, but a bitch, nonetheless. She blinked her yellow-brown eyes, picked up a hand mirror, turned around, and, holding it up so she could see her back in the vanity mirror behind her, studied the small butterfly-shaped birthmark on the back of her neck. Itchy, kinda red this morning.

She turned on her electric toothbrush, started guiding it around its circuit. Jeez, this thing's noisy. She stared at herself in the mirror. Strange dream. Strange people. Who were they? Scenes from the dream tumbled in her mind like a handful of marbles being shaken in a quart jar. When the toothbrush quit, she realized she'd held it in the same spot for the entire cycle. Idiot! She looked at her watch. Whoa! Gotta get outa here. Burnin' daylight! That was her father's favorite saying. As she splashed water on her face, dried it off, she wondered what he was doing that morning. Probably moving cows around, she thought, given they had a thousand of them on the ranch and had to rotate pastures all summer to properly utilize the grass without overgrazing it.

She walked into the bedroom, pulled off the t-shirt and flannel pants she slept in, and exchanged them for a pair of shorts and a tank top. Her body was curved and nicely sized in all the right places, had an athlete's lean tightness—like most small-town Montana girls, she'd played volleyball and basketball in high school. She'd excelled at both and kept her body in top shape; but at five three, and a hundred and ten pounds, she didn't have the size for the college game in either sport. So she'd picked up soccer and quickly developed into a consistent scoring threat in the club league she played in. Now in grad school, she played with numerous ex-college players, all of whom said she could've been a standout on any team in the conference. As she slid her feet into a pair of sandals, her cell phone rang. She checked the caller ID. "Hi, Mom. What's up?"

"Hi, Toots. How's it going?"

"Keepin' up. Been real busy, lots goin' on. How about you guys?"

"We're fine. Finishing up irrigating and fencing, moving cows around. You know the drill."

"Yeah, I do. Miss it a lot." Growing up on the ranch, Allie had done it all: fed, calved, branded, castrated, fenced, vaccinated, irrigated, moved cattle, sprayed weeds, hayed, fixed machinery, pregnancy tested, weaned, plus all the unexpected stuff that popped up every day and immediately moved to the top of the *do-now* list. Seemed like every day was two steps forward and three steps back, but you never had time to get bored with any single job because the next season was inevitably just around the corner. And with the exception of winter feeding, which seemed to never end, it was always new, always fresh and exhilarating being outdoors, even smack dab in the middle of some of Mother Nature's worst tantrums. Pulling a breech calf at twenty-five below was not a job for sissies, nor was it particularly fun, but it *did* give you a feeling of accomplishment and pride because it saved a mother and a baby, and at the same time preserved the ranch's bottom line. But most importantly, only a handful of people in the whole world could do it.

Yes, Allie missed it all. But with two older brothers, the oldest of which shared her passion for the ranch, her future had never been in doubt. She couldn't think of a daughter in their neck of the woods who had older brothers and was running a ranch, unless the brothers had no interest in ranching and the daughter was lucky enough to find a good, honest man willing to face the physical and mental challenges of ranching. So early on, Allie had resigned herself to the facts, made the decision to pursue higher education and a professional career. She had great relationships with both brothers and knew she'd always be welcome on the ranch if she wanted to be there, and this fact mitigated, to a tolerable degree, her disappointment at the inescapable realities of the O'Shay family ranch.

"I know you do, Allie. You know, Mike and Ellie are doing a really great job, I mean, *really* great; but Dad and I sure miss you being here, even after five years. I know you're busy, but I hope you can make it back more this summer. So nothing new, huh?"

"Nope . . . had a weird dream last night, but no big deal. Hey, I've got to git, Mom. I'll call you later, okay? Love you."

After a silence long enough to make Allie wonder what she was thinking, her mother said, "Bye, Allie Girl, love you too."

CHAPTER 2

The pinnace had arrived shortly after first light, unloaded more people and baggage, then taken Governor White back to the ship to parley with Fernandez. Before leaving, the governor had instructed the colonists to collect the baggage then begin repairing damaged cottages and building new palisades in case his mission with Fernandez was unsuccessful. Emily, George, and twenty other colonists walked cautiously down the pathway to the shore to retrieve the baggage. Four soldiers with ready weapons escorted them, continuously scanned the forest in all directions. Emily studied the narrow strip of sky above the pathway, thought how the clouds looked like mounds of cotton floating on an inverted sea. All around her, thin rays of sunlight sliced through the tall canopy of trees, sparkled like gem stones on the dew that clung to every leaf. Not even the queen has so many diamonds, she thought. Would that *I* had a few. She stretched her arms out to the side, executed a slow, graceful pirouette, then another, and another. "George, it's magnificent, so fresh, so free . . . so hot. Nothing like England." She stopped. "George, you look as if you're on your way to the gallows. What troubles you?"

"Oh, just thinking." He smiled. "It *is* beautiful. No smoke in the sky, no grit in the teeth." George stood five-nine, had a ruddy complexion, a round face with high cheekbones, brown eyes, and long, sandy hair which he tied in a bundle in the back, just above his shoulders. He had a man's body, which made people think he was older than he was, at least until he spoke, for he'd not yet found his man voice. He seldom smiled and always looked like he was brooding about something.

"George, what troubles you? I'll listen . . . better yet, tell me why you and your father are here."

He thought for a moment. " Everything comes back to my mother . . . her death."

"Why do I always bring up painful things?"

"No, Emily. I must accept her loss and deal with it. So when she died, Father and I were lost and depressed for a time. By the way, she, too, died of the Bloody Flux. It took Father a full two years to recover from her death. He stopped working the foundry, stopped eating, just sat and stared all day. I wasn't much better, but I did the best I could to keep the foundry going. I only had two years' experience as his apprentice, so I wasn't very good at it, but good enough to get us by. When we heard about Governor White's colony, we started thinking that perhaps we could start a new life. A colony would need all the things we knew how to make: nails, shovels, axes, shot, pikes, tools, even swords, and we heard they'd found iron here on one of the two earlier expeditions. So it all sounded quite enticing. Then it occurred to us that we might also be able to trade with the Savages, *if* they were friendly, and that we could also farm or sell our five hundred acres to someone else. So here we are. That's the story . . . and Howe and Son are ready to start work at once." He smiled, gave her a quick nod.

"George, I think you and your father are exactly what we need here: good, sincere, honest, hard-working folk." She held his hand. "I'm glad you're with us, and I'm most glad you're my friend."

George felt like warm water was trickling slowly over his head and shoulders. "Em, I . . . tell me about you and your father."

His shyness brought an understanding smile to her face. "Well, Father has dirt under his fingernails. He grew up a farmer's son, but his father didn't own anything. He was only a tenant to a wealthy lord and had to give most of his crop to the lord in payment. He wanted Father to have a better life; and in exchange for more crops, he made an arrangement with the lord to obtain an education for Father so he could teach school. So Father became a schoolmaster, and that's why I know how to read and write, which, as you know, most common women don't. I'm very grateful to him though as a child I fought it constantly . . . hated being indoors and studying all the time. He also made me—*made* me, mind you—learn French, Italian, Spanish, and a bit of Dutch; so I could teach and tutor wealthy people and their children. Well, it turned out that I rather enjoy languages, and they come quite easily to me, to the point that when I'm learning one, I eventually start having dreams in it without translating anything. That's what tells me I've become fluent . . . same with the Savages' hand signs Manteo taught me on the ship. I actually started seeing myself communicating with them and understanding them in my dreams."

"What are the hand signs for?"

"They're the signs all the different tribes of Savages use to communicate with one another when they don't know each other's language. Manteo says every Savage in the New World knows them, though some have a few unique signs of their own."

"You know everything, Emily Colman. Show me some."

"As you wish." Emily's hands and fingers moved: twists, turns, rolls, flips, flings; sometimes in conjunction with her head, arms, eyes, and mouth.

"Impressive! So did you truly say something, or were you just trying to impress me?"

"Of course, I said something. But because you doubt me, you sha'n't know what it was."

George shook his head. He never tired of hearing her voice; what she said was immaterial. "Very well, I apologize. Now will you tell me?"

"Perhaps."

"Come on, Em."

"Are you truly sorry, or just being mercenary?"

"Yes. I'm *very truly* sorry, Mistress Colman. Now please tell me!"

"I said, *I like you and your father very much, and I want to be your close friend. I'm very happy being with you and talking to you right now. And I should finish telling you why Father and I are here.*"

George blushed, felt his head muddle with warmth. "Did you really say that?"

"I did."

"Emily"—he took a deep, calming breath—"finish your story."

She smiled at him, grasped his fingers, then squeezed them for a moment. "Well, Father, though he's a fine schoolmaster, never stopped wanting to farm, always felt like he'd been denied the opportunity; so when he heard about the colony, he saw his chance—a 500acre chance—decided he could school the colony's children and farm at the same time. So here *we* are . . . strange that with all the time on the ship, we never talked about any of this. What *did* we talk about?"

"I was too sick to talk."

"Me too, now that you mention it." She recalled hours of retching over the side of the ship and other times scurrying up the steps, trying to reach her favorite spot before the big heave. She smiled as she remembered calculating exactly how long it took to make the trip and thereafter knowing in advance whether or not she'd make it in time. She also remembered the times she'd lost the race because someone was in the way and slowed her pace; she'd then had to swab the deck or the floor, which nearly made her retch again. It was particularly bad manners to retch in the hold because the smell nauseated the other passengers, with predictable results. The ship had been a terrible place, she thought: people crammed together with animals, no space to breathe, no privacy, constant rolling and pitching, horrible food, tainted water. No surprise people didn't get to know each other and were always sick, angry, embarrassed, or scared. She was glad it was over, glad to be on solid ground.

"So what about your mother and brother? Why didn't they come?"

"My brother's slightly over a year old, so my parents decided he was too young and that he and Mother would stay in England for at least another year before joining us. George, I miss them a lot and hope they come next summer, no matter what." Her face suddenly blossomed with excitement, as she reached into her apron pocket, removed her locket, which had a small hole drilled in the edge for a neck string. "Here, look at this; I've never shown it to you." She handed the locket to George. "My parents exchanged identical lockets before we sailed. Mother's holds a lock of Father's hair and this one has a lock of Mother's." Sudden tears filled her eyes, ran down her cheeks. "Look at me, crying like a baby." She held her smile, dabbed her eyes with her sleeve. "Holding it always makes me sad and teary, but it's a *happy* sad because touching it makes Mother feel closer."

"I understand very well. I feel the same way when I hold *my* mother's things."

Both smiled a knowing, wordless, lingering smile that reflected a tight, inseverable bond of shared experience. But soon Emily assumed a pensive look. "You know, George, talking about why the Howes and the Colmans are here makes me wonder why all these other people came . . . why they gave up whatever they gave up to come here."

George thought for a moment. "I suppose 'twas no different than for us. Everyone has reasons for what they do . . . but this is such a challenging and dangerous venture . . . I think their reasons, like ours, would have to be quite serious and important or else they'd not take the risk."

"That certainly makes sense; for according to Father, we have a goldsmith, a sheriff, a lawyer, a Cambridge professor, and, oh yes, two former convicts. We can guess why they're here. But then there's Governor White—a successful artist—and gentry such as Master Tayler, and a mason . . ."

"He likes you doesn't he?"

"Who?"

"Master Tayler. I've seen him look at you. He's always looking at you."

"Looking isn't a sin, George. Actually, I don't know him very well at all. Never even had a real conversation with him, but he seems like a nice man, what you'd expect for a gentleman, I suppose. Father certainly likes what he's seen of him." Emily had also liked what she'd seen, wondered when she'd have a chance to talk to him without her father or someone else around. "So, George, why would those people abandon such secure, prosperous lives for *this*?" She extended her arms out to her sides. "What could justify the risks they're taking, with so much more to leave behind than we?" She smiled. "I've often wondered if rather than running *to* something, many aren't actually running *from* something, something in the present or past they disliked or feared, some unpleasant reality, something in the mind that torments them. And yes, I think most of us probably *are* following a dream, perhaps without even knowing what it is but sensing that it will better us or improve our lot in life." They'd fallen behind the line of colonists, and Emily saw one of the soldiers look back to check on them. She bumped George's shoulder, pointed ahead, quickened her pace.

"Emily, you're a deeper thinker than I. I could never conjure such thoughts on my own." He stopped, gently took her hands, looked into her eyes, searched them. "Haunting they are . . . haunting and beautiful . . . and irresistible . . . and . . . Emily, I know there are two years between us, and that you're a woman not a girl . . . but I can't help . . ."

A crimson glow spread up Emily's neck to her cheeks. "George, the soldiers are waiting for us . . . come, I'll race you to the shore. I get a head start." She giggled, shoved him backward, then lifted her skirt to her knees and sprinted for the shore. She was halfway to the water before George took his first step.

* * *

A crew of thirty men, over half of them soldiers, felled trees around the perimeter. Cutting close to the village served two purposes: it gave the Savages less cover to sneak up on the village, and it gave the men who transported the logs a shorter distance to the palisades. However, since the last expedition had taken most of the close, properly sized trees for the old palisades, now seventy percent destroyed, the cutters were beginning to cut into virgin forest outside the perimeter.

An ideal palisade post was about fifteen feet tall and eight to twelve inches thick, so another challenge the cutters faced was that a tree long enough to make two posts would usually exceed the desired thickness and be too heavy for one man to maneuver and carry by hand. As a result, they would have to crosscut larger trees and split them lengthwise to obtain the required number of posts. Lieutenant Waters, who directed the project, calculated the task would require around five hundred oak and walnut trees, each split into two or three posts and a few cross braces, for a total of about twelve hundred posts. Without problems a thirty-man crew *might* complete the task in a little over two weeks, a length of time that troubled his maturing military mind because it meant a dangerously long period of vulnerability for the colony.

Initially, two men chopped on each tree until it was about to fall, then one man delivered the final blows after the second man removed himself from the fall line to avoid being crushed. The cutters controlled the direction of fall by making their cuts at different heights, on opposite sides of the tree. The lower cut, on the fall side of the tree, notched into the trunk about a third of the way to the tree's center and was overly wide to make space for the tree to collapse into; while the upper cut, on the opposite side, went almost to the center. The undercut notch gave the tree space to collapse in the desired direction, avoiding hang-ups with other trees and providing easier access for the sawyers and splitters. The sawyers then cut the felled trees to length, and the splitters used wedges and mauls to split them into the desired thickness. The posts were then dragged or carried to the palisades, where another crew worked on digging a continuous, four-foot-deep set trench all the way around the village perimeter, on lines laid out by Lieutenant Waters. After enough adjacent posts were stood up in the trench and buried to ground level, horizontal cross braces, ten to fifteen feet long and six to eight inches thick, were mounted across the top and bottom on the inside of the wall to bind the logs together and provide strength. The braces were joined to the logs by long, hand-hewn wooden pegs about three inches thick, driven from the inside of the wall by large hammers into hand-bored holes that went completely through the braces and four to six inches into each post. The top brace was mounted a foot or two below the top of the wall, and the bottom brace, about two feet above the ground. While no step in the process was easy, the most exhausting was that of boring the gun-barrel-sized peg holes, which required countless, forceful twists of the crossbar handle on the end of the eighteen-inch metal auger bit.

Waters, a relatively inexperienced young officer, had been trained both as an engineer and an infantryman and compensated for his inexperience with enthusiasm and a precocious degree of professional bearing and common sense. Educated and from a wealthy family, he knew he'd suffered a serious lapse in judgment when he'd questioned the governor's order yesterday; but like most young officers, he was sensitive to the fact that sergeants and conscripts generally had little respect for young, newly commissioned officers, regarded them as a threat to their survival. He was also aware that such fears were often well founded; and for that reason, he'd made it clear to the men that he'd stood up for them by resisting the governor's assignment of improper duties, wanted them to know he wasn't afraid to risk his own skin on their behalf. Foremost, he'd wanted to make that point with his sergeants: the non-commissioned officers, the implementers of orders, the buffers between officers and men, the battle-hardened survivors rich in the experience and credibility young lieutenants lacked, the gritty, up-from-the-ranks leaders who ultimately won or lost battles.

With his point hopefully made, he intended to redeem his indiscretion with White by throwing his mind and spirit, and even his muscle, into erecting as impregnable a fortress as was possible with the materials at hand. In anticipation of the possibility that there were no existing palisades, he'd taken the initiative of completing his own design during the voyage from England. It was in the shape of a polygon, with a series of cortynes—straight sections of wall with angled shooting towers, called flankers, that jutted outward from the walls like star points. The flankers joined each cortyne, or side of the polygon, to the next cortyne and allowed defenders to shoot their muskets and arrows at attackers both head-on and from the side. The latter shots were achieved by the shooters positioning themselves on the sides of the flankers and firing through narrow firing ports that exposed only a small part of their bodies, and through which an attacker could not crawl. His decision to adopt this design in lieu of parapets and scaffolding, which would require shooters to climb ladders or ramps to access firing scaffolds and probably take more time to build, gave him a deep feeling of accomplishment which he hoped the governor would share when the fort was complete.

All of the men on the palisades crew had weapons nearby, and four soldiers stood guard around the work area. Hugh Tayler and several other civilians, inexperienced at felling trees, stripped, split, and carried the logs to the trench, stood them upright, and backfilled dirt to hold them in place. When enough posts were set in line, others would bore and mount the cross braces. The heat and humidity had taken their toll on the men, drained them as if they'd been without food and water for a week. Their faces were gaunt; their clothing drenched in sweat, covered with dirt; their numb, slow movements and labored breathing vivid symptoms of their exhaustion. Having watched the pace of the operation slow, Waters now noticed the growing sloppiness in the men's movements and concluded a rest was needed to avoid an accident, particularly with so many inexperienced cutters. Experience was a relative word when it came to the colony's woodcutters, for only a handful of civilians and a couple soldiers had ever wielded an axe against a standing tree, and only one of them had done it more than a few times. So, given that a cutter's or trimmer's axe glancing off a trunk or a branch and slicing a leg was the most common tree-cutting accident, such was Waters' greatest worry.

Suddenly, he heard shouts from the tree, saw that two axe men had come dangerously close together, and someone had yelled at them to reposition themselves farther apart. He shook off a fearful tremor and recalled a long-ago day when he and his best friend, Douglas Murray, both sixteen, had been doing exactly as the two axe men were doing today. Each of the friends had been paired with another partner, and the two pairs raced to see which could fell their tree the quickest. As he caught a quick breath, Waters had glanced at Douglas and his partner to see if they were ahead of, or behind, his own team. He saw that Douglas' team was slightly ahead; but as he'd quickened his swing, a gnawing discomfort had rooted in his murky subconscious: Douglas and his left-handed partner were too close together, and their axe swings were within glancing range of each other's legs. A moment later Douglas had screamed in agony as his partner's axe glanced off the hard oak trunk into his thigh, sliced it to the bone. The three boys had knelt over Douglas, watched the blood spurt from his wound as he screamed, convulsed in wild agony. Partially unnerved, Waters had shouted at one lad to go for help, told the other to hold the leg, keep Douglas from thrashing. He'd pulled off his shirt, wrapped it tightly around the leg, but the blood immediately seeped through and under the wrap. Blood everywhere. He'd pulled the other boy's blood-stained shirt from his back, wrapped a second bandage around the wound, again to no avail. As he'd wondered what to do next, the color had suddenly drained from Douglas' face like water into sand. His convulsing had abruptly lessened, then stopped, as he lay still, eyes wide, locked in a vacant stare.

Shaking the memory from his head, Waters pondered the fact that even though one of the colonists, John Jones, was a physician, there were scant medical supplies to deal with serious injuries, and so resolved to have none such on his watch. Thus when he saw the six women and two soldiers who guarded them approaching with buckets of water, he shouted to the work crews. "Come, men. Let's have a rest. Find shade; drink and eat. We've a good start but a long way to go. Take your weapons with you to the shade."

Emily set one of her buckets down by the group of cutters, lifted her round-brimmed sunhat higher on her forehead. "Drink well, gentlemen."

Waters, who sat with the cutters, said, "Thank you, Mistress, you're an angel . . . and not just for your kind deeds." Waters had admired Emily from afar on the ship but refrained from approaching her when he'd seen how several of the male colonists eyed her. 'Twould be improper for the man-at-arms, commissioned to protect them, to compete with the colony's civilians for the favor of such a lovely lady, at least under the current, dire circumstances.

Emily blushed, sent Waters a quick smile. "You're most kind, Lieutenant." She nodded then carried her second bucket over to the transport crew which had found shade thirty yards away. Others in Waters' group gratefully thanked her as she walked toward the transporters. She turned, acknowledged with another smile and a nod.

As she approached the second group, the men gathered around her then dipped their wooden cups in the bucket. Tayler, who stood twenty feet away, his back to Emily as he leaned his musket against a tree, turned when he heard her name. He watched her, felt his heart quicken as she walked toward him.

"Master Tayler, aren't you thirsty?"

He stared at her for a long moment; his already warm face grew warmer. "I'm thirstier than ever before in my life, Mistress, but I'd rather die of it than walk away from you at this moment."

Emily felt a pleasing twinge of embarrassment, smiled, instinctively looking at the ground without speaking.

"Would you sit with me for a while in my parlor?" He pointed at the grass to his side, extended his other hand to hold hers.

"Why thank you, Master Tayler, I'd enjoy that." She held his hand, lowered herself to the grass, then spread her skirt like a fan over her quite-improperly crossed legs. When she removed her hat, her hair, which she'd stuffed up into the crown to keep her neck cooler, dropped down over her shoulders in an unkempt tangle that gave her a wild, primitive, sensuous look. She flipped it twice with her hands then settled her gaze on Tayler.

He stared at her with a gawky, awestruck hint of a smile.

"What amuses you, Sir?"

He shook his head, studied her eyes, started to speak but stuttered twice before putting a sentence together. "Mistress Colman, you honor me . . . thank you for allowing me to converse with you . . . I've long hoped for the opportunity."

"Master Tayler . . ."

"No. 'Tis true . . . and with your father's permission—and, of course, your own—I would warmly savor more such opportunities."

"I would enjoy that, Master Tayler . . . you have *my* permission." She smiled. "And, I'm quite certain, my father's, as well. I only hope the urgencies of life here permit such moments. And how do those urgencies treat Master Tayler today?" She glanced at the nearby pile of posts.

"Please call me Hugh."

She studied his face, thought how she enjoyed their quick dialogue, wanted more. "I shall. And you may call me Emily. English decorum does not fit here, does it?"

He replied excitedly, as if pleased by her response. "Indeed, it does not seem so . . . and I *shall* call you Emily . . . *Emily* . . . but forgive me if habit forces me to call you *Mistress* on occasion."

Emily nodded advance forgiveness.

"So, to answer your question, today's urgencies have been brutal and inhuman for Hugh Tayler, breaking his back and dulling his mind." He rubbed his sleeve across his brow. "I've never seen such humidity. Or heat. Devilish they are! Quickly destroy any enthusiasm a man has for manual labor. But your presence has markedly tempered their impact on Hugh Tayler."

With an inquisitive twinkle in her eyes, Emily said, "So hard labor is not for Hugh Tayler? I heard you were of the gentry, but . . ."

"Mistress—I mean, Emily—" Another smile. "See, I told you. Anyway, 'tis true, I *am* of the gentry, but gentry are no strangers to hard work. A good master knows the toils and hardships demanded of his people, and there's but one way to learn those lessons: experience them. And, sad to say, my father took his responsibilities in that regard quite seriously." An abrupt, anguished look distorted his face; he looked away.

Emily laid her hand on his shoulder. "Master Tayler—Hugh—are you . . .?"

"Sorry. I rather lost myself for a moment . . . a bad thought. I'm afraid my childhood and ascent to manhood were not pleasant. I may be gentry, but as a third son, all that buys one is, perhaps, an education and a pat on the back when you walk out the door. I got the education . . . and some money . . . but not the pat on the back . . . I apologize. This is not what I thought to discuss and bore you with. But since I've already opened the door, I'll close it quickly. My father was an evil, abusive man. Not just to me, but to everyone, including my mother, my brothers, and the people who worked their lives away under his overbearing hand. He's long dead, and good riddance it is. My oldest brother now owns the estate, and the next brother in line is his manager . . . and I'm here . . . to build a life for myself . . . and for the family I someday hope to have." He looked directly into her eyes.

She felt a pang of sympathy, extended her hand, touched his cheek. "And what of your mother?"

A damp mist covered his eyes; the shadow of anguish again swept his face. "She died when I was six, but we never discovered the cause . . . I missed her very much and for a long time . . . but that's behind me now." His heart felt like it was erupting in flames as he recalled finding his mother dead, hanging by her neck in her bedroom. He'd watched his father abuse her mentally and physically, watched him drive her insane; tried to stop him once and been severely beaten for his effort; knew she'd killed herself to escape him. After tying the rope to a ceiling beam, she'd stood on a stool, tied her hands together with her teeth and fingers, then kicked the stool away. He'd wrapped his arms around her legs, tried to lift her, screamed for his father and brothers. When they'd finally rushed into the room, they'd stood still, staring without emotion at her cocked head and white face with its hollow, wide-eyed stare.

"Hugh, I must quit asking questions. I always seem to find the worst ones to ask."

"No, no, I'm fine." He blinked twice, started to wipe the wetness from his eyes, but seemed to think better of it. "So I understand from your father that your mother and young brother are still in England but will join you sometime in the future? You and your father must miss them a lot."

"Indeed." Emily glimpsed a fleeting image of her mother as she slipped her hand into her pocket, squeezed her locket into her palm.

"Well, you may miss them, but your father could not have a more efficient or attractive assistant than you, and I can see he appreciates you greatly."

"You flatter me, Master Tay—Hugh. I'm sorry." A smile. "This is truly difficult for me." She blushed. "I'm not used to addressing older men by their given names . . . but I shall become so."

He feigned injury. "Come now. Certainly I don't qualify as an older man. But yes, you're correct. I *do* flatter you. I *want* to flatter you. You're most worthy of flattery."

Her blush deepened. "I'm not used to flattery either. It embarrasses me. And yes, you *are* an older man, much older than I. And we young damsels must be wary of who we talk to and how. An older man could take advantage of a young, naive damsel like me, lead her astray." She smiled, thought how she enjoyed teasing him.

"If you aren't careful, I'll call you *Mistress Colman*. So behave yourself, Mistress . . . I mean, Emily." They both laughed again, stared into each other's eyes. "Emily, your father told me you're fluent in four languages. Is it true? I know about four words of French, and no Spanish or other language. You impress me again, Lady."

She wasn't used to being called *Lady* either but liked the sound of it, liked the banter. "You will not woo me with flattery, *Master Tayler*. See, I beat you to it." They held their smiles, studied each other's faces, as if trying to discern the truths behind the eyes.

"You have indeed, but can you say something to me in Spanish so I can see that you truly know it?"

"Si, Señor, puedo. Es hora de volver al trabajo."

"What did you say? It sounded *very* serious."

"It *was* serious. I said, 'Yes, Sir, I can. 'Tis time to return to work.' "

He squinted, pressed his lips together, like he'd just bitten into a lemon. "No. We can't go back to work yet. I'm just beginning to get to know you. I want to sit right here, or maybe hide with you in the forest, and do nothing but talk to you the rest of the day. The work can wait."

"The cutters are on their feet; Lieutenant Waters is about to speak, see him? He'll come for you in a moment; he needs your strong back. And I must go for more water." She started to climb to her feet.

He stood first, held her hand as she rose. "I protest, Lady. I must have more time with you." His smile gave way to an earnest, almost pleading look. "Emily, I mean what I just said. I *do* want to spend more time with you . . . *much* more time. Talking to you, just this small amount today, has enflamed my passion to know you well, to know your heart, your mind. Please say that you'll allow me that pleasure."

Emily regarded him with an undecipherable look. "Hugh, I've greatly enjoyed our visit in your parlor and getting to know you, even for so short a time. So yes, we will spend more time together. I look forward to it."

Waters was on his feet, looking at the transport crew near Tayler and Emily. "Come, men. The day is fleeting. Let us—"

A distant yet loud, unnerving shriek tore through the thick, humid air. All stood, looked toward the sound, waited.

Waters said, "The stream." Another shriek, more terrible than the first, then continuous wailing, like a chorus of banshees.

Waters pulled his saber from the ground, slid it into its scabbard, quickly drew his wheel lock pistol—the only firearm in the colony that didn't require a burning match for powder ignition. "You men"—he pointed at a cluster of six soldiers sitting nearby in the shade—"stay here. Guard these people. Civilians, gather over there." He pointed at several piles of logs arranged in a loose circle. The shrieking persisted. People glanced at one another; all looked afraid, confused. "The rest of you men come with me. Now! At the quick time!" Fourteen soldiers sprinted across the clearing into the forest, toward the stream, where another group of water bearers had gone to refill their water buckets.

When they arrived at the stream, they found four women gathered around the wailing woman, their arms around her waist and shoulders, trying to comfort her. The woman's eyes focused two feet in front of her, where a decomposed body lay on the ground. A few tufts of red hair remained on the crushed skull, and five arrows lay amidst the bones. "My Jamie, my Jamie, dead. Nooo."

Waters gently eased the four women out of the way, stood in front of her, then slowly grasped her shoulders. "Madame . . . Madame."

The wailing continued; she twisted back and forth, trying to escape his grasp.

He shook her, shook her again. "Madame, stop."

She wailed on, looked Waters in the eye but didn't see him.

"Madame." The wailing unnerved him. As he held her fast with his left hand, he slapped her across the face with his right, then pulled her to his chest. He slowly relaxed his strong grip to a gentle embrace, softly caressed the back of her neck and head until only a quiet whimper remained. "Madame, is this your husband?"

She spoke softly, hesitantly. "Yes."

"How do you know 'tis him? How can you identify him?'

"He . . . he told me . . . before he left England . . . that he . . . that he was the only . . . the only redhead in . . . in the unit . . . I know 'tis him. What will become of me now? How will I . . ."

He'd anticipated finding more dead men, feared the possibility. Now he regretted they hadn't searched the entire area before allowing the people to go to the village, knew there'd be hell to pay for the governor. "We'll care for you, Madame. Do not fear." He looked at the other ladies. "Kindly help her back to the village. Then please care for her, calm her. Go to my cottage. You'll find a flask of rum in my bag. Give her some; try to get her to sleep." He motioned the women toward the village, then looked at the soldiers, who nervously shuffled their feet, glanced at the dead soldier, then the forest, then back at the soldier. "We'll escort the ladies to the village. Then, Sergeant Myllet, bring a detail of eight men back here with shovels and bury this man. He died in Her Majesty's service, and when the governor returns from the ship, we'll have a proper military ceremony." He leaned toward Myllet. "Sergeant, be vigilant, keep four men on guard while the others dig. I'm uneasy about this place."

"Aye, Sir. I feel it too."

They'd gone but fifty steps when Waters stopped, tapped Myllet on the shoulder, then pointed halfway between straight-ahead and full-right. "There . . . see them . . . about sixty yards away . . . just left of that big tree, behind the bush?"

Myllet looked, raised his musket, and aimed at the two Savages who stood defiantly tall, in plain view, readied bows in hand. "I see them, Sir. Do you want me to fire a warning shot?"

"I think not. There may be more, may be a trap . . . we need to get these women to the village quickly, prepare for an attack there; we don't want to fight here. Keep five men; follow behind us at a slow pace; keep your sights on the Savages as long you can. Fix your weapons on them, but do not shoot unless they attack . . . just watch them. They know what our weapons can do, but they also know how long it takes to reload them. I repeat. Do not fire unless they attack." Now it begins, thought Waters . . . now it begins. A sudden rush worked its way through his body, quickening his pulse, his breathing, exciting a previously unfelt exhilaration at the prospect of leading men in combat.

"Understand, Sir."

Waters held his gaze on the Savages until he lost sight of them behind the trees, but he could still see Myllet and the rear guard doing as he had ordered. Five minutes later and a hundred yards from the village, he finally lost sight of Myllet. A moment later, the colonists spied Waters and his group, immediately scrambled from the circle of logs and rushed toward him. They were halfway to him when the throaty sound of a musket shot rumbled from the forest near Myllet's position, then two more. "Damn!" Waters' mind flashed to White's cautions about the Savages, wondered if Myllet had remembered. "Go back to the palisades! Get inside the circle of logs! Take cover! Go to the logs! Run! Now!"

CHAPTER 3

Two hundred miles to the northwest of the colonists, four Savages untied their travois from their waists, set about gathering firewood for the approaching night. One pulled a stick the length of his forearm from a deer-hide bag, then a flat chip of wood half the length of the stick and the width of a man's hand. Next he removed a flat rock with a hole in it as wide as the fire stick diameter, then some tinder, which he laid around and inside a notch in the chip, adjacent to a hole that was also the diameter of the stick. Last came a short, bow-shaped stick with a loose piece of sinew attached to the ends. He looped the sinew around the fire stick and fitted the bottom into the friction hole in the chip, the top into the hole in the rock. He pressed heavily on the rock with his left hand while rapidly rotating the stick back and forth with his right hand until the friction generated smoke, then a glowing ember in the hole. He quickly laid the tinder on the ember, blew gently until it flamed, and placed it on the ground, adding several twigs, then some larger sticks, but not enough to generate a smoke column that might be seen by an enemy. Though their campsite was in a rocky, wooded, mountainous area that offered excellent concealment, they listened carefully and remained alert for any sound that might signal approaching danger.

The cool mountain air was refreshing after a complete moon cycle of days in the low, hot river country; and they savored it as they sat around their modest fire, sipping water from their large animal-stomach bags and chewing pieces of dried venison. The climb up the mountains had been strenuous, as the large, furry robes they carried were twelve hands long and ten hands wide, and weighed as much as a rock that took both hands to lift and throw. Each man carried six such robes, a heavy load, but their expected reward would more than repay their effort. The coastal tribes prized the large hides for their winter warmth and summer softness, paid dearly for them with beautiful shells and jewelry crafted from the red stones found inland from the sea, as well as with an occasional pearl. The four would use their bounty for gifts and to trade for more wealth with others of their own tribe, far to the north in their land of many big waters.

They had made good time paddling their canoes south down the Mother-of-All-Rivers, each man with his own canoe and load of robes, staying in the middle of the river to avoid enemies and stopping only after dark and in unpopulated, defensible spots on the shore. Each night they had taken turns standing guard, and all four had drunk enough water before sleeping to ensure the urge to urinate would wake them early enough to have them safely back on the water before daylight. But the level of effort demanded of them had dramatically increased when they reached the big river that flowed in on their left, for thereafter, they had to paddle upstream for many days. They had loaded all the robes into two canoes, which had then been towed behind the other two canoes, each of which carried two men. Finally, after paddling up another, smaller river that flowed in from their right, they had reached the place to leave the water and cross the mountains directly toward the rising sun. But before beginning their ascent, they had carefully hidden the canoes for the return trip and constructed their four travois, which had promptly reminded them that dragging a heavy load of hides up a steep mountainside was no easier than paddling upstream. So all four had been eager to reach the summit and begin the easy downhill drag to the flatter land on the other side, and thence across it to the Great-Water-That-Cannot-Be-Drunk. Thus, when they had finally crossed the summit, their spirits had risen accordingly, as evidenced in more-frequent smiles and lighter conversation.

The four men did not look or dress like the coastal people. All had full heads of long black hair that hung behind their shoulders to their waists and wore nothing but thin leather loincloths and rugged leather moccasins. But one looked different from the others. He had a smaller, straighter nose and less-prominent cheekbones and wore five white, black-tipped eagle feathers that protruded to the right in the shape of a fan behind his head. His dark eyes had a sharp depth to them that made them look like they could see inside a man's soul, read its contents; while his occasional wry smiles revealed a quiet confidence and easy humor that belied the fact that the exhilaration of battle and the hunt supplanted all else in his demeanor—possessed him, filled him with the fierce, unshakeable fixation of a dangerous predator. He was a handsome man by any standard, and the others treated him with a soft deference that showed him to be their leader.

* * *

Thomas and Emily Colman stood outside the cottage they shared with the Howes, swatted at the mosquitoes whining endlessly around them. As the sun approached the horizon, a dull gray slowly infiltrated the daylight and consumed it into darkness, bringing an imagined coolness to the air; but it did nothing to diminish the stifling humidity that draped itself like a heavy, wet, impenetrable blanket over every living thing. Thomas Colman said, "We saw you sitting with Master Tayler this afternoon while we were here working on the cottage. Both of you were smiling, so the conversation must have been agreeable?" She didn't reply, so he continued. "Unfortunately, young George noticed, as well, kept looking over at you. He's rather infatuated with you, you know."

"Oh?" It annoyed her that he mentioned George, had to state the obvious—the obvious being something she didn't want to hear, and *this particular obvious* filling her with guilt. She knew seeing her with Tayler would have bothered George immensely, probably even hurt him; but now it bothered *her*, made her ache for any pain she'd caused him, frustrated her because she cared deeply for George but knew she'd someday have to rebuff his infatuation. The conflict tortured her, burned inside her.

"So was it an agreeable discourse?"

"Aye, Father. '*Twas* agreeable . . . do you have to know everything? He's interesting, charming, and as clever a wit as I suspected. I like him, and I'll see him again, probably often. He'll soon be asking your permission. I've already given mine." He doesn't need to know the family background, she thought. None of his business. Between Hugh and me.

Though he was well used to her sharp responses, they always took him by surprise, set him back a step or two. "I see. A little improper . . . he should have come to me first . . . but—"

"Father, don't be so stuffy. We're not in London, and this isn't exactly a civilized place. I don't know why you think that way. 'Tis silly."

"Come now, Em, some things are core to our culture and shouldn't be discarded just because we're suddenly in the wild. There's a thin line between civilization and savagery, and we need to be mindful of it, keep ourselves on the proper side of the line or risk falling backward . . . I suppose you're already calling each other by your first names?"

"Of course." She knew he was right about civilization but resented his fixation on decorum, his intrusion into her personal life; so she replied in her favorite snippy way, the one that always annoyed him. She smiled inside as she recalled the times he'd pressed her too hard about young men who'd fancied her and to whom she'd been attracted. Rather than tolerate his probing and lecturing, she'd simply closed her lips, then sneaked out of the house late at night and met the lads elsewhere, though one time her risky brashness had nearly cost her virginity—most precious of her possessions, the prize she'd protect at all costs for the man she'd someday marry. Only her quick mind and quick feet had saved her. With a continuous stream of suitors—some young, some older; some true, some not so true—she'd developed a keen ability to read people's sincerity like a manuscript, could usually discern a devious intention from only a few words and an unguarded look. Those people—the ones who thought you were too stupid to know what they were trying to do—were the ones she detested most in the world; and because she could see through them in seconds, she didn't need her father's well-intentioned, but annoying, injection of laborious English propriety into every situation. Nonetheless, she regretted her abrupt, but seemingly uncontrollable rudeness to him, wished she could hold her tongue, treat him more respectfully, but she could never seem to resist the temptation to jab him with a verbal barb when he crossed her imaginary line. No one else had that effect on her, and it saddened her that her father, whom she loved with all her heart, had to be the only person in the world who could so quickly and unwittingly provoke her. When she thought about it, she realized that the problem was her own intolerant brashness; that she was predisposed to misinterpreting, and overreacting to, whatever he said; that she alone was responsible for making the caring, respectful relationship they both desired so difficult to achieve. She wished her mother were here; she always knew how to calm things, suppress the fiery emotions, and get them to communicate like normal people.

Colman continued, "Well, I *am* impressed with the man. And he seemed to work hard today. I believe he'll prosper here if anyone does. So, since you wish it, I shall give my permission for him to visit you." He looked away for a moment, then back at Emily. "Em, I . . . I love you, my daughter . . . and I wish you and I could . . ." He shook his head, finished his sentence with a warm hug that communicated what he was trying to say.

She replied with her own hug, leaned her head against his chest. "Father, I love you too. I hate it when I'm short with you."

After they'd savored the embrace for a moment, he asked, "How's Elyoner? I heard she was down with the morning sickness. Did you see her?"

"Aye. She's miserable, indeed, and quite ready for the little rascal to show itself, tired of puking all day. The heat makes it worse."

"Poor girl. She's quite huge, don't you think? I don't remember your mother ever being that big."

"I'm not the one to ask, but she herself thinks 'tis so, though she says the size of the mother's belly has naught to do with the size of the child."

"Indeed." He glanced at John White's cottage on the other side of the village. "I understand the governor returned from the ship with a foul countenance. Seems he made no headway with Fernandez, and then learning of the Savages lurking about, threatening the soldiers made it worse. And, of course, there was the second dead man. Unfortunate woman, finding her husband like that. My God, I can't imagine how she felt, how shocked. Then about forty people cornered him, screamed at him about deceiving us and leading us into danger and certain death. He was quite flustered by the time it was over, called a meeting of the twelve Assistants for tomorrow morning. I'm sure George will relay whatever transpires; should be a vicious gathering with all that's happened, and I shall be eager to hear about it. Perhaps you were right in challenging him about the first dead man. He *does* seem to keep secrets, which I find disconcerting, though I understand his concerns about panicking the colony. I must say, I'm mildly worried about our chances here myself . . . and there could be far more to fear than we yet know."

Indeed there is, thought Emily. "I believe you're right, Father. But we must—"

The Howes emerged from the cottage, each holding a candle. The elder George said, "Thomas, I'm ready. Good meal . . . I jest, 'twas awful. Let's find Roger Baylye and see what he can tell us of the day's events."

Colman kissed Emily on the forehead, walked off behind Howe.

Young George gawked at Emily with a look that said he yearned to kiss her, as well. "It's too hot in there. Shall we sit out here and fight the mosquitoes for a while?"

"Of course." She sat herself on the ground, swiped at the mosquito that had repeatedly attacked her for the last two minutes. "You made good progress on the cottage today. Already feels like home." She exhaled with a cynical, unladylike snort. "Pardon my sarcasm, George. Where did you find the reeds?"

"Down by the water, over there." He pointed south. "About a third of a league. We went with three other groups and some soldiers . . . always with soldiers. Father wants to go back there tomorrow, but not for reeds. He saw hordes of crabs, says it's a perfect spot. He should know: they're his favorite food, even over mussels. We used to crab a lot before my mother died, but . . ."

"Well, crabs sound a far sight better than hardtack. I hope he has a bountiful catch."

"He will. How's Master Tayler today?"

She mildly resented his query, gave him a bored look, then thought how his look betrayed his pain. "He's fine, George."

"Do you like him?"

"George, that's not a proper question. Of course, I like him. I like you, as well. But a girl can't go around explaining how she feels every time she talks to someone. 'Tis not—"

"Sorry, sorry. You're right."

Emily felt his anguish, considered telling him now that their relationship was but a *friendship*, could never be a romance, but decided against it. That discussion would come in a different setting, on a different day. "George, don't you know how much I value your friendship? Let's not let anything interfere with that."

"I understand, Em . . . guess we should talk about something else, eh?"

She nodded, gave him a soft, sympathetic smile, touched his hand.

He laid his other hand over hers, his soft smile signaling the warmth he felt flowing up his arms to his heart. "Very well. I heard about the second dead man." He paused, stared into her eyes. "You know a lot about what happened here with the earlier expedition don't you?"

Careful, Em. "A little."

"Can you tell me? I keep hearing little undertones from the men I talk to . . . only rumors, mind you, but unsettling rumors." He paused for her to speak, but she held her silence. "They said the soldiers who were here before us committed atrocities against the Savages, that they hate us and mean to kill us if we stay. Is that true?"

In half a second, she realized the events of the previous expedition would soon be common knowledge, saw no reason to hide them from George, or anyone else, any longer. Through no fault of his own, Governor White had led them into this situation; and if they were to survive, they had to know what they faced. " 'Tis so, George. Only Manteo, Governor White, and two others know these things . . . because they were here. And as you've probably guessed, since Manteo and I talked a lot on the ship, he's the one who told me what happened. He's a good, honest man and my friend, as well. So to begin, a soldier named Lane, whose name you've heard from Governor White, commanded the one hundred soldiers who were here and built the cottages and old palisades. They seem to have been a more savage lot than the Savages themselves, for they burned several villages and murdered many people along the river west of here, took prisoners, as well. Manteo said they were brutal and merciless. Well, there were Savages here on this island at that time, and they were friendly to Lane's men at first: taught them how to raise corn and hunt and fish. But the soldiers grew lazy and didn't want to work. They wanted the Savages to feed them and do everything for them, wanted them to be slaves. And as you might guess, the Savages would have none of it and soon came to hate them. Lane knew of their displeasure and suspected they were planning to attack; so he attacked them first and killed several, including their leader. They cut off his head and stuck it on a pole in the center of the village to rot, like they do at home when someone falls from grace or commits treason. Then—"

"Are they still here . . . on the island?"

"No."

George relaxed his taut look.

"But they're right over there"—she pointed west—"across that little neck of water between us and the main. And over there is not very far from right here. Those two Savages the soldiers shot at today were probably from there. 'Tis but a short canoe trip, and that's why we're at great risk, especially without a good place to defend ourselves. They hate us for what Lane did and would have us dead or gone."

"Aren't you afraid?"

"Indeed, I am. I've never had anyone try to kill me before. But fear doesn't help anything; only being vigilant and prepared will help. We need to defend ourselves or leave, like the 15 men did . . . well, now 13 men . . . *if* they escaped. Life would be much simpler, of course, if the governor convinced Fernandez to take us north to the Chesapeake, where we belong, where the Savages are friendly. But the soldiers can't get back on the boat, so there are no means of persuasion; thus, all we can do is hope the governor and the Assistants, like your father, can figure a way to avoid or deal with the danger. At least we have a standing village of sorts and a start on some palisades. And if they leave the pinnace and a shallop or two with us, as rumored, we could even sail and row ourselves up the coast to Chesapeake . . . 'tis only about sixteen leagues. There's even talk of moving into the main in the spring, but that's toward some of the tribes Lane brutalized, and I don't think I like that idea."

After a long silence mostly spent swatting mosquitoes, George picked up a couple pebbles, tossed them into the darkness. "Emily, I'd not tell this to anyone but you; but since my mother died, I've sensed a dreadful evil stalking Father and me. This place makes it worse."

"George! Stop the gloomy talk. Nothing will happen to you and your father. We've soldiers to protect us, and . . . and things are gloomy enough. Don't make it worse with such thoughts. Now cheer yourself." She held his hand to her lips and kissed it. "Know that I care deeply for you and your father."

George's eyes glassed over; he looked ready to take her in his arms, roll her onto the ground, kiss her, more; but he simply stared into her eyes. "Emily Colman, you're the most wonderful person I've ever known. I . . . I love you."

* * *

Emily awoke from an anxious sleep—anxious because her mind had never relaxed; it had churned with thoughts of her mother, her secret fears over the colony's prospects, and then the words young George had spoken to her. She lay fully clothed on her side, on a doubled-over wool blanket spread on the ground, her knees together and tucked up toward her stomach. Ground's not fit for a woman's body, she mused. No dips or hollows in the right places. The heat and humidity aggravated her discomfort. She wished she'd been able to take off her heavy wool skirt and top, strip down to her linen smock, but that would have been improper with the Howes sharing the cottage. But just the thought of it seemed to cool her perspiring body. She sat up, looked around the room. The three men lay scattered around the dirt floor, each in a different repose, all soundly asleep. Her father lay on his back, snoring with each breath. Though she'd suffered his snoring for nineteen years, she'd never gotten used to it, never learned to block it out so she could enjoy a quiet, uninterrupted sleep. She'd even heard it from three rooms away in their house in England. A candle burned by the doorway but had only an hour or so left before it would expire. Emily rose, stepped quietly to one of her bags on the other side of the one-room cottage, and felt inside. She removed a folded piece of paper that looked like it had been folded and unfolded many times before, carried it to the doorway, then carefully unfolded it, lay down on her side, and held it beneath the candle flame.

My Dearest Emily,

When you read this, you'll probably be at sea, probably sick, and probably missing me and your brother as much as we already miss you. My dear, you are the joy of my life, and being parted from you is the most painful and difficult thing I've experienced, even more so than giving birth to you and your brothers. I love you, Emily, and I miss your willing, helpful hand, your cheerfulness, your humor, your intelligence, your loyalty, your honesty, your kindness. I haven't told you often enough how much I love you, but I tell you now that I count the moments until I'm with you and your father again. No separation can dim the love I feel for you, and I pray you thrive and continue to be the fine young woman you've become.

I do not know what lies ahead for you in that new world, but I know you have the mind, the values, and the perseverance to conquer every challenge you face. I know you will survive, no matter what. Please remember everything I taught you about dealing with your father. You'll need each other to survive and prosper. And in spite of how he sometimes affects you, remember that he loves you deeply. Second, I want you to remember that your chastity is your most wonderful possession. Nothing in your life is more important. It is the very essence of you, and should be given only to the one you love more than life itself: your husband, none other. I know you understand this. Now, dear Emily, I must go. I pray that God watches over you and protects you and that our family will soon be together again. Godspeed.

I love you,
Mother

Emily dabbed her sleeve on the tears that flowed like tiny water-falls down her cheeks to her chin, onto the letter. She started crying, then sobbed, cupping her hand over her mouth so she wouldn't wake the men. When she'd settled, she reverently folded the letter, kissed it, put it in her pocket. She then removed her locket and held it to her cheek, wiped her eyes with her other hand, and stared into the flickering flames. *Mother, I miss you so.* A sudden whiff of breeze drifted through the cottage door, seemed to deposit an image of her mother in the flames. *Oh, Mother, how I miss you. Yes, I shall keep faith with my principles, with all you've taught me. I love you, Mother.* She closed her eyes, heard the sizzling of the steaming water kettle in her mother's kitchen, smelled the aroma of boiled mussels and cake that always seemed to dwell there.

A hand touch her shoulder; she sucked a loud cry into her throat. The elder George Howe said, "Emily, forgive me. Here we are with Savages about, and I'm surprising people in the dark."

"No matter, Master Howe. I was just missing my mother and feeling sorry for myself." She slid her locket into her pocket, held her index finger to her lips, then pointed toward the doorway. Outside she glanced up at the stars that covered the moonless sky like grains of salt sprinkled on a huge, black blanket.

Howe whispered, "Well, it *was* clumsy of me. I awoke and saw you by the candle, thought I'd pass the moment with another restless soul . . . it must be very difficult for you and your father. You've left two people behind. George and I have left nothing, no person or thing. You and your father, on the other hand, have left your whole lives behind. You risk much."

"I'm sorry about your wife. George misses her so. I can see he still grieves. I know you do, as well."

He looked away for a moment then back at Emily. "You see much for your years, Emily Colman. Yes, we still grieve . . . but the past *is* something we've left behind. This is our life now, and we're determined to succeed here." He snickered. "Of course, most of the citizens of England consider us daft for being here, for leaving civilization for the wilderness, for risking our lives. But a man must push himself, strive for what he wants out of life. Success is not free, not even cheap." He looked away into the darkness for a moment as if he expected it to tell him the right words to express his thoughts. "Emily, I don't know how young George truly feels about being here, but I know he's glad he met you. I'm sure you know he's quite fond of you—"

"And I of him. My close friend, he is."

"I see that. And we'll need close, trusted friends to survive here . . . yet I sense that his feelings for you go beyond friendship."

A warm flush worked its way up Emily's neck to her cheeks.

"I sense that those feelings are more romantic than yours for him . . . which I understand—you being two years older, and young ladies being more mature than young men. Truly, I don't mean to embarrass you, Emily. On the contrary, I don't want you to ever feel pressured by our circumstances to feel more for George than you would if you were back in England. Stress can play tricks on the mind and emotions, and . . . and you're a young woman unequaled by any I've ever seen. Why, if I were younger . . ."

"Master Howe, you flatter me. George is my dear friend. We share thoughts and dreams as friends do, and you're right. He does feel more than simple friendship for me. A lass knows these things. Yet there have been times when I wondered if it might be different, wondered if we could someday be more than friends. As you say, our circumstances make it more difficult to know reality from imagination. For now—"

"Emily Colman, fate and *you* will determine your future, but I have a feeling it will be *you* more than fate. So follow your mind . . . and your heart . . . and, Emily, never doubt your father's love. 'Tis true and deep."

* * *

The seething, torrid sun had not yet crested the horizon when John White and his twelve Assistants, guarded by four soldiers who waited out of earshot in the trees, arrived at the meeting place on the shore. White had anticipated a blunt, emotional, and perhaps even raucous discussion but nothing like what ensued. Lord, he hated confrontation, couldn't think under the pressure of it, never knew what to say, what to do. The colonists were rightly incensed by the events of the last two days—not only incensed but afraid, some even terrified. He understood the relationship between the two; and knowing there was no greater stimulant of irrational behavior than fear, he hoped to preclude its contagion in the colony.

William Willes shouted, "Christ Almighty, John, why did you hide these truths from us? You breached our trust, man." If there had been a table on the shore, he would have pounded it with his fist, kicked it over, stomped it into small pieces of kindling. "How can we believe anything you say now? You've squandered your credibility. 'Tis gone, man, gone!"

White's shoulders sagged as he stared at the ground. He looked like a young boy who had been caught stealing pennies from his father. What to do. What to say. "William, I . . . I acted in what I thought was the best interest of the colony."

"Bosh! I challenge that," shouted Willes.

"I, as well," grumbled John Sampson. " 'Tis simply untrue. You lied, Governor—lied to entice us here, and you're lying now to keep us here. Deceived us, you did. You even—"

Thomas Stevens interrupted, threw his walking stick on the ground. "You connived with that bastard, Fernandez, to maroon us here . . . so you could claim our land in the Chesapeake. We ought to storm the ship and hang Fernandez."

"Thomas, I resent that intimation. I've done—"

Sampson cut in. "So, Governor, why did you deceive us?"

A storm of vicious shouting erupted, pummeled White like summer hail. "Please gentlemen. Please, I beg you. Let me explain." The violent carping drowned him out, but he was actually glad of it because he didn't know what to say, had no idea what to do, how to answer such aggressive but honest anger. He wanted to run away; hide in the forest; leave the colony's governance to someone with the temperament, mind, and leadership to actually do the job—someone who could save them from the impending disaster only he knew was coming. Damn Fernandez. Everything would have been fine if the lowly bastard hadn't dumped us here.

George Howe spoke above the din. "Gentlemen, gentlemen. This is wrong. We're condemning the wrong man. We must calm ourselves, think with reason not emotion. *Fernandez* deceived us, not the governor."

Several men stopped grousing, looked at Howe.

Roger Baylye said, "Master Howe is right. This anger accomplishes nothing; it only makes our task more difficult. Please, let us show some respect for one another . . . and the governor." Baylye looked about forty years old, had a mousey look about him, magnified by a nearly nonexistent chin, permanently sad and unconfident look, and slight stature draped over a taller-than-average frame. He looked like a worrier, but had an unexpectedly deep voice that caught people by surprise and commanded their immediate attention. "You shall all have your chance to speak, but first we must act like the leaders we were chosen to be." The grousing tapered to silence. "Like it or not, we lack the luxury of choices and endless whining. As Assistants, we've naught but the obligation to advise the governor to the best of our ability. Damn it! We cannot stand here all day yelling at one another. We've work to do if this colony is to have even a meager chance of survival, much to plan and organize. We must assign tasks, create rules for governance and labor, inventory our supplies, organize hunting and fishing parties. Do you realize we've barely enough food to feed the colony for three weeks unless we supplement with other foodstuffs? But we have none. How many of you know how to hunt deer or turkey, or fish these waters? Then we've palisade construction and cottage building to plan, and much more we haven't even thought of. Have you forgotten that we'll be doing no planting or raising of crops this year? Even if it wasn't the end of July and too late to plant, how many of us have an inkling of how to plant *here*? The Savages know, but they hate us and won't teach us. Winter will soon be upon us, and we must be prepared or perish. How will we do that? Come to your senses, men. You're all intelligent, honest sorts. So cease whining and concentrate on planning the means of survival. Our situation is desperate . . . and the people don't yet realize it." He spoke quietly, with resignation, finality. " 'Tis our responsibility to guide and lead them, plan for their protection."

The ensuing silence encouraged him. "Now, I agree with George Howe. Our situation was *not* the governor's making. He may not have told us everything he knew, but I believe him innocent of willful deceit. The problems we face are related to our present location, but not at all to our *intended* location. Master White is our governor, appointed by Sir Walter Raleigh, and not removable by us. We are thus obliged to give him the opportunity to explain himself and lead us. So let us hear him and then proceed with the tasks before us. John?"

Would that Baylye were governor instead of me, White thought. Perhaps I shall propose it later. He took a deep breath, toyed with the end of his mustache. "Friends . . . I call you 'friends' because I hold you in that regard. I personally chose you to be my Assistants because of the leadership traits I saw in you. I myself have, sadly, failed to exhibit those same traits in fair measure. I have been less than forthcoming with you, and with all of the people, about the events that transpired here in 1585 and 1586. For that I am sorry. But I withheld that information with fair intentions because I had no suspicion that we would now be trying to exist *here* rather than in the Chesapeake. I thought general knowledge of those violent happenings would only create unnecessary anxiety and fear among the people but, in the end, have no effect on us, or our success, in the Chesapeake. So why mention them? Yes, Lane committed atrocities against the Savages. I witnessed and abhorred those atrocities. Yes, he enflamed their passions against us. His actions were arrogant and stupid; his men murdered, raped, burned, laid waste, brought fatal disease. But evil as they were, his actions would have had no impact upon us had the blackguard, Fernandez, not forced us from the vessel and refused us passage to our intended destination, the destination granted us by Sir Walter Raleigh and the Queen herself." He took a long breath, again toyed with his mustache.

Taking heart from a rare prolonged silence, he felt he'd regained a foothold. "But even after my lengthy pleading, and then threatening, I cannot say I know Fernandez's reason for this irrational, mutinous act. Indeed, it was most frustrating to me, for we went round in circles the entire day with him providing no explanation for deserting us here. In truth, all I can surmise is that he's been bribed by one of Raleigh's enemies, of which there are several; or as he swears, he may truly need a full month here to replenish water, food, and firewood before he departs for England, hopefully ahead of the winter gales. He says this urgent priority does not allow time for him to take us to Chesapeake; but in fact, doing so would cost him merely a day. So, I believe him to be lying to cover his intent to privateer and take Spanish prizes on his way back to England . . . certainly a more profitable venture than delivering us to Chesapeake. But whatever his true reason, 'tis irresponsible and criminal to abandon one hundred nineteen people in a hostile environment where their survival is in doubt. Unfortunately, and to my own disappointment, I believe further imploring of the man to do us justice is futile and will yield no change in his position; therefore, since we have *not* the means to attack the ship, we must find the resources and resolve to survive *here* and await the arrival of English authorities of sufficient rank to prosecute him . . . even if he's long since departed. As it stands today, he intends to abandon us here and depart with the large ship and the flyboat before the end of August."

The absence of protest gave White a surge in confidence, a parcel of gratitude that they had listened, given him another chance. "The only good fortune to come from this debacle is Fernandez's promise to leave the pinnace and two shallops here with us. If he's true to his word, this will provide us the opportunity to transport *ourselves* to Chesapeake, or perhaps up the broad river, to the west where it narrows, and thence overland into the main. Both options are preferable to remaining here."

The Assistants looked numb, depleted; none spoke, none contested. White mentally thanked Baylye for saving him, giving him the chance to compose himself and regain what little confidence he had. But he'd now confirmed their worst fears: they were in a dangerous, untenable position; the one who was to blame was untouchable and protected from retribution; and they were soon to be abandoned to their own devices. He watched their faces as they slowly regarded one another; read their concern, their fear, but also hints of embryonic determination.

As the extended silence grew awkward, Baylye cleared his throat and removed a piece of paper from his coat. "John, while you were on the ship yesterday, I took the liberty of conducting an inventory of our supplies."

White nodded. "A most urgent action. Thank you for the foresight."

"The results are *not* comforting. We've wine for a month, but the beer will be exhausted within the week. We have ingredients to make our own, and I suggest we assign that task to someone tomorrow. For foodstuffs, we have four to six weeks of hardtack, salt beef, oatmeal, rice, honey, and butter; but the cheese, currants, raisins, prunes, olives, salad oil and vinegar, turnip and parsnip seed, onions, garlic, thyme, mustard, fennel, and anise will be gone in three weeks."

A despondent shadow spread over the men's faces like the sudden smoke of a new fire.

"So, as you can see, the situation is not promising, which has led me to the conclusion that we must do two things immediately. First, we must extend the life of our existing supplies by supplementing them with fresh fish and venison. This will require hunters and fishermen, and we should begin these efforts this very afternoon. Second, we must develop and implement a system for rationing the supplies among the people so all receive their fair share. Master Howe, I'm told you've some experience with crabbing, might even qualify as an expert at it?"

George Howe flashed a proud smile. "I do indeed. A man must know how to acquire his favorite food if he's to enjoy it now and then. And if you're asking me to spend the rest of the day crabbing and call it work, I enthusiastically accept."

Hearty laughter rippled around the circle of men, fracturing the stiff tension that had gripped the assembly.

"Thank you, Sir. I'd hoped for that response. Perhaps you could choose six or eight men to accompany you and teach them the art. We'll need a bountiful harvest to satisfy the hunger of so many . . . I assume you'll instruct us in the proper preparation and cooking of these creatures, as well?"

"Certainly. Though I'm sure many are already skilled in that regard, I shall do what's necessary for all to enjoy the feast. I'll also volunteer my services for this task each and every day."

More smiles, more laughter, easing of tensions and tempers, men raising their hands to go on the expedition.

"Good. Can you also find us some fishermen? Perhaps one of the shallops could be used along with the line and hooks we unloaded from the ship, to harvest a good catch right here in the sound."

"Of course."

"And Roger Prat, you come from the country. Can you hunt deer . . . with a longbow?"

"I can indeed, Sir. Also with a matchlock. And, of course, I can also gut and butcher what I kill."

"I fear, at least until Master Howe establishes his foundry and begins producing large quantities of lead shot, we'll need to conserve our ammunition. So a longbow it must be. Can you find additional huntsmen? Again, the need will soon be great."

"I shall. I already know of two others, and I'd wager there are a couple more. My concern would be for the number of animals present on this island, which I know not the size of. That will determine how long we can rely on this food source." He looked at White.

"The island is about four leagues by one league. Will that support an adequate population of deer? There's been no hunting for a year now . . . other than what the Savages might have done."

"Not for long. With this many people, we'll soon be forced to the main, which may be a dangerous place. So hope for a large bounty of fish."

Baylye said, "Very well. Now if we're to have adequate food for the winter, we must have hearty reserves to tide us through foul-weather times when we can't hunt and fish. So we'll need to dry, smoke, and salt our fish and meat. Three problems here: we're almost out of salt, there are no friendly Savages to instruct us in the arts of drying and smoking, and we've no Englishmen who know how to do such things. We'll need salt for other purposes, as well. So John Sampson, can you and a few others begin extracting salt from seawater? You'll need to collect a large number of boiling pots; and since this water here is only brackish and won't yield enough salt for your efforts, you'll have to transport seawater from the outer banks to the island or take wood and pots with you, do your boiling over there"—he pointed at the outer banks—"then transport the salt back here. As to the second problem, Governor White, do you think Manteo's people would school us in their techniques for fishing and hunting, as well as drying and smoking?"

"I should think so. We'll have to entice them with beads or metal tools; but yes, I believe they'll help. Manteo and I are going to their island in several days. I'll ask his mother, their leader, whom I know, if they'll help us with these matters."

"Good. Now we've our livestock to consider. Six pigs, twenty chickens, and six goats. The pigs and goats were to be seed stock, and of course, the goats and chickens were to provide a steady supply of milk for cheese, butter, and eggs, but I fear the need may soon arise for them all to fill cooking pots instead. Obviously, we must defer such an undesirable action for as long as possible."

Several grumbled to each other. Sampson pointed at Baylye, shook his finger. "Roger—"

"I know. It has a foolish ring to it. If anyone has an idea how to avoid it, my ears are open. I've not found one. So breeding stock and seeds for planting are now on the resupply list Fernandez will deliver to Raleigh upon his return."

The governor was impressed with Baylye's forethought and organization, his grasp of critical needs. He has an agile mind, he thought, far more so than I realized . . . mayhap a product of his years as mayor of a small village. He's thought of everything, done my job for me, must make him my assistant governor. He's strong in every way I'm weak. Yes, he shall have that position.

The men withdrew to the forest for shade as the fierce midmorning sun began to sap their alertness and drain their desire to be in a meeting where the only news was *bad* news that further inculcated them with a sense of doom. Over the next two hours, they discussed many other needs, as well as the fact that the flow in the stream they used for drinking water had slowed markedly since their arrival on the island. Governor White told them the locations of two other streams which the water carriers would explore that afternoon. They also agreed on people to fill certain key positions, several of them direct carryovers from their employments or businesses in England. Among them were George Howe's assignment to create a foundry; John Jones to be the colony's physician; the governor's son-in-law, Ananias, a tiler in England, to explore for clay to make chimney bricks; Thomas Colman to be schoolmaster for the colony's children and any adults who wished to be educated; Anthony Cage, a sheriff in England, to be the governor's constable for civil matters; Thomas Hewet, a lawyer, to be the colony's judge; and Morris Allen, a master carpenter, to supervise the building of additional cottages. After considerable discussion and disagreement, they also decided that every person—soldier, gentleman, and common man—must apply their physical efforts to the collective good, at least until such time as the colony was secure and sufficiently established to allow individual endeavors. The governor, advised by the Assistants, would decide when that time had arrived; and until then, the penalty for failure of any person to provide a fair share of labor would be that person receiving reduced rations. Last, Governor White promised to meet promptly with Baylye, Thomas Hewet, and Anthony Cage to begin developing a code of laws and consequences for their violation.

As the meeting adjourned, Governor White proclaimed that no one was to leave the palisades area without an armed escort. Work party foremen were to notify Lieutenant Waters of their schedules a day in advance, so he could apportion his forces accordingly. This policy was to be implemented immediately.

White was feeling greatly relieved by the time the meeting adjourned, believed he'd won them back, regained their confidence; he felt immense gratitude to Baylye for cooling the hot tempers, doing the head work to begin the process of survival in their hostile environment, and for giving him a new hold on his governorship. He would reward him for this rescue, ensure he had the prestigious position he deserved in the colony. What the governor had yet to do was confer with Lieutenant Waters about the Savages, yesterday's events, and the defense of the colony. A fine lad, Waters. Seemed to have the respect of his men, though White was still disappointed that he'd challenged his order; but most important, he seemed to have good leadership qualities and a professional approach to his duties. He'd made a good start on the palisades, had created a clever design; so White felt better about the colony's defenses being vested in so young an officer, considered Waters another potential candidate for recognition and reward when the time came.

As White and the Assistants entered the village, Lieutenant Waters had just completed an instructional session with thirty of his men. When the four who had guarded the Assistants approached, he told Sergeant Smith to take them aside and inform them of his guidance. While the larger group dispersed, Smith told the four that the colony was in a very dangerous situation, one that required the utmost in professionalism, alertness, and attention to the surrounding environment, which most notably included hostile Savages. He also warned them against any temptation to lapse into laziness or take advantage of weaknesses displayed by the civilians; reminded them that they, Her Majesty's men, were trained to take care of themselves and their comrades and should set the example for the civilians in all categories of endeavor. Next he cautioned that he and the governor were the highest civil and military authorities in the colony, that their words were law, and that the same three capital offenses that applied to soldiers in England applied here: abandoning a post or sleeping on duty, drawing a weapon on a com-missioned or non-commissioned officer, and violating or abusing a woman. And last, he had stated that in order to conserve ammunition, any executions would be by hanging or beheading.

* * *

Sergeant Myllet pointed at each man as he spoke. "Bishop, Browne, Darige, Sutton, Allen—accompany these civilians to the crabbing grounds on the shore. They know where they're going, so just follow and protect, muskets ready, eyes and brains alert; watch the forest be-hind, ahead of, and beside you; spread out, no talk. Concentrate on the task, men. Protect and defend. And as I told you before, do not shoot at *anything* unless you know what you're shooting at *and* it's an immediate threat. And if you *do* shoot, reload quickly . . . and keep your matches lit. Questions?"

All five shook their heads.

"Master Howe, here are your escorts. Are you and your men ready?"

"That we are, Sergeant. Thank you. This way, gentlemen." He point-ed at a pathway into the forest, then waved goodbye to young George and Thomas Colman, who were busy attaching bundles of reeds to the cottage sides and roof. He also waved at Emily, who was talking with her pregnant friend, Elyoner. "Ladies, ready yourselves for a feast of fresh crab this night."

Emily waved back. "I shall, Master Howe. I taste them already. Good luck."

Twenty minutes later, the crabbers emerged from the forest, proceeded to the water's edge. Removing his shoes and knee socks, Howe said, "This is the place. Let's spread out and cover these shallows . . . over here." He pointed to the south where an expanse of serene water stretched at least 500 yards. A hundred yards to the north, a point of land protruded into the sound blocking the view in that direction. Always curious, Howe decided to crab his way toward the point and then go around it to see what the prospects were on its north side. Each man carried two canvas bags, one slung over each shoulder, as well as a four-foot-long forked stick to hold the crabs against the sea floor while grabbing them from behind with the other hand. Each pair of bags would hold twenty or thirty crabs and was thick enough to prevent the crabs from pinching through the sides. While the soldiers positioned themselves along the tree line, the other men removed their socks and shoes, spread down the shoreline to the south until there was enough space between them to avoid interfering with one another. They then waded into the water, taking care not to lay a bare foot on one of the strong-clawed creatures scurrying around the sandy bottom. The harvest was immediately bountiful, the men touting their success and bragging to one another with every catch.

After a half hour, George Howe had worked his way to the north point. He had taken ten crabs, but the productivity was less than he'd expected; he wanted to do better, couldn't bear the thought of one of the other men outdoing the chief crabber. He looked toward the forest, saw that the closest soldier was about a hundred and fifty yards away at the edge of the tree line, his eyes watching the forest as Myllet had instructed. Howe decided to tell the man he was going around the point for a few moments to see what was there and check the crabbing prospects. He didn't want to yell—the others were making too much noise as it was—so he started wading toward the soldier. After a few steps he decided it wasn't worth the effort, turned back toward the point. He'd only be out of sight for a few minutes, wouldn't be missed in so short a time; he could quickly return to the point and summon the entire party if the crabbing looked promising.

The water on the other side of the point was perfect crab habitat, even better than to the south. A thick blanket of chest-high reeds spread from the forest's edge to about fifty yards into the water. Howe grinned with delight as he saw crab after crab scramble through the reeds to avoid his feet. This is heaven, he thought, as he adjusted his sacks and went to work. The crabs were harder to see among the reeds, but Lord in heaven, there were a lot of them.

After a half hour, he had nearly filled both bags, had been thinking about young George and Emily, hoping in his heart that fate *would* bring them together. A finer lass he'd never seen, and the thought of them together as husband and wife sometime in the future warmed his heart, inspired him to sing his favorite tune, the one composed by King Henry the Eighth himself.

> *Pastime with good company*
> *I love and shall until I die*
> *Grudge who lust but none deny*
> *So God be pleased thus live will I*
> *For my pastance*
> *Hunt, sing, and dance*
> *My heart is set*
> *All goodly sport*
> *For my comfort*
> *Who shall me let*

"Come here, you little blighter," he said as he missed his third attempt to pin an elusive crab to the bottom. He succeeded on the fourth attempt, dropped the crab into the bag, then continued his song.

> *Youth must have some dalliance*
> *Of good or ill—*

He heard a curt buzzing sound pass his ear like a locust flying by, heard it again, but this time felt a sharp sting and a hard, forward kick in the back of his thigh, then searing pain like a severe cramp. He reached his hand behind the leg, felt the arrow shaft sticking out, the warm blood running down the back of his leg. "My God, I'm shot." He started to turn; another arrow ripped into his lower back, sliced through his stomach and four inches out the front of his belly. "Ooohh!" He looked down at the bloody arrow point, saw warm blood and stomach fluids soaking his shirt; staggered to the right; another arrow ripped through his left bicep, lodged in the ribs, pinning the arm to his side. He turned toward the shore and stumbled two steps forward, wondered why the soldiers weren't there. Another arrow hit his left shoulder, stuck in the bone with awful pain.

He cried out, but the sound vanished in his throat; he fell to his knees, looked down at the water, thought how distorted and pale his reflection was; started crawling toward the shore, wondered if he was dying. A fifth arrow cut into the top of his right shoulder just inside the collar bone, tore deep into his chest behind the front ribs. He gasped for air, none came; felt himself weakening, growing dizzy, disoriented; thought how much he loved his son, begged God to care for him; wondered what the gurgling noise was, who the people approaching him were, prayed they were soldiers. An icy chill shuddered through his torso as an arrow tore through his throat. He felt himself being dragged through the water, then onto the shore; felt a strange darkness envelope him; heard someone moan as he felt himself dumped on the ground, rolled onto his back; felt the numb thunk of more arrows piercing his stomach, couldn't breathe. Complete darkness enshrouded him, but it quickly yielded to a strange white light. He watched it grow brighter and brighter, felt himself drifting toward it, his pain gone, a light, airy feeling flooding his senses; saw his wife in the light, her arms open to embrace him. And as the Panther's stone war club smashed into the left the side of his head, imploding his skull and splattering his brains and blood onto the sand, he embraced her, held her to his breast, felt the light's glowing warmth surround him.

Another Savage crushed the back of the head, delivered another blow and another until the head was but a pile of red goo. The three

Savages then shot one arrow apiece into his genitals, dragged him into the brush, and slipped away into the forest.

***

As she dashed for the bathroom, the contents of Allie's stomach rose to her throat, driveled between her fingers into the palm of her other hand. After what seemed like an hour of gut-wrenching heaves, she wiped her hands and face with a wad of tissues. "My God," she moaned between rapid breaths. "That poor man . . . what they did to him." She hovered over the toilet for a few more minutes, then swallowed a drink of water, washed her face and hands. Still shaken, she walked slowly back to the bedroom, sat on the bed, then leaned forward and lowered her face to her hands. God, what a nightmare . . . so real . . . but it *wasn't* a nightmare; it was that same dream, same people . . . but later on, like a story that keeps moving. "What the hell's happening to me?" This is impossible. She shook her head slowly back and forth as she raised it upright. Never seen anyone die before . . . blood, brains. She paused her thoughts, covered her mouth as a dry heave rose from the pit of her stomach to her throat, hung there like a bag of lead. It was like I was there . . . felt his thoughts, his pain . . . saw the light, his wife. My God, what's happening to me? She threw her pillow across the room, stared out the window. Can't go on like this.

CHAPTER 4

Emily sat on a canvas tarp on the floor beside George, her knees pulled up beneath her chin, silently watched him in the shadowy light of the cottage. Her feet were bare, and she wore only her linen smock with the front untied and open to the top of her breasts. The faint light of two nearby candles flickered hauntingly on her face. George sat cross-legged, hands in his lap, back slightly hunched, staring without expression or sound at the dark wall by the doorway. Emily grasped George's hand, studied his face with misty, empathetic eyes. *My poor, poor friend, how my heart cries for you. Such a man, such a father. I must help you; somehow I must help you.* "Hear me, George, answer me." She rubbed her eyes then closed them. *Lord, please tell me what to do.*

Then, like a leaf floating slowly but inevitably down a meandering stream, Emily's mind drifted back to the terror of that horrible night: she and George had been in the cottage, cringing at the frequent crashes of nearby thunder, water pouring through the unfinished roof, drenching them in spite of the small canvas tarps they held over their heads. The other crabbers had noticed George Howe missing just before dusk when the storm broke, and most of the men in the colony were still out searching, calling for him. Fearing the worst, John White had ordered young George to stay behind, which had sat poorly with him. He had been unable to calm himself, worn a pale, frightened look that revealed unspeakable fears. Finally, he had stood, said, "Em, I must go," then walked out the door. Emily had raced into the downpour behind him, called futilely to him to stay, then shaken her head and jogged after him.

The heavy rain had thickened the deepening darkness to an opaque curtain in every direction, forcing them to keep a slow, cautious pace as they started down the trail the search party had taken. They had gone but a hundred yards when they heard voices, saw a glimmer of dim torchlight ahead, quickened their pace. Two minutes later they had encountered a group of men with torches, seen that several at the rear carried a tarp with something heavy in it. The men had stopped as George and Emily approached; a flash of lightning had illuminated Thomas Colman's pallid face. "George, go back."

Emily had grabbed his arm with both hands. "George, don't go there."

He had pulled away, moved forward into Colman's waiting grasp, twisted free, shoved his way through the men to the tarp, which now lay on the ground. There in the mud and rain, the faltering torchlight had illuminated a man with an unrecognizable, crushed, bloody head, his body riddled with arrows. His clothes had identified him as George Howe.

Emily had turned away, stepped into the brush, retched. Young George had momentarily stared down at his father in grim silence then fallen into the catatonic state that had gripped him like a vice ever since. He had stared at his father's shrouded corpse all night and not attended his burial the next day, then sat in the same spot, taking nothing but an occasional sip of water, for two days. Emily had been beside him most of that time, unable to reconcile her own grief and unable to console him or coax him from his stupor. She had spoken to him several times, tried to inspire a reply, but he had held both his trance and his silence. Finally, she lifted his hand, kissed it, held it to her breast, stared at him through sudden tears, questioned his expressionless face with pleading eyes. "I miss you, George. Come back to me. Be with me again."

Thomas Colman had silently watched his daughter from the other side of the room for over an hour. He sat on one of the four makeshift beds, crafted of dried grass stuffed and stitched into a rectangular canvas bag that was long, wide, and thick enough to hold an adult off the ground. In addition to the beds, the room held a crudely lashed stick

table and four stump stools, each an eighteen-inch-long, sawed-off segment of a twelve-inch-diameter log. A wool blanket hung from a rope
across a back corner to make a private place to change clothes or use
the close stool when going outside was not practical. Foodstuffs were
stacked on another lashed-stick table that stood three feet above the
ground next to two buckets of water in the other rear corner; and a
damp, stale, smoky smell permeated everything in the room. Until that
moment, Emily had not moved or spoken, had remained as motionless
as George, held his hand, waited patiently for a change, as she studied
his face.

Colman rose, walked to Emily's side, sat beside her. He wrapped his
right arm around her shoulder, tenderly pulled her to his side. Laying
his other hand gently on her cheek, he eased her head to his chest in
a comforting embrace. She spread her arms around him and held him
with all her strength, trembling as pent-up tears filled her eyes.

Several minutes passed before Emily settled to an occasional sniffle
and Colman said, "Emily, 'tis horrible what's happened . . . horrible
for all of us, for what it means to our future; but far more horrible
for young George, for he was already deeply wounded by his mother's
death." He grimaced, shook his head. "This additional loss would surely
undo him, Em, if he did not have you for a friend. Forsooth, I think you
alone can save him, and 'tis certain he'll need you now more than before, for he feels your strength. 'Tis your mother's strength, you know."
He caressed her cheek. "But I think your strength is perhaps greater
than hers—definitely greater than mine—I've admired it your entire
life. Nothing deters you from doing what is right, and . . . and your
father is very proud of you."

Emily closed her eyes, saw her mother's face, instinctively reached
for her locket, then realized her apron lay across the room by her clothes.

"Dear daughter, I cannot know what this event means for the colony
in the long term, but it gives me pause today . . . pause to wonder if we
made the right decision in coming here. George's loss may be only an
isolated incident, or it may be the beginning of a desperate struggle for
survival. I know not which, but either way, I fear I've placed us—you es-

pecially—in a circumstance that may be beyond our ability to control. And for that I am deeply sorry."

She looked up at his face, saw the candlelight reflected in his tortured eyes. "Father, you owe me no apology. I'm a grown woman, and I made my *own* choice to come here with you." She rubbed the remaining tears from her eyes. "I could have said no, but I didn't. And now it appears we're to remain here, unless, of course, we relocate ourselves somewhere. So, in fact, we've no choice but to persevere and face what comes . . . together. I love you, Father." She laid her head on his chest, snuggled in close, and tightened her arms around him.

"And I, you, dear Emily." He held his embrace, glanced at George. "Isn't it strange how the pain of others can bring people closer together?" He stared at the fire. "Em, I've seldom told you how much I love you and how proud I am of you, and I'm ashamed for that. Nor have I held you close as often as I should have." He tightened his embrace. "Like I did when you were a little girl. Fathers should never stop hugging their little girls, even when they become big girls, and my failure to do so shames me now. Why, if I were to die suddenly like poor George, without first holding you, I . . . I'd be most upset with myself in the hereafter . . . were I fortunate enough to find myself there." He smiled to himself. "You know, your mother—"

"Hello . . . Emily?" A female voice called from outside the cottage door.

Emily released her father. "Elyoner, come in."

A ripely pregnant woman about twenty-three years old waddled through the doorway. Colman rose, lifted a stump stool, and set it beside Emily. "Good evening, Elyoner."

"Good evening, Thomas . . . Emily." Elyoner was slightly taller than Emily, with a pink complexion and kind, loving, brown eyes. A green ribbon gathered her blonde, shoulder-length hair loosely behind her neck, highlighted her slightly prominent forehead. While she was not particularly attractive, her face radiated the warm glow of imminent motherhood, which gave her a calm, gentle look. "How's George?" She sat down on the stump, using both hands to support the baby in her womb.

"No change," Emily said. "And I've no idea what to do to help him either. Master Jones was by and said he'd seen such cases before but knew no treatment other than time. So I guess we wait."

Colman interrupted. "Elyoner, is Ananias at your cottage?"

"Yes, he is. He just returned from the Assistants' meeting with Father a short time ago, and he's full of news and opinions. So I'm sure he'd enjoy a visit."

"Very well. I'll be off then." Colman stood, nodded his respects to the ladies, then walked out the door.

Elyoner studied George with a compassionate look, shook her head back and forth several times. "Such a pity . . . poor man. Father said both of you saw the body. I can't imagine the horror of it."

"We did. And *horror* does not describe what we saw. Elyoner, it was unimaginably grotesque to see so kind and gentle a man brutalized in that manner. I puked my insides, and you see what it did to George. Truly, I don't know how one human being could do that to another . . . but then I think of the depredations Lane's men committed against the Savages last year. Back and forth it goes, and good souls on both sides are in the middle. You're aware, aren't you, that Manteo told me everything about the earlier expedition, on the ship?" She raised her eyebrows in anticipation.

"I am. Father told me . . . and strangely, you probably know far more than I about those earlier times, for he's kept me blind to such ugly events."

Emily smiled. "I'm sure the governor wasn't very happy with me that first night. Did he tell you of my impudence in asking him a rather embarrassing question in front of my father and Master Howe? His face turned so red I thought it was going to burst into flames. Rather stupid of me, it was." She chuckled philosophically, more to herself than to Elyoner.

"Well, in spite of your question, Father admires your spunk and calmed himself rather quickly. He has much on his mind these days."

Emily nodded. "I'm certain of that . . . Elyoner, I have George on *my* mind. Please tell me how to help him. I want so to bring him back, but . . ."

"I've no ideas, Emily. You're giving him a friend's love, and right now, I don't think there's anything else that can be done. You seemed to have a rather close relationship before this happened . . . at least I saw you together often."

"I fear he's quite infatuated, perhaps in love with me."

"And you?"

"I'm not sure. Actually, that's not altogether true. I care strongly for him, but as a dear friend, not romantically . . . yet I often wonder if . . . if in spite of our age difference, it might someday be otherwise. But I've no idea how things will be between us when he revives. Father thinks he'll need me more than before, and I guess, if that's true, his love will become deeper still. I honestly can't say how I'll feel . . . or how I'll react. But what I *can* say is that I'd give my life to save his."

Elyoner touched Emily's cheek, gave her an understanding smile. "That says much, Emily Colman." After a brief silence, she said, "And Master Tayler . . . he too appears quite drawn to you. Do you care for him?" Elyoner immediately shook her head. "Forget I asked that, Em. 'Tis not my business."

Emily smiled. "No. I don't mind talking about it, Ellie. You're my close friend—my close, *older, wiser* friend—and I value your opinion on any subject. So to answer your question, yes, I *do* care for him, though, as you know, he's considerably older than I. He's amusing and witty but can also be very serious. He's suffered difficult times, and I think there's yet much to learn about him. However, I like what I've seen so far and want to see more. Do you know him?"

"Only that he comes from a wealthy family and . . . well, I've heard some idle rumors, but I pay no attention to such. I prefer to be my own judge."

"What have you heard?" Emily raised an expectant eyebrow.

"I'm sorry, Em, I shouldn't have said anything. I really don't believe any of us should go around talking rumors. The colony's too small, and it will inevitably foster bad feelings we can ill afford."

"Very well." The two then sat in silence, watching George, until Emily spoke in a measured tone. "Elyoner, are you afraid?"

Elyoner looked flatly into Emily's eyes. "Emily, I'm terrified . . . terrified for myself, for Father, for Ananias, and especially for this little one here inside me." She patted her belly. "What happened to Master Howe changed everything. Before, we knew we were in the wrong place and that it *might* turn out to be unfriendly, but now we know death may strike at any moment. That makes a big difference: it means we can never relax and must be ever watchful. That's *not* how I want to live my life."

"Nor I."

"I assume you heard about the Assistants' meeting this afternoon? I'm told quite a few men besides the Assistants were there and voiced opinions."

"I was here with George, but I heard the shouting."

"Well, there were many cries for retaliation against the Savages, and quite a number of men were ready to man the shallops and row to the mainland to attack them that very moment. Father said he, Ananias, and Roger Baylye spoke against such action. Actually, your friend, Master Tayler, to his credit, was another calming voice."

Emily nodded twice. "Good to hear."

"As Father points out, retaliation is a rather foolish notion for several reasons. First, the Savages reside on the main; second, we've far fewer soldiers than Lane had; and third, the Savages surely watch us day and night, which makes surprise rather difficult. Another problem is that we don't know for certain where their village is. Father knows where it *was*, a year ago, after they left the island, but that knowledge isn't worth much now. So about the only opportunity for surprise would be a night attack, where the rowers could see the Savages' fires and row toward them. But if the village is inland and not visible from the water, that won't work either."

"So what are we going to do? We can't just sit here and wait for the next attack."

"No, we can't. So tomorrow, Father's taking a few Assistants and soldiers, and Manteo, to Manteo's village, down the Sound, to give them gifts and to parley. He wants to assure them of our friendship and persuade them to show us how they hunt and fish and preserve meat and fish. He also wants them to help us befriend the other nearby tribes. That was a mouthful! I need a breath."

Emily held a pewter cup of water to George's lips. "Well, as much as I miss Master Howe and detest the brutality of his murder, I think we must find peace with these people or perish. So your father's plan seems a good beginning, even though 'tis with a different tribe than killed Master Howe."

"You sense much for your years, Emily Colman. I—" Elyoner tensed, clutched her stomach. "Huuh . . . huuh . . . huuh!" She took a deep breath.

"Elyoner, are you well?"

She moaned as the air seeped slowly from her lungs. "I . . . I think so." Her face suddenly paled; sweat beaded her forehead.

Emily quickly stood while tying the top of her smock, then slipped into her shirt and pulled on her skirt. She put her arms around Elyoner to steady her. "You don't look good. Come, we're going to find Agnes."

Elyoner took another deep breath, let it ease out slowly to relax the tautness in her cheeks. "I think this little rascal . . . huuh . . . wants to see the world soon." She stood with Emily's help, and the two shuffled toward the door.

* * *

John White stood with his Assistants and Manteo at the meeting place on the shore. He had not wanted to risk another debacle instigated and enflamed by eavesdroppers, such as had occurred the previous day when they had met in the village. So they had returned to the earlier, more private meeting place; and as he had instructed, each man held a musket or a stout English longbow at his side, and most carried a sword and dagger at the waist. As before, four soldiers formed a wide semicircle around the group, while the water provided security to the rear.

White fidgeted with his mustache as he anguished over what information to relay first. Several of them already knew the results of the meeting with Manteo's people, and he surmised they had already told the others; so he hardened himself for an uproar, decided to proceed in the order things had transpired.

"Gentlemen, as some of you know, we had a most fruitful meeting with Manteo's people this morning. After they recognized Manteo, they greeted us warmly and provided us a most pleasing feast. We then offered them gifts and set about convincing them that we want nothing but their friendship and help in teaching us their methods of living here. They agreed to help us but asked that we provide them a badge of recognition so we won't mistake them for some other, perhaps unfriendly people. I must tell you that their request is well founded, for precisely the situation they fear occurred with Lane, and several of Manteo's people were wounded. Most recovered, but one remains crippled and unable to walk, which greatly burdens my mind and heart. So I agreed to provide them such means of recognition when they arrive here tomorrow. But more on that in a moment." The rare absence of protest encouraged him, emboldened him to broach the unpleasant news.

"We also learned that the Savages who reside on the main directly across from the island are the ones who killed George Howe and murdered our two soldiers last year. They further informed us that the thirteen men who survived last year's attack frantically rowed their boat to some unknown place. So, they may yet be alive and waiting for us to find them."

Several Assistants commenced an undercurrent of whispers that quickly spread through the assembly.

"These Savages are the very ones Lane attacked here on this island and whose headman he killed, and I must point out that this occurred *before* the murders of our two soldiers and George Howe. I say this so you may understand that the Savages' actions against us have not been without provocation."

The whispers diminished to a fragile silence as Thomas Stevens stepped forward. "John, I understand that Lane probably angered these Savages, but that was long ago and certainly no justification for George Howe's murder. *We've* done *nothing* to provoke them. So what action do you propose to deter further attacks against us? Truly, man, we cannot live like this indefinitely: carrying weapons and taking soldiers everywhere we go. 'Tis simply not practical on an extended basis. By and by, a man needs a good, quiet moment of reflection alone in the forest, while he does his business, if you know what I mean."

A burst of laughter erupted from the group. White grinned.

"I *do* know what you mean, Tom, and I share your view . . . most definitely I share your view. To that purpose, I asked Manteo's mother, the leader of their people, to contact the other tribes in our vicinity and summon them to a meeting with us here tomorrow when the sun is overhead. We'll bestow gifts on all who attend, as well as assurances of friendship, and we shall then ask them for their friendship and assistance in return." He assumed a somber but determined look. "We shall also use this opportunity to impress them with our progress on the palisades, and our strength. So I want every man to be present in the gathering place and in possession of every weapon he owns: swords, daggers, muskets, longbows, even hammers and axes. If we had more ammunition, I'd also demonstrate our muskets to remind them of our firepower. But with George Howe gone and his son in a stupor, we're without a foundry to cast ammunition for a time. We might, instead, demonstrate the power of an English longbow and perhaps show them a little swordsmanship. We want them to know that any attack against us will be met with force and cost them dearly."

"And what," William Willes asked, "will we do if George Howe's murderers do not come to your meeting. What do you intend to do to punish them for what they did and deter them from doing it again?"

That was the question White had dreaded all day, hoped no one would ask; for he knew there was but one viable answer, and that answer was the one he most loathed giving—the promise of an action he had sworn never to allow. "If that happens, William"—he took a deep breath—"we shall have no choice but to attack and punish them."

Most nodded agreement. Roger Baylye and a few others did not, instead looked gravely at one another then back at White, whose eyes blinked with uncertainty as he spoke. "But though I've said that, I do not wish it, and indeed, gravely fear the consequences such an action will most assuredly provoke. We are not strong; our existence is fragile and our soldiers untested. And even though I am not a soldier, I can see that such an action could unleash a chain of unintended events that culminates in our annihilation." He shook his head. "And we must, therefore, exhaust every possibility for peace before we allow that chain of misfortunes to begin."

Baylye slowly, methodically clapped his hands together. Three others joined him. "John, you speak wisely." He looked from man to man. "Gentlemen, if we take such an action, we will surely endanger our own existence. I do not know these people we speak of, and I do not know their intentions toward us. But I think we must conceive another course of action toward them—one that can produce the end we seek without threatening our lives and those of our families."

After a long silence, Stevens, who had a red, angry face, shouted, "God's teeth, John, we must teach the Savages a lesson!"

Willes said, "Aye, a strong, ruthless attack would eliminate them as a threat to the colony and send a clear message to any others contemplating trouble. To hell with your meeting, John."

White's insides churned. He knew Baylye was right but also knew the wheels of regrettable fortune had begun to turn. "Gentlemen, I implore you to aid me in finding a way to obtain peace without more bloodshed. But I reluctantly concede such a course will be difficult to conceive and more difficult to implement. So, let us pray these Savages join the others here tomorrow and that we convince them to end the bloodshed and conclude a viable, lasting peace with us."

"But John," Stevens said, "even if they come and agree with your proposal, how will we punish them for George Howe's murder, and how will we ensure they keep their word?"

"Thomas, in all candor, after my experiences here with Lane, I'm far more worried about us keeping *our* word than I am about the Savages keeping theirs."

* * *

Emily rubbed her sleeve across her sweaty brow, bent and scooped a ladle of water from the bucket at her feet, gulped it down. She picked up two pieces of firewood and laid them on the fire that burned ten feet in front of her cottage. The fire had combined with the intense heat and humidity of the day to soak her clothes with perspiration, smear sweaty soot all over her face, and make her appreciate how much more pleasant candle-making was on a cool day in England.

A large, black metal pot about two feet in diameter sat on the fire, supported by a circle of rocks, open on one side, that held the pot about ten inches off the ground and left room for new logs to be added when needed. The pot held over twelve inches of melted animal fat, while a barrel of solid fat, for replenishing the melting pot, sat several feet away. The fat barrel had been brought from England to sustain their candle-making needs until an adequate supply of local fat could be accumulated.

Emily picked up a sixteen-inch-long stick that had eight, evenly spaced, twelve-inch-long strings tied to it; and each string, from the tie point on the stick to its low, dangling end, was a partially completed candle. Holding the stick horizontally, one end in each hand, so the eight partial candles hung vertically toward the ground, she walked to the pot, checked to see that her skirt was clear of the flames, then slowly dunked the candles in and out of the fat four or five times to allow more to adhere to them. She then carried the stick to the drying rack five feet away, set the ends on two parallel, five-foot-long branches that were twelve inches apart and supported at each end by the four log stump stools from inside the cottage. Six sticks, each holding eight candles, already sat on the drying rack; she lifted the driest of them, took it to the pot for another dunking. She'd been at it for nearly three hours, and her fifty-six candles were nearly complete—one more round for each stick and the job would be done.

What a pity they smelled so bad when you burned them, she thought, though a person got used to it after a while. Fortunately, Governor White had shown Emily and a few others the plentiful bay-berry bushes that thrived all over the island. He had told them how the berries, which ripened in the fall, could be boiled in water to separate their wax, which then floated to the surface where it could be skimmed off, congealed, and added to the previous skimmings until enough was collected to make several melting pots of wax that could be re-melted for candle dipping. He had also mentioned that bayberry candles had a pleasing aroma; so Emily now had another reason to be eager for fall, the first being relief from the stifling, relentless heat and humidity.

As she placed the stick of candles on the drying rack and lifted the next, Hugh Tayler and John Bridger slid a log into the palisades trench about seventy-five feet from Emily's cottage, butted it up against the adjoining log, and held it in place while two other men deposited and set the next log. After Tayler and Bridger released their log and started back to the forest for another, Tayler veered toward Emily, waved at her, and called out. "Emily, Emily Colman."

She looked up from the drying rack, wiped her sweaty brow with her sleeve, then replied with a broad smile and a wave of her hand. "How fares Hugh Tayler this day?"

"At the top of his form and eager for more work. And what of the colony's foremost candle maker?"

"She's hot, sweating in an unladylike manner, and ready for a rest. When will you have a break?"

"One more log. May I visit you then?"

"You must ask my father first." She tried to look serious, but a slight smirk formed on her lips, then bloomed into a full smile.

"Where is he?"

"On the other side of the island."

Tayler assumed a pitifully sad look. "Mistress Emily, you wound me."

"Very well, then come and see me, Master Hugh! But put another log or two in the ground first, for I've more candles to finish before I can dally."

"Very well. I shall return; and I hope your candle making will be complete, for I will *not* sit by that fire on this hot day."

"Fear not, Sir."

Emily smiled to herself as she watched Tayler quicken his pace to catch up with Bridger, then dipped another stick of candles into the pot.

Twenty minutes later, Tayler approached Emily's cottage as she lifted the heavy melting pot from the fire.

"Emily, let me do that." He took the pot from her. "Where do you want it?"

"Over there." She pointed at the barrel of congealed fat. "Many thanks. I'm weary of bending."

"At your service. And where's Master Colman today?"

"He's with the others transporting the last of the equipment and baggage from the ship. 'Twill be most pleasant to have all the things we brought, especially the cooking wares; but"—her look suddenly saddened—"but the arrival of the last of our belongings brings with it an ominous sense of finality and aloneness . . . a bit like the Queen's headsman raising his axe over someone's head after 'tis properly positioned on the block. It means we will, indeed, be abandoned here."

"Aye, 'tis a sobering thought, and your simile is distressingly accurate. When those ships sail away, we'll be completely cut off from civilization for who knows how long." He marveled at how, in spite of sweaty clothes, disarranged hair, and a soot-covered face, Emily looked ravishingly sensuous. She overwhelmed him with the urge to take her into the cottage and make wild, passionate love to her. How could she do that to him? But it wasn't just his passion she excited. No, it had become far more than that; for ever since their first conversation, each moment he was near her, heard her voice, held her hand, he felt intense flames of affection engulf his heart—flames he'd never before felt and could not control. "So how is young Master Howe? I heard he's having a difficult time—not surprisingly, of course—and . . . oh, by the bye, I must tell you, I feel like an utter fool for speaking down about the young lad the other day. I owe you an apology for that. 'Twas quite small of me, and I hope you'll forgive me."

She smiled. "I shall, Hugh. And you heard right. He's *not* faring well. I truly do not know what will become of him. 'Twas an awful experience . . . for me, as well. Master Howe was a kind and gentle man, my good friend, and to see him like that . . ." She rubbed sudden tears from her eyes then forced a slight smile. "And how go the palisades?"

"Forgive me for distressing you, Milady." He paused, studied her face for a moment. "The palisades advance . . . but very slowly. And John Wyles suffered an axe cut to his leg this morning. He and Peter Little were chopping on opposite sides of a large tree, and John moved around the tree toward Peter to get a better angle on his cut . . . and bad fortune arrived at exactly that moment. Peter's axe glanced off the trunk and cut through John's calf muscle all the way to the bone—a very ugly wound, a lot of blood, and certainly a lot of pain. 'Twill be a difficult one to heal, for it will want to fester. Haven't seen that much blood since the army."

Emily looked surprised. "You were in the army?"

"Yes, I was."

"Actually, I wondered about that, since so many in your circumstances *do* enter the officer corps. But I thought 'twas usually a career."

"Well, it normally is . . . I shall tell you the story. When my father died, both of my brothers became drunkards, and the estate was headed for the cemetery. I suppose it just happened gradually, but after a year, I was running the place while the brothers wallowed in wine and women. Things were actually going quite well for the estate, but my brothers spent the income faster than I could earn it, and eventually we found ourselves on hard times. I was exhausted, but they wanted me to *do* more so they could *spend* more; so I left, obtained a commission, and spent several years fighting Spaniards in various places, until in '85 I found myself fighting them in the Netherlands."

"I've heard 'twas a very bloody campaign."

" 'Twas indeed. And on the first of July of that year I was on a mission to rescue a large group of our troops that been trapped by the enemy. I was with my commander and forty men." He paused, looked away from her.

"Hugh, don't tell this if it upsets you. My God, here I am again asking someone a painful question. I'm not asking any more questions."

"It *does* upset me, Emily, but I can't lock it away in a box." He paused. "So somehow, they knew we were coming and ambushed and slaughtered us like pigs in a corral. Most of the men were killed outright; and my commander was badly wounded, shot from his horse." He paused again.

"And you?"

"I took a bullet in the shoulder, which knocked me off my horse, as well; but the horse stayed beside me, as did my commander's. The commander was barely conscious, but I was able to shove him up onto the saddle and get the reins into his hands and send him off toward our lines. But then because of my shoulder wound, it took me a long time to get *myself* back in the saddle, and just as I finally settled there, another shot hit me in the hip."

"Your limp."

He nodded. "Well, I leaned forward on the horse's neck and spurred him on with great urgency until I was out of musket range. Then as I approached our lines, I passed out and again fell from the saddle."

Emily cupped her hand over her mouth.

"A number of our troops rushed out and dragged me to safety and deposited me in hospital."

"And did your commander live?"

"He did; he was already in the hospital when I arrived."

"And quite grateful, I'm sure? He should have had you decorated."

"Well, he was, and he did. But unfortunately, I couldn't walk for a year and wore a sling on the bad arm for nine months; so the army discharged me, and now I'm here with you with an interesting story to tell."

"Hugh, I'd no idea. You're certainly mum and humble about it. Did you want to remain in the army?"

"Indeed, but, Emily"—he took her hands in his, looked into her eyes—"had I not come here, I would never have met you, and meeting you is the most wonderful thing that's happened in my entire life."

A sudden blush glowed through the soot on her cheeks. "You're embarrassing me again. I'm but a common, ordinary English girl, nothing more."

"English, yes . . . common, by birth only. But ordinary? No, not in a thousand years."

"Now I'll blush again, thank you."

"You're already blushing, and it makes you even more beautiful."

She hid her face in her hands.

"Do you know that I watched you every day on the ship and racked my mind to understand why you're not married to some lord? And if not a lord, at least a country nobleman?"

Her heart tremored. "My mother told me to never talk to men, especially older ones." An impish smile appeared on her lips. "And Father enforced Mother's wish; so I've never been allowed to talk to men, and I'm therefore unable to trust them."

"Emily, that's inhumanely cruel and unfair to the men of England!"

She thought how she enjoyed their gentle teasing, his easy company, savored the strange new warmth that sometimes spread from her head to her shoulders and down her back when they talked. "And what else did you do while you were on the ship, Hugh Tayler?"

"I spent many minutes watching you lean over the side looking for fish."

She laughed as she covered her lips with her hand. "I *wish* I'd been looking for fish. Now you're *truly* embarrassing me."

"Well, the reason I saw you was because I was on the other side of the ship doing the same thing you were."

She laughed again. "Actually, now that you mention it, I *do* remember seeing you on the deck a lot . . . and by the bye, looking rather pale."

"At your service, Mistress. But 'tis true, I did wonder about you . . . and I'm very glad you're *not* married to a lord or country nobleman. Very glad indeed." He again held her hands, stared into her eyes with a deep, searching gaze, which she met with a steady, piercing look that bored into his soul.

As her breathing and heartbeat quickened, a warm twinge of alarm settled in her mind, alerted her to a sudden, unfamiliar cleft in her emotional control.

After a long hesitation, he blinked then smiled. "I saw you helping the governor's daughter to her cottage last night. How does she fare?"

"She's well, for 'twas only a false labor . . . and such matters are not to be discussed with men." She smiled. "But at that moment, both of us were quite certain her time was at hand. And then it took me considerable time to locate Agnes Sampson, who's to be her midwife. So we were in a bit of a twitter for a while."

"I can imagine. And Mistress Harvie is also due soon?"

She nodded. "It could be any time now, for both of them. Actually the two of them have a wager on who will be first. Agnes thinks 'twill be Elyoner, but who knows."

"Well, I'm glad I won't be there. Too much pain for me, from what I've heard."

Emily glanced toward a sudden clamor at the far edge of the village. "Hugh, look. Governor White and the Assistants are returning. Perhaps they've good news."

Tayler's eyes remained fixed on Emily. "Emily, might you and I walk together one day away from the village and all the eyes that spy on us when we talk?"

She wanted to say yes but knew her father would be unlikely to permit it even though he encouraged their relationship. 'Twas simply too soon, and too unconventional for Thomas Colman, even in a remote colony. "I'd enjoy that, Hugh, but with Savages about, I fear it won't happen soon. And of course, you *would* have to ask Father's permission."

"Ah, yes. The harsh realities of English decorum. Then perhaps an evening stroll around the village?"

A loud bell clanged at the gathering place in the center of the village, summoning all inhabitants. As people began to walk toward the spot, John White climbed on top of a large stump, motioned his Assistants to gather around him.

* * *

Emily, again in her smock, sat on her bed, leaned close to the candle that sat on a small stump beside the bed. Her father and George were asleep. She had read her mother's letter three times, and it now sat on her lap as she visualized her mother's face in the darkness of her closed eyes, saw her rocking her baby brother in her arms. *Mother, I so wish you could be here to guide me. I've told you about George . . . but I'm still quite uncertain about how it will be when he revives. Please help me know what to do . . . and I have something else to tell you. I'm growing quite fond of Hugh Tayler.* She wondered what Elyoner had been about to tell her about him the night before. *As you know, he's much older than I; and even though I'm well practiced at conversing with older men, he sometimes unbalances me, gives me feelings I've not had before. A few times I've even felt a little muddled in the head, and . . . and no, I'm not worried, and I will remain strong and save myself for none but my husband, whoever he may be. Yes, 'tis not inconceivable that it could be Hugh, or perhaps under the right circumstances even George . . . if he recovers . . . but 'tis impossible to say now . . . with either of them.*

She reached over to her apron, which lay folded beneath her clothes a few inches away, removed her black locket, held it to the candle, and read *MC* and *1587* engraved on the back. As a thin mist dampened her eyes, she squeezed the sides of the locket. A small stem popped out of one end. She rotated it a full counterclockwise turn, half a clockwise turn, then pushed it inward. The top of the locket popped open, revealing a folded lock of brown hair the size of her little finger. She removed the hair, stared at it for a moment, then held it to her lips. Tears rolled down her cheeks as she whispered, "Mother, please come to us soon. I need you. Father needs you. I love you." Her gaze lingered for a moment before she replaced the lock of hair, snapped the lid closed, and returned the locket to her pocket. She then placed the candle on the floor in the center of the room, lay down on her bed, and softly cried herself to sleep.

* * *

As the sun approached the treetops, Lieutenant Waters and most of his men sat near the palisades, their weapons beside them; most civilians sat immediately inside their open cottage doors, ready to assemble at a moment's notice when the Savages arrived. Ten soldiers, muskets in hand, guarded the approaches to the village. Governor White, Manteo, and all twelve Assistants sat under a canvas tarp held seven feet in the air by four corner poles tethered by rope guide lines tied to stakes in the ground. An assortment of gifts for the Savages, including glass beads, cloth, steel knives, hammers, and hatchets, lay in neat rows beside the shelter; while a stack of twelve-inch-long pieces of red cloth, for Manteo's people to tie around their wrists for identification, sat beside the gifts.

While White's plan for meeting with all the nearby Savages had received general approval, the day brought ever-rising anxiety and disappointment; for no Savage, even of Manteo's tribe, showed his face. At first he thought they were just late and would suddenly emerge from the forest later in the afternoon; but as the day wore on, he realized he was wrong, and a black fog of despair relentlessly crept into his mind. How could they ignore his offer, force him to take the terrible action he dreaded more than death itself, force him to repeat Lane's atrocities, violate his sense of humanity? Did they not know they were inviting their own deaths and destruction? How could they have so little regard for sense and logic? Indeed, the attack his men would soon mount against the Savages would completely destroy any hope of peace. He felt an icy chill on his neck, a horrible, overwhelming sense of foreboding; realized, yet again, that the vast numerical advantage held by the Savages could ultimately lead to but one outcome. He stared at the rows of gifts, drank a dipper of water from the bucket near his feet, and shook his head. While he fingered his beard, he scoured his mind for a way to avoid the attack, knew there was none.

When the Assistants began to whisper to one another, White beckoned Lieutenant Waters to join them. The civilians saw what was happening, emerged from their cottages, and gathered about ten yards outside the clump of Assistants. White knew how it would go, for Roger Baylye and the three Assistants who had supported him at yesterday's meeting, including his son-in-law, Ananias, stood together; while Willes, Stevens, and Sampson stood with the others. The soldiers remained by the palisades.

"My friends, I know many of you are as disappointed as I am about the failure of the Savages to come here today. The fact that *none* came, even Manteo's people, causes me to wonder if perhaps they misunderstood our proposal or the date or time at which they were expected."

Murmurs percolated through the men near Willes and Sampson.

White raised his voice. "And if they *did* misunderstand our intentions, how could they correctly communicate them to the other tribes? Manteo's people have always been our friends, and we've no reason to think they now feel otherwise."

Willes said, "John, we know you're against attacking George Howe's murderers, but what are you proposing? Surely you don't believe what you just suggested. My God, man, Manteo himself communicated the invitation."

" 'Tis true. But I also know something has happened to cause them not to come here today, and I think we must take every precaution to be certain of the circumstances before we resort to bloodshed."

Both Assistants and civilians, some with anger, others with contempt, shouted their opinions at one another.

Roger Baylye raised his hands to quiet the din. "Please, please. The governor's right. We don't want to start a war. We want to find a way to make and preserve peace, and I agree with John. We must make a greater effort to do so before we start something we may be unable to conclude. Do you not understand that we're alone and lack the force of Her Majesty's army to defend us? Think, men, think!"

"Master Baylye's right," Hugh Tayler said. Others voiced support for Baylye's plea but were outshouted by dissenters. White nodded his thanks to Baylye and Tayler then shook his head in despair.

William Willes raised both hands; the shouting tapered then subsided. "John, you made a promise yesterday. You told your Assistants and the entire colony that we would attack George Howe's murderers if the Savages did not come here today. Did you not make that promise?"

"Aye, I did, William, but—"

"Then you must keep it. We must attack and punish them."

Impassioned shouting exploded. White stared at the ground as if looking elsewhere would silence the tumult. He felt himself a traitor to his principles, but knowing he had no way out, finally raised his hands for silence. "We *will* attack, but 'twould be folly to simply charge off and do so without first conceiving a sensible military plan. Such planning is Lieutenant Waters' responsibility, and we should hear what he proposes." He nodded at Waters.

"The governor is correct. To attack haphazardly is to invite confusion and disaster. I will develop an attack plan and present it an hour after dark to Governor White and whoever he chooses."

All, including Willes, Stevens, and Sampson nodded agreement.

White said, "Very well, Lieutenant. We shall expect you in my cottage an hour after dark. Now, I suggest we end this gathering and proceed with our evening's affairs. It promises to be a long night."

***

Emily sat beside Elyoner, held her hand as she lay on her back panting. Her knees were bent up and outward, her legs spread apart, hair pulled back, face and smock soaked with sweat. She suddenly tensed, moaned, her features taut and pained; then slowly relaxed to a fearful, uncertain look, waited for the next contraction. Two buckets of water and a pile of rags sat nearby; and Jane Pierce and Agnes Sampson, whom Emily had summoned an hour before, stood several feet away watching, whispering to one another.

Agnes said, "They're getting closer. Won't be long now."

"I agree," Jane said as she walked over to Elyoner, lifted her smock, and looked beneath it. "Elyoner, you're nearly there. Perhaps an hour, perhaps a little less. Be strong, dear."

Elyoner tensed with another contraction. "Huuh! Huuh! Huuh! Ahhhh!" Her blanched fingers tightened on Emily's hand.

Emily shot a tense, worried look at Agnes.

"She's doing fine, lass. Doing fine . . . you, as well, Emily. Don't worry. Hold her tight; won't be long."

***

The shallop, carrying twenty-six men, cast off from the shore, glided into the darkness. As the rowers began pulling toward the main, White whispered, "Gently, men. Make no sound. We've plenty of time."

Manteo tapped White on the shoulder, pointed slightly left of the bow.

White nodded, then whispered to the helmsman, "Steer fifteen degrees left."

The man nodded as he eased the rudder to the new position.

White looked up at the stars that flooded the black sky, rehashed the evening meeting in his cottage: Manteo's reluctant agreement to guide them to the village; Waters' sound attack plan, his moral objections to executing it, followed by his dour acknowledgement that it was his duty to do so; Baylye's refusal to be part of it; Willes' and Stevens' eagerness to do the opposite; and his own persistent wish to be extricated from it altogether. As the water gently lapped at the sides of the boat, he thought of his daughter, envisioned her as a baby then as a child, was stunned that at that very moment she was giving birth to her own child. As he said a quick prayer, it struck him—the complete irony of a new birth occurring at the very moment other life would be taken away.

He shook his head in frustration and shame as he recalled when Lane had killed the leader of the people they were about to attack, beheaded him with his sword, placed the head on a pole in the center of the village. Not a night passed that, in his dreams, he didn't see Wingina's decomposing face, its half smile and questioning look that seemed to ask why he'd been treated so.

As the face faded, White's thoughts drifted to Lane's Chowanoc attack several months before he'd killed Wingina. Staring into the darkness, he saw the soldiers rushing from their boats, screaming at the Savages, firing their weapons, shooting arrows, swinging swords, killing at will. He again saw the three soldiers throw the beautiful woman to the ground, rip her clothes from her body, hold her down while each raped her in turn; saw one of them crush her head with the butt of his musket when they'd finished with her, then join others in killing her two children who lay but a few feet from her body. His stomach churned; he wanted to lean over the side and vomit but settled for squeezing the sides of the boat with both hands until they were numb.

Manteo tapped his shoulder, awakened him to his present anguish, pointed at dim firelight directly ahead, a little into the trees from the shore, and motioned to him to turn back to the right.

The helmsman saw Manteo's direction, immediately guided the boat to the new course. The attack plan called for approaching the Savages through the forest so they would be trapped with their backs to the water. The new course would take them to exactly the right spot to execute the plan.

***

Fifty miles to the north, the Panther lay beside his new wife, his eyes open and staring at the ceiling of his lodge. He'd just awakened from the dream that tormented him every night, soaked him in sweat as he again saw himself lying helpless and wounded on the ground, unable to move, watching the three soldiers rape his wife, kill her with a brutal blow to the head, then kill his sons before rushing off to kill others and torch the village. His hands clenched in unspoken rage; deliberate hate seethed in his heart; he promised his dead wife that before he left the earth he would do to a white woman what had been done to her. He rolled onto his side and gently caressed his sleeping wife's neck until he fell asleep.

* * *

Agnes pushed Elyoner's smock up above her waist for a better view, positioned a bundle of the rags under her to absorb the blood and afterbirth when they came.

"Huuh! Huuh! Huuh! Aaahhhhh! Hellllp me!" Elyoner's cold white hands squeezed Emily's hand on her left and Jane's on her right. "My God, hellllp me!"

Agnes shouted, "Breathe, Elyoner, breathe!"

"Huuh! Huuh! Huuh!"

"Now push!"

"Aaahhhhh! Going to die!" She spread her knees nearly flat to her sides, then up and back down again as if the motion would move the baby along its way.

"Breathe!"

"Huuh! Huuh! Huuh! Aaahhhhh! Make it come out!"

"I see the head . . . oh, dear Lord, 'tis a shoulder. The baby's breech. Must find the head."

"Huuh! Huuh! Huuh! Aaahhhhh!" Elyoner jerked her hands free from Emily and Jane, gripped her thighs, pulled herself up, flopped back, held her belly, tried to squeeze the baby out. "Aaahhhhh!"

Agnes shouted, "Don't let her do that. Hold her still!"

"Huuh! Huuh! Huuh! Aaahhhhh!"

Emily and Jane grabbed Elyoner's hands, pulled them back to her sides. Emily yelled, "Hold on, Ellie. Hold me tight. We'll get you through."

Agnes eased her fingers inside, gently slid them around, searching for the baby's head. "Keep pushing, Elyoner! Breathe!"

"Aaahhhhh! Huuh! Huuh! Huuh! Aaahhhhh! Caaaan't. Going to die!"

"Nay," Emily shouted. "Keep breathing. Trust Agnes. Don't quit!"

"Huuh! Huuh! Huuh! Aaahhhhh!"

* * *

The twenty-six men concealed themselves in the trees, about fifty yards from the village. Twenty-three Savages—men, women, and children—sat around a large fire talking, occasionally laughing. As the sky began to lighten, the men watched Waters, waited for the signal to attack.

* * *

Agnes panted, "There it is. I've found it. Now, come around, little one, and—"

Jane shouted, "Agnes, she's bleeding more. Hurry, dear!"

"Huuh! Huuh! Aaahhhhh! Please get it out!" Elyoner was pale as her smock, growing weak, her screams losing intensity; her head fell back on the bed. "I can't do it."

"You must!" Emily shouted. She leaned close to Elyoner's ear. "Do it! Do it! Keep working, Ellie. Push!"

"Huuh! Huuh! Faint. Huuh! Going to faint. Aaahhhhh!"

Agnes said, "I've got it, getting it straight. Almost there."

* * *

Waters raised his arm, thrust it toward the village. Blood-chilling cries rose from the concealments as the men charged the village. The stunned Savages leaped to their feet; women and children screamed as their men herded them toward the water and the thin cover of the reeds that grew there. A soldier fired at a woman with a baby on her back, swore as the shot missed. "You fool!" Waters screamed, "Can't you see that's a woman?" He bumped the weapon of another soldier aiming at the same woman.

Another soldier stopped, raised his musket, fired at a man helping a child toward the shore. The bullet tore through the man's middle, slapped him to the ground like a fallen tree; he jerked, writhed, gurgled, as blood filled his lungs.

Myllet shouted, "After them, men. Follow them into those reeds. Don't let them escape."

* * *

"There now. We're straight. I've got the head. Push again! Jane, Emily, keep on her. Don't let her leave us. Push, push."

"Aaahhhhh!"

"Here it comes, Elyoner. 'Tis on the way out. One more. One more. Keep pushing! Almost there!"

"Aaahhhhh!" Elyoner lifted her head, looked forward between her legs, then fell back on the bed, closed her eyes, melted into limp exhaustion.

"Yes. Yes." Agnes slid the baby out, cut its cord, held it upside down by its ankles. "Ah, a wee little lass, a pretty one, too. Look at that." She gave her two rapid swats on the rump, turned her quickly upright when she began to cry, wrapped her in a cloth, and handed her to Emily. Smiling radiantly, Emily cradled her for a moment before handing her to Jane and then helping Agnes with the afterbirth.

* * *

One of the Savages stopped, faced the soldiers. "John White! John White!" he shouted in rough English. "John White!" He ran toward White. Three soldiers aimed their muskets at him.

"Hold fire!" Manteo screamed. "Hold fire! These are *my* people. We've attacked *my* people, not your enemies. John, stop them! Stop them!"

* * *

Allie opened her eyes, blinked twice, focused on the ceiling. Lying still, she listened to her mind, her memory, let them take her on a journey through the events of her dream. My God! I just saw a baby being born . . . never seen that before. Lots of calves and foals, but never a real person. She remembered she'd been on a basketball trip when her high school health class watched the birth video, which had been the talk of the class for several days. She winced as she saw Elyoner writhing in pain, screaming for help—desperation, hopelessness, fear, at once racking and contorting her usually serene face—the lady groping to find the baby's head . . . a real live person being born . . . and I was there. But was it a real person? Why would I dream it, real or unreal? When was it . . . where was it? Good Lord, what's happening to me? So real—several dreams, same people, same story, goes on and on. The girl . . . Emily . . . she was there helping, first time for her too, scared . . . big smile when she held the baby. Allie smiled. Funny, but I felt her excitement and awe.

Then, like an amorphous bad memory that suddenly congeals into consciousness, the attack on the Indians appeared in her mind; she felt the anxiety, the fear, the frenzy. They shot that man, shot him in the lungs; he was breathing his own blood, suffocating . . . what a way to die . . . is there a good way? They're all gonna die, kill each other. Cruel, brutal people, all of them. But the leader didn't want to do it; he was there another time, saw another massacre when . . . oh my God, when they raped that Indian woman, killed her kids, crushed her head. Her stomach instantly rose toward her throat. They raped her right there on the ground, with people dying all around them. Her eyes misted. "This sucks! I don't want to dream anymore."

She closed her eyes, pictured Emily. I see her the most, like her a lot, feel close to her. But why? She searched the deepest recesses of her mind, wondered, probed, challenged her sense of reality. How can you feel close to someone in a dream, someone you don't even know, have never seen before? Maybe even someone in another time. Could that be? No, you can't do that . . . but I *do*. I think about her, feel her emotions deep inside me. Allie's eyes blinked open; a sudden shadow of fear swept across her face as a tide of foreboding flooded her mind, sent a tremor rippling through her body. I'm afraid for her. Something bad's going to happen. I know it. She noticed her hands had tightened into fists, relaxed them.

She rolled out of bed and plucked at her damp t-shirt. Soaked, must've sweat all night. That's another thing: it's all so real, like I'm there and I feel whatever the person I'm dreaming about feels—their emotions, thoughts, pain. But especially with Emily. This can't be. She turned on the shower, undressed. When she stepped into the shower, the cool water flowed over her shoulders, covered her body, instantly refreshing her. "Ooooooh, I could stand here all day." She closed her eyes; but an image of Emily running through the forest with a fearful, panicked look on her face immediately raced through her mind, sent a shiver colder than the water, from her shoulders to her waist. What was that about?

* * *

Allie's doorbell rang. Her mother opened the door, poked her head into the room. "Hi, Allie."

"Hey, Mom, come in."

Nancy O'Shay was fifty-one; but at five four, and one hundred twenty-five pounds, she had the well-proportioned body of a much younger woman and was remarkably limber for someone who'd had three children and spent so many grueling years working beside her husband on a ranch. Though a few thin crow's feet had recently appeared beside her eyes, serious wrinkles and sags were several years down the road; and aided by her dark, shoulder-length hair, she consistently drew glances from men of all ages, which considerably enhanced her self-esteem. A year ago, however, Allie had discovered her mother's first gray hair, taken the indiscreet liberty of pointing it out to her. She hadn't noticed another since and concluded her mother had discovered rinse.

Allie embraced her mother with a warm, lingering hug that renewed the security and comfort she'd always drawn from her. "How was the drive?"

"Uneventful and beautiful as always. Three and a half hours of head-bending scenery. And how's my favorite girl?"

"Hanging in. Having some great ideas for the dissertation." An image of Emily floated swiftly through her mind, then another chilly gust of foreboding.

"Great. Let's talk about it at dinner. How about Finley's? My treat."

"You're on, Mom. You know I'm a sucker for that place. Can't afford it unless you or Dad are here."

* * *

Two hours later, Nancy and Allie sat in Allie's living room sipping the single malt scotch Nancy had brought from home. After sharing several humorous tales of Allie's father, Michael O'Shay, their spontaneous laughter tapered to an expectant silence. Nancy stared silently and thoughtfully at the floor in front of Allie, while Allie stared at her mother and wondered what she was thinking about. As Allie started to ask, Nancy looked up worriedly. "Allie, last time we talked you said something about a strange dream. Have you had any more?" Her look and tone reflected more than casual interest.

"Why do you ask, Mom?"

"Oh, just curious. That's all."

"Well . . . yeah . . . I have . . . several, in fact. Kinda confused about them, too . . . really strange . . . unlike any dreams I've ever had before."

Nancy's face tensed. The two stared speechlessly at one another until Allie's eyes abruptly filled with tears. She stood, walked to the couch, sat down beside her mother, wrapped her arms around her and sobbed.

Nancy felt herself unraveling, held Allie close, rubbed her neck, comforted her for nearly ten minutes while her mind raced aimlessly. When she'd regained her composure, she whispered, "Allie Girl. What's wrong? Tell me, Hon." Long pause. "It's the dreams, isn't it?"

Allie nodded slowly, her head pressed against her mother's chest.

"Want to tell me about them, tell me what's happening?"

Allie sniffled. "No, Mom. Not now."

"All right. Tell me when you're ready." But her urge to help Allie overrode her caution; she couldn't sit idly by while something tormented her daughter. "Allie, do you remember me telling you about my great-grandmother?"

Still heaving sporadically, Allie said, "No, Mom, I don't."

"Well, when I was a very little girl, she used to tell me really cool stories; and she told me they all came to her in dreams—very unusual and real dreams. So when you mentioned that *you* were having dreams, I thought of her."

"What did she dream about, Mom? What kind of dreams?"

Again cautious, Nancy hesitated, scoured her mind for the right response. She desperately wanted to tell Allie all she knew, but dared not; so as her liquid courage fled her conflicted mind, she decided to lie. "That's all I remember, Hon; but hey, it's getting late, and we've both had a long day and a good bit to drink. What say we get some sleep?"

"Come on, Mom, I know there's more. Tell me."

"No, really, that's it . . . all I had to say. Just wanted to mention it. I'm really beat."

"This sucks, Mom. You know a lot more, and you're holding it back. That's not a cool thing to do, and I don't appreciate it." Allie stood, walked to her chair, picked up her glass, belted her last sip of scotch. "Anyway, thanks for dinner and the great scotch—rare treats for me. See you in the morning. Love you."

"Love you, too, Hon. Good night."

* * *

As she lay in bed staring into the darkness, Nancy wondered if Allie was the one, wondered if she should tell her *all* she knew about the dreams, try to help her deal with them before it was too late. But would it make any difference in the end?

CHAPTER 5

The grating whine of mosquitoes permeated Elyoner's cottage like a herald's trumpet stuck on a dissonant high-note, induced Elyoner and Emily to flail the space around them every few seconds to deter the demonic little vampires from approaching them and the baby. The fire smoke drifting in through the door blended with the dense humidity and the burning-animal-fat smell of the candles to give the room a dank, unpleasant aroma that was only slightly tempered by the fresh smell of the baby.

George sat ten feet from the women—emaciated, gaunt, trapped in his silent, torpid world as he stared vacantly at the wall, amidst his own private swarm of mosquitoes. The women had placed two candles beside him, hoping the smoke and foul smell would repel the pests enough to spare George the plethora of bites he would otherwise suffer. Elyoner and Emily sat on the stump stools, Elyoner nursing her baby and Emily dividing her attention between Elyoner and the floor, which she scanned for invading cockroaches.

"There's another one," Emily said. She stood, rushed to the unsuspecting insect, stomped it flat into the dirt floor. "Why are they all gathering right here, right now? Enough! That's five in the last few minutes; they're invading us."

"There do seem to be more than normal . . . filthy little creatures . . . though I've heard people quite fancy eating them in some parts of the world. Perhaps we should use them to supplement our diet."

"Faugh! Not me. Disgusting they are." She swiped at the mosquitoes.

The baby suckled loudly, contentedly, almost gulped. Elyoner smiled at her amusedly then drifted her gaze to George, nodded toward him. "What do you think, Em?"

Emily looked at George. "I'm quite beyond thinking. 'Tis simple. He eats or he dies. I led him over here by the hand like one would a goat. He just plods along wherever you take him, doesn't seem to see or hear, mayhap doesn't think either. I don't know what's going on inside his head, but he eats and drinks less than one of those roaches." Her eyes began to mist. "The last time I felt so helpless was when my brother was dying. Watched him slip away, we did. Quite depressing . . . Ellie, I truly miss George. We were together a lot, and it's like a piece of my life is suddenly absent . . . even though we're but good friends." She felt a prick of guilt, anguish that she hadn't requited his love, wondered if her reluctance had worsened his condition. Her invisible gloom deepened as she again wondered if she could love him as he loved her. But, she reasoned, pretending love is a lie; and lies always catch up with you, not worth the effort; better to be brutally honest and take what comes . . . on both sides of a relationship. She thought of Hugh Tayler, contrasted her growing affection for him with the friendship she felt for George. Different, very different. Her heartbeat quickened at the thought of Tayler.

"I can see it upsets you, Em."

The baby stopped nursing, began to sputter. Elyoner leaned her over her shoulder and patted her back, gently at first, then when she didn't burp, with more force. The child responded with a belch worthy of a grown man.

Emily laughed. "God's mercy! Most unladylike . . . Ellie, may I hold her awhile?" Emily had already developed a close bond with the baby; but there was something beyond that, something that made Emily want to hold her constantly—perhaps because she was a girl and already showed awareness of that fact in her behavior and movements, or perhaps because she reminded Emily of her baby brother back in England. Whatever it was, holding her instilled a deep warmth in Emily's heart, aroused a fierce protective instinct that made her want to never let go.

"Of course, Em. Here." She handed the baby to Emily, who cradled her as if nursing. Emily gave a hearty laugh. "Elyoner, look at that!" She glanced down at the baby as she rooted for her breast. "She's no pride at all. She'll take a handout from anyone . . . knows what she's about, doesn't she?"

Elyoner looked suddenly somber, thoughtful. "I'm actually quite glad of that, Em."

"What do you mean?"

"Well, Margery Harvie and I were talking yesterday, and—oh, by the bye, Agnes thinks Margery will deliver in the next few days—and we . . . we talked about what would happen to our babies if . . . if the ultimate misfortune befell one of us."

Emily glared at her incredulously. "Elyoner, that's not—"

"No, Em. It could happen. Think about where we are, the dangers. Truly, it *could* happen, and 'tis something we must think about . . . and if it *did* happen, how would the baby survive?" She looked at Emily, searched her eyes while her own suddenly assumed a pall of sadness.

Emily sensed something grave at hand, held her silence.

"Well, we agreed that if anything happens to either one of us, the other will nurse her baby . . . and help the father care for it."

Emily's face brightened. "Now that's a rather fine idea, Elyoner."

Elyoner nodded. "Well, there's more. Perhaps Margery and I worry too much, but 'tis not impossible that something could happen to *both* of us. Or if one of us survived, what if the other's milk was insufficient for two infants? Where would we be then with no other nursing mothers in the colony?"

Emily's bright look faded; she listened intently, uneasily, fearfully.

"Emily Colman, will you help me nurse my baby?"

Emily tried to speak, but her lips wouldn't move.

"There's no other person in the colony, or the world, that I would ask to do this." She reached out, touched Emily's cheek. "You are the sister I never had." She beamed a radiant smile, her eyes filled with tears.

Emily's eyes sparkled with tears of her own, her lips parted; her suddenly joyful face brightened like a freshly lit lantern. She laid her hands unconsciously on her breasts. "Oh, Elyoner, I . . . I don't know what to say. I'm . . . I'm so honored that you'd ask this of me. Of course, I will. Yes, yes." She promptly frowned. "But, Elyoner, how can I nurse? How can a—"

"Quite easily, in truth. I've seen it done. My cousin, who was about my age at the time, helped her sister nurse when she fell ill and later died. That's where I got the idea."

"But how?"

"Well, first you start squeezing and pressing your breasts with your fingers many times a day; I'll show you how. And the more you do it, the quicker your milk will come in. But when you first start, you won't have a lot of milk, and she won't suckle long. So you'll coat your nipples with smashed berries or something else sweet before you nurse—berries worked well for my cousin—and the sweetness will encourage her to suckle, but it could still take some time for you to produce enough milk to fill her. So you'll have to suckle more often at first, but the frequent demand will rapidly increase your milk supply. I can promise you the little rascal likes a full tummy, and she'll suckle until she gets it . . . or let you know forthwith you've failed her."

"Elyoner, I had no idea. I can't wait."

" 'Tis I who am happy, Em . . . and honored to have such a friend. 'Tis a big commitment, one that will definitely tie you down a bit." She stood, embraced Emily and the baby, then kissed Emily on the cheek. "Thank you, my friend."

While Elyoner sat down, Emily imagined herself nursing the baby, eyed her with a motherly smile. "When may I begin?"

"Today, for it could take as long as a month for your milk to come in. But it could also be much quicker. Everyone's different."

Emily looked disappointed. "Well, I wish it could happen sooner . . . I feel so close to . . ." She scowled, sternly waving her index finger up and down at Elyoner. "Elyoner, are you ever going to name this child, or do we have to call her *the baby* forever?"

Elyoner laughed. "Yes, Em. We've chosen a name but told only Father. We're saving the announcement for the christening four days hence, but I'll certainly tell *you* now if you truly want to know?"

"No, you should wait if that's what you've decided to do . . . and I'll keep guessing." Emily held the baby tight against her breast, kissed the side of her head. "I love you, little one . . . here, Elyoner." She handed her to Elyoner. "If I hold her any longer, I'll steal her and make her mine."

The baby sputtered as Elyoner took her. "She wouldn't mind that at all. See, she already loves her Aunt Emily."

"I shall count every second until the moment arrives." Emily rose, took a cup of water to George and held it to his lips. To her surprise he drank a couple sips. "Here, George, have some more." He took another sip. "Elyoner, did you see that? He heard me." But her quickened heartbeat slowed as George resumed his arcane stare. She shook her head as she walked back to her stool and sat. When she noticed Elyoner was deep in thought, she focused her eyes and mind on the baby, imagined herself holding her, offering her breast; felt a warm glow spread through her body as she wondered how it would feel, if it would hurt. She looked back at Elyoner, who remained within her own mind. "Elyoner, what troubles you? You've vanished into your thoughts."

Elyoner held her stare for a few seconds then looked at Emily. " 'Tis Father. He's different since the birth: upset, depressed, seems ashamed or embarrassed about something. I'm worried that he's having misgivings about our future, perhaps chastising himself for bringing us here. He gets reflective like that sometimes."

Emily had hoped someone else would tell Elyoner about the raid; so caught by surprise, her mind scrambled for appropriate words.

"I know Father's looks, and I know when he's upset; and he's upset now, but I know not why. Em, is there something I don't know?"

Emily stared thoughtfully at the ground then at Elyoner. "There *is*, Ellie, and 'tis nothing to do with you being here."

"What then, pray tell?"

"Your Father and Ananias told me not to tell you until you're recovered."

"Tell me what?"

"Well . . . you seem quite yourself now, so I shall tell you." Emily took a deep breath. "Just before dawn the morning you were giving birth, they attacked the Savages on the main—men, women, and children sitting around a fire talking. They charged in shouting and shooting. 'Twas like a chaotic nightmare, I'm told, and one of the soldiers gutshot a man, who then died a slow, agonizing death."

Elyoner cupped her hand over her mouth, her incredulous eyes locked on Emily's.

"As they pursued the Savages, one of them recognized your father and ran toward him, called his name. Manteo recognized the man as one of *his* people, *not* the ones who killed Master Howe, and he shouted desperately at the men to stop the attack."

"They attacked *Manteo's* people?

Emily nodded. "Aye, Ellie, they did."

"Devil's plague! But why were they—"

"The Savages who killed Master Howe abandoned their camp after the murder—so quickly, in fact, that they left many supplies there. So Manteo's people were camping there overnight to collect the abandoned supplies and take them back to their island early in the morning . . . bad luck and bad timing for them. Manteo was furious with our men but much more so with his own people. Told them it was *their* fault for not coming to your father's meeting the previous day. Well, the soldiers collected all the supplies—berries, corn, peas, tobacco—and brought them here to supplement our rations. Of course, Manteo's people want nothing to do with us now, so we've no one to teach us what we must know to survive—all the more reason to leave this island as soon as we can."

"Poor Father. He was already tormented by—"

"Greetings, ladies." Ananias and Thomas Colman entered the cottage. Ananias beamed a broad smile, proceeded directly to Elyoner, and kissed her and the baby.

Emily had not liked Ananias at first. No woman's image of virility, he was tall and lanky like a weasel standing on its hind legs; had a long, pointy nose like a woodpecker, a stress-induced blink, and occasional attacks of naïveté that worsened his periodic lapses in common sense. But in the course of befriending Elyoner, Emily had discovered and come to admire the treasure concealed beneath the mousey image: a gentle, soft-spoken man of kindness, loyal to family and friend, intelligent, dedicated, and resilient. She had then understood with great clarity why Elyoner had married the man and loved him so fervently. She also saw that though he sometimes disagreed with John White, Ananias admired him, which she thought had probably facilitated his persuading Elyoner and Ananias to accompany him to the colony. He had suggested that the colony would soon need a tiler and builder to construct sturdy permanent structures, had planted the thought that Ananias could be the man to guide and accomplish such construction and make a prosperous living for himself and his family in the process. And being one who always saw good intentions in people, Ananias had resonated with the proposal and sold his business in England to embark upon the adventure.

Stepping over to the water bucket, Ananias ladled a dipper of water and offered it to Colman.

"Thanks, my friend. Long, dry meeting, eh?" Thomas Colman had been elected an Assistant to replace George Howe, but having just completed his first meeting, he was not certain he'd made a wise choice in accepting. "Is there always so much squabbling? My God, how do they—how do *we*—ever accomplish anything?"

" 'Tis difficult. Many opinions and too many people who like to hear themselves talk, listen to their own views, and impress themselves."

Elyoner said, "What was today's talk?"

Ananias wiped his brow with his sleeve. "Well, it seems our supplies are dwindling faster than expected, so we're cutting back on everyone's daily rations and supplementing more with wild game, berries, and fish. The problem, however, is that there isn't much game left on the island, we've eaten most of the berries, and our fishermen seem to be somewhat inept at fishing these waters. Oh yes, and the water in our stream is depleting at an unexpectedly rapid rate due to the heat and drought, and we're to slaughter the first of our swine tomorrow. And last, we desperately needed the help of Manteo and his people, but since the disastrous attack on . . . oh . . . forgot . . ." He cupped his hand over his mouth.

Elyoner rolled her eyes, emitted a long sigh. "Go on, Ananias. I know about the attack. Secrets don't live long here."

Ananias and Colman gazed suspiciously at Emily, who turned her palms up and gave them a helpless, quizzical look. "Truly, Ananias, she asked, and I deemed her up to it. So . . ."

Ananias hesitated for a moment then nodded twice, proceeded as if there had been no interruption. "We then discussed abandoning the island and proceeding into the main, or perhaps sailing up to Chesapeake as we discussed when we first arrived. 'Twould be about a fifty-mile journey either way—completely by sea to Chesapeake; or on the sound, thence up a river, and finally overland to the main."

Colman said, "More argument than discussion, with no consensus, I'm afraid. Many Savages along the route into the main versus a tricky sail to Chesapeake for a company of shore folk."

Ananias nodded. "Quite true. And then"—he flicked an uneasy glance at Elyoner—"weee, uh . . . pox, you tell them, Thomas."

Colman looked equally uncomfortable, hesitated as if waiting for encouragement. Finally, he eyed Ananias then Emily and Elyoner, shook his head and sighed. "Well, Roger Baylye had forespoken to not only the Assistants but also each man in the colony about our desperate situation." He shuffled his feet and continuously rotated his hat brim between his thumb and index finger, glancing briefly and tenuously at Elyoner, then sighed. "Roger proposed that several Assistants return to England for supplies on the flyboat or on the large ship with Fernandez, who, by the way, is departing imminently, but . . . but all refused. So he . . . he suggested your father do so."

Elyoner's mouth and eyes opened wide.

"Roger then opened the cottage door to show your father that every man in the colony stood outside to demonstrate support for his proposal."

Elyoner's cheeks were vivid pink, her eyes tight, hands clenched.

Colman quickened his speech. "He cited your father's close relationship with Raleigh and how it could be used to obtain more planters and the supplies we so urgently need . . . all true, of course. Unfortunately, as you might expect, the governor would not hear him out, became enraged, actually cursed Roger, and stormed out of the meeting." He took a deep breath. "We're to try again in a day or so." He shook his head then displayed a limp, hopeless smile. "A rather unpleasant first Assistants' meeting for me."

Elyoner looked ill, disbelieving, confused, then suddenly angry again. She looked at her daughter then back and forth between Colman and her husband, shouted at them, "How can Father leave? He's the governor. He can't leave the colony." Tears filled her eyes. "How could Roger even suggest it? How could you, Anan—"

"Because," said young George Howe, "he's the only one who can accomplish what must be done. He alone can influence Raleigh and the Queen to save us."

No one spoke. They looked at one another as if wondering who had spoken, where the strange voice had come from. Silence persisted until Emily shouted, "George!" Tears rushed down her cheeks as she stepped to his side, wrapped her arms around him. "George! At last!"

The others gathered around. George wept with Emily, embraced her, and leaned his head on her shoulder, shuddering the pent up pain from his soul.

***

Arnold Archard shoved the soldier dispensing rations, yanked the food basket from his hands. "Damn it! We need more than this."

Corporal Gibbes, a young lad of about twenty, said, "Sir, you can't do that. I've my orders." He beckoned two nearby soldiers for help; they quickly seized Archard's shoulders while Gibbes wrenched the basket from his grip.

"Damn you. Take your hands off me. You can't treat me this way."

Lieutenant Waters heard the commotion, jogged to the scene. "What's happening here, men?"

"This gentleman tried to take the food basket, Sir. Demanded more than his share."

" 'Tis my right to have an adequate ration," Archard said.

"I'm sorry, Sir, there's no such right. The governor's imposed equal rations for all of us. He and his Assistants have defined what's adequate, and we must all live by that until we've more food. I and my men are to enforce his regulations. If you disagree with the ration, you should discuss it with Governor White."

"I shall. Now order your men to release me immediately. I also intend to report their rude treatment."

"Report what you wish, Sir. For my part, if you cause more trouble, the constable and judge shall know of it. Now be off with you, and mind your behavior. Let him go, men."

Archard sneered at Waters, made an indecent gesture as he walked toward White's cottage cursing and muttering to himself.

Waters was certain he had made a staunch enemy, but what else could he have done? If one person got away with something, others would do the same, and the result would soon be anarchy. "Go on with your business, men. Expect more of this behavior as people grow hungrier and more cross tempered. Equal rations for all . . . maintain your good discipline and demeanor."

"Yes, Sir," Gibbes said. "If I may, Sir, I don't think the man's himself. Just hungry like everyone else. Hopefully, the governor will calm him." He saluted Waters, and he and the other two soldiers turned to walk toward a group of civilians awaiting their rations.

"What's your name, soldier?"

"Gibbes, Sir. Corporal John Gibbes."

"You're young for a corporal. You must have seen combat."

Gibbes stood halfway between five and six feet, had a solid stature, a boyish, rosy-cheeked complexion, and large, determined green eyes. "Aye, Sir, I have."

Waters stared at him, nodded repeatedly. "You handled that situation well, maintained your poise and bearing. Well done."

"Thank you, Sir."

Waters beckoned to Myllet and Smith, who stood nearby, led the two sergeants to a secluded section of the palisades. "That man—I think his name is Archard—is selfish and arrogant, a fine example of what we'll soon see more of. I sympathize with these people and their plight—ours, as well—but as you can imagine, things are going to get worse, perhaps even ugly. 'Tis the situation I feared when I spoke to the men shortly after we arrived. They're going to be tempted to take matters into their own hands with these undisciplined fools, but we cannot allow it. We must stay on top of them, know their thoughts, ensure they control their tempers, maintain discipline. We're the backbone of order here, and we *will* do our duty. I'm depending on you two to keep the men calm, controlled, and busy. Idleness breeds complaining and contempt . . . we can't have either. We're but a short step from catastrophe and cannot permit that step to be taken. Do you understand?"

Both nodded, answered affirmatively. Then Smith said, "Beggin' your pardon, Sir, I thought I should tell you that the men are discontented about doing manual labor. They've asked me to speak to you. They—"

"Sergeant Smith, what in the hell do they, or you, think I can do about this situation. Did you not just hear me say we must keep the men busy? You know better than I that the less soldiers have to do, the more they complain. We're all stuck here together with no meaningful defenses, flimsy shelter, diminishing food, angry Savages, winter soon upon us, and weak civilian leadership. Do you . . . do they think we should sit on our arses and watch the civilians work while we just stand guard?" He looked sternly at both sergeants. "Christ, men, if the Savages attack in force before we complete the palisades, we'll be just as dead as the civilians. The Savages care not who they kill as long as they're English. So use your bloody heads and pound some sense into your men. We're all doing work we would not normally do . . . so how can they complain when you and I are there working beside them?"

The sergeants looked embarrassed, stared at the ground like guilty schoolboys caught in an errant act. Myllet collected himself first and looked at Waters. "Sir, I understand what you're saying, but I'm worried about how long these men will endure before they . . . before they . . ."

"Before they what, Myllet? Before they mutiny? For God's sake, man, we've only been here a short while; things aren't even terribly difficult yet. But they act as if we've made them fill latrines all day or make hopeless charges up a steep hill against fusillades of arrows."

"No, not mutiny, Sir . . . not yet . . . just grumbling, perhaps a little more."

Waters calmed himself. "Sorry. Didn't mean to maul you. I appreciate your informing me." He looked at both men, in turn. "What do you think we should do?"

Smith said, "Well, I think most of them are good lads trying to do their duty whatever you tell them to do. But there are some malcontents—rebellious sorts—who seem intent on disrupting the order of things, stirring the other men up. I—"

"Do you know who they are?" He knew he was putting Smith on the spot, asking a question he couldn't expect an answer to, decided to do it anyway.

"Yes, Sir, I do, but . . . but by your leave . . ."

"I understand. Forget I asked that. Keep your eyes on them, and for God's sake, tell me if it gets worse. Fair enough?"

"Fair enough, Sir."

"Very well. You're both good men, and I . . . we, the colony . . . need your help if any of us are to survive here." He expelled a lengthy, philosophical sigh, wished he was somewhere else—anywhere, fighting Spaniards—instead of swatting mosquitoes, sweating, and dealing with civilians in this miserable hole. "Young Gibbes seems a good sort. Would he make a good beginning sergeant? I know he's young, but I think we're going to need more supervision and eyes on the men, if you know what I mean."

The two sergeants looked at one another for a second, nodded, then looked at Waters. Myllet said, "Yes, Sir. I believe he would. He's a good lad."

Smith said, "I agree, Sir."

"Very well. Let's promote him. Please inform him of his new rank and responsibilities and also of the gist of our conversation. If you have any doubts after you speak to him, let me know . . . and thank you, men. I appreciate your support."

Both said, "Yes, Sir," saluted, walked off to find Gibbes.

As he walked toward the palisades, Waters' mind churned, searched for a pathway to the future that included a surviving colony. He failed, invariably arriving at the same end. *If any of us survive this debacle, it will be a miracle. If we don't starve to death, the Savages will get us: wait until we're starving, weak, pick us off a few at a time until we're so decimated they can attack en masse. Must complete the palisades quickly: assign more people to the job, work longer hours, perhaps nights*—he snorted cynically—*all on less food . . . and we must keep people in large groups, so they're not vulnerable to piecemeal attack. But we can't hunt and fish in large groups; the women can't get water or wash clothes in large groups; people can't use a privy or latrine in large groups.* He looked at the palisades—*too many problems, too many slowdowns; Wyles' accident, wound festering, be lucky to live; everyone overcautious now, slow; three large, vulnerable palisade gaps to complete; need at least ten days . . . do we have that long?*

* * *

Emily stayed with George all day, watching him, guarding him, shielding and insulating him from any word or thought that might jeopardize his fragile recovery. Hugh Tayler stopped by, visited with her father outside the cottage for a few minutes before Colman parried his request to visit Emily and led him off to work on the palisades. Emily did not speak to George, other than to ask about his well-being. The day made her feel like a wife and mother: she fed her father and

George, cleaned the cottage—as well as a dwelling with a dirt floor could be cleaned—washed the few pieces of kitchenware they had, mended torn clothes, and collected their dirty clothes so they could be taken to the stream and washed. But mostly she watched George, eyeing him furtively as she went about her chores. She wondered if he'd speak, what he was thinking, feared he'd ask her about his father. She was astounded, even shocked, at how remote, tentative, seemingly afraid of her he became over the course of the day, concluded that such behavior was probably normal after such a trauma, then resolved to give him whatever he needed to find himself.

George was alert but still internalized; busied himself sharpening his two knives, checking and re-checking his father's musket; repeatedly and obsessively rearranging their belongings, occasionally pausing to hold a lingering gaze on his father's possessions.

After several hours of silence, Emily asked George if she could get anything for him.

Without looking at her, he shook his head, remained silent.

Emily sat herself on a stool, took advantage of the silence to again read her mother's letter, caress her locket, and pray for George's recovery and the colony's salvation.

After another half hour, George suddenly stood, walked over to Emily. With a deadpan expression, he said, "Emily, where's my father?"

A frigid chill slammed into her mind, muddled her reason, panicked her. She swallowed hard, tried to think but couldn't.

George said, "Emily, please tell me where my father is."

Fear spread over Emily's face like the shadow of a fast-moving cloud; sweat dampened her forehead; her breathing quickened. He's pushed it out of his mind, too horrible to think about . . . but if I tell him, we may lose him again . . . but if I don't . . . if I don't . . . Christ, help me. "George . . . your father's dead."

George stared into her eyes, silently processing her words; he shuffled his feet, wrung his hands, lowered his gaze to the floor. "I feared such, knew in my heart 'twas so . . . saw him in my mind, lying on the ground, feared asking, wanted to . . ."

Emily rose, put her arms around him, held him tightly to her bosom. "George, please stop. Don't do this to yourself. Don't think about it."

"I don't want to think about it, but I keep seeing him. My head hurts. I'm afraid . . . I should have helped him, might have saved him . . ."

"George, you could *not* have saved him. You weren't there. No one was there. No one could have helped him . . . or saved him."

"But I should have known he needed help, should have felt it."

"No, George, that's not possible. Sometimes—"

" 'Twas the Savages that killed him, wasn't it?"

Emily stared silently at him for a moment then said, "Yes."

"I'm going to kill them, as many as I can. They're evil . . . they must pay."

"No, George, they're *not* evil. They're just afraid, like we are." She felt the turmoil within him, sensed his confusion, his conflicted, anguished heart.

"Emily, do you know where he is? Will you take me to him?"

"George, are you sure? You—"

"Yes, Em. Take me there."

Another pause. "Very well."

Many in the village observed their procession toward the grave site, stopped their work, watched silently and nodded their respects as they passed.

They walked out to a small clearing about a hundred yards beyond the wall. George Howe's grave mound was marked by a wooden cross with his name carved on it. George stopped twenty feet from the grave, stared at it for a moment, grew visibly agitated, then walked hesitantly to it and slowly knelt.

Emily watched from behind as he leaned forward, laid his hands on the mound, then lowered his face to the dirt. Her body tingled with raw emotion, felt like it floated on air.

After a minute, George rose to his feet, walked back to Emily, and looked into her eyes. His face contorted into an ugly sneer. "Emily, stay away from me. I don't want to be near you anymore."

Emily felt a knife-like jab in her heart, felt light-headed, about to faint. "But, George . . ." She extended her hands to him.

His face twisted in pain; he grasped his head with both hands like he was trying to hold something inside, glared wildly at her, shouted, "Emily, I said stay away! I don't ever want to see you again!" He batted her arms away then ran into the forest.

Emily stood stunned, watched him go, her mind numb, emotions disheveled, as if pummeled by a huge wave. She dropped to her knees, sat back on her heels, then lowered her face to her trembling hands, moaning softly as tears trickled between her fingers, onto her lap.

For five minutes, her mind tumbled, turned, twisted, grasped, tumbled again, tried to comprehend what had happened, but the thoughts vanished as quickly as they came. Oblivious to everything around her, she finally ordered herself to act. She rubbed her eyes, dried them on her sleeve, stood, and brushed her skirt with her hands. After glancing quickly at the forest where George had run, she turned and walked back inside the palisades toward her cottage.

People inside had heard George yell but had been unable to discern his words; they stood dumfounded, wondered what had happened, feared to ask. Now they watched as Emily made her resolute way to the cottage. When Hugh Tayler saw her, he read her distress, hurried to her side.

"Emily, what's wrong? What is it?"

"Go away, Hugh! I can't talk now." She didn't look at him, kept a rigid forward gaze, a steady pace toward the cottage.

"But Emily, I—"

"Go away! Leave me alone!" She knew she was on the verge of hysteria, knew she dare not stop, look at anyone, or talk.

Elyoner had seen her the same time Tayler did, had come running as fast as her weakened condition allowed. "Em, what's happened? Tell me, Dear."

Tayler said, "She won't—"

"Shh! Can't you see she doesn't want you here right now? Go away . . . I'm sorry. Please find Ananias for me and tell him to watch the baby." Elyoner didn't like Tayler; something in his manner rubbed her wrong, made her uneasy. She wondered if it was because he fancied Emily and was so much older than she. But that was not uncommon, she admitted, then decided she was being too motherly and protective of her young friend. "Thank you, Master Tayler."

"I . . . I . . . very well, Mistress." Tayler headed off to find Ananias. Weeping women and angry women unnerved him, rattled his brain. He decided he was glad he'd been sent away. Finding Ananias was something he could manage, though he marveled that Elyoner would leave her newborn baby alone, even to help a friend. Must care very deeply for Emily, he concluded. His heart warmed at the thought of Emily; he looked back to see how she fared, wondered what had happened to her, saw that she and Elyoner were nearly to Emily's cottage, quickened his pace toward the palisade section where Ananias was working. Probably something to do with the Howe lad, he thought. He felt sorry for George but still resented his close friendship with Emily, hadn't convinced himself they were just friends.

Elyoner and Emily did not speak while walking to the cottage. Once inside, Elyoner hooked the tie string on the door so no one would enter then stepped to Emily, who stood staring at the wall. Holding her by the shoulders, Elyoner looked into her eyes. "Em, what happened? Was it George?"

Emily hesitated for a moment then wrapped her arms around Elyoner, buried her face on her chest, sobbed. "Elyoner, hold me."

"Let it loose, Em. Let it out. Cry to your heart's will. I'm with you."

After five minutes, Emily's tears and moans subsided. The two sat and held hands in silence for a moment before Emily told her what had happened, how George's words had stunned and wounded her, slashed her confidence to its core, ripped her feelings like a torn piece of dry parchment.

Elyoner listened with a gentle, sympathetic expression, occasionally nodded or spoke an empathetic word.

When Emily finished, she looked depleted, haggard. She sat silently, staring at the floor, entombed in a cloud of shock.

While listening, Elyoner had delved deep into her own mind to explore and understand the possible context and explanations for George's actions, had begun crafting the words she would speak to her friend. Finally, she said, "Em, I know you don't wish to discuss this now, mayhap not for days, but I'm worried about you and believe what I have to say to you will help you."

Emily didn't reply, stared at the floor.

"Em, I think George's injury was far deeper than we imagined, and I'd wager a shilling that his mental state, even though he's no longer in a stupor, remains disturbed. I'd wager another shilling that in his disturbed state, he associates you with his horrible experience because you, his closest friend, had the misfortune to be with him when it occurred—*it* being the moment he saw his father lying there bloodied, mutilated, and dead—and being near you now reminds him, brings it all painfully back to him. 'Tis not fair to you, but 'tis also beyond his control."

Emily looked at Elyoner with a blank expression.

"Lord knows, I'm only guessing, but you"—she paused for a few seconds, studied Emily's face to gauge her temperament—"more than any other, know that George is a kind and generous young man and that you are his truest friend in this world. You also know he loves you."

After a short silence, Emily said, "I am indeed his friend, Ellie, and as you say, probably his *best* friend. And 'tis also true that he loves me, though 'tis not something I wished for or share toward him to the same degree."

"I know, Em. But I mention it because I think George was not George when he spoke those angry words to you. 'Twas some other person—one in a temporary state of disturbance—who spoke those words. And if so, with your and God's help, he'll eventually become himself again . . . but heaven knows if or when that might be."

Emily nodded, sniffled twice. "I think—actually, I *know*—you're right Ellie. 'Tis just that . . . 'twas so violent . . . so unlike him . . . so shocking. I've never hurt like this before . . . never knew I could be so vulnerable, especially with someone I'm not even in love with."

"We're all vulnerable, Em, though we often don't realize it until something like this happens."

Emily reached out, took Elyoner's hands in hers, and stared into her eyes with a sad half smile. "Ellie, you're a wonderful friend . . . a wonderful mother to me . . . and I need a mother today. Thank you for being with me. I *will* stand by George and try to help him. Yes, my feelings *are* injured, and I know not for how long. Nor do I know if George will ever speak to me again, but it doesn't matter. I'm his friend, whether or not he perceives it, and I must help him no matter what . . . and I shall."

* * *

While her father snored in bed, Emily sat beside a solitary candle, staring at the empty space on the floor where George's bed had lain. He had pitched a tent somewhere in the village and asked Robert Ellis and William Wythers, two younger lads, to retrieve his bed and belongings for him, and they had abashedly obliged. Unable to sleep, she'd reread her mother's letter three times, told her about the baby's birth, Elyoner's asking her to nurse, and George's awakening.

Then, her locket squeezed tightly in her hand like a child clenches its mother's finger, she closed her misty eyes, told her mother about George's disquieting rant, the deep pain it had dealt her; told her of Elyoner's gentle mothering, how she'd helped her understand, place it in perspective, and resolve to help George no matter what it took from her. But, Mother, she mused, if he *does* heal, how will I ever be able to tell him I don't love him? What if doing so pushes him back into derangement? How could I live with that? Mother, help me know what to do.

She opened her eyes, stared into the near darkness around her. And then there's Master Hugh. I've been so busy helping Elyoner and caring for George I've neglected him, even yelled at him today when he tried to help me. We ladies do have peculiar tempers sometimes, don't we? Must make amends. She felt a now-familiar warmth spread through her body as she thought of Hugh Tayler, realized she'd barely thought of him for several days, wondered how that could have been, then decided to talk to him in the morning.

I miss you, Mother. Please come to us soon. And pray for me, for all of us . . . especially our two babies. Help me know what to do. I love you.

* * *

Some ten miles into the main, twenty of the tribe that had killed George Howe gathered in council around a small fire in the bark-covered lodge of their leader, their damp torsos glistening in the skittering firelight. The Panther and two of his warriors had come to them from their land, which lay toward the setting sun from the great Chesapeake water to the north.

The lodge was hot, laden with a deep, thick, smoky smell; and the leader occasionally fanned himself with a bird wing as he stared into the depths of the fire, listening intently to each speaker, considering the merits and risks of each proposal. He'd been praised by all of his people for his wisdom and foresight in moving the village deeper into the main immediately after the killing of the white man on the island. He'd known from past depredations by these people that retaliation would be swift and violent. So against the persuasions of several young, impetuous warriors, he'd decided to move the village. Earlier when he'd spoken of the Englishmen's foolish attack on the only tribe that remained friendly to them, many had laughed out loud at their folly, agreed that only the English could commit such a blunder; and as in previous councils, proposals for ridding the land of them had been many and varied.

When not staring into the fire, the leader surreptitiously eyed the Panther, whose people were the most powerful in the region. Their headman, Wahunsunacock, was the paramount chief of a large, growing, tribal alliance, and this fact implicitly commanded the leader's respect and deference in all matters related to war.

The previous white men had spent time near Wahunsunacock's territory, staying for a brief time with another tribe in the area, who were tenuous, unreliable members of the alliance. And some eight moons ago, Wahunsunacock had watched as the Panther and fifty warriors overwhelmed thirteen white men who'd paddled their canoe to his territory from their island to the south—the very island inhabited by the leader's people before the earlier Englishmen arrived. They'd captured four of these men, taken them to the village, then given them the slow death they granted to selected brave enemies so they could demonstrate their strength as warriors. They'd ripped off their fingernails and toenails, peeled strips of skin from their stomachs and faces; allowed the tribe's women to use mussel and oyster shells to cut off their fingers, arms, and genitals; scalped them and cut them open so their insides fell out. They'd generously given these four the opportunity to display their courage and die great warrior deaths, but they'd died poorly: screamed like women, cried like children, begged for mercy, for quick death. And the women had jeered and spit on them as they screamed. So Wahunsunacock had little respect for these pitiful creatures or their bravery. But he knew from Powhatan witnesses, including the Panther, of their depredations against other peoples; therefore, he held a keen interest in their whereabouts, wanted them as far from his territory as possible and to eventually drive them from the land altogether. To that end, he'd frequently sent his most trusted warrior, the Panther, to represent him with these other tribes, in both council and combat.

For their part, the leader's people had an unconcealed awe for both the Panther's prowess as a warrior and his statesmanship. When the Panther spoke in council, the leader listened attentively, knew he was hearing the mind of Wahunsunacock himself, and understood that far more was at play in the Panther's words than what he heard.

The Panther had deferred to all of the warriors in the leader's council—let them speak first, genuinely considered their recommendations, been careful to give no indication of his opinion on any proposal though all present knew of his deep hatred for the English and his desire to annihilate them. Some accordingly feared he might push for a mass attack that would result in excessive casualties for them, but even those with such concerns knew that the Panther's discipline as a strategist and tactician governed his emotions. They also knew that, like all successful hunters of both animals and men, he was painstakingly patient in the hunt; ruthless, swift, and lethal in the kill. So as the Panther rose to speak, the leader shifted his eyes from the fire to the great Powhatan warrior's face, awaited the words he knew would become their strategy.

Before he spoke, the Panther looked, for a dramatic instant, into each man's eyes then thanked the leader for allowing him to speak. "My friends, as you know, Wahunsunacock knows of the presence of these white men in your territory. He also knows of their stupidity, but he respects the strength of their numbers and the power and range of their big sticks that make thunder. As you also know, he would like them to leave our lands and go back to their own land across the Big-Water-That-Cannot-Be-Drunk. But he also knows that even though their fort is not yet complete, watchers guard their camp day and night, and that without gathering many more warriors, we lack the strength for the large direct attack on them we would all like to mount. Even with the long time it takes them to load new stones into their big sticks, our casualties would be great—far greater than you or Wahunsunacock wish to bear."

The leader relaxed his taut expression, breathed a mental sigh of relief. His people were already decimated from earlier encounters with these intruders, and they were many winters from having the number of warriors they'd counted just four winters before. So the Panther's acknowledgement of the folly of a large frontal attack greatly raised his hopes for the future of his people.

"Our attack on the lone white man was successful because we were more in number, and he was unwary and unprepared to fight. These people now have warriors watching wherever they go, but their minds are not on their task. Their eyes search for things other than us and often linger on the women they protect; and when nothing scares them for a few days, they become lazy and overconfident, think they are safe, relax their vigilance. So we must combine this knowledge with patience and make small attacks, again and again, each time reducing their numbers and terrifying them a little more. We must also spread our attacks in time, so they may again become lazy and complacent before the next. And if any planned attack, even up to the moment of the first war cry, looks like it may not be a complete success, we must have the discipline to leave and attack them another day. If we do these things, then perhaps in the winter, when they're cold, starving, and weak, and we've reduced their numbers, we will attack their fort with fire arrows, burn it to the ground, and kill all who cower inside." He looked at the leader. "Many days have passed since we killed the white man on the island." He once more drifted his gaze across each man's face then looked back at the leader. "The enemy has again become complacent, and the Panther believes that now is the right time for our next attack."

Most had nodded agreement as he spoke; none objected. After a pause, the Panther sat. The leader then stood, looked at each member of his council. "The Panther has spoken wisely . . . we shall do as he proposes."

* * *

Governor White sat alone in his cottage, immersed in thought. Fernandez had announced that the resupply of fresh water and wood had been completed, that the large ships would depart within a day or two. He had asked White to provide him a supply list to deliver to Raleigh, also offered to carry any posts the colonists had for their friends and relatives in England. At least he's respectable in those regards, White thought, even though he's a blackguard for deserting us here. I'll yet see him in shackles in the Tower.

Though near noon, the light in the cottage was too dim for White to see well enough to read or write; so he lit a candle, leaned his head close to it to read the draft list Roger Baylye had made of necessaries for Raleigh's anticipated resupply voyage. He hesitated for a moment, recalled the times Baylye had rescued him, kept things on an even keel. He shook his head. Such an unlikely looking leader but a natural: thinks of everything, persuasive, honest, smart headed . . . save for his proposal that I return to England. Yes, I shall make him my deputy at tomorrow's meeting. As he looked back at the list, he compared it to his mental estimates of required supplies and skills, saw the need for but a few additions. Not enough barley for the beer we'll need, he thought. He increased the amount of barley by fifty percent. Salt beef—never have enough salt beef. He added more. And flour—need much more flour . . . oh yes, and more slow-spoiling vegetables, especially beans. He raised his head, thought, Roger's gotten a good start on this, but because he hasn't spent a year here as I have, he doesn't yet realize that supplies of everything deplete far faster than expected.

So what additional skills do we need? He looked studiously at the wall, mentally ticked off the colony's needed skills, noting existing shortfalls. We cannot yet depend on young Howe to fill his father's shoes, don't know if he'll ever come 'round, so we must have someone to set up and operate a small foundry. And medical supplies—need three times what we now have. He thought of John Wyles. Poor miserable fellow: leg's gangrenous; Jones can't help him, never cut off a leg before; and Fernandez won't take him. He'll surely die soon, and painfully . . . a good man. He hit the table with his fist. Not a just end for him, but what can I do? . . . I know what I must do: convince Fernandez to take him and hope he gets him to England in time. He pondered the idea for a moment then shook his head. No, Fernandez won't do it. John's a dead man unless Jones can do a successful amputation . . . with nothing to temper the pain. God, pray let him die quickly. But perhaps we can find a root or a berry that will dull his senses. Must ask Manteo. He said a prayer for Wyles, prayed that Manteo could help.

He again looked at the list, identified a few more missing skills. Fishermen who know how to fish, and farmers. Perhaps if we leave this place, some other Savages will show us how they farm . . . pity we never farmed with Lane . . . expected the Savages to feed us—the root of all our troubles, even now. Didn't foresee this problem. He checked the list one more time, added ammunition then bulk lead for making shot. Without a foundry to make large quantities, we'll have to make our own . . . we've plenty of molds, just not enough lead. Must have far more than we think we need . . . oh my God, and powder. He re-checked the list. Oh, there it is, plenty of powder. He doubled the order of seed stock, then tripled it. No Englishman has ever planted here; don't know what we'll need, how much won't germinate . . . very little left from initial stocks. Be safe, John. We can make bread of it if we don't plant it. He sat back, stared at the wall. I think that's all. Hope Raleigh doesn't choke on the price of it all.

He returned his gaze to the list, but his mind drifted to a vision of Cotsmur and Stilman fighting each other over a paltry little fish the day before—rolling around on the ground as if in mortal combat. Indeed, it had come to that. He shook his head disgustedly, reflected on the general shortness of tempers, the other recent fights that had broken out over seemingly trivial matters. Order is indeed beginning to deteriorate: workers running out of energy, lapses in quality and attitude, more accidents, little remaining game on the island, hapless fishermen—men of supposed skill and productivity in English waters, resounding failures here. It's all headed in the wrong direction, he mused . . . unless we leave this island . . . soon. That, and that alone, must be our priority after Fernandez leaves. Need to stop work on the palisades immediately, rest the men, begin planning and preparing an orderly departure, send emissaries to the tribes where we decide to go. But where *will* we go? The nagging question remained, tormented his mind as if he were a man choosing between two remarkably unattractive, ill-tempered women, one of whom he would have to marry. Transport into the main will require a large, noisy traverse of dangerous territory; but there is no escaping the inherent risks of sailing the pinnace and two shallops fifty miles to Chesapeake on the open sea, without a seaman among us. What to do? Even if we go into the main, we've still got to sail and row a good distance, albeit on calmer waters . . . but every Savage from here to the fall line will know of our presence and want to attack us. But on the positive side, both places should provide a better existence than here, and both will be far safer from chance discovery by a passing Spanish warship. Must discuss all of this—including the need for greater vigilance for Spanish ships—with Roger and the Assistants on the morrow, reach a decision, and move quickly. 'Tis late August and winter is coming, but perhaps the promise of a new location with better prospects will raise spirits and reduce tensions.

And Elyoner, my dear Ellie, and your baby . . . I so fear for your safety . . . the Harvie woman and her child, as well. He bowed his head, closed his eyes; thought of his wife, then Elyoner as a baby; rued the day he'd persuaded her and Ananias to join him on this foolish venture. What had he been thinking? What a huge blunder, and what a—his eyes suddenly sparkled; he raised an eyebrow, cracked a timid smile. "What if I can persuade *them* to return to England with Fernandez, be my representatives to Raleigh?" he said aloud. "Yes, that's the answer." His expression abruptly soured. But 'twould look more than suspicious if the governor sent his family back to England; 'twould truly send the wrong message, open the door to criticism by enemies . . . and an infant on a long sea voyage is a complication. Nonetheless, I shall try to persuade them . . . and in truth, 'twill probably be safer for the baby on the ship than here. But the greater challenge could be persuading Fernandez . . . perchance far more difficult than persuading Elyoner. But in any event, I must choose someone else to return in case Elyoner and Ananias, or Fernandez, refuse my bidding . . . and it must be some- one I trust, for I can *cannot* trust Fernandez. He nodded three times. Yes, Ananias and Elyoner are the perfect solution.

* * *

Emily approached the palisade section where Hugh Tayler and his workmate, John Bridger, had just finished holding a palisade post that was being drilled and pinned. As she carried her basket of food and a beer bag up to the men, Lieutenant Waters called for a supper break. Bridger nodded his respects, walked off toward the cottage he shared with several other single men. With a tentative, uncertain look, Emily said, "Hello, Hugh. I've brought you some supper. Let's find shade."

Tayler hadn't seen her approach, was surprised and pleased when he spied her. "Emily, are you . . ."

"I'm fine, Hugh. I . . . I must apologize for—"

"No, don't. 'Tis not necessary; I completely understand. 'Twas the wrong time for—"

"No, I insist. I was quite rude to you, most unfairly so. And I'm sorry. Please forgive me."

"You needn't ask my forgiveness, Emily, but granted. Now let's find that shade. Here, let me carry the basket. There's a good place over here, outside the wall. Where's your father today?" As he took the basket from her, he held her free hand, felt her warmth spread up his arm to his body then down to his loin.

"He and Ananias are finishing a final inventory of supplies for the governor. As you know, Fernandez is departing, and we must order more of everything before he goes."

"Indeed." He led her silently through a gap in the palisades then turned right, into the shade of the wall, and motioned her to sit. They were alone, out of the sight of everyone in the colony. He handed her the basket, looked into her eyes. "I've missed you, Emily. More than I can say." He felt her eyes penetrate his, as always, but this time detected a trace of sorrow.

"And I you, Hugh. It's been a most hectic time with scarcely a moment to rest or think."

"I understand." He smiled. "You've been extraordinarily selfless with Elyoner, her baby, and young Howe."

Emily nodded. "One helps those who need help." She had seen George on the other side of the green as they left the palisades, had again felt the sting of his rage. And Tayler's mention of him produced a lump in her throat, but she swallowed it before it showed. They then sat silently for a moment while Tayler debated asking Emily about George, and Emily debated telling him. Lonely out here with no others, she thought. "Here, Hugh. Have some beer. 'Tis nearly the end of our supply, but you look as if you need it." She handed him the beer skin; he took a swig, handed it back.

"Thank you, Milady. You are most kind . . ." Again the eyes, studying, probing, alive. He held her hand, felt his mind cloud as it always did. "Emily, why are you so beautiful?"

Emily choked, nearly spitting out the sip of beer she had just taken, then quickly covered her mouth and swallowed. "Stop it, Hugh. I'm not beautiful. Why do you say such things? You're teasing me again. Here, have some more beer while I think how to tease you back." She handed him the beer skin. "A bit warm isn't it?"

"Aye, a bit, but tasty nonetheless. And I am *not* teasing you. I'm speaking the truth." He took another swig. "Wait! I take it back. You're not beautiful. You're simply the most striking and captivating woman I've ever seen."

"Why do you always do this?" Though profoundly embarrassed, she admitted to herself that she enjoyed the flattery, even though she disbelieved it, and also relished their verbal sparring. "And if it were true, it would *not* be because *I* had anything to do with it. 'Twould be God's fault alone. But it matters not, for 'tis not so."

Her modesty excited him, convinced him she truly did not know how beautiful she was. "Very well, God Himself is to blame. Now tell me why you're so strong and confident."

"Hugh, stop this nonsense! Talk about something else, something serious. Lord knows we've plenty to talk about in *that* realm."

"Not until you answer me."

She sighed. "Very well. If I'm strong *or* confident, 'twould be from my mother, for she's both. My father, as well, but less so, and in different ways. And both parents always gave me much responsibility and taught me how to manage it. Now, on to something more interesting."

So different from me, he thought. I had no responsibility, no learning, no example, an abusive father. "Very well, though I'd much prefer to talk about *you*."

She opened the basket. "Have some bread and salt beef. Not much here, but enough. Perhaps tomorrow someone will shoot a deer or catch some fish."

He tore off a piece of bread, handed the half loaf back to her. "Perhaps. Oh, here. Have some more beer, Emily."

She took a swig then ate a piece of salt beef. After a short silence, she said, "Hugh, do you think we'll all be alive a year from now?"

He thought for a moment. "All of us? No. Most of us? I hope so. I can't acquire land or build an estate, or have a wife and raise a family if I'm dead. So, since I'm determined to do those things, I'll have to survive . . . and you, as well, for you're part of my plan."

Emily lowered her eyes to the ground, blushed, shook her head with a hopeless smirk. "Curse you, Hugh Tayler. You're doing it again."

"Emily, as I've told you before, no one can embarrass you. And 'tis all true. I *do* have secret plans for you."

"You must be speaking of someone else. We've not known each other long enough for you to have such plans. Truly, your resolves are too bold, beyond the possible, and quite improbable."

He chuckled. "No, Mistress, I speak only of you. You've captured my heart, and 'tis yours to do with as you wish." Though being playful when he spoke, he suddenly realized he'd pronounced the unequivocal truth—an unfamiliar, pristine truth, one never before envisioned or felt by Hugh Tayler. He then hoped for something he'd never hoped for in his life, something he'd never *needed* to hope for because he'd never loved: that his love for a woman be returned.

Emily saw something different in his eyes, something new, an urgent longing; she sensed the need for caution but didn't know why, decided to respect her instinct. "Hugh, you mustn't speak so. I'm not ready. Too many things in my head right now. Please give me some time." She waited for a response, but he remained silent, probed her eyes with his. "We should go back, Hugh. We're not supposed to be out here without guards. It makes *me* a little uneasy, if not you. And my father will have a seizure if he learns I was alone with you *and* outside the walls." She offered a weak smile. "Rogue that you are."

He held his eyes on hers, kept his silence; realized he'd moved too far, too fast; felt a thump of reality in his heart but sensed that patience would win her in the end. "Em, we can't go back now. We haven't finished supper yet. I'll starve."

She closed her eyes for a moment; considered standing, walking back inside the palisades alone; but instead gave him a deadpan look, followed by a hopeless smile and a head shake. She handed him the food basket, took a sip of beer. "Very well. Tell me . . . uh . . . tell me when the palisades will be complete."

He smiled. "Impossible to say, for our pace grows slower every day, and people are starting to grumble. We all know they need to be completed, but people are simply growing weary of it. I, as well—particularly as a former officer—but who can complain when Waters is there beside us doing his share. He's a good officer, by the way. The grumbling is what concerns me. Soldiers and others complaining about Waters, a few of them rather rebelliously. 'Tis a dangerous thing to do in the open, for the line between mutiny and griping is thin, and the right of determination between the two rests with the commander."

Emily nodded, wondered why her father and Ananias had not mentioned the discontent, wondered if they were aware, and if not, why not.

"I'm getting to know some of the soldiers—good sorts most of them, some not so good, but they all like to complain. Part of the breed, you know."

"Have you said anything to Lieutenant Waters, or the Assistants, or the governor about it?"

"No, because 'tis not too serious . . . yet. When it is, I shall. Actually, I'd rather fancy being an Assistant myself; but of course, there'd have to be a vacancy, and someone would have to nominate me, and then I'd have to be elected. No telling when or if such might happen."

"You should tell Governor White and some of the Assistants of your interest. They'll be the ones to decide."

"I shall." He abruptly frowned. "By the bye, Emily, is young Howe the reason you were upset yesterday?"

Emily looked startled, confused, suddenly unsure of herself. "Hugh, I don't want to talk about George . . . other than to say he's had a difficult time and it goes on, and I don't know when, if ever . . ." Her eyes filled with tears; she leaned against him, wrapped her arms around his middle, hid her face on his chest.

His heart raced as he embraced her, pulled her close, waited silently for her moment to pass.

After a few seconds, Emily released her hold, eased back, sniffled, rubbed her eyes, looked into his. Their eyes lingered on one another's, danced from eyes to lips to eyes; their lips drew relentlessly closer, touched, pressed together, sent a deep, flowing warmth through their bodies.

Emily pulled back, gasped to catch her breath. "I'm sorry, Hugh. I . . . I should not have done that." Her hands trembled; embarrassment inundated her mind. She realized she'd kissed him to punish George for hurting her; she felt stupid, regretted her rash behavior but admitted her action had also been fueled by a compelling curiosity toward Tayler. No, Em, too soon . . . must not encourage him until you're sure. Foolish lass.

He held a tight gaze on her eyes. "Emily, that was a wonderful moment . . . but I respect your feelings. I'm sorry if I—"

"Truly, Hugh, we must go." She stood, picked up the basket and beer. He reached out to help her. "No, don't bother. They're not heavy."

She looked at him with sad eyes as they started back inside the palisades, an uncomfortable, rigid silence between them. As they approached Emily's cottage, she stopped, faced him. "Hugh, I should not have let that happen. Please do not read anything into it." She looked away then into his eyes. "I still want very much to see you and know you. Can you come to our cottage tomorrow evening for dinner, such as it is? You can get to know Father better and, if you still wish, ask his permission to take a walk with me, perchance even out of his sight." Her lips slowly curved into an impish smile. "But he probably thinks we're still in England and will want to chaperon us. Tommy Colman does not break tradition without a fight . . . but I shall help you. What say you?"

Hugh Tayler felt resurrected, a wondrous new life before him. "Emily, I'd be honored."

* * *

All day, a thick haze had magnified the sun's intensity and thickened the humidity like a heavy, smothering fog that lingered well after darkness had fallen. John White sat with Elyoner and Emily in Elyoner's cottage and cradled the baby in his arms, looking tentative, as if he expected her to shatter into pieces if he made a sudden move. How long, he thought, since I've held a baby. What will happen to this one? He felt immediately pummeled by guilt, fear for his family's survival.

He abruptly stood, handed the baby to Emily, then looked at his daughter. "Ellie, I must ask you something. My dear, we all well know the perils we face here. And after much anguished deliberation, I've concluded that I erred and acted selfishly in encouraging you and Ananias to join me on this expedition." He glanced at Emily as if he had just noticed her, questioned his wisdom in discussing their situation in her presence, then realized that she of all people well understood its fragility.

Elyoner pursed her lips, shook her head slowly back and forth.

"Hear me out, Ellie. It occurs to me that since *I* cannot go back to England to beseech Raleigh, the next best course would be for you and Ananias to do so." Elyoner's head-shaking accelerated. "Elyoner, stop shaking your head. Think about what I'm saying. Even with the hazards of sea travel, you'll have far better chances than if you remain here. I can't command you to go, but I ask you to consider it . . . for the colony's sake, as well as your child's. The Harvie family should go, as well. This is simply not a situation for newborns, and I should have realized that in the beginning but failed to. So . . . what say you, Daughter?"

He glanced at Emily to gauge her reaction, saw none, then looked back at Elyoner as Emily said, "Governor, I shall leave so you and Ellie may speak freely. I'll wait out—"

"Stay here, Emily," Elyoner said. "I've nothing to say that you can't hear. Father, thank you for your thoughts for us. I . . . I understand the logic of your proposal, but Ananias and I are as committed to this colony as you are. I'll discuss your proposal with him, but I steadfastly wish to remain here with—"

Ananias suddenly walked through the doorway, followed by Roger Baylye, Thomas Colman, and the other Assistants. They crowded around White and the women, with Baylye directly in front of White.

When all were positioned, White said, "Well, this is an unexpected and ominous gathering. You all have rather urgent looks about you. What is it, Roger?"

"John, Fernandez sails at first light. When we heard the news an hour ago, we immediately gathered to decide how to present our plight to Raleigh and the Queen . . . without relying on Fernandez."

White's face reddened as he leaned toward Baylye. "Roger, please tell me why I, the damn Governor, was not called to this meeting? In the name of Jesus our Lord, why was I not called?"

Baylye blanched. "John . . . there was no time for argument. We knew the debate would be bitter and lengthy, knew you'd resist our proposal. I'm sorry, but there just wasn't time, and there's little now, as well. So I beg you, please hear me."

White's bulging eyes looked ready to pop from his head; his breath was quick and shallow.

"John, no Assistant will leave, but even if they did, none would have your influence with Raleigh." For the first time in their many tense discussions, Roger Baylye's eyes overflowed with uncertainty; he shuffled his feet, rubbed his fingers anxiously against the outsides of his pant legs, swallowed repeatedly. "John, we have but one course of action, and—"

" 'Tis not so, Roger. I've one you haven't thought of." He looked at Elyoner then back at Baylye. "The perfect solution is for my daughter and her family to return to England and plead our case to—"

"No, Father, I refuse!" Elyoner yelled at him. "I will *not* go . . . no matter what Ananias says."

White quivered, glared at his daughter, looked at Ananias, his eyes pleading for support.

Looking completely helpless, Ananias shook his head then glanced at Elyoner and nodded twice.

MIKE RHYNARD

Baylye said, "John, John, please listen to reason. You are the only one who can accomplish this task. Raleigh will listen to you, and engage the Queen. You are our only hope, and—"

"And what the hell do you think the people in England, especially in that political circus called London, will say when the colony's governor returns *alone*? I'll tell you what they'll say. They'll say John White lured all those innocent souls to an untenable place so he could win a reward from Raleigh, then deserted them there to die. No thank you, Roger. I'm not your man."

Elyoner said, "All the more reason for Ananias and me to stay, Father. Truly! Who could possibly think ill of you with us here awaiting your return? Don't you see? No one else can do this. 'Tis *your* responsibility."

Baylye nodded along with Elyoner's words as a glimmer of hope progressively grew in his eyes.

White thought how remarkably similar Elyoner and his late wife were to one another, how grandly Elyoner embodied her decisiveness and clarity of thought. He glanced at Baylye and a few others, gauged the determination in their faces, knew they were right, but resolved to fight on. He looked back at Baylye. "Roger, this is absurd. Even if I *did* go, what of my belongings? Would they be intact when I returned? Hell no they wouldn't! When I left the previous colony for only a few weeks, people helped themselves to my goods. No. I sha'n't do it!" A bead of sweat dripped off the tip of his cherry-red nose; he swiped at the next one with his hand.

Baylye said, "John, we understand your misgivings. So please read this." He handed White a piece of paper.

White snatched the paper from his hand, started reading.

"We agree with your concerns. So we drafted this document, all signed it—every man in the colony. It shall accompany you to England, to Raleigh, perhaps to the Queen. It says our situation is dire, that you argued to remain with the colony, that you departed only under the greatest duress and for the greater good of the colony, and that there was no other choice." White started to protest, but Baylye raised his hand to silence him. "Last, it says that all of your belongings will be cared for and preserved, even if we depart the island, and that anything missing upon your return shall be replaced or refunded by the colony."

White glared at him, gnawed on his lower lip.

"John, there's one more thing. We intend to *permanently* depart this wretched Roanoke Island, whether to the Chesapeake or to the main, as soon as we're able. Most favor the main for reasons you well know, but the Chesapeake also has certain advantages. We should decide this question now, before you leave, so you know where to find us upon your return . . . assuming, of course, we've convinced you to go."

The defiance melted from White's eyes. He knew he was beaten, had known all along the logic was irrefutable. *Lord, what will become of my friends, my daughter, my grandchild, Ananias? How will I live with myself if ill befalls them?* "Ananias and Elyoner Dare, my dear, dear family, I shall miss you and my beautiful grandchild . . . my precious Virginia Dare." He looked at Baylye. "Isn't it a lovely name?"

" 'Tis indeed, John."

White had regained his color, looked suddenly proud, relieved, stood erect. "I promise you all, I *shall* return. And when I do, I know I'll find a prosperous colony, wherever you go." He kissed Elyoner and Virginia, shook hands with Ananias, hugged Emily, touched her cheek.

Emily whispered, "Governor White, please bring my mother and brother when you return."

He nodded then eyed Baylye. "Roger, I appoint you governor in my stead. Appoint or elect a new Assistant to take your place. Act as I would to preserve and advance the colony. See it safely to the destination you choose. We've no time to discuss that now, for I must be away with haste. And Roger, thank you for your immeasurable support. You, not I, are the leader that has carried the colony of Roanoke this far. Carry it forward, my friend."

Baylye nodded, slapped White on the shoulder.

White's expression softened, grew somber; he looked around the room. "This is all happening too fast, and I haven't had time to think it through; but if you leave, carve the name of the place to which you go on a tree or post in the village, and perhaps in another spot, as well. If you leave in distress, carve a cross beside the name. Do you understand? This is very important. I must know if you leave in danger."

"We shall, John. We'll leave a second message on a large tree along the pathway from the shore."

White acknowledged with a single dip of his forehead. "I'll do my utmost to return by midwinter, for I know the need is great, but 'tis *never* easy to find seamen to brave the Atlantic in winter. Thus it may be spring. So you must hold out, no matter what it takes." He looked at each person in the room. "God be with you, friends." He shook Baylye's hand vigorously with both of his. "Good luck, Roger."

"Godspeed, John."

After a brief hesitation, he walked slowly to Elyoner, stared into her eyes, kissed her cheek then Virginia's forehead, turned toward Ananias and embraced him. He again faced Elyoner and Virginia, cast them a sad, lingering gaze, then turned and stepped out the door into the dark.

* * *

Allie's eyes opened slowly; she blinked twice, lay motionless and wide eyed in the dark as she tried to wrap her groggy mind around the breadth and content of the night's dreams. Her thoughts no longer dwelled on the bizarre nature of her dreams or *why* she was dreaming, but rather on her recollection of *what* she'd dreamed. She closed her eyes, saw Emily and Elyoner talking, the baby nursing, their discussion of Emily nursing. She put her hands on her breasts. Didn't know you could do that, cool thing to do for her friend. What's the friend's name? Heard it a million times. That baby's gonna bond with Emily as much as with her mother, but I guess that's the whole idea. Listen to me, talking like I just had a conversation with them. Emily's in almost everything I dream . . . feel real close to her for some reason . . . but why? She rubbed her butterfly birthmark with one hand and her eyes with the other. How can I feel this stuff? Shut up, Allie, keep thinking.

The Indian, the badass one, actually a good man, just pissed because they murdered his wife and kids—I'd be pissed too—gonna start killing colonists a few at a time. So how can I understand their language? Good Lord. Nothing about this makes sense. God, let it end. Oh yeah, and then the governor . . . what's his name? Heard it a lot, should know . . . John something, common name. Wh . . . Whi . . . White. John White. He's gonna leave . . . things are really bad . . . said his daughter's name, Emily's friend. Ellie, but that's short for something . . . El . . . El . . . Eleanor. That was easy. What's her last name? White said it just before I woke up. Damn. Said the name of the island, too. Come on, Allie. What was it? Did it start with an *F*? No, maybe an *R*. Yeah. That's it.

Allie rolled out of bed, walked to the bathroom. When she came back to the bedroom, she turned on the desk lamp and sat down at her computer, looked at the clock. Ouch. Three thirty . . . oh well. Okay, let's see, I know they're on an island, and it *maybe* starts with *R*. She did a browser search for *English Island colony*. A list of websites with the name *Roanoke Colony* came up. Holy shit! Roanoke. That's it! She double-clicked on a site and saw another picture of people dressed like those in the dreams. But these people stood around a big tree, pointed at the letters *CRO* carved in its side. *CRO*. What's that? Hmm. At the end of the last dream they talked about carving a message on a tree. Another picture caught her eye; this one depicted a group of men pointing at the word *CROATOAN* carved into a log that looked like a post in a fort. I wonder if . . . the leader . . . John White . . . said to carve something on a tree or post. Yeah, if they left the island for somewhere else, they were supposed to carve the name of where they were going on one of the posts in the fort . . . called it something besides a *fort* though . . . Wow! Look at that. A third picture showed a drawing of Roanoke Island with a fort depicted on it and Indian villages across the water on the mainland. Hot damn! This is it!

Allie's eyes followed the cursor as she dragged it down the screen, looked for words from the dreams. *Virginia*. I remember that. There it is again . . . place name again. *Walter Raleigh*. Heard that one. He's the guy in England who sponsored the colony, knows the queen. What else? "Oh . . . my . . . God!"

The Lost Colony.

No!

The Lost Colony is the name given to an early settlement on Roanoke Island in what is now North Carolina.

Can't be right.

The colony is called "lost" because no one has ever discovered what happened to it. Roanoke Island and North Carolina were then part of a vast territory called Virginia that extended from the present state of Pennsylvania to what is now South Carolina. The first group settled there in 1585, but because survival was so difficult, they returned to England the next year. Immediately after they left, a second group arrived, but with the exception of fifteen soldiers who remained behind, they quickly returned to England, as well.

I remember the 1585 group . . . and the guy who brutalized the Indians. They talked about it. White and the Indian remembered it, both were there when they raped that Indian's wife and killed her . . . and her kids. Oh my God. This is surreal.

In 1587, Sir Walter Raleigh sent a group of 117 settlers to reestablish the colony. John White—there it is . . . oh my God—*who led the group, was instructed to settle on the shores of Chesapeake Bay about fifty miles north of Roanoke Island. However, the pilot of the ship, for some reason that remains unknown, refused to transport the settlers farther than Roanoke Island, where they had stopped to pick up the fifteen men who were left there the year before. Not one of the fifteen was ever found alive.*

Allie looked at the wall, her mind spun wildly. I know what happened to them. Heard the Indians tell it; they killed two on Roanoke Island and the rest up north, tortured some of them. She shivered as she recalled the horrific details. How the hell could I dream this? I've never heard of it before. And now I know more about it than any historian. Or do I? Scary. She looked back at the computer.

Relations with the Indians near the island had been destroyed by the 1585 expedition, and several days after the colonists' arrival, George Howe, a member of the expedition, was brutally murdered by them. Nevertheless, the settlers remained on Roanoke Island, where in August a baby girl was born—the first English child born on American soil. She was John White's granddaughter and was christened Virginia Dare.

"Oh my God! I saw her born." She shuddered. I *did* read about these people, about Virginia Dare, in ninth grade history, or somewhere. "But I saw Virginia Dare being born." Chills raced down her back. "How . . . how can this be?"

The colonists expected to live on their supplies from England, but these soon ran out. And as the ships that brought the settlers to Roanoke prepared to leave, the colonists' situation grew desperate. They insisted that John White return to England on the ship to obtain supplies and more settlers. White reluctantly agreed, leaving his daughter, Elyoner Dare, and her baby, Virginia Dare, behind on Roanoke Island.

Where I woke up.

Immediately after White reached England, open war broke out between England and Spain (See "Spanish Armada"), and Queen Elizabeth closed all English harbors. Thus, because of the war, John White did not return to Roanoke until 1590, three years after he had left.

"Nooo . . ."

And when he landed on Roanoke Island, he found no trace of the colonists—only the letters CRO carved on a tree and the word CROATOAN, the slightly misspelled name of a nearby island (Croatan Island) inhabited by friendly Indians, carved on a palisade (log fort) post in the village. But neither carving was accompanied by a cross to signify distress, such as White had ordered if the colonists departed in danger.

Last thing he said before he left.

White returned to his ship and attempted to sail the short distance south to Croatan Island in search of the settlers and his family, but a severe storm forced the ship to sail out to sea for safety. The captain then refused to return to Virginia, and John White never again set foot on American soil.

"He never came back? How could he do that . . . his daughter . . . the baby."

Nothing certain has ever been learned about the fate of little Virginia Dare and the other colonists. Thus, unless some chance discovery or ex-

cavation yields evidence to solve the puzzle, we shall never know what happened to this first English settlement in America.

Allie stared at the page. She tapped a monotonous rhythm with her fingers on the desk. *We shall never know . . . never know.* "No! Can't be! " She glared viciously at the computer as if anger could change the words, change history. "Damn it! Why is this happening to me? Emily, George Howe, Hugh Tayler, Elyoner . . . they can't just disappear. They can't."

Stunned, numb, overcome by sudden depression, Allie turned out the light and walked to the bed. She sat on the side, stared at the wall. *It's like reading that your hometown and your family have been wiped out by a tornado or an earthquake. I know these people. But how can I? It's just a dumb dream. But somehow I'm dreaming* real *history—don't know why or how, but it's real history, and these people are real. Emily, I feel you, know you, care for you, feel like you're part of me.* With tearing eyes, she flopped onto her back, pulled the comforter over her. *Damn it! They're all gonna die.*

But they're already dead . . . lived over four hundred years ago.

"No. They're alive, I see them, know them."

Not so. They're already dead! Get it through your head, dummy. One way or another, they're already dead.

"No. They're alive in my mind. They're gonna make it. They can't die."

A pulse of excitement raced through Allie's body. *Wait a minute! There was no cross by the name in the picture. So they* weren't in danger *when they left. Said they went to Croatan Island. Maybe history's wrong. Maybe they* did *make it. Just because they weren't found doesn't mean they didn't live out happy lives somewhere. They're* gonna *make it. I know they are.*

Allie dried her tears with the end of the comforter then rolled over; buried her face in her pillow and exhorted her mind to ponder the imponderable, explain the inexplicable; whispered, "Emily . . . Emily . . . you have to make it . . . have to make it . . . have to . . ."

***

The four full-haired Indians from the far, far north were nearing the territory of the Chesapeake tribe, which was at the south end of a large, long, north-south water that most people called by the tribe's name. The Chesapeake village was on a square-cornered spit of land, the north side of which formed the south end of the large water, and the east side of which faced the Great-Water-That-Cannot-Be-Drunk. The men had spent several days with the mountain tribes, nearly all of whom spoke slight variations of their own language—variations that were close enough to allow voice communication in lieu of hand signs. But their dialect was unrecognizable to the tribes between the mountains and the large water, most of whom were members of a strong alliance led by the Powhatan tribe and their powerful leader, Wahunsunacock. The Powhatans and the mountain tribes were bitter enemies and had done much injury to one another over the years. So in their journey to the Chesapeakes, the four north men stayed well south of the large, west-to-east river that flowed into the large water by the Chesapeake village, hoping to avoid contact with both the Powhatans and their allies, most of whom resided north of the river. The Powhatans had pressured the Chesapeakes to join their alliance, even threatened them on occasion; but the Chesapeakes enjoyed their independence, preferred a less formal relationship with the Powhatans, and refused to officially join the alliance but paid significant tribute to the Powhatans to preclude being treated as an enemy.

Because of their location, the Chesapeakes were rich in a large variety of seashells which the north men and their people treasured. Though they had huge waters of their own, some too wide to see across, their water was drinkable; and for some reason, the variety and color of shells yielded by their waters were far less suitable for jewelry than those of the Great-Water-That-Cannot-Be-Drunk. So the north men planned to trade their furry robes for vast amounts of shells, as well as the red stones the coastal peoples procured through trade with certain inland tribes, including the Powhatans. The shells would be used for jewelry, while the red stones would be used either for jewelry or to craft the red medicine pipe bowls cherished by their people. Similar red stones could be found in their home territory, but their craftsmen were not as skilled as those of the coastal and inland tribes. In addition to trading, the four would spend the winter with the Chesapeakes to gather even more shells; but these undrilled shells would be less valuable than the drilled ones they procured from the Chesapeakes, for the latter were either ready to be strung on necklaces and bracelets or were already strung and ready to be draped around a warrior's or pretty girl's neck or wrist.

While most of their robes would be traded to the Chesapeakes, a number equal to the fingers on both hands would be traded with another people, the Croatans, one day's canoe trip to the south on the Great-Water-That-Cannot-Be-Drunk. For a reason understood by no one, the waters around the Croatan's island yielded uniquely colored shells that brought an even higher price in the north country. While some were the color of the red stones, others were a mix of the stone color and the color of the sand, and still others had dimples in them that made them even more attractive, further increasing their value.

The leader, who wore the five eagle feathers, and one other north man would visit the Croatans while the two who remained with the Chesapeakes began trading and building the lodge that would shelter them over the winter. The leader planned to remain only two days with the Croatans before returning to help with the lodge and the hunting and fishing required to prepare for the winter.

All four regretted leaving the refreshing coolness of the mountains for the hot, heavy-water air of the lowlands, but their vigilance for enemies was such that their minds had scant time to dwell on the weather or the punishing task of dragging their heavy travois. As they scanned their surroundings for signs of danger, the leader recalled their encounter with the Powhatans on their last visit to the area at a place not far from where they now walked. He remembered putting an arrow into one of them as he charged with a stone hatchet—a gutshot that probably killed the man in time. He'd gone down immediately, and his tribesmen had stopped, thought better of their attack, and retreated with their fallen comrade in hand. The north men had raised their weapons in the air, taunted the Powhatans as cowards and women for backing off. But the leader knew they'd been lucky that day, and though always ready for a fight, he was, *this* day, more interested in reaping the rewards of their long journey, which he couldn't do if he were dead. So he'd quietly reminded the others of last year's encounter and cautioned them to be vigilant. The days of constant alertness for battle had taken a toll on the men, left them with a mental tiredness that, together with their physical exhaustion, had created an eager longing for their journey's end. Now as they crossed a small river that flowed north into the large river, the leader knew they were in Chesapeake territory, signaled the others. He knew they could gradually relax their vigilance over the day and a half it would take them to reach the Chesapeake village; and his companions' more frequent smiles signaled their excited anticipation of an overdue rest, good food, and perhaps a pleasant evening with a beautiful young Chesapeake girl.

* * *

Shortly after sunrise the morning of White's departure for England, Emily lay in bed and imagined herself standing on the outer banks watching the two ships sail east toward the rising sun, held her breath as their sails grew ever smaller before melding into the horizon. She felt a lump in her heart, a vast, lonely, penetrating emptiness in her stomach. Then later, going about her chores in the village, she sensed an infectious pall hanging over the entire colony, a pall that could only have come from visions and feelings like her own. And after half a day of witnessing despair on every face, a skittish glaze in every pair of eyes, chores performed with apathy, she realized they all suffered the same two painful afflictions: the belated acknowledgement that since their arrival, the ships at anchor a short distance beyond the outer banks had been a reassuring comfort to them, a lifeline for escape if the worst occurred; and second, the soulful realization that they were now completely isolated from England, totally alone, with no help, no connection to home. So with no escape and no refuge, all that remained was an empty, lonely sense of abandonment aggravated by the stark comprehension of the awful peril that surrounded them. It had all drilled its way into their minds and souls and now sat like a cannon ball in the pit of every stomach until finally, just before noon, their sensibilities and the gravity of their plight were poignantly validated by the slaughter of their first pig and goat—a major, premature milestone in their consumption of the supplies they had brought from England, the supplies they had expected to see them through the winter.

After a noon meal with her father, Emily sat alone in the cottage for ten minutes, held her locket, reread her mother's letter, told her about John White leaving, the letters he carried from her and her father. She shed her usual tears of longing then told her mother of the debilitating feelings of aloneness and abandonment that had overcome the colony that morning, how she'd felt it, as well, but had now pushed it away. Finally, after putting her mother's letter under her pillow, she kissed her locket, placed it in her apron pocket. She gathered up the dirty laundry, stuffed it into a canvas bag along with some soapwort and a washing bat, then checked that her eating knife was secure at her waist and walked outside. Her first stop was Elyoner's cottage to see if she and Ananias had any laundry that needed washing.

Elyoner said, "Em, you are the most wonderful, thoughtful friend a person could have. I feel horrible letting you do this . . . but I know I cannot yet make the walk."

"I don't mind, Ellie, you'd do the same for me."

"Perhaps I'll be ready in a week or even less. You might even be nursing by then, and we'll bring Virginia with us. I'm so excited for you to begin."

"I, as well, Ellie. *I'm* ready *now* . . . but I doubt my milk is." She smiled as she took the bag from Elyoner, slung it over her other shoulder. "Better be on my way. The others are waiting. We'll talk when I return, before I fix dinner for Father and Hugh, though there really isn't much to prepare."

"Oh, that's right. Master Tayler's joining you tonight." Elyoner felt her heart bump as she spoke the words; she donned a false smile then worried that she was being preemptively unfair to Tayler. But she had long since learned to trust her intuitions, and deferred to them now but kept her misgivings to herself.

Emily saw Elyoner's hesitation, read her concern; she wanted desperately to know the root of it. "Aye, we're looking forward to it. Should be interesting to see how Tommy Colman manages entertaining his daughter's suitor. He's never had to do so before." She smiled, waved goodbye, and said, "See you in a few hours, Ellie. Kiss my baby." She then turned and started toward the far side of the village.

"I shall indeed, Em. Enjoy the cool water. I'm envious."

Halfway to the far palisades, Emily met Agnes Wood, Joyce Archard, and Audrey Tappan. One year older than Emily, Tappan had come with the colonists to meet her fiancé, and Wood to meet her husband, both of whom were among the thirteen missing soldiers. Archard was the wife of Arnold Archard, the man Waters had chastised for his greed. Three soldiers accompanied the women as they started toward the washing stream. Though the flow in the stream by the village had progressively slowed over the past few weeks, it still supplied adequate volume for drinking water; however, it lacked the swifter current and deep pools favored for washing clothes. But even the better-flowing stream could only support four simultaneous washings; so forays were limited to that number, with successive groups scheduled to depart the village every two hours. The limitation was that the stream had but one deep hole with rocks; and because the rocks served as a table for beating the clothes with a washing bat, all the washers had to use sections of that same pool. So no more than four washings could be simultaneously supported without having to wash clothes in someone else's dirty water.

Because they had only recently begun using the new stream, there was not yet a well-worn pathway to it; and the party had to work its way single file through the dense forest, with soldiers in front, behind, and in the middle of the group. Emily and Audrey Tappan walked thirty feet behind the front soldier, worked their way around briars and small trees, speaking softly so the guard wouldn't hear them. Emily had talked to Audrey several times and liked her but had not developed the closeness she had with Elyoner. Audrey was rather homely and quite shy, but as sweet and caring as a human being could be. Emily knew she looked up to her, admired her self-confidence and quickness of mind, had said as much, but such things never influenced the way Emily treated someone. She also knew the disappearance of Audrey's fiancé weighed heavily on her mind and heart, lurked just beneath the surface of fragile emotions. However, Emily doubted that any of the thirteen would ever be seen again, and she sensed that Audrey had accepted the same truth, for she had several times seen her talking to another young soldier.

Audrey said, "I think he's the best looking of the lot. He's also very nice and was just promoted to sergeant by Lieutenant Waters."

"So what's his name?"

"John Gibbes, it is. But he's not guarding us today. He's organizing equipment for the move, even though we don't yet know where we're going. I suppose you know all about that, don't you, Em?"

"Only that the Assistants are trying to decide whether to go into the main to our west or to Chesapeake Bay to the north. They voted this morning to go to Chesapeake but *only* if the Savages there, the Chesapeakes, agree to let us settle beside them. They were quite friendly to the earlier expedition, so hopes are high, even though it will require a long day's sail on the open sea, albeit only a short distance offshore. Roger Baylye's sending two assistants, some soldiers, and Manteo to visit the Chesapeakes tomorrow morning to see if they'll help us. Manteo knows them well, so let's pray for a successful mission."

"John told me they'd been ordered to stop work on the palisades, so we're obviously going *somewhere*. Do you care where?"

"No, Audrey, I don't care at all, don't know anything about either place. I just hope 'tis somewhere without Savages trying to kill us every time we step out of the village." She wondered if Audrey's lad and the other missing men had gone to the Chesapeake, how their discovery, alive or dead, might change the plan.

"Aye to that, Em."

"Oh, we're here." Emily sighed, removed her hat, wiped her brow with her sleeve. "Time to work."

The three soldiers quickly spread out around the small clearing that surrounded the washing pool, moved slightly into the timber about fifty feet from the stream to get a better view of the forest around them without sacrificing a good view of the ladies.

The four women went quickly to work, each picking a deep spot in the pool close to a good-sized rock on the bank or in the water. A few men had previously dammed the stream below the pool to enlarge it to about thirty feet by twenty feet with a depth of about two feet. The women dumped their dirty clothes on the grassy bank, removed their shoes, pulled their skirt hems up to their waists, and tied pieces of rope around them to hold them up above the knees. Their smocks, which were too short to be doubled up, hung freely to their knees.

Each then picked up a small armload of clothes and waded into the water with a few branches of soapwort in hand. The roots of the soapwort, which grew in abundance in England, as well as on Roanoke Island, produced a sudsy substance when cut or smashed, which the washers then massaged into the dirty, wet clothes. After considerable manipulation, they laid the clothes on a nearby rock, beat them with a washing bat—a paddle about twelve inches long and five inches wide with a foot-long handle slightly smaller than a sword grip. The beating permeated the soapwort through the fabric and cleaned it; thus the four women attempted to maintain an equal pace so they could beat their clothes at the same time, which allowed the residual soapwort in the pool to flow downstream and clear the water for rinsing. So after the beating, they rinsed the soapwort from the clothes and hung them on trees and bushes to drain and dry while the next bundle was washed.

Only half listening to the chatter and banter of the others, Emily glanced around the clearing to locate the three soldiers. Two leaned on their muskets, gawking at the women, while the third, musket in hand, searched the forest as ordered. She made a mental remembrance to casually mention to Lieutenant Waters that some of his men seemed to have a keener interest in watching women than in watching for Savages, but quickly decided it was an incurable soldier trait not worth mentioning. Resuming her task, she savored the fresh smell of the soapwort, the coolness of the stream on her legs. She listened intently to the sounds of birds and other small creatures, emanating from the forest around her, marveled at their number and clarity. She smiled, wondered if they were talking *to* each other or *over* each other in a lively family discussion. Emily loved the forest, had always reveled in its peace and solitude, and today felt a new freedom, a special exhilaration at being in its heart, absorbing its life, its joyful sounds.

One of Emily's pastimes at home had been to learn the voices of the birds and animals around her. She believed it strengthened her bond with nature, and she considered that bond an essential element of life. Today she'd paired three birds and one small squirrel-like creature with a short tail, with their songs; and she listened, searching for more as she rinsed a bundle of clothes, stepped out of the water, then walked the fifty feet to the tree line to hang them on branches to dry. As she stepped along, she heard a shrill warbling sound she hadn't heard before. She stopped, aimed her ear toward the opposite side of the stream where the sound had come from, heard it again. The symphony of songs suddenly ceased.

None but Emily noticed. Something's wrong, she thought, too quiet. She laid her bundle on the grass, scanned the tree line, the guards, the forest beyond them. Two guards had their eyes on her; the third watched the women in the water. As she glanced toward the pool, she heard a dull thud behind her like a rock hitting metal, faced the sound. A naked Savage with a stone war club in his hand stood over the body of a motionless soldier.

"Hiyaaaa!" He shook his war club in the air then bashed the soldier two more times in the head.

Before she could scream, three Savages leaped on another soldier, his last sound the rush of air from his slit throat.

"Hiyy! Hiyaa!"

Two more Savages overwhelmed the remaining soldier, who triggered his matchlock as he fell, firing an aimless shot into the ground.

Phffft! Phffft! Two arrows flew past Emily. She flattened herself to the ground, yelped as an arrow grazed her shoulder.

She heard screams from the pool, told herself to get up, run, but laid flat, pressed her body into the grass. Her heart raced; fear paralyzed her mind. She looked toward the water, saw a woman face down on the bank, motionless, legs in the red water, an arrow in her back—Joyce Archard.

Audrey thrashed out of the water, ran toward the forest on the far side of the stream.

Hiyaa! Hiyaaa! Two Savages churned through the water after her, but one suddenly veered off to pursue Agnes Wood, a closer target whose wet skirt slowed her pace. As the Savage struck her with his club, an arrow sliced across the top of Emily's shoulder. She screamed, rolled instinctively to the right; felt warm blood trickle down her arm, a flood of nausea confuse her mind. Bleeding, trying to kill me. Arrows thudded into the ground around her. Going to die . . . will it hurt? Get up, Em. Run! Run! *Phffft!* An arrow whizzed by her ear. She staggered to her feet, raced into the forest toward the village, her heart pounding in her ears. Can't breathe; run faster, faster, heart bursting, run; someone behind, gaining, closer, closer; run, run! A thorn bush gripped her skirt; she spun around to free it, saw a blur approaching, jerked frantically, ripped the skirt free, started to run again.

"Aah!" A vicious blow to her back tumbled her to the ground. She quickly rolled to face the attack, reached for her knife. The Savage leaped upon her; planted his knee in her stomach, forced the air from her lungs; held her right shoulder on the ground with his left hand; glared into her eyes with a burning, hateful look that froze her soul. His right hand held a stone war club above her head. She couldn't move, stared into his eyes with a defiant then submissive look that acknowledged her imminent death.

In the two seconds their eyes were engaged, she memorized his face: the curved nose, gaunt features; the right side of his head clean-shaven, covered with red paint that narrowed to a stripe down the right side of his forehead and across his right eye and cheek to his chin; on the left, a full head of coal black hair pulled behind his head and tied above the left shoulder, three long, narrow, striped feathers hanging from the hair; an inch-wide swath of black paint from the left hairline across the eye and down the left cheek to his mouth; the long, prominent scar that ran parallel to the black strip of paint from his eye to his chin—all punctuated by the crazed, malevolent look in his eyes.

She gasped for air, found none, twisted, pushed to escape his knee, take a breath.

In a sudden, swift movement, he seized her by the hands, flung her over his shoulder, jogged back toward the clearing, his shoulder jarring the air from her lungs with every step. God, help me, she pleaded. Her face banged against his sweaty back; the pungent, masculine aroma of his body flooded her mind. Can't breathe. Going to die. She saw a knife at his waist, yanked it from its sheath, thrust it into his side.

"Aah!" He threw her to the ground a few feet in front of him, quickly touched his side; looked at the flowing blood, ignored it; raised his war club, sprang toward her.

The ground's impact kicked the remaining air from Emily's lungs; she gasped, rolled to the left. His club smashed into the ground where her head had lain a quarter second before. She churned her feet to stand and run, was halfway up when he grabbed the side of her shirt and smock at the collar, ripped them apart and over her arm to her waist, shoved her brutally to the ground. As she rolled onto her back, he reached down, grabbed her hair with his left hand, swung his club at her from the right.

Emily blunted the blow with both forearms. He battered her again, and again; each time her arms blunted the blow; each time the stone came closer to her head until, exhausted, she lowered her bruised, bloodied arms to her sides, stared calmly, serenely into his eyes, surrendered to her fate, and awaited death.

But the Panther held his blow, peered deep into her fearless blue eyes, felt his soul meld with hers—her courage, her wild beauty—realized she was the one, the one he would take and use as his wife had been used. He reached out slowly, gently with both hands to lift her.

Emily felt near death; her body screamed with pain; her chest heaved as it gasped for breath that wouldn't come; she didn't move, waited for him to take her, do with her as he wished; her heart pounded like a galley drum.

He touched her chest, slid his hands over her bare breasts, lingered for a moment, then reached under her shoulders to lift her. When she was nearly to her feet, a musket shot crackled through the air, then another. He dropped her to the ground, looked toward the shots then back at Emily; his frenzied look returned, he abruptly swung his club at the left side of her head.

She again raised her bloodied forearms, felt the club smash into the bones; knew she'd moved too slow, felt the stone thud into her head; saw a brilliant white light, then darkness and oblivion.

* * *

Allie screamed, bolted upright in bed, gasped for air; tears filled her eyes. Emily! No! Oh my God. No! Don't let this happen. Not her. Please, God. Not Emily!

CHAPTER 6

A t first there was total blackness, as black as the inside of a womb, followed after a time by gray until the black returned. The cycle repeated itself until an hour into the fifth gray period, when a faint haze appeared then slowly yielded to a fragile light; and out of the hazy light appeared a sleek, graceful ship, a fierce dragon head atop its tall prow, a single square sail pushing it nimbly through rhythmic ocean swells. As the ship drew closer, a row of colorful shields became visible on each side above lines of stowed oars that protruded from her sides. Rugged-looking, bearded men—some sitting, some standing, some wearing metal helmets—talked to one another or looked silently out at the gray sea. At the prow of the ship stood a sturdy, determined-looking man about twenty-five, his long, light brown hair flowing behind him with the wind. His blue eyes had a strong set but also a touch of sadness that hovered quietly behind the resolve. After a while, he turned toward the men behind him, looked at one who sat in the second row, and motioned him to come forward. "Bjarni, let us talk about the large freshwater seas."

Bjarni rose and walked toward him. "What would you like to know, Tryggvi?"

Total darkness engulfed the scene.

∗∗∗

A darkening gray sky melded with a narrow band of dirty, faded blue dotted with puffy pink clouds that seemed to float on the western horizon, where the endless black sea had just swallowed the sun's last, shrinking rays. Rising into the thickening darkness, the dragon head on the ship's prow seemed to search the horizon and point the way for the pilot at the tiller. And except for small spaces at the stem and stern, the entire deck was covered by a red- and white-striped tent, its ridge pole extending fore and aft with lingering drops of rainwater occasionally dripping from its sides.

Other men sat under the tent engaged in various endeavors: some sharpening swords and axes, some eating or drinking, a few fishing, some staring forward at the horizon, some staring aft toward home, and some watching the school of porpoises that followed the ship. All of the men wore knee-length tunics and cloth pants covered by fur leggings which were held in place by spirals of ribbon wrapped from the ankles to the knees, and a few wore round metal helmets with nose plates in front. Tryggvi, Bjarni, and a third man sat in the front section of the ship, just inside the tent, engaged in animated discussion, occasionally motioning toward a roughly sketched animal-hide map held by the third man. As he pointed at a line on the map, Tryggvi said, "So, Hefnir, if the Skraeling stories are true, there will be many portages before we reach the largest freshwater seas. But first, my friends, we must find the bay. And I think we've drifted a little south of course, so"—he looked at Bjarni and Hefnir—"do you think you can find it if we make landfall on the coast to the south?"

The two nodded. Bjarni said, "Aye. The huts and fortifications will still be there, and it's a unique-looking place with a large island in the entrance to the bay, so you have to sail north or south of it to enter the bay and reach the river. Also, the camp was on the north tip of the island, on a long peninsula that runs northeast from the west side of the island—an unusually long and straight peninsula . . . like my poker." He pointed between his legs, smiling proudly. "Then you have to—"

Tryggvi and Hefnir snickered at one another.

Bjarni pretended surprise. "What? What's so funny?"

Tryggvi said, "It must be a very short island, indeed, if it looks *your* poker, Bjarni." He punched Bjarni's shoulder as all three burst into laughter. "Go on."

"Well, the mouth of the river is at the northwest corner of the bay."

Hefnir said, "The river flows into the bay from the southwest; so we go upstream and then portage a great waterfall before we find the first freshwater sea, which is smaller than the others. And after that, all the seas are connected by short rivers until we reach the last, largest sea, which extends back up to the northwest . . . I think. Everything *was* on the map, but as you've seen, it's too faded and smudged to be of much use. Besides, I think Albrikt was drunk when he made it; and remember, all the directions were from the Skraelings, and none of them had ever seen a map, so . . ."

"Well," Tryggvi said, "I'm still undecided whether it's best to explore Vinland or find the freshwater seas. How many days' sail to Vinland from the bay camp?"

Bjarni said, "At least four days south with good wind, and . . ."

The scene vanished.

* * *

Ananias Dare, Thomas Colman, and George Howe sat on stools in front of Colman's cottage. Though the brutal summer temperatures had begun migrating toward those of fall, it was still too hot and humid to sit close to a fire; so the three sat some ten feet from the flames, dark shadows and firelight comingling on their faces in a primitive, wavy dance.

Ananias said, "But Thomas, there are too many angry Savages between here and the main for us to simply sneak our way there undetected. They watch our every movement. No, I think going to the Chesapeake was the right decision . . . the *only* decision. The governor spent a winter with the Chesapeakes on the last expedition and found them friendly and helpful, as did our recent emissaries. On the other hand, we know nothing of the tribes in the main; and even if we successfully bypass the belligerent tribes along the river, who knows what we'll find there? No, Chesapeake was the only real choice. And don't forget that the Chesapeake *is* where Raleigh granted our charter and acreage. 'Twould be rather presumptuous of us to think we can take our charter and settle wherever we please. Again, Chesapeake was the correct choice."

Colman shook his head. "I understand, Ananias, and I basically agree with the vote, but going somewhere other than where the governor *thinks* we're going is risky, makes me wonder if he'll find us when he returns."

George Howe said, "But didn't he know we might go to Chesapeake when he left?"

"Aye, he did," Ananias replied, "and I think we've devised a foolproof plan to inform him of our decision, one that follows his instructions precisely."

Colman frowned. "But, Ananias, that's the part that worries me. There's no such thing as a *foolproof* plan . . . something can always go awry. And leaving carvings that imply we went to Croatan Island instead of Chesapeake will send him in the wrong direction . . . and what if misfortune overcomes the three people we leave on Croatan Island, and there's no one there to guide him to our Chesapeake village? In that case, he'd have to rely on the Croatans; but they'll know only our *general* whereabouts, and that's no different from telling him we went to Chesapeake in the first place. So you see, there's a risk, my friend, and I'd prefer we simply tell him we went to Chesapeake in the first place and then let him locate the village when he arrives there."

"Well, I agree there is a slight risk, Thomas, but there's always *some* risk in everything. However, with only modest luck, at least *one* of the three at Croatan will be alive to show the governor *exactly* where we are. Think about it. He may return as soon as three months from now"—he counted on his fingers—"and certainly no later than seven or eight months from now. So really, how much can happen to the three at Croatan in so short a time?"

"But, Sir," George said, "though I have no vote, I agree with Master Colman. Why not simply tell him we're going to Chesapeake?"

Ananias said, "Here's why. Who knows where we and the Chesapeakes will be when the governor finally arrives? What if it *is* eight months, or longer, before he returns? Their territory is large, and we may move. Why send him searching all over Virginia when he can simply sail down to Croatan Island, a safe place he knows well, pick up the three men, and sail directly to our exact location? By the bye, thanks to Manteo, the Croatans have already agreed to let our three men live with them until John returns."

"But how will those three know where we—"

Ananias nodded. "Well, since we're moving people and supplies to Chesapeake over a period of days, we'll take the three Croatan volunteers up to the Chesapeake village on one of the early voyages. We'll then take them down to Croatan Island on the return voyage. 'Tis only a short distance south of here and not far out of the way. So all three will know exactly where the new village is; and if for some reason we and the Chesapeakes move from that location to another, we'll simply leave John a message at the first location telling him where we've gone, or we can sail the pinnace down to Croatan and tell the three people where to find the new site. Thus"—he looked at Colman and George—"if ill befalls one, or even two, of the three, someone will still know our exact location . . . and the Croatans will know our general location. By the way, we'll carve the word *Croatoan*, rather than *Croatan*, here at Roanoke, since that's what the governor knows it by, even though 'tis incorrect. And as Roger promised the governor, we'll carve it on a palisade post here in the village and on that large tree on the pathway from the shore."

"Well," Colman said, "though I see the logic of it, it also worries me that we're not leaving a cross of distress by the word *Croatoan*. He told us to do so if we leave in danger—emphasized it, in fact—and"—his voice suddenly cracked with emotion—"and I *do* believe we're in danger." His eyes sparkled with sudden tears; he blinked, looked away, rubbed his eyes. "Sorry, gentlemen, thinking of Emily . . ."

George's eyes misted, as well, as he and Ananias waited for Colman to regain his composure.

When he looked back, Colman said, "My apologies."

"None needed," Ananias said. "We share your feelings about Emily."

Colman continued. "Anyway, I think we should carve crosses by the words."

"I agree," George said.

"Well," Ananias replied, "I can't disagree that we're leaving in distress, but I also agree with Roger and the majority that by the time the governor returns, we'll be out of danger and safely settled with the Chesapeakes. So why unnecessarily alarm him and, more importantly, the new colonists with him. Think about it; if they get off the ship *here* and find crosses of distress, they'll be terrified, probably reboard immediately and sail back to England."

Colman nodded slowly. "Hmm. Well, I can't disagree with *that* logic, but—" He saw Elyoner and Virginia approaching. "Elyoner. Here, take my seat." He rose, pointed at the stool.

"No, Thomas, sit down. I came to see how my best friend fares. Here, Ananias, hold Virginia while I visit her. Any change?"

"None," Colman said. "Let's go inside and sit by her. 'Tis cooler now, and time to bathe her wounds.

The three men lifted their stools, followed Elyoner inside, then set them near the doorway to enjoy the light breeze that drifted in from outside.

Colman went to the bucket, poured some water into a bowl, and started tearing two-inch strips of cloth for bandages. George collected three candles and set them beside Emily, who lay unconscious on her bed at the rear of the cottage. She had a sheet over her body, and her forearms and head were completely covered with bandages that had several red splotches where blood had seeped through.

Elyoner knelt beside her then looked at Colman. "I think the bleeding's slowed, don't you agree, Thomas?"

"Aye, but not enough." He handed the water and bandages to Elyoner, turned away, rubbed his eyes. Seeing his vibrant daughter helpless, battered, and nearly dead tore at his heart like a wild beast. Normally a reserved, dispassionate man, he struggled to contain his emotions; had remained by her side, leaving only for the most necessary matters; prayed as never before while she clung to life by the thinnest of threads.

Even now, when she appeared to be improving, he couldn't escape the horrible guilt of having caused her suffering and near death solely for his own gratification. He'd been a selfish fool, and though he hadn't told anyone, he'd resolved to return to England at the first opportunity, even if his wife and son arrived with White and had to immediately reboard the ship to sail home.

Elyoner stared at Emily with misty eyes, shook her head. "My friend, my friend, my poor, dear friend. You must return to us." She leaned forward, kissed Emily on the cheek. "Here, George. Hold her head up—right here, under the neck—while I unwrap the cloth."

After George did as she asked, Elyoner gently unwrapped the bandage, winced, swallowed hard as she saw where the stone club had hit on the left side of Emily's head and the physician had cut away enough hair to see and stitch the gash. "Well, 'tis still ugly but definitely better. I think she's improving . . . at least the wound is. We won't know how she is inside until she wakes . . . and she *will* wake. God will answer our prayers."

Elyoner began to bathe the wound with a slow, feathery touch. It was a two-inch-long cut surrounded by a purple-black bruise that covered the entire side of her head and the left front of her face, all the way to her black left eye. Careful to do no more than caress with the wet cloth, Elyoner cleaned the dried blood away, rinsed the cloth, and repeated the process until the blood was gone. Then as a trace of new blood appeared, she held the cloth against the wound with a slight pressure until it stopped.

The men watched the process with twitchy, empathetic eyes, grateful that Elyoner, rather than they, was treating the wound.

When she had stopped the bleeding, Elyoner put a bit of tree moss on the wound, wrapped a new bandage around it, and nodded at George to ease her head back onto the pillow. "Good, George. Now hold her left arm up a bit . . . that's good." She unwrapped the cloth from Emily's purple-black forearm. Elyoner shuddered at the horrific punishment the arm had taken, agreed with Physician Jones that there would likely be shattered bone beneath the bruises. "The arm's improving, as well, though it still looks horrible . . . hurts me to look at it. She'll be in pain for a good while, but it *will* heal . . . she has ferocious determination." She cleaned the wounds, rewrapped the arm, and repeated the procedure on the right arm. "Much better here. She obviously took most of the blows with the left arm."

When she had finished, she kissed Emily on the cheek, stood, stared down at her friend's expressionless face. "I so miss your bright eyes and smile, Em. Please heal." She caressed Emily's cheek, dabbed the tears that had formed in her eyes, then faced the men. "Come, gentlemen, let us sit with her and pray."

In a silent pall, the four sat glumly in a circle by the door, prayed privately for five minutes, then looked at one another in painful silence. With a morose expression accented by a forced smile, Elyoner looked at Colman and George. "This *will* pass. She's *going* to live. I *know* she is."

After Elyoner put Virginia to bed, she returned to the Colman's cottage, and the three took turns reading Bible passages. George had read three lines when, from the back of the cottage, a faint voice whispered, "May I have some water?"

George stopped; the four regarded one another with quizzical looks, their eyes wondering who had spoken.

Elyoner looked toward the back of the room, saw Emily's tired blue eyes peering at her between the top of the sheet and her head bandage, instantly thought how she looked like a sick, helpless little girl in need of her mother's love. "Emily!" She dashed to the bed, knelt beside her, crossed herself, caressed Emily's cheek, kissed her, caressed her again. "Oh, Em. You're here. Thank God!" Tears rolled down her cheeks faster than she could catch them with her sleeve. "Someone bring a cup of water."

Emily looked back at her with exhausted, glassy eyes and a tepid smile, whispered softy and slowly, "Hello, Ellie."

Colman knelt on her other side, fought his tears, touched her cheek, then kissed her.

"Father." Tears filled Emily's eyes.

Elyoner took the water from George. "Thomas, hold her up a little . . . gently now . . . too high, back down a bit. There." She held the cup to Emily's lips while she sipped. "Slowly, Em, slowly. Not too much."

When she had finished, Emily noticed George standing behind Elyoner. Her face immediately filled with sadness, uncertainty, caution. "George . . . are you . . ."

He knelt beside her, eyes damp and red. "Emily . . . I'm here. I'm myself now . . . I . . ." He kissed her cheek, held the hand she'd raised to him. He leaned down to her ear, whispered, "Emily, I love you. Praise God, you're alive."

Emily answered with a faint new glimmer in her eyes and a soft smile, then looking at each of them in turn, whispered hoarsely, "Why am I like this? What happened to me? I remember nothing. Why do I hurt so?" She winced as she moved her left arm, then rubbed the back of her neck with her right hand.

The four looked at one another. Solemnly, Elyoner said, "You've been lying here on your back for eight days, Em, eight days unconscious."

"Eight days? But . . . but why? What happened? I don't remember anything."

Again they glanced at one another, each pair of eyes begging another to tell the tale, none accepting the challenge.

Emily's eyes suddenly widened with a spark of remembrance. "I *do* remember something . . . a dream . . . unlike any I've ever had before . . . a ship . . . a Viking ship, I think . . ."

* * *

A frigid chill rushed through Allie's sleeping body.

* * *

"and some men talking . . . I felt their thoughts and feelings, understood their language . . . smelled the sea air . . . they were deciding something . . . something about freshwater seas . . . 'twas so strange. I've never given a thought to the Vikings in my entire life. I know they raided us for many years and left much of their blood in our veins, but . . . but why would I dream about them? Never had a dream like that before . . . and I remember everything."

Elyoner said, "I don't know, Em, but nothing would surprise me after your ordeal."

Emily touched her bandaged head, looked at her wrapped forearms, moaned as she tried to move, then glared at her attendants. "God's blessed mother! Will one of you tell me what happened!" Her cheeks reddened, she kicked her legs up and down like a child in a tantrum. "Ow!"

"Emily Colman! You stop that right now!" Elyoner said. "You'll hurt yourself, make things worse."

George said, "I'll tell you, Emily." He sat down beside her, held her hand, took a deep breath. "You, Agnes Wood, Joyce Archard, and Audrey Tappan were washing clothes. Three soldiers guarded you. Then Savages—the Roanokes, who killed my father—and another, different-looking Savage from some other tribe, surprised and killed the soldiers and Joyce Archard. They tried to take Audrey with them, but she resisted and they clubbed her . . . she died that night."

"And Agnes?" Emily's eyes were a wide, fearful blue.

"They took her."

"Did you try to rescue her?" She looked at each man.

All three shook their heads. Elyoner's hands covered her face.

Colman said, "It grieved us, Em, but we'd not the strength, the means, or the will to rescue her . . . and shame be upon us . . ." He sighed. "Her existence, if she has one, will be one of unspeakable horror."

Emily's eyes misted; she looked toward the wall. After a long, reflective pause she said slowly, "I remember him . . . the different-looking one! His face, its hateful look . . . he was the only one with hair . . . long hair on the left side . . . pulled back . . . three thin feathers. I shall never forget him." Her breathing quickened as if she were again running for her life. "Wanted to kill me." She closed her eyes for a moment, opened them; looked at her arms, touched her head; began to cry, slowly rocked her head back and forth, panted loudly. "He hit me . . . then must have decided to take me with him . . . his hands on my breasts . . . then picking me up . . ."

"Em, this pains you. Enough for now."

She stopped, grabbed George's sleeve, stared at him with sad, spent eyes. "Go on, George."

He stared at her for a moment. "As you wish, Em. We heard a shot in the village. I seized my axe and ran toward the sound. Twenty men and soldiers were behind me; and when I saw you about a hundred yards away, the Savage was clubbing you like a berserk. You blunted his blows with your arms . . . mostly your left arm . . . again and again. I don't know how you kept the club from your head."

Emily's eyes widened in terror. She pulled the sheet up to her nose, closed her eyes, sighed. "I remember."

"Should I stop?"

"No! Tell me everything."

"Truly, Em, you need not—"

"George, go on!"

"Very well. He suddenly stopped pounding you, reached down to lift you up . . . I think he wanted to take you with him like they took Agnes. Then two soldiers fired their muskets; I yelled and ran toward him; he looked, saw us, swung his club at you, hit your arms, then your head . . . you went limp." George pressed his lips together, looked away, dabbed his eyes. "He raised his club to hit you again, crush your skull . . . like Father's . . . but the soldiers shot again and he ran off." He faced her. "Em, I thought you were dead . . . covered in blood and dirt . . . lying still as the earth, barely breathing. I screamed your name . . . cried . . . Lord God, how I cried . . . the thought of you dying before I could beg your forgiveness . . ." He touched her cheek.

She laid her hand over his. "George, if you hadn't come, I'd . . ." She held his hand to her lips.

Elyoner said, "Let her rest. This is too much."

As George slid his hand along her right cheek and stood, Emily reached under the sheet, assumed a frantic, panicked look. "Where's my apron?"

George reached behind her, picked up her apron, and handed it to her. "I found it on the ground near where you fell."

She snatched the apron from George, thrust her hand into the pocket, searched with her fingers. " 'Tis not here. Where is it?"

"Where's what, Em?"

"My locket! I want my locket! It was here in the pocket." She grabbed his sleeve, pulled herself up.

"Em, I . . . I don't know. We searched the area for anything that might have been dropped, but—"

"Mother!" A flicker of insanity flashed in her eyes. "I must find it! I'm going now!" She rolled to her side, braced herself to rise.

Elyoner held her down. "No, Em. Not now. You're not strong enough. Tomorrow. Perchance I'll take you tomorrow . . . *if* you're ready."

"No! I won't wait! I want it now!" She tussled with Elyoner.

Colman held her right arm. "Emily! Stop this! You don't need the locket. Your mother will join us soon, and we've scant time to search anyway."

"*Scant time?* Why?"

Colman looked flatly at Elyoner then at Emily. "Because in a fort-night, we depart this wretched island for the Chesapeake country."

"Then I'll find my locket now." She rolled off the bed onto her knees. "Ahhhh!"

"Emily Colman! Enough!" Elyoner said. "You can't leap about like this." All three eased her back onto the bed.

Like a little girl telling her mother about her skinned knee, Emily blubbered, "That hurt . . . bad."

"The ribs," Elyoner said with a mother's scolding look. "Physician Jones said you may have cracked a few in the back; so by my troth, you stubborn, rebellious lass, lie still! You've only just awakened, and you're not ready to walk. And you're not going anywhere . . . yet. If the locket's there today, 'twill be there tomorrow. So rest awhile, and then I'll help you stand if you must. And perchance in a day or two, we'll take some soldiers and go look for it." She waved her index finger up and down at Emily. "We've an entire fortnight, so do as I say, girl!"

Emily closed her eyes, curved her lips into a pouty curl then looked up at Elyoner. "You act like my *mother*. I want my locket! I can walk *now*."

"You *need* a mother, Emily Colman, and I'm her! You *cannot* walk yet, so lie still and behave yourself. You're *such* a troublesome lass." She thought how diminished, fragile, and frail Emily looked, thanked God she was alive, still spirited—nothing could take that from her.

Emily glared at Elyoner, snorted like a swine. "Very well then. Tell me about departing for Chesapeake."

* * *

The next day, Emily sat tenuously on a stool beside Elyoner, her bandaged left arm in a cloth sling. As Virginia sucked assiduously on her breast, Elyoner said, "Well, Em, the three of them, and the soldiers with them, searched the area again, found nothing. So perhaps in a day or two, you and I can get some soldiers and look again. It's got to be there somewhere . . . but the way you ran . . . you covered a lot of ground, and who knows? Emily, do you have the stomach to go back there . . . it was such a terrifying experience."

The massacre squeezed its way back into Emily's mind as it had routinely done since her awakening, made her shudder with renewed terror as every detail again unfolded before her: the dash for the forest; the Savage pursuing, pushing her to the ground, his knee on her stomach; gasping for air, his face. His face . . . never forget his face: curved nose, gaunt features, red and black paint, wild, malicious eyes. She again felt herself slung over his shoulder, his jog jarring the air from her lungs like a bellows. That's it! That's where it is. When I stabbed him, he threw me to the ground; it must have fallen from the apron pocket. "Ellie, I know where it is . . . if I can . . . if I can find where he dropped me." A solitary tear tracked haltingly down each cheek as a shadow of fear crept across her face. "But you may be right, Ellie. Perchance I'm *not* yet ready to go back there. Perchance . . ."

Clutching Virginia with one arm, Elyoner stood, stepped over to Emily, gently pulled her head against her side, and caressed the back of her neck. "They say tears and time are the greatest healers, my friend, so let them flow. I cannot imagine how you feel, your memories, your terror. But I'm with you, and I'll stay with you and help you. You *will* persist, dear Emily. You *will.*"

A few seconds later, Emily looked up with passive, mournful eyes, wondered how it could ever be so; then before the thought faded, re-solved that it *would* be so, that she would *make* it so. "Ellie, thank you for being my friend. We *will* go to the place. We *will* find my locket." She closed her eyes. Mother, I promise you I shall find it.

After Elyoner returned to her stool, she smiled at Emily. "Em, I must tell you a story. The year Ananias and I were married, I was help-ing him dig post holes for a small fence we were building. My wedding ring was hurting my finger on the shovel handle, so I took it off and laid it on the ground near one of the holes. Well, that night after supper, I stuck my hand out to admire the ring as I frequently did in those days, and to my horror, it was gone. I couldn't sleep that night, cried and worried that Ananias would notice, think the worst of me, that I didn't love him and was declaring my independence. At first light, I rushed to the post and searched for the ring; and when I couldn't find it on the ground, I concluded we'd buried it in the post pole. So there I was on my hands and knees, digging and sifting dirt with my hands, when Ananias came outside and saw me." She chuckled. "You can't imagine how embarrassed and tongue-tied I was when he asked me what I was doing."

Emily smiled. "Just trying to do a better job of setting the post, right?"

"That's *exactly* what I told him; and to my utter surprise, he nodded and walked back inside, quite impressed by the diligence of his new bride. Anyway, I dug up and reburied that post three times—in secret, of course—before I gave up hope. Then I went inside and cried all day—fortunately, Ananias was away. So the next morning, I went back to the beloved post one more time and searched the ground around it; and by the saints of Christendom, there it sat on the ground exactly where I'd put it." She held her hand out, looked at the ring, her smile broad, proud, and radiant, as if she were about to delve into a dish of plumb pudding. "And the moral is that one should never give up. Never! And that's my story. And don't *you* ever give up, Emily Colman."

"I sha'n't, Ellie. I'll search until I find it." After a pause, Emily flashed a more somber look. "Ellie, have you seen Hugh Tayler?"

Elyoner frowned instinctively at Tayler's name then quickly recovered her smile. She still had misgivings about the man, felt an uneasy ripple in her heart when she saw him; but she'd noticed heartfelt concern in his eyes when he looked at Emily, prayed that her apprehension was misplaced, that he *was* as he appeared to be. "Have I seen him? My Lord, he was practically living here the whole time you were unconscious. Came by twice a day to see how you were doing, spent hours talking to your father, who's quite impressed with him, by the way, and . . . oh, that's right, you wouldn't have known. Master Tayler was with the men who ran to the . . . to the site, helped George and two others carry you back, and I'm sure he'll be here as soon as he hears of your awakening."

"Really?" Emily's eyes brightened with the delight of a young girl receiving her first piece of jewelry.

"Aye. 'Tis true."

Emily studied Elyoner's face, noticed the shadow of misgiving that always appeared there at the mention of Hugh Tayler's name. "You still don't like him, do you, Ellie?"

Elyoner frowned again, this time through a weak smile. "Truly, Em, 'tis not that I don't *like* him. 'Tis . . . 'tis just something I sense . . . and your age difference doesn't help. But 'tis only me, I'm sure. He seems genuinely taken by you, and I'm being a dunce by scowling every time I hear his name. So please forgive me and think nothing of it."

"You don't need to ask forgiveness. I know you're only thinking of my well-being, and one must respect one's intuitions. And Ellie, please understand that though I'm attracted to Hugh and enjoy him, I've much more to learn about him before I could ever say I loved him, though I confess I *do* have strong feelings for him, even now." She felt a twinge of guilt at understating the depth of her attraction, justified it by telling herself that Elyoner would be all the more concerned if she knew the full truth; but she respected Elyoner's unspoken intuition, resolved to be cautious with Hugh. "So did Father tell you anything of his talks with Hugh? He'd never discuss such matters with me, other than to encourage the relationship."

"Not a lot. Only that he retains considerable holdings in England and will someday receive a rather large inheritance, possibly including the family estate under certain circumstances. For sure, *if* he's spoken the truth, he already is, or will be, a wealthy man."

Emily wondered why Elyoner had questioned his honesty, stowed the thought in her subconscious for later consideration. "Interesting. I've never had such discussions with him; but regardless, my feelings are independent of any wealth the man has or may acquire in the future. When *I* fall in love and marry 'twill be for love of the *man*, not his money. I know some think those priorities are reversed, but I guess I'm just a simple, naïve young lass."

"Emily, your priorities are exactly as they should be. The love of money leads nowhere. Only the true love of another person can sustain one through life's challenges, though a little money certainly helps. Anyway, I'm just happy you're alive and recovering well, and I'm anxious for the time—soon, I hope—when you can begin nursing Virginia. And speaking of Virginia, I must take her back to the cottage for a change of clothes and a nap. A nap would suit you, as well, my friend, keep you on the rapid mend." As she rose to leave, someone tapped on the cottage door.

"Come in," Emily said.

Hugh Tayler poked his head into the room. "Emily! I heard . . ." He rushed through the door, knelt beside her. Looking into her eyes, he shook his head slowly back and forth, seemed awed that she now sat alive before him. "Emily . . . I'm . . ." He started to put his hands on her shoulders, noticed the sling, then grasped her right hand with both of his, held it to his lips. "Emily, I'm so happy you're alive. 'Twas unbearably painful seeing you unconscious, not knowing if you'd live or die. I . . ." His eyes glistened with a thin dampness; he thought how vulnerable and helpless she looked with all her bandages and her black eye, marveled that even in her helpless, wounded state, she remained striking beyond description, stirred his soul and emotions to their deepest depths.

"Hugh, I . . ." Familiar warmth surged through Emily's body. She reached up, touched his cheek, began easing her head toward his, looked alternately at his eyes and lips; her heart and breath quickened.

Elyoner coughed. Hugh and Emily stopped, pulled back with knowing smiles.

Emily took a deep breath, mentally thanked Elyoner for rescuing her from another emotional lapse she might have regretted; admitted she was no longer confident of her ability to control herself with Hugh Tayler, knew she must avoid situations that could imperil her chastity—her mind flashed to her narrow escape with the young lad back in England. Even if she were truly in love, she could allow no compromise of her morals before they were married. Stupid girl, she thought, why are you thinking marriage? You haven't even decided that you love the man . . . must ask Ellie again what she heard about him.

Elyoner said, "Master Tayler"—she couldn't bring herself to call him *Hugh*—"I don't wish to sound like a nagging mother, but I suppose that's what I am. I was just telling Emily that she's been up too long and needs to rest if she wants to continue mending. I'm sure you understand. Perhaps you could come back this evening, when Thomas is here, and have a lengthy conversation with my *young* friend." She couldn't resist expressing her disapproval of their age difference.

Emily showed a pouty look but was again relieved at Elyoner's intervention, knew it would have been improper to be alone in the cottage with Hugh; she agreed her father's presence would be a perfect, though somewhat awkward, solution, one that would also allow her to assess the relationship between the two men. The last thing she needed was her father and Hugh striking a secret betrothal agreement; her presence with them would surely preclude such an occurrence.

Tayler rose, swallowed his disappointment. "An excellent idea, Mistress Dare." He turned toward Emily. "With your permission, Emily, I'll return this evening. Your father and I have actually become quite good friends, even talked about him nominating me to be an Assistant. So I shall enjoy the visit on two counts. Good day, ladies." He bowed to both women then walked out the door.

Elyoner, instinctively unsettled by Tayler's comment about the Assistants, stared at Emily without expression. "I'll see you later this afternoon, my dear friend. I expect George will be by to visit you sometime today, as well. Em, I trust George completely; but on other matters, please take care . . . and I speak not of your health."

* * *

Emily didn't sleep. Rather, she lay on her back, relived the massacre, grieved for the dead; imagined Agnes being raped again and again, beaten, led about by a rope around her neck, treated as a slave, visualized herself there instead of Agnes; saw Audrey Tappan, Joyce Archard, and the three soldiers enshrouded, being lowered into their graves; thought how quickly the graveyard was filling, shuddered when she thought how close she'd come to being there herself. As her hand slipped into her empty apron pocket, she blinked at the fresh tears in her eyes, again promised her mother she'd find the locket. In a day or two, I'll be strong enough, and Ellie and I will go there and find it. Yes, Mother, it *was* awful . . . but I didn't have time to be afraid . . . even when I knew I was going to die. With a moan, she rolled to her right side, stared at the cottage wall, thought about all that had befallen them in so short a time, and again felt the wispy twinge of foreboding that had haunted her since their arrival.

No, Mother, I don't know what I'm going to say to George. He told me he loves me again. I'm so torn, don't want to hurt him; but in truth, I don't have a passionate love for him . . . yet someday . . . he's such a good young man. And Hugh . . . he actually helped rescue me and . . . I like him, Mother . . . and my passions are rising, and I may be falling love with him, so I think I must guard myself carefully. But on the other hand, there's so much happening in my life right now, there's little time for daydreaming about love . . . daydreams, and Hugh, may have to wait until Chesapeake . . . Oh! Elyoner also told me Manteo was here to see me several times while I was unconscious, paddled his canoe all the way here from Croatan Island. A true friend he is, and I regret that I've seen so little of him. Yes, Mother, he's shown me that Savages aren't at all what we think they are—at least *he's* not. I expected an ignorant, unfeeling, ferocious animal, like Savages are said to be; but I found him intelligent, witty, honest, and with feelings and values like any good Englishman. No, Mother, the one who nearly killed me was *not* like Manteo . . . but I think 'tis because his people have suffered at English hands, and they believe they're fighting for their existence . . . the same as we would. As a man, he's probably as noble as Manteo. She trembled, imagined his ferocious glare hovering above her, his club on its way to her head. With a painful moan, she rolled onto her back, closed her eyes. Anyway, Mother, we'll soon be away from here . . . and I *shall* depart with my locket in hand. So pray for me to find it . . . and to find the words I shall say to George. I love you, Mother. Come to us soon.

* * *

Baylye continued, "and as you know, we're critically short of nearly everything we need to eat and drink." The usual grumbles floated around the room as he unfolded his list. "Fortunately, the modest success of our hunters and fishermen has enabled us to stretch our shipborne rations considerably further than estimated. But even at that, people are quite famished and tempers short; and with the end of our supplies now in sight, the issue is whether the last of them occurs *here* or at Chesapeake. If we fill our bellies here, we'll arrive at Chesapeake well-fed but with no food to initiate our new existence there. I doubt that the Chesapeakes—

fine, friendly souls that they are—will greet our arrival with platters of fresh fish, oysters, and deer . . . and they certainly have no beer."

Snickers floated around the room.

"No, I think they'll be expecting us to acquire those delicacies on our own. I would also call your remembrance to the fact that in 1585, Lane demanded that the Savages here at Roanoke feed him and his men, and that demand has been the root of nearly every ill that's befallen both sides ever since. We have a chance for a new start with the Chesapeakes, and arriving with enough food to establish ourselves will stand us in far better stead than expecting them to provide for us."

He looked from man to man, gauged their thinking, their feelings. They were restless, he thought, but more from frustration with events than anything else. "So, if you agree, we'll stretch what we have to cover the first week of the entire colony's presence at Chesapeake . . . and that means we go hungrier here or drastically increase our success at hunting, fishing, and foraging, all of which are complicated by the threat of attack." He paused for comments, none came; wondered if the grim reality of their situation had finally sunk in, convincing them that they were precariously close to disaster and needed to take actions that matched their circumstances. "Fishing, of course, offers less exposure to the Savages, but in two days, the pinnace and one shallop will be completely engaged in transporting people, belongings, and equipment to Chesapeake, and thus will be unavailable for fishing. We also need boats to get to the mainland to hunt, given that little game remains here. But the Savages there have probably already taken most of the local animals, so we'd have to sail or row far up the river to find any measurable amount of game, which would waste much valuable time with no promise of success and far greater risk of attack." He shook his head. "So I think before we depart, the only course is to harvest every animal we can find *here*, including small ones like squirrels, hare, the big-eyed animals with rat tails that hang from tree branches, and the mischievous ones with striped furry tails, and we must use arrows and other means to do so lest we expend our ammunition too quickly. At the same time, we must also fish with *all* of the boats for the remaining two days and with the unengaged shallop after that. We must also clam and crab like zealots until the last voyage departs for Chesapeake twelve days from now. However, even though Manteo showed a few of us how to salt and dry fish and venison, we haven't enough salt and time to do so. So we'll eat the fresh food first and save the preserved food for Chesapeake."

After general concurrence by the Assistants, Baylye observed that supplies of grain and yeast for beer brewing were nearly depleted because they had been used for food, which meant that until John White returned with more, they would have to use grain made from corn they bartered from the Savages, *if* the Savages were willing. He then proposed they cease making beer immediately, to avoid adding bulky cargo to the voyages, and take only what was already brewed, which would provide a modest initial supply at Chesapeake, where they would begin brewing with corn. He next discussed the salt-making operation on the outer banks, which, though laborious and logistically challenging, had met the colony's seasoning needs at a fundamental level. He directed that the operations continue but at an accelerated pace, with all three vessels transporting salt crews to and from the outer banks each morning and evening, and fishing the rest of the day. Then when the pinnace and one shallop departed for Chesapeake, the remaining shallop would carry on until the final departure.

Baylye's insides churned when he thought of the challenges ahead, the complication of approaching winter. One such challenge, a monumental one, would be the building of palisades. He had no idea how he'd persuade them to do so, given their weariness of palisade building, but at least they were now experienced and could perform the task much faster. But, he acknowledged, winter would probably preclude serious progress before spring and allow him plenty of time to concoct a compelling argument. It would have to be a good one, for many would counter that because they were with friendly Chesapeakes, palisades were unnecessary. Perhaps they'd be right; he hoped it would be so.

"Two more items, friends: the Chesapeake transportation plan and the election of a new Assistant to fill my former position since

I've now replaced Governor White. Let's discuss the move first. The plan has little flexibility for adjustments because the objective is to get most of the supplies and equipment, and a goodly number of people, up there on the first two voyages. The first voyage will be two days from today—ten days before our final departure—and the second voyage will be five days before the final departure. John Hemmington will pilot the pinnace, while Peter Little and John Cheven will pilot the shallops. These three are our most experienced sailors, and I want them to know the sound and offshore well in case the weather turns on us. The first voyage will take thirty men and women, some with particular skills, as well as heavy equipment and enough personal belongings and supplies to sustain them for a few days. Twenty-four people will remain at Chesapeake with the five who are there now, to lay out the new village and begin building cottages. Six, including the three going to Croatan Island, will sail back here by way of Croatan. Henry and Rose Payne, and Charles Florrie, have volunteered to be our people at Croatan Island, and the returning voyage will deposit them there since they'll then know where the Chesapeake village is. Sergeant Smith will head the contingent of soldiers; and John Bright, Cuthbert White, and William Willes will be the three Assistants responsible for governance.

"As I said, the second voyage will go to Chesapeake five days before our final departure and will also consist of thirty men and women and a large amount of baggage and equipment. Lieutenant Waters will be on this voyage; and Roger Prat, John Sampson, and Thomas Stevens will be the Assistants." He looked at Thomas Colman. "Thomas, I thought it best to assign you and Emily to the last voyage to allow her as much recovery time as possible before traveling. Will that be acceptable?"

"Aye, it is, Roger. Thank you for the consideration."

"Very well then . . . Oh, Dyonis and Ananias, since you've both welcomed new family members—" He frowned as a sudden surge of compassion flooded his mind. "Dyonis, please excuse me, I can't begin to tell you the sorrow we feel over Margery's death. My God, man, you bear it well. I could not be so strong in such circumstances." He paused while the others offered their condolences to Dyonis Harvie. "But since you now have a fine, healthy young son to raise, I think it fair that you choose the voyage that best suits your needs."

Dyonis rubbed his bloodshot eyes. "Thank you, Roger . . . all of you. I shall miss her greatly, but somehow young Henry and I shall persevere. Thank you for your support." He paused, collected himself. "So, since Elyoner Dare is nursing and caring for the boy, I'd like to send him with her and Ananias on whichever voyage they choose. I myself would like to go on the third voyage, so I may spend as much time as possible with Margery at her gravesite . . . probably the last times I'll be with her."

Baylye nodded, laid his hand on Dyonis' shoulder. "So be it." He looked at Ananias. "And you, Ananias?"

"We've discussed it and would prefer to go on the second voyage though when Elyoner hears Emily will be on the third, she may change her mind. But plan for us to be on the second voyage."

"Done." Baylye's eyes then surveyed the entire group. "I will be on the last voyage with the remaining fifty-one; and by the bye, while the people on the first voyage are working on building the village at Chesapeake, we on the last voyage will be hunters, fishers, gatherers, and salt makers here at Roanoke."

The last item of discussion was the election of a new Assistant. The nominees were Lieutenant William Waters and Hugh Tayler. There had been some concern about soldiers being involved in the colony's governance, but Baylye had convinced them that it was appropriate, if not absolutely essential, given the colony's circumstances. Thomas Colman had been unaware of Waters' nomination when he nominated Tayler, and subsequently decided there could be no better candidate than Waters, making his selection unanimous.

When the meeting adjourned, all of the Assistants lauded Baylye on his thorough planning, expressed their joy at leaving Roanoke, their eagerness to get underway. After they departed his cottage, Baylye congratulated himself for conducting his first non-contentious meeting then cynically concluded that their situation was so severe, their choices so few, there really wasn't much to contest; nonetheless, he felt a sustained uplift in spirits as he rethought the transportation plan, again acknowledged its soundness. As he chewed on a small piece of overcooked venison and swigged water instead of beer, he agreed with himself that the plan was as close to perfect as it could be, given their circumstances. Then with a slight shiver, he regretted the thought—bad luck to be prideful, for perfect plans seldom go perfectly. And as he stared at a small sketch of his wife, who was back in England, he wondered what would go wrong with *this* plan.

* * *

Emily, her father, and Hugh Tayler had just finished dipping their eating knives in a bucket of warm water and wiping them dry on their sleeves. Though it was still warm in the cottage, a clean, fresh smell in the outside air hinted at a shift in the weather toward fall. Emily, who now wore only small bandages on her head and left arm, listened quietly as her father divulged his feelings about Queen Elizabeth.

"She's been quite a good queen, I believe. Wouldn't you agree, Hugh? Certainly, there have been the usual sendings of people to the Tower, and the headsman seems as busy as with her father, Henry, but she appears to be more of a people's monarch than he was. What do you think?"

"Well, I would agree. But I also think the success of a monarch has much to do with who they choose as their close advisers; and perhaps more importantly, how well they filter the truth from all they're told. Most advisers, it seems, work for their own good rather than the good of all. King Henry is a fine example, from what I've heard—well advised during the first part of his reign but later drifted off course due to the bad advice of certain advisers—but there's no way we non-courtiers will ever know the truth of such matters. If anything, the Queen seems to be less easily misled than her father, which is good, though I'm told she *does* have her enemies; and as we all know, the bloody Catholics would have her gone in a breath if they could."

"Yes, that's true; and I find it interesting that there's now such a sharp divide between us of the Church of England and the Catholics, given that most of us—our parents at least—were Catholic to begin with. I believe those who say that nothing divides like religion are quite correct, and—"

"Well, Father," Emily interjected, "I think the entire idea of popes *or* kings telling people how to live is foolish. Jesus Christ Himself told us how to live, and I think we can follow his teachings on our own."

Colman said, "Emily, you shouldn't say such things. People have been burned at the stake for less. You're lucky you're here instead of in England."

Tayler had never found religion but was nonetheless amazed at Emily's candor—amazed and awed that a woman could be so forthright. But then again, he thought, maybe he wasn't surprised after all. He'd seen enough of Emily to know she had her own mind—a deep, decisive mind, capable of surprises and sound judgments—admitted that her quickness of thought was one of the attractions that had plunged him ever deeper into the whirlwind of passion and love that possessed him.

"I don't care, Father. I *do* agree there's value to attending church to remind us of our responsibilities to the Lord and each other, and to receive Him in communion; but in the end, 'tis our *individual* relationships with God that are important and should guide our way."

Tayler said, "Well, Thomas, speaking of individual relationships, I think it's no secret that I have a deep interest in Emily and would like to ask your permission to court her, such as our circumstances allow."

Emily tensed, felt a rush of caution rise to her head. Tayler's request had caught her completely off guard, and her instincts screamed at her to move more slowly. But then, was he really asking for anything more than what the two of them had already discussed? Probably not, she decided, though she hadn't expected him to pose the question this soon, or in her presence. Relaxing, she turned her attention to her father, watched him with an impish, expectant grin; awaited his reaction, knew he was completely unprepared to respond.

Colman glanced at Emily then looked at Tayler. "Um . . . this is rather sudden, Hugh, especially with Emily present; but uh . . . even though *I* have no objection, I'd like to discuss it with Emily before I respond, if that—"

"No need, Father. Hugh and I have already discussed it; I'm quite agreeable." She chastised herself for speaking rashly, again cautioned herself to move more slowly, make no commitments until she was sure of her feelings.

Colman looked at Emily, shook his head with a helpless, resigned look. "I should have known . . . but very well, I grant my permission . . . but only in the village . . . in plain sight of others." He looked at Tayler.

"Aye, sir. I'd have it no other way."

Though mindful of lingering caution floating in her mind, Emily smiled at Tayler, delighted in the thought of spending more time with him, perhaps some of it hidden from observers. He stirred her heart and body more than any man in many a day, and she wanted to see where their relationship would lead. Still, she warned herself, *I must protect my virtue.*

Colman glanced quickly at Tayler then back at Emily. "So, uh . . . Emily, Hugh and I have something we must discuss, man-to-man. Would you mind waiting here for a moment while we step outside?" As soon as the words left his tongue, he knew they were awkward, knew Emily would resent them and respond in her usual acerbic way, braced himself for the inevitable storm.

Emily met his expectations with the force of a cannonball. "And what if I do not, Father? What then? Since it's something I'm not to hear, it must involve *me*. So by what leave do you treat a grown woman this way?"

Her fire excited Tayler but intimidated Colman, who said, "I'm sorry, Emily. I didn't say that well." He looked at Tayler. "Sometimes there are things men must discuss alone, and this is one of those things. I promise you it has nothing to do with—"

"Fine, Father. Do as you wish. Good evening, Hugh. I'll see you tomorrow." She turned away, began tidying the cottage.

Tayler had hoped to prolong the evening with a walk around the village but read unmistakable finality in her tone. "Until then, Emily. Thank you very much for the supper. It was a most pleasant evening."

As the two men stepped outside and closed the door, Emily wondered what they'd talk about. She knew she'd been abrupt with her father, regretted it as always; but even as she struggled to soften her ire, her alarm heightened as she imagined the two crafting a betrothal agreement for her marriage. *He's no right to do this, no right at all,* she steamed. *And I sha'n't abide it no matter how I end up feeling about Hugh Tayler.* She sat down on a stool, crossed her arms, fumed, pouted, waited for her father to return.

A minute later, Colman walked into the cottage, looking like a man about to be burned at the stake. While Emily glared at him, he spoke haltingly. "Em . . . please allow me to . . ."

Emily stood, walked to within a nose of him, her eyes like flying daggers on their way to a target. "How dare you insult me like that, Father! How dare you bargain with my life! How much did he agree to pay you for my hand? How could you do this to me? I don't even know if I love him."

Colman's sad, mournful eyes, downturned lips, and pink nose made him look as if mortally wounded. "Em, my dear loving daughter, I could *never* do as you suggest. In twenty lifetimes, I could never bring myself to barter your future. Your future is yours and yours alone, and decisions regarding it are also yours alone."

Emily's outrage evaporated like a drop of water on a hot, windy day. She embraced her father, pulled him as close as she could. "Father, forgive me. I thought the worst . . . an impetuous fool, I am."

"Nay, Daughter, my delivery was at fault. As so often happens when I speak to you, the well-intentioned words that depart my lips are poorly chosen and therefore poorly perceived. 'Tis my fault alone."

Emily held him close, whimpered softly. "No, Father, I was rash and presumptive . . . but at least we can be honest about our shortcomings, and we both know we love each other deeply." She pulled away to arms' length, looked into his eyes with a smile. "Perhaps we'll never learn the art of communication with one another, but our love is all that matters in the end, and we're both secure in that. I love you, Father."

He put his arms around her, pulled her to him. "And I, you, dear Emily. May God be with us in the days ahead." After a few moments of silence, he said, "I should tell you what I discussed with Hugh as I'm sure it will come up when you walk with him. When we voted for the new Assistant, we elected Lieutenant Waters; and even though I nominated Hugh, I voted for Waters. 'Twas actually unanimous because everyone, even the usual malcontents, agreed that it was an oversight that he was not an Assistant from the beginning. He's a most capable young man of good judgment and character . . . well worthy of the position. So, I told Hugh what I've just told you . . . thought he should hear it from me rather than someone else."

"That was good of you, Father. How did he take the news? He *was* rather keen on the idea . . . but how could anyone quarrel with the choice."

"He took it quite well, actually. A bit upset at first, but as you say, the logic is irrefutable to any sane man, and I believe Hugh to be such. I think he understood and felt better by the time we parted. I do like him, Em."

Emily wondered if it were true, if Hugh had really accepted the decision, wondered where their relationship would go in the coming months. Would they fall hopelessly in love, or would their circumstances and the dramatic events ahead forge a different outcome?

* * *

As Hugh Tayler walked back to his cottage, he thanked the God he didn't believe in but was afraid to ignore, for allowing him to know and love Emily Colman. Yes, he admitted, for the first time in his life, he was deeply, passionately, headlong in love, and that love was growing ever deeper. This vivacious, vibrant young woman has changed my life, he thought, given me new breath, a chance to rise above my past—all of the many things I've done of which I'm not proud, have run away from, closed my eyes and conscience to. She's provided me the opportunity—nay *inspired* me—to become the noble human being I've always *wished* to be . . . but lacked the courage and character to *actually* be. Her mere presence has made me a different man, and I *shall not* let her down. I love her.

He then thought about his unanimous defeat in the Assistants' election, saw the logic of their choice, resented it nonetheless; vowed to yet become an Assistant, knew it wouldn't be long before another vacancy occurred.

***

Lieutenant Waters and his three sergeants huddled just outside the palisades. Waters looked at Smith. "About a third of our force will sail on each voyage, and you, Sergeant Smith, will command the men who go on the first, the day after tomorrow; I will command those on the second; and"—he looked at Myllet and Gibbes—"you two will command those on the last voyage, with you, Sergeant Gibbes, acting as deputy to Sergeant Myllet." Turning back to Smith, he said, "There will be but twenty-eight souls with you at Chesapeake, civilians and soldiers combined; and though the Savages there seem friendly enough, take *nothing* for granted. With that few people, you *will* be vulnerable. So you must plan and act from a defensive perspective. Be alert, ready for anything. The five who are already there should have the village laid out and perhaps a start on cottages, but you should expect to live in tents initially, and I want you to first place piles of logs around the site for defensive cover. Whether we build grass mat cottages like here or bark cottages like the Savages prefer will depend on the availability of materials, which translates into time; and the time before winter being scant, we shall have to adopt the approach that yields the quickest winter-worthy shelter. The five there now have likely already made that decision. Also, Sergeant Smith, there will be three Assistants on your voyage, and they are Governor Baylye's representatives, the decision-making authority, and are to be obeyed in all but pure military matters." He glanced at Myllet and Gibbes. "Same for you two with regard to the Assistants who remain here for the last voyage."

All three nodded assent.

"Now, men, we're unfortunately exactly where I feared we'd be: hungry, under the constant threat of attack, and winter soon upon us. We will therefore need *all* hands to do whatever is necessary to ensure we have shelter and food for the winter." The three sergeants looked at one another. "Time is against us, and nothing short of full cooperation and obedience will be tolerated from the men. Further, our already inadequate rations will grow more so in the days ahead—at least until we begin hunting and fishing at Chesapeake. So I anticipate that discipline and order, with both the troops and civilians, will be severely taxed in the days ahead, which means we soldiers must continue to lead by example, however difficult that may be. And on that note, how is morale, and what's the level of discontent?" He drifted his gaze expectantly to all three in turn.

After a long silence, Myllet said, "Not good, Sir. The issues are the same as I mentioned before: lack of food and manual labor; but the intensity of the grumbling has become more severe, more open. So perchance our new start in Chesapeake will somewhat divert their minds."

"And is the discontent universal or limited to a few?"

"As before, they *all* grumble . . . but a few are beyond grumbling and approaching that line that cannot be crossed. Again, I'm hopeful that new surroundings and more food will help the situation, but at the moment 'tis not good."

"Well, I appreciate your candor, Sergeant. You all know where duty compels me to stand on this matter, and you must stand with me." He looked into each man's eyes, paused to let him grasp his intensity and resolve. "Nothing's changed in our response to insubordination or mutiny—death by hanging or the axe—and public flogging by one of their mates for lesser offenses; and I expect you three to ensure the men understand this, and that you'll promptly inform me of any who are about to cross the line. None of us want to carry out punishments against our own, so better that we *preclude* violations than deal with them after they occur."

The three nodded agreement, but Waters read their faces, saw unspoken thoughts and words behind them, then concluded that a few men had already crossed the line. He realized the day would soon arrive when he'd have to demonstrate his resolve, make an example of some poor bastard who didn't have the brains or maturity to understand the bigger picture: that all of their lives were inextricably entwined, that weakness of resolve by any jeopardized all. He thought back to his training, to how his instructors had repeatedly pounded the importance of unbreakable discipline into their heads, insisted that breaches could *never* be tolerated in Her Majesty's army, demanded they be met with firm, swift punishment when they occurred. Yes, he dreaded that inevitable, inescapable day, but knew he had no choice, that anything less than immediate, harsh punishment would permanently undermine discipline and destroy the colony.

* * *

The first voyage had been gone for two days. They had sailed the short distance to the gap in the outer banks a little south of Roanoke Island, then out to the sea and north up the coast toward Chesapeake. The salt crew at work on the outer banks had watched them until they blended into the horizon. And though only thirty had sailed, it might well have been three times that number, for those who remained at Roanoke were wrapped in the same blanket of isolation, despair, and fear they had felt when John White and Fernandez departed for England. Though all were eager to see the last of Roanoke Island, they felt a persistent flutter of apprehension in their bellies, the ever-present fear of the unknown; so they'd busied themselves by carefully packing cups and saucers, candlesticks, dishes, pots, pans, bedding, clothes, linens, and more; collecting furniture, trunks, lead shot, weapons, tools, and small amounts of food in the assembly area.

The Assistants had assigned personal belongings to specific voyages; and many second-voyage people had sent their belongings on the first voyage, while many third-voyage people, including George and the Colmans, would send theirs on the second voyage three days hence. Since the cottage George shared with several other bachelors was rather crowded, the Colmans had retained most of his and his father's belongings in their cottage. The three had just finished a meager noon meal and were about to resume packing when Thomas Colman was summoned to an Assistants' meeting. Perhaps because George was younger than Emily and Colman knew Emily was not romantically inclined toward him, he had never had misgivings about the two being alone together and so, said a casual goodbye then stepped outside.

George and Emily had not been alone together since before the massacre, and there was a nervous, awkward tension in the room as they resumed packing. Emily's head bandage had been removed, and her facial bruises were nearly gone, but because it was still tender, her left arm remained covered in a thick wrap of protective bandages. She had tried fewer bandages, but had frequently bumped the arm painfully on various objects and therefore decided it needed heavy padding to protect it until it was better healed.

After five minutes of silence, George faced Emily, took her hands in his, stared into her eyes. "Emily, I want to tell you how very sorry I am for the way I treated you that day. I . . . I was not myself. My head was spinning, aching, screaming at me to run from everything associated with Father's death . . . and sadly, you bore the brunt of my insanity. I can't imagine how horrible you must have felt. I know I said awful things . . . I cannot even remember what they were; but I *do* remember they were terrible, hurtful, unjust things." He hesitated as his voice cracked and tears found their way into his eyes and down his cheeks. "Em, I'm so sorry." He wrapped his arms around her waist, pulled her to him, felt her warmth flow through his body.

Emily leaned her head against his chest, felt his heart pounding, as soft, compassionate tears glazed her eyes like morning dew on a crisp fall day. "George, you need not apologize. You were possessed, overcome by grief. Yes, I *was* hurt, but Ellie helped me understand what you were going through, and I then felt only deep frustration that I could not help you." After a silence, she said, "You know, George, we've gone through a lot in our short time here, and other than our relationships with each other, and Virginia's birth, most of it has been sad. Our courage and fortitude are about all we have left; but with God's help, perhaps we'll prosper at Chesapeake."

George pulled back slowly, looked into her eyes. "Emily, you're so strong and courageous. Would that I had half your courage."

"But you do, George. Else you wouldn't have come to my rescue and probably saved my life. For certain, another blow to the head would have killed me."

"That's different, Em. 'Twas *spontaneous* courage... not the strength of character *you* have. But I told Father when I prayed at his grave that I'd do everything I can to help this colony succeed and prosper, no matter what the dangers, and thus it shall be. Emily"—his look hardened as his eyes probed deep into hers—"as I told you the day you awoke ... I love you. I love you more than my own life, more than anything I can imagine in this world. I know you don't feel that same love for me; but Emily, I will wait until you do ... even until the last moment of my life. I shall always love you."

They embraced, held each other in silence. George felt her breasts pressed against him, their smooth rise and fall with her breathing. His mind swam in a sea of emotion filled with the flush of her warmth, the depth of his love and commitment, the absence of hers, his desperate hope that time would win her.

Emily's heart writhed with anguish as she wrestled for a response. She wanted to tell him she really *did* love him, but couldn't lie; wanted to say she loved him enough to give it time to grow, but knew such faint encouragement would be unkind; considered telling him that it could *never* be, but refused to hurt him. In the end, she decided he already understood her feelings and reaffirming them would only worsen his pain, decided to say nothing, and responded with the firmness of her body against his.

After a moment, George said, "Em, I must ask you something."

"What is it, George?"

" 'Tis awkward asking you this, but . . . is it true Hugh Tayler's courting you?"

* * *

The Assistants had decided that when the colony arrived at Chesapeake, the women, like Savage women, would be responsible for dressing the wild game shot by the colony's hunters, thereby allowing the hunters more time to hunt. The women's training was to begin immediately; so when three men led by Roger Prat, the colony's most experienced hunter, shot a pair of does and a fawn, Emily, Elyoner, and several other women began their instruction by watching Prat as he gutted the animals prior to hanging them for curing. None had seen the process before, so moans and gasps filled the air around Prat as he cut a doe's throat to allow the blood to bleed out. He then cut out some dark, bulgy areas below the hind knees. "These are the scent glands . . . very smelly . . . ruin the meat if you don't get rid of them." He promptly buried them in a hole and washed his hands in a bucket of water that sat by the deer. Next he cut around the animal's anus and cut the skin upward the length of the belly to the neck. "We'll leave the skin on until after the animal's cured and we're ready to butcher and cook it, a few days before we depart. Now here's how you gut it. Remember, you must have a very sharp knife for this." Prat had a mischievous twinkle in his eye and seemed to be enjoying the ladies' disgust at having to observe the process.

He cut the belly open from in front of the anus up to the rib cage. The stench from the cavity drifted out, hit the women like a sharp slap in the face. All but Emily turned away, covered their mouths and noses. "You'll either need a man with a knife, or a saw like this one, to cut through the chest." He held up a short, pointed saw with fine teeth. "And always go to the side of the chest plate, or you'll never get through it."

After he completed the cut, he said, "Now all of you gather in close so you can see this part." Only Emily did as he asked. "Come, ladies, 'tis not that bad. You'll soon be doing this yourselves, and you must do it properly, so please give me your attention." The others reluctantly inched closer. "There are a few things to cut before you can take the innards out: two places where the lungs attach to the rib cage, this tube from the throat, and these canals that go to the heart." He had made the cuts as he pointed out each piece. "Now I want each of you to put your hands on all of the guts so you get used to the feel of them . . . and the smell. You'll think nothing of it after a few times. So, who's first?"

Most of the women groaned in disgust.

Emily knelt beside Prat. "I'll do it." She no longer wore her forearm bandage but had attached her long sleeves for protective padding; so she pulled up her right sleeve, ran her hand over every piece of the innards, smiled at Prat. " 'Tis not so bad, still warm."

"Good," he said. "Now pull the guts out."

Without hesitation, she reached inside the cavity and pulled the innards onto the ground.

"Very good, Mistress." He then pointed at several items in the gut pile. "This is the stomach, the bladder, the liver, and the heart. And these are the intestines—we clean and save them for making sausage." He smiled at the looks of revulsion on their faces. "Now this is very important. You don't want to rupture the bladder or the intestines while they're still in the animal, for 'twill ruin the meat. Now I'm told the Savages use stomachs for water bags, and we can do the same if we become short of water buckets though you'd probably want to use a buck's stomach because it's larger. Also, the heart and the liver are very good to eat when properly cooked."

Emily asked, "So how do you cut the heart and liver free?"

"Ah, you're a good student, Mistress Colman . . . right here." He put his hand around the heart and pointed at the canals leading into it, handed Emily his knife. "Here, go ahead and cut it out."

Again without hesitation, Emily took the heart in her left hand and the knife in her right, cut the heart free, then held it up with both hands for the other women to see. "Manteo told me the Savages eat the heart and liver raw and drink some of the blood because it gives them the strength and spirit of the animal that's sacrificed its life. I want to do it."

Disgusted moans again rippled through the group.

Elyoner said, "Emily Colman, are you turning savage? Perhaps that blow to your head did more than we thought."

Emily laughed. "I'm serious. I want to try it."

Prat looked shocked. "Well, it wouldn't be for me, Mistress . . . and I wish I could tell you to go ahead, but Governor Baylye instructed me to put all the meat together, so it can be cooked and rationed. Perhaps you'll have your chance at Chesapeake when we've more game. So, if you will, pass the heart around to the other ladies, so all can feel it." More disgusted groans. "Mistress Dare, why don't you kneel where Mistress Colman is and touch the innards a bit. You other ladies should do the same."

Emily passed the heart to Jane Mannering then washed her hands in the bucket of water.

Elyoner said, "I don't think I can do this. I'm going to spill my *own* guts."

"Elyoner, show some courage," said Emily. " 'Tis really nothing—just gooey, slimy, bloody, and sticky. Don't be a coward!"

Elyoner frowned, knelt beside Emily, touched the guts, manipulated them a little, then stood to let the next woman do the same. "You're right, Em. 'Tis not so bad . . . certainly no worse than dealing with a baby's bottom."

Prat said, "Very good, ladies. Now the last thing is to take a rod like this"—he held up a two-foot-long iron rod—"and stick the ends between these tendons, here, and the legs—behind and just above the knees—to hang the animal to cure. And if the ends of your rod aren't hooked like this gambrel, to keep the rod from going all the way through, you'll need to tie them tightly with something to keep them in place, so the legs remain spread. You can use a sturdy piece of green wood if you don't have a rod. Next you tie a rope to the middle of the rod and call a man or another woman to help you; then throw the rope over a sturdy tree limb, hoist the animal up high so other animals can't reach it, and tie the end securely to the tree trunk. And that's the end of your training for today, ladies. Those of you who are still here a few days before the final voyage can help me skin, butcher, and cook these deer for our first meal at Chesapeake."

"Thank you, Master Prat," said Elyoner, "for turning our stomachs. But 'twas indeed informative."

Emily said, "Thank you, Master Prat. I'll help you do the skinning when 'tis time, if I may. And Elyoner, please speak only for your *own* stomach. Mine's quite settled."

Roger Prat smiled, nodded at Emily, then dragged the deer to a tree and hung it to cure. The women then dispersed to other activities. As Emily and Elyoner neared Elyoner's cottage, Hugh Tayler approached, nodded, tipped the brim of his hat. "Good morning, ladies. Only seven days until the final voyage. Doesn't the very thought of it raise your spirits?"

Emily said, "Hello, Hugh."

Elyoner nodded. "Indeed it does, Master Tayler." She looked at Emily. "Time to feed Virginia and Henry. We'll talk later, Em."

Emily nodded then faced Tayler, who said, "Emily, you've been very difficult to locate these last few days. Seems like a year since we talked."

Emily had avoided Tayler since George asked her if he was courting her. Something about the word *courting* was wrong—perhaps the feel of it, the newness, or the implied commitment and surrender of freedom. Regardless, the sound of the word gave her a strange, uncomfortable sensation, like a pair of too-tight shoes. She'd wanted more time to think, to decide if courtship was what she truly wanted, to crystallize and confront the disquieting uncertainty that hovered in the back of her mind. "Sorry, Hugh. I've been busy preparing for the voyage . . . and learning how to gut deer." She held up her hands, which still had specks of blood on them. "I've also been a bit upset at your telling people we're courting. I realize 'tis not a secret, but I thought 'twas between the two of us."

"I'm sorry, Emily. I was quite excited . . . mayhap *too* excited. I only told a few people, but 'twas apparently big news and spread quickly.

And you're right. It *is* between you and me. Can you walk with me awhile?"

She smiled. "Of course."

As they walked toward the most uninhabited part of the village, he took her hand in his, immediately felt the familiar, warm rush to his head and loin; he marveled that she still affected him so, like the first time they'd touched, wondered what would happen when they were truly alone together. "Did you and Elyoner find your locket?" He felt Emily's hand tense.

"No. We looked everywhere, crawled around on our hands and knees where . . . where the Savage threw me to the ground and hit me. Not there. Not anywhere around the . . . the massacre site. We could still see Joyce and Audrey's blood on the grass where they fell." A knot of nausea grew in the pit of her stomach, started to rise as she visualized the two lying dead on the ground. But an empty void displaced the nausea, and an ache squeezed her heart when she thought of her locket, gone forever.

"I'm sorry to hear that, Emily. Will you look for it again before we leave? I'd be happy to help."

"Perhaps. It has to be there somewhere . . . but our search was very thorough . . . to the point of pushing blades of grass back and forth. But yes, I *would* like to search one last time. And thank you for offering, Hugh. If they can spare the soldiers to guard us, we'll try again."

"At your service, Milady. And did your father tell you what he and I talked about outside that night?" He frowned as he spoke the words.

"Indeed, he did, and I'm sorry 'twas bad news . . . also sorry I was so rude to Father . . . and in front of *you*, as well."

He chuckled. "I knew what you were thinking, so I wasn't surprised you reacted that way. And as far as the election, I was angry about it at first, but I've swallowed my disappointment. Lieutenant Waters is a fine young officer, and all respect him. So I've no complaint about the choice."

His concession surprised Emily. She'd expected anger, resentment, wondered why there was none. "No offense, but I have to agree. 'Twould be difficult to argue against the choice."

He nodded. In truth, it piqued him that they'd considered Waters superior to him, though he painfully acknowledged it was true. But *I'll be an Assistant in time*, he thought. *Something will happen to one of them—a resignation, an untimely death. Whatever it is, I'll be there.*

They had reached the palisades behind a solitary cottage at the south end of the village. Tayler faced her, held her hands, smiled. "Shall we sit and talk, Milady?"

"Certainly, kind sir," she said with mock formality.

When he had guided her to the grass and seated himself, he said, "Emily, have you ever been in love?"

He'd surprised her again. "Well . . . I think so, but I was quite young, and it may have been infatuation." She again visualized her risky escapade with the young lad she'd lain with in the warm, soft moonlight of a summer night—flushed with desire and curiosity, kissing, exploring each other's bodies, heart and breath racing, risking her virginity in a moment of steamy passion. Yes, she well knew how quickly the best of judgment, the most heartfelt of moral commitments, could melt away in the frenzy of passion.

"What happened?"

"He went with his family to another part of England, and that was the end of it. And you, Hugh Tayler?"

He looked away from her, stared at the ground. "We were deeply in love, were to be married in several months, but . . . but she caught a strange sickness and died in a week's time. I was heartbroken for more than a year, unable to do anything but think of her, dream of what might have been. 'Twas painful, Emily." He saw the girl in his mind, felt a twinge of guilt for the way he'd treated her, repressed it, telling himself that had been the *old* Hugh Tayler, that the *new* Hugh Tayler was a different man. He also pushed away the nagging fear that upon his death, he *might* be held accountable for his sins, and it was this nagging uncertainty that made him desperately afraid of death, for though he didn't believe in God—or at least told himself so—the possibility that he *could* be wrong ate at his soul like a slow cancer consuming a life.

Emily shook her head. "Hugh, I continue to ask you things that bring back horrible memories and hurt you to talk about. Your life seems to have been one painful moment after another. Tell me something good that's happened to you."

He turned slowly toward her, his face suddenly sharp and alive with sincerity. "Emily, the best thing that's ever happened to me was meeting you, and I'm deeply in love with you, uncontrollably so, unable to be without you."

Emily maintained a steady, expressionless gaze. "Hugh . . ."

"Emily, 'tis true. When you were wounded, I was destroyed, ready to die, ready to kill myself if you died. I . . . I've made no secret of my plans for our future together here in Virginia, and I—"

"Hugh . . . you mustn't speak so. I . . . I don't mean to sound like I don't feel strongly for you . . . I do, but . . . but 'tis just too fast for me. I haven't discovered my true feelings yet, and I . . ." Emily felt trapped, enclosed in a box with all six sides closing in. It was too much, too soon; she wasn't ready for such declarations nor for the reply she'd have to give. It had been difficult with George, but this was worse because she was strongly attracted to him.

"I understand, Emily, and I don't know why I blurted out the truth like that . . . except that I'm an impatient sort. A mature man should be coy and aloof . . . and I usually am, but I simply can't be that way with you. You strip away every facade I ever had, make me feel like a bumbling young schoolboy."

"Now you've embarrassed me again, Hugh Tayler."

"I'm sorry, Em. But I had to say it, and I understand your hesitation. You *are* much younger than I, and this *has* been quick . . . too quick for you to know where your heart stands. Truly, I *do* understand; but Emily, I will wait for you to know your heart . . . as long as it takes. And I know in my own heart that one day, you and I will be man and wife."

***

The fishermen had fished the sound with limited success, and to their disquietude, the crew on the shallop had twice seen Savages watching them, both from dugout canoes and from the mainland. They had found the Savages' presence unnerving and thus rowed around to the east side of Roanoke Island, fishing north and south up and down the sound rather than in the sound at the mouth of the river to the island's north. On a third occasion, three dugouts had followed the shallop into the sound and approached to within fifty yards before stopping. The Savages had raised their bows and taunted the colonists, further unnerving them because they had only a single longbow on-board. After that every fishing sortie carried at least three longbows, a healthy supply of arrows, and one matchlock. Then the day before the second voyage, two dugouts approached to thirty yards, suddenly turned broadside, and sent a swarm of arrows flying at the shallop, two of which found their marks—one hitting Richard Kemme in the chest, just inside the shoulder, and the other grazing Martyn Sutton's neck. The dugouts immediately turned away and paddled for the mainland.

While Kemme screamed and Sutton groaned, John Cheven, the helmsman, turned the shallop broadside to the fleeing Savages and said, "Nock your arrows men, and let 'em fly before the bastards are out of range." The three longbowmen loosed two quick volleys of arrows at the narrow dugouts, which were separating rapidly from the shal-lop; and though the distance had widened to fifty yards, the powerful longbows imparted enough energy for the arrows to strike with lethal impact, hitting one Savage in the neck, throwing him overboard, and two others in the back.

A cheer rose from the shallop, drowned out the Savages' taunts. Cheven said, "Maybe that'll give 'em some respect for English long-bows . . . filthy jackanapes."

After the encounter, Roger Baylye decided that even though they had held their own and the two wounded men would recover, the risk of losing the shallop or having more people injured or killed outweighed the benefit of several more days of marginal fishing. He therefore halted fishing, except for crabbing and oyster gathering from the shore with guards present; but with seeming inconsistency, he allowed salting operations to continue. He then ruminated about his decision—admitted they needed both food and salt, decided they could manage without more fish but could *not* manage without additional salt to preserve the meat and fish they would harvest at Chesapeake for winter, noted that the shallop could row or sail from the east side of the island to the outer banks undetected by the Savages to the west—concluded that the greater need justified the risk.

***

Thomas and Emily Colman placed their belongings with those of the Dares at the baggage marshaling point for loading and transport to Chesapeake on the second voyage. While Ananias and Thomas spoke with several other men, Emily walked to Elyoner's cottage to say her goodbyes.

Staring pensively at Elyoner, Emily watched her nurse Virginia, imagined herself doing the same as soon as they were all safely at Chesapeake. She thought of her excitement that very morning when she'd expressed several solid streams of milk, then hoped the time would go fast, that the two remaining voyages would be uneventful, that the Chesapeake would be everything they so desperately needed it to be. She then thought of her lost locket, felt a prick to her heart as she admitted she'd never see or hold it again. The day before, she and Hugh Tayler had searched vainly; concluded that someone had stepped on it, forcing it into the ground beneath a clump of grass; realized it was gone forever. She felt she'd betrayed her mother's trust, knew the pain of its loss would remain long after they were reunited in a few short months.

With a spacey, unseeing look on her face, she thought of George then of Hugh Tayler; she felt an anguished tightness inside, a tightness born of aggravated frustration over her relationships, frustration because she was loved but unable to return that love in like manner.

Elyoner said, "Emily! Are you asleep with your eyes open, girl? I've been talking to you for ten seconds . . . you haven't heard a word."

Emily shook her head quickly as if to wake herself. "Oh. Sorry, Ellie. Too deep in thought, I suppose."

"I see that. And what troubles you, my dear friend?"

"Men . . . two men . . . both of whom say they love me and want to marry me, and neither of whom I'm able to love in return . . . at least not in the same way they love me. I told the first I love him as a friend, and the other that I *may* love him but am not yet sure. Both vowed to wait as long as it takes, and I'm here thinking 'tis all far too fast." She shook her head. " 'Tis so frustrating, Ellie. Why is this happening to me . . . and what am I to do?"

"Well, the first part's easy . . . because you *are* who you *are*: a beautiful, intelligent . . . and yes, sensual young lass who doesn't know she's that way, which, of course, makes you all the more attractive. By the bye, many women go a lifetime without such attention. So that's the *why* of it. But the *what to do* part is more difficult, and I don't have an answer other than to follow your heart and your mind and let it unfold with time." She knew George had made no secret of his adoration of Emily, and she was very comfortable with the thought of him and Emily together someday, but Tayler was a different song. She realized she'd just frowned when she thought of him, quickly cast a smile, wondering if Emily had noticed. Elyoner wished she hadn't heard the gossip about Tayler before leaving England; she wanted desperately to tell Emily but had no substantiation of the hearsay, so refused, in spite of her intuition, to interfere with what could be an innocent, fulfilling relationship. On the other hand, she thought, what if it *is* true? Then she'd be saving Emily from an unsavory, perhaps dangerous, situation. What to do?

"I saw your hard look, Ellie Dare. You must have been thinking of Hugh and the secret you know about him. Please, Ellie, what is it? Honestly, it could be something that would sway me, change my thinking. I wish you'd tell me and let *me* bear the burden instead of it tormenting *you*." She knew it had to be serious, or Elyoner would have told her, but she also knew the noble Elyoner would *never* tell her unless she was *sure* it was true, and concluded such was the case."

"You're too perceptive, Emily Colman. But forsooth, 'tis not something I'd feel right talking about because I've no idea if 'tis true, and I refuse to be an instrument of slander if 'tis in fact false."

"But what if 'tis true, Ellie?"

"Em, this is very difficult for me, and I don't know what to say . . . and I feel horrible talking about it because it's agitated you so and made me feel small and petty. So I beg your indulgence and beseech you to forget I mentioned it and—Ow! This one's sucking me dry." She glanced at Virginia. "She's a greedy one, and young Henry Harvie has an appetite, as well. So I'm probably more excited about you nursing next week than you are."

"I doubt *that*, Ellie. I'm so *very* excited. May I hold her for a while?"

"Of course."

She handed Virginia to Emily, who laid her on her shoulder and started burping her. "Don't fret about your secret. I understand, and I respect your judgment in not wanting to tell me. Meanwhile"—she smiled at Elyoner—"I'll just continue being tormented and wondering what it is."

Five minutes after Elyoner had laid Virginia down for a rest, Emily said, "Well, Ellie. You'd better get some rest, as well. Tomorrow will be a long day for the four of you. I'll miss you, my dear friend, though we'll only be apart for five days." She extended her arms to Elyoner, who took her hands, pulled her into a tearful embrace.

"My Emily. I shall miss you, too . . . more than you'll ever know. Though we're all excited to escape Roanoke, there may yet be much danger ahead—the voyages are not without risk, and what awaits us at Chesapeake is something only God himself knows." She held Emily at arms' length, looked into her stunning eyes. "Be safe, my friend. Virginia and I shall await you."

Emily's heart and mind churned with anxious emotion while a flutter of foreboding tickled the pit of her stomach; she slowly pulled Elyoner toward her, and the two kissed on the cheek, quickly hugged again. "Goodbye, my friend. Fare thee well."

"And thee, as well," Elyoner said, rubbing her eyes.

Emily turned, walked out the door, wondered if she'd ever see Elyoner again.

* * *

Emily and her father had been asleep for two hours when someone scratched on their cottage door. Thomas Colman continued snoring, but Emily stood, walked to the door. "Who is it?"

Elyoner said, " 'Tis I, Em. I must speak to you urgently. I'm so sorry to wake you, but 'tis very important."

Emily quietly opened the door, slipped outside in her smock. "Ellie, what is it? Is something wrong with Virginia?" Even in the moonlight Emily could see that Elyoner's eyes were red from crying, her face strained with anxiety.

"Emily," she whispered, "I couldn't sleep, been crying all night, agonizing . . . agonizing about telling you what I heard of Hugh Tayler. Even though it might be false, I can't keep it from you any longer. Your safety may be at stake. "

A chill raced down Emily's spine. "Ellie, what is it?"

Elyoner took a deep breath, rubbed her eyes. "Father told me before we left England that Hugh was . . . was on the run from something, that he *had* to leave England; but he never told me why, and I'm not sure he knew. Father didn't want to bring him, but someone higher up insisted. I didn't think much of it until the day we departed England, when I overheard that young sergeant, Johnny Gibbes, talking to another soldier." She took another deep breath.

Emily's eyes were taut with concentration, lips pursed.

Tears welled in Elyoner's eyes, rolled onto her cheeks. "Emily . . . I feel so terrible telling you this."

"Go on, Elyoner."

"He said . . . before Hugh was in the army, he . . . he forced himself on a young lass, made her pregnant, then beat her, abused her in other ways . . . then abandoned her when she was on her deathbed, and ran away. Oh, Em, I've been so afraid for you when you were alone with him. But"—she held her shoulders, looked into her eyes—"what if 'tis not true? What an awful thing for me to say about someone."

Emily shook her head repeatedly back and forth; tears filled her eyes as she embraced Elyoner, held her tight, spoke in a broken whisper. "My dear, dear friend. Thank you for telling me. I know how difficult it was. But now you're free of it, and 'tis *my* burden to deal with, as it should be, and deal with it I shall. Thank you, Ellie. I love you, my friend. Now get some rest." She felt as if a huge weight had been lifted from her, but another dropped in its place. How can I ask him? What will he say? What *can* he say? What will he think of me if 'tis not true? What will he do if it *is* true? My Lord, please help me know what to do.

As Elyoner nodded, started to walk away, she stopped, turned and said, "Em, please be careful."

* * *

The pinnace and shallop returned from the second voyage on schedule, two days before the third voyage was to depart, reported an uneventful trip and smooth disembarking of people and equipment. The two pilots, John Hemmington and Peter Little, reported that the new village was laid out about a hundred yards from the Chesapeakes' village and that work had begun on cottages. Since winter was near, they had decided to build grass-mat cottages, as at Roanoke, and then replace them in the spring with either bark-covered lodges like the Chesapeakes used or perhaps more permanent log buildings. Unfortunately, while grass mats were the quickest pathway to shelter, they were the least effective at holding a fire's heat, and with only a smoke hole in the roof rather than a chimney, the fire had to be kept at a modest level to prevent rising sparks from igniting the grass.

Soon after the boats arrived, Roger Baylye, the remaining Assistants, and Sergeants Myllet and Gibbes held an impromptu meeting at Myllet's request. As a veteran of many battles, Myllet had learned to trust his instincts; and they now pummeled him with discomfort at the fact that only half of their total number remained at Roanoke, including but a third of the soldiers. The fishing incidents with the Savages further aggravated his discomfort, for he recognized that the colony's obvious reduced strength had emboldened them. So when the group assembled in Baylye's cottage, Baylye immediately turned the meeting over to Myllet, who spoke somewhat nervously of their vulnerability, strongly urged the Assistants to change the departure plan and leave the island as soon as possible rather than on the planned departure day.

Baylye, who'd had similar discomforting feelings, immediately saw the wisdom of Myllet's proposal, put it to a quick vote, which passed unanimously. They would consolidate equipment and belongings that very afternoon, start loading an hour before first light, and be on their way by early morning, a full day before the planned departure. As the meeting adjourned, Baylye asked one of the Assistants to tell John Cheven to quickly gather a few men to take the shallop to the outer banks and retrieve the salt crew. He then asked another to assign young Robert Ellis the task of carving *CROATOAN* on the large tree on the pathway between the shore and village. The lad had done a sharp, legible carving of the word on the palisades post, and Baylye wanted him to do the pathway carving, as well.

***

It took five gallons of seawater to yield four cups of salt; and the task of producing it was labor intensive: the water had to be held at a boil for hours and frequently stirred, which meant firewood had to be pre-positioned so it could be fed to the fire as needed, to maintain the boil until the water evaporated and the residual salt was the consistency of wet sand. Then at the end of the day, before the shallop returned the crew to Roanoke, the salt was bagged and driftwood collected and stacked to dry for the next morning's fire.

William Dutton was around the small point to the south of the salt fire, gathering driftwood for the final day's burning. As he pondered how much he was going to enjoy a few days' respite from the job, he looked up, gazed down the outer banks to the south. He abruptly dropped his load of wood, shook his head as if to clear his mind, rubbed his eyes, looked again. "By the saints in heaven and God o' mercy! 'Tis a ship, a big ship . . . with three tall masts . . . too far away to see the colors, but . . . but it *must* be the governor. My God! Governor White's returned!" He turned around, ran a few steps back toward the fire, stopped, frowned; can't be Governor White. He hasn't had enough time to reach England, gather supplies, and return. No. Can't be him. But who cares? 'Tis a ship, mayhap a supply ship. Praise God. He started off at a headlong sprint, rounded the point to where he could see the rest of the salt crew. "A ship! A ship! We're saved! A ship!"

***

Inside her cottage, Emily heard shouting and cheering, walked outside to see what it was about. Most of the people were gathered in the village center, hooking arms, dancing in circles, singing *halleluiah*, praising God, proclaiming their salvation. She queried the first person she came to, a soldier, "What is it, soldier? What's happened?"

" 'Tis a ship, Mistress. A ship's at anchor down by the southern outlet to the sea. Not Governor White but some other ship, a supply ship sent by Raleigh, we think. Governor Baylye told us to cease preparing for tomorrow's departure, said that if the ship's crew doesn't come to *us this afternoon*, he's taking both shallops out to *them in the morning* to discuss supplies and passengers who may want to go to Chesapeake with us. Oh, yes, he's also asking them to transport us to Chesapeake, so we don't have to squeeze onto the pinnace and shallops. 'Tis a happy day, Mistress."

"Indeed it is." Emily smiled at the young man, nodded. "Indeed it is. Thank you."

***

Since Elyoner's revelation, Emily had avoided Hugh Tayler, was unsure what to say to him or how to approach him. She had searched for opportunities to surreptitiously speak with Sergeant Gibbes, query him about Tayler in some roundabout manner, but had found none. Tayler and Emily had crossed paths several times during the intervening days, but each time she had quickened her pace, pretended to be deeply engaged in some task, and told him that perhaps they could talk later.

A while after hearing of the resupply ship's arrival, Emily proceeded to the marshaling point to retrieve the small bag she had placed there earlier in the day, saw that John Gibbes was alone at the site. He had been there all afternoon preparing the cargo manifest for the next day's voyage, but because they were no longer departing the next day, he had been crossing off items as their owners retrieved them. When he saw Emily approaching, he smiled at her. "Good day to you, Mistress Colman. And a happy day it is."

Gibbes always seemed to have a smile on his face and a pleasant disposition, which inspired a broad smile of equal quality from Emily. "Good day to you, Sergeant Gibbes. How's your task progressing? You look quite busy."

Gibbes had never spoken to a woman as stunning as Emily, and his knees tried to buckle beneath him as he searched for a response. "Well . . . well, Mistress, most of it's been collected, and I suppose the owners of what's left are too busy celebrating to worry about baggage at the moment."

Emily was tense, uncertain what to say. "Well, I'm here to get my bag and . . . and Sergeant Gibbes, may I ask you about something rather sensitive?"

He assumed a serious, quizzical look, hesitated for a moment. "Of course, Mistress. What would it be?"

"Well, I hope you'll keep this between you and me, but a friend of mine told me something she heard about Master Hugh Tayler's background in England and said you might know something of it. I feel terrible asking you such a thing; but you see, Master Tayler and I have been seeing each other, and it's quite important that I know the truth of this matter because it *could* affect our relationship. Again, I feel very awkward and improper asking you such a thing, but 'tis of great importance."

He frowned, looked around to see if anyone was watching. "Mistress Colman, every time I've seen you and Master Tayler together, I've wanted to tell you about him, but I didn't think it proper to do so, me being a soldier and all. But yes, there *are* things you should know about him, and since you've now asked, I'm obliged to tell you the truth."

Emily bubbled with cautious anticipation. Gibbes clearly knew something, and it wasn't good, but how could she know if it was true or simply the slander of a disgruntled soldier. No, she thought, he's not the sort to slander. What he tells me *will* be truth. "Thank you, Sergeant Gibbes. I'm very grateful to you."

"Well, Mistress, I'm afraid it isn't happy news, but for your own good, here's the story. When Hugh Tayler was—" He suddenly stopped talking and said, "Good afternoon, Master Tayler."

Emily spun about as Hugh Tayler walked up behind her.

Tayler ignored Gibbes. "Good afternoon, Emily. I see you've met Sergeant Gibbes."

Emily tensed, glared at him with a mix of contempt and fear. "Aye, I have, Hugh."

Tayler shifted his gaze to Gibbes. "Well, please continue, Sergeant. I don't want to interrupt."

"We were just discussing how pleasant it will be to be rid of this island and live where we're not in constant danger. But we've finished . . . and I must be about my duties." He looked at Emily. "Perhaps we can continue our discussion another day, Mistress."

"I'd like that, Sergeant Gibbes. I enjoyed the conversation." She smiled a false smile, told him with her eyes that she was desperate to hear what he knew.

Tayler said, "Well, Emily, it looks as if our salvation has arrived. May I carry your bag for you?"

Emily was now convinced that Tayler had a past—one that could threaten their relationship, that now made it impossible for her to be at ease around him, and that instilled an instinctively cold formality to her disposition toward him. "If you wish, Hugh."

They walked silently for a minute before Tayler said with an edgy voice, "Emily, something bothers you. What is it? Can I help?"

Emily wanted to confront him but realized she wasn't ready. "No, Hugh. I don't think so, but . . . but . . . Hugh, someone told me something I must ask you about." She stopped, faced him.

Tayler looked at her with an intense, challenging look. "And what might that be, Emily?"

"When you were back in England, did you—"

"Emily! Emily!" Thomas Colman shouted as he ran toward his daughter.

Tayler and Emily turned toward him, saw an urgent flurry of activity in the village behind him.

"What is it, Father?"

"Manteo's arrived with terrifying news. The ship at the inlet is *not* an English supply ship. 'Tis a Spanish man-of-war; he saw the cannon ports and flag. He also watched for a good while but saw no one leave the ship, probably because of the late hour. But certain danger awaits us in the morning. So come. We've little time." He tugged her toward the gathering place. "We've decided on a course of action, and Roger wants all to hear it; for as you can see, chaos has already descended upon us."

As her father pulled her toward the village center, Emily glanced back at Tayler without expression, read a new, tense, anxious look in his eyes. In her heart, she wanted Elyoner to be wrong, wanted Tayler to be the gentle, honest man she'd known, but she now feared it would not be so.

Roger Baylye said, "My good people, at this moment, we face the gravest peril of our lives. A Spanish warship lies just outside the inlet through the outer banks to our south. Either the men aboard her already know of our presence and will soon attack, or they'll discover us on the morrow to the same end."

Whispers, then protests, buzzed through the crowd. Worried faces looked toward the inlet, glanced at other anxious faces.

"Therefore, I fear we've but one choice, and that choice is to depart Roanoke under cover of darkness—tonight."

"What do you mean, Baylye?" a man asked. "We can't sail out of here in the dark."

"We should stay and fight," shouted another.

Yet another said, "Why didn't the governor warn us about Spaniards?"

Baylye raised his hands for quiet, spoke softly, urgently. "Please! Please! Don't shout! The Spaniards have ears. 'Tis not that far to the outer banks, and sound travels a great distance. They may not have detected us yet, and we daren't hurry that moment." Like eager school-children who'd spoken out of turn, they fell silent. "We've no time for discussion or argument, so please listen to me. Since the Spaniards block the only passage through the outer banks to the sea, we're now trapped in the sound and cannot sail to Chesapeake on the open sea. Thus instead of an easy, familiar voyage up the coast, we now face a shorter but far more perilous sail up the shallow sound."

Suddenly gaunt, fearful faces watched Baylye in silence as the realities of their plight seeped into their minds like water into sand.

"Darkness will greatly heighten our risk; and 'twill take a full day's overland journey after the voyage, to reach our destination. But if we can—"

"Why don't we stay here and fight?" a man said. "We've palisades and weapons, and mayhap they won't discover us or even come here." Several agreed.

"Nay!" Baylye said. "The Spaniards are a trained fighting force, probably four or five times our size. We'd be slaughtered like swine. No! We must make a silent escape tonight and avoid discovery and contact at all costs. We cannot win a fight; so I ask you, would you rather try to escape or be a Spanish slave for the rest of your life? Forsooth, we"—he paused for a moment as a sudden, grim silence, such as occurs in the second after the headsman's axe falls, descended upon the gathering— "forsooth, we enjoy a nearly full moon; and with fair winds and luck, we can make the north end of the sound before sunrise. Further, our pilots are well used to sailing the sound and know her shallows and sandbars, as well as how to hold a compass course." He cleared his throat, swallowed hard. "However, we *will* have to leave many belongings behind lest we overload the ships and create too much draft for the shallow waters. The pinnace has a six-and-a-half-foot draft, fully loaded, and that's too deep for some places in the sound. She'll strike bottom. On the other hand, the shallops have only a two-foot draft, so we'll put *all* of the remaining baggage and equipment on the shallops. But to be safe, we'll leave the spare lead, cannon, extra shot, iron bars, and Governor White's three chests behind; and we will bury these items in concealed locations, so the Spaniards and Savages cannot find them. We can then return and retrieve everything after the Spaniards depart. Now, to further lighten the pinnace load, all women and their men will go on the pinnace. Soldiers will be assigned to vessels by Sergeant Myllet. Next all single civilians, including me, will draw from this bundle of sticks to determine who goes on which vessel." He pointed at a bundle of twigs held by Sergeant Myllet; it was wrapped in a cloth to conceal their lengths. "We've calculated the maximum number of men that can fit on the two shallops, and there are exactly that number of short sticks in the bundle. So if you draw a short stick, you're on a shallop, and a long stick puts you on the pinnace. Last, my friends, there must be no fires or noise. We must accomplish everything in candlelight and silence, and as rapidly as possible."

All the single men then drew a stick from the bundle. George and Baylye drew the pinnace, and Tayler a shallop. Tayler threw his stick to the ground, glared at Baylye, then looked distraughtly at Emily.

Baylye said, "One last thing. We must dismantle our dwellings to deceive the Spaniards into thinking we abandoned Roanoke and returned to England some time ago; and hopefully, this ruse will discourage them from searching elsewhere for us. We will also cast all of our fireplace ashes into the sound and conceal the latrines."

Thomas Colman said, "A good plan, Roger." Others nodded assent.

Baylye nodded at Colman, took a deep breath, scanned the crowd. "Friends, as your leader, 'tis my duty to tell you that navigating the sound is challenging in daylight. 'Twill be far more so in darkness, and few of us are skilled sailors, but we *will* do it. My friends, we've only an hour until dark, so let us now pray for our deliverance and then prepare to meet our fate."

All but Tayler and one other dropped silently to their knees, held each other's hands, prayed silently, then together, that the Almighty would guide them through the night and see them safely to Chesapeake and a reunion with their comrades. After a moment's hesitation, people began to rise, scurry about, dismantle cottages, carry belongings to Sergeant Gibbes at the marshaling point, while the soldiers quickly dispersed and started burying the items that would be left behind.

Roger Baylye beckoned to Robert Ellis, who jogged over to him. "Robert, did you finish carving *CROATOAN* on that big tree on the pathway?"

"Oh! Beg your pardon, Sir. I'm afraid not. I was working on it when the salt crew returned with news of the ship, and I was so excited I followed them back here to celebrate."

"Well, I understand your excitement, lad, but how much did you complete?"

"The first three letters, Sir. The carving says *CRO* instead of *CROATOAN*, but—"

"That's good enough, Robert. Governor White will understand it." Baylye suddenly wondered if the Spaniards might understand it, as well—particularly *CROATOAN* on the palisades post—and go to the island and seize the three English colonists, torture them into disclosing the colony's whereabouts. Too late now, he concluded. Too late for *everything*. We shall have to take our chances . . . God be with us. He shook off an icy chill as he started for his cottage, saw Hugh Tayler approaching, stopped, faced him. "Hello, Master Tayler. You look as if you've something on your mind."

"I want to go on the pinnace."

"Why? What difference does it make?"

"Not that it's anyone's business, but I'm courting Mistress Colman, and I want to be with her in case . . . in case there are problems."

"Well, Hugh, we haven't the time to negotiate changes. The draw is done, and we must *all* abide by its results; so I'm sorry, but I can't help you." He turned, walked toward his cottage.

Tayler glared at Baylye's back as he walked away. Devil take you, you foolish ass. I'll even *this* score someday, and you won't like it when I do. He started toward his cottage, saw Emily approaching hers, jogged as fast as his limp allowed to her side. "Emily, I *must* speak with you."

Emily stopped, regarded him with a blank look; she wanted to confront him, hear his response, so they could either end or resume their relationship, but knew George would arrive in a moment to take her for a last visit to his father's grave. She spoke in a dry, curt tone. "I'm sorry, Hugh. I'd like to, but I've too much to do before we depart. 'Twill have to wait until Chesapeake . . . when we've more time. We've *none* now." She stared into his eyes with her most penetrating look, noticed him blinking repeatedly, and thought he seemed different, less confident. "Fare thee well, Hugh. I hope you—all of us—have a safe voyage. See you on the shore in the morning." She turned away, walked the twenty feet to her cottage, which her father had already begun dismantling, stopped for a moment to visualize the good and bad times they'd had there, then realized that in spite of all, it *had* been their home for two months.

As he watched her walk away, Tayler wondered what she'd heard. Whatever it was, if it was true, it was *past*, a part of the *old* Hugh Tayler, nothing to do with the *new* Hugh Tayler—the Hugh Tayler who deeply loved this fair young woman who'd taken his heart and soul, meant everything to him. She *will* be mine, someday, somehow. May whatever gods exist protect her this night since I cannot.

**

Emily and George stood hand in hand at George Howe's grave. They stared in silence for several minutes before George turned, pulled Emily into an embrace and held her to him, felt her breasts, the warmth of her body, the soft texture of her cheek against his. "Emily, I miss him so, and I fear this will be the last time I stand beside him."

"No, George. When we're at Chesapeake, you can return when they come to pick up the things we leave behind. Perhaps there will be other trips, as well. We can't know those things, but we *can* know and remember that your father was a wonderful man and that he'll live in our memories and hearts until we ourselves join him."

He sighed. "You're right, Em. You always see things clearly. I promised him I'd give my all to help this colony succeed, and I shall. And, Emily"—he held her by the shoulders and looked longingly into her eyes—"I still love you more than anything on earth, and I shall forever. I must also tell you that I pray every day for you to love *me* in the same way. Em, I'll do *anything* for you." He spoke slowly, clearly. "I love you . . . I love you . . . I love you."

Emily again embraced him, laid her head against his chest; prayed that it would someday be as he wished, wanted with all her heart to love him. Someday . . . someday I shall. She kissed him on the cheek, looked up at him. "George, we must go."

* * *

Thomas Colman saw Emily approaching from the other side of the village, called to her with an urgent voice. "Em, where have you been? Come quickly. I need your help."

"I'm coming, Father. I was with George at his father's grave. I'll be—"

"Emily!" said an accented voice behind her. She turned around, saw a Savage, instinctively pulled back in fear, then realized it was Manteo. "Whew! Manteo. You startled me. I haven't seen a . . ."

He held her hands. "Emily, my friend. I heard of the Roanokes' attack . . . I'm glad you escaped . . . I do not know why they kill women. I came to see you twice while you were asleep. You must hate them very much for what they did to you."

"I *want* to hate them, Manteo . . . I *should* hate them. But truly, I can't, for they act as we would if *we* were threatened . . . and as you know, Lane gave them many reasons to feel threatened."

Manteo nodded. "Emily, your wisdom is great. I'm honored to be your friend, and I'm sorry we must part."

"Part? Are you not coming with us?"

"I cannot. It would endanger my people."

"Why?"

"Because I've heard from my friend"—he motioned toward a different-looking Savage beside him, whom Emily ignored—"that the Powhatans, who live inland from the Chesapeakes, were with the Roanokes when they attacked George Howe and you. They wear their hair on one side, pulled back over the shoulder, and some—their greatest warriors—wear feathers in their hair to commemorate their great deeds. Did you see any such people?"

Emily's eyes widened; she saw again the vicious, painted face, the hair and feathers as Manteo described. "I saw one of them, Manteo . . . the one who tried to kill me . . . he had several feathers." She shook the image from her mind. "But, Manteo, your people—"

"The Powhatans hate your people and will kill anyone who helps you. They know we Croatans, and the Chesapeakes, are friendly to you; and that puts all of us in danger, for the Powhatan chiefdom is strong and has eyes in many places. So you see, I cannot go without endangering my own people. We're already at risk with your three people on our island . . . we hid them today in case soldiers from the Spanish ship come looking for you." His face stiffened. "Emily, you may find more danger at Chesapeake than you escape here; I've told your leaders this, but they do not listen."

Emily chilled at his words, flashed the frightened eyes of a child expecting a night of terrifying nightmares. Will we ever be safe? she wondered.

"But I shall miss you, Emily, for no white person knows and respects our ways better than you." He again motioned toward the different-looking Savage at his side. "And I've told my friend about you."

Once more, Emily ignored the man. "Manteo, you flatter me."

He shook his head. "No, Emily. I taught you much on the ship, and you learned well, especially your hand signs . . . Oh!" He looked at the other Savage again, then at Emily. With hand signs, he said, "Practice your signs with my friend." Then he said out loud, "His name is Isna." It sounded like *eee-shnah*. "He's here to trade with us and the Chesapeakes, and he and his three tribesmen will live with the Chesapeakes until spring."

Emily glanced at Isna, started to look back at Manteo; jerked her gaze back to Isna, stared intensely into hypnotic ebony eyes; lingered, felt as if warm water were pouring down the back of her head and shoulders.

Except for a thin braid on either side of his well-proportioned face, Isna's full-headed black hair hung down his bare back to his waist, while five large eagle feathers, arranged like a fan, protruded to the right from behind his head. He had a smaller, straighter nose and less-prominent cheekbones than any Savage she'd seen; and his lean, muscular body, clad only in a leather loin cloth and moccasins, had the tight, explosive look of a predator about to attack its prey.

"Man . . . Manteo . . . wh . . . why does he trade here?" His eyes . . . so deep, dark . . . can't look away . . . searching my soul. Blushing, she turned her face slightly toward Manteo but held her eyes and mind on Isna.

"His people are called *Lakota*, and he and his men trade the furs of big-horned animals that live in their land many weeks to the north, near the headwaters of the Mother-of-All-Rivers. They trade for shells we gather from the sea and the red rocks we get from the mountain people." Manteo held up the red stone that hung on a thong around his neck, but Emily's eyes remained fixed on Isna. "He came with me today so he could see what a white man looks like. He's never seen one before but says the grandfathers of his people tell stories told by their grandfathers, and their grandfathers' grandfathers, of tall white men with long, light colored hair, who came to their people from a great freshwater sea where they then lived—a different place from where they *now* live.

He says these men came in ships with tall wolf heads in front, and they wore hard hats, like your soldiers, but of a different shape . . . and their blood is in his veins.

"Emily looked at Manteo, her face enlivened with excitement. My dreams, she thought. The Vikings. "When did—"

Thomas Colman walked up and put his arm on Emily's shoulder. He nodded at Manteo. "Come, Emily, you *must help me*. We cannot leave until all the cottages are down, so please come now." He pulled her toward the cottage.

"Fie, Father!" She twisted free, glared at him with daggery eyes. "Don't treat me like a child."

He stared at her for a moment, shook his head, walked away.

Emily turned back to Manteo, hugged him. "Thank you for being my friend, Manteo. Tell Isna I shall see him at the Chesapeake camp."

"You should tell him yourself, Emily."

I dare not look at him, she thought as she impulsively stared into the depths of his eyes, then spoke with her hands. "I shall see you up north . . . soon."

"And I, you," he signed with a wry little smile.

Emily's heart flamed with unfamiliar, breathtaking passion; she stared into Isna's eyes but spoke to Manteo. "I shall miss you, Manteo." She sniffed the air. "Rain coming."

Manteo's thin smile faded to a frown as he glanced at the small clouds building to the west. "May the spirit above, the one you call *God*, go with you tonight. The sound is no place to be in a storm. He looked back at Emily, whose eyes were still locked on Isna's, smiled. "I shall miss you too, Emily, my friend. Perhaps we'll meet again someday."

Emily forced her gaze to the sky then Manteo, as a sudden breeze swept the stagnant air, whipped her hair like fine thread. "Goodbye, Manteo." She waved slowly then walked away; told herself not to look back at Isna's piercing black eyes, stopped, looked over her shoulder at him anyway; wondered if Lot's wife had suffered the same compulsion. His eyes awaited hers; chills raced through her body; she felt a damp warmth between her thighs, a dizzying fog in her mind. His eyes . . . his eyes.

As she forced herself to turn away and walk toward the cottage, she saw the bright, high-riding moon, a sparkling, solitary star beside it. Both glowed like beacons, unwilling to yield to the approaching clouds. Do not leave us, Mother Moon . . . stay . . . guide us through this night. George, I want so to love you . . . Hugh, I don't know what to think of you, a thousand knives stabbing my heart. Mother . . . Mother, what should I do? His eyes. She looked back where Isna had stood, but he was gone. "God help me . . . help us . . . please let us survive." She put her hand in her empty apron pocket. Gone forever. Mother, I love you. His eyes . . . never seen such eyes, never felt this way. When she reached the cottage, the first dark clouds reached Mother Moon and her star, began to swallow them like demonic forces of evil enveloping the forces of good at Armageddon. The wrong winner, she thought. "Lord, please be with us this night. Destroy the evil that stalks us."

***

They had slipped away from Roanoke Island at deep dusk, in a gentle rain, and with only enough light to find their way across the large estuary to the north and into the five-mile-wide sound that led north-northwest toward Chesapeake. Once into the northerly sound, the smaller shallops had hung lanterns on their sterns for the pinnace to follow; and in spite of the steady rain, the pinnace crew had kept them in sight. The two shallops sailed in a spread formation about two hundred yards apart, using sounding ropes with ten-pound weights attached to the end and knots tied every foot, to measure the water's depth and ensure that the deeper-drafted pinnace, which steered between the two shallop lights, would always have the deepest possible channel.

After an hour and a half, the rain stopped, the temperature warmed, and the wind subsided to a gentle breeze; the brilliant moon then reappeared, spread its beams over the calm water before them, illuminating the mainland on their left and the outer banks on their right. In spite of the rain, the entire company had remained above deck, the hold having been configured for cargo and not a comfortable place for passengers. On deck they either sat on newly constructed plank seats or stood at mid-deck to avoid being thrown over the low side railings by a sudden heave of the ship. All were wet and chilly from the cool rain and the evaporative effects of the breeze; but when the rain stopped, their subdued spirits rose like hot smoke; and they began to celebrate their escape from Roanoke Island, voice their emerging optimism for the times ahead.

After three hours, most on the pinnace sat silently on their seats, wrapped in thin blankets, leaning against one another, trying to sleep while the newly trained crew made subtle adjustments to the sail configurations and watched the moonlit water slide by with a smooth, steady whoosh. Two men at the prow had the job of keeping sight of the two shallop lanterns in case John Hemmington, who manned the tiller, lost sight of them. There had been several anxious moments during the rain when one or both lights had been extinguished by the wind before being quickly relit. Hemmington estimated another two hours to the north end of the sound, and it couldn't pass too quickly to please him. He was a part-time, small-boat, coastal sailor; and the fifty-foot pinnace was a new experience for him, one he found disconcerting with so many people depending on him and mistakenly thinking he was competent. He thanked God the rain had stopped and the moon would be with them for the remainder of the voyage. Encouraged, he acknowledged to himself that he *was* beginning to get the feel of the ship though her lighter-than-normal weight gave her a reduced draft and a correspondingly higher ride on the water, which, when combined with her relatively flat bottom and shallow keel, gave her a nimble but sensitive, almost-tippy feel. "Stay with me, Lord," he said as he glanced at the stars overhead. As he looked back to the front to reacquire the shallop lights, one of the crew at mid-deck on the left side shouted, "By Jesus Himself! Look at that lightning! Ho . . . ly Lord!"

Hemmington and others who had heard the man looked toward the western horizon, saw nearly continuous lightning the entire length of a north-south line that stretched as far as they could see in either direction. He shook his head, shuddered. Nothing so frightful and monstrous in England. He felt the sudden chill of a rising southwest wind graze his left cheek, smelled fresh moisture in the air. He looked at the sky, judged from the speed of the thin clouds drifting past the moon that the line of thunderstorms would hit them in about thirty minutes and, judging from the expanse and severity of the lightning, would likely pummel them with heavy rain, hail, and wind that would roil the serene, shallow sound into a churning cauldron of vicious, choppy waves higher than the freeboards of their boats. He took a deep breath, then another, looked at the moon, tried to slow his racing heart, calm his impulse to panic.

Suddenly, the right shallop light disappeared, and a moment later, the left. Probably the last we'll see of them before morning, he thought . . . if we *see* morning. Damn! Worst possible timing: approaching the narrows, two-and-a-half-miles wide for five miles. He checked his compass: three-five-five. Maintain this course, and you'll be alright, John . . . but don't forget, wind will push us toward the outer banks . . . got to compensate . . . hold three-*four*-five when the wind rises . . . but compasses don't work well in lightning storms. Damn, Damn, Damn . . . maybe we should anchor here, ride it out . . . no . . . anchor will drag or rope will break . . . keep going . . . fast . . . get through the narrows before it hits. Got to be close. Lord Jesus, I don't want to be here . . . keep moving . . . wind from the southwest . . . keep the tiller and sail angles constant to maintain course when the compass quits . . . but wind will shift in the storm . . . but perhaps lightning will illuminate the shorelines enough to see them . . . but what about depth . . . could run aground. Damn it! Got to pass through the narrows before it hits . . . already at top speed. Christ Jesus. Help us.

Thirty-five minutes later, Hemmington's compass was a useless trinket, its pointer flicking randomly in aimless directions; but as he had hoped, bright lightning flashes told him they were now in the narrows, but too close to the outer banks. Dangerous, he thought as a needling, wicked chill raced down his back. He estimated the wind at more than thirty-five knots and rising, still from the southwest; he increased his tiller angle to steer back to the center of the channel. Rumbling, shrieking black clouds suddenly enveloped the ship, pelted her first with huge, heavy raindrops then with hail the size of radishes. A churning cauldron of malicious waves and towering swells tossed and battered the ship, crashed onto the deck; tumbled screaming people who hadn't tied themselves to something, like pebbles tossed onto a cobblestone street; flung those who *had*, to the ends of their tethers, where the violently pitching deck pounded them like a man being drug on the ground by a runaway horse.

Hemmington leaned into the tiller with the full force of his body but couldn't hold it, called one of the crew to help; heard people screaming, crying, praying. As the howling, shrieking wind pounded his ears, he yelled at the two lantern watchers to look outboard for the shorelines when lightning flashed, realized they couldn't hear him. He'd never had the bad judgment to remain at sea in a storm like this, knew he was beyond his capabilities. He shuddered as a deep, burning fear gripped his insides, planted the gnawing realization that they would not survive the night.

Suddenly, the aft mast snapped like a twig, fell partially overboard, trapping those beneath it in rigging, like flies in a spider web. It entangled Hemmington and his helper, pulled several screaming people into the water. The top of the mast and its sprit sail sank, flowed with the current; acted like a sea anchor, tried to drag the stern to the right and the prow farther into the wind. Hemmington's helper lay on the deck, tried to climb to his feet. Hemmington wrapped both arms around the tiller, leaned his chest into its left side; but even with the submerged aft sail trying to drag the stern to the right, the force on the main mast, with its large spritsail and smaller, square topsail, was too great for him to maintain course, and the prow turned relentlessly downwind toward the outer banks. Hemmington's mind tumbled in chaos: if we strike the mainsail we'll drift backward, run aground; anchor won't hold, no choice but to hold fast and pray; but we're listing too far over, may capsize, or the main mast may break. "Damn it to hell, what should I do?"

One of the crew crawled over to Hemmington, screamed, "John, I think I saw one of the shallops off the port side . . . belly up, adrift, no people in sight."

Hemmington's heart pounded; he stared at the man, his mind and lips frozen in a rigid stupor.

Emily—drenched, disheveled, exhausted, gasping for breath—knelt and clutched the plank bench she was bound to on the left side of the ship; her father and George knelt beside her. A wall of water crashed over the side, bludgeoned the three to the deck, swept them to the ends of their rope tethers.

"Father! My arm."

"Hold on, Em!"

George grabbed her waist with one arm, wrapped his other around the bench.

Roger Baylye yelled at Hemmington, "John, strike the damn sail before we capsize. Let her drift to ground, take our chances." The whining roar of the wind swallowed his words.

Another deluge crashed over the side, again pounded Emily to the deck and the end of her tether. She coughed up a mouthful of seawater, rolled over, grabbed George's leg. "George, hold me."

George and her father pulled her back to the plank.

"Hellllp!" Elizabeth Viccars and her young son washed over the right side.

"Elizabeth!" Ambrose Viccars yelled as he leaped after them.

"Father, did you . . ."

"What?"

Emily again wrapped her arms around the plank, grasped her weak left arm with her right hand. George and her father each held a handful of her shirt in their free hand.

Another wave pounded over the left side. Emily saw Robert Ellis struggling to hold on to the seat in front of her. "Father!" Another wave.

"Help Robert!" She looked back toward Ellis; he was gone. "God help us!"

Suddenly, the ship gave a mighty moan, abruptly stopped as the right front rammed into a sandbar like a careening carriage hitting a stone wall, sent untethered people flying across the deck, knocking several unconscious. A huge swell lifted her stern to the right, threw people against the right side, or to the ends of their tethers, or overboard. A loud cracking sound ruptured the shrieking of the wind; the main mast snapped in two, fell across the deck, its top hanging over the right side. The rudder slammed hard right, smashed the tiller into Hemmington, throwing him against the left stern railing then overboard.

The mast thrashed around the deck; splintered a man's leg, crushed Dyonis Harvie's head like a melon hit by a boulder; spread its rigging over the screaming passengers, bound them to the deck like a cargo net. A moment later, a large swell lifted the ship off the sandbar, slid her into a deep hole; she rolled onto her right side where she groaned, creaked, began to drift downwind and sink. The screaming, terrorized people on the high, left side hung from their tethers or fell into the water, while those tethered on the right were thrust underwater to drown.

Hanging from her tether, Emily struggled to untie the wet knot that bound her to her plank and the sinking ship. "George! Father!" Thomas Colman hung unconscious beside her.

George grabbed Emily's rope with his left hand, pulled out his knife with his right, cut into his own rope. "Emily! Hold my waist!"

The ship moaned and warped; the plank seat broke in half, tore loose from the deck, which freed Emily's rope but sent George and Emily tumbling into the convulsing nightmare below. Colman's section of plank remained attached to the ship, suspending him from his snagged tether ten feet above the rising waves. In the water, George grabbed the plank; reached for Emily with his other hand, missed, saw her disappear below the surface; grabbed her rope as it snaked after her, pulled, kicked, drug her to the surface. "Emily!" He lifted her onto the board.

"Aaaarghhh!" She gagged, vomited a stomachful of water.

George twisted and kicked the plank through tangles of rigging until they were free of the wreck. He seized a piece of rigging secured to the ship. "Here! Hold this. I'm going for your father. If she goes down before I return, let go and kick away as fast as you can."

"No, George! I won't leave you!" Dizzy, hold fast, Em.

A few moments later, George returned with a groggy Thomas Colman, pushed and shoved him onto the plank beside Emily, then looked back at the drowning ship where tangled people screamed, pleaded for help. A huge swell suddenly rolled the ship onto her top-side; the stern dipped beneath the surface; the prow began to rise.

George looked into Emily's eyes, thought how blue they looked even in the dead of this dark, evil night. "Emily, I love you! Remember me! Now let go and kick. Go! Now! Hold on to your father. Kick! Kick! Go!"

"No, George! No! I love you! Please don't go back!" She reached out to restrain him. "No! No!"

He yanked the rope from her hand, kicked and shoved her plank away, then swam back toward the ship.

"George! Come back! No, George. No!" Emily kicked her plank a short distance, looked back for George, realized there were no more screams. A flash of lightning illuminated the small part of the prow still above water. "My God. George, please come back!" she screamed, stared in dazed horror as the next flash revealed only black, angry water where the prow had been a moment before.

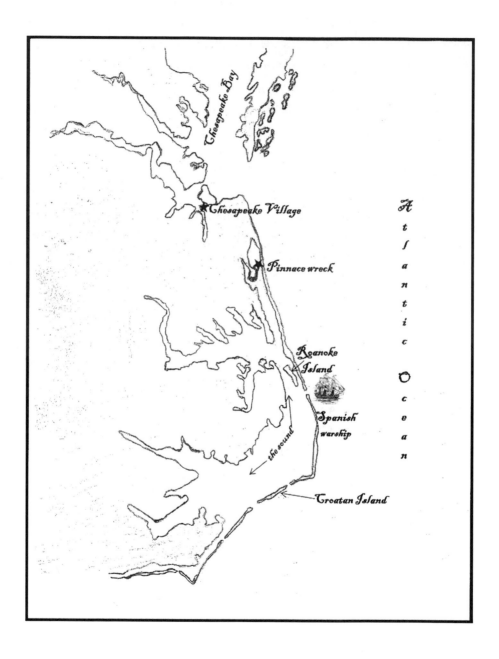

CHAPTER 7

As the sun passed its zenith and slid toward the western horizon, a heavy, salt-fish smell permeated the narrow outer banks like morning mist. The measured roar of ocean waves breaking onto the eastern shore overwhelmed the soft swoosh of gentle waves from the sound as they lapped at Emily and Thomas Colman's feet. They lay face down, motionless on the sand, small crabs skittering about on their bodies, gulls waiting patiently nearby for the imminent feast.

Emily stirred, rolled to her left side; the gulls flapped grudgingly into the air; the crabs scurried onto the sand. She looked down the shoreline with blurry, exhausted eyes, saw boards, pieces of rope, other debris littering the beach, nothing on the water. Sand covered her cheeks and forehead like grainy powder; and her hair was a tangled, sandy mop that hung down over her face as if she had just awakened from a weeklong sleep. So sticky and damp, she thought. She rolled right, onto her forearms, propped herself up, pushed the hair from her eyes, then looked to the left. "Father!" She pulled her knees under her, started to crawl toward him. "Father!" She pushed shakily to her feet, stepped toward him, staggered, dropped back to her knees, crawled the last yard. She pushed his shoulder. Nothing. Pushed again, harder. "Father! Wake up!" Is he breathing? She rolled him onto his back, wiped the sand from his face. His eyes were closed, face pale as the sand, chest flat and still. She snatched a fluffy gull feather from the sand, held it an inch from his nose and mouth, saw it flutter softly. Breathing. He's alive. "Father! Wake up!" She pushed his shoulder again.

Thomas Colman opened his eyes, blinked twice. "Emily . . . where are we?"

She sighed, smiling weakly. "I don't know, but . . . but we're alive." She kissed his cheek, closed her eyes; saw the seething black cauldron of water, she and her father clinging desperately to their board; saw herself pulling him back onto it when he'd passed out and slid off; kicking, screaming at him to hold on; saw herself slipping beneath the surface, exhausted, nearly drowning, refusing to surrender to the waves, grabbing the plank again; kicking, praying, fighting the evil water, her injured arm screaming in pain. She saw the lightning flash, the emptiness where George and the ship had been, remembered her scream, her desolate despair, her frantic cries. She raised her head, again looked up and down the shore, scanned for survivors. "George! George!" She cried softly, then wailed, shuddered; slowly lowered her face to the wet sand, dug her fingers into its soft, warm, claylike texture.

Colman rolled onto his side, put his arm around her. "Emily, what happened to George?"

She sobbed on.

He pushed her shoulder. "Emily, where's George?"

"He's dead, Father. Drowned. Dragged down with the ship . . . saving others . . . saved you and me. Gone, Father. He's gone. Don't you remember?"

Colman pushed himself close to her. "No, Em, I *don't* remember. I don't remember anything after the mast broke."

Emily stopped crying, sat up, wiped her eyes. "George saved you, Father. You were unconscious. He brought you to that board over there." She pointed at the six-foot plank lying on the shore behind him. "I was already there—he saved me, too. Then after he rescued you, he went back for others who were caught in the rigging . . . then everything was gone." She looked out at the sound. "They're all out there somewhere . . . under the water, tangled with the pinnace . . . I want to go back and find George. I can't bear the thought of him dead out there in the water. I'm going out to find him." She stood, walked to the plank, lifted the end, started dragging it into the water.

Colman watched for a moment with hanging jaw and dumfounded eyes, then rose, walked to her, gently put his arm around her shoulder as he gripped the plank with his other hand. "Em, you cannot go out there. You've no idea where to look, and there's nothing to be done, even if you find something. Nay, Daughter, there's naught you can do for George but thank God for his bravery and pray he's in heaven." He guided her down to the sand. "And I must thank you, my dear, brave daughter, for somehow holding me on that board all night and getting me to this shore."

She looked at him with numb eyes, saw nothing, tried to grasp his words; leaned her head against his chest, wrapped her arms around him as she'd done as a little girl, closed her eyes; moaned softly, hid herself in the solace of his embrace. But her mind returned to George—his surprised, smiling face when she'd shoved him and run away on the pathway to the shore their first day at Roanoke, his lingering sorrow at the loss of his mother, his breathless grief at the brutal murder of his father, the adoring honesty in his eyes when he told her he loved her more than life itself. As she sobbed and pulled her father closer, she suddenly saw George tethered to the ship, floating underwater, blank eyes staring at her, begging for help. She moaned softly as she blinked the vision away.

After a long silence, Colman said, "Come, Em, we must pray for George . . . and for ourselves, I fear." With a damp stiffness, he guided himself and Emily to their knees. They looked like out-of-place sculptures wrapped in a tight-fitting cloak of silence. He held her hand, looked skyward. "Almighty Lord, we, your children, offer you profound thanks for our deliverance from the wicked jaws of the sea. We also thank you for any others you may have spared." He coughed. "Lord, we also commend to you the spirits of those who perished in this terrible storm . . . especially that of young George Howe, who sacrificed himself that others might live. No finer soul have you ever put upon this earth."

Wailing and trembling, Emily sank back on her heels, lowered her face to her sandy hands.

"And may he revel in your grace in paradise. Last, Lord, please guide us as we seek our deliverance. And when we've been reunited with our brethren, protect us as we struggle to survive in this hostile land, so all may serve your will. Amen."

Colman lowered his gaze to Emily, then leaned forward and touched the back of her head, glided his fingers through her hair, softly caressed the back of her neck.

When she had quieted, she took a deep breath, looked up into his eyes. "Amen, Father." I've nothing left, she thought. Wonder if any others survived? How will we find them? How will we find the village, Elyoner, Virginia? How can we survive the coming winter and the Savages who would kill us? How can I live without George?

As the two sat in silence, staring out at the water, Colman looked across the sound, saw the main to the west; he followed it north to the hazy distance, where it merged with the outer banks. That's where we must go, he thought, but 'tis more than a day's walk. No fresh water here on the banks, only rotten fish to eat unless we catch some crabs. He wondered if the people at Chesapeake would search for them. Alas, he thought, we left Roanoke over a day early; they won't expect us until tomorrow night. We're alone . . . unless one or both of the shallops survived, arrived safely, told them of our ill fortune. How calm and placid the water looks now, so different from the hellish tempest of last night. He again scanned up and down the waterway, wondered how many had perished, how many bodies they'd find on the way north, how many besides themselves had survived?

Emily surveyed the panorama before her; focusing on sections of water, she searched for remnants of the ships, bodies. She wondered why she'd been unable to love George as he'd loved her, succumbed to the smoldering guilt that billowed in her mind—feel so alone without him, like part of me is gone, empty, dead; wish I'd perished with him, lay entombed beside him in the water. God, why did you take him, the noblest soul on earth? Why him? Why not someone else? Why? You erred, Lord. She quickly crossed herself. Forgive me, Lord . . . 'tis not for me to judge . . . please care for my George; tell him how much I miss him . . . and love him.

Her eyes drifted to the birds above and on the water. So carefree, so content, she thought. So unlike me. She watched the tiny waves glide gently ashore from the sound, run their course, slowly recede. Like the joys and sorrows of life, she mused. Will we ever feel joy again? Can we ever live in this land? I think not. I think we must leave. I think God is *telling* us to leave, abandon it to the Savages . . . I *want* to leave . . . want my locket . . . my mother, my brother. She slid her hand into her empty apron pocket. I *shall* leave . . . when John White returns . . . return to England . . . and a safe life . . . where people and things aren't trying to kill me every day; where I can live without fear, like my friend Jane back home; where there's real food, beer, wine; where I can be courted by a good man, fall in love, marry, have children . . . but there *is* a certain excitement and exhilaration to living perilously, narrowly escaping death. Perchance it gets in your blood . . . like the warriors of old times . . . like the Vikings. She suddenly thought of Hugh Tayler, realized her usual warming at the thought of him had been displaced by chilly indifference. She shook her head. God's blessed will, Emily, how can you condemn the man on hearsay—albeit your best friend's—without giving him a chance to speak for himself? Most unjust . . . but I feel what I feel, so what am I to do?

After minutes of vacant wandering, Emily's mind replayed the disasters that had plagued them: George Howe's brutal murder, the attack on the Croatans, White's departure, the massacre, Manteo's disclosure of the Powhatan threat at Chesapeake, the wreck . . . her last glimpse of George. Then for a fleeting moment, she saw the penetrating black eyes of Manteo's Savage friend. She couldn't remember his name but felt a sudden, new warmth spread through her body, between her thighs, a disorienting rush to her mind. Oh . . . such a stirring inside me . . . why? Forget him, Emily. You'll never see him again . . . he's a Savage, a heathen. You've nothing in common . . . but Manteo's a Savage, and you found much in common with *him* . . . perchance . . .

"Emily, we must be on our way." Colman pointed to the north, where the outer banks met the main. "We must go there, then somewhere beyond and inland. 'Tis a long walk, and we shall have no food or water until we are there . . . so we must start now. I am already famished and thirsty. How are you?"

"The same . . . so let us go, Father." She looked out at the sound, said another prayer for George. "I want to forget this place . . . but I'll never forget George."

"Nor shall I, my dear." He embraced her, kissed her cheek, gazed into her eyes, then grasped her hand and started north.

They had walked a quarter mile when Colman abruptly raised his arm, pointed ahead. "Look there!" A hundred yards up the shoreline, several bodies lay on the sand.

Emily stopped, stared ahead with an anxious look. Perchance 'tis George, she thought . . . mayhap he . . . she raced ahead. What if . . . what if . . . oh, God. She stopped. "Father, do you recognize anyone?"

Colman shook his head.

Emily walked slowly ahead. George's shirt . . . looks like his shirt. "Father, I think I see George!" She quickened her pace.

Thirty feet from the bodies, she stopped, looked out at the sound.

Colman caught up, paused, then walked forward as he covered his nose and mouth with his hand. Flies and small crabs covered the bodies. One corpse was a woman who lay face up, her eyes already devoured, her body naked and bloated. The other two were men lying face down. One, indeed, looked like George. Colman hesitated, then stooped, rolled the body over, looked at Emily without expression, shook his head. "Come, Daughter, we've a duty."

***

Two hours later, Emily and her father patted the sand on the last of the three graves. The burials had been difficult, for they'd had only their hands and driftwood sticks to dig with. Depleted, hot, desperately thirsty, they sat on the sand, stared at the graves and emptiness around them. Only the lapping water of the sound, the periodic crash of an ocean wave, and the cry of an occasional gull violated the silence.

Finally, Colman said, "They came so far, Em, but for what? For this? To be buried on an empty shore in a hostile land? Why, I ask? Why?"

"At least they're buried, Father. I can't say that for George. He died for us . . . I feel so guilty . . . wish I'd died with him." She closed her eyes, crossed her hands over her chest.

"Don't talk like that, Em. You're alive because God has a plan for you. Life seldom proceeds the way we expect, but 'tis God's plan, nonetheless."

She opened her eyes, looked at him.

"Em, our burial of these good souls has made me think . . . made me realize what a fool I was to bring us here. I'd hoped to better myself, achieve a lifelong dream . . . but all I've done is put us at risk, perhaps doom us to certain death. You know, my dear, sometimes God tells us what his plan is, and I think He's telling us now that it doesn't include us living here."

"Father, you—"

"I was truly selfish to leave your mother and brother, and risk you, my only daughter, for selfish ambition. I see that now."

"Father!"

"I should've been happy with what I had in England, been content as a schoolmaster. My self-indulgence has almost cost you your life twice; and now we may never see your mother and brother again, and they'll never know our fate."

Emily thought of her lost locket; her fingers instinctively explored her apron pocket. Elyoner, pray thee protect Mother's letter.

"Emily, I will also tell you I'm a total failure at expressing my feelings to those I love. I'm clumsy and awkward, and cannot easily say to you that I love you more than anything in this world, but I do. I cannot say to you that your safety is my obsession, but it is . . . and here we sit."

She grasped his hand.

"We've no chance for survival here. We're more alone than any civilized people have ever been. The Savages and this dangerous land will overwhelm us in time, and I cannot allow that to happen." He looked into her eyes. "After the massacre, I decided that when John White returns, we shall board the ship and return to England with your mother and brother if they're aboard. And if another ship finds us before he returns, we'll leave with *them*."

"No, Father! I thought the same earlier today, but now I see 'twas wrong. What of the sacrifices made by George and his father, and those who died at the massacre and in the storm, and those who've survived? We'll desecrate it all if we run away. No, Father! We *cannot* leave! We *will not* leave. I *refuse* to leave! We must stand and rely on God and ourselves to overcome whatever lies ahead. We must, Father!"

Colman stared at the ground with empty eyes, shook his head. "Emily, you are the bravest of girls, but—"

"What's that?" Emily looked south, sudden alarm in her eyes, put a finger to her lips, then rolled flat onto her stomach, motioned her father to do the same. "There it is again."

"What? What is it?"

"Voices. I heard voices."

The two lay flat. Emily's heart pounded against the sand; her mind spun with fear. Two heads appeared over the top of a sand dune a hundred feet to the south.

A voice said, "There they are. Looks to be Master Colman and his daughter. Hello! Are you alright?"

"Father, 'tis Sergeant Gibbes and Roger Baylye." Emily and her father looked at each other, sighed, smiled; they climbed slowly to their feet and held hands.

"Praise God! That we are," Colman said, brushing the sand from his clothes. "Have you seen any others?"

"Not alive," Baylye said. "And you?"

"Nay." He pointed at the three grave mounds.

Baylye and Gibbes hurried to the Colmans; all four hesitated, stared awkwardly for a moment, then embraced. Baylye said, "Good to see you alive, Thomas, and you, Emily. *Very* good to see you alive." He looked at the graves. "Could you identify them?"

Colman said, "Richard Arthur, Thomas Scot, and Margaret Lawrence."

Baylye nodded. "Since we've nothing to write with, all of you must help me remember the names of those who've perished. Sergeant Gibbes and I buried Morris Allen and William Sole. There were also five others, four men and a woman, we couldn't identify. We'll have to determine who remains when we reach Chesapeake and check the manifest." He shook his head. "It has been a long, tiring day, Thomas, and—"

"Excuse me, Sir," Emily said, "were any of those you found dressed like George Howe? He rescued Father and me . . . and others. He was wearing a—"

Baylye and Gibbes looked at one another, shook their heads. "I'm afraid not, Emily. I saw him helping others, as well. A courageous lad. He would have made you—"

Emily covered her face, turned away.

"I'm sorry, Emily. Please forgive me."

* * *

By the time the sun sat two hours above the western horizon, they had advanced but two miles, buried eight more people, found five alive. Two of the dead had been with Gibbes on the shallop that had sailed to the right of the pinnace, closest to the outer banks, while the remaining dead and the survivors, three men and two women, had been on the pinnace. As the nine made their way slowly up the shore, they scanned the sound and the banks for more bodies and survivors, searched for debris that might reveal the fate of the second shallop. Most had lost their hats, shoes, jackets, and weapons in the storm; and though the early fall sun was slightly cooler than the debilitating August sun, it remained hot enough to burn exposed skin and gravely aggravated their thirst. So Emily and the other woman had torn their aprons and part of their skirts into sections of cloth for themselves and the others to drape over their heads and necks for a measure of shade.

Wary of surprise by Savages, Baylye had cautioned all to watch the banks, sound, and sea, both north and south, for Savages on foot or in canoes; for without weapons or cover to hide themselves, they were nakedly vulnerable to discovery and attack, their only hope being to spot an enemy before being seen and lie flat on the opposite side of the small rise that formed the spine of the outer banks. Although they had seen nothing but small pieces of debris on the shore and in the sound, they *had* discovered six sets of footprints heading north, including a set made by shoes.

As he walked with Thomas Colman, Baylye said, "Thomas, I think 'twould be wise to walk through the night and try to reach the main by morning . . . we *must* have water. Another day in this sun will shrivel our chances of survival like spit on a hot rock."

"Aye, Roger; and remember, Lieutenant Waters won't consider us overdue until tomorrow night. So we've no choice but to go on . . . Emily and I had planned to do so."

Baylye nodded, scanned the sound for a few moments, then looked back at Colman. "Thomas, I've been fretting all day over how many critical skills we might have lost in the storm and what we'll have to work with at Chesapeake. Physician Jones will be irreplaceable, and—"

"Our three sailors, as well . . . but with nothing left to sail . . ." His voice trailed off, then he flashed a hopeful look. "Actually, Roger, we don't yet know the fate of the second shallop, and 'tis not impossible that they survived and are looking for us."

"I suppose there's a chance, but 'twould indeed be a miracle if 'twas so."

Emily and Johnny Gibbes walked thirty feet behind Baylye and Colman. She had told him of George's heroism, her hope they would yet find him alive. "I suppose you felt the same when you heard about Audrey after the massacre. 'Tis natural to keep on hoping, even when you know there's no reason to it." She studied him with empathetic eyes.

"Aye, Mistress, I did . . . but fortunately, there's much to think about now: survival and starting a new village." They walked silently for a few moments before he said, "I imagine you're in no mind to hear about Master Tayler . . ."

Emily stiffened, looked at him in fearful anticipation. *I so dread this . . . the end for Hugh and me . . . but why should I fear it? If Johnny can affirm Elyoner, why wouldn't I* want *to know it, and why would I* ever *want to see Hugh Tayler again? And if he* can't *affirm her, then I'll know* that *truth . . . and be able to go on with my life and my relationship with Hugh. So what do you fear, Emily Colman? Forsooth, I fear knowing I was deceived and must face my deceiver and confront him . . . and hear him deny what's been said . . . and then face a dreadful dilemma: my own uncertainty, the possibility of my own indecision . . . and the difficulty and pain of doing whatever I must do. So the problem is mine . . . mine alone, and* I *must face it and resolve it. But by Christ's suffering death, I* do *dread facing Hugh Tayler if 'tis true . . . wonder if he's alive.* "I suppose he could be dead."

"He *may* be dead, but in case he isn't . . . and because you're in danger if he isn't . . . I feel a duty to tell you the truth about him before 'tis too late."

Emily squeezed her lips together, looked at him with tight eyes. *Hear him, Em . . . hear with your heart but react with your mind.* "Very well." She gazed up the shoreline.

"I know much about him, Mistress, but I should start with whatever your friend told you."

She glanced at him. "How do you know so much?"

"Because we grew up together in the same place, his father's estate. *My* father was a tenant farmer there; and though Tayler's a bit older than I, I grew up hearing of, and witnessing, his deeds. So if it be your will, Mistress, I shall tell you all I know . . . and 'twill be God's own truth."

A wave of apprehension burst into Emily's mind like flood waters through a broken dike. With a quaver in her voice, she said, "My friend heard something about him forcing himself on a young maiden."

Gibbes flashed an angry look, then one of sadness. "He did indeed, Mistress, and more than once. But the occasion your friend likely spoke of was when he seduced a young lass of fifteen, made her pregnant, then abandoned her, left her alone when she was in labor . . . she bled to death with no one to help her. The baby died, as well . . . and Tayler denied even knowing her."

Emily's heart tightened like a hangman's noose as grim acceptance chewed its way into her exhausted mind. "Forgive me again, but how did you or anyone else come to know such private matters?"

With a look beyond painful, he said, "Mistress, the young lass was my sister."

Emily gasped, cupped her hand over her mouth. "Oh, no! How horrible, how . . ." Her eyes misted with tears.

"Do not be concerned, Mistress. 'Twas long ago."

"I'm so sorry."

"You must hear the rest. There's much more."

She took a deep breath, nodded, felt a surge of anger, then embarrassment that she'd been deceived by a womanizing bounder. She imagined the girl writhing in agony, screaming for help on her blood-soaked bed, suddenly saw *herself* in the girl's place, felt the agony, the abandonment, despair, life seeping from her body. "Can you tell me what happened at the estate?"

"His father was a firm, fair man, but they never got on well. Nonetheless, his father respected tradition and, while he was still alive, placed Master Tayler in charge of the estate, even though both of his younger brothers were, and still are, far better beings than he."

"He told me he was the youngest of the brothers and that the older brothers ran the estate . . . ran it into the ground . . . and he had to step in to save it."

"On the contrary, Mistress Emily. Hugh Tayler was successful only at drinking and womanizing; and 'twas *he* who ran the estate into the ground . . . to the point that his father threw him out and disowned him on his deathbed, gave the estate to the brothers . . . and that is when he joined the army . . . as an officer, of course . . . and that is yet another story."

Emily shook her head. A fool, I am. "I want to hear about the army, but first, what of his mother? He told me she died when he was very young."

"No, Mistress. His mother was always on the border of insanity; and though I believe he loved her, he'd no wish to have her survive his father and meddle in the estate; wanted everything for himself, he did. And this part I cannot verify, but 'twas said he encouraged her to take her own life; and being of unsound mind, she did as he suggested, hanged herself from a ceiling beam. Strangely, I believe his grief was genuine, though I don't know if it was because he feared going to hell or because he loved her and truly regretted what he did."

Emily stared into empty space. Strange, but I feel sorry for him ... yet how shall I ever face him or speak to him again ... perhaps 'twould be better if he'd died in the tempest. She shook her head. Shame upon you for such thoughts, Emily Colman. "What of the army?"

Gibbes glanced at her with a somber look. "Worse than his earlier years, and since I was in his unit, I know the complete truth of it, even though I was but a simple soldier and he, an officer. The entire company knew." A worried look suddenly spread across his face like night shadows following the setting sun. He looked around as if to ensure no one was listening. "Before I continue, I must tell you that Hugh Tayler knows I know everything about him . . . and as you know, he saw us talking at Roanoke. With no uncertainty, my life will be in danger if he ever suspects I've told you the truth about him. So I pray, Mistress, please keep all I've told you secret."

"Johnny, surely you don't believe he'd—"

"Aye, he would, and without hesitation. He's a brutal, selfish, evil man, and he'll destroy anyone or anything in his way. And Mistress Emily, if he even suspects I've turned you against him, he'll kill me dead, as sure as there's a sun in the sky."

She looked away. "I cannot put you in such danger. Tell me no more. We must tell Master Baylye. We cannot simply sit by and—"

"Tayler's clever, and telling Baylye may be worse than simply taking my chances."

She shook her head. "Johnny, you should not have said anything to me, shouldn't have risked your life on my behalf."

"Nay, Emily. I did so because you're in danger of falling prey to his evil . . . like my sister. I did it for both of you—her memory, and your future—and I beg you, please, never again allow yourself to be alone with him . . . never."

Emily's teary eyes glistened in the sunlight; her stomach churned. She shuddered, nodded, wished she'd never met Tayler; wished she wouldn't have to bear the grim truth about him, fear for herself, fear for Johnny Gibbes. She took a deep breath. "Tell me the rest."

He nodded. "Very well. When we engaged in our first battle in Holland, Tayler—Lieutenant Tayler—was—"

Roger Baylye yelled, "Hello! Hello over there!" He and Thomas Colman quickened their pace toward six colonists who had gathered a small pile of driftwood and were laying a fire. Two lay motionless on the sand, their backs bare, their shirts pulled over their heads.

Christopher Cooper replied, "Roger. Thank God. We prayed there'd be others . . . we're building a fire for the night in case we find some fish on the shore . . . Roger, we're *very* hungry and thirsty, and two of us"—he waited for Baylye to reach him, leaned close, whispered—"two of us are sick . . . rapid heartbeats, short breath . . . as if they've run a great distance. They're very hot; and both have headaches, cramps, dizziness, and who knows what else." He glanced at the two. "They also seem lost in their own heads . . . and I know not if they can go on."

Baylye said, "I've seen this before. 'Tis the sun that does it . . . and in God's name, I don't know what we can do for them without shade and water."

Sergeant Gibbes said, "Governor, we can find some sticks and make them a tent with our shirts . . . at least for the remainder of the day."

"That's a splendid idea, Sergeant Gibbes . . . as are the ideas of waiting for others to find us and building a fire to cook fish . . . excellent ideas, and I'd gladly embrace them . . . if we weren't in the situation we're in." He looked at each person in turn, gauged their expressions, read little but raw, numb exhaustion. "Unfortunately, there may be hostile Savages about, and a fire would tell them our location . . . we've naught but one sword and our eating knives among us." He glanced at the two sick men. "Of greater concern is the possibility that without shelter and water, some could die tomorrow. Thus I fear we must walk through the night, so we can find water and shade as soon as possible in the morning." He looked north to where the sound ended and the outer banks merged with the main, estimated the distance at ten miles. " 'Tis less than two hours until sunset; so until then, I propose we do as Sergeant Gibbes suggested—shield the two who are ill; then at dusk, we shall head north with all the haste we can summon. We shall carry these two, if necessary. At least we won't get lost out here on the outer banks, and—"

"Hello! Hello there!" a voice to the south yelled.

All but the two sick men looked south. Cooper said, "Looks to be Master Tayler and Sergeant Myllet."

Thomas Colman glanced at Emily, saw the frightened look on her face. He walked to her side and put his arm around her waist. "What's wrong, Em? You look horrified. Are you not excited to see Hugh alive?" He started toward Tayler, then looked back at Emily, wondered what dismayed her.

Emily watched Tayler and Myllet approach the group, shake hands with the men. Gibbes and Myllet embraced, smiled at one another, hit each other on the shoulder, embraced again.

Tayler spoke to Colman then spied Emily standing behind the men.

Her body stiffened as his eyes found hers, lingered, searched. She fought to conceal the anger, fear, revulsion, and confusion that swirled in her mind.

Tayler walked briskly to her, held his gaze on her eyes, opened his arms to embrace her.

She stepped back, held her hands up in front of her chest as she gave him an inscrutable look.

He leaned forward to kiss her.

She looked away. "No, Hugh, I cannot."

He whispered, "Emily, what's wrong?"

The others watched in curious silence.

"George perished in the storm, Hugh . . . after he saved Father and me. I'm not able to think of anything else yet."

He hesitated then nodded. "I understand . . . but I'm so glad you're alive. I . . . I had horrible fears you'd . . ." He again stepped toward her.

"No, Hugh. I cannot. I thought about you, as well . . . but I'm not ready. Please understand."

He forced a smile. "Emily, can we talk somewhere?" He motioned his eyes toward the others. "I'm so thankful you're here before me; and I desperately need to hold you, tell you how much I love you, talk to you. My soul aches for you. Please, let me . . ."

In her periphery, Emily saw Johnny Gibbes, his hand on his dagger, glaring intensely at Tayler's back. "Hugh, I'm here because of George and no other reason but God's mercy; and 'tis true, we've much to talk about . . . but not now, not here. Please forgive me . . . I need time . . . perchance when we reach Chesapeake."

He hesitated, wondered what was behind her sudden coolness, the same coolness she'd shown just before they left Roanoke. *She's heard something about me, but what? And from whom?* He looked behind, surveyed the watching people with an innocuous glance that abruptly hardened into a hateful glare when it stopped on Johnny Gibbes and Michael Myllet.

* * *

The Panther and his wife lay naked, panting, beaded with sweat on a bed of soft deer pelts. She was a striking young woman about nineteen, with sharp features; mysterious, intense, dark eyes that admiringly studied his face; full lips that curved gracefully into an exhausted, satisfied smile. Her long, black hair spread like a fan beneath her shoulders, complimented her breasts, which still had a firm, erect look and melded proportionately with the gentle curves of her lower body.

The Panther's sinewy, muscular body had a spent look as he gently massaged her inner thigh where it met her triangle of hair. His eyes blankly stared at the top of the lodge while he euphorically savored the lingering aftertaste of their passionate love. Then for a moment, he thought of his first wife, his lost children, felt a ripple in his heart as he remembered the pure, intense love they'd shared, their plans for their family, their joy at the births of their two sons. He didn't think he could love his new wife as deeply and unselfishly as he had the first; but her beauty and ability to make wild, frenzied love—love that nested in his mind for hours or days afterward—would carry their relationship a long way. He'd suspected for a few weeks that she carried their child, and believed its birth would strengthen their love, move them closer to that lost first love. But he knew he could never draw his mind completely into the present until he severed the final tie to the past, and that could not happen until he did to a white woman what the white warriors had done to his first wife. With the whites moving to the Chesapeakes' country, he knew that the arrival of that moment was at hand, and he knew exactly with whom it would be.

He'd earlier considered exacting his revenge on the captured white woman from Roanoke, but she'd been claimed by another warrior who'd taken her as his wife shortly before she killed herself. No loss, he thought, for she was unworthy, lacked the courage to satisfy his thirst for revenge. But the one he'd nearly taken at Roanoke—the one with hair like the night and eyes the color of a cold, clear winter sky—was the most beautiful woman he'd ever seen. Not only was she beautiful, she was more courageous and defiant in the face of danger than any woman he'd ever encountered in his world, and *that* he respected above all else, and *that* placed her above all others as the choice for his revenge. He'd thought he killed her; but Roanoke watchers, one of whom had been with him at the attack, had recently reported seeing her in the village. He smiled imperceptibly, felt a twinge of excitement surge through his body as he reached down to his side where she'd stabbed him, touched the nearly healed wound; understood for the first time why his heart had stirred so forcefully when he'd looked into her eyes, wondered in the course of a heartbeat how a white woman could have such power, the power to touch his deepest soul. Even her look of exhausted submission at the end had moved him; she'd fought to the limits of her strength, exhausted herself, then serenely faced her fate. He knew he'd again see her fierce determination, her will to live, and ultimately, her look of submission when he took her body and then ended her life to sever his tie to the past . . . but perhaps . . . perhaps . . .

He looked at his wife, captured her eyes with his, rolled toward her, kissed her, probed her mouth with his tongue; he heard and felt her breathing quicken as she embraced him, felt her hand slide to his loin, caress his manhood. He felt himself becoming aroused but suddenly decided he had too many important things on his mind to make love a second time this night. His first duty was to the people, and he had to think on their behalf. He touched her cheek. "I love to love you, my beautiful, wild young woman . . . but I have much to do tomorrow, and you've already exhausted me." He smiled, kissed her gently on the lips, again touched her cheek, then rolled onto his backside and laid his left hand on her breast, forced his mind from the soft sensuousness of her body to that evening's council held with Wahunsunacock.

As always, the entrance to the great chief's council hall had been imposing: first, a walk through the long quarters, which were longer than nine men lying head to foot, half as wide, and constructed of a framework of arched, bound saplings covered with large panels of tree bark; then the approach to the narrower council hall at the end; and finally, the entrance to the hall and arrival before Wahunsunacock's seat of honor, which was an elevated, wall-to-wall bench at the end of the narrow hall, upon which had sat the paramount chief of the Powhatan chiefdom and his two favorite wives. The lesser chiefs, other trusted warriors, and more of Wahunsunacock's wives had sat in two parallel rows that ran from the hall entrance all the way to the great chief. A small fire had crackled and burned near the entrance to the hall, at the head of the two rows; and as always when he held a council, Wahunsunacock had worn his finest jewelry and headdress, which consisted of nearly as many skyward-pointing turkey feathers as there were people in the hall. He'd greeted each person's arrival with a nod at the spot where they should sit; and when the Panther had arrived, the dim, fire lit hall had already been thick with musty smoke and quiet whispers; he'd felt a surge of warm pride when Wahunsunacock had met his gaze, nodded at the spot immediately below his right foot at the end of the line—the most honored position, other than his own, in the hall. The Panther had returned the nod, sat in his place, looked up and down the lines, acknowledging the other council members, then fixed his eyes on the ground in front of him to summon the words he'd speak when called upon by the great chief.

Moments before the council had begun, the Panther's mind had drifted back to his many exploits in battle, most against the Monacan people, their bitter enemies who lived toward the setting sun where the mountains rose. They spoke a different language from the Powhatan peoples, a language similar to what he'd heard from traders from many moon cycles to the north, where there were rumored to be huge lakes with drinkable water—lakes nearly as large as the Great-Water-That-Cannot-Be-Drunk. He'd killed eight Monacans in his twenty-six years, some easily, some with great difficulty, nearly lost his own life several times in the process; but fighting brave, dangerous enemies was life's greatest challenge and its greatest honor . . . even if one died. And he knew his intense bravery and the wisdom that guided it were the reasons Wahunsunacock had chosen him as his most trusted and valued advisor.

Several lesser Powhatan chiefs had spoken first. They'd told how the Roanokes had seen the English leaving Roanoke Island, how visitors to the Chesapeakes had learned that these people were coming to settle with the Chesapeakes by the big bay; and they'd spoken about new incursions into their territory by the Monacans, the latter having resulted in the killing of two Powhatan warriors when Monacan and Powhatan hunting parties unexpectedly encountered one another several days before. Then another lesser chief, from the Nansemond people, who bordered the Chesapeakes, had called for a punitive raid against the Chesapeakes for their refusal to become full members of Wahunsunacock's chiefdom and for allowing the English to live with them. Many mouths had buzzed and many heads had nodded at the comment, but Wahunsunacock and the Panther had shown no reaction.

The next speaker had been Wahunsunacock's shaman, a man of great honor—not for his exploits in war but for the remarkable accuracy of his visions and prophecies. He'd previously told of a dream he'd had of a nation rising from the Chesapeakes' land to destroy the Powhatan chiefdom. He hadn't been able to accurately identify the people in the risen nation but had assumed they were the Chesapeakes; so though the Powhatans *never* decided for war without serious consideration of the potential gains and risks, the council had immediately voted to rub out the Chesapeakes if they ever grew in strength and belligerence toward the chiefdom. But this night, the shaman had spoken of a new dream: a vision of white men growing strong in the Chesapeake land, rampaging through Powhatan villages, accompanied by Chesapeake warriors, killing, raping, forever destroying their world. He'd concluded that this dream confirmed that the white men were the nation he'd dreamed of in his first dream and that the Chesapeakes were merely their allies; and though his dream had not shown him *when* the destruction of the Powhatans would occur, a voice in the dream had told him that the Powhatans could avert the danger only by attacking and annihilating the white men first. A stunned silence had filled the great hall. The Panther had studied the shaman's face to discern whether or not he was exaggerating, taking liberties with his dreams as shamans sometimes did, but he'd seen only the face of an old man worried to the core of his soul.

After a prolonged silence, Wahunsunacock had looked at the Panther. "Wahunsunacock would hear Kills-Like-the-Panther."

The Panther had risen, nodded at the great chief, drifted his gaze to the eyes of every other man in the room. "We have heard many voices tonight. All spoke with wisdom and with the good of the people in their hearts. I have listened and heard and thought on every word, and asked our spirit leader, Okeus, to guide my thoughts. This is what he has told me. The English and their fulfillment of our great shaman's prophecy are the greatest threat we face. They remain strong, with many big sticks that make thunder, and a direct attack on them *now* will bring many weeping women and children among us. For that reason, we should bide our time, let winter take its toll, let them grow hungry, fight with each other, perhaps kill each other; then nibble at them like small fish, kill a few when we can do so with little risk, capture a few, torture them, test their bravery as they die slowly, leave what remains of their bodies where the others can find them, and feel their hearts fill with fear. Then when they're weak, diminished in numbers, and without the protection of a fort, we shall attack and annihilate them and their Chesapeake friends." He'd paused, again looked into each man's eyes, thought of his first wife and children lying dead, his new wife, the child in her womb. "They will not have the strength or heart to build a fort in winter. They may begin it, but they will wait until spring to complete it, which means we have until *then* to attack. So we have time to be careful, choose the right moment, the right weakness, the right vulnerability; we can then rub them out without losing more of our own people than we can suffer to lose, for we must expect to face other white men in the seasons ahead and must preserve our strength and will to do so."

He'd paused while private discussions of his words rippled around the lodge, then glanced at Wahunsunacock, who'd nodded at him without expression. A moment later, he'd looked back at the council, raised his arms for silence. "We have heard that the Monacans are encroaching on our territory. We've always fought these people and always will. But they pose far less danger to us than the English, and we cannot fight two big wars at the same time." He had watched the nods of approval ripple their way down the two lines, like small waves. "So I tell you that Okeus has let me see that we must first make a *little* war on the Monacans to keep them from our hunting grounds. At the same time, we must harass the English with small attacks as I proposed a moment ago. Then when most, or perhaps all, of the right conditions are in place, we will attack the English and Chesapeakes with all of our force and rub them from the earth."

The Panther had barely seated himself when Wahunsunacock had said, "Kills-Like-the-Panther has spoken with wisdom and concern for the people. He has spoken the words Okeus gave him, which are now in his heart . . . and in my heart." He'd then looked at each man in the two lines, had nodded his acknowledgement as each had nodded his assent. When finished, he'd said, "This council has decided to proceed as Kills-Like-the-Panther has proposed. We will begin tomorrow."

As the council's war cries and howls of approval faded to the present, the Panther suddenly felt the warmth of his sleeping wife's body flowing through his arm to his heart, her life force melding with his. He looked at her, feathered his hand slowly across her belly to feel the soft rise where their child grew, gently touched her cheek, smiled, rolled to his back; and as the tunnel of his mind narrowed toward sleep, he saw the white woman's piercing eyes, her wild raven hair, her face tight with raw, defiant determination to live.

***

Bright moonlight flooded the white sand around Emily as she knelt beside Griffen Jones' prostrate, writhing body, eased a wet cloth over his forehead. She thought of herself two years earlier doing the same for her twelve-year-old brother; remembered praying with every stroke, wishing with all her soul he'd live, knowing he wouldn't; replayed her emotional unraveling at his painful death. She didn't know this man, but it didn't matter. He was a human being who needed help, and she would do her best to provide it, as her mother had taught her. Mother . . . oh, dear Mother, how I miss you . . . so tired, sore, arm hurts . . . hot, sticky sand all over me . . . thirsty, hungry, mouth dry as a ball of yarn, can't swallow . . . stomach groaning, barefoot, bruises from the sand, so hot, so thirsty . . . my locket . . . oh, Mother, I long for my locket. Hope Ellie has your letter. Ellie, I miss you and Virginia . . . more than I could ever have imagined, and it's only been a week. Pray for us, Ellie, we—

Thomas Colman arrived with a rag saturated with the warm, brackish water of the sound. "Here, Em. Give me yours, and I'll wet it again." Hugh Tayler and Roger Baylye stood several feet behind Emily, watching her treat the man.

Emily took the rag, handed hers to her father. "He's burning with fever, Father . . . keeps trying to vomit, but there's nothing but blood . . . he then convulses for a few seconds and lies still." As her father turned to walk back to the sound to wet the rag, Emily looked at Tayler. "Hugh, can you rub this across his forehead while I check on Master Burden?"

"Emily, I don't—"

"Fie, Hugh Tayler! Come here and take this rag . . . Father, I need another wet rag for Master Burden . . . quickly." She lifted the bottom of her skirt, tore out a large square, and handed it to him. *Why did you snap at Hugh, Emily? Do not force your own afflictions on others . . . even if . . .*

Tayler looked as if he'd been slapped in the face, stepped hesitantly toward her.

Emily placed the rag on Jones' forehead, looked at Tayler, beckoned him to kneel; she rose, walked the twenty feet to John Burden, and knelt beside him to touch his cheek. "Oh, no! Master Burden, wake up." She shook him gently, laid her palms on his cheeks, then grasped his wrist and searched for a pulse. "I think he's gone. Master Baylye, can you . . ."

Baylye stepped to her side, knelt, checked the pulse, looked at Emily, shook his head.

Emily stared at him, moonlight sparkling on her damp eyes. "I'm sorry. I . . . I didn't know how to help him, what to do."

Baylye grasped her hands. " 'Tis not your fault, sweet Emily. None of us know what to do. You did the only thing you could . . . tried to make him comfortable. I'm afraid the ending was inevitable. You're a kind, gentle soul, young mistress."

Emily tried to force a smile but couldn't. "What can we do for Master Jones?"

Emily and Baylye stood, walked back to Jones, where Tayler knelt, dragging the cloth back and forth across his forehead as if it were a rock. Tayler rose, handed the cloth to Emily. "I'm not very skilled at this, Emily."

Emily looked at Jones; took a fresh, wet cloth from her father, handed him the warm one; knelt beside Jones, resumed her task. After a moment, she looked for Baylye; she saw that he, Tayler, her father, and several others were digging a grave for Burden. Jones suddenly moaned, twisted his body back and forth several times, heaved, then faded to unconsciousness. Emily shook her head. "Stay with us, Master Jones. Don't let go. We'll get you to water and shade in the morning."

After twenty minutes, Baylye and the others approached Emily with gaunt, somber expressions. Baylye said, "Emily, you've made a valiant effort . . . but he's slipping away . . . just as Master Burden did."

Emily ignored him.

"We've discussed our situation and the best course of action for all." He paused, blinked several times, rubbed his fingers and thumbs together. "The welfare of the entire colony is my responsibility, and I must base my decisions on its best interest."

Emily paused, looked up at him; she glanced at her father then back at Baylye.

"We've decided our first responsibility is to get as many of us as possible to shade and water. Unfortunately, whether or not we stay with Master Jones will not affect his chances of survival. He's going to die, with us or without us, and remaining with him longer may cause others to suffer the same fate. We've no idea what awaits us further up these banks, and we'll likely encounter unforeseen obstacles. So, for the good of all, we must tarry no longer."

Emily thought again of her mother's teachings to never abandon the helpless, to care for the sick until their end. Mother, what should I do? No one spoke. She heard only the crashing of ocean waves behind her, felt as if the entire group of survivors awaited her response, as if the decision to abandon the dying man was hers alone. She stood, whispered, "Master Baylye, we cannot leave him here to die alone. 'Twould be unchristian. I shall stay with him until he is gone if that be his fate. Then I shall bury him and make my way north behind you." A breath of breeze ruffled her tangled hair as her eyes held steadfastly on his.

Baylye blinked, said nothing.

Johnny Gibbes said, "I shall help her, Governor."

Hugh Tayler gazed at Gibbes. "I, as well."

Thomas Colman shook his head, frowned. "Em, you *cannot* do this . . . 'tis not . . ." He hesitated, knew he'd again bungled his choice of words.

She glared at him, snapped, "Father, I *can* do this . . . and I *will* do this." She walked toward him, looking ready to spit in his face, held her teary eyes on his for a moment; suddenly wrapped her arms around his waist, pulled him close; laid her head against his chest, sobbed. "You're right, Father. I cannot. 'Twould endanger others . . . but it pains me so to . . . to . . ."

"Emily, my dear Emily. You're such a good, kind soul."

As suddenly as she had embraced him, she pushed back, composed herself. She looked down at Jones then at Baylye. "Master Baylye, I'm ready to go. But first we must pray for Master Jones."

Baylye nodded, looked at the others, said a brief prayer for God to exert his will quickly, then turned and started north. "Come, friends. We've a long way to go."

Emily started after the line following Baylye, looked back at Jones. As the darkness swallowed him, she saw him squirm in the sand, heard him quietly plead for help. She stopped, closed her eyes, whispered, "Forgive me, Master Jones; forgive me, Lord," then walked on.

***

The group of fifteen huddled together against the chill of a steady rain. Most men had temporarily removed their shirts to hold them over their heads as shelter and to soak up drinking water, which they wrung from the cloth into their mouths. Emily and Emme Merrimoth, the young woman who sat beside her, had done the same; and when Emily tilted her head back to catch the water, her soaked smock pressed against her chest, revealing the curves of her breasts in unimaginative detail.

Hugh Tayler stared at her, breathless, lips agape, realized the sight had aroused him. Wild, ragged, beautiful, exciting—the thoughts circulated through his mind like the relentless turning of a waterwheel. I must have her, he thought, but it must be because she loves me. She owns my soul and my mind; she's my salvation from myself; she must be mine. I must . . .

William Clement of the latest group of survivors said, "Baylye, why don't we try to build a fire before we all get the shakes and die?"

Baylye looked at him. "Because we don't know where we are, and a fire might attract Savages if any are about."

Clement, who was larger than most of the men, had a permanent, intimidating sneer on his face that guaranteed no one would befriend him. He spit on the sand, uttered a sarcastic grunt. "In this?" He looked up at the rain. "Are you daft, man?"

"No, Master Clement. I am not daft, merely cautious. We cannot take the chance. The wood's probably too wet anyway."

"Well, I think you're a fool, Baylye. I'm building a fire."

"No, Clement, you're not. I order you to stand down."

"To hell with you. I'll do as I please." He stood, sneered at Baylye. " 'Tis you who put us in this situation. We should've stayed at Roanoke, taken our chances with the Spanish. You're the reason so many are dead and our boats underwater. Fool!"

Myllet said, "Sit down, Clement. Your time in prison must have shrunk your brain. Do as the governor says."

"I'll not. And just what will you do about it?"

Myllet stood and walked toward Clement. Gibbes and two other soldiers rose, stood beside Myllet.

Clement leaped at Myllet, tackled him to the ground, and reached for his neck.

Myllet slammed his fist into the side of Clement's head as the three soldiers pulled him off and held him fast. Myllet climbed to his feet, stood before Clement, who teetered groggily. "You keep your mind to yourself, Clement. We've no time or tolerance for fools here. Now sit down and shut your mouth."

Clement sneered, sat down, rubbing the spot where Myllet's fist had hit him, then pulled the tail of his shirt over his head.

Baylye stepped closer to Myllet and whispered, "Thank you, Sergeant Myllet," then glanced around the group before continuing. "I think we've rested enough and should move on. The labor of it will warm us and dissipate tempers. What think you?"

"Aye, Governor. I'm for it."

As the grumbling people stood and started north, Emily's mind drifted back to George and his father. Only death and strife, she mused . . . but it *will* get better . . . it *must* get better. This is the low point. We *will* survive. *I* will survive . . . even if no one else does. She noticed Tayler watching her as she trudged along holding her father's hand, noticed Emme Merrimoth talking to Johnny Gibbes. She's pretty, short like me, trim and pleasing to look at—lovely blond hair and haunting brown eyes, always smiling and bouncy—seems very pleasant; I must get to know her better. She definitely likes Johnny . . . he seems to fancy her, as well. I like them both . . . especially together. She glanced at Tayler, resisted the temptation to smile at him, then leaned her head back and opened her mouth to catch a few drops of rainwater. 'Twould be so perfect if—

A loud cry came from the front of the line. Emily and the others rushed forward, saw Roger Baylye being swept away by a rushing stream of water that flowed swiftly from the sound to the sea, blocking their pathway up the outer banks. Myllet and Gibbes sprinted at full speed along the side of the channel until they were slightly ahead of Baylye, clasped each other's arms as Myllet leaned out over the water, seized Baylye's flailing hand, and pulled him ashore.

"Taking a swim, eh, Gov'nor?"

Baylye trembled, shook his head. "Whew! Thank you again, Michael Myllet . . . 'twas a complete surprise. Stepped off that bank right into deep water . . . never saw it. When we sailed up here on the sea side, there were no gaps in the banks." He thought for a moment. "But there *were* some low valleys between the dunes . . . must be a tidal inlet, and the tide's on its way out . . . damn strong current. How the hell are we going to get all these people across?"

"Well, Sir, how deep is it?"

"I hit bottom twice, so 'tis not *too* deep—mayhap four feet—but very fast and very strong . . . pulled me off balance, and I couldn't get a hold with my feet."

Myllet looked across the channel. "I think you're right, Sir. 'Tis an inlet that opens and closes with the tide . . . 'tis indeed going out now, which isn't good if anyone gets swept away like you did." He wiped the rain from his face with his sleeve, squinted toward the far side. "Looks to be forty or fifty yards across—hard to say in the dark—but it may be deeper in the middle than here on the side. Actually, we could probably wait for the tide to go completely out and then walk across." He looked at Baylye. "But we sure as hell can't wait long. When that sun comes up, we'll bake again, and . . . and, well . . . some of these folk might not last another day."

Baylye nodded. "Could we make a hand-to-hand chain and work our way across?"

"Might work . . . but we better alternate tall and short people in case there be holes out there." He glanced at the channel. "You know, Sir, I hesitate to say it, but there may be more of these inlets in front of us, and some may be deeper; and if so, we'll want to cross them when the tide's out. So all the more reason to be quickly on our way."

"You're right. So let us be about it."

Moments later, Myllet, the last man in the human chain, stepped into the channel. Baylye was the lead link, and all between him and Myllet walked cross-current rather than facing the current and side-stepping across it. This resulted in better stability against the swift current, even though it shortened each person's reach by the width of their torso and forced the chain to have a ragged, weakened, offset structure. Emily was in the middle, with John Starte, a tall, strong man, in front of her and Hugh Tayler behind. Thomas Colman's periodic dizziness since the shipwreck had prompted him to reluctantly ask Starte to take his place holding Emily, lest he lose his balance or his grip on her.

As the chilly rain fell harder, the chain crept across the channel; but with each step, the force of the current pushed their feet a little farther downstream toward the sea. When Emily reached the middle of the channel, the front of the chain was twenty feet farther seaward than the rear, which weakened it and increased the effects of the current. She thought how strange it felt to have the warm water of the sound flowing across her body from her feet to her chest while cold rain drenched her head and shoulders and laid tangled, itchy mats of hair over her face. She wanted to let go of Starte or Tayler for a second to brush the annoying hair from her eyes but dared not.

Suddenly, John Starte sank beneath the surface, lost his grip on the man in front of him, pulled Emily after him into a deep hole. As her left hand slipped from Tayler's grasp, she tried to break Starte's hold on her right but couldn't, felt herself pulled under, swept by the current. She swallowed a gulp of brackish water, felt her lungs burning, exploding, begging for air; she kicked, twisted, jerked, tried to free herself from Starte. Suddenly, his grip released; she tumbled with the current, dark terror flooded her mind; she kicked, paddled, felt herself drifting faster, her mind numbing, darkening. God, forgive me my sins; she thought of her mother—never see her again—head burning, drowning. Father! When her feet hit bottom, she pushed upward with all her strength, paddled for the surface. In a remote corner of her mind, she sensed a grip on her wrist, then an arm across her chest; felt herself being dragged across the surface—air, a deep gasp, coughing water—more air, sweet, wonderful air; she kicked toward the pull of the arm. As her feet found ground, she heard yelling, screaming; found her balance, stood, opened her eyes, saw Hugh Tayler's desperate face; felt him wrap his arms around her, pull her to his chest.

"Emily, Emily. My God, Girl. I thought you were gone." He squeezed her, kissed her wet hair. "Couldn't find you. Thank God I bumped your arm . . . you were down so long." He walked her onto the bank then upstream, where the people from the back half of the chain had regrouped on the shore. "Are you recovered?"

Am I, she wondered? Gasping, trembling, legs buckling, dizzy, she whispered, "Yes, Hugh . . . I think so . . . barely . . . thought I was drowned."

"So did I." He looked at the others then back at Emily. "Are you able to try again? I'm afraid we must do so quickly."

"I think so. I doubt there's any choice to it . . . no matter how I feel. But hold me close for a moment . . . until I stop shaking. Don't let me go." She buried her face against his chest, found comfort in his arms, thought to herself, whatever else, he loves me with all his soul . . . would that I hadn't heard what I heard. Would that it could be untrue.

"I love you, Emily. I shall never let you go." He kissed her hair, her neck, her forehead, her lips.

Emily's body warmed; her heart raced; she felt a hand on her shoulder.

Thomas Colman said, "Emily. My God, you scared me." He looked at Tayler. "Thank you, Hugh. Thank you for saving my little girl." He leaned forward, kissed her on the cheek.

Tayler said, "She needs to rest a moment, Thomas. Then I'll lead the rest of us across. Could you find Starte?"

"Nay. Never surfaced. Must have been swept out to sea."

Fifteen minutes later, Myllet, the final link in the chain, climbed ashore on the far side of the channel. The rain stopped, and the fourteen huddled together for a brief rest before proceeding north. In the next two hours, they crossed two more inlets, found and buried six more bodies, and caught up with four survivors from the second shallop.

As the comforting sun cleared the horizon, warming rapidly toward another blistering day, Baylye estimated the main to be five miles distant. He wondered how many would fall before they reached it, before they found the forest, shelter from the sun, water to quench their stifling thirst.

"Look there!" someone shouted. "Dead fish . . . a big, dead fish." Half the people rushed to the ocean shore, gathered around the three-foot-long fish. Its smell said it had been dead a long while; nonetheless, William Clement and several others started tearing at the loose flesh, stuffing handfuls into their mouths. Suddenly, Clement stood, picked up a four-foot-long piece of waterlogged driftwood, held it over his right shoulder with both hands, growled, "Get your hands off my fish. I found it, and I'll eat it. Get back . . . all of you."

All but George Martyn backed away from the fish.

"I told you to get back, Martyn. Do it!" He stepped closer to the kneeling man.

" 'Tis not *your* fish. It belongs to all. Drop the club."

Baylye said, "Put it down, Clement." He, Myllet, Gibbes, and several others eased toward Clement.

Myllet slipped behind Clement, reached for the club; he was an inch from touching it when Clement swung it at Martyn's head, slammed it into his left temple, knocking him onto his side, where he lay still, blood trickling from his nose, mouth, and ears, his startled eyes wide in a lifeless stare.

Myllet, Gibbes, and two soldiers tackled Clement, yanked the club from his hands, held him face first to the ground, and pulled his arms behind his back. Gibbes produced a piece of rope rigging he had found on the shore, quickly wrapped it around his wrists, then tied it tight.

Baylye felt Martyn's pulse, stood before Clement. "Stand him up, so he can face me."

The men pulled Clement to his feet in front of Baylye.

"William Clement, I charge you with the murder of George Martyn. As governor, the urgency of our circumstances permits me to sentence you to death at this moment . . . but we have no proper means of carrying out the sentence."

Clement sneered. "He got what he deserved."

"Drown him," someone yelled.

"Cut his throat," another shouted.

Baylye said, "Nay. Executions will be by hanging or the axe, and we've the means for neither. So we shall wait until we reach Chesapeake and let Thomas Hewet try him. With so many witnesses, the outcome is not in doubt."

Clement said, "Fuck the lot of you. You'd better kill me now, Baylye, for I shall find a way to get free, and I mean to kill you when I do."

Myllet pointed at a soldier who had a six-foot coil of rope in his belt. "Tie that rope around his neck and keep the other end tied around your wrist at every moment . . . even if you sleep. If he tries to escape, all of you kill him any way you can. And if we encounter Savages who attack us, use him as a shield, or offer him in exchange for your lives and let the Savages have their way with him."

* * *

Emily wished her throbbing headache, body aches, foot bruises from the sand, and cottony-dry mouth would go away . . . also, the incessant rubbing of sticky sand on the insides of her legs, which had created a painful rash, made her wish she wore pants like the men. She had tried to fold the front of her skirt and smock between her legs as she walked along, but they had slipped out after a few steps. Another female burden, she decided with a private smile. Bear it and move forward: one foot, then the next, keep moving. I'm no slower than anyone else; keep moving, Em. So hot . . . why am I not sweating? Mother, Ellie, I miss you. I want my locket, my letter. She glanced at the blazing sun hovering at its zenith, felt thirst and hunger devouring her insides. She looked toward the north end of the sound and the main, noticed swampy marshlands along the banks to her left, tall clumps of grass covering the narrow banks themselves, and a half mile ahead, perhaps another half mile inland on the main, a thick forest. Her heart rippled with hope at its sight: salvation, shade, water, mayhap food. The thought of it made her empty stomach churn and rumble, but she thanked the Lord she hadn't eaten any of the dead, rotting fish they'd found along the way. Those who'd gorged themselves had quickly vomited and been queasy ever since.

Her eyes on the sand five feet in front of her, she thought of her mother's kitchen: its warmth, the sizzling kettle beside the fire, the ever-present smell of cooking food—delicious food—beer, water. She saw herself and her mother preparing a feast of pig pie, her favorite meal. They first skewered the small pig and cooked it on the spit—a hot, sweaty job for Emily, the spit turner—and when it was cooked, they removed the skin and rubbed hog's lard over the meat. Before applying the seasoning, they looked at one another questioningly, then shrugged their shoulders, giggling as they sprinkled generous, unmeasured dashes of pepper, salt, nutmeg, and sage over the meat. She smiled as she recalled how, in spite of their guessing, it always seemed to turn out perfect. They laid slices of the seasoned meat on a bed of butter in the bottom of the pie, rubbed mace and more butter over the top of the meat, closed the top of the pie, and baked it. Emily closed her eyes, imaginatively inhaled the satisfying aroma, licked her lips, saw herself enjoying the delicious feast.

Johnny Gibbes said, "Hello, Emily. How fare you? God was surely with you last night."

"He was indeed." She smiled, crossed herself. "God and Hugh Tayler. And I see glorious forest ahead . . . with shade and water."

"Do not drink too fast when we find the water. Take little sips at first . . . else you'll toss it all back up."

She looked at him. "Truly?"

"Aye." He smiled. "We learn such things in the army."

"Well, thank you for telling me that. I'd surely have gulped it like a fish if you hadn't." She tried to swallow, gagged, shook her head, then imagined herself kneeling by a stream, her cupped hands raising sips of cool, clear, delicious water to her lips. She suddenly thought of Tayler holding her by the tidal inlet. "Johnny, I . . . I don't want to sound like I doubt you. I don't, but I must ask . . . are you completely sure of the circumstances we spoke of?"

He gave her a quizzical look. "That I am, Mistress. And to prove it, Hugh Tayler has watched me like a spy since he saw us together . . . and he's watching me now, so I dare not talk much until we can do so beyond his sight. I'm probably a fool for speaking to you right now."

Emily glanced behind, saw Tayler walking beside her father, his eyes on her and Gibbes. She nodded. "I believe you . . . the difficulty is mine, for I've been foolishly hoping there was some mistake, that what you told me wasn't true, that it would go away . . . because . . . because now I must face the fact that in spite of whatever *was* between Hugh and me, he's *not* who he appeared to be, and *such* invalidates our relationship, and as you say, may also endanger me. So there's no choice to it. I must either cast him from my life now or confront him and give him a chance to defend himself."

"I understand, Mistress Emily. And to worsen it, he seems to care deeply for you . . . and caring for another is a quality I've never before seen in Hugh Tayler. Forgive me for intruding, Mistress, but do you love him?"

She studied his eyes, again read only naked sincerity. "I do not know, Johnny. I truly do not know. I thought I might . . . until Elyoner, then you, told me your secrets. But now I truly do not know. I'm confused between my heart and my mind, and the fact that he saved my life last night worsens the confusion. If he hadn't acted so bravely, with complete disregard for himself, I'd be decomposing in some shark's belly right now; and that means something, Johnny. It truly *means* something . . . about *him*. But whatever's to betide Hugh and me can't be determined until later, for we're in no place or clime for the parley that must occur between us." She looked away at the sea for a moment then back at Gibbes. "Do you think people can change?"

"I've not been on this earth long enough to know for certain, but I suppose they can . . . still, I'd be surprised at such from Master Hugh Tayler . . . though it could be *you've* changed him. I don't know." He looked into her eyes. "Mistress Emily, I can see you don't want to let go; and perhaps he *has* changed; but until you're certain, I plead with you to *never* allow yourself to be alone with him. Please . . . always be in sight of others and—"

"Hello, Emily, Johnny," Emme Merrimoth said. "I hope I'm not intruding."

Emily smiled. "Hello, Emme." As her expressionless, unseeing eyes watched Emme and Johnny converse, her logical, decisive mind grappled with her feelings over Hugh Tayler. Perhaps he *has* changed, she thought. Perhaps I should go on as if nothing has happened, see where it goes. I *do* care strongly for him . . . at least I did. But Johnny fears for me, says there's much more to tell. Can I take the chance? But what if I confront him and he claims it isn't true, as he'll probably do. What then? I know what. I'll have to decide who's telling the truth. But I already know that, so why complicate it by giving him the chance to deny it? Accept the truth, Emily, the pain of having been deceived; be done with him now . . . even if it hurts.

She thought of George—again wished she could have fallen in love with him—conjured her fading hope that he might somehow have survived. *We would've been quite good together. Love would've come to me eventually; for no more honest, caring man ever lived on the earth. Still, I never felt the raw passion and delirious love I expect to feel for the man I marry; and while I felt considerably more for Hugh, 'twas still short of my expectations. So perhaps as Master Howe told me that night on Roanoke, our situation has played tricks on us, made us feel things we wouldn't otherwise feel. Lord, please guide my heart and mind to the right decision.* A sudden image of Manteo's friend, whom she'd met at Roanoke, raced through her mind, spread an unexpected warm glow through her body and mind. *I wonder if I'll see him at Chesapeake.*

As they reached the main and headed west toward the forest, Emily took a last glimpse of the sound, envisioned George and his father smiling at her, then Elyoner and Ananias anxiously awaiting her arrival. She shuddered as she thought of the Savage who'd nearly killed her, then thought of the storm, the wreck, the ordeal on the outer banks.

A half hour later, they entered a forest as dense as that at Roanoke and soon after came to a gentle stream about twenty feet wide.

Baylye, who was in front, yelled, "Water!"

They raced to the stream, plunged wholesale into the cool current, lay or knelt on the side, buried their faces in it. Emily knelt on the bank, a little off from the others, leaned over, took a sip as Gibbes had suggested, then another, and another, then abruptly plunged face first into the water, rolled to her back, kicked her legs up and down to wash the sand from between them and sooth her rash. *Blessed Lord, this is heavenly.* She rolled onto her knees, hands on the bottom, dipped her face into the water again and again as she sipped with each plunge; swooshed the water through her hair; stood to remove her shirt and the remnants of her skirt, then fell back into the water; lay on her back with her legs spread upstream, reveled in the refreshing coolness that flowed to the tops of her thighs; laid her head back, swallowed water as it flowed over her face. When she finally stood again, oblivious to the presence of others, she let out a loud whoop, extended her arms, twisted her torso back and forth, then splashed up and down with the jubilance of a child on Christmas morning.

Suddenly she felt eyes upon her and stopped. Glancing down at her front, she saw that her wet smock clung like a second skin to every curve and indentation of her body, revealing her firm, round breasts, her nipples erect from the cool water, the small mound between her legs. She felt her tiny waist, the small, tight curves of her bum and hips. "God's blessed mother," she whispered, "I'm as good as naked." She plopped back down into the stream, looked around giggling, slipped back into her outer garments, then sat in the water, smiling a mischievous smile to herself. A rather bawdy display, Mistress Colman . . . but how delightful . . . pray Father didn't see. She laughed out loud. He'd surely die of embarrassment. She looked around, ensured no one was watching; laid back, leaned her head on a smooth rock, closed her eyes; softly eased her hands over her breasts then across the insides of her thighs, suddenly thought again of Manteo's friend, and again felt unfamiliar warmth permeate her. She shook her head. Lord, prithee someday give me a true, loving man with a gentle touch, to summon forth, and then drown himself in, the passions hidden within me.

Her inner voice broke her trance. "Emily! You daydreaming twit! Gather your wits. Quit thinking like a hussy." She thought of her mother. Yes, Mother, 'tis our ordeal . . . lost my good sense for a moment. Fear not. I remain chaste . . . the fair young woman you raised, and—

"Friends," Roger Baylye said, "thank the Lord for your deliverance, then rest yourselves. We'll remain here until morning and use the remaining light to search for food. Sergeant Myllet, would you see to the prisoner? Then post some sentries, including civilians, around us. Every man shall stand a shift . . . no matter how tired we are."

"Aye, sir." Myllet and two other soldiers shoved Clement rudely to his knees, pushed his face into the water, and held it there until he began to squirm and try to raise his head for air. Myllet pulled his head up by his hair, let him gasp twice, said, "We ought to drown you now, Clement, save the judge the trouble of hanging you. They used to do that, you know." He stuffed Clement's face back into the water, held it until he again squirmed for air.

* * *

In spite of Baylye's and Myllet's misgivings, they built a fire to cook the frogs they caught. They also killed three of the animals that hung from trees by their rat-like tails and were bigger than a large, plump tomcat. Then three soldiers who had hiked back to the marshes at the north end of the sound returned, their shirts laden with frogs and oysters. They had also encountered a large, aggressive snake with a big, triangular head and a thick, yellowish body with black-edged, triangular bands over its entire length. It had struck at one of the men as they walked beside a swamp, but its fangs had gotten caught in his baggy pants; one of the others had quickly grabbed it by the tail and torn it free, flung it away, then killed it with a heavy branch and a big rock. They had cut its head off, pried its mouth open with their knives and found it to be cottony white on the inside, with a pair of long, curved fangs; they decided it was poisonous like the adders of England. When it had stopped writhing, they had skinned it and brought it to the camp to be roasted along with the other meat; even those who were squeamish about eating frog and snake were hungry enough to relish the savory meal.

Immediately after the meager feast, most scattered around the clearing, stretched out on the ground, and fell asleep. But as darkness encroached, another chilly rain began to fall. Many retreated to the shelter of large trees and resumed their exhausted sleep; while others remained by the fire, added wood to grow the flames and dry their clothing, even as the rain dampened it, until they, too, fell asleep, oblivious to the steady downpour upon them.

Roger Baylye stood under a tree with Myllet, Gibbes, Thomas Colman, and Christopher Cooper; all wiped rain from their foreheads and faces. Baylye said, "When I went to Chesapeake for the initial meeting, we sailed around a horn into the south part of the bay, and along the south shore past two large estuaries with a small one in between. We then sailed a mile or two south into the westernmost estuary and landed near the Chesapeake village. I'll recognize that estuary if we walk back to the coast, follow north, and go around that horn to the west. But I fear the first estuary will be impassable on foot, which will force us to march back south to a favorable crossing point and waste much time." He brushed the rain from his forehead with his forearm. "Still, 'tis the only way we'll know our bearings for certain, and 'twill be far less risky than searching our way through an unknown forest without a compass, with the possibility of encountering hostile Savages—especially with no weapons to defend ourselves. But on the other side, following the coast, while safer, will take several days longer than going straight through the forest . . . if we can keep our bearings in there." He surveyed their faces, read no opinions. "But remember, Lieutenant Waters and the others don't know we came up the sound or that we were wrecked by the storm; so when they finally decide we're overdue—probably not before tomorrow morning—they'll search for us along the coast with canoes, *not* in the forest. If we can capture their attention with a fire or some other means when they pass, I think we'll have a good chance of being rescued before we walk too far. Considering all factors, I therefore believe the coastal route to be our safest choice, as well as the one that offers the *only* chance of rescue.

Myllet sleeved the rainwater from his brow. "I see your logic, Gov'nor, but in addition to being a much shorter distance, won't the forest offer us more drinking water, shelter, and food?"

"Aye. There's no question about it." Baylye squeezed his lips together, nodded several times, studied the ground for a moment, then looked up. "So perhaps there's another approach: send two or three back to the coast to prepare a signal fire and wait for the rescue party's appearance to light it, while the rest of us remain here in the shelter and shade of the forest and periodically resupply or replace the three on the coast." He saw doubt in their eyes then the light of an idea on Myllet's face. "What are you thinking Michael?"

"Well, Sir, I'm thinking we might be smart to do two things. I agree they'll search for us along the coast; but instead of the main body waiting *here*, what if we proceed through the forest . . . the village can't be more than a day away, if that far. Meanwhile, the three on the coast can do as you propose, taking turns resupplying each other from the forest. If and when they're rescued, they can tell the lieutenant to send searchers into the forest to find the rest of us . . . if we haven't yet found *them*. That way, if the search party along the coast is delayed or misses the three, the rest of us will be ever closer to the village. Verily, we've no perfect choice, but I think most would rather take their chances in the forest than suffer more days on that bloody hot shoreline without shelter from the sun."

Baylye nodded, glanced at Colman and Cooper. "Thomas . . . Christopher . . . your thoughts?"

Colman said, "Sergeant Myllet's idea is sound . . . certainly the best of a distasteful lot. I say we do it."

Cooper said, "I, as well, Roger. I like the idea of moving toward the destination better than waiting."

Gibbes said, "I'll wait on the coast."

Baylye nodded at Gibbes. "So be it." He then eyed Myllet, who was about to speak. "Sergeant Myllet, I know you're about to volunteer to wait with Sergeant Gibbes, but we can't afford to have both of you on the coast. One of you must remain with the main body and the other soldiers."

Myllet smiled. "You've caught me, Sir."

Baylye grinned. "Then we're agreed. Pick two soldiers to accompany Sergeant Gibbes . . . actually, if a civilian wants to go, I'm agreeable with that, as well."

Cooper raised his hand. "I'll go, Roger."

Baylye smiled, nodded, thumped Cooper on the shoulder. "Good, Christopher. Thank you." He looked at Myllet. "Now pick another soldier, and we'll be on our way at daybreak." He drifted his gaze from man to man, nodded. "Oh! One last thing. We've no weapons other than two swords, and we cannot face malevolent Savages with bare hands.

So every man must arm himself with a club of some sort. My friends, we've suffered greatly these last days. So pray this ordeal soon comes to an end. Now, let's all find a leafy tree and try to get some rest in this damnable rain."

Myllet pulled Johnny Gibbes to him for a brief hug. "Godspeed on the morrow, my friend."

"Thee, as well, Michael."

***

Lieutenant Waters, the other Assistants, and Sergeant Smith stood in a small cottage in the dim light of three flickering candles, trying to dodge the raindrops that trickled through the grass-mat roof. Waters' eyes were tight, his lips curled between clenched teeth. He flicked a water droplet from the tip of his nose. "Something's happened to them . . . something terrible. I feel it."

Ananias Dare said, "Perchance the storm's delayed their preparations and departure until tomorrow."

Waters looked at him, nodded. "A possibility, but I worry nonetheless. I suppose we could wait another day before searching . . . but what if they left on time and they're shipwrecked and stranded somewhere without shelter or water or provisions or armament? Can we take that chance?"

John Brooke said, "I think not."

After all had spoken in favor of an immediate search party, Waters said, "Very well. At first light, I shall take a small party of volunteers and four Chesapeake canoes and follow the coastline from the big bay, around the horn, and down the coast toward Roanoke. We'll need water, food, tarps for shelter, and weapons. If they were simply delayed, we'll meet them somewhere in between; and if they wrecked . . . if they wrecked, we'll do whatever is necessary. So let us—"

"Beggin' your pardon, Sir," Sergeant Smith said, "but mightn't it be wise to also send a search party southeast through the forest toward the north end of the sound and the coast . . . just in case they met trouble, landed on the banks, and proceeded overland hoping to reach us more directly? We could take a handful of Savages and a few troops, travel at the quick-time, and—"

"A good plan, Sergeant Smith, but dividing our strength worries me. We don't yet know our relations with other Savages in the vicinity, and we must be cautious until we do. True, it could take us two full days, or even longer, to search the coast and return . . . with or without them . . . and that will greatly delay the departure of a forest search party, but I fear we've no choice. Also, Master Baylye has seen the coast but not the forest, other than here at the village. So I think if the worst has happened . . . and if he's alive . . . he'll choose to follow the coastline. Your thoughts, gentlemen?"

All nodded concurrence.

Ananias said, "I'll accompany you on the morrow."

"I, as well," John Bright said.

Smith asked, "What would you have *me* do, Sir?"

"First, choose five men to accompany us. I know you want to go with the search party, but I need you here with the men to maintain a sharp vigilance and guide the construction."

"And if you don't return as planned?"

Waters took a deep breath, exhaled slowly. "We *will* return as planned . . . but if ill should befall us, the troops will have a new leader named *Lieutenant* Thomas Smith." He smiled, slapped Smith on the shoulder.

Smith grinned. "Thank you, Sir, but I'd rather remain a sergeant, if you please. So good luck and good hunting."

"As you wish, *Sergeant*. I shall do my best."

Moments later, Ananias stepped into his new cottage. Elyoner, hands clasped in prayer, rushed toward him, her face distraught, strained with worry. "What will they do, Ananias? Tell me. I'm destroyed with fear for Emily . . . and the others, of course. Something awful's happened. I know it! I just know it!" She looked at Virginia and young Henry Harvie, both asleep in crude cradles made of branches lashed together with vines and stuffed with grass; she then stared at Ananias, wrung her hands, struggled to hold back looming tears.

He embraced her, leaned his head on hers as she began to whimper softly. "I share your fears, Ellie. I share your fears."

* * *

Emily had curled into a fetal tuck under a large tree, draped her shirt over her head to keep raindrops from her face. She'd slowly dissipated the knotted, pent-up tensions she'd accumulated over the last two days; and her last tether to consciousness had been cloudy thoughts of her lost locket and her Mother's letter, which she'd prayed Elyoner had safeguarded. Now she dreamed of George, her last sight of him; she heard herself scream, saw the empty, churning water. She then saw another dream: herself lying in a place of thin darkness, in the arms of a man, both of them naked; hot, sweaty, bodies entwined; panting, wild with passion, anticipation; kissing, touching; but she couldn't see who the man was. As he gently eased on top of her and she parted her legs to receive him, her subconscious felt a touch to her shoulder. She at once bolted from her sleep, pulled the apron from her head; she sat up, saw her father asleep on one side and Hugh Tayler staring into her eyes on the other. She rubbed her eyes, brushed raindrops from her forehead. "Hugh . . . what's wrong? Why aren't you sleeping?"

He whispered, "I'm sorry to wake you, Emily; I *cannot* sleep. As exhausted as I am, I cannot sleep knowing not why you so suddenly shun me." Rain trickled down his cheeks, made him look like he'd been crying. "Can we go to that tree over there to get out of this rain and talk for a moment?" He pointed to a large tree about thirty feet behind him where no one slept.

She nodded, glanced at her father, engaged in his usual snoring, then stood and followed Tayler to the tree as chilly rain ran down her hair and neck, beneath her smock, and onto her chest and back, which sent a sudden shiver through her body. She thought of Johnny's warning. And here I am doing exactly what he told me not to do. Stupid girl!

Tayler noticed her shivering, reached out his arms to hold her.

She held her hands in front of her, shook her head. "No, thank you, Hugh." She shivered again, rubbed the rain from her face, looked skyward, felt no drops. "Drier here . . . Hugh, I haven't properly thanked you for saving my life. I don't know what to say other than, were it not for you, I would not be here now . . . standing soaking wet in the rain." She flashed a sudden, heartfelt smile. "You acted with unthinkable courage, and I thank you for it."

"No courage, Emily . . . only the desperate instinct to save the one I love above all things on this earth." He felt his heart glow with warmth as he spoke the words, then a sting of disappointment that something beyond his control had chilled her toward him.

Emily felt her eyes fill with tears, her hands tremble, her heart quicken.

His look softened. "Emily, please tell me what's happened between us. 'Tis horribly unfair of you to condemn me without a trial, without telling me what I'm accused of, without letting me answer whatever charges have been drawn against me. Please give me a chance to defend myself."

I *have* been unfair, she thought. I *have* treated him poorly . . . cold-ly . . . with no explanation. Most cruel of me . . . whether or not what's been told me is true. He says he loves me, and he's proven it by risking his life to save mine. How can I treat him so? She rubbed tears from her eyes with the backs of her hands, took his hands in hers, whispered tenderly, almost affectionately, "Hugh, you're right. And I shall tell you what troubles me, I promise you. But it cannot be here, and it cannot be now. 'Twill be a lengthy talk between us, and we've not the privacy or the time or the freedom of mind to do it here. Please understand . . . please be patient with me . . . and as I told you on the banks, I'm still grieving for George, my dear, dear friend, George, and 'twill be so for some days yet. But when it's passed, and we've settled into a semblance of ordinary life, I shall think of you, Hugh Tayler . . . and we shall again share our minds with one another. 'Pon my faith, I swear it."

He stared at her in silence with sad eyes, lips drawn down like a disappointed child's; his heart churned with passion, desire, love; the touch of her hands filled him with gentle warmth, the hopeless longing that she'd never let go. "As you wish, Milady. I shall love you always; and so, I shall wait at your pleasure until we again share our hearts."

As they started back to Emily's tree, Tayler stopped, pulled her back under the shelter of the tree. "Em, I must ask you something else. I saw you talking to Johnny Gibbes back on the banks. Did he—"

Emily bristled, yanked her hand from his. "Hugh, I'll speak to whomever I wish. You cannot go 'round telling me who to talk to. 'Tis—"

"I'm sorry, Emily . . . but I must speak to you about him, for there's something of dire importance you must know."

Emily had started to relax, but her body again stiffened as waves of fearful anticipation and confusion surged into her mind. She stared at him without expression, waited for him to speak.

"Did Johnny Gibbes tell you anything about me?"

"Hugh, that's not your affair!"

He shook his head. "Emily, please hear me. 'Tis most important . . . important to you. Did he tell you anything about me?"

She hesitated. "No! And why is it so important?"

"Because Johnny Gibbes and his entire family are liars and thieves; and since the day we threw them off our estate for stealing us blind over ten years, they've held grudges against me and my family, told bold, hateful lies about us. We should have had them before the magistrate and put in prison, but we were merciful and only expelled them. Even the mother was an accomplice, and Johnny himself was in the thick of it all. We also believe that . . . that they murdered my mother because she uncovered the truth about them. We couldn't prove it, so we didn't pursue it. But I know the truth . . . and Johnny knows I know. So Emily, please, for your own sake, believe nothing Johnny Gibbes tells you; for he'll do anything, stop at nothing, use any person, any opportunity, to destroy me; and you are now the best opportunity of his life to do so.

Emily Colman, by my sacred honor and my undying love for you, I swear this to be the truth."

* * *

Even in the rain, the previous night's rest had renewed their bodies and souls, instilled a visible urgency to complete their odyssey, reunite with their more-fortunate brethren at the new village. Throughout the late morning and early afternoon, occasional openings through the treetops had allowed thin lines of sunlight to strike the forest floor, reveal patches of deep blue sky above, further lift their risen spirits. At midafternoon the small band stepped slowly, cautiously, quietly through the thick undergrowth, whispering softly and tentatively to one another, scanning the forest for signs of danger, searching for a stream by which to pass the night. Emily walked with her father, held his hand as they meticulously picked their way through interminable thickets. Both had wrapped and tied large pieces of Emily's skirt around their feet to shield them from the sharp thorns and twigs that carpeted the forest floor; and the makeshift shoes had functioned far more effectively in the forest than they had on the coast, where sand quickly worked its way beneath the wraps and between their toes, rubbed sores on their feet.

Instead of scanning the forest for birds and matching their songs and images, Emily had all day dwelt on the unsettled churning in her stomach, anguished over what she'd heard from Johnny Gibbes and Hugh Tayler; she carefully recounted their every word, tried again and again to visualize their faces, gauge their verity. *What should I do; who can I believe; who* dare *I believe?* She mulled it all again for the hundredth time. *How can I know the truth?* Her heart and brain wrestled for control of her mind, her emotions, her convictions, her soul. *Lord, I'm but a young lass . . . far too young for these desperate complications and decisions. Why can't my life be simple, straightforward? Please tell me what to do . . . let me know happiness again.*

Thomas Colman coughed twice, jostling Emily's hand and mind as he did so. "Emily, you've had a face of stone all day, and your pretty lips have scarcely uttered a word. What ails you, Daughter?"

"Nothing, Father . . . just thinking about our life here in Virginia, all that's happened."

"Well, you've given me a lonely day in the process, and—"

A loud thumping sound like a sharp, treble drum ruptured the silence a few feet into the thicket beside them. All jumped sideways, tensed; men raised their clubs, held them ready with both hands.

Myllet smiled, "A turkey, friends. Naught but a flapping turkey . . . would that we could have him on a spit tonight."

Nervous snickers and sighs of relief trickled through the group as they resumed their trek. Emme Merrimoth touched Emily's shoulder. "Were you scared, Emily? Chased the wits right out of *me*."

"I, as well. I saw you jump, Emme . . . we were in the air at the same time." Both chuckled.

Roger Baylye said, "Friends, let us rest here awhile." He glanced at the tiny patch of fading blue sky above them. "With the Lord's help, mayhap we'll be without rain this entire day."

Emily and Emme whispered, occasionally giggled to one another as they sat by a tree. Emily thought, I like Emme . . . could become good friends with her . . . it shall be so. She glanced at her father and Hugh Tayler as they spoke with Roger Baylye, wondered what they were discussing, concluded it wasn't her since Baylye was there, but her heart suddenly quickened when Baylye nodded at Tayler and Colman then walked away. She strained to hear Tayler and her father, sighed with relief when Tayler said, "Well, at least we finally had a pleasant day, eh, Thomas?"

"Aye, a pleasure 'twas, without rain."

The two regarded each other in silence for a moment before Tayler said, "Thomas, I've been wanting to speak to you about something . . . could we step over here?"

Emily's heart pounded like the drums that summon people to a hanging; a gust of panic swept into her mind like a fast-moving summer storm.

"Certainly."

Tayler led Colman to a large tree beyond Emily's hearing, resumed speaking in a hushed tone. "Thomas, the disasters and near disasters that have befallen us these last days have made me think deeply about many things, but most urgently about Emily."

Colman turned his head away, coughed twice, choked slightly when he started to speak. "Excuse me, Hugh. This damnable cough is getting the better of me . . . I've always time to talk about Emily."

"And rightly so." He looked around to ensure no one could hear, leaned closer to Colman. "We all know our life here is overflowing with risk and danger, and . . . and . . . forgive me for intruding, but have you ever thought about what would happen to Emily if ill befell you?"

"Aye, I have, Hugh . . . but not nearly enough."

"Well, Sir, I've made no secret of my affection for Emily and the future I envision for us. And you *have* granted your permission for Emily and me to court."

Colman nodded.

"Thomas, I love your daughter more than anything on earth, more than life itself, and I'll do anything for her. Truly, Sir, the happenings of these days have convinced me that life is too short and dangerous, particularly here, to delay decisions of the heart and soul. So I respectfully and humbly ask you for Emily's hand in marriage."

Colman stared mullingly into Tayler's eyes, wondered why the request hadn't shocked him. Perchance he'd expected it, he thought. His heart suddenly thumped with guilt as he remembered his promise to Emily that he'd never arrange her marriage; but he quickly discarded the thought, decided the situation had changed, that all of their lives hung by a thin thread, that his own thread had nearly been severed a few nights before . . . not to mention the three times Emily had almost perished. Yes, the situation *was* different now, which meant that considerations that had been inconceivable a short time ago were now at the forefront of his responsibilities as a father, and foremost among such considerations was the assurance of Emily's well-being if anything happened to him. And who better than Hugh Tayler to fill that role? Certainly, the Dares would take Emily in, but it would strain the privacy of their young family, especially now with the orphaned Harvie infant to care for. No, Hugh Tayler loved her to the depths of his soul, and he'd proven it; and she, in turn, seemed quite taken by *him*; so there could be no better choice. Yes, he thought, Emily *shall* marry Hugh Tayler . . . and she'll do so as soon as we reach the village. He smiled at Tayler, extended his hand to seal the agreement with a handshake. "Hugh, I—"

"Hieeeeeeeeee!" A solitary, piercing, chilling cry arose from the forest; all sprang to their feet, faced the sound, reached for their knives and clubs. A dissonant chorus of horrible, unnerving wails and shrieks, filled the air around them. Anxious, unsure feet shuffled toward the center of the small clearing; hollow, gaunt eyes searched the forest, dithered from face to face, tree to tree. Women moaned, some cried, a few screamed; some men whimpered, two knelt, hid their faces on the ground, covered their heads with their hands. The wails became louder. They squeezed closer together, women in the middle, the eight soldiers on the outside. The wailing grew louder, closer, louder still; a ring of twenty Savages, bows and war clubs at the ready, suddenly emerged from the forest, closed around them.

CHAPTER 8

In a tearful, half-hour phone call, Allie told her mother every characteristic of her dreams: their color and vividness, how she sensed peoples' thoughts, heard their dialogue, felt relationships and emotions; that the dreams were orderly, not chaotic like most dreams; that the story moved relentlessly forward, even when she wasn't dreaming; that the dramatic, movie-like events had steadily drawn her in, entwined her mind and emotions with the story and characters—the massacre, Tayler's advances, the escape from Roanoke, the shipwreck, George's death, the struggle for survival on the outer banks, and especially Emily. She stated the historical fact that the colony had vanished; then admitted that she'd developed a craving, almost an addiction, to know what would happen next, wanted to sleep all day so she wouldn't miss anything. She started to mention the sleeping pills she planned to take that night but thought better of it.

When she finished, her mother said, "Allie, there's something I need to tell you, and when you hear it you're going to think we both need to see a shrink. Wish I could do this in person, but—"

"What, Mom?"

Nancy sighed. "Something I should've told you when we were talking about my great-grandmother's dreams."

"Tell me!"

"Well, there's a family tale—actually, far more than a tale as I see now—that every four or five generations, a woman in the family inherits this gift, or curse, of dreaming the past."

Allie squinted. "The past? Like me? Are you kidding? Jeez, Mom, why didn't you tell me?"

"Hhrumm. Well . . . I guess I wasn't sure it was real. You see, your great-great-grandmother told me about these dreams of the past being in the family. By the way, we called her Great-Grandma *Ian* because we couldn't pronounce her real name. Anyway, she had dreams like yours her entire adult life; but I never thought about telling you earlier because until you mentioned dreams on the phone that day, I'd actually forgotten all about them."

Allie's mind spun like a potter's wheel. "So *you* didn't dream?"

"No. Great-Grandma Ian was the last one to dream. She was in her nineties when I was a little girl. Everyone thought she was loopy, didn't believe her stories . . . but I did. In fact, I hoped in my heart of hearts I'd be the next one to dream . . . but I wasn't—not enough generations between us, I guess. So, as time went on, I forgot about the dreams and got over the whole deal. But when you were born, I remembered and wondered if you'd be the one. Your generational timing was perfect *and* Great-Grandma always told me that if I had a little girl, she'd be the next one to dream." She smiled wistfully. "*My little girl . . .* but even then, it drifted into oblivion until I heard you mention strange dreams on the phone that day. Then it clicked, and now . . . and now, I have to believe everything Ian told me." And, Nancy thought, it's the *everything* part that worries me.

After a long pause, Allie said, "So she—my great-great-grandma Ian—dreamed history . . . just like me. This is wild."

"Indeed, it is."

The knowledge of *not* being the only one to dream history both awed and excited Allie, made her wonder anew why and how the dreams happened to only a chosen few—perhaps a mutation of some type. She wondered if Ian had dreamed about Emily, about the Lost Colony, had seen what she'd seen. "Mom, did Ian dream *real* history? Like, were her dreams *validated* somehow?"

Before her mother could reply, Allie said, "Wait, Mom. Don't answer that. I'm trying to get my head around this, and I'm not making myself clear. What I mean is: there's the basic historical events, and then there's all the stuff that happened to individual people, like their feelings, loves, hates—all the behind-the-scenes, interpersonal stuff that actually *made* the history. Like, how could *any* historian ever know or validate such things? And how could Ian or I ever know if what we dreamed was true or just vivid imagination? Do you see what I'm saying?"

"I . . . I *do* see what you're saying, but . . . but I don't know the answer."

"Mom, are you okay? You don't sound like yourself."

Pause. "Yes, Allie. I'm . . . I'm fine."

"Well, you don't sound fine, and I don't think you've told me everything you know. You're holding something back again, aren't you?"

"No, Hon. Honestly! That's all I know."

Allie shook her head in frustration. "Did she tell you where the dreams come from? Or why every four or five generations? Seriously, it sounds like a fantasy tale, or sci-fi, or something."

"No, she didn't, and I don't think she knew."

"But what about the accuracy thing? Did she ever say if the dreams were true or not?"

"She . . . she . . . yes! She told me they were *absolutely* true, and . . . and . . ."

"Come on, Mom! And *what*? Tell me, for God's sake. And how did she know? And where does it end? I mean, do the dreams go on forever? Will I spend my whole life watching history unfold and seeing people I've come to love suffer and die? And when it gets to be too much, will I finally have a nervous breakdown and shoot myself, or go permanently crazy and get put away in a nuthouse? Is that what happens?"

Nancy clapped her hand over her mouth; her mind flailed wildly for a response.

"Mom, what's wrong? Something bad happens with these dreams, doesn't it? And you know what it is, and you're not telling me . . . because it's something you're deathly afraid of." After pausing for a reply that never came, Allie said, "It's okay, Mom. I know you're not telling me for my own good . . . but . . . but I'm scared . . . scared of what might happen when I go to sleep . . . also scared of what might *not* happen . . . like what if I don't dream because Emily's dead? Do you understand what I mean? The dreams—*these* dreams—have taken hold of me, pulled me in, made me part of them by making me part of Emily, almost like I'm her. And what happens if one night I see her lying dead, or being buried? Will the story go on without her? Or will I dream another history dream, or just some dumb normal dream, or nothing at all? I'm afraid, Mom; and . . . and . . . I don't want to dream anymore, but I'm completely addicted . . . gotta know what happens to Emily."

Nancy's body tightened; she felt a shiver of déjà vu hover in the back of her head, a wave of panic flood her mind. "Allie, what the hell are you saying? You're scaring me." Damn it! This is going exactly where Ian said it would go. Maybe I should tell her . . . no, it would push her closer to depression, perhaps make her do something rash. But she's headed there anyway. Maybe knowing what's ahead *now* will help her get a grip before it's too late.

"Don't worry, Mom. I'm not going to do anything stupid." She cringed at her lie, wished it could be otherwise, but knew it couldn't. "You know, it might help if you told me what scares you so much about the dreams . . . and how Great-Great-Grandma Ian knew they were true . . . and what happens when someone dies. And how do you keep it all from blowing your mind and taking over your life? Come on, Mom. Tell me what you know."

Nancy held her silence.

"Mom, are you there?"

"Yes . . . I'm here. I don't know the answers to most of your questions, but I'll tell you what I know." Most of it anyway. "Ian never told me *how* she knew the dreams were true, but she said she was absolutely certain they were. Remember, I was a little girl, so she didn't go into a lot of adult detail. She said that when one series of dreams ended, she *always* had another, but not necessarily right away; she was still having them when I knew her . . . in her nineties. And I kind of remember her saying that stressful events brought them on, but I'm not sure of that. Again, I was so young." An image of the old woman's haggard, wrinkled face, sad eyes flashed through Nancy's mind; she then saw the family gathered around her coffin, talking to one another about her dementia. A twinge of sadness overcame her, sent a tear down each cheek as she remembered being the only one who'd shared intimate moments with her in her last months. No, she hadn't suffered from dementia . . . she was all there; the others were wrong, simply couldn't bring themselves to accept what she'd told them about the dreams and their burden—too big a leap—so they'd written it off as insanity. She closed her eyes, again savored the memory of Ian's warm, reassuring embrace, the sincerity and honesty in her eyes; shook off a pang of grief as she thought of her sad end, the end she wasn't supposed to know about. And now, Allie was following in her footsteps, perhaps sprinting inescapably toward the same end. God forbid!

"Mom . . . Mom!"

"Sorry . . . just thinking. You know, I just remembered something else. Ian had a butterfly birthmark just like yours—same place, same shape and size. She showed it to me once, and I remember being *very* impressed. Funny, but I didn't think of it when I first saw *your* birthmark—never made the connection. Pretty dumb of me. I wonder if—"

"No kidding! Just like mine? Does anyone else in the family have one?"

"No. Just you and Ian. So maybe it's something the dreamers in the family share."

"Mom, this is crazy . . . actually kind of spooky." She paused to process a thought. "What was Ian like? Did she die of old age?"

Nancy's body stiffened; her mind fogged with confusion.

"Mom! What's going on?"

"Dad's calling me. Gotta run. See you soon, Kiddo. Bye!"

＊＊＊

Tryggvi stood at the aft right of the dragon ship, manning the tiller, which consisted of a vertical rudder attached to the outboard side of the ship, ten feet fore of the stern, and a handle that extended about five feet inboard at a square angle from the rudder. Bjarni sat on the side of the ship, in front of him, his feet on the deck, his right hand gripping the top edge while his huge left hand made a spread-fingered cup shape. "And that's how big her tits were, but she squirmed so hard I could barely keep my hands on them. And I tell you, by Freya's beauty, instead of enjoying my company as she should have, she screamed like a demon the whole time. No! English wenches are no match for our Viking girls who know a good man when he mounts them."

Tryggvi studied him with a serious, contemplative look, a mild smirk behind his thick beard and mustache. "Well, Bjarni, perhaps it was the suddenness of your approach that upset her. Perhaps instead of just ripping her clothes off and jumping on her, you should have told her how beautiful she was . . . *then* ripped her clothes off and mounted her."

Bjarni raised his bushy eyebrows, curved the ends of his lips downward. "Do you really think so?"

Tryggvi punched him in the shoulder. "Of course, you big oaf. Every woman likes to hear how beautiful she is, even if it's not true . . . but especially if it's from a stranger who's about to take her. But it's also true that my opinion of English women is not unlike your own . . . except for one." He looked out at the gray sea to his right; sensed his heart pulsing with sudden warmth, longing, regret; visualized her stunning dark hair and brilliant, penetrating blue eyes, her small, lithe body; he reflected on the depth of their love, their mutual despair at parting. Yes, she could have come with him to the northland, been his wife, let him help raise the child he knew she carried. But her religion, that mental distraction that possessed the English like a curse, had precluded her following him, even though he himself was no great believer in the Norse gods. True, he thought, he could have taken her against her will, but he'd loved her too strongly to do so. And now her memory tormented him every day; made him long for her touch, her smile, the warmth of her body, a glimpse of his child; made him lament his kindness. He smiled as he recalled teasing her about her strange dreams, then nodded to himself. I must return and find her one day . . . perhaps when this voyage is done . . . take her and the child with me . . . no matter what.

"and," Bjarni continued, "I've often wondered how many children I have in England." He thought for a moment, counted on his fingers.

"Could be as many as twelve. But far more important than the number is the way in which I've improved the handsomeness and intelligence of the English people."

Tryggvi smirked at him. "Bjarni, I doubt there's enough space in England for so many handsome, intelligent people as you might father, so—"

* * *

Emily lay on a pile of dry grass covered by a blanket. She opened her eyes, looked briefly at the ceiling of the grass-mat cottage, then answered young Henry Harvie's sputtering by climbing to her feet, walking to his makeshift stick crib, lifting him into her arms, and rocking him back and forth. She glanced at Elyoner, asleep on a grass bed beside Virginia's crib on the other side of the room. *Thank God she's getting some rest.* "Shhh, little one . . . shhh now. You'll be fine." Henry rooted for her nipple, which he had located beneath her smock. His face grew ever redder as he tried unsuccessfully to suckle through the cloth, until he finally closed his tiny eyes, took a deep breath, and emitted a loud, demanding cry, followed by another breath and an unrestrained, red-faced tantrum. Emily rocked him faster, kissed his forehead. "Shhh, little Henry. You'll wake Ellie, and she's very tired from feeding the two of you all night. Come now, be a good little lad." *Lord, what am I to do? Perchance I shall start nursing today.*

Elyoner rolled over, opened her eyes. "Emily"—she yawned—"let me wake up for a moment, and I'll take him."

"Ellie, I'm so sorry. I tried to quiet him, but I don't have a mother's touch yet."

"Oh yes, you do, my dear. He's just ready to eat, and only one thing can calm him." She stood, walked to Emily, took Henry and carried him to a log stool, where she sat and untied her smock, lowered it over her left shoulder and breast, then began nursing.

"Ellie, you must be exhausted. Is it like this every night?"

"Aye, I fear so. Mayhap you—"

"Ellie, I'll start this moment if you'll let me. I think I have milk, and I'm eager to try. Tell me what to do."

"You're my savior, lass. Bring your stool over here, then go over to the food trunk and get the crock of honey I brought from England. The berries are too ripe and have lost their sweetness, so we'll try honey. I've seen it used, and I think we'll fare well enough . . . oh, put that other stool in front of the door, so no one intrudes on us."

Emily smiled broadly as she placed one stool in front of the door and the other beside Elyoner, retrieved the honey; she sat down, lowered her smock over her left shoulder and breast. "Now what? Do I rub the honey on my nipple?"

"Aye. And you may as well do both sides because you won't have much, if any, milk today, and you'll have to go back and forth several times on each side, so your body senses the demand and produces more. You can do Virginia, as well, when she wakes. And if you do the two of them as often as possible for the next week, I should think your milk will be flowing quite well."

Emily dropped her smock to her waist to bare her other breast, rubbed a healthy dab of honey on each nipple. "I'm ready."

"By the saints, I can see from your breasts that you're making milk. Here, take him and hold his face to a nipple. He knows what to do." Henry's lips made a popping sound as Elyoner pulled him off her nipple and handed him to Emily.

As he started to crank, Emily situated him, placed her nipple at his lips, smiled as he began suckling. "Whoa! The little rogue's got strong jaws; glad he's got no teeth." Her eyes sparkled, lips parted in a broad grin. "Tickles . . . a strange feeling, but it warms my whole body . . . rather excites me."

Elyoner smiled. "You'll make a fine mother, Em."

After a minute, Henry started cranking, and Emily switched him to her right breast while she re-honeyed the left. After three more quick rotations, Emily's milk was exhausted, and the honey no longer pleased Henry; he again began to sputter, which woke Virginia. But she was of a more pleasant disposition than Henry had been, so Emily handed

Henry to Elyoner to finish nursing while she untied Virginia's diaper, replaced it with a clean one. She pulled the folded, narrower front of the doubled-over cloth between Virginia's legs and up over her belly, tied a double knot at each side with the front and back corners. She then honeyed both breasts, picked Virginia up, and let her suckle. After three short cycles, Virginia performed her own hunger tantrum; and Emily passed her off to Elyoner, took Henry, laid him over her shoulder, and tapped his back to belch the air from his stomach. She honeyed her nipples and again let the now-contented Henry suckle their sweetness.

"Ellie, look at him. He's smiling at me . . . must like me, eh?" She savored his warmth and clean, fresh baby smell, cuddled him closely as he watched her eyes. Feels like my brother . . . so many times I held him like this, wished I could nurse him though it rather embarrassed me to think such thoughts . . . wasn't sure if 'twas proper or not, but I craved doing it nonetheless. Feels so warm and close.

"I think you're right, Em. 'Pon my honor, if the two of them keep up like this, your lovely breasts will grow even more tonight, and you'll have full milk by morning."

"Ellie, I'm so happy and honored you've let me do this. It feels quite wonderful . . . and you certainly need the help."

"You *are* my savior, and . . . and, Emily Colman, know that you are the *only* one in the world I would let do this. You are my dearest friend for life, and you shall be Virginia's second mother . . . and her *only* mother if anything happens to me."

The two smiled misty eyed at one another with a silence that wanted no words, then spread a blanket over a pile of grass on the floor and laid the two infants upon it, began preparing the morning meal. Elyoner said, "I suppose Thomas and Ananias will be here any moment, expecting us to be cheerfully ready with breakfast. 'Twas indeed good of them to stay with the bachelors and allow us privacy for nursing. I'm told your house will be finished in a few days, so we'll have to figure out a good pattern for the feeding after you've moved in . . . and, Emily"— she walked to Emily, put her arms around her, pulled her close—"I'm unthinkably happy you're here . . . that you survived all that's befallen you . . . poor George. What a fine young man he was. I know you miss him terribly, and it pains you to think and talk about it, but . . ."

Emily felt warm tears on her cheeks. "I miss him, Ellie, and . . ."

"I know. You feel guilty that he died without knowing your love. I know how you must feel; but, Em, you can't force your feelings. They are what they are. I'm just so thrilled you've come back to me. I feared the worst . . . we all did . . . you've certainly had to face far too much for a young lass your age." She held Emily at arms' length, looked into her eyes. "Oh, I nearly forgot." She reached into her pocket, held out Emily's letter from her mother. "You'll be wanting this right away, I'm sure."

Emily took the letter, stared at it for a moment, kissed it, slowly laid it against her heart, then closed her eyes. "Thank you, Ellie. I prayed with all my heart you'd still have it." She opened her damp eyes, leaned toward Elyoner, and kissed her on the cheek. "Thank you, my dear, dear friend." She smiled a contented smile. Thank you, Lord. Mother, I'm here. I've survived. I await you. Please come to me . . . I so miss my locket, the remembrance of you inside it. "And, Ellie, you're right. I *am* too young for what's befallen me. Would that life could be normal and simple and happy, free of unyielding pressure from suitors and the risk of imminent death that seems to hang over me like a low, dark cloud. But truly, Ellie, nursing the babies will surely help. I'm so happy you've allowed me."

Elyoner smiled. "*Auntie Emily* we shall call you." She took Emily's hands in hers, looked into her eyes. "You know, my dear, we've barely spoken since your arrival. So let us talk now."

"Truly, I remember nothing from yesterday or the night before. I know we talked, but I was completely exhausted—in every way—I've no idea what we said."

"You told me of the storm and nearly being swept out to sea with the tide; and then you fell asleep until yesterday afternoon when you awoke, had a nibble of food, and fell asleep again. So tell me of the rest of your journey . . . if it doesn't pain you too much . . . all of it must have frightened you near to death . . . especially when the Savages surrounded you."

"It did indeed . . . I nearly piddled down my legs when we heard them. 'Twas far worse than the massacre because I had time to think about what was happening, time for fear to seize my mind . . . though that's becoming rather commonplace. But when the Savages stopped closing in on us, and one of them said *Chesapeake*, it eased my terror a bit; and I walked up to him, started using the hand signs Manteo taught me: asked him how they found us and whether you were all safe, and why they nearly scared us into our graves, and . . . listen to me blather on. Anyway, he told me about the two survivors from the second shallop, straggling into the village after Lieutenant Waters had departed with the search party, and Sergeant Smith—he didn't know his name—asking the hunting party to search for us because he wasn't allowed to send any soldiers away from the village. Then he told me why they surrounded us and let out such horrible, blood-chilling shrieks. I guess it makes sense . . . if you're a Savage . . . but they didn't know we were without weapons, and were afraid we'd shoot them if they didn't make noise and show themselves to us." A sudden smile brightened her face. " 'Twas probably fortunate we *didn't* have guns, for some jumpy fool would surely have shot one of them if we had."

"Aye. No question there."

"And, Ellie"—she again embraced Elyoner—"I truly believed I'd never see you again."

Elyoner held her close, patted her back as she would a distressed child. "Em, I feared for you more than I can ever tell. 'Twas most strange, but the night of the storm and the night you were nearly swept out to sea—though I believed you were still at Roanoke—I had a flood of fear flow into me; dizzied me like a blow to the head, it did. It wouldn't leave, and I knew you were in danger, feared you were dead . . . just laid there on my back all night staring at the roof, crying."

"I thought I was dead, as well . . . I *was* dead but for George, and then Hugh." Her face grew abruptly somber. "And what am I to do about Hugh?"

"I don't know, Em; but in spite of my misgivings about the man, praise God he risked his life to save you."

"Indeed, but how shall I ever know the truth about him?"

* * *

Surrounded by his nine Assistants, Roger Baylye stood under a large tree halfway between the colonists' village and the Chesapeakes'. "Before we start, I must tell you all that the hanging of William Clement this morning turned my stomach. In the unfortunate event we have to perform another execution, we must be certain that the knot works properly and delivers swift death. Though there was little sympathy for the man, no one should slowly strangle like that . . . kicking, writhing, gasping."

Baylye waited silently for the nods and somber looks to abate, then traded his compassionate expression for a formal one. "John Bright will now give us a tally of our remaining strength. John . . ."

Bright pulled a piece of paper from inside his shirt, unfolded it. "We had one hundred eight souls when we began the move. Three are at Croatan Island; seventy-two of us are here; and . . . and thirty-three perished in the storm or on the . . ." He covered his mouth with his left hand, turned away.

Every man stared silently, dejectedly at anything but the face of another. Finally, Bright collected himself, wiped his drippy nose with the back of his hand. "We've twenty-one soldiers and fifty-one civilians, and—thank the Lord—all of our leadership save Dyonis Harvie. On the other hand, we've lost several critical skills, including our physician, John Jones; our sheriff, Anthony Cage; and Professor Thomas Harris. Fortunately, our skilled farmers and hunters, and our magistrate, Thomas Hewet, survived. Ananias Dare will conduct a remembrance ceremony at midmorning on the morrow for those who perished."

Baylye said, "Thank you, John. Now to the task of electing a new Assistant. When we elected Lieutenant Waters, I made the decision to hold the number of Assistants at twelve rather than the thirteen we started with, and I would like to maintain that number because 'tis more proportionate to our diminished numbers. Besides, Fernandez, the thirteenth Assistant, never really participated in our proceedings. Further, as you all know, the colony's charter states that the advice of the Assistants is precisely that—advice—and the governor is the final decision authority. So it matters not if we have a tie vote on some issue, for a split vote will convey the mind of the Assistants as well as an uneven vote. However, I make this promise to you: on grave matters, such as the election of a new Assistant, should we have the misfortune to have to do so again, I will abide by the Assistants' decision unless 'tis a tie, in which case I shall cast the deciding vote. Speak now if this be not acceptable to you." He looked at each man, saw no dissent. "Very well. Proceeding then, the names of Thomas Hewet, our magistrate, and Hugh Tayler have been placed in nomination, and I should like to entertain your thoughts on both."

Thomas Colman coughed, doubled over with one hand on his mouth, the other on his stomach. "Excuse me . . . gentlemen . . . I'll . . . return . . . shortly . . . please continue." He began walking away.

Baylye said, "Certainly, Thomas."

Lieutenant Waters raised his hand. "Sir, while in general I think it best that members of the judiciary and the military *not* be part of government, I realize our situation and numbers demand a somewhat different view . . . at least temporarily until Governor White returns with more planters. I also believe we've difficult times ahead . . . times that may require creative deliberations . . . and collaborations . . . to maintain the rule of law, good order, and discipline in the colony. Therefore, I believe Master Hewet's legal experience makes him a good choice."

*Aye*s rippled through the group until Thomas Stevens spoke for Hugh Tayler, recommended him as a man of good breeding and sound judgment. Again several voices of assent wafted toward Baylye.

After several seconds of silence, Waters again raised his hand to speak. "Two of my men, whose judgment and probity are beyond question, asked me to speak on their behalf should Master Tayler be nominated and seriously considered."

Even those who had been looking elsewhere immediately focused at Waters.

"I do not wish to be specific on this occasion without him being here to defend himself; but I *will* say my men challenge Master Tayler's character, and I've good reason to believe their misgivings are valid; and I shall say no more at this moment."

Dubious looks spread through the Assistants.

Baylye surveyed them for a moment; he wondered what Waters had heard, made a mental note to ask him after the meeting. "Any more comments?" He used the pause to search for Thomas Colman, whom he spied leaning against a tree at the edge of the forest. "Very well. Let us vote. Master Colman appears indisposed at the moment, but he may certainly vote when he rejoins us, if necessary to break a tie." After the lopsided vote, he said, "Thank you, gentlemen. Thomas Hewet is our new Assistant. Now to the subject of palisades."

Groans instantly filled the assembly.

Thomas Stevens said, " 'Tis too late in the season to begin palisades."

Several said, "Aye! Aye! True words!"

John Brooke raised his hand. "Roger, we've not the manpower to build palisades. God o' mercy, man, the Roanoke palisades nearly killed us when we were at full strength. How can you expect us to undertake such a huge endeavor with our *current* numbers?"

Cuthbert White shook his head. "Out of the question, Roger."

Baylye nodded at Waters, who had raised his hand to speak. "Gentlemen, from the military view, 'twould be insane *not* to build palisades . . . no matter what the cost. Without them the colony is indefensible; and for anyone to think this land is a safe haven, rather than the violent, dangerous place it is, would be utter foolishness. Rather, we *must* build palisades, and we must begin now to complete them before deep winter . . . it simply *must* be done . . . even if only my men and I have to do it." He cringed at his own words, knew too few of his tiny contingent would ever be free enough from guarding the colony to accomplish such a feat, knew their morale would plunge even deeper at the mere suggestion of it, knew that even with the entire colony on the task, completion before winter was impossible. But perchance . . . just perchance . . . with a total commitment and long days, perhaps even some nights . . . and with a bit of luck and good weather . . . they *might* complete enough to mount a semblance of a defense against a Savage attack. But, he admitted, morale already sits at the bottom of the bay . . . many will be diverted to procuring food for the winter . . . cannot depend on the Chesapeakes . . . cannot use them to help with the palisades. Mayhap we can trade with them for food, save ourselves the time of hunting and fishing . . . but trade what? We've little left. Good Lord, there's no way . . . but we must try. "But we can do the job far faster if *all* lend their effort. So I beseech you, gentlemen, help my men and me do what must be done, for nothing less than the survival of the colony is at stake."

None spoke. All stared at Waters, weighed his words.

Baylye read their eyes, sensed their hearts denying Waters' words, their minds acknowledging their truth. "What say you, men? Will you support us?"

Ananias voiced the first *aye*, followed by Thomas Colman, who had returned in time to hear Waters' plea. Then White and Brooke added their *ayes*, as did the remainder except William Willes and Thomas Stevens.

Baylye said, "Thank you, men. We *shall* build palisades . . . commencing as soon as all the cottages are completed, which should be in a few days." He paused for a moment. "In addition to cottages and palisades, we've an enormous amount of work to do to lay in stores for winter. The Chesapeakes' harvest, with the exception of corn, will not likely yield enough to help us, so we're on our own, which means we must procure fish, venison, and any small game we can catch." He looked at Christopher Cooper. "Christopher, would you choose three men—perhaps those that George Howe worked with—to be our lead fishermen. Then take Mistress Colman with you if she's willing, to the Chesapeake village. As you know, she's fluent in the Savages' hand signs and can speak with their fishermen, learn their skills, and communicate them to you. Our own skills fell quite short at Roanoke, and we must do better here. Mistress Colman might also relate their drying and smoking methods."

"Certainly, Roger."

"And, Roger Prat, can you collect your surviving hunters and put them to work? We also need *you* to visit the Chesapeakes with Mistress Colman." He glanced at Thomas Colman. "Thomas do you think Emily will be willing to help us with all this? We need her rather desperately."

"Of course, Roger. I think she'll be quite eager to help."

"Excellent. Thank you. So, Roger, to continue, take Mistress Colman and have her talk to the Chesapeakes about where the best hunting grounds are, as well as their methods for hunting, and preserving venison."

"Aye, Roger. And by the bye, Mistress Colman was by far my best student at dressing deer at Roanoke; I should think she'd be an excellent teacher for the other ladies since they'll now be performing that duty."

Thomas Colman glowed, thought how proud he was of Emily.

"Good idea," Baylye said. He glanced at Colman. "Thomas, your daughter has become the most valuable asset in the colony." He smiled then eyed Cuthbert White. "And now, Cuthbert White, I'm told you enjoy great favor with the ladies." He paused for the volley of snickers that rippled through the assembly, recognizing White's five-foot stature and ponderous, unseemly girth. "So could you find a couple of willing ladies—" More laughter. Baylye frowned. "That is not what I meant. I meant *willing to lead* the soap- and candle-making tasks. There's plentiful bayberry here for making wax, and we'll have considerable animal fat if our hunters are successful. And soapwort abounds. Mayhap you could find two ladies to be in charge of soap and candles, and help them organize the others."

White nodded stoic agreement.

"And, William Willes, can you find three people to make salt . . . men or women. We've good stores on hand from Roanoke, but we'll eventually need more."

"Aye."

"Now for our most important task. John Brooke, you've some experience at brewing beer."

" 'Tis true, Roger."

"Then would you deal with the Chesapeakes, again with Mistress Colman's help, to barter some of our few remaining trade goods for as much corn as you can acquire? Then set aside some for making flour as the Savages do and begin making beer with the rest? We've abundant wild hops about for preservation and flavor."

" 'Twill be a pleasure, Roger, as long as I can guarantee the quality with frequent tasting."

Laughter.

"So ordained, John." He paused, looked slowly from man to man. "Gentlemen, our situation is such that with all men engaged in building cottages and palisades, fishing and hunting, and defending the colony, we *must* rely on our women, as well as any youngsters old enough to help, to perform *all* other tasks . . . including water and firewood gathering, cleaning our dwellings, and preparing and cleaning up after our meals. Would that it were not so, but it *is*; for as we all know in our hearts, our situation remains desperately fragile . . . at least until John White returns; and with our diminished numbers, we *cannot* survive without extraordinary cooperation and effort from all." He exhaled slowly. "And that's enough dismal talk for one day. Let us adjourn and be about our tasks. Thank you all."

* * *

Cloaked in cool, dry fall air, Emily walked toward the edge of the village closest to the Chesapeake camp. When she had passed the last cottage, she stopped to remove her mother's crinkled letter from her apron pocket, unfolded it, read it again. She stared at the letter, fought the tears trying to rise in her eyes, unconsciously searched her apron for her locket. Mother, I miss you, want to be near you, feel your touch, see your smile. Dear Lord, I know 'tis impossible, but I pray you'll help me find my locket . . . somehow . . . someday . . . even if I have to walk and swim back to Roanoke to do so. Please, Lord. An image of her desperate fight for life at the massacre flashed through her mind. She folded the letter, kissed it, slid it back into the pocket; stared blankly at the forest, then looked at the deep blue sky dotted with small, puffy clouds. She focused on two, watched them slowly drift together then apart. Like people, she thought. We come together; then whether by death or happenstance, we inevitably drift apart . . . sometimes to be reunited, sometimes not. Pity 'tis so . . . quite painful . . . but a burden of humanity, I suppose. I miss you George, pray you're with God. How wonderful and simple it would've been if everything had worked out for us at Roanoke . . . no murders, no massacre, harmony with the Savages, food. We would've fallen in love, married, had children—the first English children to be conceived on this continent—enjoyed all life has to offer . . . rather than the sorrows we now endure . . . and those that lie ahead. She gazed at two more clouds that were moving together. I wonder what makes clouds . . . beautiful, soft clouds . . . would that I could fly up and touch them, mold my own images, then quickly glide back to earth like a bird and admire my work.

She glanced at the twenty cottages in various stages of completion. Going up fast, she thought. Bark sides would be warmer than grass mats, but no time to make them now . . . perchance in the spring . . . mayhap even split rail siding. She closed her eyes, imagined a mature, thriving colony with permanent wood or brick homes, brick chimneys, and ten times the population they now had. 'Twill be exciting to be part of it. Prithee come soon, Mother. Her gaze then shifted to the Chesapeake village with its bark lodges, smoke wafting through smoke holes; women gathered in small groups, visiting with one another, skinning game, scraping hides, smoking fish and meat, cooking. No different from us. I wonder how many thousands of years they've done things that way . . . as we did before the Romans . . . I shall soon know how to do all of it. Strange, but even though their ways seem backward from ours, I think I shall enjoy learning them . . . in truth, the idea of it rather excites me. Perhaps I shall learn their language, as well. Yes—

"Emily!" Hugh Tayler limped rapidly toward her from the village. "Emily, how fare you, lass?"

Her body stiffened. "I'm well, Hugh. Good to have some sleep in my bones. And you?"

"Good as new. Ready to move forward with life . . . and, Emily, with all my soul, I long to speak with you as you promised back on the banks . . . *speak our hearts*, as you put it. I cannot go on not knowing what's come between us. I beseech you, Emily, please tell me now."

"Hugh, I haven't the time now. Masters Cooper and Prat are meeting me in a moment, so I can interpret for them with the Chesapeakes. I . . ."

He stared at her with crestfallen, pleading eyes, downturned lips, said nothing.

His look and silence sliced into her heart like a knife, filled her with guilt, crumbled her will. "Very well, Hugh. I shall tell you." She took a deep breath then related all that Johnny Gibbes had told her.

When she had finished, he looked away, fixed his gaze intently on the ground as if waiting for it to bore a hole in the earth, then looked back at her with a quizzical look. "You must know in your heart that I could never do such things. Only John Gibbes would accuse me of such travesties."

"No, he did not." She cringed at the lie but knew she dare not speak the truth . . . or could she?

"Then who?"

"I cannot tell you, Hugh. I'm sworn to silence."

She'll never tell, he thought. Don't push it. "Emily, I've not the heart nor will to go against you, but it had to be Johnny Gibbes, for no one else bears me such ill will."

She kept her silence, her flat look.

"So I shall tell you that he is indeed a liar and a thief, and I can prove it."

Be careful, Em. "I care not, Hugh, for 'twas not Johnny, but if you—"

"I've written proof from the magistrate . . . proof that identifies him, and others, as deceitful blackguards. John White himself knows the truth though he's loathe to admit it, for he dislikes me. Yes, he knows— from the lips of a benefactor of mine—and by King Henry's soul, I shall force him to tell you the truth when he returns."

She watched his eyes for any betrayal of falsehood, found none. More confused than ever, I am. Mother, help me. I was nearly in love with this man . . . I can't discard him like old clothing based on what may be a lie . . . nor can I trust him. Must stand my guard and wait for the truth to reveal itself . . . as it will in time.

"Emily, my love for you has not diminished. It shall never diminish. You are the love of my life, and I shall patiently await your learning of the truth . . . and learn it you will. And when you're ready, I should dearly love to walk with you in the forest . . . perhaps take a small meal with us . . . talk of pleasant things . . . and as you said, again share our hearts . . . as we did at Roanoke."

A gust of caution swept her mind, then a wave of compassion; she smiled faintly. I can ill learn the truth by avoiding him, must gauge him directly. "We've little time for such pleasures these days, Hugh, but if chance permits, let us speak of it again." She glanced behind him. "Master Cooper and Master Prat approach. Please be patient with me, Hugh. I need more time to—"

"Hello, Mistress Colman," Christopher Cooper said. "Master Tayler." He shot a rancorous glance at Tayler.

Prat said, "Good day, Mistress Colman. Are you ready to proceed to the village?"

"Aye, I am." She glanced at Tayler. "We shall speak again, Master Tayler."

Tayler returned Cooper's glare with one of his own then nodded at Emily. "Indeed we shall, Mistress Colman. Good day to you."

***

Emily sat by a meandering stream, stared at her image in a small eddy by the bank. Well, Mistress Colman, you've still got black hair and blue eyes, but that's all that hasn't changed with you. You're certainly no longer the carefree young lass who arrived from England a few months ago. She looked up, surveyed the forest around her, mentally cataloguing the different types of trees. Some of you are changing colors. You'll soon look like a rainbow . . . red, orange, yellow . . . still some green . . . in only a fortnight or so. She closed her eyes, inhaled a deep breath of cool air. How wonderful it feels after breathing water like a fish these last months. She took another deep breath, opened her eyes, fixed them on a small clump of purple flowers with six wide, pointy pedals, a yellow core, and a short, reddish runner in the middle. "Aren't you a pretty sight . . . and just why might you be still in bloom in this late season? I'm glad you are though, for you brighten my day and my life. I shall visit you as often as I can . . . until the snow hides your pretty faces. Would that—" A branch cracked behind her; she spun about. "Ellie, you startled me."

"Sorry, Em. I should have announced myself."

"Babies still asleep?"

"Aye, but we'd better check them soon. They'll be awake and hungry." She frowned. "Henry's a bit colicky today. Pray it passes quickly." She replaced the frown with a broad smile. "And Mistress Colman, I'm amazed at how quickly your milk's come in. A boon to me, you are." She looked around the small clearing. "You've chosen quite a lovely spot for your thoughts. I should not intrude on you here."

"Nay, Ellie. I'm always eager for your company. Sit . . . share the peace of it with me. I was talking to that clump of lovely flowers over there . . . look like crocuses, they do, but rather late for such."

She sat beside Emily. "I would agree. And how clean and refreshing everything is since the weather's cooled . . . much fresher than England . . . and how does the skirt fit?"

"A bit long but well otherwise. We should hem it after we nurse." She smiled. "My feet get tangled up every time I turn about quickly . . . nearly spilled me on the ground a time or two. But thank you again for the gift of it. 'Twas quite foolish of me to pack so many clothes on the shallop instead of sending them with you."

"Well, you didn't know the shallop was going to sink. I have other things you can have, as well."

"Many thanks, Ellie. Actually, I suppose we'll all be wearing Savage clothing by spring unless your father returns before then."

"You're probably right . . . and I do not think we dare expect him before then. Not many captains and seamen are willing to venture across the Atlantic in winter. So I think we're on our own for a good while . . . by the bye, you seem to enjoy your translating with the Chesapeakes."

Emily smiled again. "You know how I love languages. They've taught me many new hand signs and quite a few words; I made friends with some of them, as well, and learned much about how they live. *And*"—she smiled— " 'tis delightful having two English *men* anxiously awaiting my every word, for the Savages told me all their secrets of hunting, fishing, preserving, fleshing, and tanning hides. Of course, the women do the dressing and preserving, as we will; but, Ellie, I must tell you 'tis exciting learning it all . . . a completely different way of life . . . admittedly primitive by our standards but undoubtedly similar to how we lived in ancient times. Nonetheless, I wager many will abhor lowering themselves to such ways; but truly, we've no other choice if we're to survive . . . and that's why 'tis so thrilling to *me*, for I now know I can exist in this land . . . without English wares and civilization . . . and"—she assumed a guilty look—"I think I'll actually quite enjoy doing so. I shall tell you about all of it in time, but"—her eyes glistened with excitement as her hands moved in continuous motion with her lips—"the most clever thing I saw was their fishing weirs. They make a fence of sticks stuck into the bottom of the bay and draped with nets made of wild hemp and deer sinew, that runs from the shore out into the water nearly a hundred yards and into the top of a heart-shaped enclosure with an opening in it. The fish then swim along the fence, trying to find the end of it to swim around it; but since the end is inside the heart-shaped enclosure, they swim into the enclosure and can't get back out because more fish are always swimming in and blocking them. So they swim toward the bottom, pointy part of the heart, but it opens into yet another heart-shaped enclosure, and that into a big, square one with no outlet, where all the fish remain trapped until the fisherman comes with a net, scoops them out, and takes them ashore to be cooked, dried, or smoked. And . . ."

Elyoner's eyes were wide as shillings, vacant as an empty glass of water, her jaw agape.

Emily pointed at her, snorted, then giggled girlishly, covering her mouth with her hand. "God o' mercy, Ellie. You should see your face. You look ready to faint . . . I'm so sorry. I've rambled on like an old crone with nothing better to do . . . bored you to oblivion, I have."

Elyoner shook her head. "Zounds, Em! You are truly taken by your experiences . . . I hope I can match your enthusiasm, for I fear you're right. Their ways will soon become ours . . . and will remain so for considerable time to come."

" 'Tis true, and I've no doubt you'll do it well, Ellie." She glanced up at the sun. "And shouldn't we be returning to the babies?"

"Aye. Let's fill the water bags and be on our way."

They stood, filled two deer-stomach water bags each, started toward the village. After a few steps, a dark cloud of anxiety drifted over Emily's face. "Ellie, I must talk to you about something."

Elyoner looked at her expectantly.

"I told Hugh everything Johnny Gibbes told me though I denied it was from Johnny's mouth. I hated lying, but I couldn't put Johnny at risk. And, Ellie, I'm more confused now than ever. He denied everything . . . again declared his love for me, and I know at least that part 'tis true, and he then told me he has written proof Johnny's a liar and a thief."

Elyoner stopped, faced Emily. "Em . . ."

"He also told me your father knows the truth but won't admit it because he doesn't like him . . . says a benefactor of his told your father the truth . . . perchance 'twas the high official who made him bring Hugh on the voyage . . . and, Ellie, I don't know what to do. But I *do* know I'll never know the truth unless I give it a chance to reveal itself . . . and to do that, I must be with Hugh."

"Emily, the one who told Father to bring Tayler on the voyage was none other than Lord Walsingham himself, the Queen's favorite . . . and rumored to be Raleigh's ardent enemy. . . and no friend of this colony. 'Tis said he tried to turn Her Majesty against Raleigh, and Father thinks he

- 283 -

insisted Hugh Tayler be on the voyage so he'd have a spy among us. You see, Hugh's father was close friends with Walsingham, and Walsingham owed him a debt for some service he'd performed before he died. Hugh called in the debt to extricate himself from whatever shadowy trouble he was in shortly before we departed England. But Father mentioned nothing of Walsingham being associated with Johnny Gibbes, or his family, though he did confide that Walsingham admitted Tayler had an ignominious past then told Father to disregard it and give him a fair chance. And for Father's part, he never heard of Hugh Tayler before someone—possibly Raleigh—warned him to beware of the man."

＊

Emily and Elyoner were nearly to Elyoner's cottage when a man's voice behind them said, "Emily."

Emily stopped, spun about in a single motion; her too-long skirt wrapped around her feet, sprawled her on the ground. "Oh!" Lying on her stomach in a puddle of water, she saw a pair of wet moccasins inches in front of her. She awkwardly pushed her torso up on her elbows and forearms like an infant in a crib, rolled slightly onto her left side; gazed up tan, muscular legs, past a deerskin loincloth and a sturdy chest, to a wry smile and a pair of dark eyes that peered amusedly down at her; the eyes and smile were strikingly framed by a full head of black, waist-length hair with five large, black-and-white eagle feathers arranged like a fan, extending to the right from behind the head. Dearest Lord. 'Tis him . . . his eyes.

Elyoner helped her to her feet. Heart's pounding . . . he'll hear it. Lord, help me! She stared into his eyes, felt herself unraveling, melting, hypnotized like a snake's prey. My soul's bare . . . can't move. What's wrong with me? She rubbed her wet hands on her skirt. "I . . . I . . ."

His eyes sparkled; his wry smile bloomed into a full one. He pointed at her and said, "Emily," touched himself on the chest, said, "Eee-shnah." He made the hand sign for *people*, said, "Lakota." He then pointed to the north and made the *far away* sign. Emily watched his hands as he quickened his movements, nodded her head with each sign, but shook it and motioned him to repeat when she didn't understand.

"Isna will stay with the Chesapeakes for the winter and return to his people in the spring, near the birthplace of the Mother-of-All-Rivers. His land is by big seas like that"—he pointed east toward the ocean—"but the water can be drunk. And from here, it is *this* many suns' journey"—he flashed all ten fingers five times—"first by foot, then down a large river to the Mother-of-All-Rivers, and then up to her birthplace." He stopped for a moment, looked into her eyes. "Isna heard of the sinking of Emily's people's canoes in the storm . . . and of her friend's courage. It is a great honor to die for one's people. Such bravery must be remembered."

Emily's eyes misted; she bit her lower lip.

"Isna will visit Emily again." He smiled his wry smile, turned, walked away.

Emily stood silent, motionless, stunned; heart racing, panting, head flushed with feverish confusion; watched him walk toward the Chesapeake village. Body's aflame, tingling, clammy, legs like butter, can't think, can't move, can't do anything! She shivered. How can he do this to me?

Elyoner tugged at her sleeve. "Are you ill, young lady?" She took Emily's hand, led her toward the cottage. "Let us be along. I hear hungry voices."

Emily glanced over her shoulder, watched Isna as Elyoner tugged her along.

"Emily. Watch where you're going . . . Emily! Pay attention! Are you asleep, lass?"

Emily stopped, looked at her with a dazed, bewildered look. "Ellie, what's wrong with me? I've never felt like this before."

***

Emily walked back from the Chesapeake village with Thomas Prat and Christopher Cooper. While the men were discussing what they'd learned that morning, Emily wondered why she hadn't seen Isna in the village. Strange, but I've thought of little else since seeing him. Perhaps he's hunting. How odd that he should haunt my mind like this. Foolish lass. What's wrong with you? He's a Savage, and—

Johnny Gibbes hurriedly approached the three, glanced behind him every few steps. "Emily, may we talk for a moment?"

"Of course." Emily stopped. "Until tomorrow, good sirs."

Prat said, "Aye, Emily. Thank you for your help. You've been indispensable."

"Indeed you have, Mistress," Cooper said.

Emily nodded, faced Gibbes. "What is it, Johnny? You look as if you've seen King Henry's ghost."

"Tayler's had his eyes on me most every moment, but he's off with the wood cutters for a while. Your father, as well. Emily, I must finish telling you what I know of Hugh Tayler if 'tis your wish." He looked at her with the eager anticipation of a hungry puppy.

Emily nodded. "Yes."

"Back on the banks when we last spoke, I was telling you about the army . . . when our unit was in Holland . . . our first battle." He hesitated.

* * *

Thomas Colman and Hugh Tayler had just finished chopping branches from a downed tree, now sat on the log for a rest. Tayler said, "Thomas, I'd like to finish our discussion of Emily's and my betrothal . . . if you're willing. The happenings of these last several days have precluded such talk, and your response weighs heavy on my mind."

Colman nodded slightly, held his silence for a moment while he organized his thoughts. "Hugh, when we last talked, our future looked completely bleak, without hope." He abruptly turned away, coughed for a moment. "Excuse me. This dammed cough won't leave me." He cleared his throat. "To continue, when the Savages came upon us, I was in the process of granting my approval of Emily's betrothal to you. In all honesty, Hugh, I think you'd make Emily a splendid husband, and I'm *for* such a match." He coughed again. "On the other hand, our situation is now more stable, perhaps more secure, and . . ."

* * *

"The battle was horrendous, and we were being overrun by the enemy. Lieutenant Tayler was riding beside our commander when the commander was shot from his horse; he lay on the ground bleeding to death, shouting at Tayler through the roar of the battle to help him. But Tayler sat on his mount, watched the approaching enemy, did nothing. The commander yelled at him again, told him he was dying and to take command of the troops, lead an immediate counterattack."

* * *

"hopefully less urgent. But danger still stalks us, and all of us are at risk. Forsooth, I've no greater care in this world than Emily's safety and well-being. So I now . . ."

* * *

"Lieutenant Tayler stared at the dying man for a moment then at the enemy, spun his horse about, and galloped to the rear."

Emily's eyes narrowed, softened with disappointment; her lips parted. "Johnny, he told me he saved the commander's life and was commended for bravery."

* * *

"grant my permission for you and Emily to marry."

"Sir, you honor me. My lips are incapable of telling you how deeply I love her and how relentlessly I shall care for her. I—"

"Hugh, we must first overcome an obstacle."

Tayler frowned.

* * *

"On the contrary, Mistress, he was tried and found guilty of cowardice; but some high-ranking, influential person close to the Queen arranged for the finding to be discarded on some point of order, which I do not know the facts of, and Tayler was allowed to retain his commission. He *was*, however, strongly *encouraged* by his superiors to resign . . . but he refused."

* * *

"Hugh, if I tell Emily I've betrothed her without first obtaining her consent, a fury such as God himself has never seen will descend upon me, regardless of the degree of esteem in which she holds you. So while I enthusiastically agree to your betrothal, and indeed pray for it, our best—our only—chance for *realizing* it will be for me to approach her in a subtle, gentle manner that ensures her willing concurrence." But how shall I ever do so? I know not how to influence my daughter with any grace or chance of success whatsoever . . . but I must . . . her life depends on it. Only Hugh will love her and protect her if I should die.

* * *

Emily said, "And what of his wound, his limp?"

Gibbes snickered. "That, dear mistress, came from his *next* commander, a major, in a pistol and sword duel several months before we sailed from England . . . after the major found out that—forgive me for discussing such matters with a lady—that Tayler had been having a lengthy lovers' affair with his wife and that she'd become pregnant by him. When Tayler and the major faced each other, Tayler tried to back away and run; but as he turned, the major fired his pistol, hit him in the back of his leg, and laid him on the ground. The major had too much honor to kill a fallen man, so he told him, with sword in hand, to be gone from England as soon as he recovered and that he'd kill him if ever he saw him again. Tayler then resigned his commission, hid out for several months as he looked for a means of escape. He eventually heard of Governor White's search for colonists and secretly arranged passage."

Emily looked away then back at Gibbes. "Johnny, these are damning accusations. Are you absolutely certain of them?"

"I am, Mistress, for you see, I and two others of our *current* company, who shall remain unnamed, were present as witnesses. Saw it all with our own eyes, we did . . . and that is yet another reason Tayler wishes I were not here."

Emily stared silently at him, nodded twice.

"Emily, there's more, but 'tis of such a serious nature that it should be divulged only under the most dire of circumstances, so I shall retain it until such circumstances occur . . . and hopefully, they will *not*. But I *can* tell you—and this is hearsay from my parents, from when I was a young child—when he was a lad, Tayler abandoned a friend of his in the fog of the moors, ran away to save himself while the lad drowned. Tayler lied that he'd searched for him and tried to save him. So you see, Tayler's deviance began at an early age."

Emily looked into his eyes. "Johnny, thank you for these truths . . . and I know they are such. I'm deeply hurt by his deceit . . . and embarrassed by my own foolishness . . . but thank you. You are a true friend."

"Indeed, Mistress, I care truly and deeply for your safety. You are the kindest and most gracious lady I've ever known, and I shall do all in my power to protect you."

"Thank you, Johnny."

* * *

Tayler's face distorted with frustration. "Very well, Thomas. I cannot say that I disagree with your conclusion. In addition to loving Emily to the depths of my soul, I well know the vigor and spirit that reside in her and know you speak the truth about her response to an *arranged* betrothal. Thus, I shall wait for you to win her concurrence . . . Thomas, my friend, your cough alarms me. I hope it soon subsides and departs you. Emily needs her father, and she would be unspeakably vulnerable without him." She was falling in love with me, soon to be mine . . . but I fear that moment is lost, and I do not believe Thomas Colman can rescue it or influence her to marry me . . . unless she decides to do so on her own, and that I now doubt. So I must convince her myself . . . somehow . . . at whatever cost.

CHAPTER 9

A t the edge of the Chesapeake village, Emily knelt beside a young Chesapeake woman about her age, leaned over a spread-out deer hide, its perimeter staked, fur side down, to the ground. She repeatedly scraped a flat, three-inch wide, serrated piece of deer bone hafted to a wood handle, across the hide to remove the flesh, so it could be tanned for clothing, moccasins, or other uses. As Emily scraped, she thought how fitting the girl's name, Shines Like the Moon, was; for the girl's face seldom displayed anything but a wide, gleaming smile. Emily called her *Shines*; and she had already taught Emily the Chesapeake words for her name, as well as *deer, hide, flesher, tool, brains, tanning, clothes, and moccasins.* She had also explained with hand signs how, after the hide had been de-fleshed and the hair removed by burying it in ashes for a time, deer brains would be rubbed on both sides to preserve and soften it. Two women would then repeatedly pull it back and forth over a tightly stretched piece of sinew or a green vine until the desired softness had been achieved. Shines, who like all Chesapeake women wore a wrap-around, fringed-on-the-bottom apron around her midsection and nothing above, often forgot that Emily wasn't fluent in Chesapeake, and *spoke* her instructions, at which time Emily would stop scraping, hold up her hand, and sign for her to repeat the instructions with signs. Each time, Shines smiled, shook her head at her oversight, then signed the instructions while speaking some of the words.

Emily had carefully concentrated on Shines' demonstration, but when she began fleshing on her own, her mind drifted from her task to Isna. I've not seen him for several days . . . but why should I care? I don't even know him, and he means nothing to me . . . only a Savage.

She imagined herself and Isna walking hand in hand in the forest. They stopped, faced each other, stared into one another's eyes; their lips moved compulsively, slowly, relentlessly together. She shook her head. What's wrong with you, Emily Colman? Concentrate, lass.

A shadow suddenly spread across the deer hide in front of her; she saw Shines look behind her. She stopped scraping, looked back over her shoulder; instant warmth flooded her mind and body when she saw Isna standing behind her, his wry smile in bloom and his dark eyes regarding her with an amused sparkle.

"Emily does well for a beginner," he signed.

Emily smiled, climbed to her feet, then wiped her hands on her apron; she looked into his eyes, signed, "Why does Isna always find Emily on the ground?" His eyes see my soul. She tried to look away, couldn't; rubbed her fingers against her palms, again wiped her hands on her apron.

He stared into her eyes for a moment then broadened his smile. "Mother Earth must love Emily . . . for she often calls her close . . . but Isna sees that Emily's dress now stands above Mother Earth, so Emily will no longer fall and spill water upon her."

A flush rose from Emily's chest to the top of her forehead; her bosom heaved with each breath. She stared into his eyes, fidgeting for a moment, then pulled up her skirt, grasped the hem, and showed him where she and Elyoner had shortened it by three inches and stitched it in place. She immediately thought, stupid girl, why are you doing this? He cares naught about the hem of your dress.

He extended his hand toward the skirt.

Emily abruptly pulled back, then realized he wanted to feel the cloth; smiling, she held it out to him.

He rubbed it slowly between his fingers, returned her smile. "Soft . . . like Emily's cheeks . . . and her eyes."

She blushed a deeper red. Lord, help me, I'm burning up. What should I say? What should I do? What does he want with me? Why does he look at me so? She nodded, said, "Eee-shnah," then signed, "Did Emily say it right?"

He nodded.

She signed, "What does *Isna* mean?"

"*Alone*. But Isna's full name is," he signed then said aloud, "Takpe Toka Isna."

"What does it mean?"

He signed, "Kills Enemy Alone."

Emily's jaw dropped; her eyes widened with dismay. God o' mercy, he's *killed* people. She paused while the thought imprinted her mind, then signed, "Kills Enemy Alone?"

He nodded.

She said, "Top Kay . . ."

He shook his head. "Tah-k'pay."

"Tah-k'pay."

He nodded.

She said, "Toe . . . Toe . . ."

"Toe-ka."

"Toe-ka," she repeated.

He nodded.

"Tah-k'pay Toe-ka Isna. Takpe Toka Isna."

He again nodded, proffered a modest smile.

She tilted her head slightly forward, looked innocently, questioningly up at him, signed, "Kills Enemy Alone?"

He nodded, touched his chest, said, "Ah-kee-chee-tah," then signed, "Great warrior . . . *killed* many enemies . . . *touched* many enemies."

He's certainly proud. She shook her head, thought for a moment, then signed, "*Touched* many enemies? What does it mean?"

He stood erect, assumed a proud, dignified look. "To touch an enemy is braver and more worthy of honor than killing him."

Emily's eyes widened as her hands asked, "How does Isna *touch* an enemy?"

"With his hand or bow or club . . . but without killing him. And the greater and more fierce the enemy touched, the greater the bravery and honor."

Emily's face was a picture of fearful anticipation, as if she dreaded his answer to the question she was compelled to ask him. "How . . . how many enemies has Isna . . . has Isna killed?"

"Nine. Their scalps hang in Isna's lodge. He was thirteen when he killed the first." He recalled his fear, his excitement at loosing his arrow at the Little-Shell warrior charging him at a full run, the surprised look on the man's face when the arrow ripped through his neck and his body failed him, collapsed him to the ground. Before the man had hit, Isna had nocked another arrow; but he hadn't needed it, had walked slowly up to the man, laid the bow and arrow beside him, pulled out his knife, then bent over him to take his scalp. But he'd been hunting alone and had no one to show him the proper method of scalping this first enemy kill; so he'd not made a clean cut, but it had been good enough for a youthful warrior . . . good enough for the people to honor his bravery with a dance and give him his first feather and his adult name . . . the name he now bore with pride. He smiled. "But when Isna cut the first one's scalp, he did not cut all the way into his head bone, and—"

Emily raised both hands to stop him then cupped them over her mouth, turned away. After several seconds, she took a deep breath, composed herself, again faced him. "How dreadful," she said in English.

He gave her an inquisitive look.

She shook her head, signed, "How many has Isna touched?"

"Seven . . . but one wounded Isna." He pointed at a scar on his left shoulder. "Isna cannot count that one, so his touch stick has but six notches."

'Pon my faith, he must do nothing but fight. "Isna must be greatly honored by his people."

"It is so."

No modesty. "Tell Emily again what your people are called?"

He spoke, "Lakota."

Emily said, "Lah-ko-tah."

He nodded, signed, "It means *allied*."

"Lakota," she repeated then signed, "What do Isna's feathers mean?"

He gave her a long, stolid look, then smiled. "Emily asks many questions for one so young."

Emily's blush reappeared; she pressed her lips together.

"Each feather is for an act of bravery . . . killing or touching an enemy." He re-crafted his wry smile. "And now Emily will ask why Isna wears only five feathers instead of fifteen."

She smiled, nodded.

"Because fifteen is too many to wear at one time . . . unless they are in a headdress . . . and headdresses get in the way. Isna's other feathers hang beside his scalp pole and his touch stick."

She tilted her head slightly to the right and studied his eyes, his face, let her look linger, opened her soul to the questions flowing from his eyes. "Why do the Lakota fight so much?"

His visage hardened. "The Lakota have enemies . . . and the safety of the *people* is more important than all else . . . far more important than any one person. But know that every Lakota is both peaceful and warlike . . . peaceful and gentle *within* the circle of the Lakota . . . courageous and ruthless *outside* the circle . . . peace and war . . . life and death . . . it is the story of man."

Emily stared at him, felt a prickly chill dance down the back of her neck. How terrible . . . but how starkly true . . . and not only for his people. How can a Savage understand this?

"And for the Lakota, it is a great honor to die in battle."

She cupped her hand over her mouth. How brutal . . . primitive . . . like the Vikings. "Does Isna wish to die in battle?"

"If it is meant to be . . . and gladly, to protect the people . . . or for honor."

Emily took a deep, contemplative breath, let it drift out slowly between parted lips. I shall never understand this. "Where does Isna travel?"

"He travels many places . . . to know different people and lands. He also travels to trade for things, like large shells and the furs of the great horned beasts that roam the grasslands in huge herds beyond the mountains toward the setting sun."

Emily raised her hands. "Slower. Return to the horned beasts."

He nodded as he signed more slowly, "These horned beasts"—he said, "*Tah-tonka*," made the sign for male then said, "and *P'tay*" and made the sign for female—"roam the grasslands in endless herds. The grasslands take many days to cross, but on the other side, tall, snowy mountains . . . much taller than those here . . . reach to the sky. Beyond the mountains, though Isna has not gone so far, lies another great water that cannot be drunk, like the one Emily and her people crossed to come here." Isna studied her for a moment then touched his lips with his fingertips, nodded at Emily, and one by one, repeated many of the signs he had just made, spoke the Lakota word for each as he did so, exaggerated the pronunciations, and waited for Emily to repeat each word several times. He then repeated the signs randomly, paused after each for Emily to say the Lakota word. When they had finished, he nodded, gave her an admiring smile, and signed, "Emily learns quickly."

Their intense, deliberate eyes held on one another's. Emily wondered, how can he beguile me so? "Lakota words are lovely . . . they sing like the birds."

"Isna will teach Emily more. Her pronunciation is very good, and she will soon speak like a Lakota."

A sudden, childlike delight sparkled in her eyes, flowed to his like a soft, gentle breeze. "Emily would like that. Will Isna teach her often?"

"He will . . . but Emily will also teach Isna more of her words, to add to those Manteo taught him."

She gave him a slight tilt of her head and the beginnings of a smile. "What did Manteo teach Isna?"

He signed, "Emily has two names. Her second is"—he said, "Col-man."

Emily said, "Yes."

"Emily's friend is"—he said, "El-a-nor."

"Yes."

"Elyoner's man is"—he said, "Ann-na-nigh-as." He studied her, thought, her heart and soul glow in her eyes without fear. She warms my heart.

"Yes, Isna." Her eyes remained on his; she trembled, felt a pulsing warmth flow through her body, her mind.

He slowly extended his hand as if to shake hers but raised it toward her cheek, hesitated, asked with his eyes if he could touch her.

She nodded slowly, willfully.

He gently laid his fingers against her cheek, held them there, gazed into her eyes.

Her heart raced; her breathing quivered. Unable to move her eyes or lips, she laid her hand over his, closed her eyes. *My heart . . . my soul . . . spinning.*

He held his touch and gaze for a long moment then slowly withdrew his hand and spoke measuredly, "Emily lifts Isna's heart like an eagle in the sky. He will see her again soon."

Emily whispered slowly, lingeringly, "Yes." *Dizzy, going to faint. My heart, my heart. Is this what love is like? Am I falling in love . . . no . . . I'm* already *in love. But how . . . how can . . .*

***

Emily's complexion was three shades livid, her eyes tight and focused, her hands alive, abrupt, angry. "Father, how dare you betroth me without my agreement! Fie upon thee! By the saints, you've no right to do so . . . 'tis ardently against my will. I'm not a swine or a goat waiting to be paired for breeding. How dare you?" She picked up a pewter pot from the table, flung it across the room into the fire, sending a cloud of sparks and smoke into the air, compelling her to look at the smoke hole to be sure she hadn't started a fire. She pushed the table onto its side, walked to the wall where her shawl hung, snatched it, flitted toward the door.

"Emily! Please. Calm yourself. You'll burn us down."

"I don't care. How could you betray me so? Tell me, Father!"

Colman coughed three times, then once more, clearly for sympathy. "Emily, I sought only to protect you. Our lives are fragile . . . and I have this worsening cough . . . I don't know what will befall me . . . I wanted only to ensure your protection."

A twinge of compassion flirted with her heart. He's indeed growing more ill . . . 'tis now a deep, vicious cough. "Elyoner and Ananias will protect me if anything happens to you . . . but you'll soon recover, so that's no excuse for treating your daughter like a piece of livestock, and I sha'n't abide it!"

"But, Emily, do you not care for Hugh?"

"No. I do not."

He looked confused, off balance. "This is sudden. Why not? You seemed quite taken by him."

"There are things . . . things you don't know . . . about his character . . . other things, as well. But even if I *did* love him, betrothing me without first asking *me* would remain a grievous transgression I would never accept. *I* shall choose my husband . . . not you or anyone else . . . and that's the end of it. So you can go back to Hugh Tayler and tell him—"

He shook his head; despair and frustration contorted his face. "Emily, my dear . . . there are necessities that outweigh love . . . marriage will provide security for you . . . Hugh loves you deeply . . . he'll protect you, care for your every need."

"No! I refuse. I shall kill myself . . . or go live with Elyoner . . . or Emme . . . or the Chesapeakes. I'll simply not accept it."

"Emily, don't say such things." He coughed again. "I'm loathe to say it, but arranged marriages remain quite legal and binding under English law, and—"

"Try it, Father! I dare you!" She opened the door.

"Emily, please. Hear me. Consider the benefits."

She looked back at him, said, "Goodbye, Father," walked out the door.

"Emily. Come back. Don't begrudge Hugh. He came to me openly and honestly . . . as a gentlemen *should*. Emily!"

Emily walked briskly toward the edge of the village and her special place beyond. *I'm too enraged to think.* She kicked at the ground as she walked. As she passed Elyoner's cottage, Elyoner walked outside.

"Emily. What ails you, lass? You look furious."

"I am!" She held her forward gaze, crossed her arms, and stomped into the forest as if she were walking through foot-deep snow.

When she reached her special place, Emily sat by the stream, stared at the water swirling in a lazy eddy beside her. Her blue shawl covered her shoulders, and she wrapped her chilly hands in the long ends that hung across her chest to her waist. *I was too harsh . . . unkind.* Tears rolled down her cheeks. *Father cares only for my safety and well-being, and I should not treat him so. His cough is truly worsening. Please, Lord, let it leave him. Still . . . I cannot abide what he did, and I cannot . . . will not . . . marry Hugh Tayler . . . even if what Johnny's told me is untrue, which I know 'tis not. Oh, Mother, help me. Help me know what to do. Yes, Mother, I'm finished with Hugh Tayler . . . yes, Isna is a Savage, but . . . no! He's a Savage only because that's what we in our ignorance have chosen to call people we judge less civilized than ourselves. In truth, he's a Lakota warrior . . . a brave man . . . with values, gentleness, honor, dignity . . . more genuine than most English gentlemen I've met . . . and being with him excites me like nothing I've ever known.*

She stared at the center of the stream. *I must apologize to Father . . . but I shall hold my position.* She looked up, surveyed the orange, red, yellow, and green leaves around her; listened to the soft whisper of the stream; heard three different bird songs, the screech of a hawk, the gentle breath of the light breeze rustling the treetops; savored the refreshing chill in the air that invigorated her with every breath. *How beautiful you are today, my world. How free from my tribulations. My Lord, I see your face in all around me. What better way to know you and worship you than to admire and delight in the beauty you've provided. I wish I could know your mind, for you know what is to become of me . . . of us . . . whether we'll be alive a year from now . . . how I shall resolve my trials . . . whether I shall know happiness or sadness in the days ahead. Please let me choose my actions in a way that pleases you. And let me know how to govern my feelings, my emotions . . . yes, my passions . . . with Isna. I don't know how to proceed with him, for in spite of my feelings, he is a Lakota, and he will return to his people.*

And I am English and must be with *my* people, my family. So I fear that giving my heart, which I cannot control, can lead only to my deep sorrow at his parting . . . but so be it, for I cannot be without him if he is near . . . I shall simply bear the pain of his one day vanishing from my life. As for now, I shall enjoy my time with him to the fullest.

She drew her gaze back to the eddy, smiled at herself. Seems to be a rather boastful sort . . . but perchance 'tis a *warrior* trait rather than a personal flaw. No matter . . . I warm at his presence. So let yourself be free, Emily Colman. Dream of him now; let your mind imagine what it will.

She closed her eyes. Isna and I are here by the stream . . . talking with signs and words. He looks into my eyes and . . . she shook her head. "Don't be a twit, Emily Colman! Do something useful." Practice your Lakota words. Yes. Practice.

"Man . . . wee-chah-shah.

Woman . . . ween-yahn.

Father . . . ah-tay.

Mother . . . ee-nah.

White men . . . wah-see-chew.

Friend . . . tee-blow.

Water . . . m-nee.

Yes . . . hahn.

Sky . . ." She sensed a stiff, new silence around her. Birds stopped singing . . . like at the massacre. Her body tensed; her neck tingled with a sudden chill; she studied the forest for movement, clutched her knife, listened, waited. After half a minute, she looked back at the water. Seconds later, Isna's reflection appeared beside hers.

"Oh!" She sprang to her feet, faced him. Something different about him, she thought.

His hair was parted on the right side of his head and hung freely to his waist on that side and behind; while to the left, it was clasped at shoulder height by a four-inch-wide strip of leather which gave it a neat, formal look. In spite of the early fall chill, he remained clad in only a buckskin loincloth and moccasins. But what caught her attention was his eagle-bone choker made of five separate necklaces stacked on top of one another, each a ring of end-to-end, tubular, white eagle bones an eighth-inch thick and two inches long, arranged with the bones of each necklace in perfect alignment with those of the adjoining necklace, so they could be tied together at the ends of each bone with vertical strips of sinew to form the choker.

Emily's pulse quickened. Want to touch him, hold him . . . Em! Control yourself! Trembling, she stood straight and formal, looked into his eyes, whispered, "Isna," then signed, "Isna scared Emily . . . she was visiting Mother Earth again."

He smiled, reached out, held her hands, studied the intricacies and graceful lines of her face as he thought, her eyes shame the sky . . . their brightness outshines the moon and the sun. "Emily." His face grew suddenly grave as he signed, "There are many dangers in this forest."

"Yes, but Isna will protect Emily."

"Isna is not always here."

"But every person needs a place to be alone . . . to think."

"Perhaps there is a place closer to Emily's village where she can think alone. And perhaps she will come here only with Isna or some other protector."

"Emily will think on Isna's words." Starting to talk like him.

He nodded, guided her to the grass, where they searched each other's eyes until his hands spoke. "Does Emily mourn her friend who died saving her?"

Sudden tears appeared in her eyes; her voice quivered. "Hahn."

"Isna is sorry he upset Emily," he signed, "but . . . why does Emily not slice her arms with her knife for this friend?"

She looked confused for a moment then said, "Emily does not understand . . . hee-ya okah-nee-zhay."

"Lakota women slash their arms and legs, cut off their hair, and wail when in mourning. Do white women not do this?"

Emily's lips parted; her eyes looked like big, white bird eggs with a small dot of blue in the middle. She shook her head, said, "No . . . hee-ya." She dabbed her eyes with her shawl, signed, "White women weep and moan . . . and Emily weeps for her friend . . . and her heart aches for him . . . but she loved him as a friend . . . not as a . . ."

He nodded. "Isna understands."

She signed, "Emily knows he is now at peace with"—she said, "God."

"Who is this person?"

How can I explain this? I know no sign for God. She raised her right index finger, assumed a thoughtful look, then smiled. "God." She spread her arms wide and looked at the sky.

He signed, "Sky."

She shook her head, said, "Hee-ya," and signed, "higher than the sky . . . everywhere."

He smiled, nodded, said, "Wakan Tanka." He lowered his forehead slightly toward her, assumed a serious demeanor, signed for her to watch carefully, then moved his hands slowly so she could follow. "There are three types of peace. The *first* peace—the greatest peace—enters men's souls when they escape the things of this world and look *within* to become one with the great powers of the universe. And when this happens, they see that Wakan Tanka is at the center of all, that there are no limits to his presence, and that he lives within each man's soul and everywhere in the universe. There is no greater peace than this first peace, and the other two are but images of it—like seeing one's face in the water—for this first, great peace must exist before the second and third can come to be. The second peace is the peace between people who know the first peace, and the third is between nations who know the first peace. So Emily will see that the first peace must live in each man's soul before it can grow to peace between people and nations."

Tears glistened in Emily's eyes. "Isna, this is beautiful. Emily thinks Wakan Tanka and"—she said, "God"—"are the same. And her people believe as the Lakota do . . . but Emily has never heard it explained so well, so clearly." She smiled, nodded quickly several times. "Strangely, Christians have been taught that the people who live in this land do not believe in God, have no honor, no values, kill each other at will."

Isna smiled. "It is true that the third peace, the peace between nations, is often not attained by the Lakota or their enemies. But still, the

Lakota believe in the harmony of all things in the universe because Wakan Tanka lives within each of these things—the forests, each piece of grass, rocks, waters, hills, sky, moon, sun, the two-legged and four-legged and winged peoples. And because of Wakan Tanka's presence, all of these things have spirits and life . . . yet Wakan Tanka is also *over* all these things, and has allowed man alone to be the determiner . . . and sometimes man determines poorly."

"Isna, Emily's people know these same things to be true, but they have a *church* with a chief . . . a *queen* . . . at its head to tell them how to live."

"How can any person tell another how to live? Isna does not understand this. A human being must believe and feel and live every day on his own . . . in harmony with himself and the universe around and inside him. It must be something he knows on his own and holds sacred . . . not something he does because he is told."

Emily nodded, considered his words for a moment, then smiled. "Most people ignore the Queen and do as they please, and some are good and some not so good. And some are truly evil."

"This is the nature of man, and so it is with the Lakota . . . but truth is the Lakota way of life, and they rub out those who speak *untruth* or *withhold* truth because such people will also break customs and rules and will eventually hurt others to gratify themselves, which makes them a danger to *all* the people."

"Truly?"

He nodded.

"Most of Emily's people . . . white men . . . don't think of harmony . . . they think only of themselves, their work, their own lives. So I see good in the Lakota way of thinking, for when one is at peace with oneself and the universe, one will be at peace with God . . . Wakan Tanka." I want to hold him close . . . feel his heart beat with mine.

Isna glanced at something behind her, sprang to his feet.

Emily spun about, stood, grasped her knife, searched for danger.

Realizing he'd frightened her, he smiled, held up a hand, then stepped a few feet away to a purple flower that held its head proudly above the colorful carpet of leaves. He picked the flower, returned to her, held her right hand with his left.

Her breathing raced with her pulse; they searched each other's eyes.

Slowly, measuredly, he held the flower to her parted lips, leaned forward, and touched his lips to the petals.

She closed her eyes as he lowered the flower, felt his breath, then his lips as they met hers with the lingering softness of a gentle summer breeze. He again gazed into her eyes, laid the flower in her hand and touched her cheek with the lightness of a down feather, then led her into the forest, toward the village.

As they approached the village, they stopped, faced one another. Isna touched her cheek, turned toward the Chesapeake village, and walked away.

Emily stared after him, waiting for him to look back so she could see his face one more time. When he did, she waved inconspicuously with her right hand, smiled, kissed the air.

He repeated her gestures then walked into the Chesapeake village.

As Emily entered the village, Hugh Tayler spied her, hurried toward her, raised his hand. "Emily, wait . . . may we speak?"

Emily's heart raced with alarm; she gauged the distance to her cottage, realized she couldn't reach it before he overtook her, took a deep breath, faced him.

As he approached, he said, "Emily . . . Emily . . . it's been days since we've spoken. May I—"

"No, Hugh. I do not wish to speak to you. Father told me of the bargain the two of you struck . . . and I despise you for it. Leave me!"

Tayler frowned, lowered his gaze to the ground. "Emily, I . . . I only sought to—"

"I said leave me . . . be gone from me this instant."

"Emily, please let me explain—"

"No . . . you knew my mind on the subject of betrothal, and you willfully ignored it. I'll have nothing to do with you."

"Emily, you treat me unjustly. How can you thusly wound the man who loves you so?"

"Your going behind my back makes it easy."

"When we last spoke, you told me you would meet with me again, let me defend myself against the frivolous, wrongful charges levied against me by your . . . your secret source. Do you not intend to keep your word?"

Emily glared at him, took another deep breath. "No! I do not!" She turned, walked away.

* * *

Virginia suckled Emily's breast with fervor; while Henry refused Elyoner's, turned away, sputtered, coughed, then tentatively nursed for a moment before repeating the cycle. Both women cringed each time he did so. Emily said, " 'Tis like Father's cough . . . deep and chesty, a lot of phlegm. Seems fine one moment, then he's doubled over the next. At least this one's not so bad . . . at least not yet."

"Aye, but it's hung on far too long, and I think he's losing weight, do you not agree?"

"Indeed I do. And it matters not which of us nurses him. He's simply got no appetite . . . he's a most discontented little lad. And I know not what we can do to help him; and sadder still, there's no one for us to ask. Grieves me to see him suffer so and be so incapable of helping him."

Elyoner studied the wall for a few seconds, looked at Emily. "Perchance you could query some Chesapeake mothers to see what they do for colic . . . if they even have it?"

Emily nodded. "I shall, Ellie, this afternoon. I shall."

"Thank you." She smiled. "Meanwhile, mayhap we could lull him with a gentle tune. Do you know 'Green-sleeves,' my favorite?"

"Of course. 'Tis mine, as well. Same for the Queen's court, I'm told. Oooh! Virginia's hungry today. Sucking hard, she is . . . are you ready?"

"Aye, I am . . . but let's skip the chorus after the first time through."

Emily nodded as they began floating their mellow notes toward Henry.

Alas, my love, you do me wrong,
To cast me off discourteously.
And I have loved you so long,
Delighting in your company.
Green-Sleeves was all my joy
Green-Sleeves was my delight,
Green-Sleeves was my heart of gold,
And who but my Lady Green-Sleeves.
I have been ready at your hand,
To grant whatever you would crave,
I have both wagered life and land,
Your love and good-will for to have.

A pall of sadness appeared on Emily's face with the first words of the song, deepened with each verse. Pox upon me. It may as well be Hugh Tayler singing this song. Swirls of compassion, then guilt, drifted through her heart.

If you intend thus to disdain,
It does the more enrapture me,
And even so, I still remain
A lover in captivity.
My men were clothed all in green,
And they did ever wait on thee;
All this was gallant to be seen,
And yet thou wouldst not love me.

Emily's mind filled with images of the good moments she and Hugh had passed together, joking, teasing, touching, sharing their intimacies.

Thou couldst desire no earthly thing,
but still thou hadst it readily.
Thy music still to play and sing;
And yet thou wouldst not love me.

Elyoner looked at Emily. "Psst." She nodded at Henry, who had settled and was nursing with conviction, then she suddenly shot her gaze back to Emily. "Em, you look ill. What afflicts you?"

"Nothing, Ellie."

"Are you sure?"

"No . . . in truth, those lyrics saddened me, made me think of Hugh. Am I not *his* Lady Green-sleeves? Forsooth, I've heard some of those same sentiments from his own lips."

Elyoner nodded. "I understand. 'Tis only natural. But you would truly be insane to be with him . . . and to be brutally frank, that he tried to trap you into marriage is . . . well . . . nakedly despicable, and I'm aghast your father agreed to it."

A moment later, the babies finished suckling; Emily and Elyoner lifted their smocks over their shoulders, buttoned their shirts, lifted the babies over their shoulders, and gently jostled them up and down as they thumped their backs.

"Well, as angry as I was when Father told me, I can't blame him, Ellie; and indeed, I've forgiven him, for I know he cares only for my safety." A sunless look spread across her face. "Though he hasn't said so, I think he believes he's dying; and it saddens my soul, for I fear he may be right. Every day he coughs more and seems weaker; and now he sometimes gets chills and muscle aches with the cough, and . . . and, Ellie, I can't suffer the thought of Father dying . . . being without him. I love him so"—she smiled faintly—"though you wouldn't know it from our frequent arguments . . . and my awful rudeness to him."

Elyoner walked to her, held her hand, looked at her with compassion. "My poor Emily. I think your father will heal in due time; but should the worst happen, you'll have a home with Ananias and me . . . and Virginia and Henry, of course."

"Thank you, Ellie, but let us pray he recovers."

They laid the babies in their cribs, returned to their stools. Emily said, "Let us speak of something besides Hugh Tayler and Father's illness." Her face beamed with a wide smile and sparkling eyes.

Elyoner shot her a knowing smirk. "And what might that be, Mistress Colman?"

"Isna, of course. But mind you, 'tis only a *casual* relationship . . . mostly educational, for I scarcely know him, though I do greatly relish learning about him and his people." Emily thought of Isna—his wry smile, piercing eyes, dignified presence, his Lakota pride, his gentleness and patience. Yes, her entire body—mind, soul, heart, newly discovered passions—all simmered in a hot, tingly, dizzying cauldron whenever she thought of him.

Elyoner smirked. "Indeed! Is that why you light up like a lantern when you hear or speak his name?"

Emily glanced at her with furrowed brow, hard, tight eyes, fought the sheepish grin that wanted to creep across her face.

Elyoner's round, rosy cheeks mushroomed over a perky, knowing smile. "Not being blind, I *have* noticed you spend considerable time with him . . . and seem to take far more than educational pleasure in it."

Emily's wooden look unexpectedly burst into an ear-to-ear smile and an unrestrained giggle. "You've found me out, Ellie Dare. 'Tis true. I delight in every second I'm with him, and I greatly enjoy learning of his peoples' beliefs and their legends . . . so many things are so close to what we believe. Listen to this. Yesterday he told me about P'tay-sahn-ween and—"

"Who?"

"*Ptesanwin*, the White-P'tay-Cow-Woman. *Pte* means bison, like the bison that used to roam the plains of Europe in ancient times. Isna says that to the west of the mountains, they're as many as the stars, and that his people use them for nearly everything: shelter, food, clothes, tools, water bags, string, thread, and many other things. But to the story, Ptesanwin brought the Lakota—and others of their larger group, the *Da*-kota—a sacred pipe."

"A pipe?"

"Aye. And I think they revere it . . . and follow the teachings associated with it, much as we do the Eucharist."

"Oh. Interesting. Go on."

"Well, Wakan Tanka, who as far as I can tell is exactly like our *God* but without Jesus Christ, sent a magical bison cow, or *pte*, who turned herself into a beautiful woman dressed in white buckskin and delivered the sacred pipe to them. Actually, though I hadn't thought of it until just now, it *does* sound a lot like God the Father sending Jesus Christ . . . but without the crucifixion and all . . . to save humanity."

Elyoner nodded reflectively. "Most interesting. I'm listening."

"Well, as she approached, two young men, one of whom who had impure intentions, met her; and she immediately turned the bad one into a pile of bones, which taught the Lakota and the other Dakota peoples to revere the sanctity of women and honor them forevermore."

"I rather like *that* story."

"She then gave them the sacred pipe, which has a red stone bowl meaning *the earth*, a long wooden stem that signifies everything growing *on* earth, including people and animals, and twelve eagle feathers that signify everything that flies *above* the earth. She said that all of these things, together with people who smoke the pipe, speak to Wakan Tanka . . . God. She also told them to walk the earth *with* the pipe and that the earth is their Grandmother and Mother and very sacred, and that every step taken upon her should be a prayer . . . that every dawn and every day are holy, and that each day's light comes directly from Wakan Tanka."

"A rather beautiful notion . . . but how can so many smoke one pipe?"

"Well, I'm not certain they do . . . I think it may be symbolic, in the sense that *walking the earth with the pipe* means living a good life, at peace with all people and things in the universe . . . like Christians walking the Bible's *straight and narrow path*. And—"

"I see what you mean about similarities . . . quite mystical, it is."

Emily rippled with enthusiasm. " 'Tis beyond mystical . . . 'tis completely *astounding* . . . two cultures an ocean apart, with no contact, having similar views of God and how he wants us to live. Think about it."

"I completely agree, but where does the *white* bison enter the story?"

Emily raised her right index finger. "Before she left, Ptesanwin said that as long as the pipe was kept and honored by the people, they would live; but if they ever forgot about it, they'd be without a center and would perish." She smiled. "Is it not a beautiful story?"

"Aye, it is, Em."

"And now to your question . . . as Ptesanwin departed, she turned back into a bison cow . . . but it was a *white* bison cow . . . and that's where she got her name . . . White-Bison-Cow-Woman."

"Zounds, lass. You've been a busy student, and . . ."

Emily sat quietly, an impish smirk on her face, thought how Isna always seemed mischievously annoyed when she asked him to explain things . . . as if he had more important things to do than answer a woman's incessant questions. He probably did, but he always smiled at her, spoke gently, touched her with the softness of fine linen, then displayed rising yet measured excitement as he told her of his people and their beliefs.

"Emily Colman . . . are you in love?"

Emily looked directly, piercingly into Elyoner's eyes, smiled. "Ellie, he stirs my blood and soul like nothing in this world."

Elyoner looked at her, lips slightly parted as if to speak, but without words took a deep, pondering breath. "Em, I see how you feel; I *feel* how you feel . . . you sparkle at his name . . . and I see a man in Isna with every attribute a woman could desire. But I cannot part my mind from the reality that he's of a different culture. Yes, his culture and—"

Emily raised her hand. "Ellie, I know what you're about to say. And I've already had that conversation with myself and made my decision. I shall delight in every moment I pass with Isna . . . for as long as those moments last."

"But, Em, how can you torment yourself so? You're placing yourself on a cliff above a bottomless emotional pit into which you can do naught but fall. Hear me, lass, I—"

"Then so be it, Ellie. I *must* be with him, and I will bear whatever happens when he leaves."

Elyoner bit her lips, sighed. "Very well." She walked to Emily, knelt beside her, pulled her close. "Em, I cannot suffer to see you hurt. I love you, my dear friend, and I shall stand beside you in whatever lies ahead."

"Thank you for caring about me, Ellie. I shall manage . . . somehow. I've a long winter ahead to know Isna and decide what to do when he departs." She stood, held Elyoner's hands, kissed her on the cheek. "I see the sun is high; I must be off with Master Cooper to the Chesapeakes. I shall ask them how they treat colic." She glanced out the window. "Here come Father and Ananias, and they look quite intent upon something."

"I'm sure they've some new crisis on their minds. I'm told the Assistants are fearful we've not enough provisions for the winter."

" 'Tis true, and they've traded beads and other trinkets to the Chesapeakes for help hunting deer. Isna and his three Lakota are going with a group of them this afternoon to hunt for a few days . . . somewhere near the mountains. It seems that's where most of the deer are . . . but it's a place sometimes frequented by Powhatans and their enemies, the Monacans, who live near there and speak a language similar to Isna's. And that's why he's going . . . he said it could be dangerous." She opened the door.

Elyoner hesitated for a moment then scowled like a scolding mother, wagged her right index finger up and down at Emily. "Before you leave, I have something I must say. Mistress Emily Colman, I well know you intend to do something with regard to Hugh Tayler . . . some fair gesture you think you owe him . . . something that will put your mind at rest . . . even as you cut yourself free of him. Know you that I do not believe him worthy of such." She paused. "But if you insist on such a noble, merciful gesture, remember thee well your promise to me. Do not be alone with him."

Emily faced her with a guilty smile, gave her a quick hug. "I promise, Ellie."

***

The ten Powhatan warriors moved swiftly, silently through the dense forest. Each man wore only moccasins, and a fringed, thigh-length apron across his front; while lines, swirls, and splashes of paint adorned their bodies and the shaven right halves of their heads. Each carried a painted-bark shield on his arm, a long bow, an un-nocked arrow in his shield hand, and a knife and stone war club at his side. It was *not* a hunting party.

The Panther had three parallel stripes across his face on each side, that ran from the ridge of his nose across each cheek to the bottom of his jaws—red on top, black in the middle, and yellow on the bottom. Every man had a red design of some sort on the right side of his head; the Panther's was a collection of lines, in a shell shape that emanated upward from just above his ear to the hairline at the top, where his long hair hung down the left side.

As he jogged at the front of the band, his mind reviewed their plan to surprise the Monacan hunting party they knew was hunting deer in their territory. They'd made two previous raids against the Monacans and on the first had killed two and taken one prisoner for torture. But the Monacans had pursued, and they'd had to kill the prisoner because he'd slowed their pace; the Monacans had outnumbered them and would likely have won an encounter in which the Powhatans did not have the advantage of surprise. The glow of any victory was dulled by heavy losses, and such were to be carefully avoided. He ground his teeth together when he thought of the second raid, led by another warrior, who'd stumbled headlong into the Monacan hunting party; and again outnumbered, they'd lost two warriors: one killed and another taken prisoner. They'd found the prisoner's body days later, after he'd been tortured and dismembered, his body left where the Monacans knew the Powhatans would find it. He smiled, for the captured man had been a close friend, an exceptionally brave warrior, and the Panther knew he'd laughed in their faces and taunted them as they tested his courage, knew he'd died a warrior's death because the Monacans had left his weapons with his body: testimony that he'd died bravely and earned the respect of his tormentors.

As the memory of his friend faded from his mind, the Panther thought of the young white girl with eyes the color of the sky and black hair like their own. He'd been unable to keep her face and the thought of her courage from his mind. Even when he thought of his very pregnant wife and her still-ferocious passion for lovemaking, Blue Eyes displaced her in his mind, captured his desire and his longing, filled him with visions of her naked body tight against his own, their wild, frantic movement together. The fact that a white woman could influence him so, still confounded, even troubled him; but he'd finally concluded it was what he'd known all along: it had been her raw beauty and courage that together captured his mind and now convinced him to take her for his second wife when they annihilated the whites in the spring or perhaps sooner. However, his present wife's possible reaction to his plan troubled him, for she was aggressively possessive, not the kind to share love with anyone. But she'd have her hands full with their new child, perhaps be more tolerant of his decision. Then again . . . who could predict the emotions of an angry, jealous woman . . . certainly not him. But he had plenty of long winter days ahead to think more on it; it was time *now* to think about the fight at hand, how they would inflict great pain on the enemy while escaping it themselves. He'd done so many times—led lopsided victories, killed many enemies, taken many prisoners, lost few of his own warriors. This fight should be easy because they knew where the Monacans would come from, where they would hunt: deer-rich Powhatan territory where there was excellent cover for ambush. But to think any fight would be easy was to invite defeat, and he cautioned himself to leave nothing to chance, to demand the utmost discipline and fighting skills from his men. A little more time would bring them to the place he'd chosen for the ambush, with enough time for the good concealment and positioning that would ensure their victory.

***

Afternoon shadows had begun lengthening from the foot of the narrow section of completed palisades when Emily returned from the

Chesapeake village. Hugh Tayler spied her from the village green, hurried toward her. "Emily!"

* * *

Isna was glad for his short Lakota bow. It was far less cumbersome than the long bows used by the Chesapeakes, allowed quicker movement through the forest. He and Soft-Nose, one of the other Lakota warriors, were therefore ahead of the two Chesapeakes who accompanied them, and he calculated that he himself led Soft-Nose by perhaps the length of three bow shots but wasn't sure. The hunting party had split into two groups because too many hunters in a band was counterproductive, created too much noise, alerted the prey and forced it from an area. So the two other Lakota and several Chesapeakes hunted elsewhere to increase the harvest, which they would combine at the end of the day.

All day Isna had tried unsuccessfully to keep Emily from his mind. Visions of her had persistently quickened his heart, drawn his mind from his task. Too dangerous to think of this now, he thought. He forced his mind to the deer's track. Fresher now, shallow in the leaves, not afraid, not running, close. Slow the pace, be more silent, don't want a *running* deer I can't catch. He took one of the four arrows he held in his left hand along with his bow's handgrip, nocked it, held the bow up in firing position. A few more steps . . . there he is, too much brush, can't see him well, move slowly, be careful; he pulled the bowstring back, aimed at the shape, advanced slowly, cautiously, one silent step at a time. No sound, breathe slower, quieter, move slowly, feel the earth, touch it before you step; his foot felt a stick; he stepped slightly, cautiously to the right, felt leaves and earth, thanked Wakan Tanka they were damp. Quiet, closer, better view, big buck, no wind, don't shoot yet, another step, slow, quiet—he slid noiselessly under a low tree branch—almost ready, two more steps. His heart began to race like it always did before a kill—two or four legged. He moved right, slipped behind a large tree, paused, breathed deep, exhaled slowly, did it again, took a third breath, let half out, held the rest, eased slowly from behind the tree, aimed, released.

As the arrow left the bow, a bolt of fear shot down his spine; he instinctively jerked back behind the tree, began to nock another arrow. Deer's sideways, looking right; something's there. "Phffft!" An arrow zipped by the tree. "Phffft! Phffft!" Two more. "Phffft-thunk!" One into the tree. He leaned around the trunk, let his arrow fly where the deer had been watching, heard a moan, pulled back behind the tree, nocked a third arrow.

"Hieeeeeeeeee!" War cries rose from the forest where he had shot, began to spread to either side. Silence, then a long, piercing, solitary cry. They come now. He leaned around the tree, loosed his arrow at the lead warrior, saw it hit his side; but he kept on coming, others behind him. Isna dropped his bow, pulled his war club and knife from his waist, shouted, "It's a good day to die," charged the ten Powhatans.

* * *

Hugh Tayler shifted his deadpan gaze from Emily to the bottom of the palisade section where they stood together.

Emily watched him with a stern, suspicious look.

He faced her, started to reach for her hands, but she withdrew them. He took a deep breath. "Emily, in all you've told me, there's but one truth. When I was twelve, I did indeed leave my good friend, Charlie, alone in the moors; and he did, in fact, drown. 'Twas a shameful act of cowardice on my part, and I give no excuse for it beyond my own youthful fear of being lost in a dark, foggy, haunting swamp, an unspeakably terrifying experience. I dream about it every night, and it will torment me until I die." He shook his head. "No matter that there was really nothing I could do to save him. What matters is that I didn't *try*, and I lied about it to his and my parents . . . and I shall forever regret my actions."

Emily's eyes saddened with unwilling compassion. "Hugh . . ."

"But, Emily, the remainder of what you've been told is completely false, and I shall refute each charge in turn."

Her hard look returned. "Go on."

"First let me say that I detest the people who've slandered me, but I respect your wish to conceal their identities; nevertheless, I know who they are, and I'll now tell you the truth about *them*. All *three* of them are shameless knaves who've made a pact to undermine and destroy me."

Emily held her silence. Three? Who besides Johnny? She felt a discomforting seed of uneasiness worming its way into her mind.

Tayler's face began to redden; his eyes filled with a fiery anger Emily had not seen before, an anger that frightened her. "I've already told you about Johnny Gibbes. Now let me tell you about William Waters and Michael Myllet." He spoke with disgust.

Emily's eyes widened. Cannot be, she thought.

"Waters courted my younger sister; and when she spurned him, he beat her . . . broke her nose, cut her cheeks, blackened her eyes. When I heard of it, I called him out; but he refused to face me, ran away and joined the army, which I would have denounced had I known about it, for I had many influential army friends who could have blocked his commission. But as it turned out, by the time I found out, he was already in and established, and 'tis most difficult to force an officer out once he's in service. And as for Myllet"—he shook his head, flashed a disgusted sneer—"he's but a vagabond who had the fortune, or misfortune, to know Waters' family, and was able to exploit the connection in the army to rapidly ascend to sergeant's rank . . . which he ill deserves. He's a churlish lunkhead, incapable of independent thought . . . a mere dancing puppet for Waters . . . does his bidding like a dog."

Emily's mind spun in confusion; she felt as if the earth beneath her had suddenly vanished, left her tumbling through the air.

"I shall now speak of each charge that's been brought against me, beginning with Gibbes' sister. Please forgive my bluntness, but she was a whore." He frowned. " 'Tis true I spent a night with her . . . lost my head in several tankards of ale and fell prey to my own distorted judgment. 'Tis also true that she became pregnant, but there were so many who'd been with her that it was impossible for anyone to say who the father was. So the Gibbes clan seized the opportunity to accuse *me*, attempted to extort a vast sum of money from me in return for their silence. I refused, but . . . but of my own volition, I paid for the girl's care until she died . . . even though I was certain the child was not mine."

Emily shuffled her feet, squeezed her hands into fists, wanted to speak but didn't know what to say. God o' mercy, this challenges my mind. I'm adrift in a sea of confusion . . . who to believe? She glanced around the village, saw several people watching.

Tayler spoke louder, mirrored his emotions with his hands; more people cast their glances upon him. "The battle in Holland occurred exactly as I described to you. I can show you my honorable discharge papers, which clearly state it was due to wounds incurred in the line of duty. I can also show you the citation they gave me for bravery. Anything else you've been told of that battle is a bold lie. Then there's the myth of the duel with the major . . . the most outlandish assertion."

* * *

Two Powhatans lay on the ground, one motionless, one twisting in pain. The one with the arrow in his side stood ten feet from Isna, raised his hand for the others to stop.

Soft-Nose whispered to Isna from behind, "Isna's Lakota brothers are here."

Isna nodded, held his position, watched as surprise then uneasiness crept into the Powhatans' eyes . . . all but the man he'd wounded. The man hung his club at his waist, glared hatefully, defiantly into Isna's eyes while he reached behind his back, snapped off the front of the arrow, pulled the shaft forward and out of his side, threw it on the ground, then looked slightly to Isna's left, spoke angrily in a language similar to that of the Chesapeakes.

One of the Chesapeakes approached Isna from behind, signed that their attackers were Powhatans, that their leader, the one he'd wounded, was called the Panther and was a great warrior. He said the Panther had told him they were trespassing on Powhatan land, so the deer belonged to them.

Isna regarded the Panther with a casual, disdainful look, signed, "The land belongs to no man. The Lakota will keep the deer."

The Panther's eyes tightened into tiny black dots fixed on Isna while he again spoke to the Chesapeake.

The Chesapeake looked back at Isna, signed, "The Panther wants to know why the Chesapeakes hunt with outsiders, enemies of our peoples and the Powhatan paramount chiefdom. I told him the Chesapeakes are not full members of their chiefdom and hunt with whomever they please. I also told him that while the Lakota speak a language like their enemies, the Monacans, they are from far away and came in peace to trade. He then told us to go away so they can kill the Lakota, but I told him we will fight *with* the Lakota if they attack."

Isna nodded respectfully then looked at the Panther, who seemed oblivious to the steady trickle of blood running down his right side and leg. He smiled, signed, "The Lakota are warriors such as the Powhatans have never seen . . . but the Lakota come to trade, not to fight. Still, if the Powhatans *want* a fight, the Lakota will oblige them." This man is worthy and brave. I shall touch him with my bow one day.

The Panther smiled a stiff, tight smile, twisted with frustration and stifled rage; thought, two dead, one wounded, too many losses, not a good fight; these two strangers fight well, have humiliated us today . . . I shall kill them slowly, painfully when we next meet . . . and the Chesapeakes, though they have not fought us, shall be punished for helping them. He nodded at Isna then signed, "This Lakota wears many feathers. The Panther has seen that he is unafraid and a worthy foe. He and the Panther will meet again one day . . . but when the sun sets that day, only *the Panther* shall live."

Isna answered, "If Isna and the Panther meet again, the Panther's puny half-a-head of hair will hang in Isna's lodge on the *bottom* of his scalp pole . . . a *new* scalp pole because the old one is already filled with enemy scalps." Isna stepped slowly toward the dead deer.

The Panther leered at him, lifted his weapons from his waist, eased forward.

Isna held his pace, grasped his club and knife. The two groups closed toward one another, weapons drawn and ready. It will be a swift, deadly fight, thought Isna. It's a good day to die.

***

"Waters, Myllet, and Gibbes contrived the entire story of an affair. 'Twas naught but a fabrication they perpetrated to wound and discredit me; and their dishonesty was soon discovered . . . by my benefactor, as well as by the major. But as is the custom with the army, when someone sins, but not grievously enough to warrant court-martial, they're banished; and so it was with these three slanderers . . . banished to Roanoke Island, they were . . . and they now continue to defame my character here at Chesapeake." He looked at her with eyes as sad as those of a man at his true love's burial. "Emily, everything I've told you—the good and the shamefully bad—is true. I swear it to you. And I swear to you that my love for you is undying, deeper than the sea, and it begs earnestly for your acceptance."

Emily's mind spun in confusion. "Hugh, I . . ."

Two ladies working at the closest cottage had been watching the discourse. One said, "Are you well, Mistress Emily?"

"Aye, I am. Thank you." She rubbed her eyes.

"Well, you certainly don't look so." They glanced back several times as they whispered quietly to each other, glared at Tayler.

Emily thought, 'tis impossible to know the truth. He's heartfelt, sincere, seems nakedly honest. What am I to do?

"Emily, there's something more I must tell you . . . something of the gravest nature and greatest importance . . . more so than anything we've yet discussed. It too will eventually come from the lips of these three liars, and I must inform you of the truth of it before they speak it."

Emme Merrimoth ran up to Emily and Tayler. "Emily! Emily! Come quick! Elyoner needs you immediately."

"Emme, what is it?"

"I don't know. She's in a desperate frenzy over something, shouted to me from her window. Perhaps 'tis one of the babies."

"My God!" Emily started after Emme, looked back at Tayler. "We shall finish later."

"Emily, we *cannot* finish this here in the village. We *must* speak privately somewhere . . . anywhere, outside the village . . . without intrusion. Please, I beg you. 'Tis of the greatest urgency."

She stopped, regarded him with a tormented look. "Very well, Hugh. I shall go with you." She quickened her pace toward Elyoner's cottage.

As she approached, she heard Elyoner scream, "Nooo! Lord, please don't let this happen. Nooo!"

CHAPTER 10

The cat-o'-nine-tails, with three knots at the end of each tail, ripped long, deep gashes in Richard Taverner's bare back. He groaned as his flesh splayed open, beaded with blood that ran down his back and onto the ground. His body trembled; he struggled to stay on his feet, braced for the next blow.

Sergeant Myllet dangled the whip limply at his side as he glanced questioningly at Lieutenant Waters. Waters nodded subtly, at which Myllet stepped a long pace backward, jiggled the whip to untangle the four-foot-long strands, and flipped them behind him; he stepped forward with an abrupt, forceful stride, threw the full weight of his body into his next stroke.

Nine new gashes appeared: more raw flesh, blood. Taverner cried out; his legs buckled; he hung by his wrists, which were bound to a tree, turned his head partially to the side. "I'll kill you, Myllet. God damn you to hell. I'll kill you."

With the exception of the perimeter guards, the entire contingent of soldiers stood at attention behind Myllet and Waters; civilians, including Emily and Elyoner, watched from around the green. As Myllet prepared for another blow, Waters held an expressionless stare on Taverner, let his mind drift, wondered where the discipline and morale of his men would be in another month. It was only fall, and they were already acting like they'd been through a full winter of starvation and deprivation. Tempers were short, grumbling rampant; he wondered how the hell they'd survive the long winter ahead. The Chesapeakes had told them that strange animal behavior, the premature departure of certain birds, the sudden, early falling of leaves, and the calm, crisp evenings meant that the winter would be severe. He prayed it would not be so then wondered how many more times he'd have to mete out punishments to maintain discipline. Taverner had been a clumsy thief, gotten himself caught. Waters was certain there'd been other, more careful or lucky thieves who *hadn't* been caught, knew there'd be more, knew he'd inevitably have to judge a capital offense, impose a death penalty in the face of deteriorating morale and discipline. He then admitted to himself the disquieting but inescapable plausibility of a total breakdown in discipline, knew only John White's timely return could preclude or salvage such a situation.

Taverner screamed as the fourth lash ripped into his mutilated, bloody back, which looked like a piece of raw meat being sliced for stew. Spontaneous, breathless gasps rippled through the civilians.

Waters doubted Taverner could survive another sixteen lashes, decided to end it after six more . . . *if* he remained conscious that long. How convenient, he thought, that Taverner was so disliked by the other men—he'd been suspected of stealing before and frequently started fights over foolish matters. No, there'd been no grumbling from the men, and Myllet hadn't blinked when ordered to deliver the punishment. How much more difficult 'twill be, he thought, when a *popular* man has to be disciplined. Yes, that day—and he knew it was coming—would challenge his leadership; for he'd heard of entire units refusing to participate in punishments of popular soldiers, which then left their commanders no option but to do it themselves and prosecute those who'd refused for insubordination; and that action, in turn, had inevitably prompted a death plunge in discipline. His stomach felt like a bag of down feathers fluttering in the breeze; he nibbled on his lower lip, acknowledged that the small size of his unit fostered uncommonly close personal ties among the men, greatly enhanced the potential of a *death plunge* scenario. So he prayed that John White would soon return with a bevy of enthusiastic colonists and a large contingent of uncynicized soldiers to save them from seemingly inevitable disaster.

Myllet winced with involuntary compassion as he struck Taverner the fifth time, splattering blood on the front of his own shirt and pants.

He glanced at Waters, who again nodded for him to continue, then stepped back to prepare for the sixth blow.

Waters' mind swirled between pity and his resolve to make a convincing example of Taverner, but how much was enough? Taverner was still able to pull himself to his feet, so Waters decided he could suffer a few more lashes to solidify discipline, further establish his authority and credibility with the men. But to escape the discomfort gnawing at his heart, he drifted his mind to the previous night's Assistants meeting—another unpleasant, worrisome affair—at which he'd reported that palisades construction had fallen behind schedule and completion now looked improbable, if not impossible, before winter. 'Twas only October, but they'd already seen snowflakes, and he'd grown increasingly uneasy about the impact of the food shortages Baylye forecast. So since the existing palisades provided a modest amount of cover—an amount that was unlikely to increase materially before deep winter—he'd proposed they reallocate their manpower to increasing the winter food supply. The Assistants had voiced immediate, unanimous assent, and the proposal had been adopted. But while the Assistants had celebrated their reprieve from the detested palisades, Sergeant Smith had knocked on the door, called him outside, reported that James Lassie, a member of a hunting party, was missing, then explained what had happened.

Waters had asked, "Did you return to where he was last seen?"

"Aye, sir."

"Very well. Too dark to do any more tonight. Let's take ten men and search a wider area in the morning." He'd stared at Smith while his mind raced through possible reasons—all unpalatable—for the man's disappearance.

"Well, Sir, I know what you're thinking, but it could have been something besides Savages. Remember, he had no weapons, so mayhap he hurt himself, and a wolf or bear or panther got him."

"Possible, but . . ." Waters had nodded, turned to step back into Baylye's cottage.

"Excuse me, Sir. I should also tell you that Master Prat feels 'twas his fault. I told him it wasn't, but you know how—"

"Not his fault, Thomas, and you can tell him I said so. Every one of us would have allowed Lassie to take a moment alone in the bush. No one needs an audience for that particular task. Don't worry. We'll find him."

"Hope so, Sir."

Waters had turned again, reentered the cottage. "Excuse me, gentlemen. It seems we have a missing man, James Lassie." Several Assistants had looked surprised. "Late this afternoon, the hunting party he was with, which was led by Roger Prat, was about five miles away when they started back toward the village. Lassie told Roger he had some *personal* business to attend to . . . by a log over in the trees . . . if you know what I mean. Said he'd catch up as soon as he finished his business, gave his gun and sword to two other men to carry, so he could catch up quickly. It must have been urgent, as I'm told he started loosening his belt as he trotted toward the edge of the forest." Several Assistants had started to chuckle but quickly realized the impropriety of doing so and held silence. "Master Prat told him 'twould be safer if they just waited there for him, but Lassie asserted he was a grown man and could handle the job alone, said everyone needed a little solitude now and then. Well, they started back toward the village at a slow pace; but when he hadn't overtaken them after twenty minutes, they went back to where they'd left him, found no trace, no signs of a disturbance in the grass or leaves." He had shaken his head. "Nothing! Our search parties also found nothing, so I'll take another party tomorrow and search a wider area. By the bye, Master Prat has been off with the main search party all afternoon, which is why he's absent from this meeting. Seems to be taking the incident rather personally, which is, of course, absurd."

Roger Baylye had said, "That's alarming news, Lieutenant. I suppose you suspect Savages?"

"Certainly a good possibility, Sir, but could also have been an animal attack, an injury, or simply getting lost." He'd noticed the dismay that had suddenly appeared on their faces, betraying vivid remembrances of George Howe's disappearance and demise, as well as their frustration that after only a brief respite from fear, the all-too-familiar feeling of impending doom haunted them again.

Baylye had looked at each Assistant. "Well, good luck. All of you please pray for Master Lassie's deliverance from whatever's befallen him; but meanwhile, Lieutenant, do you think we should restrict people to the palisades area . . . at least until we discover what's happened to him?"

"That might be wise, Sir; but I should think we'd be safe within a quarter mile of the village, wouldn't you? Especially if we travel in groups?"

"I suppose, but—"

The whip tore into Taverner's back the tenth time. He hung unconscious from the rope, his shredded back oozing blood and tissue fluids onto his stained pants and the ground below. Nearly all of the civilians had turned away, pressed their hands over their mouths; those who had not done so had closed their eyes, while a third of the soldiers had pasty complexions and glassy eyes.

"Enough," Waters whispered. He turned around, faced the ranks. "Men, what you just witnessed was unquestionably brutal. But understand you, our situation here is akin to martial law, and we cannot and *will* not tolerate the slightest deviance from good discipline and behavior. Violations *will* be dealt with swiftly and harshly." He pointed, in turn, at three men. "You men. Release the prisoner and treat his wounds. I expect him back in ranks on the morrow. That's all. Dismissed!" He turned, walked toward Baylye's cottage as he wondered how long it would be before the next incident.

* * *

Emily stared into the fire at the back of Elyoner's cottage, its quiet, rhythmic crackle the only sound. She watched the yellow tongues wrap around the log, creep slowly up its sides until, like clasping fingers, they joined over the top, enveloped it. Relentless, she thought, like the march of fate. She watched the blue flames beneath the log, admired the intensity of their color. Even *looks* hot . . . lying down there below, distributing heat to the rest of the log. She heard a loud pop, watched a stream of sparks rise to the smoke hole in the roof, shook her head. Unnerving having a fire inside a grass house. She glanced at Elyoner, who slept soundly, then at Ananias' empty bed and the crib that sat close enough to the fire to overcome the slight chill that hung in the room. Ananias must be growing weary of me . . . fortunate he and Father are such good friends. She looked back into the fire, thought of Richard Taverner, unconscious, hanging by his hands, his back a bloody, shredded, gooey mess. She breathed deeply, exhaled slowly, stifled the sudden nausea that rose to her throat. She'd nearly retched at the end of the flogging, had rushed away with Elyoner close behind. The two had walked briskly to Emily's cottage, stopped, looked at one another in silence for minutes before they spoke. Yes, it had been a difficult moment, but not nearly as terrible as little Henry's death and burial, after which they'd both dashed behind trees and vomited, then sobbed in each other's arms. She closed her eyes, felt her heart knot as if twisted by a pair of giant hands, felt Henry's soft, still-warm, lifeless little body pressed against her bosom, his cheek gently touching her own. She'd rocked him back and forth, thought of the hours they'd shared together, their bonding, his instant smiles at the sight of her face; she'd blinked at the tears filling her eyes, trembled, asked God why he'd taken such a helpless, innocent young life, berated him for doing so. She'd then laid him in his crib, stared at him: pale, still, silent. She and Elyoner had embraced, held each other close, then cried on each other's shoulders until Virginia had awakened, diverted them with hungry sputtering. Now Emily slowly shook her head, drifted into a comatose state as she again slipped under the fire's magical spell.

When her mind awoke, Emily realized the big log had burned down to coals before her oblivious eyes, her senses having been thoughtlessly submerged in the fire's mysterious heart. Bewitching it is . . . as if taunting me . . . telling me it holds all the primordial secrets of the world—past, present, future—but it refuses to yield those secrets, abandons me to my heart. She thought of Tayler, thanked him for staying away while she grieved for Henry. Clearly, he had some decency, but soon she must meet with him, end their relationship. And Father . . . poor Father . . . his gut-ripping cough, lost weight, frequent fevers, ever-increasing time spent lying exhausted on his bed. Where will it end? Mother, please come soon, or I fear you'll ne'er see him alive. And Mother, please ask God to let me find my locket.

She put another log on the fire, again stared into the flames, saw her parents, her deceased brother, herself holding her baby brother and Henry on her lap, all beside the fireplace in a new frame house in Chesapeake. Her father smoked his pipe and between puffs joined them in verses of *The Keeper,* one of their favorite songs. She smiled as she mouthed the words, saw their laughing faces, their bodies swaying to the music, felt their joyful hugs, their warmth.

> *The Keeper did a-hunting go*
> *And under his coat he carried a bow*
> *All for to shoot at a merry little doe*
> *Among the leaves so green, O.*

> *Jackie boy! Master!*
> *Sing ye well! Very well!*
> *Hey down, ho down,*
> *Derry, derry down,*
> *Among the leaves so green, O!*

> *To my hey down, down,*
> *To my ho down, down,*
> *Hey down, ho down!*
> *Derry, derry down,*
> *Among the leaves so green, O.*

Mother, I miss you so. Her smile melted away as her eyes bored deeper into the fire. She allowed it to pull her inward, beyond the surface of the flames, into its hidden soul, the sanctum of knowledge. Suddenly, she saw flashes of her strange dream of the night before: the huge brown bear walking side by side with a little white fawn as if protecting it, then many brown and white fawns walking behind them before scattering in all directions. What does it mean? Why would I dream such a thing? Isna's face appeared in the fire, his wry smile, his intense warrior's glare, then a different smile, a smile of warm affection, adoration, tenderness. Her heart sizzled with desire; within a single beat, a warm glow flowed through her body, down her legs. Her breath quickened; she felt a sudden, damp warmth between her thighs. Isna, I must be with you . . . my life, my all.

She'd not seen him since the hunting foray to Monacan country and Henry's passing, but Shines had told her of the encounter with the Powhatans, how Isna had charged ten Powhatans alone, how he and Soft-Nose had killed two, wounded two others, including their leader, held them at bay until the Chesapeakes arrived. The Powhatans had demanded the Lakota and Chesapeakes relinquish Isna's deer, but he'd refused, stepped forward to claim it. The Powhatan leader had moved to stop him; but as the two grasped their weapons, the second Chesapeake and Lakota hunting party had arrived with bows drawn. And since the Powhatans had left their bows in the forest when they charged Isna, the Chesapeakes and Lakota now had the advantage in both numbers and armament. Shines had measured up to her name when she proudly told Emily of the Powhatan leader's fury at being outmaneuvered, his promise to kill Isna when next they met. But her smile turned to awe as she described Isna's calm courage in standing a breath from the Powhatan's face, smiling at him, telling him not once, but twice, that his scalp would hang in his lodge at the bottom of his scalp pole. She'd beamed with pride when she'd told how the Powhatan leader, whose name was the Panther, had glared at Isna for a long while then turned his back, motioned his men to leave, walked away. The Chesapeakes and Lakota had kept their bows aimed at the Powhatans until they'd picked up their dead and their bows and disappeared into the forest. After a tumultuous victory cry, the hunting parties had gutted the deer and started back to the village with advance and rear scouts, bows ready, in case the Powhatans returned to fight. The Chesapeake warriors said they'd never seen such courage as Isna's in charging ten Powhatans alone, killing one and wounding the Panther. Emily had stared at Shines, wide-eyed, speechless, her hands trembling, a sudden sweat beading on her forehead. Fie on him, she'd thought. How can he do this to me, risk his life as though it means nothing, and charge into certain death. I can't bear it. How can I love a Savage . . . but, dear Lord, I do. You know I do, with all my heart and soul. I must see him.

* * *

While the other three Lakota slept, Isna stared into the small but intense fire in the center of his lodge. His gaze penetrated to the fire's heart, pulled his mind and soul along to search for answers to the questions that haunted him. I love her, he thought, but how can it be so? She's of a different people with strange thoughts . . . yet *she's* not strange. She understands the Lakota, thinks more and more like us, will soon know our language, more of our ways. Perhaps . . . he shook his head . . . no, it can never be. So am I not foolish to remain with her? Perhaps I should leave now, spare us both the pain of leaving later, when that pain will certainly be greater, for my love and desire grow with the speed of a bounding deer. He saw her face in the flames, her raven hair, features that captured and held a man's eyes, her own eyes of blue fire that enflamed his soul, harvested its secrets, enslaved him, filled him with wild desire. No! I cannot leave her, must be with her, hold her, feel her heart beat with mine, her warmth, her touch, her kiss, her . . . but she will be mourning the death of the child she nursed. Nothing strikes a woman harder than a child's death, and it will be of no matter that the child was not her own . . . the pain will be the same. Unfortunate that Isna knows not how these people grieve . . . but could it not be the same as the Lakota? Perhaps . . . but not likely, and would it not be bad manners to do the wrong thing and increase her pain . . . and would not a kind person stay away for a time, let her mourn, strengthen her soul from within? Yes, but it could take many days, perhaps an entire moon cycle, for she has seen much death for one so young; Isna must give her time . . . but how much? Even tomorrow is too long.

* * *

Virginia's whimper broke Emily's trance, sent an alarming shudder through her mind. She climbed to her feet, walked quickly to the crib, lifted her out, sat on a stool, then dropped her smock and began to nurse. She looked at the sleeping Elyoner. Thank you, Ellie, for letting me be with this little one. Were it not for her, I'd cry myself to death and worry myself into my grave. May God care for our little Henry . . . and help Father recover. And, blessed Lord, please let me see Isna tomorrow.

* * *

Emily and Shines laid strips of venison across thin, green tree branches supported at either end by tall, vertical, forked stakes which held the meat high over a smoky, slow-burning fire outside Shines' lodge. When the new meat was in place, they collected the dried, brittle meat they had removed from the fire and laid it beside two thick, flat rocks a foot in diameter, sitting on a tanned deer hide spread on the ground. Emily watched attentively as Shines laid several dried strips in a single layer on top of one of the rocks, began pounding them with a second rock, which had a flat bottom and a top that fit comfortably into her small hand. She pounded vigorously until the strips were pulverized into a fine powder which she then brushed off the stone and heaped around it.

Emily covered her own rock with a layer of dried meat and started pounding along with Shines. After twenty minutes, Shines raised her hand for Emily to stop, covered her rock with dried, purple berries, and resumed pounding. Emily mimicked her until after an hour, Shines again stopped, laid her two rocks aside, and retrieved a wooden bowl of melted animal fat that had been sitting beside the fire. She then sprinkled in the powdered venison and berries, stirring the mixture into a thick paste with a wide stick whittled flat on one end and carved into a handle on the other.

Emily raised her hand to stop Shines, held a finger over the paste, and asked with her eyes if she could sample it. Shines smiled, nodded at the bowl; Emily scooped up a blob with her index finger; licked a bit, judged the taste; smiled, nodded, licked the remainder from her finger.

Shines widened her perennial smile, reached behind for a rawhide pouch into which she spooned the remainder of the mix before laying it aside and telling Emily it was to be stored until midwinter when fresh food was scarce.

Emily signed, "How long will it keep?"

"Many years."

"Long time. What is it called?"

"Pemmican."

Emily said, "Pemmican."

Shines nodded.

"Good. I shall make much pemmican and show the others how to make it. It tastes good, and I think we will need it." Not something I'd want every day, she thought, but methinks 'twill be wonderful when 'tis all we have.

"Yes, you *will* need it. It's usually all we have at the end of winter, except for fish . . . and fish grow tiresome."

Emily nodded. "Shall we make more? I have all day."

"Yes, I can help you for a while, but then I must help my mother. You do very well."

Emily smiled. "Thank you. And tomorrow, will Shines show me how to make the rawhide bags?"

"Yes. I like helping you," she signed then said, "Em'ly friend."

Emily smiled, nodded, then said, "And you are *my* friend, Shines." She stood, checked the strips of meat drying over the fire, then knelt and resumed pounding. An hour later, she sat back on her heels, surveyed the Chesapeake village, and signed, "Shines, where do the Lakota live?"

MIKE RHYNARD

"In that lodge over there." She pointed to a different-looking lodge that sat at the edge of the village, not far from the forest. "Do you seek Isna?"

"Uh . . . no . . . well, yes. I haven't seen him since the hunting party, and . . . and . . . have you seen him today?"

Shines' smile broadened again. "I saw him this morning but not since then."

Emily spoke slowly, inquisitively. "Shines . . . may a girl visit a warrior at his lodge?"

"No. It is not done." She giggled like a little girl with a secret. "But you are not Chesapeake . . . so you may do as you wish."

Emily smiled. "Hmm. 'Tis true." She thought for a moment. "But 'twould be bad manners for my people, as well . . . but then . . . mayhap I don't care." She looked at Shines, smirked impishly.

Shines laughed again. "Em'ly will do as Em'ly wishes."

An hour later, Shines went off to help her mother, but Emily continued making pemmican and flashing frequent glances both at the Lakota lodge and around the village in the hope of seeing Isna. When the sun neared the treetops, she collected the remaining meat, berries, and fat and placed them at the door of Shines' lodge. She gathered her pouches of pemmican, stuffed them into a large canvas bag, and started toward the colony. As she passed the last Chesapeake lodge, she stopped. I must see him. She turned around, walked to Isna's lodge; stopped in front, hesitated, looked around to see if anyone was watching; took a deep breath, extended her hand, scratched on the door, as was the protocol. She waited for a long, anxious moment, sighed, then turned to leave but immediately ploughed into Isna who stood directly behind her. "Oh . . . Isna! Emily . . . Emily was looking for—"

"Isna is here." His wry smile appeared.

"Emily . . . Emily has not seen Isna for a while . . . she . . . she wanted to see him again."

"As Isna has wanted to see Emily."

She smiled excitedly. "Emily has practiced her Lakota words . . . but she must still use a few signs to—"

He nodded, grinned proudly. "Isna sees this is so and that Emily will now sign only when she does not understand a word." His eyes suddenly softened. "Emily, Isna heard of Emily's little one." He reached out, held his hands on her cheeks. "Isna does not know how Emily's people grieve, but Emily will perhaps know that Isna's heart suffers with her. The loss of an innocent little one is the greatest of all losses."

Her eyes misted. She dipped her head once. "It has been difficult; but he is now with God, Wakan Tanka, and will be spared the troubles and pain of this world. And Emily has shed her tears and is ready to continue her life." She smiled weakly.

He nodded. "It is said tears of grief purge sorrow from the soul and strengthen it. Isna believes this to be so."

"It *is* so, Isna. Emily *knows* it is so."

He smiled. "Will Emily walk with Isna?"

Her smile deepened shamelessly. "She will." She laid her pemmican bags on the ground then walked with Isna toward the forest.

When they had walked a short way into the forest, they stopped, sat on a bed of leaves, looked at one another in silence. The sparkle in Emily's eyes suddenly yielded to an uneasy, concerned look. "Isna . . . Emily heard of the fight with the Powhatans." She paused to allow the anxious quaver in her voice to subside. "Even though it has passed, it frightens Emily that Isna did what he did. He could have been killed."

He grasped her shoulders. "Isna *would* have been killed had he not fought. A warrior does not run like a scared rabbit to be caught from behind by the fox." He shook his head. "A warrior must die a warrior's death . . . or die of old age; and of those two, Isna will prefer the warrior's death."

She shook her head. "Oh, Isna . . ."

"Would Emily respect Isna if he died running from an enemy?"

She looked at the ground. I hate this . . . damnable pride, total disregard for his life. "Emily would have Isna alive under any condition."

"It cannot be so with a Lakota warrior. Perhaps with other peoples, like these Powhatans, who fight only when they have greater numbers, but not with the Lakota. And Isna is Lakota."

She swallowed hard, looked into his eyes. "Yes, it is so. Emily understands this . . . but Isna should know that this is difficult for Emily . . . that it scares her . . . for she knows Isna will do this many more times . . . and that she must accept it."

"Emily, Lakota warriors live by four virtues; bravery is the first and most important."

"What are the others?"

"Fortitude, generosity, and wisdom. No man masters all of them, but most strive to do so. Wisdom is most elusive—like the clever creature that always evades capture—and very few acquire it. But without bravery, nothing else matters, for the people will not be protected, and all will die. So every warrior will give his life to defend the people."

She looked at him glumly, silently. "Is Isna ever afraid?"

"All beings are sometimes afraid, just as all beings sometimes grieve . . . and it is these things—fear and grief—that make us whole. We cannot be so without them . . . bravery is meaningless without fear . . . as is inner strength without grief."

She pondered his words for a moment, nodded. "Emily sees that this is so . . . and are there virtues for Lakota *women*?"

"Yes. They are bravery, generosity, truthfulness, and childbearing. But there is also an unspoken virtue."

"What is it?"

"Lakota women will obey their husbands in all things."

"*All* things?" She flashed an indignant look.

He nodded but looked confused by her reaction.

"Emily does not think she could live *that* virtue."

"Emily, Lakota men provide for and protect the people against all threats—enemies, creatures that walk the earth, the weather that descends from the sky. But women must *be* protected. So, since men are the protectors, *they* decide all matters. But remember, Lakota men respect and honor their women, seek and consider their counsel before making decisions . . . at least in matters other than hunting and war."

Emily's cheeks flushed, but a hint of a smile appeared as she recalled her mother's words of a year before.

Always let your man think he's in charge. 'Tis easier that way. But 'tis we women who truly decide the direction of things through our influence.

It must be the same with Lakota women, she thought. "Emily understands this. In truth, 'tis no different from our ways."

He nodded. "Do Emily's people have virtues?"

"Yes. They're called the Ten Commandments, and they came to us from God, Wakan Tanka, himself, but they're the same for men and women."

"Are they of equal importance?"

"No. The most important is to love Wakan Tanka above all things and worship none but Him; and the second greatest is to love others as yourself, including your enemies."

"How can this be done?"

" 'Tis very difficult, but it is a very important part of that commandment."

"Perhaps many ignore this part?"

Emily smiled. "They do."

"And will the people obey the other virtues?"

"Sometimes yes and sometimes no. Most try to honor their parents and not steal or kill or lie, but two other virtues—to not desire the possessions of another and to not desire the wife or husband of another—are more difficult for people to keep."

He nodded. "Hmm. It is the same with the Lakota. And such wanting is thought to be a sickness that will destroy the people if those afflicted by it are not quickly banished or killed."

"That is sometimes true with us, as well." She looked away, pondered for a moment, then faced him. "Another important commandment is to not commit adultery."

"What is this?"

Emily blushed. "It . . . it is what . . . what a man and a woman do to make a baby . . . but with someone other than the one to whom they are married . . . or . . . or *before* they are married." An involuntary surge of carnal warmth flooded her body but was immediately followed by a wave of guilt.

He stared at her intently. "The Lakota also believe a man and a woman are to be married before they make a baby, and they are to do so only with the one they are married to. But it is not always so."

" 'Tis the same for us." She felt her cheeks warming, looked away for an instant, wondered how they could be discussing such matters; she felt a tantalizing twinge of curiosity, a closeness, a sense of belonging with him. Then suddenly, for no reason, she remembered her strange dream. "Has Isna ever seen a large brown bear?" She spread her arms wide apart. "A *very* large brown bear, larger than five or six deer?"

Wry smile. "Yes . . . these bears roam the grasslands toward the setting sun from our land . . . and at a certain time, one also roamed in Isna's dreams."

"In his dreams?"

"Yes. Why does Emily ask this?"

"Because . . . because Emily had a dream about such a bear. He walked with a little white fawn and seemed to be protecting it."

Isna's smile vanished; his eyes queried hers with sudden awe. "Isna had such a dream . . . many summers ago, when he undertook his vision quest as a boy becoming a man."

"Vision quest?"

"Yes. Each boy, when he and the seer think he is ready to become a man, prays to Wakan Tanka for a vision that tells him what he is to be and what his spirit creature is. This praying is called crying for a vision and is undertaken with the help of the seer, who knows the holy ways. It can go on for several days, without food or water. The crying is then followed by more praying in a small shelter made of twelve or sixteen willow branches covered by hides, in which the boy sits, often for several more days, with hot, steamy rocks and his pipe while he contemplates his inner self, asks Wakan Tanka to purify and cleanse him of all worldly influence, so he may receive his vision. He offers his pipe to each of the four directions, the sky, and Mother Earth, and adds a pinch of kinnikinnick tobacco for each. The pipe is then sealed with animal fat until after the vision quest. The young man goes alone with his pipe and without clothing, food, or water and sits and stands on a rock ledge on high ground far away from the camp for three days and nights by himself, shunning sleep. And during this time, he disregards his bodily wants, prays to Wakan Tanka, all the creatures of the earth and sky, and the spirits of his grandfathers to send his vision, and he listens to and speaks with all creatures and spirits who wish to tell him something."

"What does he think about?"

"Isna thought of his father and grandfathers and the things they taught him as a child and young man: the languages spoken by all the winged and four-legged creatures, the signs they leave with Mother Earth, their habits, how they hunt; the disguises used by creatures to conceal themselves from enemies and prey; how to read the signs of the sky and Mother Earth; how to suck on a cold stone to keep his side from aching when running; how much water to drink before sleeping, so the need to urinate might wake him at a certain time; the ways and beliefs of Lakota enemies, how they think and fight; how to make and use weapons; how to confuse and conquer an enemy by being unpredictable; and many more things, including those taught by Isna's mother. All these things hovered like a bird in Isna's mind for three days and nights of praying to Wakan Tanka for his vision; and finally, on the third night, it came."

"The large bear?"

"Yes. This bear is called Grizzly, the *Four-Legged-Warrior*, and he is the most feared creature on Mother Earth . . . even more so than man himself, for he knows not fear and is known by all as the killer of all enemies. He came to Isna and told him he would be his spirit creature and that he would allow him to possess his powers—his ferociousness in defending all who need his protection, his kindness and gentleness to those he loves—but he said Isna could only obtain these powers by finding Grizzly himself on the plains and taking his life and his spirit with his hands and bringing them both inside his own."

Emily's eyes were wide, an intense blue like the late afternoon sky; her lips parted in wonder.

"He then told Isna to wear his token—his claws—in battle, that he would protect him, and that Isna was to paint his face and shield with Grizzly's symbols and the symbols of his vision. He told Isna to travel Mother Earth and that one day a little white girl fawn would come and that Isna was to honor her and protect her from all danger for all of his life. And many brown and white fawns then appeared and followed the bear and the little white fawn for a while; but then they went off in different directions on their own until finally, everything vanished except for one brown fawn that turned into an old woman who wore two black stones around her neck and held Isna's vision pipe. But then a little white girl fawn appeared beside the old woman, and she placed her hand on its head; and a moment later, the old woman, along with the two black stones and Isna's pipe, vanished, leaving only the little white fawn. And suddenly, the fawn grew into a mother blacktail with a little white girl fawn of her own; and then the two black stones and the pipe suddenly appeared around the last little white fawn's neck, and Isna awoke. He then climbed off the ledge, returned to the village, told the seer what he'd seen, and smoked the pipe with him; but the seer could not explain any of the fawns or the old woman with the two black stones and Isna's vision pipe. So Isna yet waits for that knowledge to be revealed to him."

"Did Isna kill Grizzly?"

"Yes. But he did not give his powers easily; he nearly killed *Isna* before yielding. And that, Isna now knows, is because he wanted to teach Isna that things of great value are not easily earned."

"Isna, this is a great truth . . . but how . . . how could a single young man kill so great a bear? Was Isna not afraid?"

"Yes . . . at first . . . even though the great bear himself had told Isna to do what he was doing; but then his spirit started coming into Isna's, strengthening it, and Isna lost his fear."

"But how did Isna take his life?"

"With many arrows, three strong spears, and finally, when Isna himself was about to die, with his knife. But before he yielded his spirit, he knocked Isna to the ground with his huge paws and tore at his head and shoulders with his teeth and long claws, which were nearly as long as Isna's forearm."

Emily's hands covered her mouth then reached out, held his, her eyes wide with astonishment as she spoke carefully, measuredly. "Isna . . . the bear . . . the white fawn . . . the other fawns . . . the old woman . . . the last white fawn . . . all were in *Emily's* dream as well. How can this be?"

He stared silently at her for a long, thoughtful moment. "I know not." He glanced at the sky then slowly back to her eyes as if pulled there by an invisible string. Illumination crept slowly across his face like a gentle wave rolling onto the shore. "But *this* Isna *does* know: Wakan Tanka acts in mysterious ways, and that he sent Isna's spirit vision to *Emily* means he has made Emily and Isna a dreaming pair . . . and a dreaming pair is bound together for life."

They stared into one another's eyes, mulled the implications of his words. Chills rippled down Emily's back. Without speaking, they touched hands, embraced, rolled onto the leaves; their lips met, spread, tongues touched, caressed, explored; breath and hearts raced; bodies pressed together, moved as one on the forest floor; restraint evaporated like a snowflake in a flame.

Suddenly, Isna stopped, drew back, looked into her eyes, waited to catch his breath. "Emily, this cannot happen now. Our blood flows too warm . . . we must not let it be so."

She took a deep, quivering breath, stared into his eyes. "Isna is right. Though Emily would willfully yield to her passions, Isna is right. We must not." She closed her eyes. Mother, help me. Such temptation I've never known. I know not how to control it; and if ever I am to break my vow 'twill be here, now, with this man who stirs my blood like no other.

* * *

Thomas Colman lay in bed on his side, propped up on his elbow coughing blood onto a rag which he quickly shoved inside his sleeve when he heard Emily open the cottage door. She carried a tankard in each hand, wore a bright, airy smile on her face. " 'Tis ready, Father. Here, you shall have the first taste." She put the tankards on the table, poured a cupful, and handed it to Colman.

"I know not if I dare, my dear. I'm probably too weak, could send me to sleep. You go ahead. We'll toast your mother and brother." He coughed.

"Very well." She carried the cup to his bed, sat on the stool beside him. "Been a long time, Father. I've indeed missed my beer."

"I, as well." He studied the cup for a moment, abruptly smiled, slapped the bed with his hand. "Alack, I say! I care not if it puts me out. Bring me a cup of that brew, Daughter. Live hearty, for tomorrow, we may—"

"Father! Don't say that! 'Tis bad luck. I don't want to hear that word . . . heard it enough, seen it enough." Her frown softened, a gentle smile took its place. "But I see no harm in a glass of ale." She poured another cup, handed it to him. "So here's to Mother and Brother Johnny, along with our prayer that they're on their way to us soon. Eh?"

"To their health and safe journey." Both took a sip. "Not too bad for corn beer." He chuckled. "But John White had best return with as many beer kegs as people."

Emily took another big gulp. "I rather like it, Father. But mayhap that's because we've been so long without."

"Go slow, young Em." He coughed again.

Emily giggled. "Of course, Father."

An hour later, they'd finished one tankard and half of another. Colman sat on a stool beside Emily as they completed a rousing verse of *The Keeper*. Suddenly, tears filled his eyes; he stopped singing, stared at the fire in the back of the room, rubbed his sleeve across his eyes.

"Father, what is it?"

"I'm afraid, Emily. Your old father's afraid. Afraid he'll die before he sees your mother and brother." He shook his head. "One day I think

I'm improving, but the next, I know not. I'm so weak, tired, filled with aches, so unlike myself. And the cough. The damned cough."

Emily knelt beside him, held her arms around him. "I've seen it, Father, seen you coughing blood, as well. I'm gravely worried." This can't happen . . . not to Father . . . not without Mother here . . . but, God, I fear it is. Please stop it.

"I thought 'twas but a passing thing when it started back at Roanoke, but now . . . now I'm truly afraid, Emily . . . and mostly for you, for I fear I shall *not* recover; and more than all else, I dread leaving you alone in this land. So 'tis my sacred duty to ensure you know what *could* befall me and prepare you for what may come if it does."

"Father. Don't talk like that. You'll not die." Her eyes tried to fill with tears, but she held them back. "I sha'n't let you. I simply sha'n't. You're going to get well. I know it. I shall ask the Chesapeakes, and Isna, if they have any cures for such an ailment. We'll find something. Perchance you could sweat it out in a sweat lodge like the Lakota use to purify themselves for a vision. Or perchance—"

"For a what?" He coughed.

"A vision. Never mind. I was just speaking my mind."

"Well, it *does* seem that you spend much time with those Savages. And I truly don't approve of it. Forsooth, they're naught but primitive heathens. I can't imagine you could find anything interesting or attractive about them." He nodded. "Yes, Emily, in truth, it bothers me deeply."

" 'Tis not for you to like or dislike, Father. 'Tis for me alone." She felt an immediate jab of remorse. Be calm, Em; be kind. His illness magnifies his lack of grace. Understand; be patient.

"Well, you know my thoughts, Daughter. You should, at this moment, be married to Hugh Tayler, and . . . Emily, please give me another cup of that beer. It actually makes me feel a bit better."

Mayhap it will divert him. "Surely, Father." She poured both of them another cup, handed one to him, sipped the other.

"As I was saying, Hugh Tayler's the right man for you. He's a gentleman through and through, educated, of good family, and . . . *and* . . . he has wealth, and a young lass should never underestimate the importance of wealth. It can solve many a problem in a marriage." He hesitated, took a swig of beer, stared at the fire for a moment, then looked back at Emily. "My dear Em, now that I think more deeply of it, I *insist* you marry Hugh Tayler, for such is my right as your father. Truly, I see no other way to ensure your safety. 'Tis a perfect match, and your mother will be delighted, and I can then go to my maker knowing you're cared for. Yes, Emily Colman, you *shall* marry Hugh Tayler as soon as arrangements can be made."

Emily stood, glared at her father with parted lips as if she was about to spit. "The beer has softened your mind, Father. You've lost your senses, and I'll have none of it. And I'll have none of Hugh Tayler either."

"Why not?"

"Because, as I told you, I have knowledge of his character which you do not."

"Such as?"

"Such as nothing you'll hear from me. 'Tis my business, and it shall remain so."

"This is foolishness, Emily Colman. Tell me now, or obey my wishes!"

"I'll not." She gulped the last of the beer, grabbed her shawl, started for the door. Three crisp knocks halted her. She walked slowly to the door. "Who is it?"

"Hugh Tayler, Emily. May I speak with you?"

"Hugh, this isn't a good—"

Colman said, "Come in, Hugh. Come in."

Tayler opened the door, stepped inside.

Emily flipped her shawl around her shoulders, started for the door. "Hello, Hugh. I was just leaving. Father would love to visit with you."

He whispered, "Emily, we must talk." He looked at Colman. "How are you today, Thomas?"

"I think I'm better . . . probably this excellent beer." He lifted his cup. "Emily, remain with us, lass."

"Goodbye, Father . . . Hugh." She walked out the door.

Tayler followed her outside. "Emily, please. Pardon me for intruding. I can see 'tis an awkward moment. But I wanted to express my deepest sorrow over the young Harvie lad. I truly grieve for you . . . and Mistress Dare . . . and the lad himself, of course."

Emily stopped, faced him with a neutral cast. "Thank you, Hugh. I accept your sympathy . . . I know 'tis sincere. And I— "

"Emily, I can no longer suffer the sorrow of being parted from you. My love grows stronger even in your absence, and I shall be loosed from my mind if I cannot soon enjoy your company for long enough to clear my good name and show you by my actions that I'm worthy of your affection. So I beg you, fair lady, please oblige me as you said you would. Meet with me in a private place where we may speak our souls without intrusion and interruption, for what I must tell you is of the direst importance. Please, Milady, oblige this poor suffering soul before 'tis too late."

She held her stoical look, let his words drift through her heart and mind. I told him I would meet him, hear him; I must honor my word . . . though I would joyfully avoid it. "Hugh, I gave you my word, and I shall keep it. I cannot meet you tomorrow or the next day but three days hence."

He smiled humbly, spoke slowly, appreciatively. "Thank you, kind lady. Might we meet just outside the palisades gate at midafternoon on that day?"

She feigned a smile. "Aye, we shall, Master Tayler. I shall see you then."

"Until then, my fair one. Now I should like to visit your father."

"He would enjoy that, Hugh. Goodbye." She turned, walked away.

* * *

Though the southern sun tempered the afternoon chill, traces of ice clung stubbornly to the banks of the stream where Emily sat on a log at her special place. She'd spent the day slicing fish into strips to be smoked over a fire covered with smoldering green bark, but barely a moment had passed without oppressive guilt tormenting her heart. Though her father's spirits and combativeness had risen with yesterday's fresh beer, he'd been unable to roust himself from his bed that morning, and she was now convinced he was failing but wondered why the prospect no longer terrified her as it once had. Yes, the thought of him absent from her life deeply saddened her for the simple fact that he *was* her father, and she'd never been without him in life; but her fear of the unknown, the uncertainty of existence without him, no longer distressed her. She knew she could survive on her own, be it with the colonists or with Savages; but rueful regret tore at her insides for her snippy, tart replies to his innocently inflammatory statements. She knew the root of the problem was naught but his personality and inherent tactlessness, so she vigorously decried her lack of self-restraint and inability to overlook trifling shortcomings. She took her mother's letter from her apron pocket, opened it, skipped to part about her father. Tears dampened her eyes as she vowed to hold her tongue and prayed God would preserve him long enough for her to show him the deep love she harbored for him, the respect he truly deserved.

She glanced around the forest. Leaves gone, beginning to look stark; a few birds remain but not many. Wonder if the stream will freeze, how much snow we'll have . . . surely far more than at home . . . home . . . Mother, when will you come to us? She reached into her pocket, searched for her missing locket as if touching its place would return it to her. She visualized her mother lifting her young brother from his bucket bath, wrapping him in a large cloth, dabbing him dry while singing a soft lullaby, then folding him into a blanket, rocking him gently in her arms. When he started to fuss, she sat, lowered her smock, nursed him. She saw herself holding Henry, then Virginia, cuddling, nurturing, bonding. Oh, Mother, would that you could know that I, too, am nursing a child. She ached at Henry's loss, thanked God for Virginia's life, told him she'd delighted in sharing herself with both of them, wondered if the bond could possibly be any stronger if they were her own, thought not.

The birds stopped singing. Emily instinctively searched the forest, smiled when Isna soundlessly emerged from the brush. She sprang to her feet, ran to his waiting arms, met him with a lengthy kiss, pressed her body against his, and savored the sudden euphoria that glowed like a warm fire in her mind. She pulled back, looked into his eyes, smiled. Something different. She pulled back further, looked him up and down. That's what it is.

He wore a soft, tan buckskin shirt that reached to his thighs; the long sleeves, shoulders, and chest were painted a light blue, the bottom fringed all around, and the entire underside of the sleeves adorned with a line of thin, foot-long tassels of black hair. Buckskin leggings, fringed from waist to foot on their outside seams, covered his legs from his waist to the bottom of his moccasins; and his hair hung long and loose down his back to his waist, with his five eagle feathers protruding to the side in their usual fan shape. Emily gawked wide-eyed at the large necklace of sixteen, six-inch-long bear claws that hung loosely about his neck. "Isna, those claws are huge. Are they . . . are they from . . ."

"Yes. They're from the great bear." He grasped the longest ones, which hung in the center. "These are the ones he used to tear at Isna's head."

Emily stared at the necklace, her eyes wide with awe. "Isna, Emily cannot imagine something so big as this bear. Wakan Tanka watched over Isna that day."

"Yes. But remember, the bear had told Isna in his vision that he must take his life and his spirit. So he knew he would eventually yield to Isna and could not do so if Isna were dead. He fought hard, so Isna would respect and honor the value of his gift and use his strength wisely. And this Isna strives to do."

"Emily knows this is so." She smiled, looked again at his shirt and leggings. "Isna looks warm. Is this what he wears in winter in his land?" They walked hand in hand to Emily's log and sat.

"This and much more. It is very cold there. Much *wah*." He extended his arms upward, fluttered his fingers as he lowered his arms to shoulder height, then moved them back and forth horizontally.

"Snow . . . wah. Very deep?"

He nodded. "Also *kha-gha*." He pointed at the ice clinging to the stream bank, held his hands palms down in front, spread them back and forth. "Hard water, kha-gha, covers the Mother-of-All-Rivers."

"What does Isna do in such cold?"

He smiled. "Hunt a little . . . but mostly sit in the lodge by a large fire and tell stories."

Emily chuckled.

"The Lakota also paint stories on large skins to remember the important things that happened that year . . . it is called the winter count."

Like a book. "Who else lives in Isna's lodge? Does he have a . . ." She grimaced at her words.

His look saddened. "No. Isna has no wife . . . he nearly did, but she, and Isna's parents and young brother, were killed by our enemies, the people who call themselves *the first peoples* . . . two half-brothers now share my lodge."

Emily looked embarrassed, ashamed. "Isna. Emily is sorry. Forgive her. She—"

"But Isna found the people who killed them, and it is their hair that hangs from his sleeves." He held his arms out to his sides. "And their scalps, with the rest of their hair, hang in his lodge."

With wide eyes and parted lips, she looked at his sleeves, pointed. "That is *their* hair . . . *human* hair?"

He nodded.

"My God," she said in English, looked away, hand over her mouth. How barbaric . . . yet, they *did* kill his entire family . . . and his—

"Why is *Emily* not married? No woman is as beautiful . . . or wonderful as she."

In less than a breath, Emily's cheeks turned sunburn red. "Some . . . some girls Emily's age are married, but . . . but Emily has never loved anyone enough to *want* to marry him . . . until . . ." She stared into his eyes with a sensuous, lusty look, fought the urge to pull him to the ground and entangle his body in wild passion. What's happening to me? Such feelings, temptations. She swallowed hard. Chastity used to be easy. Her body shuddered, breasts heaved with her breath. But now . . . now I can't restrain myself?

He took her hands in his, met her gaze with a desirous look, pulled her close until her breasts were against his chest, then kissed her with the softness of a butterfly. Pulling slightly back to study her eyes, he smiled softly, gently, silently, took a slow, deep breath. "Emily, there will be dancing tonight. The Chesapeakes will thank their gods for the harvest. The Lakota will dance with them. Perhaps Emily will come to the village and watch . . . and perhaps dance."

"Yes, Isna. Emily would like that. She *will* come."

"Come when you hear the drums. Isna will await you."

She smiled. "I shall. And do the Lakota dance like the Chesapeakes?"

"Yes. But we dance for many reasons: to celebrate the harvest, bravery of a warrior, the taking of scalps, victories, a good hunt . . . a good marriage. Everyone dances. It is part of our life. Do your people dance?"

"Sometimes. Emily likes it very much, but her people don't dance to thank God for things; they dance because it makes them happy. And they laugh and tell stories and play games and drink beer and wine."

"What are these things?"

"They are drinks that make one feel very good and happy, but too much can make one's mind soft and make one act like a different person from who they are. So one must take care."

"Perhaps a warrior will not take such a drink, for it would be a bad thing if he had to fight while his mind was soft."

Emily chuckled. "That is so, Isna."

"And games? Does Emily play games?"

"A few, but mostly we sing—my family, especially." She smiled to herself, visualized her family sitting in front of the fireplace at home in England then dancing arm in arm around their small gathering room. Such fun we had . . . and God willing, will have again.

"The Lakota sing much but mostly when they dance. And they play games."

"What kind of games?"

"Many, but the people most enjoy the kicking-ball game."

"And how is it played?"

He raised an eyebrow; his lips curved into a mischievous grin. He raised his index finger in front of her, stepped to the stream; reached in, scooped up a handful of mud, plopped it on the bank; then tore off several handfuls of long, dry grass, squeezed it into the mud, shaped it into a ball about four inches in diameter, and wrapped more grass around the outside. Next he walked to a close-by tree, cut out three narrow strips of thin bark about two feet long, wrapped and tied them around the ball. He handed the ball to Emily, walked a few feet into the forest to a fallen tree; broke off two, four-foot-long sticks that were curved on the bottom, broke the curved parts to about a five-inch length; returned to Emily, handed her a stick.

She smiled at him suspiciously. "What would Isna have this young girl do?"

"First, she must rise to her feet. One cannot play this game sitting on Mother Earth." He walked to the side of the clearing, placed two short logs about three feet apart, then did the same at the opposite side of the clearing. He pointed at the first pair of logs. "Emily must use her stick to hit the ball between those logs to score a point." He pointed at the other end. "And Isna must do the same with those logs. One may also kick the ball but cannot touch it with hands."

"Emily can do this easily. What's the sport of it?"

"Will this young girl be able to do it when Isna tries to stop her?"

A trace of concern crept over Emily's face. "Oh . . . and will this young girl also be allowed to stop Isna from hitting the ball between *his* logs?"

He smiled devilishly. "If she can. Let us see if Emily plays Lakota games as well as she speaks Lakota words."

She gave him an arrogant, nose-in-the-air look. "Emily is ready. How do we start?"

He nodded, took the ball from her, placed it equidistant between the two goals. "Emily stands there on that side of the ball, facing her logs; and Isna stands here on this side, facing his; and when the first winged creature makes its song, we start. Emily will also understand that it is fair to bump into another player if he is in your way."

"That is *not* fair. Isna is much bigger and stronger than Emily."

"Isna will be gentle."

She smiled. "Emily won't. Let us begin."

Both held their sticks beside the ball, waited for a bird to sing. They waited . . . and waited . . . until finally, Emily said, "Perhaps we should—"

A bird chirped; but before Emily could react, Isna batted the ball to her side, raced to his logs, knocked the ball between them. He looked back at her. "Isna did not tell Emily that he is very good at this game. She will have to move quickly to make a goal."

"Humph! Very well. Emily now sees how to play. It will not be so easy for Isna the next time."

Isna placed the ball in the center again, but as he let go, a bird chirped, and Emily whacked the ball with a hard blow that caught the tips of his fingers between her stick and the ball. He groaned, shook the sting from his hand while Emily darted around him after the ball, pushed it toward her goal. He leaped after her, thrust his stick at the ball as she was winding up to shoot. His stick knocked the ball to her right; but she stuck her foot out, stopped it, quickly pushed it between the two logs for a goal, then raised her hands and stick in the air as she jumped up and down. "Emily told Isna it would not be so easy this time."

Isna said, "One is not allowed to hit another with his stick . . . but Isna will forgive Emily since she is new. Emily may keep her point."

She gave him a smug look then a devious smile, retrieved the ball, returned it to the center of the clearing. "Emily must nurse Virginia. Next point wins."

"Women do not set rules. Lakota men are the deciders . . . but Isna will allow it this time."

She frowned. "Start on the next winged voice."

A bird chirped; Isna smacked the ball to Emily's side, started after it; but she stuck out her stick, tripped him, chased after the ball as he fell. He leaped to his feet, caught up, then stepped in front of her as she pushed the ball toward her goal. She lowered her shoulder, charged into his stomach. As he fell backward, his feet tangled with hers; she tripped, fell laughing to the ground on top of him. They looked into one another's eyes, hesitated, pulled into a tight embrace, kissed. She wrapped a leg around his, pressed her middle into his groin, fondled the back of his neck, moved her hand to his side as he did the same—heart racing, panting, passion flooding her mind.

Emily thought, can't stop. Lord, help me. Mother! Emily, stop! She pulled her face back from his, stared at him with a sad, exasperated look, her heart pounding against his. "Oh, Isna. Emily wants you."

"And Isna, you. But this must not be the time . . . and Emily . . . it is also possible that the time never comes . . . but even so, *now* cannot be the time."

They sat up, stared at each other for a quiet moment, caught their breath. He rose, backed away toward the edge of the forest. "Wait here. Isna will show Emily something."

What's he doing? She watched him intently as he approached the forest, leaned behind a bush, picked something up, then backed toward her while masking whatever it was with his body. What *is* he doing?

When he reached her, he set the items on the ground. On the bottom was a round, brown object about two feet in diameter, made of thick, tough-looking hide, and on top of it, a light-tan, soft-looking leather bundle folded neatly into a two-foot square. He slid the round object from beneath the bundle, turned around to face her, flipped it over. He watched her eyes as she studied the painted figures on its face, the five eagle feathers hanging equally spaced across the bottom edge. "This is Isna's war shield. It is made from the thick hump of the man pte, the bull pte, called *tah-tahn-ka.*"

"Tatanka."

"Yes. It protects Isna from enemy arrows and spears. And here"—he laid it flat so she could better see the painted figures—"this is the great bear . . . *tah-blo-kah*, the Four-Legged-Warrior."

"Tabloka."

He nodded. "Now see here where the little white fawn walks beside him . . . and here walk the many brown fawns and white fawns. And then one brown fawn that turns into the old woman who carries Isna's pipe and wears the two black stones around her neck." He slid his hand further to his left. "And here a new white fawn stands beside the old woman, but then the old woman vanishes along with the black stones and the pipe. And here the little white fawn grows into a white mother blacktail with a little white girl fawn of her own. And here the stones and the pipe reappear around the neck of this last white fawn, and that is the end of the vision. It is Isna's vision and"—he looked into her eyes—"Emily's dream. And Isna now knows what some of it means."

Her wide, shining blue eyes stared deeply into his, waited for him to speak.

"Grizzly is Isna's spirit creature, and his soul is in Isna's; he and Isna are one in this vision . . . and Emily . . . is the little white fawn who walks beside Isna. Wakan Tanka has told Isna this . . . and he has also told Emily . . . in her dream."

Volleys of chills raced down Emily's back. "Isna, it *must* be so. Isna and Emily *are* bound together; Emily's heart tells her so; and nothing in her life has felt more right, more true, more natural."

"It is the same for Isna, my little white fawn."

They leaned slowly together, joined their lips in a soft, lengthy kiss, pressed their bodies together until, after a long moment, Isna whispered, "Of the little white fawn, Isna is certain, but he knows not the meaning of the other fawns or the rest of the vision. But perhaps . . . perhaps the many brown and white fawns are . . . are . . ."

Emily said, "are the children of Isna and his little white fawn . . . and their children . . . and their children . . . for many generations."

He held her by the shoulders, again stared into her eyes. "Isna prays to Wakan Tanka that it is so."

"As does the little white fawn." She laid her head on his chest. "But, Isna, how can this ever be? Isna is Lakota and must return to his people. And Emily is English and must be with *her* people, her family, her father, her mother, and brother . . . and her religion. Isna cannot stay, and Emily cannot leave. And she cannot ask Isna to stay."

"As Isna cannot ask Emily to leave."

"And Emily's heart is now heavy with the sadness of knowing it can never be as both of us wish it to be or as the vision and dream have foretold. Oh, Isna, we are one day to know the great sadness of parting, but . . ."

"but for now, let us live."

"And love each other fully until that day when . . ."

"when we must part."

"But we shall always remember each other, always love one another. Oh, Isna, Emily loves you so." She pulled him close, trembled as she held him with all her strength. '*Tis* so *meant* to be, yet so *impossible* to be. As deep is my love, so complete will be my anguish and pain when we part. Oh, Mother, what am I to do?

Isna slowly eased away, again turned his back to her, knelt while he did something with the leather bundle that sat beside his shield. Emily stood, leaned sideways to see what he was doing, but he sensed her impatience and turned his body to block her view. Suddenly he turned, held up a light tan doeskin dress with a three-inch-wide band of intricate red, blue, and yellow designs across the top of the shoulders and down the arms to the elbows; three parallel, stacked, horizontal rows of twelve small sea shells each across the chest; and a hem and cuffs of six-inch-long fringes.

Emily's eyes bloomed like brilliant blue flowers; her lips spread into a broad smile; her eyes darted from the colorful bands to the shells, to the long fringes, then back to the colors. "Oh, Isna, 'tis beautiful."

"Here. It is for Emily . . . so she will no longer trip and fall on her water bag."

She laughed; her eyes brimmed with humble gratitude as she glanced at the dress then stared into his eyes. "Isna! 'Tis so beautiful! Emily knows not what to say." She took the top of the dress, held it to her shoulders, looked down at her feet to check the length, tried to swallow but couldn't. "Isna, Emily will now cry." She laid her head on his shoulder, closed her eyes. "Thank you, Isna. 'Tis *so* beautiful."

He held her close. "Do not cry. The dress was to make Emily happy . . . Isna's little white fawn."

She looked up into his eyes. "She is *so* happy, Isna, so very happy."

* * *

Emily sat on a stool, nursing Virginia, her doeskin dress untied at the shoulders and laid down to her waist. As Virginia suckled with her usual wolfishness, Emily thought of her special place, savored the day's joyful moments with Isna: the kicking-ball game, falling on top of him, laughing, embracing, kissing, her beautiful dress, his shield with its depiction of his vision, her dream, their bond . . . their commitment to love one another forever . . . forever. A twinge of sadness tore at her heart as she envisioned Isna kissing her goodbye, walking into the forest to begin the long trek home to his people. She saw herself standing alone like a statue, tears streaming down her face, her heart rending with anguished yearning. *I cannot think of this yet. Too happy. Must revel in every moment I have with him, push the inevitable, awful ending to the dark future . . . yes . . . and pray it never comes to be.* She saw herself and Isna lying naked together, their bodies as one, moving in a slow rapturous rhythm. The vision abruptly vanished as her mother's words on chastity appeared in her mind.

Oh, Mother. What can I do? I love Isna far more than I can ever love any human being. He is my life, my everything . . . but the way for him to become my husband is unclear, indeed unlikely to be found. But this does not diminish my love . . . my passion . . . truthfully, my lust, my sinful lust . . . to be with him, have his child, whether we are ever married or not. Oh, Mother, when he leaves, I shall never see him again, and I must have something to remember him by for the rest of my life . . . I know 'tis shamefully immoral, but I must do this. It must be so; I must let it be so. Forgive me, Mother. Forgive me, Lord, for my sin will be great, and I shall likely never marry . . . but it must be so.

Elyoner slid the hooked end of a metal rod under the handle of an iron pot, removed it from the rocks on which it sat in the heart of the fire. She set it on the ground, removed the lid, sniffed the aroma rising from within, then glanced at Emily with a broad smile. "Can you smell it, Em? Zounds, it smells tasty."

Emily didn't reply.

"Em, are you there?"

"Oh . . . no . . . actually, I wasn't; but Lord in heaven, that smells good. What is it, Ellie?"

Elyoner smiled. "Oysters, mussels, and clams, all in the shell and mixed together with some slices of garlic I carved off one of the cloves from home. The Dares and Colmans shall dine like royalty this night. And by the bye, my dear friend, you seem to be floating around in the air this evening. Is it your love for Isna or the beautiful dress he gave you?"

Emily smiled. "Why both, of course. Oh, Ellie, I so love him . . . so want to spend my life with him, but . . . but I know it can never be . . . for the reasons you and I, and Isna, have discussed. But that doesn't stop me from loving him with all my heart and soul, for no other has ever warmed my blood as he does. We are meant to be together. Wakan Tanka . . . God has ordained it." She frowned. "But I know not how it can be." She looked at Elyoner with forlorn, misty eyes that begged her to find a way.

"Well, my dear friend, what will be will be, and you've a long winter ahead to let God work his will. So please don't cry, Em." She walked to her side, pulled her close, kissed her forehead. "Meanwhile, I don't think I've ever seen such a beautiful dress. 'Tis completely unlike how Chesapeake women dress, with their aprons, no tops, and capes when the cold comes." She smiled. "I've often thought their naked tops would feel wonderful in the summer heat, imagined myself . . . never mind. So the dress must be like those Isna's people wear?"

"Aye, but sometimes instead of shells the Lakota use the teeth of an animal that looks like a deer but is much larger and lives on the grasslands: *hay-khah-kah*." She looked down at the shoulders of the dress, which lay on her lap. "And those colorful patterns on the shoulders and sleeves are many small, painted quills from a short, four-legged creature about two feet long whose entire body is covered with them. Isna says they're very sharp and can stick into you, which keeps other animals from attacking them. This four legged is called *pah-heen*, but I don't think there are any here. The Lakota fold the ends of the quills under, sew them onto their clothes, and then paint them different colors made from bear grease mixed with berries or roots or finely crumbled, colorful rocks. Aren't the colors brilliant?"

"Aye, they are. So who made it for Isna, and where did they find the quills?"

"Shines did. He showed her what it should look like and gave her the quills and paint . . . he brought some with him to trade for shells and red rocks, and he gave all that were left to Shines as a gift for making the dress. Did she not do beautiful work . . . especially for her first time?"

"Aye, she did."

Emily smiled. "She liked it so much she's making one for herself, to wear in winter."

"Do you think she'd make one for me? I just love it, Em."

"I shall ask her. Perchance we could give her some sort of trade goods, like a pot or a knife, in return. I'm giving her my spare eating knife for all her help, and I think I shall give Isna a hatchet and a large knife . . . and some flint and steel. And . . ."

***

After supper Emily helped Elyoner clear the table and clean the dishes and eating knives. Thomas Colman sucked on a long-stemmed pipe, and between coughs chatted with Ananias Dare about the deterioration of the colony's discipline since their arrival at Chesapeake. Emily and Elyoner listened silently as they worked.

After a chest-rattling cough, Colman looked at Ananias. "Ananias, do you realize tonight is the first time I've been outside my cottage for anything but nature's necessities in a week?"

"You've been missed, Thomas. Good to see you up and about."

"Well, I thank you and Elyoner for such fine fare. By the bye, has there been any word of James Lassie? My Lord, the man's been missing for nearly a week. He couldn't just vanish into the air."

"That's what worries us, Thomas. We fear the Savages abducted him—possibly Powhatans."

"That would be most unfortunate. From what I've heard, the Powhatans—"

"Enough, Father! We just ate a fine meal. Let us discuss something else."

He gave Emily an insulted look, pouted for a moment, puffed on his pipe, then coughed three times. "Very well. Excuse me, Elyoner, Ananias. My fair daughter, who looks more like a Savage than an Englishwoman these days, is quite correct . . . 'twas a poor choice of after-dinner topics, for surely, no good could have befallen the poor man."

Emily and Elyoner glanced at one another with raised eyebrows.

"I've also noticed my dear daughter keeps close company with that Savage Manteo introduced her to at Roanoke. What's his—"

"And what if I have, Father? What would be the wrong of it?"

Colman coughed again. "No wrong, my dear. 'Tis simply not proper. These people are good, friendly stock, but their ways and beliefs are heathen, uncivilized."

Elyoner tugged at Emily's sleeve. "Emily! Shhh!"

"I'll not!" She slammed a wooden plate on the table, leaned toward her father. "They're more civilized than you'll ever understand, Father."

"Nay, Daughter. We must never forget our roots and values. Else we'll be absorbed and lose our heritage forever."

"Fool's talk!"

Elyoner wrung her hands. "Em. Shhh!"

Colman coughed again. "Well, it won't be our worry. We're returning to England when John White returns, and I'll not have you looking like a Savage when we do."

Elyoner, still wringing her hands, looked at the ceiling, rolled her eyes, sighed.

"And what if John White *doesn't* return, Father? What then?" She paused. "I'll tell you 'what then.' We'll become one with these people or die. And the sooner you and others realize it, the better."

"Emily, that's—"

"We're a greedy, selfish lot, but these people are in harmony with themselves and the world around them. Yes, some have attacked us, but that's because they fear us. They also attack each other, but so do we. And I'll wager we're the bloodier by far. If we—"

The eerie thunder of drums rose from the Chesapeake village.

"What is that?" Colman asked.

Emily started for the door. " 'Tis the harvest dance, Father. The Chesapeakes are thanking their gods for the harvest. I'm going."

"You're what?"

Emily removed her apron, stepped to the door, opened it. "I'm going to the harvest dance."

"You'll do no such thing, young lass! I forbid it!" He snapped the stem of his pipe in two.

"Don't dictate to me, Father. I'm a grown woman. I shall make my own decisions. Elyoner, Ananias, good night, thank you for dinner." She slipped out the door and ran into the dark toward the drums.

* * *

From beyond the circle of singers and rhythmic, deep-pounding drums, Emily watched nearly naked men and women step and whirl around the roaring, crackling tower of flames, felt the hypnotic pulse of the drums impregnate her, throb within, possess her soul, mesmerize her. Haunting . . . the drums, the chants. She stepped closer.

Oblivious to her surroundings, she eased through the watchers, approached the ring of rapturous dancers. Smoke, sweat, body on fire . . . drums, pounding inside me, dizzy. Shadows and firelight flickered on her face like primeval spirits at the dawn of time. She stared into the fire, let its bewitching spell pull her in, arouse primitive passions hidden beneath thousands of years of rising civilization. The drums . . . throbbing, shaking my soul . . . on fire . . . the fire, go to the fire.

As she stepped toward the flames, Isna touched her arm. She stopped, but the fire held her gaze. He touched her again. She looked at him with glazed eyes that didn't see.

He took her hands, held them to his lips.

She blinked, blinked again as recognition flashed in her eyes. "Isna." She leaned her head on his glistening chest. "The fire . . . the drums . . . Emily . . . Emily was in a trance." She stared into his eyes, touched his brow, drifted her fingers softly down his damp cheek, feathered his chin. "Isna has been dancing."

"Yes." His breath raced as if he'd been chasing a fleeing deer.

"Does Isna thank Wakan Tanka for the harvest?"

"Yes . . . and for his victory against the Powhatans." He smiled. "But mostly for the little white fawn who forever owns his heart."

* * *

Near midafternoon Emily walked out the palisades gate, saw Hugh Tayler standing at the edge of the forest fifty yards away; she felt the persistent ember of apprehension she'd carried in her stomach all day instantly flame into blatant dread. Don't want to do this but promised I would. Don't let it show, Em. But how can I speak of heartfelt things when I'm lost in love with Isna. The thought of Isna momentarily lifted her spirits, brought a thin smile to her face. Perchance I'll see him tonight or tomorrow. So happy, alive with joy when I'm with him. What will Hugh tell me? No way to know the truth of things . . . yet I know in my heart Johnny Gibbes does not lie. But Hugh . . . how could Hugh—any man—be as immoral and contemptible as Johnny portrayed? How could Hugh present such great lies so convincingly? But does it matter? Do I care? Hugh and I have no future. My future, at least until spring, is with Isna, and that's as far ahead as I can see now. A warm glow transfused her mind and body; her smile deepened then gradually withered as she approached Tayler. Ready yourself, Emily.

"Good afternoon, Emily. You look lovely, as always."

"Good afternoon, Hugh. Thank you, but I feel rather disheveled from the day's toil. 'Twas a step back into summer with that warm sunshine." Her hair was somewhat unkempt, her sleeves rolled up, and the front of her shirt unbuttoned down to her breasts.

Like Emily, Tayler's sleeves were rolled up and his shirt unbuttoned. "It matters not, fair lady. You're always beautiful. Shall we go?" He extended his hand, but she didn't take it.

"Where are we going, Hugh?"

"Oh, I thought we could walk a slight distance into the forest . . . far enough to be beyond earshot and prying eyes."

"Are you sure 'tis necessary? In truth, is there that much more to discuss, and can we not talk here at the edge of the forest?"

"Emily, what I must tell you is of such grave importance I dare not risk being overheard." He took a deep breath, looked into her eyes with a pleading, desperate look. "Please trust me, Emily. We won't go far."

She sighed, again wondered what could be so dire. "Very well, Hugh. But I must tell you that while I'm deeply conflicted over what I've been told by you and others, I don't think there is anything you can tell me that will restore our relationship to the course it was on at Roanoke. Truly, my feelings, as well as certain influences in my life, are not what they were back then, and . . . and this is very difficult for me, but what I wish to say is that I believe the relationship that was then maturing between us is no more . . . and 'tis only fair to tell you so."

He studied her silently for a moment. "Emily, I thank you for your openheartedness, but Hugh Tayler does not give up easily, and I believe that what I will shortly tell you will vindicate my honor and convince you to renew our relationship. So I beg you to please come with me and give me that chance."

She sighed, flashed a bland expression. "So be it, Hugh. Let us be on our way." She turned, started into the forest.

Tayler blinked at her abrupt departure, double stepped to catch her, then walked along beside her. "Let us follow this trail over here." He pointed to a pathway into a deep thicket. After a few steps he said, "Emily, while we walk, I should like to tell you a sad tale, one that—"

She stopped, looked at him. "Verily, Hugh Tayler, have we not enough sadness about us already?"

"Yes, Milady, we have, but this tale serves an important purpose if you'll hear me."

She held her bland expression, hesitated a moment, blinked. "Very well."

"Thank you, Milady." He pointed down the trail. As they resumed walking, he said, "My mother had a cousin she was very close to, and one day a close friend and business partner of his was found murdered. The third member of their partnership accused Mother's cousin, swore he'd witnessed the murder. The cousin proclaimed his innocence in private and in court, but no one listened, and he was condemned and hung. Six months after his execution, his accuser, who had taken sole control of their business, lay on his deathbed and confessed to the murder just before he died."

"How awful."

"Yes, Emily, 'twas awful; and I told you the story because the slander committed by your informant, or informants, places me in exactly the same position as my mother's cousin: innocent and wrongly condemned . . . and in my case, condemned by the person I love more than my own life. And this is why I am driven to tell you what I'm about to say. Shall we sit?" He extended his hand to her.

Emily glanced around, noticed the dense wall of brush that completely encircled the small clearing in which they stood. "Yes, Hugh, though it seems we're indeed quite isolated." She took his hand, sat down on the bed of richly colored leaves that blanketed the clearing. She felt a brief wisp of anxiety that quickly surrendered to a smothering surge of empathy. *I have been summary toward him, especially since I'm uncertain of the truth. So I must give him his moment.*

Tayler sat close beside her, stared at the leaves for a moment, then looked into her eyes. "Emily, do you know who Sir Francis Walsingham is?"

"Of course. He's the Queen's Principal Secretary and her Secretary of State, the most powerful and influential person in England, next to Queen Elizabeth herself."

"That is correct. But I'll wager you *don't* know that Sir Francis Walsingham is my father . . . not the late Richard Tayler as everyone thinks."

Emily's eyes bloomed wide.

"You see, when he was twenty-seven, Sir Francis had an affair with my mother, who was already married to Richard Tayler, and I was the result. Richard Tayler eventually found out about the affair and that I was not his child, and he hated and resented me for it until the day he died. He also thereafter resented my mother and abused her for the rest of her days, which ended with her suicide."

Emily laid her hand on his arm, stared at him with compassionate eyes, parted lips. "Oh, Hugh . . . I . . ."

Tayler swallowed hard. "Well, throughout my youth, Sir Francis kept himself informed of my life . . . from afar, of course. But when Richard Tayler died, he sought me out, told me the truth, and pledged to be my benefactor. John White knows this because Sir Francis told him when he insisted the governor bring me on the voyage. And now for the important part."

"Hugh, what could be more important than what you've just told me?"

"You'll soon see, my dear Emily." He looked away for a moment, took a deep, dramatic breath, looked back into her eyes as a sudden sadness shadowed his own. "Sir Francis detests Sir Walter Raleigh, the sponsor of this colony—first, because Raleigh is a commoner who has the Queen's ear, and second, because Raleigh's influence challenges his own. And what do people in high places in England do when they feel threatened by other people in high places? They find a way to discredit them and, if possible, have them charged with treason and executed. And such is Walsingham's design with Raleigh; the failure of this colony is the first step in his plot."

"Hugh, how can that be? Walsingham wouldn't scheme against an English endeavor, his own innocent countrymen. Nor would he sacrifice our lives for his own benefit."

He stared at her in silence for a long moment. "Em, unfortunately, such is not the case. Rather, such actions are everyday occurrences for the powerful. Naught but power and influence drive them. But there's more."

"Good sir, I do not know that I can bear more."

"You must hear what comes next, Emily. 'Tis everything that matters to *us*."

She cringed at his use of the word *us* but took a deep, calming breath. "Proceed."

"Before we left, Walsingham himself approached me with his plan, told me he wanted me to be his spy and lead three others who'd already agreed to undermine the colony and perpetrate its failure. He didn't tell me their names but made the uncharacteristic mistake of telling me they were all soldiers: an officer, a sergeant, and a corporal." His look hardened. "He also said he'd arranged for the colony to be outfitted with inadequate supplies and had bribed the pilot, Fernandez, to abandon us at Roanoke rather than bringing us here to Chesapeake. He well knew the history of Roanoke and that our chances of survival there would be greatly diminished by the hostility of the Savages." He paused, looked away then back into her eyes. "He knowingly sent us to almost certain death . . . but he then assured me we'd be rescued at an appropriate time." He snickered. "However, he neglected to address the reality that many of us might already be dead by that time."

Emily's chin dropped to her chest, her eyes billowed with astonishment. "Hugh . . . what did you say to him?"

He looked at the ground with lifeless, despairing eyes. "I refused."

"Oh, Hugh, what did he say?"

"He was not happy, and he commanded me to remain silent on the matter . . . or face most serious consequences. So, Emily, I've now defied him, and I shall tell you further that I know who the three soldiers are. Truly, 'twas not difficult to deduce since we started the voyage with but one officer and two sergeants, one of whom I floated with on a board the night we left Roanoke. He was certain we wouldn't survive and foolishly revealed his role in the plot to me."

Emily stared at him with tight eyes. "And the corporal?"

When we sailed, we had but one corporal, and he's now a sergeant . . . Johnny Gibbes."

"Lieutenant Waters, Sergeant Myllet, and Sergeant Gibbes."

"Yes, Milady. And now you know why they seek to discredit me: I know of their plot, and they fear I'll accuse them."

Tears of frustration, guilt, conflict at once rushed to Emily's eyes. She shook her head, started to extend her hand to touch his, held back. "Hugh, this . . . this is astounding. I don't know what to say."

"Aye, 'tis, Milady, but every word is truth."

She stared silently at him, grappled with a flood of discordant thoughts, intuition, convictions. "Hugh, I haven't told you where I heard the things said against you. How do you know 'tis one of these three?"

"No you have not, Lady; but I *know* 'tis one of them, and my wager is on Johnny Gibbes; for as I've told you, he hates me and my family and has an obsessive passion to harm me." He took a deep breath, let it waft slowly between his lips. "But the greater misfortune is that regardless of what I know of their plot, I cannot say or do anything until one of them makes a conspicuous move to execute it. And, of course, all of this ignores the grim reality of my father's wrath toward me if I'm party to uncovering his conspiracy. So for obvious reasons, 'tis fruitless to pursue any course against these three until the governor returns, hopefully with additional soldiers and some loyal officers."

"You could go to Roger Baylye and the Assistants."

"Aye, but to what avail? They're powerless without the soldiers, and the conspirators command the soldiers."

" 'Tis true." She stared into the forest, heard her heart tell her to believe him, her mind plead for caution. I know not what to do . . . so confused. Yet . . . 'tis almost too outlandish to be untrue . . . and what if *'tis* true, and I've believed slander? But could Johnny Gibbes simply compose the intricate tales he's told me? I think not. And are there not two issues: the welfare of the colony and my own heart? And is the latter not given to Isna . . . my dear Isna. How I love him. Oh, Mother, what should I say? She looked squarely into his eyes. "Hugh, your revelation frightens me . . . yet . . . yet I can conceive of nothing I can do, for I'm but a young lass with no power to influence anything of the consequence you describe. And you're right. We must wait for

John White to return . . . and pray we survive until he does. Truly, Hugh"—a sudden deluge of caution pummeled her mind—"I want to believe you . . . but I know not what to believe. Nor do I know what *not* to believe. So I can do nothing, believe nothing until some future event—one more persuasive and demonstrable than *anyone's* spoken words—reveals the certain truth."

He looked at the ground for a moment then back at Emily. "And what of our relationship, fair lady. Does the truth I've presented persuade you enough to allow us to step back in time and rekindle the relationship that once grew between us? Do I receive a reprieve or remain condemned?"

Emily's heart pounded; her mind staggered in confusion; anxiety burned in her stomach. She swallowed, stared silently at him, blinked. "Hugh, what you have told me is indeed dire and of great import to the colony." She swallowed hard again. "And when the truth of it is confirmed, 'twill truly embarrass me for hearing falsehoods and certainly compel me to think differently of you. But"—her face assumed a soft, tender, almost apologetic look—"it can have no influence on what was between us . . . for . . . for I love another."

The ends of his lips curved downward; his eyes clouded with sadness, disappointment. He held his breath, stared vacantly into her eyes. "And might I ask with whom you are in love?"

With a bland look, she said, "Hugh, I do not wish to be cruel, but that is immaterial to this discussion."

His eyes flashed a crazed glare; his lips twisted into a harsh sneer; his face flushed red. " 'Tis that Savage, is it not?"

Emily held her inscrutable look, as a wave of fear careened down her back.

"I know 'tis so, for I've seen you with him."

Her body tensed; her intuition screamed at her to stand and run, call for help.

"So I've lost to a Savage. How can this be? An uncivilized, mindless, primitive heathen? How can it be?"

Her hands and fingers trembled; she pressed them against the sides of her legs, so he wouldn't see.

He again looked away, stared at the forest for a moment then back at Emily, now with a soft, composed, admiring look. "Emily Colman, you know that I love you with all my heart and soul . . . and that you mean more to me than anything in this world. We are meant to be together . . . and we *will be* together . . . and you will learn to love me as I love you."

Fear gripped Emily's face. Why had she been so foolish, let him lead her so far into the forest, away from help? She shook her head slowly, ignored her mind's command to remain silent. "No, Hugh. It cannot be so."

He canted his head slightly to the right as if to see her better, stared at her with intense, focused eyes, sneering lips, said nothing.

Emily sensed his agony, his churning mind, knew he was deciding something. Fear raced through her like an invisible wind; her senses swirled in disarray. "Hugh, the sun is nearly down; we should start back."

His crazed expression returned; he canted his head to the left.

Emily started to stand. "Truly, Hugh—"

He seized her shoulders, pulled her into a tight embrace, his right arm around her back and left arm, his left elbow over her right arm and his left hand behind her head and neck; he pressed his lips to hers. She tried to twist free, but he held her fast. His right hand slid down her back to her waist; he pulled her shirt and smock from her skirt, slipped his hand beneath them, caressed her soft back and side.

Terror flashed in Emily's eyes; she twisted, squirmed, tried to free herself, felt his wild panting, her heart racing, pounding, her own breath quickening; she screamed, heard only a muffled moan.

He laid her on the ground, moved his right leg between hers, again feathered her soft body with a slow, lingering touch that unhurriedly drifted to her breast and nipple, tenderly fondled them like fragile works of art. His warm, rapid breath blew against her cheek; he reached down to the hem of her skirt, pulled it up to her thigh, smoothly caressed the outside of her leg and buttock then the soft inside of her groin, found the patch of hair above, the soft lips that shielded her virginity. He eased his fingers between the lips, spread them apart, found her entrance, gently explored inside, smoothed and spread the dampness within, touched the tiny organ at the top where the lips met, brushed it briefly, softly, teased it with repeated, wispy touches, again . . . and again . . . yet again.

Shock and panic flooded Emily's mind; she pulled her left arm free, pounded his shoulder, thrashed, squirmed, screamed another silent scream, felt his hard prick through his pants, throbbing against the top of her leg, wondered how something that large could enter a woman. She sensed her own involuntary arousal: gasping breath, pounding heart, tension, firm beasts, erect nipples, a warm craving in her body and mind, dampness where his fingers touched, the swelling of the organ as he gently caressed it, the strange anticipation of ecstasy rising within her. Her mind raced. How can it feel good? He means to rape me. Can't feel good. Can't happen to me. I'm a virgin. No! Dear God, make him stop. Must remain a virgin. Don't want this. Only my husband. Isna. Mother, help me. She saw her mother's words: *chastity . . . most wonderful possession . . . essence of you . . . given only to the one you love more than life.* His hands are gentle. Feels good. Can't think. Can't do anything. She pounded his ear with her fist, reached behind his head, grabbed a hank of hair, pulled his head back far enough to get her teeth around his lower lip, bit it with all her strength.

Tayler groaned, pulled his head back, rolled completely on top of her, sat on her stomach, pulled her arms under his knees, then pressed his left hand over her mouth. He noticed the blood dripping from his cut lip onto her shirt, wiped it with his forearm. "Emily, listen to me! Stop! You *will* be mine, and you *will* learn to love me. Fight me no more." He wiped the lip again, held his right forearm against his mouth.

His weight forced the air from her lungs; she gasped for breath, twisted, tried to roll to her side. Can't breathe; someone help me. This can't happen. Please, God. Make him stop. I'm a virgin. Cannot do this. Isna, please!

He leaned over her, his face but an inch from hers. "Emily! Emily! Stop! Hear me! Listen carefully." He held her chin with his right hand, forced her gaze to his eyes.

She stopped twisting, stared at him.

He spoke slowly, almost inaudibly. "Emily . . . I regret what I'm to tell you, but you've left me no choice. So hear me . . . and listen *very* carefully . . . I'm going to remove my hand from your mouth and get off of you. But if you scream or do not submit, something terrible . . . something unthinkable . . . will befall one you love dearly . . . one who is very small and helpless . . . and her death will torment you the rest of your days."

Another frigid chill ripped through Emily, doused her involuntary glow of arousal; she felt as if a sword had been thrust through her heart. Virginia. He means to kill Virginia . . . no . . . he'd never do such a thing . . . yes, Emily . . . yes, he *would*. Oh, Lord, God, Mother, Isna. Help me. What am I to do?

Tayler felt his lip, saw that the bleeding had nearly stopped. "You see, Emily, my love is such that I shall let *nothing*, including an innocent young life, prevent me from having you." He swallowed hard, looked suddenly unsure of himself. "And if I must, though I would detest it, I *will* hurt you. But one way or another, I mean to have you, and when you are mine, we will be bound together forever, for no other will have you once I've taken your soul and your body. So you see, you shall have no choice but to love me." He paused, glared into her terrified eyes. "Now think of that beautiful young child whose life now lies in your hands. . . and make your choice."

Emily stiffened, her numb mind swirled like grains of sand in a windstorm. No one can save me. Virginia, my dear Virginia, so precious, so helpless. Must protect her. Oh, Isna, I wanted this for you. Please forgive me, find me, save me . . . now. Virginia must live. He'll do what he says. No choice . . . my virginity, my life, my Isna, gone forever, unworthy of him . . . but I shall *never* love Tayler. Never. I shall kill him, be a whore . . . yes, and go to hell when I die . . . perhaps I should die now. Fight him, make him kill me . . . no . . . for then I'd be deprived the joy of killing him. Tears filled her eyes, flowed down her cheeks to her hair; her heart pounded. No escape. She took a deep, trembling breath, exhaled slowly, closed her eyes, nodded.

Tayler's hard look softened to a compassionate one. He looked suddenly unsure, hesitant. "I shall be gentle, Milady; I shall *not* hurt you."

She held her eyes closed, trembled; her voice cracked as she spoke. "And I shall *never* love you, Hugh Tayler. Do you hear me? Never! And one day, I shall kill you . . . now have your way with me and leave me."

He looked at her silently, uncertainly, then slid off to her side; unbuttoned the remaining buttons of her shirt, the tie strings of her smock; bared her chest, stared at her full, erect breasts; leaned down, gently kissed her neck then her chest. His right hand caressed her stomach then her left breast and nipple. He eased his lips down her chest to the other breast, kissed it, caressed it with his tongue, sucked gently on it as it stiffened further.

Emily lay still, sobbed, trembled with dreadful anticipation; she felt her heartbeat and breath racing, the wet warmth inside her, the hardness of her breasts and nipples. How can I feel so? I'm sinning, giving myself to a man I hate, ruining my life. Forever a whore. Hell awaits me . . . body, mind drunk with uninvited pleasure, must resist, hate him, love Isna . . . Mother . . . dear Lord . . . please help me.

His hand again lifted her skirt and smock, this time to above her waist. He caressed her inner thighs, found the lips, the small, firm organ, fondled it sparingly, tenderly, then continuously, spread the rising dampness inside her entrance.

Emily panted, sensed her hips moving with his touch, the wetness inside her, the lips swelling tight around his fingers as they probed within her, her heart's runaway pounding, tension gripping her entire body; she reviled the moment but couldn't exorcise the insatiable, burning desire that flooded her mind, heightened her senses beyond pleasure. She craved something but knew not what. Losing my mind, something must yield inside me lest I die. My God, make it stop. Forgive my indulgence. My senses, no control, can't stop the feeling, wild ecstasy, something *must* happen. Oh, God, don't let me enjoy this so. Make me hate it. I'm a whore.

Tayler suddenly removed his hand from between her legs, hastily unbuttoned the small flap at the front of his pants that covered his throbbing cock. As it burst free of its enclosure, he rolled over her onto his forearms, gently nudged her legs further apart with his knees, moved forward until he touched the wet lips of her entrance, moved the tip of his prick in a slow, small, circular motion, then pressed it gently forward until it entered her.

Emily felt him inside, felt herself moving with his motion, wondered why it didn't hurt. Hate myself. God, stop him. She felt him increase the pressure as he penetrated deeper, met a barrier, felt him push harder but enter no further, then withdraw slightly. Perhaps God stopped him; perhaps he cannot enter me; perhaps—a sudden, hard thrust pressed into her maidenhead, jarred her senses with a stab of pain; she groaned loudly as the barrier tore, allowed him to surge deep within her to his groin; their bodies pressed firmly together as one. 'Tis done, a virgin no more, a slut. God save me. She moaned again, felt him pull back, nearly withdraw, then thrust forward again as far as he could go, then again, and again, and again, quicker, ever quicker. She felt their panting, their hearts pounding together, her insides tightening about him, her hips rising to meet each thrust, heighten the pleasure. She gasped for breath, unthinkingly squeezed his back, clawed him with her fingernails, wrapped her legs around his. Sweat drenched her body, rolled off her forehead and cheeks; she sensed a strange, acrid odor, heard herself moan loudly, felt her mind and senses suddenly falling through the air. She arched her back, pulled him close with all her might, felt his warm, surging seed shoot deep within her. A euphoric sense of well-being immersed her body and mind like a gentle flood of warm water; her tension yielded to limp exhaustion.

Tayler emitted a long sigh, delivered four more slow, weak strokes, lay silent for a moment, then rolled to her side.

A moment later, wispy inklings of anxiety drifted into Emily's mind like the opening scenes of a bad dream; tears again filled her closed eyes, trickled down her cheeks; she whimpered softly as she pushed the front of her skirt down to her knees. Betrayed you, Mother . . . Isna . . . Father. Betrayed myself. Should have fought, died. A filthy whore without worth. Never face you again. Life . . . future . . . gone forever. Must die . . . shall die.

* * *

Allie screamed, sat up. Her hair was wet and matted, clothes soaked with sweat. She hung her feet over the side of the bed. "That dirty bastard! He raped her . . . just pinned her to the ground and raped her." She sighed, started to stand. "Whoa . . . dizzy."

She steadied herself, sat back on the bedside. "That rotten sonofabitch! Damn him to hell!"

CHAPTER 11

Emily wore a clean smock, sat by the fire in her otherwise dark cottage, glanced at her sleeping father. Breathing fast, she thought. Strange gurgling, rattling sound . . . like he can't breathe. She looked back into the fire. He must never know what's happened to me. She still felt dirty, emotionally spent, morally barren, permanently fouled, damned to hell without hope because of the pleasure she'd felt. For the twentieth time in the two days since the rape, she mentally replayed its final moments: her dramatic release, Tayler on top of her, then rolling to her side.

He'd lain quietly beside her while she cried softly and both caught their breath. Finally, he'd turned toward her, reached over, caressed her cheek. "Emily . . . my Emily, I . . . I love you, and I'm deeply sorry this happened the way it did. I didn't want it to be like that. I truly love you and need you . . . but at least you seemed to pleasure in it . . ."

Her eyes had flipped open; she'd looked toward him, spit at him.

He'd recoiled, stared at her in surprise.

She'd rolled away, again closed her eyes, whispered, "Leave me, Hugh Tayler. Never touch me again. I hate you, and I shall kill you."

He'd hesitated, finally stood, buttoned his codpiece. " 'Tis nearly dark. I should escort you back to the village."

"Leave me. I shall find my own way."

He'd stared at her for a long moment, finally turned away, then looked back at her. "Emily, you must tell no one what's happened here. It cannot be disclosed, and I shall do what I promised if *anything* is said to *anyone*. I know you understand. Again, I'm very sorry about the manner of this." He had turned, walked away toward the village.

After he'd left, Emily had climbed to her feet, tied her smock, buttoned her shirt; flipped the dried leaves and grass from her hair, smoothed it; for the first time, sensed pain between her legs. She'd fluffed her dress, started slowly toward the village, staggering the first several steps; cried, moaned, nearly fainted; then vomited when she thought of what had happened to her. Cringing with shame when she thought of her unwanted pleasure, Emily had shivered with guilt, despair, decided to kill herself. She'd tremored inside and out, decided to do it then. *Yes, I can hang myself from a tree branch with my shirt.* She had looked for a tree with a high, sturdy branch and low branches she could climb on, found one, removed her shirt, walked toward the tree, stopped, and looked up at the branch. *No. 'Twould be a greater sin and the way of a coward. I am not a coward. I shall face my sin, suffer, do penance for the rest of my life, perchance save myself from hell . . . but how can I do penance if I'm a whore?*

Before entering the cottage, she had again tidied herself, noticed Tayler's dried blood on her shirt, decided to tell her father she'd cut herself and used the shirt to stop the bleeding. Taking a deep, quivering breath, she had opened the door, sighed her relief when she saw her father sleeping. She'd immediately stepped to the water bucket, quietly removed her clothes, washed her entire body, praying that the feeling of filth that racked her like a fever would rinse away. But it had not, so she'd washed herself again, then two more times before she'd donned a clean smock, walked to the fire, thrown her clothes upon it, sat beside it, then stared numbly into its soul as the clothes flamed then quickly collapsed into ashes. *Like my life,* she thought.

What will become of me? What will I say to Ellie, to Isna . . . Father? My guilt, my unworthiness will show. My dear Virginia. What if someone discovers what he's done, and he does what he said? What if he comes and takes me again . . . and yet again? Oh, Mother, what am I to do? She sobbed quietly, trembled, searched the flames for answers until almost imperceptibly, a new, diminutive seed of anxiety rooted in her mind; it quickly bloomed, chilled her as if she were standing naked in frigid night air. *I could become pregnant, have his child. Oh, Lord,* please forbid it. What would I do? Would have no choice but to be with him, be his wife . . . his whore. Dear God, save me. Please don't let it be. She rose, walked to her bed, reached beneath it, and pulled out a small, thin stick with notches on it. She picked up her knife, cut two notches. That's for the last two days. She then tallied a total of fourteen notches on the stick, stared at the wall with a dazed look. Heaven help me! If I'm early like I usually am, I should start in seven days. Please, Lord, let me bleed. Please. She replaced the stick, walked to her duffle bag, opened it to view her supply of neatly folded rags. Must keep these close and ready. Lord, I beseech you, please let me bleed.

***

On the morning Emily cut the twenty-first notch in her period stick, she and five other women, escorted by two soldiers, carried buckets toward the water hole. Twenty yards outside the palisades, they found James Lassie. Emme Merrimoth saw him first, stopped still as a boulder; started to cover her mouth with her hands, hesitated; screamed, then screamed again and again and again. Others joined her while some, including Emily, simply stared in speechless horror at the pile of bloody body parts before them.

The two soldiers hesitantly approached the pile, looked at one another. One leaned close to the other, whispered, "Find the lieutenant . . . or a sergeant. Tell them what we've found . . . has to be Lassie . . . no way to tell for sure. But who else could it be?"

The other soldier said, "By the saints, what a death he must have had." He nodded toward Lassie. "Hard to see how *that* was once a man."

"Aye." He shook his head. "Better be on your way . . . and get those women out of here if you can. I'll stay and keep people away until the lieutenant comes." He stared at the hideous mess, suddenly cupped his hand over his mouth, puked between his fingers, then wiped his mouth with his sleeve as he glimpsed others approaching from the village.

Lieutenant Waters arrived first. He stopped, stared at Lassie. "God's blood!" Lassie's legs and arms had been pulled from their sockets, piled on top of the man's disemboweled torso, which had been completely skinned. His toes and fingers, all missing their nails, had been chopped off and stacked on top of the arms and legs like small pieces of kindling. His scalped head sat atop the pile, its severed ears, nose, lips, and gouged-out eyes stuffed, along with his genitals, inside his open mouth. Except for the four Powhatan arrows stuck in the forehead, the skull's empty eye sockets and thin circle of residual hair, below where his scalp had been, conjured the image of a vacantly staring monk in song.

Waters turned away as more soldiers approached. "Myllet, Smith, form a detail; get a tarp, remove this poor man to the cemetery, and bury him; then post guards all around the perimeter . . . inside the palisades, where possible. No one is to leave the village until I say so. Gibbes, summon Governor Baylye. Tell him what's happened and that I propose an immediate Assistants' meeting."

"Aye, sir." The three spoke in unison but stood fast, their eyes locked on the morbid scene before them.

"Move out, men!"

* * *

Emily sat by the fire, the image of James Lassie's mutilated body vivid in her mind; but as the image slowly faded, she again looked at her period stick, tallied the notches, prayed she'd miscounted . . . nay, twenty-three again. She looked at her sleeping father. Chest rattle worse: louder, thicker, gurgling, as if he's drowning. Dying, he is . . . so jaundiced and weak. Naught I can do but comfort him. Pray, Lord, let this pass him by. She hid her face in her hands, felt tears on her palms. When she finally looked up, she glanced at the stick again. Two days past my time, tired, weak, muddled in my mind, so afraid, sick to my stomach. She held her hands on her midriff. Tight, some cramps but not like usual, not nearly as many or as bad. Mayhap I'm late . . . no. Never late, always early. Afraid, punishment for my pleasure. Doomed to be with a man I despise for all my days, naught but a lowly whore, now condemned to be used at will—all just retribution for my sin. God, have mercy on my soul. I'm so sorry. She looked back at the fire. Ellie knows something's happened, see it in her face, asks where my spirit and smile are, commands me to smile. Tush! And what might I smile about? My dishonor? Being a harlot? Alack! I should have hung myself from that tree. She shook her head. Ellie must never know, for Virginia's sake. But what will happen when I show? How will I conceal it, hide my shame? Should I tell Tayler of the baby when he comes for me again? I think not. No, not until I show . . . if I haven't ended my life by then.

Dizzy . . . sore. She rubbed her groin. Still some bleeding, probably from . . . from the rape. She visualized Tayler lying on top of her, her legs wrapped around his, their bodies moving in unison. She sobbed quietly, shook her head, trembled inside. Unworthy of any decent soul. Naught but a slut now. She saw an image of her mother's anguished face. Oh, Mother, I've betrayed you, your trust, shamed myself and my family. And now . . . now I'm with child, condemned to be with a man I hate, be his whore . . . or a whore to any man who'll pay to use me. Oh, Mother, I'm so sorry. Please forgive me. Lord, let me bleed. Suddenly a vision of Johnny Gibbes' pregnant sister appeared in her mind: the young girl lay alone in her bloody smock, her hair matted, soaked in sweat; writhing, screaming in pain, bleeding to death in desolate agony; finally, lying still, her suddenly vacant eyes staring directly into her own as if warning her what lay ahead.

She pushed the thought from her mind, replaced it with one from long ago, one of her mother with a pained expression on her face. Over the previous weeks, Emily had seen her occasionally grip a piece of furniture to steady herself, abruptly clutch her abdomen. She'd also noticed other irregularities: more frequent visits to the close stool and privy, abrupt mood changes, unusual tiredness, and sudden dashes outside to gag or vomit. When Emily had asked if something was wrong, her mother had composed herself, smiled softly. "My dear, 'tis naught but the burden of pregnancy . . . I shall have a baby in the spring." Emily's face had beamed with excitement as the two had hugged, kissed, laughed, danced around the room. Then with deepest conviction, her mother had told her that the burdens she bore were nothing compared to the joy of bringing a baby—a baby conceived in love—into the world. And now as Emily acknowledged with a chill that she herself was experiencing those same symptoms, she whimpered quietly, again touched her abdomen. Lord, how will I treat this child born of sin? How can I love it? Will I not hate and despise it for the way 'twas conceived? She opened her eyes, stared at the fire. No. I could never do such; I shall love it as God intends. But how shall I not lament that 'twas not conceived by the man I love, my dearest Isna, but rather by the force of a deceiver and blackguard I hate. A breath of hope suddenly brightened her face. But perchance . . . perchance I'm just late, will yet bleed. She glanced at the period stick again then stared into the fire, shook her head. No, 'tis not to be; I *know* 'tis not to be, for I feel another life within me.

Emily stared thoughtlessly into the fire for twenty minutes until, for the first time in a month, an image of George congealed in her mind. You were such a good, kind soul, George, but I've betrayed your memory, your sacrifice. How strange that in a day's time two men saved my life: you, who were truer than true and gave your life for mine, while the other forcibly invaded my body and stole the life you saved, along with my eternal soul. And you, Isna, my love, now banished from my life; nay, I cannot bear it . . . but nor can I bear the pain, the shame of facing you now that I'm . . . oh, Isna, how I miss you, how I love you. You must be wondering what's happened to me, why I've abandoned you. I love you, I love you, I love you. She closed her teary eyes, moaned softly. My life is done. She thought of Isna's vision, her dream, the white fawn, the brown fawns. Never to be. She looked at her doeskin dress hanging on the wall. Must give it away or destroy it lest its presence torment me all my days by reminding me of what was and what might have been. Must also forget *you*, my Isna . . . now . . . even before you leave in the spring. She felt a surge of nausea rise to her throat, stood, started for the door. But it settled as quickly as it came; so she returned to the fire, sat, tried to calm herself with slow, deep breaths.

As Emily visualized Isna handing her the doeskin dress, her father moaned, tried to raise his head from the pillow but couldn't; his lips moved but without sound. She rushed to his bed, knelt beside him.

His gaunt face was a pasty, pallid color like old, icy snow, had the texture of an empty, crinkled, rawhide bag, and a deep, thick cough rumbled in his lungs with every breath. He covered his mouth with a blood-soaked rag, pressed his other hand against his chest, again tried to speak, managed only a faint, broken whisper. "Emily . . . my . . . my dear . . . Emily . . . Oh, Em . . . look at me. Shall . . . soon die . . . so much . . . to say . . . to you . . . no time . . . so weak." He moaned, lay back on the pillow, closed his eyes, trembled.

Emily rubbed her eyes on her sleeve, leaned over him, whispered, "No, Father, please don't leave me! I beg you."

He opened his eyes, again mouthed words without sound. Emily leaned her ear close to his mouth, whispered, "Speak slowly, Father. Take time, don't tire yourself. I'm here."

He wheezed, rattled, coughed; his voice quivered as he spoke. "Nay . . . my dear . . . few . . . moments left . . . must tell you."

She sobbed, held him, moved her ear closer. "Yes, Father. Tell me."

"You . . . must be . . . strong . . . my Em . . . as when . . . brother died . . . you . . . were strong . . . Mother and I . . . broke . . . remember?"

"Aye, Father. But that was different."

"No, Em . . . same . . . same . . . you're strong . . . stronger than I . . . stronger than Mother . . . you will survive . . . must survive . . . live."

"Father, don't leave me."

"Emily . . . tell Mother . . . I love her . . . always . . . loved her . . . even when . . . she was . . . angry at me."

"Yes, Father. I shall."

A faint twinkle appeared in his eyes, a hint of a smile grew on his lips. "Before . . . you . . . were born . . . I forgot . . . anniversary . . . Mother . . . angry . . . I knew not . . . why." He closed his eyes, rested a moment, panted, intermittently coughed. "When I . . . realized . . . why . . . brought . . . fat goose . . . flowers . . . knelt . . . before her . . . proposed . . . again . . . she smiled . . . kissed me." He forced a weak smile. "You . . . were conceived . . . that night . . . and what . . . a joy . . . you have . . . always been . . . to us . . . so proud . . . of you." He closed his eyes, again rested, coughed; his body writhed violently from side to side as if to expel the cough.

So helpless . . . be strong, Em. She blubbered through heavy tears, "Father, I love you so. I'm so sorry for the things I've—"

"Emily . . . survive . . .tell Mother . . . how deeply . . . love her . . . so sorry . . . brought you here . . . sorry for . . . leaving you . . . here alone . . ."

"Father, please forgive me for—"

"Hugh Tayler . . . loves you . . . good man . . . gentry . . . marry him . . . Emily." He seized her sleeves, tried to lift himself. "Emily . . . marry him . . . survive . . . only way."

She eased him back onto the bed. "You must rest, Father. Don't speak."

He nodded weakly, relaxed his grip, closed his eyes, then resumed his rhythmic chest rattle.

Emily moaned, cried quietly beside him. *Such a kind, well-meaning man, and I treated him so poorly.* She took her mother's letter from her apron pocket, looked at it, held it to her cheek. *Thank you, Lord, for sparing him the pain of knowing what's befallen me at the hands of this man he would have me marry.* She stared emptily at him for several minutes before a repugnant thought took shape in her mind, hovered there like a stale kitchen smell. *In the end, I've no choice but to go to Tayler . . . but as wife or whore?*

* * *

Tayler sat alone in his cottage, stared at the embroidered kerchief Emily had given him back at Roanoke when their relationship was on the ascent, when her growing affection had warmed his heart, nurtured and encouraged his hopes for the future. He spread it open, read the inscription—*Savor Each Day the Lord Provides.* A thin mist hung in his eyes as he recalled their moments together, the afternoon in the forest when she'd smiled, handed him the kerchief, then held her hand on his for a long moment. *What have I done?* He bit his lip, stared at the ground with mournful eyes. *The love of my life . . . the most wonderful, kind,* gentle, innocently stunning woman in the world . . . and I despoiled her. He laid his face in his hands. Ashamed. My future, my pathway to salvation, all gone, for she spoke the truth. She *will* always hate me. But yet, he squinted, raised his cheeks in a puzzled look, she showed the rapture of one lost in passion. Perchance, she *did* find pleasure but battles guilt within. Or mayhap she had no control at all over how her body responded. Women are indeed complex, confounding creatures. Either way, I was disdainful of her honor . . . but it was my frustration that prompted it—her abandonment of our relationship, her foolish infatuation with that Savage.

A half hour later, he looked back at the kerchief. I love her as no other, but beyond that I have an obligation to her for what I did, for 'tis likely true that no worthy man will now have her. But mustn't I also fear she will tell another what I've done? And if that should be, am I not then bound to do what I threatened to do to the young Dare child? He nodded. Yes, I *am* so bound, and though it would grieve me to do so, I *will* take her life if I must. But most importantly, Emily must *know* that I will do so; for if others learn what I've done, my future and my mission will be in peril. He shook his head. Fie on these thoughts. They torment me without mercy. He thought for a moment. There's but one way to rid myself of this torment and at the same time satisfy both my love *and* my obligation to her: make her my wife. He looked at the candle burning beside him. And if that cannot be, then I shall force her, by way of my threat, to become my mistress; and if, in the end, *that* should fail, as well, then I shall indeed take that young life. He frowned as an unsettling thought infiltrated his mind. If I take the child's life then all will know of my transgressions; I shall pay dearly, and my future and my mission will be at an end. So my plan must not end there. No, the young one's death must be but the instrument that convinces Emily I will forever do whatever I say. There must be more, and the *more* will be the death of her Savage if she fails to keep her silence and do my will. He put another log on the fire, watched the flames take hold, slowly shook his head. Though I've gravely wronged her, the great irony is that my taking of her body did naught but enflame my lust to new heights—new heights that demand I soon lie with her again.

* * *

Emily stared at the floor of Elyoner's cottage with a glum, detached look as she held Virginia to her breast. She glanced briefly at Virginia, offered a thin, fleeting smile as she began to nurse; but the baby soon stopped nursing, began to squirm and sputter. "Ellie, I think you'd better take her." She shook her head, glanced furtively at Elyoner, shrunk from her probing glare. "I don't know what's wrong with me. My milk seems less each day." She looked at the baby. Your mother suspects something, little one, but she must never know. And you must keep your life at all costs. Pray she stops staring at me like a barrister. She forced her gaze back to Elyoner, broached a false smile as she handed Virginia to her. "Ellie, why do you look at me so?"

"Are you well, Emily? You . . . you seem most unlike yourself these last days . . . as if something troubles you deep within."

She feigned a smile. "Of . . . of course, I'm well." She shook her head. "You're imagining things, Ellie."

"I think not. Your thoughts are elsewhere, mayhap up there on a star." She looked skyward, lifted her hand toward the ceiling. "I don't know what it might be, but something is different; 'tis as if you carry a great burden you're unable to confide. 'Pon my faith, lass, I'm not blind; I'm your dearest friend and know your manner."

Emily swallowed hard, again shook her head as her dulled mind drifted in a sea of apprehension. What should I say? "Truly, Ellie, there's nothing."

Elyoner held her rigid glare. "Come now, Em. I'm not fresh from the womb. We women know when something's amiss, and you've not been *you* for a week now. Forsooth, lass, none of us carry secret burdens well; and there's great relief in telling others when something afflicts us, great comfort to be gained from another helping us endure our trials.

And who better than the friend who loves you so dearly she'd give her life for you?"

Emily felt her composure crumbling from within. "Truly, Ellie . . ."

"Em, do you realize how much you've cried of late? People don't do that unless something troubles them deeply." She paused. "Is it Isna? Has something happened between you? Have you even seen him?"

A gust of pain stabbed her heart; her hands trembled; tears filled her eyes. "No, I . . . I have not."

"Did you quarrel?"

"No."

"Then why haven't you seen him?"

Emily bit her lower lip, felt warm tears on her cheeks, her heart shattering like broken glass. "I don't love him anymore." She lowered her face to her hands and moaned.

"Then why are you crying? I don't believe you for an instant, Emily Colman. 'Tis something else." A compassionate look abruptly took her face. "Oh my Lord! 'Tis your father! How stupid of me. How callous. Oh, Em. Pardon my blindness. Yesterday when I saw him, he . . . I understand your distress." She laid Virginia in her crib, pulled her smock over her shoulders; hurried to Emily, leaned over her, held her close; kissed her head, caressed her neck.

Emily whimpered, trembled. "He's near death, Ellie. What shall I ever do without him?" Father, Isna, losing both of you at once.

"You shall come and live with us. That's what you shall do."

"Nay! I could never do that. You must have your privacy."

"It matters not."

"Aye, it does. And I shall not intrude upon you. I'll do quite well on my own. But Ellie, I shall miss him so. I never truly appreciated him; and now . . . now when he's slipping away, I feel so guilty that I wasn't a better daughter. So many times I was brash and short with him. Ellie, give me a kerchief. I can't stop crying."

After a lengthy cry, Emily dabbed her bloodshot eyes, gave Elyoner a faint smile. "Thank you, Ellie. You're such a dear friend. I . . . I don't know what I'd do without you and your relentless solace."

"Dear Emily, you are the sister I never had. And it shall always be thus. Your sorrow is *my* sorrow, and it *will* pass, and I will *help* it pass."

"I love you, my sister." She smiled a genuine smile, took a deep breath, then looked at the door. "I should return to Father. Thank you, Ellie."

"I shall come over and stay with you as soon as this one's asleep." She nodded at Virginia. "Call me if you need me sooner. Oh, by the bye, did you meet with Hugh Tayler?"

Emily blanched, trembled, couldn't speak.

"Em, you look as if you've seen a dragon."

"I . . . I . . . yes . . . I saw him."

"You did!"

"Yes."

"In the village, of course?"

Emily nodded. "Of course." She bit her lower lip. "Actually . . . actually, Ellie, 'twas in the forest."

Elyoner frowned. "Was someone with you?"

"No, we were . . . we were alone." She turned away, rubbed her teary eyes, looked back at Elyoner.

Elyoner gasped, held a long silence. "Emily, did something happen?"

"No, nothing happened. Ellie, I . . . I must go." She stood, turned away, covered her mouth with her hand, rushed outside, a muffled wail trailing behind her.

* * *

Myllet said, "Well, Sir, we've no disagreement on the threat posed by the Powhatans, but with only twenty-one men, counting you and us three sergeants, we lack the manpower to do as you suggest. If we have four men guarding the village at all times, how can we also have four guarding the water gatherers, clothes washers, hunters, fishermen, and woodcutters? Right there, we're up to twenty-*four* men."

Waters nodded. "Then we must invent a means to meet our need. For example, we could combine water and washing parties. No one washes their clothing *or* their body very often anyway, so that might help a little. I admit, the other situations are more worrisome; though when the fishermen are afloat, they probably don't need four guards; two would likely suffice. In any event, I think 'twould be wise to train a few civilians to augment our men, mayhap as a fourth member of each detachment of three soldiers. What do you think?"

The three nodded agreement. Smith smiled. "There's no doubt we'll have a bevy of volunteers from the ranks of the woodcutters. They'll see standing guard as far easier work than cutting trees, which *could* be troublesome if they don't take the duty seriously. Of course, 'tis *our* job to see they *do*, and also that they know how to fight, if necessary."

Waters nodded. "Well said, Thomas. And I think you're the best man to train them."

Myllet said, "Good idea, Sir." He and Gibbes snickered as they jostled Smith.

Smith smirked at Myllet. "Some things never change."

Waters smiled. "Well, you *do* have the most experience training recruits."

He smiled. "Aye. Unfortunately, that is quite true; so I suppose I be your man, Sir."

"Good. Then let us choose the men and begin training today."

"Aye, sir."

Waters looked away, pondered for a moment. "I've another thought on our defense. What if each group of four guards had mixed weaponry—say two matchlocks and two longbows? Then they'd have the range and killing power of the muskets combined with the long range and high firing rate of the longbows. So while the musketeers were reloading, the two longbowmen could maintain fire at the same rate as the Powhatans; but because of the greater strength of our bows, they could do so from greater range than the Powhatans, thereby overcoming, or at least reducing, our vulnerability during matchlock reloading. What do you think?"

Myllet said, "Should help, Sir, as long as we're not vastly outnumbered." He nodded repeatedly. "Another advantage to it is that we can make new arrows from now until Christ's second coming, but we can only make shot until the lead runs out."

Smith Smiled. "What ho! Prithee listen to the brilliant ideas flowing from that ancient head."

Waters snickered. "Agreed. So let us effect this change immediately." Waters again paused, looked intently at each man. "I have a question for you. If you were the Powhatans, and you hated us and wanted to be rid of us, what would your strategy be?"

The three grinned slyly at one another. Myllet spoke. "Well, Sir, happens that the three of us discussed that very question after Lassie's burial, and we agreed the Powhatans have seen enough Englishmen come to know we intend to keep coming. So we think they plan to annihilate each group that comes; and we think what they did to Lassie was but the beginning—meant to scare us half to death, which it did. And we think they'll attempt to do more of the same, which means no single person, or even small group, is safe. We must *always* do what we're planning to do: have larger groups defended by enough firepower to deter attack. By the bye, several woodcutters and hunters have reported seeing what they thought were Savages watching them, though they weren't certain, saw only fleeting, ghostlike shadows in the brush. Precisely what one would expect from these Savages."

Waters nodded. "But at some point, if they mean to annihilate us, they'll have to attack in force; and to that point, the Chesapeakes say the Powhatans have many alliances which provide them more than enough warriors to handily do so. Therefore, a massed attack is my greatest concern; for in our current circumstances, I know not how we could withstand it." He fashioned a painted-on smile. "Any ideas?"

Myllet said, "We're of like mind, Sir; we discussed this as well." He paused, took a breath. "This resembles our situation in Holland, where we faced a greatly superior Spanish force. There we relied on deception to make the enemy *believe* we had far more men than we did. And it actually worked . . . for a while. We built extra campfires at night and conducted extra drills in plain sight during the day, but they eventually realized it was a ruse and attacked. Fortunately, our reinforcements arrived the second day of the battle, and we eventually won the field. And the delay in their attack, caused by our deception, was what saved our arses. But there were many frightening, uncertain moments along the way. So to your question, we think such a deception is, for now, our only hope against the Powhatans; but that brings us back to our fundamental weakness: too few men—soldiers *and* civilians. For if we're to create this illusion, we'll need to show the Powhatans more woodcutters cutting wood for more fires, more hunters, fisherman, and guards out doing their jobs in plain sight far more often." He wrinkled his brow. "And unfortunately, there's a further weakness: methinks Powhatans are better, smarter scouts than arrogant Spaniards are and won't be so easily deceived. Why, I'd even wager they already know our true strength, or lack of it."

Waters nodded with a frown. "Indeed, they may, Michael. A grim picture, painfully grim." He sighed, looked at the ground for a moment. "Still, we must hold on until Governor White returns, and that means resumption of palisades construction as soon as spring arrives. Then with more men and a fort around us, we'll perchance be able to not only deter a large attack but also repel one and possibly, just possibly, win the fight. Let us all think on this for a few days then talk again to see where we are. Said another way"—his eyes sparkled as he broke a sarcastic smile—"it remains for our fertile military minds to conceive a way out of the impossibly deep hole we're in, eh?" As he looked at each of them, he thought for a misplaced moment of his parents in England, then of Rebecca Roberts, who he prayed still waited patiently, lovingly for him. He saw her smiling at him, wondered if his eyes would ever behold her again, then wondered how quickly the Powhatans would grow bolder, attack larger groups.

Myllet pointed at Gibbes and Smith. "You two sluggards are overdue for a good idea. So get to work and save our skins."

Waters laughed. "Well, at least *our* morale is high. Let us now—oh, on that subject, how are the men? What's *their* morale? What do you see?" He looked at Myllet.

"A bit worse in the last ten days or so, same malcontents—Taverner, Dutton, Allen—but they seem a bit more open in their whining, mayhap finding a bit more sympathy with the others."

"Hmm. Anything that requires immediate action?"

"Close, but not yet." He pressed his lips together, tightened his gaze. "There *is* one thing." He took a contemplative breath. "I've several times noticed Tayler, a few of his friends, and Taverner engaged in guarded conversations." He looked at Gibbes and Smith. "Have you two seen anything?"

Smith nodded. "Aye, I have."

"I, as well," Gibbes said. "And they clammed up as soon as they saw me. Of course, Tayler *always* has his eyes on *me* for reasons you well know."

Waters nodded, as a quick chill slide down the back of his neck. "Useful information, Michael. May be something amiss. Watch them closely but subtly—Allen and Dutton, as well. If they're hatching something, we must be onto it and gather good evidence to damn them. Understood?" His mind sprang instinctively back to the day John White had departed for England. Just before he'd stepped onto the boat, White had waded back ashore, summoned him and Roger Baylye to the shoreline; he'd huddled closely with them, told them that shortly before they'd sailed from England, he'd met with Raleigh. White had then lowered his voice to a breathy whisper, said that Raleigh suspected that his arch competitor, Sir Francis Walsingham, had secretly engaged someone to undermine the colony and abet its failure. Raleigh had not stated why or whom he suspected; but because of Walsingham's forceful intervention when Hugh Tayler had been stricken from the ship's manifest, White had believed *Tayler* to be Walsingham's agent. So, Waters reasoned, perchance White was right, and perchance 'tis time for Baylye and me to reassess this suspicion. Then there's the other matter Raleigh had mentioned to White, also involving Tayler—a sticky one, indeed, and so serious and damning that it had to wait for White's return, hopefully with a warrant in hand and enough evidence to hang him. Waters considered disclosing both matters—one a suspicion, the other an apparent fact—to his sergeants but decided against it for the moment.

The three spoke in unison. "Aye, sir."

***

Roger Baylye and Lieutenant Waters ceased their whispering when the other Assistants, absent Thomas Colman, filed into Baylye's cottage. After the usual pre-meeting courtesies, Baylye said, "Gentlemen, let us begin." He took a deep breath, looked at each man with somber eyes and downturned lips. "You all either saw or heard of the discovery of James Lassie's remains this morning. So you know that what befell him was so gruesome it would have sickened King Henry's Master of Persuasion, who's better known as his Captain of Torture. What you may *not* know is that the arrows in Lassie's skull were Powhatan arrows, so we know they perpetrated this poor man's torture and death. This discovery, however, is far more significant than one man's demise. 'Tis significant because it further signals the intention of these Savages to destroy us. And with that introduction, I'd like Lieutenant Waters to present his plan for our survival; and gentlemen, make no mistake, nothing *less* than our survival is at stake here. Lieutenant?"

"Thank you, Governor." Waters presented the plan he and the sergeants had contrived, with the addendum that he'd already chosen four citizen augmentees. With seemingly clear understanding of the colony's dire circumstances, the Assistants quickly approved the proposal.

Baylye said, "Very well, gentlemen. Understand that we cannot suffer any lapse in vigilance. We suddenly find ourselves in a most desperate situation." He paused, drifted his gaze from man to man. "Another contributor to that desperation is our food supply. Now into winter, we're reasonably well supplied from the bay, but we remain deficient in our meat supply. We must, therefore, weather permitting, increase the number of hunting parties until we acquire adequate venison for the remainder of winter. So, Roger Prat, realizing you'll have to draw men from other tasks, I ask you to organize additional hunting parties with reliable leaders, to bring our deer harvest closer to what we need."

"God's teeth, Roger, I shall try but know 'twill be a daunting task; for we remain challenged by the large distance we must now travel to find game, much of it through unfriendly, dangerous territory. And that means we should probably be accompanied by even stronger guard contingents than what the lieutenant proposes."

Waters said, "What Master Prat says is true, but to do as he suggests will require an even greater number of civilian augmentees and will further decrease the basic labor force, though we clearly must eat before we can work. I should also say that we'll soon face a shortage of shot and powder and must take care to preserve enough of both to fight off a large frontal attack against the colony—perhaps more than one. So I suggest that, just as we plan to do with our armed escorts, we employ more longbows in the hunt. We can retrieve arrows that miss or strike, and make new arrows, but not so for lead and powder. Bows also offer the added benefit of silence, which should remedy the problem that constantly plagues us with matchlocks: scaring twenty deer away by shooting at one."

Baylye said, "A fine point, Lieutenant. So, Roger, see what you can do. Any more thoughts on this subject . . . anyone?"

No one spoke. "Good. Now to the next subject." Baylye cleared his throat, glanced furtively at Waters. "With great sorrow, I announce that Thomas Colman appears close to death. I know we shall all miss him, not only as a friend but also as a sound-thinking contributor to this council. Thus, we arrive yet again at the need to elect a new Assistant, and I now ask you for up to three nominations."

Roger Prat raised his hand. "I nominate John Stilman, a man of fine character and judgment."

Christopher Cooper said, "Second."

Thomas Hewet raised his hand. "I nominate Brian Wyles."

No one spoke.

Baylye said, "Is there a second?"

Cuthbert White said, "I'll second."

Baylye said, "Stilman and Wyles, both good men. Is there a third?"

William Willes said, "I nominate Hugh Tayler."

Thomas Stevens immediately seconded.

Baylye and Waters glanced at one another, then Baylye took a deep breath, looked at each man. "The Assistants shall now vote, treating Thomas Colman as an abstention, which gives us a total of eleven voters. I shall log each vote with a charred stick on this tablet of tree bark." He scratched an *S*, a *W*, and a *T* on a piece of white birch bark, turned to John Brooke, who stood to his immediate left. "John, you're first."

"I vote for Stilman."

After each Assistant had voted, the tally was three for Wyles, four for Stilman, and four for Tayler.

Baylye gave Waters another stoical look, studied the others, in turn, searched their eyes. "As you know, our procedures now call for a second vote, between Hugh Tayler and John Stilman. Since it appears we could have a close vote, 'twould be a good time for anyone with anything to say to do so."

Waters raised his hand. "Sir, I should like to repeat the caution I gave when we last voted on Master Tayler to be an Assistant. I have unfavorable information about him, which unfortunately, I remain unable to disclose. I also have persuasions from two impeccable sources against Master Tayler's character, persuasions that would cause any righteous man to vote nay. I apologize for my lack of presentable evidence, but I'm bound by duty at this time to say no more, so I ask that you place your faith in my judgment.

Willes and Stevens grumbled quietly, shook their heads.

Baylye said, "Do you gentleman wish to speak?"

Willes said, "Only to say that such unsupported allegations should not be permitted, and the lieutenant's words should be disregarded."

Baylye said, "Well, we shall leave that to the conscience of each man. Does anyone else wish to speak?" After a brief, uneasy silence, he said, "Then let us vote. I shall start to the right this time. He nodded at Christopher Cooper.

"I vote for Stilman."

Roger Prat said, "Stilman."

Thomas Stevens said, "Tayler."

With one vote remaining, the tally was five for Stilman and five for Tayler.

Baylye faced John Brooke for the deciding vote.

Waters' mind danced on the edge of panic. No surprise with Willes, Stevens, and Sampson, but White and Bright? Good men who'd never vote for Tayler unless . . . unless bribed or threatened. He looked at the pair, adjudged both faces wallowing in guilt. We've trickery at play here.

John Brooke hesitated, looked at Baylye, who looked back with desperate, pleading eyes. "I vote for"—he then glanced at Willes, who glared threateningly at him—"for Hugh Tayler."

Willes, Sampson, and Stevens smiled, slapped each other on the shoulder while White, Bright, and Brooke stared at the floor, seemed afraid to look at Baylye or anyone else.

Willes said, "So Hugh Tayler it shall be."

Baylye's face was red, his lips pressed firmly together. He raised his hand. "Wait a moment. As governor, I retain the ultimate decision-making authority, and I . . . I will *not* have Hugh Tayler as an Assistant."

Willes said, "But, Governor, a few weeks ago you promised you'd abide by the Assistants' vote on grave matters. You used the election of future Assistants as an example of such matters. Did you not say this? Do you now go back on your word?"

Baylye paled, looked flatly at Willes then hopelessly at Waters. He swallowed hard, looked back to Willes, hesitated. "No, I shall not go back on my word. Hugh Tayler will be our new Assistant."

* * *

The Panther stood to Wahunsunacock's right, faced the council, and held up James Lassie's scalp, which held Lassie's pierced finger-nails and toenails dangling like ornaments around its perimeter. "You watched this man die poorly—a screaming, begging coward unworthy of manhood, weaker than a young child of our people, unworthy of a warrior's piss. I say to you that this is the nature of these people. They lack courage; they lack honor; they are soft, filthy; they do not know how to fight; but above all, they fear us. And because they fear us, we will defeat them—defeat them in a way that discourages all whites from coming to our land again." Amid the council's nods and words of agreement, the Panther's mind drifted to Isna, imagined him bound to a tree and stripped as Lassie had been, women cutting his flesh with shells, his body burned with torches, his skin then stripped away, his guts spilled to the ground as he watched them fall, his limbs yanked from their sockets and burned on the fire before him, his eyes gouged out, and the head and torso roasted on the fire—all without screams of agony or fear, nothing but one piercing war cry. I know this man's courage, he thought. I shall give him the death he deserves, a brave warrior's death, and his courage will show all of the people that Kills-Like-the-Panther faces none but the greatest of enemies. And we will then honor this man's courage with a dance. His mind drifted to his young wife; but as he began to mentally caress her now-large belly, Wahunsunacock spoke.

"And does Kills-Like-the-Panther still believe we should attack these people in small bites and reduce them to a size we can destroy in force?"

He met the chief's gaze, nodded. "Yes, Great Leader." He turned and looked into the eyes of each man before him. "We should capture and kill any other foolish ones who stray from protection, and at the same time, watch the movements and behavior of those who gather their water and wood, and those who hunt our deer and take our fish. They do not know how to defend themselves; for they rely on the big sticks that bark, which take too much time to ready for a shot. So at the right time, when they again become lazy in their vigilance, we shall ambush one of these groups by showing ourselves and tempting them to shoot at us. We will then hide ourselves while their stones fly through the air; and when they've passed, and while they put new stones in their sticks, we shall attack them with bows, shooting them in the legs, arms, and face if they wear their hard shirts. We will finish them with clubs, hatchets, and knives, capture the ones they seek to protect, and bring them here for their deaths." He again drifted his eyes around the lodge, listened to the cries of assent. "But to make them fear us more, we will do this to a party of their women collecting water; and after we've killed their guards, we will bring them here to use for our pleasure and to produce our children, for as long as they remain alive. We will also place some of their clothes and light-colored hair outside the fort, so the whites will know we use their women. And this knowledge will fill them with anger toward us, but their anger will remain inside them and further demoralize them, for they know they cannot attack us." He restrained a smile as the council voiced enthusiasm.

Wahunsunacock nodded, then raised his hands for silence. "And when would Kills-Like-the-Panther make such an attack?"

"Before the half-moon of the cycle just begun, Great Leader."

The chief looked uncertain.

"I propose this because we are in the cold-air moons, and the white men will not expect an attack."

Wahunsunacock nodded, stood, raised his hands. "It shall be so."

The Panther nodded at the leader then turned and started to follow the others from the lodge. He had gone but a few steps when Wahunsunacock spoke his name. He stopped, looked back.

"Kills-Like-the-Panther, my trusted friend and advisor, I fear that more and more of these people will come to our land even as we kill them." He held his gaze on the Panther, but his eyes showed his mind to be deep within his thoughts. After a few seconds, he blinked, refocused his eyes on the Panther, and sighed. "The prophecy says that a people from the land of the Chesapeakes will destroy us."

"Yes, Great Leader."

"When the time comes to attack these white men in force, we must spare no one . . . including the Chesapeakes, who befriend them. And after we have rubbed *all* of them out, we will destroy every sign that they were ever here. For when the next white men come, they will look for these people and surely blame *us* if they find any trace of them in our territory. Even then, we must be prepared to fight them each time they invade us, until we finally convince them to stay away forever."

"You are wise, my chief. I will do as you say. And you are right; the Chesapeakes should also die, for they are unworthy allies. But I shall first use them to gain information about the whites. I shall be in their village, so I can watch the Whites, know their numbers and habits, even until the moment we turn on them." The Panther made a slight bow then turned, left the lodge.

As he walked across the village, each step found him more troubled about his plan, for *his* plan did not include killing *all* the white people. There was one he'd planned to spare, so she could be his second wife— she, the brave, young white girl he'd dreamed of and desired every day since the Roanoke attack, the one who'd aroused wild, new passions in him. So he would now have to devise a way to obey Wahunsunacock while somehow saving the girl for himself. A few steps later, a smile creased his lips. Wahunsunacock will honor my victory by giving me the girl to use as I wish; and then in respect for his great wisdom, I shall promise to kill her and burn her body if white men ever again come to our land. And though I will not wish this, I will do it.

***

Emily wore a heavy wool shawl and Shines a fur cape as the two sat silently on a mat beside the fire outside Shines' lodge, weaving baskets. The bases of the baskets were eight-inch-wide circles of thick, interwoven strips of corn stalk. Multiple rod-like pieces of vine were woven two inches apart into the bases, like spokes of a wheel, then bent upward into the desired vertical shape for their intended use and held in the proper form by succeeding layers of weaving material. Shines wove with thin strips of cornstalk, while Emily used long, thin sections of vine thinner than the rods. Emily stared intently, yet emptily, at her work; Shines regularly rotated her concerned gaze back and forth between her basket and Emily, as if waiting for her to speak. Suddenly, she took a deep breathe, set her basket on the mat, stared at Emily with a look that invited a response. After several seconds with no response, Shines said in English, "Em'ly makes no talk."

Emily continued working for a moment, finally looked up at Shines with a strained, fragile look that seemed ready to erupt into tears. She hesitated then spoke with her hands and a few English words. "I'm sorry, Shines. I worry about my father. I must return to him soon."

Shines replied with hand signs and a few English and Chesapeake words. "Em'ly thinks too much these days. Something else troubles her." She patted her heart. "Something hurts her here. Perhaps Em'ly will tell Shines, so Shines can help her be happy again."

Emily half smiled. "No, Shines. Shines cannot help Emily . . . no one can help her."

Shines shook her head. "Let Shines try."

Emily paused for a deep breath. "I can't . . . 'tis really nothing. I—" She saw Shines look at something behind her, glanced over her shoulder, saw Hugh Tayler approaching. A jolt of panic addled her mind. She whispered, "Shines, you should—"

"Good day, Emily," Tayler said.

She stood, whirled around to face Tayler. "Go away, Tayler. I've nothing to say to you."

"I must speak to you, Emily."

Emily's face flushed; her tight eyes glared with hate. "I said go away!" She glanced at Shines, who was easing slowly toward her lodge.

Tayler's look softened. "Emily, I . . . I apologize for what happened. I . . ."

Emily screamed hysterically, "Leave me! Leave me now! Do you not know what you've done to me?"

Tayler's eyes filled with remorse; his voice cracked. "I *do* know, and I deeply regret it." He swallowed hard. "Emily, please, I love you, and—"

"You've ruined my life, taken it from me, taken my soul, my honor, everything. Do you understand? I hate you! Go away, you wretched scum!" She looked for Shines, glanced around the village, saw several Chesapeakes and colonists watching. She backed away as Tayler approached. He reached for her shoulders; but she pushed him away, stepped back.

He lunged forward, seized her shoulders, pulled her close. As he looked into her eyes, he spoke quietly, fervently. "Emily, I'm sorry. I know 'twas wrong. I love you. I want you to marry me. 'Tis the right thing for both of us."

Emily twisted, tried to push away, screamed at him, "Let *go* of me! Someone help me! Damn you to hell! I hate you! I hate you! Let go of me!"

He pulled her closer.

Emily kicked his shins, again tried to push away.

He flinched, warped his face into an angry scowl, shook her twice, then a third time. "Emily, you *must* be with me. There's no other way. 'Twill preserve your honor. You must." His eyes suddenly refocused on something behind Emily; he slacked his grip.

Emily looked back over her shoulder, saw Isna approaching behind her at a fast walk, with vengeful eyes and his stone hatchet in hand. He motioned Tayler away with the hatchet, motioned again, raised it above his waist for a strike.

Tayler's face filled with terror; he released Emily, stepped backward, held his hands up as if to blunt a blow.

Isna stepped faster, closer.

Tayler stumbled, nearly fell, caught his balance, turned, and ran toward the village. Halfway there, he stopped, glanced back at Isna for a moment, then resumed his hasty retreat.

Isna turned to Emily, stared at her with sorrowful, aching eyes that begged her to speak.

Emily, still as a sculpture, tried to speak, couldn't. Want to hold him, kiss him, cry, die in his arms, escape my sorrow and despair. She stood as still as a hot summer night, felt her eyes fill with tears, her heart melt, burn like boiling water. Must hold him, feel him in my arms again. Lord, let me die now, can't move, can't do anything. Unworthy, ashamed. She spoke in Lakota. "Isna, go away. Emily never wants to see Isna again. Leave her . . . now . . . please!"

He said nothing, held his ground, his anguished stare.

Tears rolled down Emily's cheeks; her body trembled. She whispered in English, "Oh, Isna, please, I beg you, my love, go before I die of sorrow and a broken heart. I cannot bear to see you. I love you, I love you, I love you."

Slowly, he turned, started to walk away; stopped, looked back at her with pleading eyes, spoke a silent message; then turned and walked into the forest.

Emily stared after him for a moment then dropped to her knees, sat back on her heels, and buried her face in her hands.

A moment later, Shines knelt beside her; she touched her gently, pulled her close with both arms, and whispered softly as Emily wept, trembled, abandoned her composure.

* * *

Thomas Colman's eyes opened slowly, had a dull, spent look as they feebly focused on Emily as she entered the cottage. He lay on his side on the dirt floor, several feet from his bed, unmoving, gasping for air as if suffocating.

Upon seeing him, Emily dropped her shawl on the floor, rushed to him, knelt; she rolled him onto his back, held her hand under his head. "Come, Father, I must get you back on your bed."

He mouthed words, but none came forth.

Emily shook her head, leaned her ear next to his mouth as he tried again.

Faint whispers came in labored, broken phrases. "Emily . . . you're here . . . can die . . . peace with . . . God . . . saw . . . Mother . . . told her . . . sorry . . . for leaving . . . her . . . she smiled . . . kissed me . . . said I . . . could go . . . if God . . . called me . . . ooooooh . . . so tired."

"Rest, Father."

"No time . . . told . . . your brother . . . sorry . . . left him . . . never . . . knew him . . . love . . . him." He closed his eyes, took three gasping, gurgling breaths. "Now . . . goodbye . . . my Emily . . . dear Emily . . . love you . . . so."

Emily whispered, "I love *you*, Father. Must tell you how sorry I am for—"

"No time . . ." He smiled faintly. "We . . . had . . . good times . . . some bad . . . most good . . . love you . . . survive." He closed his eyes again, gasped a few more times. "Pistol . . . powder . . . shot . . . in bag . . . you know . . . how to use . . . protect yourself." He grasped her arms, looked into her eyes. "Emily . . . marry . . . Hugh . . . now . . . fine . . . husband . . . give you . . . children."

Emily closed her eyes, lowered her face to his shoulder. Oh, Father, thank heaven you shall never know.

"So glad . . . you met . . . him . . . protect you . . . promise . . . now . . . marry him . . . Emily . . . promise . . . promise . . . now . . . please."

Emily's thoughts whirled in confusion; she shook her head; tears dripped from her cheeks onto his chest. "No, Father, I cannot. You do not know what you ask me to do."

He again gripped her arms, looked feebly, pitifully into her eyes; his breath quickened. "Emily . . . Emily . . . now . . . please . . . promise . . . marry him."

"Father"—she wailed, covered her face with her hands—"do not force me to do this. Please, I beg you. I . . . I . . ."

"Now . . . Emily . . . please."

How often and easily she'd defied him, refused his bidding, but all that had evaporated with the life force that seeped steadily and rapidly from his body. "Father, I cannot. Please! God save me." She paused, closed her eyes. "Yes, Father, I will marry him." She lowered her head, tried to expel the despair that smothered her mind.

He gasped, gasped again.

Emily's eyes snapped open; she cradled his head.

His wide, desperate eyes gazed into hers; he squeezed her arms, shook with a violent tremor, released a long, flowing breath, then lay silent and still.

Emily stared at him, her mind and body numb, stunned, racked with anguish and guilt. "Go to God, Father . . . and God save me." She reached across her chest, gently pulled one hand then the other from her arms, looked into his vacant eyes. "Goodbye, Father. I love you." She touched his eyelids, eased them closed, then leaned her head on his chest, wept quietly. *Oh, God, what will become of me? Mayhap I should end my wretched life now.*

After a long while, she sat up. Too drained to think, she stared numbly at his lifeless body until her mind drifted to comforting, youthful memories of them together, memories that had been lost for years. They came in quick glimpses, made her smile: her father carrying her on his shoulders; hugging her after she'd cut her knee on a cobblestone street; showing her how to prepare the soil for planting; teaching her the gentleness owed by human beings to all other beings; holding her on his lap while the family sang Christmas carols; showing her how to pray, how to talk to God directly without the clergy; teaching her his appreciation of the simple joys of life, the land, its creatures, being alone; and lastly, showing her, by example, the value of honor and integrity.

Despair suddenly tore at her heart as she wondered what value such memories and lessons would have in the life that awaited her—a life of shame and dishonor, without love or hope. She looked down at his motionless body. *I promised you I'd marry a man I hate, which is the same as being a whore, yet I already am a whore and condemned to hell. But I shall have a child to love and raise despite the sin of its conception.* A faint smile creased her lips. *And I shall love it with all my heart. Will it be a boy or a girl? Who will it look like? Me, or Mother, or Father?* Her smile abruptly faded as she remembered the apology she'd been unable to give. *'Twill haunt me all my days, and—*

Someone knocked on the door; Emily whispered, "Who is it?"

"Elyoner."

"Oh, Ellie, Ellie, come in." She stood, rushed to the door as Elyoner entered, stopped a foot from her.

Elyoner glanced at Thomas Colman then at Emily's gaunt, teary face.

Emily nodded then lunged to Elyoner's waiting arms.

"Oh, my Em, my dear Em. What you've endured."

* * *

Three inches of snow lay on the ground in the Chesapeake village as Isna and the other Lakota sat around a modest fire inside their lodge. Isna stared into its blue heart, oblivious to the animated discussion beside him. He'd done little that day but mull the incident with the white man and Emily, try to mold what he'd seen into something he could understand and act upon. But the ache of seeing Emily with another man, particularly one who'd touched her and appeared to mistreat her, had hung sourly and heavily in the pit of his stomach like the aftermath of a bad meal. When he finally pushed his pain to the background, he wondered what had occurred between Emily and the white man, what had caused Shines to seek him out, summon him to help her. She'd told him Emily needed him, but hadn't said why. He'd then seen the man seize Emily's shoulders, shake her, speak rudely to her. The remembrance quickened his heart, enflamed his anger. He'd seen Emily scream at the man, kick him, try to escape; had decided at that moment, to kill him and would have, had he not released Emily and backed away.

Certainly, this man was trying to force her to listen to him, hear something she didn't want to hear, do something she didn't want to do. Certainly, she dislikes him; for she screamed at him, tried to push him away. And *most* certainly, there is something between them, perhaps something deep, deeper than Isna will know from afar. And why does she suddenly avoid Isna, tell him to leave her, never see her again, but then shed tears of sadness even as she commands him away? What did she say to Isna in her own tongue? Perhaps something she felt inside, in her mind or her heart, that she didn't want Isna to hear. These things . . . these things fit together like a great bear with the head of a deer and legs of the little white four-legged that hops.

He poked the fire with a long stick, laid another log on top. And this white man . . . is he not a weak, troubled one, one with an evil fire burning within him? For none but a self-doubting coward forces his will on a woman. His gaze hardened; he pressed his lips together as he saw Emily's tearful face, felt the now-familiar ache in his heart. Emily, the little white fawn who forever owns Isna's heart. Emily, who cries even as she sends Isna away. Isna's heart burns for you, my little one, and his mind and senses tell him that even as you push him away, you need him desperately in a way not yet understood by either Emily *or* Isna.

He took a bite of smoked fish, glanced at the others without hearing their words, then looked back into the fire, saw Emily's anguished, pleading look as she spoke to him in English. Is it not true that a woman will often say the opposite of what she feels? And is it not also true that she will do this most when something pains her deep in her heart . . . or when she hides something . . . or protects someone from something? And is it not so that her *true* heart can be read in her face like one reads the signs of the forest . . . as when Emily speaks to Isna in Lakota, tells him to leave her, then speaks something in her own tongue while tears flow like a river from her eyes. And when those eyes, the deepest color of the sky, tell Isna she wants to hold him, feel his heart beat with hers, feel his strength, his love, does she not at that moment bare the truth in her heart? Can Isna not read these signs as clearly as he reads the trail of a deer or an enemy? And when she shows Isna these things, does she not tell him without speaking it that a great pain dwells within her—a pain she believes she must bear alone, a pain she fears telling Isna of, a pain she does not know Isna will gladly bear with her, help her lessen, help her destroy? And does she not shield Isna from this pain or perhaps fear it will force him away? His look suddenly relaxed, softened, as if some reassuring thought had taken hold of his mind; a slight smile creased his lips. Emily's love for Isna lives . . . Isna's love for *Emily* lives and will always live. Isna must discover her pain, help her place it on the pathway behind her, help her know that his heart burns for her and that he will love her forever, no matter what befalls her or him, and that he will willingly give his life for her. And as surely as only the rocks live forever, this evil one who is without honor is the cause of her pain. And if so, he will know a Lakota death, and Isna's hand will deliver it. He took another bite of fish then a swig of water, again stared into the soul of the fire.

Shines is her friend. She knows white women, knows some of their words. Would it not be wise for Isna to talk to Shines, learn what she knows of Emily's heart and her pain, and *then* find Emily and know *her* mind? And would it not also be wise for Isna to watch this evil one? His mind churned for a moment as he tried to consider arguments against his plan, but he soon shook his head. No, these things Isna must do.

* * *

The naked, towering trees at the edge of the forest beside the graveyard rose starkly above the snow, rendered a gloomy feel to the small, pole-fenced plot and its nine graves. The melting snow had left the ground soft and muddy, particularly in the grassless graveyard; and while a steady, misty rain relentlessly consumed what remained of the snow and worsened the gloomy atmosphere, Elyoner and Emily, their hooded wool capes already heavy with water, held hands, huddled together beside Thomas Colman's grave.

Graveyards had never bothered Emily, but this one was different. The wintry gloom and her intimacy with two people at rest in *this* graveyard magnified her grief and discomfort as she glanced between her father's grave and that of baby Henry Harvie. She'd visited Henry every day before the rape, but her condition and that of her father had since precluded such visits, a negligence that pained her when she thought of it. She relived her father's last anguished moments, the promise she'd resisted but known was inevitable. Thin tears, masked by the now-pouring rain, filled her bloodshot eyes as she looked at Elyoner with a despairing look. "Ellie, what's to become of us?"

Elyoner sighed, shook her head. "None but the Lord knows that, my friend. But I fervently pray Father returns with the first breath of spring."

"Aye to that. Have you ever—oh!" Emily abruptly clutched her stomach, took several deep breaths.

"What is it, Em?"

Three more quick breaths. "I'm fine. Just . . . just a sudden cramp."

Elyoner smiled. "Oh, is it your time?"

Emily looked at her with guilty eyes, quickly lowered her gaze. "Yes." She hesitated then looked up at Elyoner. "No, Ellie, 'tis actually *not* my time. Ellie?"

Elyoner shed her smile, frowned at her. "Yes, Em."

Emily hesitated then shook her head. "Sorry, I . . . I don't know what I was thinking." She took another deep breath, clutched her abdomen again, felt a wave of nausea rising to her throat, turned away.

"Emily Colman. Pray tell, what is wrong with you? By the saints, you are quite obviously *not* well. What ails you?"

"Nothing ails me. Why do you hound me like an old crone with nothing better to do?" Her eyes immediately saddened; her lower lip protruded like a pouting child's. She took a deep breath, exhaled slowly. "Forgive me, Ellie. That was most cruel of me. I didn't mean it at all. I'm truly sorry." She shook her head. "You're right, I am *not* myself. I should leave." She turned, started to walk away.

Elyoner grasped her wrist, gently restrained her. "Emily Colman, this is not about your father. Something else is gravely wrong, but I can't help you unless you tell me what it is. Truly, lass, your milk has withered, and you're someone other than yourself, and I've seen you look and act as if . . . as if you're in a condition I know you can't be in. I see quite clearly that something is wrong. So please tell me what it is." She waited expectantly, but Emily said nothing. She assumed a stern pose, spoke as if scolding a child. "Very well then. I heard there was an incident in the Chesapeake village, an incident with you and Hugh Tayler, and then Isna. I heard 'twas quite unsightly: that you screamed at Tayler, that he seized you and shook you, and that Isna approached him, threatened him by his very presence, and drove him away."

Emily stared at her with a horrified look, covered her mouth with her hands.

"And then you spoke to Isna in his language then in English, but no one heard what you said."

Emily began to tremble, felt herself unraveling toward hysteria.

"Then Isna walked away, you fell to your knees and wept, and Shines came to you and comforted you."

Emily sniffled, rubbed her eyes. "Ellie, Ellie." She pulled herself into Elyoner's arms. "I don't know what to do. I'm so confused, so afraid." The rain intensified, splashed off their hoods and shoulders.

Elyoner closed her eyes, hugged Emily, rocked her back and forth, then whispered softly to her as if she were a child, "Em, my dear Em, you must let me help you. Please tell me what destroys you so." Neither spoke until Elyoner held her lips to Emily's ear, whispered over the roar of the rain, "Emily Colman is a woman of great strength, and she *will* persevere and overcome her trials. But first, she must share her burden with her dearest friend. Please, Em, let me help you. And since I already know what happened in the Chesapeake village, pray begin there. What was Tayler doing? Why did you scream at him?" Emily remained silent. "You told him to leave, asked him if he knew what he'd done to you. Emily, what did he do to you? Did he . . . did he force himself on you that day in the forest?"

Emily covered her face with her hands, turned away, sank to her knees in the mud. "Noooooo . . ." My God, Mother, I so want to tell her. How can I bear this?

"Then what *did* he do?"

Emily sat crouched, shivering in the mud and rain.

"Please, Emily, release your burden; tell me what happened!"

"I can't!"

"So he *did* do something."

No answer.

"Emily, you *must* tell me." She shook her head as rain dripped off her nose. "There's but one thing that could upset you like this. So I'll ask again, did he . . . did he force himself on you?" Elyoner dropped to her knees beside her, put her arm around her, leaned close to her ear. "Emily, did he *rape* you?"

Emily screamed through a sudden rush of tears, "No, Ellie! No. He didn't. Now leave me alone. I don't want to talk anymore. I must go." *Lord, make her leave me.*

"You're lying to me, Emily Colman. I know you are. You're hiding the truth. He did something terrible to you and has scared you into silence. And by the saints above, I shall find out what it is and make him pay. Rape is a capital offense, and if it has happened to my dearest friend, there will be hell to pay. That I promise." A flash of alarm swept Elyoner's face. "Emily? Are you . . . are you with child?"

Emily moaned softly then whispered with a submissive, quavering voice, "Ellie, please leave me alone. Please, I implore you. Don't ask me this."

Elyoner knelt in the mud beside her, put her arm around her; gently pushed her wet, matted tangles of hair aside, brushed the dripping rain and mud from her face; pulled her close, kissed her cheek. "My dearest Emily, you *cannot* bear this alone. I know what's happened; your silence confirms it. And I shall do something about it."

Emily opened distraught, desperate eyes. "No, Ellie. You mustn't do anything or say anything to anyone. Promise me, please, Ellie. Much depends on it." *Lord, make her listen.*

Elyoner looked at her with wondering eyes and parted lips.

"Please, Ellie. Promise me."

Elyoner held her look and her silence, finally said, "Very well, Em. I promise, but 'tis only for today. This is not the end of it. I *shall* be an old crone, and hound you until you tell me what's happened and let me help. Do you hear me, Emily Colman?"

Emily sniffled. Her voice was a weak, broken whisper. "Yes . . . I hear you."

"Now I've something to tell you."

Emily looked at her with hopeless eyes.

"I talked to Shines today. She's difficult for me to understand, but she told me to tell you that Isna talked to her, that his heart is sick with love for you, and he doesn't understand why you turned away from him. She also said he knows some great pain afflicts you, and he would help you bear it and place it behind you no matter what it is or what it takes."

Emily again planted her face in her muddy hands, shrieked, "Ellie, I love him!" Her body trembled wildly. "I can't live without him . . . but I cannot face him."

"Yes, you can, Emily. And you must. You must go to him. He loves you, and he's shown himself to be the only man in this world worthy of you. He's certainly changed my notion of . . . of these people *we* call Savages." Elyoner leaned down, again pulled Emily close, kissed her cheek. "Emily, you must go to him."

"I can't, Ellie. I can't, ever. I'm so ashamed, so unworthy. Oh, Ellie, what am I do? My life, my hopes, everything, all of it gone."

"You can't speak like this, lass. Whatever's happened was not your fault, and you bear no shame or dishonor for it. You must purge such notions from your mind." She shook her head. "We shall cross this river together. Now come with me. We're soaked to our bones. Let us escape this rain to my house. And I want you to move in with us immediately."

Emily shook her head. "No, Ellie. I can't. 'Twould be a terrible intrusion."

"Now you listen, little sister. Though you hide it and deny it, I've no uncertainty what's befallen you. And what's befallen you is the most pressing reason to do as I say. So if you lack the good sense to care for yourself, I shall provide it; and you, Mistress Colman, are coming to live in my house. And that is final!"

Emily rubbed her eyes, smeared mud over her cheeks and forehead. "Ellie, there's something I must tell you."

Elyoner leaned back with a skeptical look.

"Father's last words were a plea—a desperate plea—that I marry Hugh Tayler."

"No, Emily."

"Ellie, I refused him again and again, but he persisted, *begged* me, almost with his dying breath, and . . . and Ellie, I *had* to say *yes*."

"No, Em."

"Yes. I'd no choice."

"Em, you *do* have a choice. You don't love Tayler; and if he's done what I fear he's done, marrying him will only worsen things. Trust me, sister. You'll only condemn yourself to misery and pain." She placed her hands on the sides of Emily's head, pulled her close, focused intently on her eyes. "You love Isna not Tayler. Do not do this to yourself. Denounce Tayler; go to Isna."

She looked at the ground. "But, Ellie, I promised Father even as he died!"

"God forgives promises forced by threat or duress . . . and you are most certainly under both. You've no obligation to honor that promise."

"You don't understand. I've no choice. If I don't do as . . . Ellie, I must marry him."

"Do as what?"

"Nothing."

Elyoner shook her head. "Em . . . 'tis wrong as wrong can be. But enough! You're a muddy mess. To my house and dry clothes. I want you near me . . . at least for the remainder of this day and night. So come now, 'tis time to feed Virginia. We shall continue this later."

* * *

Ananias greeted them as they entered the cottage. "Ah, you've returned, ladies. Looks as if you've been bathing in the mud. I despise this damnable rain. Reminds me of home." He took a breath, looked somberly at Emily. "Em . . . again . . . my deepest sympathy. Thomas was such a fine man and an incomparable friend. The Assistants will truly suffer his absence." He shook his head. "I'm sure you've heard Hugh Tayler's been elected to replace him."

Emily and Elyoner glanced at one another with evident surprise.

"I know Thomas thought a lot of Hugh, as you do, but I must confess I've never been comfortable with the man. Something doesn't feel right about him. Have you ever had that perception of someone?"

Emily tensed, struggled to retain her composure; Elyoner scowled.

Ananias saw both, offered an innocent look. "What did I say? I appear to have upset both of you somehow. Please forgive me if I have. I was only trying to—"

Elyoner shook her head. "Please continue, Ananias."

"Very well. As we went into the election, there were quite strong feelings for and against Tayler; but the grand surprise was that Cuthbert White, John Brooke, and John Bright all voted *for* him, when all three were known to previously be *against* him. So Waters, Baylye, and I discussed it afterward and verily, could think of no reason why they would vote for Tayler and against Stilman. But I will tell you that all three looked ready to crawl out of their skins for fear of something; and Waters suggested that mayhap there was bribery or some sort of intimidation at play, either by Tayler or his cohorts: Stevens, Willes, and Sampson." He shook his head. "He also said he and a few of his men know very disquieting things about Tayler; but he couldn't divulge the details, which frankly, makes me suspect there's a very long thread to this tale, and all we've seen is the first inch of it."

The color fled Emily's face like dissipating fog. *Waters must know: Walsingham, the conspiracy, even that Hugh's the leader. So Johnny spoke the truth, and Waters has the sound judgment to remain silent until the right moment. And meanwhile I, Emily Colman, have sworn to marry the head conspirator. Dear Lord, save me. I know not what to do.*

Elyoner grabbed Emily's wrist, led her to the fire. "Emily, you're pale and tottery again. Please sit down."

Emily nodded, sat shakily on a stump stool, then looked blankly at Ananias while her mind rambled in circles.

Ananias said, "Well, I have to say the whole affair rather upset me; for I'm told Tayler has outlandish ideas on how things should be done, such as less work for us and more for the Chesapeakes. 'Tis as if he's completely blind to the history of English expeditions in Virginia. And at this point, being an astute husband, I can see my presence is unneeded, and you two have something important to discuss without my counsel." He stood, lifted his coat and hat from the table, and walked toward the door. "So I shall bid you farewell and cast myself out into the rain. Oh, one other thing. There was an incident this morning. Seems that someone caught a Savage—a Chesapeake man—stealing something from his house. We're to have a meeting momentarily to decide how to deal with the situation, and plainly, our decision could have vast implications. Also, 'twill be Tayler's first meeting and an opportunity to gauge him and his judgment directly." A resigned look appeared on his face as if he'd suddenly reached a momentous conclusion. "But truthfully, we do owe the man a fair chance to show his capabilities and intellect, or lack thereof, without prejudging him. So, with that great observation, I bid you adieu." He bowed, put on his coat and hat, and walked out the door.

Emily looked despondently at Elyoner. "I must leave, as well, Ellie."

"Em, I think you should sleep here tonight and reconsider moving in with us. Ananias and I have discussed it, and he's quite comfortable with the idea."

Emily shook her head. "I cannot, Ellie."

Elyoner's look hardened. "You challenge my patience, little sister, and I remain direly concerned about you. Please be wise in your decisions; and, Em, please, please, forget your promise to your father. He himself would release you from it if he were here and knew the truth. Forsooth, he'd no doubt be the first to call for prosecuting and punishing the filthy swine."

Emily battled rising tears as she hugged Elyoner. "Thank you, dear Ellie. See you on the morrow." She turned, flung her cape over her shoulders, started for the door, then abruptly stopped, looked back at Elyoner. "Oh, I nearly forgot. Ellie, because of the experience of caring for my baby brother, I think you should no longer leave Virginia alone as you're accustomed to doing. She's old enough to . . . to get herself into trouble if she isn't watched. So I think you or I or Ananias, or someone else you trust, like Emme, should always be with her. 'Tis very important, and I know of which I speak."

"Well, I hadn't thought about it, but I suppose you're right. Still, we're all so busy . . . I don't know how we'd find time to watch a sleeping child . . . even my precious Virginia."

***

Emily didn't want to answer the knock on her door. Nor did she want to tell whoever it was to enter. So she held her silence, hoped they'd go away. They knocked again, then again. Still she held her silence, rubbed the tears from her eyes, looked back into the fire, and wondered who it could be at such a late hour. Another knock. She stood, walked to the door.

"Who is it?"

" 'Tis Hugh, Emily. I must speak with you."

Emily bristled, remained silent.

"Emily, may I please speak with you?"

"Go away, Hugh. I've nothing to say to you."

He spoke with a soft, contrite tone. "Emily, I beseech you, please hear me for a brief moment."

No response.

"Please, Emily."

No response.

His voice was a near whisper. "Emily . . . I am deeply saddened by your father's passing. And I know this is a terribly difficult time for you. I do not wish to add to your sorrow. Please believe me."

"I believe nothing you say, Hugh Tayler."

"You've every right to feel that way, and what I did grieves my soul. I'm truly ashamed, and I know I've stolen what you valued most in life. And in so doing, I've cast you into a different world: a hopelessly unforgiving world that will wrongfully condemn you, hold what happened between us against you, and forever deny you the decent life you would otherwise have enjoyed and truly deserve. 'Tis my doing, and I deeply regret it."

Emily closed her eyes, bowed her head. 'Tis true, and I'm now but a whore.

"And my transgression places upon me the obligation to care for you, an obligation I gladly accept and will faithfully execute. There's truly no other way for you, Emily." He paused for a moment. "And I am certain you will learn to love me. Also, it should be of no small consequence to you that my family is wealthy, and you will share that wealth and want for nothing."

Emily sat on her stump, pressed her face to her hands; she wanted to cry but couldn't.

"Emily, I felt your pleasure when we made love, and—"

"Fie, Hugh Tayler! We did *not* make love. You raped me."

"Nay, Emily. It may have begun that way, but I felt your passions rise, felt your climax with all the ecstasy of my own. So I *know* you can love me."

Emily seethed with anger, frustration, then guilt as his words seeped into her mind. I *did* feel pleasure. Didn't want to, but I did; and so I *am* a whore, a slut, a sinner, condemned to hell. So why then, though I hate him, should I not marry the man who fathered my child, so it will have a name, a father . . . and at the same time rescue myself from the shame of being shunned by respectable men because I'm not a virgin? She thought of her father, her mother, Isna, Elyoner. I've failed you all; but from now forward, what choice have I if my baby and I are to have a life?

"So, Emily, please marry me now, as soon as we can arrange it with the governor. 'Tis truly best for both of us, and you will not regret it."

She hesitated then started to speak, held her words. No escape. My tragedy is inescapable. She sighed, whispered slowly, quietly, "I shall marry you, Hugh . . . but I shall *never* love you; rather, I shall hate you to the end of my days for what you've done." And you shall not know of your child until I can no longer hide its presence within me; and then I shall tell you 'tis from another, that 'twas conceived after the rape, and after our marriage.

"I love you, Emily. And despite what you think, I shall always love you, and I shall be a perfect husband to you."

Silence.

"Emily, will you please open the door and let me see you? I desperately need to hold you in my arms. Please, since we are now to be married."

She jerked the door open, glared at him with venomous eyes.

"May I kiss my bride to be?"

"If you must."

He leaned forward, laid his hands gently on her shoulders; kissed her softly on her cheek, her neck, then her lips; eased his tongue inside her mouth, found hers, teased it gently then firmly. He lowered his hands to her waist then suddenly shrank back, looked into her eyes, and slowly shook his head. "Emily, you arouse my passions and fuel the fires of my heart. I must lie with you again . . . soon . . . even now, this very night. And I ask you, what would be the wrong of it? Our marriage is consummated. Let us begin our life together, here, now." He caressed her sides, started to draw her close.

Emily stiffened; her eyes filled with panic. "No, Hugh, not here, not now." But the marriage *is* consummated, and I *am* pregnant with his child. So the marriage *is* but a formality. And is a wife not bound to do her husband's will even as she loathes doing so? And am I not already condemned? Her mind flailed in a sea of guilt like someone who can't swim trying to float in deep water. She looked at him with a resolute but not unkind look. "Please, Hugh, not yet. My father's death still weighs heavy on my mind. I need more time. This is all too fast."

He sighed, thought for a moment. "I understand, but, Emily, prithee remember the promise I made to you that day in the forest. Regrettably, it must remain in place." He looked sternly into her eyes. "I know you understand and will do what is necessary to protect that beautiful child."

Scum! I know you'll do as you say, but perchance I can delay this. "Hugh, I cannot yet do as you wish. Besides my grief, 'tis my time of the month. Truly, I am ill, and . . . and I'm"—she made her herself blush,

look pained, anxious, embarrassed to be speaking of such things—
"certain you understand my hesitance?"

His face paled; he fidgeted, swallowed twice. "Yes, I understand."
He nodded repeatedly. "We shall wait, and meanwhile I shall visit
Governor Baylye and inform him of our intention to marry with all
haste." He leaned forward, kissed her sealed lips, bowed, said, "Be well,
Emily, my love," and departed.

Emily closed the door, walked to her stump, sat; she stared dry-eyed
into the fire, saw Isna's face, his longing, sorrowful look. Isna, my love,
I love you, I love you, I love you. How I wrong you. How can I betray
you so? Please forgive me.

* * *

Baylye said, "Come in, Master Tayler." He pointed at a stump then
sat on another beside it.

Tayler sat, glanced around the room, looked anxiously at Baylye.
"Well, Governor?"

Baylye pursed his lips, stared at Tayler for a moment. "Master Tayler,
I'm afraid I've disappointing news for you. I've received information
that prohibits my marrying you to anyone."

Tayler stood, glared at Baylye. "Devil take you, Baylye. What in hell
do you mean? You can't do that! And pray tell, who speaks against me,
and why are they not here to speak their lies to my face?"

"They *are* here, Master Tayler." He glanced at the door. "Gentlemen,
please come in."

Lieutenant Waters and his three sergeants entered the cottage,
stood in a half circle facing Tayler and Baylye.

Baylye said, "Please inform Master Tayler of the reasons."

Waters nodded at Baylye then Myllet, who studied Tayler with a
loathsome look as he began to speak. "Master Tayler, you well know
what I've spoken against you, but I shall repeat it. After the shipwreck,
you forcefully pulled Robert Wilkinson from the board to which he
clung, so you could save yourself, and you then watched him drown.

'Twas no less than murder, Master Tayler, and I witnessed it as I swam toward that same board—a board large enough for all three of us to have safely survived the night. I suspect you would have tried to drown me, as well, were I not a soldier and armed. And mark me well, had more eyes than my own seen your crime, you'd have been long since hung for what you did."

Tayler leered at him. "That's a lie, Myllet. I did no such thing. You simply want to ruin me. 'Tis your word against mine and nothing to do with marriage." He looked at Baylye. "What else have you, *Governor*?"

Baylye said, "Forget not, Sir, that 'tis against the law for me to knowingly marry someone of low character; and albeit 'tis his word against yours, Sergeant Myllet's accusation raises serious doubt about your character." He nodded at Gibbes while Tayler stewed, held his silence.

Gibbes said, "Master Tayler, as you are aware, I know most of the despicable things you've done in your shameful life, so you shouldn't be surprised that I know you abandoned a wife and two children in England."

Tayler's eyes and nostrils flared; his breath quickened as tiny beads of sweat formed on his forehead. "Damn you, Gibbes. I've no wife or children, and you're naught but a lying scoundrel who wants to destroy me and has made a crusade of attempting to do so."

"I wish not to destroy you, Master Tayler, for you're doing that quite well on your own. I seek only justice."

Tayler quickly faced Baylye. "Again, 'tis my word against his, so his testimony is without merit. Is this the best you can do, Baylye?"

"We've not finished."

Waters said, "In addition to Sergeant Gibbes, Sergeants Smith and Myllet, and I myself, know of the family you've abandoned in England, also that you abandoned them a considerable time before we sailed for Virginia and successfully eluded the authorities who sought to hold you responsible before we sailed."

Smith and Myllet nodded.

Waters said, "Do you still deny this?"

Tayler scowled. "I can see you've all conspired against me, so it matters not what I say. You all clearly seek to deny me the pleasure of marrying Mistress Colman, an event both she and I deeply desire. Could it be you're jealous of the favor she shows me?" He recaptured his sneer as if his insinuation had bolstered his confidence.

Baylye said, "Mistress Colman is a fine young woman of the strongest character and kindness. And from what we know of you, Hugh Tayler, 'tis impossible to understand why she would favor you over *any* rival, under *any* circumstance, unless illicitly compelled to do so. But before you leave, there is yet another grave charge against you." He again nodded at Waters.

Waters walked to within six inches of Tayler, leaned closer, glared into his eyes. "Before he returned to England, Governor White told Master Baylye and me that there is yet *another* active warrant for your arrest back in England."

Tayler paled, looked ready to vomit; he spoke weakly, without his usual bravado. "For what?"

"For the rape and murder of the wife of a friend of yours. Governor White informed us that as we sailed from England, your former friend arrived on the dock and pleaded with him to stay the departure until the magistrate, who was on his way to the ship, arrived with the warrant and removed you to prison. Governor White agreed to do so and directed the pilot, Fernandez, to hold the vessel in place, but Fernandez ignored the order and hastily set sail." A sudden chill raced down Waters' spine. How had he missed this? A volley of questions he'd never thought to ask suddenly burst into his mind like a band of frightening apparitions: Why had Walsingham intervened when White wanted to remove Tayler from the manifest? Why did Fernandez blatantly disobey the governor to protect Tayler, a man wanted for murder? Why, on the voyage, did he try to elude and then abandon the flyboat, which carried part of the colony's supplies and people? Why, when we stopped at that bountiful island on the last leg of the voyage, did he not allow us to take on the additional supplies we needed? And lastly, why did he abandon the colony at Roanoke, a place of known hostility and danger, instead of bringing it to Chesapeake as mandated by the charter? The questions churned in his mind like vultures circling their prey. You fool, Waters. 'Tis plain as a portrait. Walsingham, Tayler, Fernandez— all together in a plot to undermine the colony, ensure its failure. God's teeth, man, Governor White said it all in a single breath, and we never tied it together. Fernandez was there in plain sight all the while, the stage setter of the conspiracy. So now what, Waters? Stay mum, that's what, lest we scare Tayler from making the move we need to hang him. 'Twill indeed be more difficult now that he knows we're onto him, but mayhap he won't suspect we know of the conspiracy.

Tayler meticulously leered at each man in the room. "Governor White's a liar. He hates me and will do anything to discredit anyone he sees as a competitor or threat."

Waters said, "And why would Governor White consider *you* a competitor or a threat?"

"Because . . . because . . ." He scowled. "If you know so much and have sound cases, why do you not arrest me and prosecute them? I know why, and so do you—because they're contrived and without merit."

Baylye said, "I think not, Master Tayler. The true answer is that because those alleged crimes occurred in England, 'twould be illegal to arrest you without the due process of the warrants in hand. And while we *are* in a condition of martial law here, where I can legally hear and judge cases committed *within* the colony, I may *not* do so with regard to alleged crimes committed *outside* the colony. So we will wait until Governor White returns with the two warrants and *then* arrest and prosecute you. And meanwhile where will you escape to? The Powhatan village? I think you'd find their measure of justice considerably more painful than ours."

Tayler held his glare. "You're all out to discredit me; and mark my promise, I shall even the score with each of you." He turned and stomped out the door.

Waters looked at Baylye and his sergeants. "Would that we could have saved that for later when we have additional evidence, but Mistress Colman is the finest and noblest of ladies. As gentlemen, 'twas our duty to protect her with the truth. And by the saints above, we *shall* discover the compulsion he holds over her and hold him accountable."

Baylye said, "Well said, William, and thank you all."

"A pleasant duty, Sir." Waters looked at his sergeants. "Men, continue to keep your eyes on Tayler and our other malcontents. I also ask you to watch Mistress Colman, for I fear—nay, I know—Tayler's the sort to satisfy his inadequacies and disappointments by bullying a lady."

* * *

As Tayler walked briskly toward his cottage, his mind churned with possibilities, none good. If White knows of the warrant, he may also know of Walsingham's plan. But how could he? Nay, he couldn't know of that . . . or could he? He may be half a fool, but he's not a total fool, and . . . fie! He knows Walsingham kept me on the voyage, and Walsingham's messenger said Raleigh spoke to White shortly before we sailed. Indeed, he *could* know; but even if he *does*, he lacks the conspiratorial instinct to take it seriously and act upon it. So I think I remain safe on *that* endeavor. But the warrants—the damn warrants—they're a different matter. What if White returns with them in hand? What then? I know. My father, Sir Francis Walsingham, will secure my acquittal on both counts. Yes, that's it. And still better, he'll likely have the warrants dismissed before White even sets sail. He smiled. So I am safe . . . and must now reward my benefactor by completing my mission . . . and reward myself by taking the woman I love to my bed as my *unlawful* wife.

* * *

Emily knelt beside her father's grave, prayed for him and Henry Harvie, prayed for herself, her mother, George, and Isna. Finally, she crossed herself, stood, turned, and walked toward the palisades gate forty yards away. She was halfway there when she spied Tayler limping hurriedly toward her. His face was flushed, eyes tight and focused, his jaw jutting out in a stiff pose as if locked in a permanent overbite. She stopped, felt a surge of anxiety abruptly numb her mind.

Tayler looked back over his shoulder to see if anyone watched, then stopped in front of Emily. "The devil take those colluding jackanapes. They've conspired against me, refused to marry us."

"Who has?" An absurd irony hit Emily. *I may not have to marry him, but now my child and I shall never have even a pretense of legitimacy.*

"Baylye, Waters, and those three fools who do his bidding."

"Why have they done so?"

"On the contrived grounds I told you of. 'Tis naught but an underhanded plot to embarrass me for not joining their conspiracy. And now they've got Baylye with them. I swear I shall kill all of them."

And now he'll want me to be his . . .

"But to hell with them. We need not be married to live together and enjoy the *pleasures* of marriage."

For a moment, Emily's mind swam in the same frantic confusion she'd felt when being swept out to sea on the outer banks; but suddenly, a thin thread of defiance emerged from somewhere, began to weave itself into her thoughts. *Being his wife would have been painful enough; but how shall I ever endure being his whore, a toy for his pleasure? And what of my child? It will have no status but that of a bastard. So all that was to be gained is now lost, and would it not be better to live alone in shame than to further degrade myself by being a slave to an evil son of the devil who would own my body and soul?*

"And to show our contempt for their authority, you shall be with me this very day. So come, let us go now to your cottage and in plain sight, move your belongings to mine." He put his arm behind her back, started to nudge her toward the palisades.

Emily held fast. "Do not push me! I will *not* be your whore, and I do not want you anywhere near my house ever again. Now leave me."

He looked startled for a second, but a sneer slowly slid across his face. "Perchance you've forgotten something. You've not the choice of *deciding* to be my mistress. You *will* be my mistress, or young Virginia Dare will perish. And 'twill be on *your* conscience; for you see, my obsession for you is such that her death means nothing by comparison." He leaned his face to within inches of hers, showed her the same crazed look as the moment before he'd raped her. "And make *not* the mistake of thinking I cannot or will not do as I say, for I can, and I will."

Raw fear and despair again burrowed into Emily's heart and mind, throbbed in her head. No escape. No choice. Her mind crafted words of submission, relayed them to her tongue; but before she could speak, a sudden impulse told her to wait; and as if an invisible butterfly hovered by her ear and whispered to her, she remembered Isna's words: *bravery is a virtue of Lakota women.* A sudden sense of freedom and a swell of resolve to resist him swept into her mind; she took a deep breath, hardened herself. "Hugh Tayler, because you are the dregs of humanity, I've no doubt you'll do as you say. So since I am not compelled to test your resolve with the life of one so dear, you may *discreetly* have your way with me and use my body as you wish, but you will *never* own my mind or my soul, and I will *not* live with you and justify your crime against me. I further refuse to go to you or permit you to come to me for your pleasure until my grief for my father is complete and my monthly curse is ended. And if you try to force me or harm that child, I shall take my own life in the village green while shouting to the colony the reason why." She spat in his face and ran toward the palisades gate.

He stood still, watched her with a stunned look as her spit ran down his cheek. "Five days, Emily. No more. Do you hear me?"

She ignored him, ran through the gate into the village. Lord, what have I done? Please save me; please save Virginia.

＊＊＊

Lieutenant Waters announced himself as he knocked on Emily's door.

She stood, rubbed her damp, bloodshot eyes, flipped her hair, then walked to the door, opened it, presented a nervous smile. "Good afternoon, Lieutenant. How may I help you?"

Waters looked suddenly embarrassed. "Are you well, Mistress? I see you've been . . . I can speak to you another time."

"No, I'm fine, Lieutenant." She sniffled.

"Very well. My reason for coming is twofold. First, Governor Baylye and I wanted to ensure you understand why the governor is unable to marry you and Master Tayler. I'm sure you're quite disappointed, and if you don't want me to . . ."

Emily tensed. "No. Please go on."

He told her of Myllet and the shipwreck, Tayler's wife and children, and his arrest warrant for the rape and murder of a married woman.

Instantly dizzy, Emily felt her knees weaken, begin to buckle.

Waters steadied her. "Here, let me help you." He walked her slowly to the closest stump, sat her down, then scooped a cup of water from the bucket and handed it to her.

Emily sipped the water, took a deep breath, composed herself. "Thank you, Lieutenant. Please go on."

He explained why they could not legally prosecute Tayler before the governor returned. He then took a deep breath, looked more embarrassed than before. "Mistress Colman, if I am wrong in what I am about to say, and you do not want me to continue, please say so." He paused for a response; none came. "It seems plain to Governor Baylye and me that you are not the type of young woman who would marry Hugh Tayler unless you were compelled in some illicit manner to do so, if you understand me."

A thin film of tears glossed Emily's eyes. *Dear Lord, I want so to tell him. They could arrest Tayler now for rape, but he'd deny it, and the entire colony would think me a slut. But they'll know anyway when the baby shows. So why not accuse him now? Because there's no jail to put him in, and he'd still be able to . . . to kill Virginia. Can't take that chance. But what if . . .*

Waters studied her with mindful eyes that couldn't miss her tears and anguished expression, decipher the agony behind them. "Mistress, I do not ask you to tell me if you are under threat, if you fear doing so; but I do urge you to consider it, for Hugh Tayler has shown himself to be the sort that—please forgive me if I offend you—that would mistreat a lady. The governor and I want you to know that you do *not* have to do what he says and *should* most definitely not do so. I know not if he holds something over you; but if he does, please know that my men and I, and every decent man in the colony, will help and protect you. And the sooner you inform us of any wrongs, the sooner we will be able to help." He paused for a moment then smiled. "Mistress, I've admired your beauty of person and soul, also your enthusiasm and bravery, since we left England. You are indeed an angel among women, and I will die to protect you. Please know that."

Emily sniffled, rubbed her eyes. "Thank you, Lieutenant. I doubt I look like an angel at the moment, but thank you." *I know not what to do. How could they protect Virginia? Without that, they can't help me. No one can help me. Must bear this alone.*

"You are wrong in your doubt, Mistress." He held his eyes on hers, seemed unable to move them. "I apologize if I've upset you; I should leave now."

She smiled faintly. "Lieutenant Waters, you have not upset me. My plight upsets me, and I know not what to do about it, for 'tis too late for anyone to help me." She again rubbed her eyes. "But thank you. I shall consider what you've said. You're a good, kind man for seeing my distress and trying to help. And if you've an intended one back home, she is a fortunate lady."

He gave her a deep, questioning look, his eyes inviting an explanation of her plight; but when none came, he smiled. "Her name is Rebecca Roberts; I pray my eyes behold her again someday. And I pray the time soon comes when you'll permit me to help you." He bowed, took his leave.

* * *

Elyoner said, "Praise God and the saints, lass. You're free of him, and—"

"Ellie, I'm *not* free of him. I—"

"What do you mean?" Elyoner slammed her hand on the table then shook her finger at Emily. "What does he demand? You must tell me. Enough of this mystery! I'm going to Baylye and Waters."

Emily paled. "No, Ellie. Please."

Elyoner threw her towel on the floor. "Why not, Em? Sit down; you look pale again. In the name of the saints, what does he hold over you? What can it matter if he's already done what I suspect he's done? And what can it matter if the worst that could result from *that* has already come to pass? None of it matters in the end. All that matters is that you are the most wonderful, kind, and courageous of young ladies and that you will rise above the outrage that's been done you. You *cannot* allow yourself to be menaced by him. So tell me now why we should *not* go to the governor."

Emily stared at her, pleaded with her eyes and urgent tone. "Pleeeease, Ellie, listen to me. Do not do this. I beg you, trust me. I cannot tell you why, but please say nothing. Please."

Elyoner's face was a sketch of frustration; she stared at Emily then shook her head, sighed. "As you wish, Em, but know that the time approaches when I shall no longer abide the pain of watching you suffer so."

Emily stared at her, lowered her gaze to the floor, closed her eyes. "I understand." And what will you and I do when that time comes?

Elyoner went to her, held her close for nearly a minute before Emily eased back, looked into her eyes. "Thank you, Ellie. I'd better go now."

"Well, Em, prithee tell me your secret soon. 'Twill be the first step in the rebirth of Emily Colman, the beautiful young lass Isna and I adore." She helped Emily don her cape. "Oh . . . Em . . . I nearly forgot." She reached into her apron pocket, removed a kerchief. "Is this yours? I seem to remember you embroidering it back at Roanoke. It bears a very nice sentiment, indeed."

Emily snatched the kerchief from Elyoner, looked at the words: *Savor Each Day the Lord Provides.* "Where did you find this?"

" 'Twas in Virginia's crib. I thought you might have dropped it there by accident."

CHAPTER 12

Allie led her mother to the computer, pointed at the monitor. "Read that, Mom."

It has long been known that dreams frequently include events and feelings the dreamer has experienced. But new theories hypothesize that it may be possible for experiences and feelings of one generation to be passed to subsequent generations of the same family through their genes and DNA, and perhaps, through genetically guided access to selected information stored in what Jung described as a "collective unconscious"—a sort of window through which we're able to access such information from the whole of mankind from its beginning to the present. It is thought that these experiences and feelings could manifest themselves in the form of dreams that portray the actual events and feelings experienced by those earlier generations.

"Oh my God!" She silently shifted her gaze to Allie, put her hands on Allie's shoulders, pulled her close. "Hon, there's something else I need to tell you about Ian . . . something I dodged on the phone that day."

Allie's eyes bloomed wide. "Mom, why are you doing this to me? What is it?"

Nancy swallowed, took a deep breath. "Well, two things. The first is that in addition to her telling me her dreams were true, she told me they were *always* about our family's ancestors. Again, I don't know *how* she knew, but she did . . . same for the dreams being true history. So maybe that's why you feel so close to Emily . . . could also relate to what we just read. You know, you and Ian are the only ones I've ever heard of who dreamed like this, and you're the only ones with that butterfly birthmark. So I'm wondering if you two were somehow endowed with some special gift that enables you to do what that article says, while those of us without the gift can't."

Allie stared blankly at her mother, tried to process what she'd said. "Mom, you just told me that Emily's my great-great—many-great— grandmother. I'm a goose bump."

"I guess that's what I'm saying, isn't it?"

"Holy shit! Did we know we had an ancestor at Roanoke?"

"No, but we really don't know much about the family before Ian's time. Obviously, if *she* knew, she didn't share it . . . probably because she didn't think anyone would believe her, which is a real shame."

Allie reflected for a moment. "Wouldn't it be something if she had the same dreams I'm having? Sonofabitch! No wonder I feel so close to Emily."

Nancy's look hardened; she shook her head. "Allie, don't forget what history says: the entire colony vanished. So even though you now understand some of the *why* of it, the outcome probably won't change. I mean, that's the way it is. You can't change history."

Allie's eyes suddenly glowed with excitement. "But, Mom, wait a minute. If Emily's my many-great-grandmother, she *can't* die now, because she hasn't had any kids yet. And if she died before she had kids, we wouldn't be here today, would we?"

Nancy submerged herself in long-forgotten thoughts, grasped for a fragment she knew was there.

"Hot damn! Emily's gonna make it . . . at least long enough to have a baby . . . and that baby has to make it, too, because we're here." Allie's relief and satisfaction turned abruptly to a scowl when she thought of Emily having Tayler's child. She promptly shed the thought. "The history books are wrong, Mom. Emily's gonna make it."

"Allie, hang on a second. I just remembered something else . . . and you're not going to like it . . . I remember Ian telling me her dreams weren't always of *direct* ancestors . . . some were of *siblings* of direct ancestors . . . and . . . and some of them died young."

Allie's smile vanished; she squinted tight-lipped and speechless at her mother.

"And here's the part I *really* didn't want to tell you on the phone." She took a deep breath. "Ian became addicted to her dreams and the people in them, just as you have to yours. And when some of the people died, she . . . she basically went into withdrawal, deep depression, and . . . and . . ."

"Here we go again! And *what*, Mom?"

"And she had several emotional meltdowns . . . and . . . and they say she tried to kill herself a couple times."

"I knew it." She shook her head. "I can relate, Mom. I can really relate. You can't imagine how attached I am to Emily . . . how I love her . . . how she's part of me. I've been afraid *with* and *for* her, sad and happy *with* and *for* her. And I don't know what's gonna happen when she dies . . . or what I'll do . . . or if I'll be able to handle it. I'm scared, Mom." Sudden tears filled Allie's eyes.

"Allie, you're scaring the hell out of me."

"I know, but the more I understand what's going on, the better I can deal with it. So it's really important that I know *everything you know*."

Nancy studied Allie's eyes; tears filled her own as she meekly sniffled her surrender. "You're . . . you're right . . . Hon. Knowing what happened to others has . . . has got to help you deal . . . deal with this better than Ian and . . . and some others did."

"Others? There were other dreamers besides Ian?"

"Yes. Ian told me so, said they were all way before her—you know, the four or five generations thing."

"Jeez. This gets deeper by the second. Oh, by the way, did you ever learn Ian's real name?"

"No, but I know where I can find out, and I'll check it out before you come home. You know, Ian was—"

"Great. So the next question is how did Ian and the other dreamers keep the dreams from dominating or ruining their lives?"

Long silence. "They didn't."

Allie felt as if a gust of frigid winter wind had slammed into her back. "They didn't?"

"No."

"What happened to them?"

Another long silence. "My mother told me Ian's great-great-grand-mother killed herself. Don't know how, or even if it was because of the dreams. It was back in the early 1800s."

Allie swallowed hard. "I knew it!" What a great thing to look forward to. "And what about Ian?"

More silence, another sigh. "They said she died from . . . from a sleeping pill overdose, but no one knew for sure if it was accidental or planned. Like I said earlier, most of them thought she was crazy because she talked about the dreams, and they didn't believe they were real. But *I* know they were real because we had a special relationship, and she told me so. I'm also convinced—but without real proof—that if she *did* die of an overdose, it was accidental, but we'll never know. It could just as well have been suicide. And Allie, that's what frightens me now. "

Allie stared at the desktop for a moment, then whispered solemnly, "Me too, Mom."

"Aw, don't tell me that."

"It's true. The dreams are totally addictive, like a TV series you just can't miss; and I feel as strongly for Emily as I do for anyone in the family. But don't get me wrong. I'm only saying I see *how* it could happen. It's probably like working with terminally ill people day after day—you probably get depressed, but you can't escape. Then you either go crazy or . . ."

"Oh my God!" Tears filled Nancy's eyes.

"Mom, please don't cry. I'm not saying I'm there . . . only that I see how someone *could* get there. And as far as the sleeping pills go, if I had to guess, I'd say Ian *accidentally* overdosed; because before she ever got to the point of suicide, she'd have been so addicted to the dreams that she'd have done everything possible to dream more—like taking sleeping pills. And I doubt there was much savvy about the dangers of sleeping pills in those early days." Déjà vu in spades. Damn. Said too much. Now she'll worry more. Dummy!

"Well, that makes sense. But Allie . . . *you* aren't taking sleeping pills are you?"

"No, Mom." Allie cringed as she thought about the new drug she'd discovered and was about to try—a drug normally used for treating Myasthenia Gravis—that could induce more frequent and longer dream periods. She wondered what she'd do when the samples a med-student friend had given her ran out. "So enough on that. What more do you know about how the dreams end?"

"Only that Ian told me they sometimes end badly, very badly. But she also said some end happily. She never said how far into an ancestor's life they go. I mean, if you dream of someone long enough, they're eventually going to die; but maybe, like real life, it doesn't get you down as much when they're real old and had a full life."

"That fits. So do you know more about how Ian knew the dreams were real and that they were about our ancestors?"

"Nope. She never told me; but when I look through the box of her stuff before you come home, maybe I'll find the answer."

"You have a box of her stuff?"

"I do. My mother put it away after Ian died, and frankly, I forgot all about it until this very moment. Don't know why I haven't thought of it, but there could be some interesting things in there. Maybe we can do that together when you come."

Allie pulsed with excitement, while her mind trembled with angst at what they might find. "That'd be awesome, Mom. Let's do it."

"Deal. I'll dig it out before you come."

"Great. I can't wait."

* * *

The Panther and ten warriors left the Powhatan village amid war cries and whoops of encouragement from the people. Each man was without his jewelry, wore face paint, and carried a bow, full quiver, a war club or hatchet, and a knife. Despite the cold, all were naked but for loin cloths and thick-soled moccasins, and each carried a rolled-up deerskin strung across his back, for warmth during the cold night they would spend in forest. As they passed the village perimeter and entered the forest, the Panther stepped into a measured jog toward the narrow upper waters of the large river they would soon cross. After the river, they would turn in the direction from which the sun rose during the cold-air moons and continue to the end of the large bay where the white men dwelled with the Chesapeakes. He thought of his dead first wife, his dead children, felt a pang of sadness, then smiled as he considered that this raid was the first step in their planned annihilation of the white men, the true beginning of his revenge. For a moment, his mind drifted to thoughts of his wildly passionate second wife and the child in her womb; but a few steps later, an image of the white woman's beautiful face stole into his mind, filled his body and senses with the warmth of desire, but also a pang of frustration at having to wait to quench the burning passion that consumed him. Perhaps she will be among those we attack. He smiled again, quickened his pace.

***

Roger Baylye's face was redder than a rooster's comb as he glared at Tayler. "We can't hang a man—especially a Savage—simply because someone caught him trying to steal something. In the name of Christ the Almighty, we've caught several of our *own* people stealing food and other items. Do you propose hanging them, as well?"

"Of course not. Our people are civilized. A simple lashing will do for them. But these Savages need to be taught a lesson before they steal us bare."

Baylye shook his head. "Master Tayler, you obviously fail to grasp the fragility of our existence, especially our dependence on these people for their knowledge and friendliness. Your proposal would gravely worsen what's already becoming a dire situation. The man knows he did something wrong in our eyes, and the threat of a sound lashing for any future transgression will quite suffice."

Tayler whispered something inaudible then said, "Mark my words, Baylye, this is but the beginning of their treachery. These Savages are born thieves, and sooner or later, we must show them the limits of our tolerance."

"At the moment, Master Tayler, *you* press the limits of *my* tolerance; we shall have no more discussion of this topic. The next item is . . ."

Tayler, Willes, Stevens, and Sampson whispered busily to one another as Baylye spoke.

Baylye stopped, stared at the four until they felt his gaze, looked self-consciously at him, and ceased their chatter. "If you men wish to comment, please wait your turn, then speak so all may hear."

The four smirked at one another like contemptuous school boys.

"The next item is the food supply. 'Tis now late January, and we've barely enough food to get through February, much less to the harvest; and frankly, the reason for the deficiency is the laziness of many of our men, particularly we civilians—insufficient time hunting and fishing, indifference to the tasks at hand, and lack of responsibility. By the saints, we've no room for such behavior by anyone. Indeed, it appears that several believe their former status in England excuses them from their fair share of work here; but I assure you, such is not the case. And 'tis our responsibility—we, the council of Assistants—to lead by example. We—"

"Governor Baylye," Tayler said, "it may surprise you, but I came here for land and wealth . . . not to work like the vassal of a feudal lord, yet most would agree that I've not slacked in contributing my share of work. But the truth is, your friend John White lied to us about conditions here, and—"

"First, Governor White did *not* lie to you; and second, while I acknowledge your contribution to our efforts, I reiterate that *all* in this colony must share equally in the labor—and the fruits of that labor—without exception until our survival is assured."

Tayler snorted, shook his head. "Many of us disagree with you on this, Governor."

"Disagree, you may, Master Tayler, but the policy stands . . . and that is the end of *this* discussion. And with regard to slackers, the situation is simple. We cannot and will not tolerate them, and I therefore expect all of you to inform me and Lieutenant Waters of such offenders, so we may appropriately reduce their rations."

Tayler glanced around the room, appeared to discern little support, silently returned his persistent glower to Baylye.

Baylye nodded at Waters. "Now we shall discuss a most grave matter. Lieutenant Waters will provide the background."

Waters stepped forward, glanced at each Assistant, then fixed an onerous gaze on Tayler. He felt simultaneous bursts of excitement and anxiety at what was to come, knew, for better or worse, it would have an abiding impact on the effectiveness of the Assistants and the colony as a whole. "As Thomas Colman lay dying, I spoke to you of unspecified but disqualifying character flaws in Hugh Tayler."

Tayler growled, "I protest."

"Continue, Lieutenant," Baylye said.

Waters nodded. "I shall now specify those flaws. The night of the shipwrecks, Master Tayler murdered Robert Wilkinson . . . murdered him to save himself. He forcibly pulled him from the board to which he clung for his life, and shoved him away to drown."

Tayler shouted, "Waters, you're a lying knave! You've no evidence, only the lies of one man who hates me." He looked at the other Assistants. "Do not believe him. He seeks only to discredit me for selfish purposes, and—"

"I speak but the truth, gentlemen—the truth provided by Sergeant Myllet, who witnessed the event." He took a deep breath, again looked at each man. "The next charge against Master Tayler is well known by several of our soldiers, including me."

"Fie, Waters, you lying churl." He clenched his fists, took a step toward Waters.

Waters gripped the pistol at his waist, dared Tayler with his eyes, hoped he'd advance so he could end it there, but Tayler stopped. Waters glared at him, again challenged with his eyes. "Before leaving England, Master Tayler abandoned his wife and two children and escaped to the colony only by evading the high sheriff who sought him with a warrant for non-support."

Soft murmurs floated around the room like parishioners' whispers before Mass.

"Damn you, Waters, this is a sham." He looked at the others, shook his head repeatedly. "Do *not* believe him."

Waters' hand remained on his pistol. "Enough, Tayler. You're out of order. Any more and we shall have to remove you."

Tayler's right cheek twitched, and he nervously shuffled his feet as he stared angrily at his followers.

"And last, as we set sail from England, another high sheriff arrived at the pier with a warrant for Master Tayler's arrest, this time for rape and murder."

Most Assistants shook their heads in disgust, while Willes, Sampson, and Stevens glanced skittishly at one another.

"And he's here today because of the treachery of our ship's pilot, Fernandez, who disregarded Governor White's order to stay the ship's departure and hand him over." Waters marveled at how quickly he'd come to despise this man. *Would that I could disclose the conspiracy now; but too soon, need* real *proof rather than suspicion and conjecture to hang him. Now that the men know, mayhap we'll catch him at his game. But it must be soon.* He nodded at Baylye. "Governor."

Tayler watched Baylye, shuffled his feet, frequently glanced at his supporters.

Baylye eyed Waters, communicated something with his eyes, then looked at the other Assistants, spoke with a slight flicker in his voice. "So, now that you've all heard the truth about Hugh Tayler, you understand our misgivings the night of Tayler's election; and because that election occurred under false pretenses, or at best, misconceptions of his character, I now declare that election void and John Stilman the new Assistant."

Tayler laughed out loud. "You can't do this, Baylye."

Willes, Stevens, and Sampson booed. Willes said, "You can't overturn our vote, Governor. 'Twas done in good faith, and you're *not* a king."

Baylye lifted a paper from the table, held it up so all could see. "No, I'm not a king; but this document, our charter from Sir Walter Raleigh, expressly bestows upon the governor of this colony the power to remove Assistants he considers unfit to represent the best interests of the colony. And based on what you've just heard, Hugh Tayler is plainly unfit; I therefore declare him no longer a member of this body." He looked squarely at Tayler. "Master Tayler, you must now leave."

Tayler shouted over the din of cheers and protests, "I refuse, Baylye! Now what?"

Waters walked slowly to the door, admitted Sergeant Smith and two other soldiers. They walked to Tayler, seized him by the arms, and pulled him toward the door.

Tayler shook loose; his cronies surrounded him, held the soldiers away from him.

Waters pulled his pistol, cocked the hammer, aimed at Tayler's head. "Now, Tayler! Now!"

Stevens grabbed Tayler's arm, looked him in the eyes, shook his head.

Tayler thought for a moment then nodded at his men before looking at Waters and Baylye and flipping his middle finger at them as he walked out the door.

Sampson said. "Governor Baylye, we'll not be party to this treachery." He turned toward the door, beckoned Willes and Stevens to follow.

Almost to the door, Willes stopped, turned, glared threateningly at those who had voted for Tayler in the election. All had ashy, milksop faces, shuffled their feet, but held fast. Willes nodded three times, turned, started out the door.

As he exited, Baylye said, "You men depart of your own free will, and I remind you that any measures passed by those who remain will be binding. I further remind you that if you willfully miss another meeting of this council, you will be permanently removed."

When they had left, Baylye turned to those who remained. "Men, I am obliged to tell you there is more at play here than meets the eye—things that must, for now, remain undisclosed. But I beseech you to resist any approach or threat from those who just departed, or their surrogates. Please be vigilant for seditious behavior and be prepared to protect yourselves. I fear perilous times lie ahead."

Ananias Dare beseeched Baylye and Waters with a pleading expression. "Verily, Roger, can you not disclose what begets your fears?"

"I cannot, Ananias, not yet, but I believe the time will soon arrive. And I promise you—all of you—that when it does, I shall do so immediately."

All but Baylye and Waters then slowly and silently filed out the door, each carrying with him a look of baleful apprehension. Waters closed the door, faced Baylye. "Governor, I fear things deteriorate faster than expected. We must be clever and thorough in determining the loyalty of every person in this colony. Tayler and his men mean to destroy it, and they'll buy or intimidate the weak and malleable among us to do so."

Baylye nodded, pondered for a moment. "I wonder if Walsingham's promised to rescue them." He shook his head, pounded his fist on the tabletop. "My God, does it not anger you what men do for power?"

"Aye, it does, Sir, and I have the same question about Walsingham. I also fear we're dealing with something far bigger than we thought." The two stared quietly at one another, absorbed their words, contemplated their implications. "Perhaps we should build a jail—a sound jail—several stocks, as well. 'Tis true there is nowhere to escape to here, but I sense the time has come to remove conspirators and other criminals from contact with the populace—isolate them, limit their influence, and reduce the damage they can do. What say you, Sir?"

"I say that's a splendid idea—one whose necessity saddens me, but a necessity nonetheless. Have you—"

Someone knocked on the door.

Baylye said, "Who is it?"

"Ananias."

"Come in."

Ananias wore an anxious look as he entered the cottage; he glanced behind to see if anyone watched, then looked at Baylye. "Roger, I must inform you of something Elyoner told me. It may be pertinent to your concerns."

Waters and Baylye eyed each other quickly. "What is it?"

After Ananias related what Elyoner had told him of her father's suspicions about Walsingham and Tayler, Baylye said, "William, I think we have a new confidant."

"Indeed, we do. Ananias, have a seat while we tell you what's amiss."

* * *

Emme Merrimoth and Emily held their capes and hoods tightly around them, panting as they trudged through six-inch-deep snow toward the Chesapeake village. Each step produced a squeaky crunch in the dry snow; while each breath blew a white cloud in front of them. Emily squinted, shielded her eyes with rag-wrapped hands as the sun suddenly slipped from behind a cloud, elegantly decorated the snow with dazzling sparkles of red, green, yellow, and blue. Beautiful, she thought, as if God crushed a handful of gemstones into thousands of grains of sparkling sand and sprinkled them over the snow. Oh, look at that . . . 'tis like a crystal . . . colors change when you move your head. She shifted her head sideways then back again, giggled with delight.

Emme laughed. "Emily Colman, pray tell, what are you doing?"

Emily giggled again. "Being a little girl. That's what. Look at that, Emme. Move your head back and forth . . . see how the sparkles change colors?"

Emme copied her movements. "Oh, I see what you mean—so many colors. Aw! Come back, sun! Pity . . . brief but beautiful, eh?"

"Indeed, like so many things in life." Like George . . . and Isna . . . and Father. But at least it put a smile on my face for a moment, and . . . fie, today is the fifth day, the day I must go to him. Don't think about it. But, Em, you *must* think about it, must think of Virginia and decide what to do. She shivered as she imagined his hands on her naked body, touching, probing. No! Not now. Lord, let me have a moment of peace.

"and Johnny says Tayler's an unsavory sort, and he worries about you whenever he sees you with him. He's quite convinced you don't see him by choice, but—"

"What does he say, Emme?"

"Says he can't tell me . . . but he's certain Tayler somehow compels you, and he's quite concerned."

"I like Johnny very much—a good, honest man, he is—and I've noticed *you* like him, as well." Her smile invited a response.

Emme grinned coyly. "I do indeed, Em. We've grown quite close . . . don't have much time together because of his duties, but we savor what we have . . . even talked about—"

"About what?"

"Can you keep a secret?"

"Of course." Her own dreadful secrets flashed through her mind.

"I'm not supposed to say anything, but . . . we've talked about marriage . . . he doesn't want anyone to know, says he has enemies who would hurt *me* to hurt *him*. So please don't tell anyone, Em, especially—" She looked suddenly frightened.

"Especially Tayler?"

"Yes."

Emily nodded. "Be certain. I won't."

Emme stopped, held Emily's hands. "Emily, Johnny's desperately afraid for you. He thinks Tayler has . . . has used you in an improper way . . . by force . . . like he did Johnny's sister, but—"

"You know about Johnny's sister?"

"Aye, I do. He's told me about her many times—still grieves, mind you—and seems frightened when he talks about Tayler. Says he's a coward and extortionist who will do *anything* or hurt *anyone* to gain what he wants, as long as he can do so without risking himself." Emme's misty green eyes saddened but then sparkled in a sudden burst of sunlight. "Emily, I fear for Johnny . . . and for you . . . but I pray every day those fears are unfounded."

Emily shook her head. "I fear they are not, Emme."

After a few silent steps, Emme said, "Emily, you've . . . you've seemed to be carrying a weighty burden these last weeks. I know you would tell me of it if you could; so know that when you're able, I . . . I will share it with you and help you in any way I can."

Emily smiled, hugged her. "Thank you, Emme. You're a good friend . . . and a patient one."

Emme kissed her on the cheek. "We'd better move along before we freeze, eh?"

"Aye. My toes are already numb . . . fingers, too. Would that the ungracious sun would share its warmth with us and—ahhhh! Snow keeps packing into my shoes, and . . . and my legs are frozen. Why are we out here in skirts?"

"Because we're women, I suppose. I've never worn a pair of breeches, have you?"

"Certainly not, though at this moment, I wish I could."

As they proceeded toward the village, Emily heard Emme speaking but didn't hear her words. Her mind dwelt instead on the chilling implications of Tayler's kerchief in Virginia's crib, her dearth of choices, and the inevitability of the most repugnant among them. *Yet 'tis true. It must come to pass . . . 'twill come to pass . . . though I dread it more than death itself. But how can I give myself to a rapist and murderer, a man who deserted his wife and children? Adultery is a grave sin, and 'twill condemn me to hell for eternity. God help me, what shall I do? No choice before me is without grave sin. Mayhap I can delay him again, make him believe I will take my own life if his demands are too great. Perhaps I should do more than threaten . . . perhaps I should end this horrible dream now . . . hang myself . . . or cut my own throat. Yet if I take my life, I shall also take my child's life, and I cannot do that. So I must now live for my child and no other—not me, not* even Isna . . . nothing else matters. But what will God think of me, and Father, and Mother, and George . . . and Isna when he sees me with child . . . Tayler's whore? Perchance he'll return to his people before then. A cloud of sorrow drifted through her mind like a soft breeze. *I shall never see him again . . . my Isna. What if I should see him today in the village? What will I do? Oh, my soul.* She reached into her apron pocket, touched her mother's letter. *Would that I had my locket, as well. Mother, forgive me.*

Emily stopped, tensed, grasped Emme's wrist, parted her lips, stared ahead with piercing, unblinking eyes. The man stood ten yards away, wore a large fur around his shoulders, and fur leggings that rose from his moccasins to his knees. His dark eyes bored into Emily's, questioned her, waited patiently, expectantly for a reply. Her chest pounded, legs buckled, breathing quickened. *My God, must go to him, hold him; need him so.*

"Emily."

"Isna." Tears filled her eyes, ran down her cheeks; she trembled, moaned softly. *Want to run to him, hold him. No. Cannot dishonor him, must bear this alone, ashamed, unworthy.* She tugged on Emme's hand, turned, started back toward the palisades, moaning softly as she walked. She suddenly stopped, looked back with mournful eyes, saw him watching her; she turned, sobbed as she trudged back toward the palisades.

***

Tayler sat on a stump a foot from the fire at the back of his cottage, a heavy cloak wrapped around his shoulders. He laid a pair of logs on the fire, watched them catch. *Fie on grass houses in winter, damn heat goes but a foot or two before the cold swallows it. Back's freezing.* He shivered, wiggled his stool a little closer to the flames, tucked his hands under his armpits. *Acted impetuously today . . . stupidly . . . not cleverly, as I* should *act. Too much attention, they watch me now, who I talk to, how I behave. Made them more suspicious, jeopardized my mission.*

Fool. Keep your head down, bide your time, and keep your mouth shut for a while; let things settle, appear to be your old loyal, dedicated, hard-working self. He took a bite of smoked venison. Don't need to be on the council of idiot Assistants to complete my task . . . work through Willes and the others; let them bear the suspicion and distrust while I muster more support and guide their actions from afar . . . easy to per- suade people when they're weary of work and starving. Promise them anything, and they believe it . . . and all accept a good bribe. Thank you, Lord Walsingham—Father—for your foresight. A consummate conspirator you are for provisioning me with such a bounty of funds. He wondered what his life would have been like if he'd been raised in Walsingham's household, wondered if he'd have been happier, been a better man, mayhap even one whom people looked up to rather than despised. He shook his head. No. I *am* who I am. So I must make the best of it and have my way with life, do what I want, take what I want, no matter who from, and let nothing stand in my way. But what if there *is* a God and a hell? He shuddered, quickly cast the thought from his mind.

He thought he heard a sound at the door, turned, stood, hoped it was Emily. No, no one there. Hearing things, Hugh. He sat, squiggled closer to the fire. So when things have calmed . . . when they believe they're in control again . . . then . . . then we will act. Meanwhile, what do I do about Gibbes and Waters and the other two? Though all be fools, I think they know I'm up to something . . . but they can't possibly suspect the truth . . . not yet. But what if they do? What then? Perhaps 'tis why they watch me so closely, especially that son of a whore, Gibbes. Would that I could put a ball in his brain this very moment. And Waters, as well. Curse the day those two entered my life . . . but must be cautious . . . both excellent marksmen . . . far better than I . . . and fearless. Dare not face either of them, or Myllet or Smith, in a *fair* fight. He smiled. The credo of your life, Hugh Tayler: do *nothing* fair. Fairness is for fools.

He tossed another log on the fire. Burning too fast. Damn cold out there. "Brrr." Damn cold in *here*. And what of Emily? Must soon feel her close to me again. My God, I crave her . . . not just her body but her whole being . . . truly love her. He smiled, imagined her lithe, exquisitely proportioned body standing naked before him. 'Tis blissful to know that none but I have had her . . . to know I own her forever . . . to use as I wish—the only person in this world who can turn me from my ways, make me the person I long to be but cannot become on my own. He took another bite of venison. Must make her love me, convince her to give me a chance. Yet, despite the ecstasy of being the first to have her, 'twas another foolish mistake. Should never have done it . . . terribly wrong. Should have been patient, rebuilt our relationship, regained her trust. He shook his head. Blather, patience is for fools. I want her *now*; and if I'm to *have* her now, I must use whatever means are necessary. But what of the consequences? What if I kill the young child and am discovered? "Christ, 'tis cold in here." He eyed his shaking hands, again thrust them under his armpits. They'll draw and quarter me . . . there will be hell to pay. *Hell. Hell.* The word again conjured up his recurring horrific vision, planted it in his mind. He trembled as he visualized himself writhing in everlasting flames.

When the image faded, he again thought of Emily. Days since I've seen her . . . avoiding me. But today is the day she *will* come to me. His heart quickened at the thought. But what if she doesn't? He stared at the fire for a moment. If she doesn't, then I shall go to her and . . . careful, Hugh, you dare not attract *more* attention. 'Tis not the time for a noisy argument *or* to be smothering the governor's granddaughter. But my need is great, uncontrollable. The thought of Emily's firm, tight, naked body, warm and sweaty against his own, stiffened his prick, made it throb with anticipation while warming his blood and quickening his heart. Pox on caution, I must have her now. But this time . . . this time 'twill be different: gentle . . . slow and loving. She'll savor the slow rise of her passions, the wild release, the rapture. True, she felt it last time, but this will be better: endless; she won't be so afraid and will therefore al-low herself to savor the ecstasy I bring her—and, yes, let herself drown in the glorious intoxication that follows. And she *will* beg me to do it again and again and again, and the joy of it will make her begin to love me.

He suddenly scowled as his idyllic daydream yielded to shadows. She will not come to me unless forced, and . . . and she still loves her Savage and will *continue* to love him, at my expense, until . . . until I kill him. So I must do so soon. He stirred the fire with a stick, added another log. But what of today? How do I *quietly* force her to satisfy my passion?

He stood, walked to his chest, opened the lid, and removed a quill, an inkwell, a thin, six-inch square board, and a small piece of paper. When he'd reseated himself in front of the fire, he laid the paper on the board, placed the board across his knee, dipped the quill in the inkwell, and wrote:

My dearest Emily,
It has been an unbearable . . .

***

From his hiding place behind a large tree, the Panther had an unobstructed view of the white warrior's back. This one was well within bow range; the others, who stood around the four women gathering firewood by the frozen stream, were longer shots but within easy range for his men across the clearing. He nodded at the other warriors near him, drew his bow, then stepped from behind the tree, aimed, and released.

Phffft! The arrow ripped clean through Johnny Gibbes' neck. He fell forward into the snow, felt a warm wetness flowing down the front and back of his neck onto his chest and back. Shot . . . groggy, mind spinning, want to sleep. He heard a woman scream, then a bevy of loud, chilling cries behind him, more on the side. He heard someone crying, felt hands on his shoulders, felt himself being rolled over, prayed it wasn't a Savage. He blinked, looked into Emme Merrimoth's desperate eyes, heard her scream. *Phffft-thunk!* She screamed again, but the sound caught in her throat as she lurched forward, fell limp and silent upon him. He felt the arrow graze his cheek as she fell, her blood dripping steadily onto his face. More war cries, screams from across the clearing. He gripped Emme, rolled her over, saw the front half of an arrow sticking through her chest, just below the shoulder and inward from her armpit. He shielded her with his armored back, snapped off the point, lifted her limp torso with his left hand, and pulled the rest of the arrow out through her back. *My God, she's dead, saved me, my Emme.* He jerked his helmet off, laid his ear on her chest, thought he sensed a faint pulse but couldn't be sure.

* * *

Emily removed the note attached to her cottage door, stepped inside, unfolded it.

> *My dearest Emily,*
> *It has been an unbearable period since that wonderful and matchless moment when we shared the deepest pleasure of each other's company. My heart now yearns to relive the grandeur of that moment, and I pray your heart, being of like mind, will persuade you to meet me tonight at the place we've frequently discussed. I shall prepare a warm, hearty fire for you as I eagerly anticipate your complete pleasure and satisfaction at the time we pass together. But alas, if some unforeseen misfortune prevents your presence, be certain that I shall bear my boundless misery graciously, and in the manner I have so often described to you. With highest affection and hope, adieu until tonight.*
> *With undying love,*
> *Hugh*

A wave of despair flooded her mind as she stared at the note quivering in her hand. *What am I to do?* As she walked slowly and thoughtfully toward the fireplace, she heard the rumble of a distant matchlock, then another. Chills raced through her body. "The firewood party, Emme, Johnny, under attack." She stuffed the note in her pocket, rushed out the door, saw Myllet and Smith, five soldiers in tow, jogging out the palisades gate.

Myllet shouted at some soldiers standing in the village center, "Find Waters, take cover, prepare to defend, may be a trap!"

* * *

Gibbes looked across the clearing to where he'd heard two match-locks discharge, saw one of his men lying face down and motionless on the ground—an arrow in his neck, one buried to the feathers in his side where his front and back armor met, and yet another in his leg. Gibbes rolled to his knees, stood. *Phffft!* He ducked at the sound, grabbed Emme's hands, pulled her farther from the tree line. "Fie!" He let go of Emme, stumbled back to where he'd fallen, retrieved his matchlock, then crouched and inched back to Emme. He heard the other soldiers yelling, glanced at them. One was reloading his matchlock while the other two pumped arrows at the tree line as fast as they could nock them. Must organize fire, hold for help. "Over here, men." He lifted Emme over his shoulder, grabbed his matchlock, plodded awkwardly to the stream; he dropped the gun then laid Emme gently on the snow-covered ice of the streambed, a foot below the banks.

Emme's eyes slowly opened to narrow slits. "Johnny, I . . . I'm dying."

"Don't talk, Emme. Here." He pulled his matchlock pistol from his waist, cocked the hammer, handed it to her, butt first. "If any come for you, wait until they're close then point at them and pull the trigger, like I showed you. Hold it with both hands if you can, and keep your hand off the trigger until you're ready to fire."

She slowly took the weapon, smiled faintly, whispered, "Stay alive, Johnny . . . goodbye."

"No, Emme! No! You can't die; *pretend* to be dead, keep the pistol ready. He looked at her with an agonized look. "I must rally the men. Don't die. I'll return. Do you hear me? Don't die!"

She smiled weakly, closed her eyes, slowly laid the pistol at her side. "Farewell, Johnny, I love you."

Gibbes stared at her for a second, prayed she'd live, then crept toward the three men further down the stream bank. He realized the Savages had stopped shooting. "Getting ready to come again, men; spread out, make low, small targets. You women, hide on the ice in the stream, get below the bank, scream if they come for you. Archers, slow your fire, save arrows, don't shoot unless you have a good target. We're at the limit of their range; they must cross the clearing to get to us. Keep checking behind for flankers."

Six Savages emerged from their trees with blood-chilling cries, drew their bows on the soldiers. The other musketeer lifted his matchlock, aimed, pulled the trigger as Gibbes yelled, "No! No! Hold fire. 'Tis a ruse."

The Savages leaped back behind cover, waited until the shot whistled past them into the trees.

"Damn it. Reload quickly. Archers, be ready, they're coming. Don't shoot until they're in the open and coming toward us, then shoot fast."

Screams from the streambed. Gibbes turned, saw a Savage standing over Emme, a stone hatchet in his hand. He lifted his gun, aimed at the man's chest, began to squeeze the trigger but saw Emme lift the pistol, fire into his gut. The man lurched backward, lay motionless on the ground, blood spurting from his wound. Gibbes noticed a circle of red snow around Emme. Bleeding badly, must help her. More screams from the streambed. He fired at a Savage dragging a woman by her arms, saw him fall sideways, then climb to his feet, stagger toward the far tree line. "Berrye, put arrows on those Savages." He pointed at the streambed. "Only clear shots. Toppan, Johnson, cover the front." As he dropped the butt of his matchlock to the ground, he heard a chorus of war cries from the front but kept his eyes on the women. He blindly poured a charge of powder down the barrel, dropped a ball behind it. Just as he yanked the ramrod from beneath the barrel and jammed it inside, he saw a Savage disappear into the far tree line with a shrieking, flailing woman over his shoulder.

"Help me! Help me!"

"God damn it!" Gibbes pumped the ramrod twice, jerked it from the barrel, saw another Savage dragging a frantic woman from the streambed. She twisted, squirmed, pulled free an instant before Berrye's arrow ripped into his stomach. He lurched backward, spun around, dropped to his knees, grasped the shaft that stuck from his stomach, fell forward and still.

Phffft! Phffft! Phffft! Gibbes glanced toward the front, saw six Savages running toward them. He glanced back at the streambed, saw another Savage reach the far tree line with a young woman on his shoulder, watched him stumble when Berrye's arrow slashed into the back of his thigh and lodged in the bone. He dropped the girl, tugged on the arrow but couldn't remove it, then bent down and grabbed the hysterical girl by her wrist, drug her several steps toward the trees before releasing her and limping into the forest.

"Good shot, Berrye!" He heard Toppan's matchlock rumble, turned toward the front, raised his own, and fired at the closest Savage. The man kept coming but suddenly stopped, aimed and fired an arrow at Johnson, who was releasing an arrow at another Savage.

"Ahhhh!" Johnson dropped his bow, yanked the arrow from his shoulder where it had hit bone; he picked up his bow, resumed firing.

Suddenly a fierce-looking Savage in the middle of the clearing stopped, calmly raised his hand while he glared at the soldiers. He then turned slowly, walked indifferently back to the tree line, the other Savages following behind. At the tree line, he stopped, faced the soldiers, raised his bow, shook it defiantly as he and the others shrieked their cries then turned and vanished like ghosts into the forest.

Gibbes panted, stared after the Savages, winced as he touched his neck where the arrow had entered and exited a half inch from his throat. He stared for a moment at his blood-soaked hand, felt a wave of dizziness numb his mind. As he wrapped a scarf around his neck to stem the blood flow, he looked at his men, saw only Toppan and Johnson, their eyes locked on something behind him. He heard a thudding, crunching sound, turned, saw Berrye pounding the butt of a matchlock, again and again, into the skull of the Savage he'd killed by the streambed. Each blow splattered blood and brains on the snow, his breeches, and his tall socks; the two wide-eyed women watched in frozen horror from the streambed, their hands cupped over their mouths. Gibbes looked at Toppan and Johnson. "Stop him, then help the women." He turned, saw Emme lying motionless in the snow. "Emme!" He dropped his matchlock, ran toward her.

* * *

With trembling hands and a pain-twisted face, John Chapman pleaded with a quavering, cracking voice, "Roger, we're losing time. We must move quickly, muster a rescue force, pursue them. They've already got several hours' start. I beseech you." He shook his hands up and down in frustration. "My Alis . . . my dear Alis . . . out there with those heathens. Damn it, Roger! Hear me, please pursue them. Have you no feelings? She's one of our own. How can you abandon her?"

Baylye's eyes glowed with misty compassion, but his thin features were taut as old shoe leather. He shook his head slowly, put his hands on Chapman's shoulders. "Please, John . . . try to understand . . . we must consider the safety of the entire colony. Forsooth, I know how you feel. I—"

"No. You *can't* know how I feel, Roger. You *can't*! She's my wife, my love, the mother of our children. My God, do you know what they'll do to her?" His body trembled. "What will I tell the children? That we abandoned their mother to Savages who ravished her to her death? No, Roger. I cannot do that. I must try to save her, even if I go alone." He started for the door.

Baylye tightened his grip. "John. Wait." He stared at him, sighed. "Lieutenant Waters will be here any minute. I shall ask if he can spare a detachment to pursue. But understand, he lacks the forces to do any more than deal with—"

A sharp knock. Waters entered, saw Chapman. He bowed his head, shook it slowly. "John, terrible about Alis. I'm so sorry. Sergeant Gibbes is most distraught, blames himself."

Chapman shook his head. "No, no. 'Tis not his fault. He and your men mounted a valiant defense, gave sound measure of themselves."

"They did indeed. But Gibbes takes Alis' loss personally, and—"

"William," Baylye said, "can we spare enough men to pursue the raiding party and attempt to rescue Alis? Perhaps they'll stop somewhere for the night and allow us time to catch them."

Chapman's tenuous composure crumbled; he stared at Waters, whimpered softly, "My Alis, my love . . . pleeeease, Lieutenant, I beseech you. Find her before 'tis too late, I *beg* you."

Waters grimaced as he glanced at Baylye then Chapman. "Master Chapman—John, my friend—my heart grieves with you." He again glanced at Baylye, swallowed hard, parted his lips as if to speak but silently shook his head, his eyes dull, cloudy with frustration. He looked back at Chapman. "Sir, our military situation is dire, and our fighting force perilously small, even if we count all the civilians." He sighed. "If we withdraw a sizeable portion of it from the village, for *any* purpose, the colony will be dangerously vulnerable; and as you know, most civilians know nothing of warfare or military practices. Even if we *were* to pursue, we do not know where the Powhatan village is or therefore the route taken by the Savages to return to it. We are not skilled forest trackers, and they move swiftly . . . far more swiftly than we. Nor do we know their territory."

Baylye said, "William, the Chesapeakes know the Powhatans' territory *and* where their village is."

"Aye, they do, Governor, but they won't tell us for fear of retribution by the Powhatans. And even if we found their village, the Powhatans and their allies would outnumber us at least twenty to one. We'd have no chance against them and would be overwhelmed, leaving the colony defenseless—a situation the Powhatans would promptly exploit to a disastrous conclusion. Believe me, Sir, were it not for our partial palisades, with most of our force always within and at the ready, they'd have attacked and overwhelmed us long ago. Make no mistake—either of you—we've but one hope of surviving, and that is to hold out *here* until Governor White returns with reinforcements."

Baylye sighed, clasped his hands behind his back, studied the floor for a moment before looking at Waters. "I agree, William, and I appreciate your clear understanding of your duty and our situation. But what if you did no more than pursue the raiding party with enough force to defeat it and rescue Alis? Gibbes estimated that only eight or nine Savages remain."

"I do not believe we can catch them, Governor; and the farther we go from here, the deeper we'll move into their territory, with the ever-increasing likelihood that they'll discover and ambush us, with the result I just described." He took a deep breath, exhaled slowly, lowered his gaze to the floor, then looked at Chapman. "John, my commission from Sir Walter Raleigh and Governor White is to protect the colony, and I would be negligent in that duty if I ordered a blind pursuit of a superior force and put the colony at greater risk. So, though my heart and soul beseech me to pursue and try to save Alis, who I know to be a most kind and gracious lady, the weight of my duty forbids it. I'm gravely sorry, Sir, for were it *my* choice alone, I would instantly and gladly risk my life to save her." He turned away, twice brushed his sleeve across his eyes, cleared his throat.

A stiff, pregnant silence hovered in the room like a musty smell. Chapman silently lowered his gaze to the floor; tears fell from his cheeks; he whispered, "I understand, Lieutenant, but I cannot abide my *own* inaction." He quickly spun about, bolted out the door.

Baylye yelled, "John, wait!" He glanced at Waters, who was on his way to the door. "Hurry, William!"

* * *

Johnny Gibbes turned his head stiffly toward Emily. "Thank you, Mistress Colman. You are indeed an angel."

Emily smiled meekly, finished wrapping a long strip of cloth around his neck, secured it with a knot, then stepped back to judge her work. "How does it feel?"

He mustered a tepid smile. " 'Twould be a lie to say it doesn't hurt, but you've greatly eased the pain."

"Well, you're quite fortunate, Johnny Gibbes. A stick's width closer to your throat and you'd not be here talking to me."

" 'Tis true," Elyoner said. She stood beside Johnson, the other wounded soldier, wrapped a strip of cloth around his shoulder as Shines watched attentively.

"Aye, I know." He touched his neck, smiled at Emily, then grasped her hand, held it to his lips. "Thank you again, Emily. I should be healing in a few days." He glanced at Emme, who lay sleeping beneath a blanket on Thomas Colman's bed. "Do you think she'll prevail?"

Emily smiled. "I'm certain of it. While you were tending to your men, she delivered endless bawdy exclamations over her condition then fell promptly and soundly asleep. She's definitely retained her spunk, but 'twas most fortunate the point went cleanly through her chest, else we'd have had to push it through . . . horribly painful. 'Twas also fortunate it went where it did; a little further inward and it might have passed completely through her ribs into her heart, or something else, and been impossible to remove . . . if she wasn't instantly dead. But as it was, she bled a lot, and she hurts, but 'tis under control, and she now needs a long rest. I shall keep her here with me for a few days, so I can treat the wound and watch her."

Gibbes nodded, stood to take his leave, beckoned at Johnson. "Well, she's in good hands with you, Milady, and I am deeply grateful. Could not have forgiven myself if she'd died helping me." He looked suddenly forlorn. "And I shall *never* forgive myself for the loss of Mistress Chapman."

Emily replied quickly, curtly, "Johnny Gibbes, do not blame yourself; you did everything you could to protect her, and what happened was *not* your fault."

Gibbes shook his head abashedly. "Would that it were so." He sighed, bowed, took his leave.

Johnson followed but stopped at the door, faced Elyoner. "Many thanks, Mistress Dare. You, too, are an angel."

Elyoner smiled, nodded, then led Shines to the fireplace and a large pot of bayberries immersed in boiling water, began skimming berry wax from the water's surface with a thin, rectangular piece of wood the length of a woman's shoe. After several swipes, she held the board over a smaller pot, also on the fire, used a knife to scrape the accumulated wax from the board into it, then motioned Shines to repeat the process.

Emily rolled her stump over to Emme, knelt beside her, touched her forehead, then watched the rhythmic rise and fall of the blanket covering her chest. Satisfied, she walked to her own bed where Virginia lay squirming and rooting, preparing to demand a meal. She picked up the grass doll Shines had brought Virginia, held it in front of her, watched her eyes glow, her hands animate excitedly, then grasp it and thrust it into her mouth. "No, no, little one. We don't eat our dolls . . . especially this clever, beautiful one Auntie Shines made for you." The doll was three inches wide, eight inches long, and crafted from a doubled-over tuft of grass bound by a tight piece of sinew at the neck to make the head. She had small tufts of grass—bunched together, cut to proper lengths, and bound—at her sides and bottom for arms and legs; her eyes and nose were small pebbles held in place by dried sap, as were her smiling lips which had been fashioned from a curved twig. She wore a soft doeskin dress and moccasins and had a neat tuft of long, black hair tied in a tail behind her head. Emily stared at her for a moment, felt a twinge in her heart as she thought of her own doeskin dress, which she'd started to burn after the rape but had instead folded and placed in her chest. She turned, smiled at Shines, who watched with a wide grin, then nodded and lifted Virginia from the crib. "Come, baby, time to eat." She carried her to the stump stool beside Emme, sat; unbuttoned her shirt, lowered it and her smock over her shoulders; offered a breast, which Virginia ravenously accepted. Emily pulsed with excitement as she felt the warm, flowing sensation in her breast, smiled at Elyoner. "Ellie, my milk's returned. You've no idea how I've missed this."

Elyoner smiled. "I knew it would, Em. Forsooth, you seem more yourself today in every way."

Emily nodded, looked down at Virginia. *I love you, my little one . . . as I shall love my own child. And I shall let nothing harm you. I've decided what I must do, and I feel the better for realizing it though 'twill not be the life I'd expected for myself. But for you and the one within me I shall give my life, and the peace brought by this decision must be why I have milk for you today. So eat hearty, dear Virginia. Verily, I'd forgotten how wonderful the pull of your lips feels upon me.*

She looked up, glanced at Elyoner and Shines, saw them whispering to one another, their faces but a few inches apart. "What ho, you two, what's amiss?"

Elyoner pulled back. "Oh . . . uh . . . I was telling Shines what a wonderful mother you are."

Emily gave her a suspicious look. "You lie, Elyoner Dare, I see it in your face. Truly, what were you saying?"

Elyoner looked at Shines then Emily. "Indeed, that is precisely what I said." She looked back at Shines, turning her head so Emily couldn't see her right eye, then spoke with her hands and a few English and Chesapeake words, followed by a wink. "I said Emily's a wonderful mother, yes?"

Shines nodded, first at Elyoner then at Emily.

Emily raised an eyebrow, replied with her free hand and some Chesapeake words. "I do not believe you either, Shines. But very well, keep your little secrets." She looked down at Virginia. *They're plotting something; but no matter, I shall watch your pretty little face instead of them.*

Elyoner started pantomiming the steps of making bayberry candles to Shines: fluttered her fingers to describe the wax melting; grasped both ends of a two-foot stick with five wick strings attached, pretended to lower it into the wax pot; hesitated; removed it, set it aside on two elevated supports as if to let it solidify. She repeated the procedure with the other three sticks then returned to the first and pretended to dip it again. Setting it aside, she made a circular motion with her right hand to convey repetition. Finally, she picked up a lit candle from the table-top, held it in front of Shines, whose dark eyes immediately glowed with childlike delight.

Later, as Elyoner and Shines skimmed wax, Emily burped Virginia, listened as Shines, with a shadow of fear on her face, told Elyoner that before the attack at the streambed, the Powhatans had been watching both villages, which had greatly discomfited the Chesapeakes; for though they disliked the Powhatans, they *had* sworn allegiance to their powerful chiefdom and agreed to be their allies. So there had been nervous talk of moving the camp away from the colony to avoid aggravating the Powhatans and incurring their wrath.

Elyoner said, "More good news, eh, Em?"

"Aye, indeed . . . Ellie, when do you think your father will—"

Emme moaned, pushed herself up on her elbow. "Ooooh! Hurts." She fell back to the bed.

Emily said, "Emme, be still." She hurriedly carried Virginia across the room, laid her in her crib, then picked up a bundle of fresh cloth, returned to Emme, joining Elyoner and Shines, who already knelt beside her.

"I want to sit up."

Elyoner said, "Very well, here, let me help you. Move slowly." She and Shines grasped Emme's arms, pulled her up to a sitting position as the blanket fell away from her bare upper body. "Chilly in here. Let's get something on you before you freeze to death."

Emily said, "Wait. I must change the bandage; 'tis quite bloody."

Shines raised both hands, signaled Emily to wait. She stood, rushed outside.

Emily and Elyoner watched her go; then Elyoner quickly retrieved a shawl, laid it across Emme's shoulders while Emily unwrapped the bandage and Emme groaned.

A moment later, Shines returned with a handful of mud and moss, knelt beside Emme. She looked at Emily and Elyoner, pointed at the mud and moss then at Emme's wounds, looked for approval. When Emily nodded consent, Shines laid the moss over Emme's wounds, packed a layer of mud on it, and nodded at Emily, who waited with her bandages.

Emme said, "Ooh! 'Tis quite chilly, but feels good."

Shines smiled. "Make better."

Elyoner and Shines held Emme's arms as Emily re-wrapped the wounds then pulled Emme's smock and shirt over her shoulders. "A most stylish shirt, Emme Merrimoth. Those bloody holes are quite attractive. Perhaps you'll start a new style in London." She smiled. "I'll get a fresh one from your cottage when I change the bandage."

"Aye. Thank you, Em. Did not expect to lose a good shirt to an arrow. Can I get up now?"

"No. Stay where you are. In fact, I'm keeping you here for a few days to ensure you behave yourself, for I know you to be a villainous sort . . . like me."

Emme smiled impishly. "I'm no such thing." Her smile slowly receded. "How is Johnny?"

Emily said, "Fine. He's returning to see you later."

Emme stared somberly at the blanket covering her legs. "Happened so fast. No time to think or be afraid . . . just threw myself on him . . . protecting him was all that mattered." She looked at the others. "You know, I love him, and . . . and . . . I'm not supposed to tell anyone, but you are my best friends . . . and I have to tell someone." She smiled. "Governor Baylye secretly married us yesterday."

Elyoner and Emily immediately leaned over Emme, congratulated her, hugged her, kissed her on the cheek. Emily then explained the excitement to Shines, who replied with a broad, toothy smile. Elyoner said, "Why secretly? 'Twould have been a rare, grand opportunity for some merriment in this morose colony."

Emme grinned for a moment then reclaimed her somber expression. "I should not have said anything; but we married secretly because Johnny fears Tayler will try to harm *me* to harm *him*, as you and I discussed, Emily. So please guard our secret." She shook her head. "I tell you, Johnny fears no man face-to-face, but a craven's strike to the back from the shadows is another matter, and such is Tayler's way."

Emily looked surprised. "You must know far more about Hugh Tayler than what he did to Johnny's sister."

"Aye. I know of his murder of Robert Wilkinson, his cowardice under fire, his affair with his commander's wife, his abandonment of his wife and children, and his rape and murder of a friend's wife. But there's something else. Johnny and the other sergeants, as well as Lieutenant Waters and Governor Baylye, believe Tayler leads a conspiracy to undermine and destroy the colony."

Shines said, "Tayler . . . bad man." She slid her index finger across her throat in a cutting motion.

The three Englishwomen gawked at her with wide, incredulous eyes and gaping lips.

After an awkward silence, Elyoner cleared her throat. "Well . . . Father knew there was something between Tayler and Lord Walsingham, but he knew not what. Pray he's put the puzzle together and returns prepared to deal with it."

Emily said, "And soon, I hope."

" 'Twill be soon. I'm certain of it, for I know he longs to see Virginia." She paused a moment. "Perhaps we should now enjoy a feast of smoked fish and pemmican."

After a meager meal, the three sat around Emme in silence until Elyoner nodded subtly at Emme and Shines, and all three promptly looked at Emily.

Emily said, "Why are you all looking at me like that?"

Elyoner again cleared her throat. "Emily, Emme told me you saw Isna a few days ago."

Emily tensed; her heart raced then pounded. "Yes . . . I did."

"But you fled him, didn't speak to him."

"Ellie, am I on trial? You know I no longer wish to see him, and I refuse to discuss it further."

After a long pause, Elyoner said, "I do not know Isna other than through your voice, but I know you love him. All of us know it. And Shines knows that *he* loves *you* and will do anything to help you."

Emily swallowed, looked away, fought the tears welling in her eyes. "It matters not." She closed her eyes. Oh, Isna, I miss you so. My heart, rending in two.

"But it *does* matter, Emily; and *you* matter, beyond measure, to all three of us . . . and to Isna. So we shall no longer abide your carrying this burden alone. You must share it with *us, now*." Shines and Emme nodded.

Emily's eyes lingered on Elyoner, read her resolve. She glanced quickly at Shines and Emme, saw the same, then looked back at Elyoner as her fragile composure began to melt like an icicle in a warm spring sun. Her eyes misted; her lower lip jutted forward and curled downward; tears rolled down her cheeks, dripped onto her lap; her hands trembled. "Ooooooh." She lowered her face to her hands, sobbed, shuddered.

The three stared helplessly at one another with anguished faces.

Emily sputtered, "You were right, Ellie . . . right about . . . about everything . . . he . . . he raped me . . . took my . . . my virginity . . . my life, my soul . . . and I hated it . . . but I pleasured in it . . . and now I am naught but a whore . . . a condemned sinner . . . a worthless slut . . . unworthy of a good man, if any were fool enough to want me . . . and a disgrace to any who might. I cannot do that to Isna, for I love him with all my heart and soul. Ooooooh. I want to die."

Elyoner rushed to her side, enveloped her in a tight embrace, then shook her head. "Please do not say that, Em . . . my poor, dear friend. How have you borne this alone?"

Emme whispered, "Emily you are wrong. 'Twas not your fault. You bear *no* guilt, *no* shame. 'Twas all *Tayler's* doing, and believe me, many a good man will want you, love you, understand what's befallen you, and think naught of it—see beyond to the wonderful, kind, innocent person you are."

Shines spoke in broken English. "Isna say"—she touched her heart, shook her head, motioned Emily to watch her hands—"Isna loves

Emily . . . more than his own life. He will do *anything* for her if she will let him."

Elyoner said, "What did she say?"

Emily again buried her face in her hands, moaned. "She said . . . Isna . . . loves me . . . oooh." She lifted her face from her hands, rubbed her eyes. "There's one thing more I must tell you. I've . . . I've missed my period . . . had the sickness, bleeding, dizziness, weariness . . . and I feel it inside. I *am* with child."

Elyoner said, "Oh, Em, my dear Em." She exploded with an angry, venomous look. "Damn him to hell, Em, you've tolerated too much, too long. By God himself, I shall see that filthy miscreant pay—slowly and painfully."

Emily stared grimly at her, shook her head. "Ellie, you mustn't say anything."

Elyoner's face was red, her eyes wild with rage. "The devil with that, Emily Colman. Tayler's a plague, and he must be treated so."

"No, Ellie! You must say nothing!" She paused, looked at the floor, composed herself. "Since the rape, I've thought of nothing but my situation and future; and I now know that for the good of my child, I must make my life with Hugh Tayler . . . though I detest the very thought of it."

Emme and Shines moaned; Elyoner stared glassy-eyed and dumbstruck.

"My child and I must have a means of support other than me selling my body." She watched their pained, sympathetic, faces.

Elyoner said, "Does he know of the child?"

"Nay. And I sha'n't tell him until I can no longer hide it. But, Ellie, I know for certain he loves me and will care for me; so mayhap I can change him for the better, perchance learn to love him . . . or at least tolerate him."

Elyoner shook her head wildly, shouted, "Nooo, Emily, can you not see? Being with him will solve nothing. 'Twill make matters worse. You'll hate and resent him every moment of every day. And forget not, he's a wanted man, a lying, murderous blackguard; and a sheriff or some angry husband, father, or brother will one day end his stinking, miserable life with a pistol ball or a noose." She leaned her angry face close to Emily's. "And where will you be then . . . the former mistress of a dead criminal? No, Em. Do not do this!"

Emily waved her hands, shook her head desperately at Elyoner, screamed, "Ellie, *I have no choice!* What am I to do? I must think of my baby, live for *it*, sacrifice my life for it, and forget about myself, Isna, my past life, my dreams, my everything. Why do you not understand?"

Elyoner started crying. Emme whispered, "And what will you do when he grows tired of you and the child, seeks other pleasures, other women, casts you out or abandons you as he did his wife and two children in England? What then, Em?"

Emily calmed, yielded to a stifling wave of despair, felt her intricate tapestry of self-delusion unraveling around her. Deceived myself, no future, especially with Hugh Tayler. "My God, Emme, I know you're right, but what else can I do? How can I live . . . how can I end this hideous nightmare?" She paused, again looked at the floor, sighed, then looked up at the others. "I'm to go to him tonight, please him . . . and I know in my heart he'll demand the same every night hereafter. So you see, I'm trapped . . . and I *must* go."

Elyoner waved her hands in the air. "Ahhhh! What are you saying, Emily Colman? God forbid it!"

Emme said softly, "Emily, you must not go to him!"

"Emme, I must, or . . . or. . ."

Elyoner said, "Or what?"

"Nothing."

Elyoner shook her head angrily. "Or what, Emily? What does he hold over you? How does he govern you like this? 'Tis insane." She stood, started for the door. "Enough! I'm telling Ananias."

"Noooooo, Ellie." Emily lunged after her.

Elyoner turned as Emily dropped to her knees, wrapped her arms around her legs, and sobbed hysterically. "Please, Ellie, please! Hear me! Do not do this! Please trust me."

Elyoner burst into tears, knelt, laid her hands gently on Emily's cheeks, then hugged her. "Emily, how can he do this to you? Your father's dead, and you're far too strong to be intimidated by threats against *yourself*. What is it, Em? Tell me."

Emily blubbered, "Please, Ellie, don't ask me this, I *beg* you, for I dare not tell you."

Elyoner studied her for a long moment before her face suddenly flashed a glimmer of discovery. " 'Tis Isna, isn't it?"

Emily looked away, rubbed her eyes, said nothing. Lord, what if he harmed Isna? Could he? No. He fears Isna, and he's a coward. But what if he had help, ambushed him? He could, dear Lord, he could.

"Emily! Is it . . . is it me? Or . . . or . . . dearest God in heaven, is it Virginia?"

Emily shrieked, buried her face on Elyoner's shoulder, shuddered, sobbed. "No, Ellie, no. Please stop."

Elyoner, Shines, and Emme looked at one another, their faces overflowing with anguish and frustration. Emme spoke softly, calmly. "Elyoner, Emily fears that if Tayler thinks she's told others of his threat, he will *carry it out* rather than be deterred from it." She looked at Emily. "I understand your fear, Em, but I believe you wrong. I think if all know the truth, he will be afraid to act; for he is, in the end, a coward."

Emily looked at her with a suddenly tranquil expression. "Emme, he is an *irrational, obsessed, likely insane* coward, and he will *not* act predictably. He also has henchmen who do his bidding." Her mind whirled, wobbled. We cannot assuredly protect Virginia, and Isna alone cannot defeat a band of assassins. So a momentary lapse could mean the end for both . . . and 'twould be my fault, and mine alone, plague my conscience for the rest of my life. And what matter if I then killed myself to spite him? They'd still be dead, and . . . and 'twould murder my child, and I'd have even *more* grave sin on my soul. In the end, I've no choice but to quietly and secretly bear this burden God has given me and do his will, for such will protect the lives of those I love and limit my sin to adultery.

Emme held a long, thoughtful gaze on Emily then sighed. "Emily, you may indeed be right." She glanced at Shines, then Elyoner, sighed despairingly. "God forgive me for saying this, but perhaps Shines was right." She sliced her index finger across her throat. "Perhaps we *should* kill Hugh Tayler?"

* * *

"So all in all," Waters said, "the men fought a courageous, effective fight against superior numbers." His face abruptly saddened; he bowed his head. "But the loss of Alis Chapman was a terrible blow, even though there was naught anyone could do to prevent it. And—"

Terse, accusatory, John Sampson interrupted, "Why did you not pursue the Powhatans and try to rescue her?"

"For the reasons I explained to John Chapman." He presented the case against splitting his command, leaving the village weakly defended. All but Willes, Stevens, and Sampson nodded understanding.

Sampson said, "Well, I disagree with your reasoning. The Powhatans will *never* attack these palisades. They'd suffer unbearable losses, and they know it. So I find your logic against pursuing the raiding party flawed and unsound. There's another reason why you didn't pursue, and I know what it is."

Waters smiled, crossed his arms across his chest. "Do you, indeed?"

"Aye, I do."

"Well, since you seem reluctant to reveal your secret to the rest of us, I shall say that you have less military training than that large spider climbing up your leg."

Sampson frantically bent over, brushed his legs, shuffled his feet; finding no spider, he glared at Waters amidst a sudden din of hearty laughter.

Waters gnawed on his lower lip to avoid smiling. "With all due respect for your intelligence, Master Sampson, please consider the possibility of a Powhatan strategy that draws a large portion of our force away from the palisades, so they can then strike the weakened, remaining force with overwhelming strength."

"Foolery! Savages are not that intelligent." He glanced down his legs, again checked for spiders.

"On the contrary, Master Sampson, such thinking is common among them; and I suggest that you, and perchance others of your persuasion, would scream the loudest when hordes of Savages came pouring through the palisades, bent on your annihilation. And I doubt, at that moment, you would see the merit of having dispatched a large part of our force in cold, blind, nighttime pursuit of a swifter force that knows where it's going . . . oh yes, and our force with the matches on its matchlocks glowing in the dark like small torches."

"You insult me, Waters, because I disagree with you, and you can ill tolerate it. I hold that you should have sent a contingent to help Master Chapman find his wife rather than forcibly returning *him* here and abandoning *her* to the pleasures of Savages." He looked around the room. Willes and Stevens mumbled support; others shook their heads dismissively. "He preferred dying, trying to save her, to being brought back here *without* her. So the truth, Lieutenant Waters, is that *you* were *afraid* to pursue."

Waters spoke emotionlessly. "It may be true that he preferred dying while searching for her; and had we not found him, he would surely have had his wish. But that aside, we shall remember your spoken preference for James Lassie's fate over being rescued if you should ever become lost in the forest as Master Chapman was."

Sampson blinked several times, glanced at his cohorts with a nervous dither in his eyes, then looked back at Waters and promptly dropped his gaze to the floor.

Waters studied him for a moment. "Master Sampson, I truly wish you no ill will. My duty is to protect the colony and ensure 'tis prepared to defend itself when the time comes, and I fear that time may come sooner than any of us think. But *whenever* it comes, we will need every man and woman, able-bodied and otherwise, to defend—to the death— whether or not they agree with Governor Baylye and me . . . and that includes *you* men." He eyed Stevens and Willes. "There is no alternative but certain death."

Waters floated his gaze from man to man, waited for replies, wished the scene he'd painted wasn't so frighteningly probable. "Now I shall discuss the ugly aftermath of the fight with the Powhatans. The mutilation perpetrated by one of our men was disgusting and intolerable, and such behavior will not be tolerated again. The man who committed the mutilation is a highly skilled, dependable soldier who was in a fit of anger over the death of his closest friend . . . which helps *explain* his behavior but in no way *justifies* it." He paused. "He has been dealt with privately by me; but any further deviance of this type will be dealt with by the lash, or if warranted, more extreme measures. Are there any questions? Governor Baylye?"

Baylye shook his head; no one spoke.

"Very well. Then what did we learn from this encounter? We learned that our tactical changes were effective but cannot completely overcome superior numbers—a lesson of great value since we will always be outnumbered, at least until Governor White returns. So how do we survive until then?" He paused, let the sobering reality of his question permeate and challenge their minds. "First, we must exercise greater precaution and vigilance in all we do; second, we must double the number of escorts for all outside work parties, which will require additional trained civilians; and third, we must complete the palisades." Loud groans inundated the room; Waters raised his voice. "In addition, we will post four guards high on scaffolds around the inside of the palisades, all day and all night; and last, until I state otherwise, there will be *no* unescorted sorties by *anyone* outside the palisades unless directly between our village and the Chesapeakes' or less than thirty yards into the forest beyond the clearing around the village."

After a brief silence, Thomas Stevens said, "Lieutenant, some of your measures seem reasonable and appropriate, but others are excessive and wasteful." He glanced around the circle of visibly anxious men. "The truth is that the Powhatans met their match in that fight and now understand we can hurt them." He shook his head. "They will *not* chance further losses by attacking us again."

Loud *ayes*, louder *nays*, raucous din.

Stevens shouted, "And most importantly, they will never risk an attack against the palisades, which are quite adequate and intimidating as they now stand. Further, we civilians have no interest in becoming soldiers *or* in unnecessary palisades construction. Protection is *your* job, and palisades construction is part of protection—also your job—for we civilians will soon have crops to plant. And last, restricting us to such a narrow band around the palisades is unreasonable and impractical; for as I've stated, the Powhatans have learned their lesson and will not return."

More *ayes* and *nays*.

Ananias Dare raised his hands, waited for silence. "Thomas, I disagree with you. That fight was naught but a skirmish in the Powhatans' minds. They've a huge number of warriors to send against us, and 'tis absolutely certain they'll return in force."

Stevens and his cohorts scowled.

Waters said, "Protest if you wish, gentlemen, but at this moment there are seven gaping breaches in the palisades wide enough for five or six men to pass through shoulder to shoulder. That condition is far from what any military mind would call secure. And the *only* advantage the palisades provide is the ability to shoot down at the Savages, both inside and outside the wall, from high scaffolds, or from ground level from behind the palisades, on both sides of the breaches as they pour through the gaps. But that *latter* tactic will surely result in our people on opposite sides of the breaches shooting each other while they're shooting at Savages." He paused, sighed a lengthy sigh. "There are but four ways to bolster the effectiveness of our palisades. The first is to complete them as designed."

Moans.

"Well, thank you all for telling me precisely what you think of *that* alternative."

Laughter.

"The second is to cover the breaches with horizontally stacked logs to a height taller than a man and place elevated platforms on the ground behind them for our shooters to stand on. The third is to, instead, build several log barricades thirty or forty feet inside the breaches, so they can be manned by shooters with a clear field of fire at the Savages as they concentrate through the breaches. And last is to build front barricades across the breaches, *and* rear barricades inside them so that if the Savages scale the *front* barricades, we can withdraw to the *rear* ones and shoot at them while they're scaling the front ones and unable to return fire. The obvious advantage of two, three, and four is that no time-consuming holes must be dug, no braces and pegs constructed, and no peg holes bored. We can simply cut and drag the trees to the proper locations and stack them. Of course, we'll also have to complete construction of the gate, so we can enjoy easy passage under normal conditions but lock it shut under threat." He surveyed their faces, felt an unexpected surge of assurance when he heard no objections. "Comments?"

Silence.

Baylye said, "Lieutenant Waters' proposal is an excellent one and achievable with the resources at hand; and those resources include *all* of us though I must point out that our soldiers are here to *protect* us . . . *not* for colony building, as some seem to think. And 'tis only through their good graces, and Lieutenant Waters' fine leadership, that they've worked with us every step of the way."

*Huzzah*s from all but the three.

"So I direct that we resume palisades construction—alternative four—as detailed by Lieutenant Waters, without further discussion."

Willes shook his head. "A breech of protocol, Governor. We are supposed to vote on proposals like this, and I'm certain I am not the only one who thinks building palisades for a non-existent threat is a foolish waste of time and manpower."

"I'm afraid you are quite wrong, Master Willes. The charter clearly states that the governor, with the counsel of the military commander, has sole responsibility for security decisions. Thus, as I said, this matter is closed. Now let us—"

"I care not, Baylye. That charter was written for a fully populated colony with enough manpower to build palisades. As this colony now exists, it has inadequate manpower to even gather the food we need, much less build palisades. I refuse to obey any order to—"

"If we're all dead at the hands of the Savages, we won't need food, Master Willes. Secure defenses must be our first priority, so do as your conscience demands, but know that I shall do as I say with regard to slackers."

Willes stepped forward, leaned his flushed face toward Baylye. "Are you suggesting I—" Sampson and Stevens gripped his shoulders. He glanced at both, read their eyes, stepped slowly back, scowled at Baylye then Waters. "We shall see where your proclamations go, Baylye."

Waters wondered why the trinity of conspirators had suddenly grown so openly disruptive and belligerent, why they'd not taken a more subtle, cunning approach to their sedition. The puzzle ignited his curiosity, vexed him, convinced him it was time to infiltrate the conspiracy and learn its intentions and strategy. Damn it, Waters . . . should've done so long ago.

Baylye continued, "As I said, the palisades will be completed as stated, with logging beginning as soon as the rain and snow slacken, and movement and placement of logs when the mud has dried. Meanwhile, we must focus, yet again, on our most pressing need after defense: our inadequate food supply." He paused, took a deep breath. "As I look around, I see faces far more gaunt and drawn than they were two weeks ago. In addition, we've witnessed shorter tempers, frequent altercations, and a rise in food theft. Gentlemen, I fear we approach the threshold of starvation; and though I understand hunger prompts men to do things they would not otherwise do, we can no longer tolerate the theft and hoarding that have recently occurred. Therefore, henceforth, ten lashes will be given to any man caught stealing or hoarding, and five to any man guilty of starting a fight. In addition—"

"And I suppose," Sampson snorted, "you will be the judge and jury?"

Baylye stared at him with a flat expression. "Indeed I shall, with the advice and assistance of Lieutenant Waters."

Stevens, smirked, flashed a glance at Willes and Stevens, then murmured, "Ah. King Roger and Prince William. Is that it?"

Ananias stepped forward, slowly eyed the trinity. "I know not what prompts you three to such blind, contentious opposition to every constructive thought proposed in this council; but I, for one, have seen and heard enough of it. 'Tis time for you to either help solve our challenges like responsible gentlemen or remove yourselves and leave the rest of us to do our duty."

All but the trinity shouted assent. Stevens' face flushed; he swallowed, shuffled his feet, flicked glances at Willes and Sampson, then looked meekly around the room like a scolded child.

Baylye nodded respectfully at Ananias then drifted his gaze from man to man. "To continue, partly due to the weather and partly to our own shortcomings, which I detailed in our last meeting, the food supply continues to lag our need. If we are to survive to plant our crops, we must take more drastic steps to remedy the situation. First, I have the names of three men, all of whom have been confirmed as slackers by at least three Assistants. They are Masters Kemme, Spendlove, and Wotton, and all three are hereby placed on half rations"—he eyed Waters—"for one week, or longer if their productivity does not improve."

Grumbles from the trinity.

"I must tell you that in the long term, I do not favor the forced cooperative endeavors necessitated by our present situation, and I eagerly anticipate the day when each man can be responsible for his *own* welfare and do as he pleases about providing for it. But that day is far in our future, so I cannot overstate the importance of all doing their share to ensure the colony's survival during this difficult time." He waited for dissent, heard none, quickly continued. "Therefore, despite the cold, the driving wind, and rough waters on the bay, we *must* increase our fishing intake. There's simply no other way to survive; for the deer population moves farther away each day, which will soon force us to hunt dangerous territories. If for a time we reduce the pressure on the deer by relying more on fish and shellfish, perhaps they will return."

Willes shook his head, rolled his eyes as if upset at having to endure Baylye's oratory. "Baylye, you miss, or choose to ignore, the obvious. The solution is to take food from the Chesapeakes, either outright or by making them hunt and fish for us, or both. They've vast stores of corn and other crops, as well as smoked venison and fish, which they've hidden from us. So we must force them to—"

"William," Roger Prat said, "that's profoundly absurd. The Chesapeakes don't have enough food for *themselves*, and they, too, suffer from our over-aggressive deer hunting. I know so because I hunt with them every day and have witnessed their desperation and concern. So—"

"Then we should immediately seize what they have. They're un-civilized heathens, without value compared to we Christians. Even God himself would not care if they perished."

Most cast incredulous glances at one another. Baylye said, "Master Willes, are you ignorant of the fate of the previous colony when they attempted to do exactly as you propose? No. I shall not lead us down that pathway under any circumstance."

Willes said, "No, Governor Baylye, I am *not* ignorant. But you clearly are if you cannot see the merit of my proposal. 'Tis plain as day to the rest of us." He glanced at his companions. "Yet you refuse to consider it because 'twas not your idea. Forsooth, you act more like a king than a governor, and we think you unfit to lead this colony." He again eyed Sampson and Stevens then the other Assistants, except Waters. "And I propose we elect a new governor."

Angry shouting erupted. Baylye's face flushed; he folded his arms across his chest. "Master Willes, as you well know, the governor of this colony was designated in Sir Walter Raleigh's charter; and that gover-nor, John White, duly appointed *me* to represent him and perform his duties until his return. So there will be *no such* election, and you will either cease your disruptions or depart . . . now!"

Willes' face twisted in anger. "By God's teeth, I'll not suffer this tyranny." He placed his hand on his dagger, stepped menacingly toward Baylye.

Prat, Hewet, and Waters quickly stepped in front of him. He pushed Hewet sideways, but Hewet pushed back. Willes drew his dagger, thrust it at him; Waters seized Willes' wrist with one hand, thumped his pistol soundly on his head with the other.

Willes dropped the dagger, staggered half a step, fell to his knees, and clutched his head as Stevens and Sampson caught him by his shoulders. Stevens leaned down, whispered, "Steady, William. Come, let us be away from here." He and Sampson lifted him to his feet, placed his arms over their shoulders, then turned him around and started for the door.

Waters said, "When he regains his senses, inform him he's under arrest for assault and that Sergeant Myllet will take charge of him. And if such is not to his liking, tell him to seek justice with the Powhatans."

Baylye stoically watched the three approach the door. "Master Willes' conduct leaves me no choice but to permanently remove him from the council of Assistants. You may inform him of *that* fact, as well . . . and due to the imminence of John White's return, we will not replace him, for I will again become an Assistant at that time. I now warn you two gentlemen that any further disruption of the sort witnessed today will place you in the same status as Master Willes. Do you understand?"

Stevens and Sampson sneered at Baylye, nodded subtly.

"Good. Then I bid you care for your friend, and pray the knock on his head put some sense into it."

Before moving, Sampson shot a hateful scowl at each Assistant, lingered on Baylye then Waters. "This is not the end of this." He and Stevens then turned Willes toward the door, half-led, half-dragged him from the room.

***

An hour after the other Assistants had departed, Waters, Baylye, and Ananias Dare sat by the fire in Baylye's cottage. Waters whittled on a stick, stopping now and then to toss the shavings that had missed the fire into the flames. Ananias rested his chin on his clasped hands, his elbows on his thighs. He watched Baylye intently as he spoke over the crackling of the fire. "So we agree their strategy is to instigate the colony's failure by first fracturing the council of Assistants, then the colony, into irreconcilable factions that refuse to cooperate, perhaps coming into physical or armed conflict with one another." He shook his head. "But how do they expect to survive such a self-imposed catastrophe? Forsooth, if half of us starve, the other half will starve, as well; and if the Powhatans charge through the palisades, they'll kill all in their path without regard to their loyalties. Yet they act as if God himself will rescue them before that happens."

Waters stopped whittling, looked at Baylye. "Not God, Roger, Lord Walsingham."

Baylye's eyes blossomed; his jaw dropped.

"I've pondered this for days, and *that* is the only answer that makes sense. Walsingham must be secretly sending a ship at a pre-determined time to rescue Tayler and his confederates, while the rest of us are left here to die by starvation or massacre. And that"—he gazed at Baylye then Ananias—"my dear acting governor and my dear son-in-law of the *appointed* governor . . . is why they've become so brazen in their disruptions. They must accomplish their mission *before* the rescue ship arrives, and *that* convinces me its arrival will be in the near future."

Ananias stared numbly at the fire then at Waters. "But what about John White? Walsingham's ship can't cross the Atlantic any earlier than John's can. A winter crossing is too risky, and Raleigh will surely outfit and dispatch John at the first hint of spring, so how—"

"Walsingham, Ananias. Walsingham. Forget not that he is the most powerful man in England, second only to the Queen herself. He will intercede in some manner to delay, or even prevent, John White's sailing; and by the time John finally arrives, if he ever does, the conspirators will be gone, and we'll be dead."

Baylye looked as if his favorite dog had died; he shook his head, rubbed his thumbs and fingers together. "My God, William, you paint a dreadful picture . . . unfortunately, one that has an unwelcome and chilling reality to it." He paused. "But how will the pilot of Walsingham's ship find us?"

Ananias smiled. "He'll go to Roanoke . . . and as you so carefully planned, he'll see CROATOAN and CRO on the tree and post then go to Croatan Island, retrieve our people, and come here." He snorted cynically. "And when John White arrives at Roanoke, if he ever does, he'll do the same; except when *he* arrives at Croatan, no Englishmen will remain. And unless Manteo happens to be there to tell him where we are, he'll never know our whereabouts. Even if a blind guess sends him here, we'll already be dead."

The three looked silently, reflectively at one another for nearly a minute before Waters spoke. "Gentlemen, here's what we must do."

* * *

Elyoner cradled Virginia as she and Emily walked briskly through the palisades gate toward the Chesapeake village. Virginia smiled with the rhythmic sway of her mother's step, chattered continuously. Elyoner said, "Well, aren't you the happy one today." She smiled at Emily. "Listen to her, Em. Quite a conversation she's having with herself."

"Aye, like a little squirrel, she is."

Elyoner sniffed the air. "Em, I know 'tis only February, but do you not feel a touch of spring in the air?"

Emily sniffed, smiled. "I do, and it lifts my spirits."

"Indeed." Elyoner peered ahead for several steps, progressively rearranged her smile into a frown, then abruptly stopped, faced Emily. "Em, you . . . you were to meet Tayler the other night. May I ask if . . ."

Emily's smile withered to a hollow stare. "No. I did not."

Elyoner grinned. "Thank God. How did you—"

"When I went out for water, I saw him from the corner of my eye watching me, but I pretended not to see him. And when he started toward me, I stopped, clutched my stomach as if I had terrible cramps, doubled over, knelt and moaned for a few seconds before continuing with a pained look on my face . . . I even staggered a bit. He looked aghast, immediately changed direction and walked away." She shook her head. "But I doubt 'twill work again, for he surely knows the length of a woman's period."

Elyoner held Emily's shoulders, kissed her on the cheek. "You've a quick wit, Em. No man relishes a tempestuous, bleeding woman, so perhaps 'twill work again. I myself have been cursed for two weeks on occasion. But 'twould be far better if you'd simply tell me how the lowly varlet compels you, so we can prosecute him."

"Ellie, you know I cannot tell you more; and though I despise it, I'm resigned to my fate and must face it." She thought of her friend Mary Thomas in England, who'd become pregnant at seventeen. She'd been shunned as an adulteress, disowned by her parents when she showed, and had hanged herself a short time later. Emily shuddered. The same will surely happen to me. I've but two choices: be an outcast whore, alone with my child, or be a whore to Tayler. But if I don't become Tayler's whore, then—

"Fate, shmate! 'Tis wrong that *you* pay for *his* crime. It infuriates me, and I'm loathe to promise I'll maintain my silence." She shook her head, again faced forward, resumed her course.

After a few steps, Emily said, "Ellie, pray tell, where are we—"

"To meet Shines, but I must first ask you something else. I've thought much on Emme's proposal. Have you?"

"Aye, and it scares me; for though I would savor Hugh Tayler being punished for what he did, I doubt *I* could deliver the punishment . . . and who but *I* could claim self-defense? Then too, while rape is supposed to be a capital offense, it seems the authorities often decide the *woman* was at fault; so in the end, I could be without a defense and tried for murder. And where would that leave my child? Oh, Ellie, my life, my choices, my future—all suddenly changed, vanished because of Tayler."

Elyoner stopped, faced her with a sad, thoughtful look, then pulled her into an embrace, leaned her head on Emily's, closed her eyes.

Emily whispered as if thinking aloud. "Worst of all, murder is a more serious mortal sin than adultery, and who am I to judge that *my* preservation"—and that of Virginia and Isna, she thought—"justifies the death of another . . . even Hugh Tayler? And what if God disagrees with my judgment? Verily, the truth is that every course before me is a grave sin, and my future is now narrowed to choosing the least of them. Still, the day may come when I've no choice but to defend myself in spite of all my reasoning. And then my life will be in the hands of a magistrate, and my soul in the hands of God."

Elyoner looked at her philosophically. "That may be true, but I've not a crumb of doubt that God would view your defending yourself against Tayler as self-defense."

"Ellie, even if that is so, I'd have to kill him in *my* house; for in *his* house, I would certainly appear to be a seductress. But I never want him to set foot in *my* house again. So . . . yet another dilemma." And, she thought, *wherever* I did it, Virginia and Isna would be saved, but I would leave a motherless child when hanged for murder. In truth, I've no escape.

Elyoner sighed. " 'Tis indeed an impossible situation." She hesitated, stared vacantly into Emily's eyes. "But mayhap there is another way." She crossed herself, looked suddenly afraid. "God forgive me for suggesting this, but I can see a time when, in spite of everything we've considered, there's no choice but for the *three of us* to dispatch this bastard to hell; and if it comes, Emme and I shall be at your side." She shook her head. "But Emily Colman, I state again that the only way to completely free yourself of this agony is to seek the aid of those who will help you . . . now . . . before the rest of this story has a chance to unfold." She looked abruptly ahead, proceeded another twenty yards, then veered off the pathway into the forest.

"Truly, Ellie, where are you taking me? You're being most mysterious about this. I thought we were going to meet Shines."

"We are, but in the forest . . . we have a private matter to discuss."

She sighed. "Very well, but we're not supposed to go this far."

Elyoner tugged her along with her free hand. " 'Tis only a short way farther, not far beyond the restriction."

Emily's eyes suddenly brightened. "Ellie, this is the way to my . . . my special place." A sudden pain pricked her heart as she visualized Isna in his buckskin leggings and shirt, white choker, long black hair, feathers, entrancing dark eyes, wry smile.

"Aye, it is, Em; we're to meet Shines there."

Emily shook her head. "You confound me, Ellie."

They entered the small clearing that was Emily's special place; Elyoner stopped, looked suddenly angry, frustrated. "God's teeth, Em, I'm getting forgetful . . . or stupid." She sighed. "I forgot the food I was supposed to bring . . . and I'm famished. Wait here. I'll be back in a moment." She turned, jogged back into the forest.

"Ellie, wait. Leave Virginia. I can . . ." Gone.

Emily sighed, looked around, smiled. *Feel the memories here.* She spontaneously spun around in a circle, her arms extended like a little girl twirling her dress. *Haven't done that since I walked down the pathway with George our first day at Roanoke. George . . . thank heaven you cannot see me now, though I gravely mourn your loss.* A feeling of sadness swept through her as she plopped down on the leaves by the stream bank, watched the water ripple over the rocks, and listened to its soft, reassuring purl. *Love that sound, free and endless. No ice now.* She thought of Isna. A lump grew in her throat; a sudden ache squeezed her heart. *So long ago, so many memories, beautiful memories . . . loving memories I shall never live again. Lord, how I miss him, love him so.* She surveyed the forest around her, brushed some leaves from the grass beneath them. *No green yet . . . and no buds on the trees.* She sniffed the air. *But Ellie's right, there is the smell of spring in the air. Won't be long . . . perchance another light snow or two, a little more cold, but green and warmth will soon overtake us . . . if we don't starve first. And John White will return, and my child will grow within me, soon show itself to the world, and . . . and*—tears trickled down her cheeks—*and Isna will return to his people . . . and I will have naught but his memory for the rest of my life, and*—

She heard a branch crack behind her, tensed, looked back over her shoulder, and slid her hand over her pistol grip. "Elyoner?" No, can't be Ellie, wrong direction, too soon. She stood, strained her ears for another sound, heard nothing. Stream's too loud. A chill raced down her back as she recalled the moments before the Roanoke massacre; she pulled the pistol from her belt, gripped it with both hands. No birds to warn me this time . . . shouldn't be here, stupid girl. After a soundless minute, she relaxed, replaced the pistol, again sat on the leaves watching the forest where she'd heard the sound.

Her gaze eventually wandered back to the stream then to the place where she and Isna had played the kicking-ball game. She smiled as she remembered smashing his fingers with her stick, tripping him, falling on him, their sensuous embrace, her abandonment of restraint.

Suddenly sensing a presence, she whirled around, sprang to her feet, gripped her pistol. Isna stepped from the trees at the edge of the forest. Her heart and mind fluttered with fright, passion, shame, joy; her legs trembled like flimsy sticks. Tears rolled down her cheeks as her eyes locked on his. She suddenly turned away, took a step; stopped, turned back; held her eyes on his, her resolve melting as she felt their pleading, their pain, their love.

He took a step toward her, stopped.

Her heart raced, hands quivered. "Isna!" She ran to him. "Isna, oh Isna." Their bodies met, embraced, melded to one. Their lips pressed together, hearts pounded like the drums of the harvest dance.

"My little white fawn."

"My Isna. Forgive me. I've hurt you so. I . . . I . . ."

"Do not speak. Hold Isna; let him hold *you*, feel your heart."

Emily sobbed, pressed her body tighter against him, kissed him frantically again and again. Her chest heaved with quick breaths as she whispered, "Isna . . . never let me go, never leave me . . . never, never, never." But a moment later, her body tensed; she eased her head away, looked emptily past him into the forest, visualized Tayler forcing himself inside her. She trembled; her eyes filled with fear. I'm a whore, unworthy, ashamed, destined to be with Tayler . . . but I love Isna; he stirs my soul, my blood; feel safe, secure; must never leave his arms, but . . . but . . .

"Emily fears something."

She nodded slowly, turned toward him with a heartsick look, whispered, "Yes."

He stared into her eyes, laid his hands softly on her cheeks, leaned forward, kissed her forehead, slowly pulled her into a gentle embrace. "Emily will be afraid no more. She is with Isna." He leaned his head on hers, held her close as she moaned softly.

When she'd calmed, she eased back, stared into his eyes; held his head in her hands, pulled his lips to hers; felt her heart racing, her breasts heaving with each rapid breath. She again eased back, smiled faintly. "Perhaps Emily and Isna will sit." She led him to the stream, pulled him to the ground beside her, looked at the water for a moment, then smiled at him, kissed him again. "How did Isna find Emily?"

He smiled his wry smile, held his silence for a moment. "Shines . . . Elyoner. They worry for Emily . . . worry for Isna. They know Emily suffers . . . they want to help her . . . and they know Isna wants to help her . . . but something keeps Emily *from* Isna . . . though her heart commands her to go *to* him." He paused. "In his heart, Isna knows something has happened to Emily." Another pause. "And Isna now tells Emily that he loves her above all things under Wakan Tanka and will give his life to end her pain. But first, he must know what causes it."

Tears ran down Emily's cheeks like hot wax down a candle; she stared into his eyes, couldn't speak, swallowed, took a deep, quavering breath. "Emily will tell Isna all that happened." With frequent tears, she told him of Tayler's courtship, his past, his love and desire for her. "And . . . and the day after the harvest dance, Emily walked with him to tell him she loved Isna, and . . . and . . ." She buried her face in her hands. I cannot tell him this.

Isna reached out, pulled her gently into his arms, held her head tenderly against his chest. "Isna will hold Emily until she is no longer afraid."

A minute later, Emily sniffled twice, whispered, "The white man, Tayler, took Emily's body . . . against her will." She started sobbing. "He took her life, her soul, her honor."

Isna pulled her closer, kissed her hair, held his cheek against her head, swayed her gently back and forth like a small child. "Did Emily believe Isna would turn from her?"

Her voice shimmered, cracked as she spoke. "Emily is . . . is dishonored . . . shamed . . . unworthy of Isna."

"*Emily* is not dishonored . . . nor is she shamed. Only the *coward* who forced himself on her is dishonored and shamed."

"No, Isna, Emily is unworthy, for though she hated what he did, she . . . she felt pleasure in it."

He paused a moment. "Only Emily's *body*, which could not hear the hate that screamed in her mind and heart, felt pleasure." He slid his hand under her hair, gently caressed the nape of her neck. "Perhaps Emily will also know that this evil one took *only* her body . . . *no one* can take her honor or her soul. These things were given to Emily by Wakan Tanka and will remain hers for as long as she breathes the air."

She looked into his eyes, blinked her tears away as they formed. "But Isna, Emily is . . . is no longer a virgin."

He shook his head. "Isna loves Emily all the more for her courage . . . and he will love her so forever." Again he pulled her into his arms, kissed her cheek.

"And Emily will love Isna until the sun no longer rises and sets."

"Isna knows this is so." He paused, feathered his cheek softly back and forth against her hair. "Isna now tells Emily that he will kill this evil one and take his hair from his head. But since there is no honor in keeping the hair of a coward, Isna will burn it, so Tayler walks without it in the next life and is scorned by all who see him."

Emily tensed. "Isna's words frighten Emily."

"Why do they do so?"

"Because if Isna kills Tayler, other white men will try to kill Isna . . . too many white men for Isna to defeat."

"These men must find Isna before they can attack him, but they will not find him because they do not know the forest or that it is Isna's friend . . . and if Isna is no longer here . . ."

Emily pulled away. The color fled her cheeks; she gaped at him with sad, fearful eyes. "Isna will leave the Chesapeakes . . . and Emily?"

"The warm-weather moons approach; Isna must lead his men back to the Lakota."

Emily turned away; tears filled her eyes. "Emily understands. Isna said it would be so." She rubbed her eyes. "But Emily was foolish. She hoped . . . and prayed . . . that Isna would . . ."

"Isna's heart is *also* troubled by this. His vision, Emily's dream—the bear and the little white fawn, the great bear's instruction to protect the little white fawn forever, the many brown and white fawns, and the old woman with the two black stones around her neck—how can the vision and the dream be fulfilled if Isna and Emily are apart?" He shook his head. "It is something Isna and Emily must think about, try to understand."

She looked at him with desperate eyes.

"And even if these white men find Isna before he leaves, he will kill many before dying a great warrior's death."

She shook her head rapidly. "No, Isna. Please. Isna does not understand these men."

"Isna understands, yet he wonders why these men befriend one such as Tayler . . . a coward whose heart burns with hate for himself . . . an evil man. Surely, they are like the people Ptesanwin spoke of when she told the grandfathers that as long as they kept and honored the pipe, they would live; but if they forgot it, they would be without a center and perish. Have these white men not lost their center? Do they not follow a path *away* from the one you call God?"

"Yes, Isna. They do, but—" She clutched her abdomen, bent over, took several deep breaths, smiled. " 'Tis my time." Would that it were so. She looked away for a moment then back at him. "There is something else Emily must tell Isna."

He looked perceptively at her, canted his head, eased her into his arms. "Be silent; find comfort in Isna's arms, the arms that will forever protect the little white fawn from all evil . . . as the great bear commanded."

They held each other in silence until Isna said, "Isna has learned that Emily's father has gone to the spirit world . . . he remembers when his own father and mother went there . . . he knows Emily's pain, and his heart aches for her."

She looked tearfully into his eyes. "Did Isna cry for his father and mother?"

"Lakota women wail and slash their arms and hair . . . Lakota warriors mourn in their hearts."

Emily nodded. "Nor does Emily slash her arms, but she misses her father and mourns him every day . . . and every day she regrets words she spoke to him in disrespect when his words angered her, though they intended no harm."

"It is proper to each day think of our fathers and grandfathers . . . our mothers and grandmothers . . . bring their wisdom into our souls as we do with the wisdom we acquire from our own mistakes. And Emily must also know that regret is part of grief. As Isna once told her, *all* people sometimes grieve . . . as they are also sometimes afraid . . . and it is these things—fear and grief—that make us whole."

She smiled. "And help us live the four virtues of Lakota men and women . . . the greatest of which is bravery."

"Emily remembers well . . . and she will also remember that fear and grief teach us bravery and inner strength, and that we must therefore experience them and then place them in their proper places in our minds." He smiled. "The little white fawn understands this because she has the gifts of the north and east."

Emily tilted her head. "What are *gifts of the north and east*?"

"Isna will tell Emily, but first he must explain the order of the world and how it determines these gifts." He crossed his legs, sat erect, assumed a scholarly pose, then brushed a two-foot-wide clearing in the leaves, scraped the yellow grass away so only bare earth remained. "All things in the world are in *rounds*, except the rock. Animal bodies and legs, plant stems, trees and their branches—all are round . . . as are the sun, moon, earth, and sky. Day, night, the moon, and the year all circle the earth, as do the four winds. But the world is *also* in fours. Four things sit above the earth: stars and sky, sun and moon; there are four parts of time: night, day, the moon cycles, and the year it takes them before they repeat the cycle; there are four pieces of each plant: flower, leaves, stem, and the roots that provide the water of life; four seasons: summer, fall, winter, and spring; four animal types: those who crawl, those who fly, the two-leggeds, and the four-leggeds; four virtues of men and women; the four seasons of life: that of the baby, the child, the mature adult, and the aged; and last, the four directions: north, south, east, and west."

Emily smiled. "Emily has never thought of the world in this way, but . . . but it is true."

He picked up a small stick, drew a circle in the damp dirt, scratched marks at its top, bottom, right, and left, then pointed with the stick as he spoke. "Just as the world is in rounds and fours, so is this circle, the circle of life, which represents the universe and everything within it—all animal families, human beings, the seasons, the earth, and all things upon it. The four marks are the four directions: north, south, east, and west. And each direction holds a certain gift. The north holds the gift of wisdom; the east, the gift of enlightenment; the south, the gift of innocence; and the west, the looks-within place, holds the gift of introspection."

Emily nodded as her eyes alternated between Isna and the picture in the dirt.

"Every human being is born somewhere on this circle or within it, and their position determines which of the four gifts they receive at birth." He pointed at the mark on his right. "So a person born here is a person of the east, with the gift of enlightenment." He then pointed at the bottom mark. "And one born here is a person of the south, with the gift of innocence; and here, a person of the north, with the gift of wisdom; and here, a person of the west, with the gift of introspection."

"But Isna said Emily is a person of the north *and* east. How can she have two gifts?"

"Because some people are born with two or three gifts, and Emily is one of these . . . she was born *here*." He touched his stick to the circle, halfway between the north and east marks. "But the strength of the gifts depends on where on the circle, or inside it, one is born, and the gift that one is closest to will be stronger than another." He pointed the stick closer to the north mark then closer to the east mark. "To be whole and balanced and more like Wakan Tanka, we must seek *more* than one or two gifts, and these additional gifts must be acquired as we walk through life. Emily will understand this; for she knows that if a person is only a wise person of the north, they will be wise but will lack the illumination that brings understanding. They will also lack both the introspection that lets them see within themselves and the innocence that allows the understanding and trust of other beings. So they will be a wise but cold person—one without feeling."

Emily nodded. "Emily understands. She has met people like this."

Isna then drew a line between the north and south marks, and another, between the east and west. "If a person is on one of these lines, they are on a pathway from their birth gift to the other three gifts, and their position on the line determines the strength of the other gifts in relation to their birth gift. So a person here"—he pointed at the middle of the line segment between the center of the circle and the west mark—"would be *introspective* but would also have lesser gifts of wisdom, innocence, and enlightenment. And one here"—he pointed halfway between the center and the north mark—"would be *wise* but would also have lesser gifts of innocence, enlightenment, and introspection; while one in the center of the circle, where the two lines cross, would share all four gifts equally and, like Wakan Tanka, be in perfect harmony with himself and all things in the universe. No human being can achieve this position, for it represents the spirit, Wakan Tanka himself, who is everywhere and in all things yet above all things. This center is the place of the pure heart and truthfulness, from which love and goodness radiate like the warmth of the sun—a secure, guarded place that is the center of goodness for all the universe. And even though no human being can *enter* the center, *every* human being should strive throughout life to touch and understand each of the other gifts, thereby becoming closer to the center, closer to being whole, and closer to Wakan Tanka."

Emily looked away, mused for a moment, then looked back at Isna. "Emily likes this, for it explains God's gifts better than she has ever heard. And . . . and Isna is right: no human being can enter the center of the circle; but . . . but most of my people believe that God, Wakan Tanka, long ago, sent his son to the world as a human being, to save us from ourselves; and since he was the son of Wakan Tanka, he too was at the center of the circle."

He looked at her with a pensive look, a soft smile. "The Lakota do not know of this man, but Isna would like to learn more of him."

She smiled impishly, nodded. "Emily will someday tell Isna about Him; but now, she wants Isna to show her where *Isna* is on the circle."

He looked embarrassed, slightly annoyed, pointed quickly to the top left of the circle, between the west and north marks. "Isna was born here; but like Emily, he is no longer on the edge of the circle." He made a new mark inside the circle, between the north and west lines but more to the east than the south, then looked back at Emily. "Isna's travels *started* him on the pathway to enlightenment, but knowing and loving Emily has taught him far more and also allowed him to learn from her the gift of innocence." He quickly made another mark inside the circle, this time between the north and east lines but closer to the center than his own. "But Emily has grown far closer to the center than Isna; for she has a strong gift of innocence, which she may have had at birth; and she also has touched the gift of introspection, which causes her to look deeply inward in all she does." He smiled, touched her cheek. "Emily has traveled far down the pathway to Wakan Tanka."

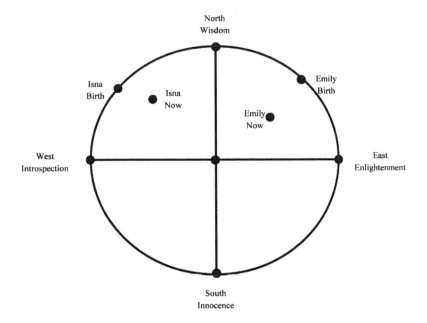

They held hands, stared silently into each other's eyes. Tears tumbled down Emily's cheeks; she smiled, leaned slowly forward, placed her hands behind his head, then pulled his lips to hers. He embraced her, eased her gently to the ground, where they held their lips and bodies together while their love-fueled passions rose toward the threshold of flames.

*　*　*

A pang of sadness gnawed at Emily's heart as, hand in hand, she and Isna approached the edge of the forest by the Chesapeake village. She glanced silently at Isna several times, and he at her. They'd stepped but two feet into the clearing when Emily stopped, pulled him back into the forest, threw her arms around him in a frantic embrace. They stared longingly at one another, kissed, smiled. "Emily's heart will cry until Isna is again near her."

"As will Isna's." He nodded once, turned, walked away toward the Chesapeake village. Emily watched him for a moment then started toward the colony. She was halfway there when a staggering thought bludgeoned her mind: Tayler . . . surely furious with me. A chill raced down her back. My God, what if . . . what if he's made good on his promise, hurt Virginia. Good Lord, please don't let it be. She lifted her skirt above her ankles, ran as fast she could. Virginia, Virginia, must find you. Lord, let her be safe. She gasped for breath; her heart pounded. "Oh!" She tripped over a root, sprawled front first onto the ground, gasped for air, found none. More gasps, then finally breath. She struggled to her feet, sprinted for the palisades as new images flashed through her mind with each gulp of air. Virginia . . . please . . . be there . . . please . . . please. She envisioned her lying in her crib, face blue from strangulation, eyes bulged wide, unmoving, sightless, her body still. Oh, God! She raced through the palisades gate, saw no one on the green; her throat burned for air. Keep going . . . Em . . . hurry . . . Virginia . . . be there. She reached the Dares', burst through the doorway. No one here. She dashed to the crib. Gone! Dear God! Where can she be? She turned, ran to the door, imagined Virginia lying dead, bloodied in the forest. She stepped outside, looked for people, saw none but the sentries. Ellie, Ananias, where are you, must find you. My God, save her! My fault . . . all my fault! Dear Lord, where is she?

CHAPTER 13

A s Waters sucked in a big gulp of air, he savored the fresh, lingering smell of the previous night's downpour, decided it was the
cause of the spring-like feel in the air that had invigorated his usually
reluctant loggers. But at the same time, he wondered if he'd been hasty
in restarting the palisades work on such wet and muddy ground—too
much slipping and sliding, and the wet bark increased the risk of an
axe glancing off a tree trunk into someone's leg. He stood with a small
group of sawyers and limbers on the far side of the clearing from the
palisades, watched two axemen vigorously attack a sixty-foot tree from
opposite sides. Deciding they were exercising proper caution, he forced
his mind to the unpleasant reality that it was now unlikely the palisades
would be finished before John White returned—too many now hunting, fishing, guarding—only a small contingent left for palisades work,
and most of them ill fit for the task. Nonetheless, even though the work
was slow and laborious and the heavy, green logs had to be carried
ever farther, each new log brought added protection to the village. So
persevere, persevere, persevere.

He then daydreamed of Rebecca Roberts—her smile, long brown
hair, green eyes, somewhat plain yet captivating face, and slightly
buxom body. It had been her smile that attracted him; and when he
thought of her, it was always the first thing he saw, a permanent fixture
of her visage. They'd fallen in love immediately; but her father had
harbored nagging doubts about his daughter marrying a soldier—not
because he had anything against soldiers, especially officers of good
breeding, but because he didn't want his daughter to be a young widow.
So he'd withheld his blessing for a time—too long a time—and the day

before he'd given it, Waters had accepted the Virginia command, which was a career opportunity he could not pass up—a lieutenant in sole command of a contingent that would normally be commanded by a senior captain. His superiors had told him if all went well, he'd be immediately promoted upon his return—perhaps two ranks—a prospect that somewhat lessened the pain of Master Roberts' awkward timing. But now he was beginning to wonder if he'd live to see England and Rebecca Roberts again.

Peripherally conscious of the rhythmic thuds of the two axes striking the tree, his thoughts drifted to something that had nagged him all day: Elyoner Dare's curious reply that morning when he'd asked her about Emily Colman, voiced his distress at seeing her with Hugh Tayler. Elyoner had told him that when she'd seen Emily the day before, she'd initially been quite distraught over something but had calmed when she'd found Virginia with her parents at Governor Baylye's cottage. Elyoner had then started to tell him something else but stopped in mid-sentence. The entire exchange now chewed on his mind like a dog gnawing on a bone. What had Elyoner started to tell him? Why had she held back? Why had Emily been so frantic about finding Virginia? He rubbed his chin. What was she afraid of? He stared at the ground for a moment then raised an eyebrow. Perhaps Tayler's threatened to harm Virginia . . . or . . . or worse . . . if Emily does not do his bidding, and . . . and the poor lass bears the entire burden alone. He shook his head, stared dejectedly at the forest. So what did Elyoner start to tell me? He rubbed his chin again. Perhaps she knows something of Emily's plight . . . and . . . and she's sworn to secrecy but started to tell me anyway because it torments her to keep it inside . . . then she changed her mind . . . and two shillings says Tayler's taken advantage of Emily and will do so again. He stared vacantly for a moment. "Bastard." I cannot abide this, must somehow persuade her to tell me what's happened, so we can prosecute this swine and give him what he deserves . . . protect her. He sighed, shook his head. 'Twill be an arduous task to draw her out . . . unbearably painful for her to speak of it, but I must try. He

glanced at the two axemen, thought they'd moved too close together, particularly since one was left-handed.

A loud crack ripped through the air as the tree snapped from its stump, plunged toward the ground, and crashed with a muffled thud into the mud. Taking a deep breath, Waters looked around, saw Thomas Stevens, Private Taverner, and Humfrey Newton whispering secretively to one another as they approached the tree to trim limbs. It had not escaped him how quiet Tayler and his miscreants had been of late; but he'd wondered about Newton, who'd previously been little more than a shadow—yet a shadow with a reputation for sudden, stupefying displays of rage. Ah! He smiled faintly. Forgot he's one of the two former convicts—not surprising to see him with Tayler's bunch after all . . . wonder what they're plotting. He picked up his axe, looked around the clearing; accounted for each of the four guards, ensured they were alert, looking in the right directions; then walked toward the far end of the tree just as several ladies arrived with smoked fish, water, and pemmican.

The men received their rations, dipped their cups in the water buckets, then walked back to the downed tree, sat wherever they found space between the branches. Several picked up sticks that had broken off when the tree fell, used them to scrape the huge globs of stick mud from their shoes before they ate. Stevens and Taverner sat ten feet from the other six men, but Newton sat barely four feet from Cuthbert White, who meticulously removed not just the *big* globs of mud from his shoes but *all* of it.

Waters watched White with amusement from a hundred feet away thought how, despite always being impeccably dressed, and wrong voting for Tayler in the election, he seemed a good man—ever willing naturally helpful, in spite of being gentry. Waters smiled as he watched him shift his food and stick between hands to avoid dropping the food as he experimented with stick positions to effectively remove the mud Finally, he seemed to tire of the endless juggling, carefully set the food and cup on the log beside him to concentrate on the muddy shoes.

Waters looked back at Stevens and the other two, saw nothing to arouse his interest, started to look toward the palisades, but his periphery caught Newton sliding down the log toward White.

Newton looked back at Stevens and Taverner, smirked knowingly, then turned to White, said something Waters couldn't hear.

White stopped scraping, stared incredulously at Newton, mouthed something.

Newton responded with more words and an angry glare. The other loggers stopped eating, focused on the two as White suddenly snatched his food from the log, placed it in his lap, covered it with both hands as if to protect it, again spoke to Newton.

Newton sneered, barked loudly, "Perchance you didn't hear me, White. I said give me your food, now!"

White shook his head, again spoke too softly for Waters to hear. Waters started toward the two.

Newton stood, reached for White's food; but White pulled it to his chest, turned his back to Newton.

Newton grabbed White's collar, yanked him off the log, shoved him to the ground, then kicked him twice in the back.

White groaned, rolled toward the log, still clutching his food.

Waters pulled his pistol, broke into a run. "Newton, stop!"

Newton stepped over White, turned about, kicked him in the stomach.

White groaned, dropped his food, grabbed Newton's foot with both hands, then twisted until Newton, a slight man, spun about to avoid disjointing his leg, dropped to his knees, and tried to kick free. "Let go of me, you son-of-a-whore!" He wiggled back closer to White, stood, and twisted toward him; whipping a dagger from his belt, he stabbed it into White's shoulder, then into his back.

"Ahhhh!" White flattened onto his stomach.

His leg freed, Newton grabbed an axe from the log, lifted it overhead, started to swing it downward at White's head, but stayed the blow when the bore of Waters' pistol pressed harshly against his head.

"Drop it, Newton!"

Waters summoned three soldiers, who tied Newton's hands behind his back while several of the loggers attended to Cuthbert White. The soldiers then placed a rope around Newton's neck, led him behind Waters to Roger Baylye's cottage, where they waited until Baylye and Ananias Dare arrived, followed by Myllet and Smith. Waters motioned the sergeants to take charge of Newton and follow Baylye and Ananias inside. He turned to the soldiers. "Find Sergeant Gibbes. Tell him I said to post four guards around this cottage, fifty feet out from it. Let no one in or out. We'll be conducting a trial. Understood?"

"Aye, sir." Two soldiers immediately took up positions fifty feet from the cottage while the third trotted off to find Gibbes.

Waters entered Baylye's cottage, nodded at Baylye and Ananias, then spoke to Myllet and Smith. "Sit him down; don't let him move." He looked at Baylye and Ananias, flicked his head toward the door, led them outside.

Newton watched them leave then anxiously eyed the two sergeants. "What are they going to do to me?"

Myllet said, "They're going to try you for assault with intent to kill ... perchance also for stupidity in doing so in front of the lieutenant and the others."

Newton spit on the ground. "I care not, been tried before."

Smith said, "For a hanging crime?"

"What ... what do you mean ... hanging crime?" He swallowed hard. "I ain't killed no one."

Myllet said, "Matters not. You should read the charter, Newton ... if you can read. Says assault with intent to kill, and several other things, are capital offenses under martial rule ... which we are under." He slowly eyed Newton from top to bottom with a studious glare. "You're not a heavy man, Newton ... probably kick a long time before you strangle and die."

A sudden pall of fear spread over Newton's face.

Waters, Baylye, and Ananias re-entered. Waters walked to Newton, glared down at him. "Master Newton, as a witness to your crime, I charge you with assault with the intent to kill; and since we are now under martial rule, we've no need of further discourse. Accordingly, the tribunal, composed of myself, Governor Baylye, and Master Dare, has judged you guilty and hereby sentences you to be immediately hanged or beheaded, as you choose. We'll not waste good shot and powder on such as you." He looked at the sergeants.

Newton looked shocked; he panicked then scowled. "You can't do this, Waters."

"No?" He looked at Myllet and Smith. "Very well. Hanging it shall be . . . cleaner than the axe. Lead him outside to the tree where we hanged Clement. I shall meet you there with the rope in a moment. Have the guards accompany you, and tell one to bring a tall stump to stand him on while we adjust and tighten the noose. We'll then draw straws to see who kicks the stump over. Meanwhile, Master Dare and Governor Baylye will summon the colony."

"Aye, sir." The sergeants seized Newton's shoulders, stood him up while Myllet tightened the lead rope around his neck, tugged him toward the door behind Waters.

"Wait, wait! I wasn't trying to kill him. I only wanted his food. I'm hungry, starving."

Waters looked back. "So are we all."

"But, Lieutenant. This ain't fair. 'Tis not right."

"Was it right for you to stab Master White?"

Pause. "No. No, sir. I . . . I was angry, lost my senses for a moment. Please . . . please don't hang me. I didn't mean to hurt him. Please! I'll do anything. Don't hang me!"

Waters stopped, faced Newton, stared at him for a long moment, then looked at the sergeants. "Sit him down."

The sergeants led Newton back to the stool, pushed him roughly onto it. Waters stared at him intimidatingly until he began to fidget, then said, "We know Tayler's plan and who's behind it. We also know about the ship Walsingham is sending to rescue all you conspirators. But your rescue is overdue . . . is it not, Newton?"

Newton blinked, swallowed hard, shifted himself around on the stool, avoiding Waters' eyes. "How could you know such things?"

"Not for you to know, Newton; but I tell you now, your rescue ship will *never* arrive, and all of you will hang from that big oak tree out there when Governor White returns." As he extended his arm and index finger to the left, he held his gaze rigidly on Newton's eyes, watched his anxious face contort while he digested the words. "That is, all will hang except *you*, Newton, for you'll already be hanged . . . if you do not do as we tell you. But if you *cooperate* and help us thwart Tayler's plot, you will live and receive a pardon from Governor White."

Newton's face immediately brightened with hope; he almost smiled. "Can you guarantee my safety? They'll kill me if they learn of this."

Waters glanced at Baylye then back at Newton. "We will do all in our power to do so, but you must keep your wits and not do anything stupid to betray yourself."

He took two deep breaths. "Very well. I shall do as you ask . . . but they'll be wonderin' why I'm free without even a flogging. What do I tell them?"

Waters nodded. "Good point." After a brief contemplation, he said, "If they ask, tell them we discovered White had stolen food from you yesterday, and we therefore ruled that your action was partially justified and required naught but a warning. Now, tell me what Tayler promises the men he recruits."

Newton stared blankly for a moment then swallowed. "Money . . . and land . . . when we come back to start *Walsingham's* colony."

Waters glanced at Baylye then back at Newton. "Tell me about Tayler and Mistress Colman."

Newton shook his head minutely, blinked several times. "I know nothing of that."

"Come now, Newton, this is not my first interrogation. Tell us what you know . . . now! Or the bargain's off."

Newton glanced around the room. "Truly, I know nothing of it."

Waters grabbed Newton's shirt with both hands at the chest, yanked him from the stool to within an inch of his face. "Newton, you tell me now, or you're a dead man."

Newton trembled; his breath quickened to a near pant. "He . . . he wants . . . wants to marry her but knows he can't while he's here . . . so he'll take her any way he can, if you know what I mean. But I think he truly loves her . . . for he plans to take her back to England . . . marry her there when his other marriage is annulled . . . with Walsingham's help."

Waters relaxed his grip. "She hates him. How does he force her to do his bidding?"

"I . . . I know not, but . . . but . . ."

Waters grabbed his shirt, again yanked him off the stool. "But what?"

"He . . . he holds something grave over her . . . but again, I know not what."

"Hell's fire, you don't. Tell me! Now!"

Newton swallowed. "He . . . he's threatened to kill people . . . people she loves . . . if she doesn't do as he says."

"Which people?"

"I know not."

Waters shook him twice, again held him an inch from his face, hissed softly, "Yes, you do, Newton; now tell me!"

"I promise you, Sir. I know not."

Waters dropped him back on the stump, glanced at Baylye, Ananias, and his sergeants, then back at Newton. "Find out. I want to know by this time tomorrow. Understand?"

Newton shook his head. "How can I do that, Lieutenant? No one but Tayler knows."

"Find a way! And for encouragement, imagine yourself hanging from that tree, slowly strangling, kicking your legs and pissing your pants while your sorry life slips away." He paused, leaned over Newton, glared down at him with beady eyes. "Now, this is what you must do."

***

The Panther wore a gloomy frown as he stepped briskly across the village toward Wahunsunacock's lodge. Most unusual for the leader to summon him in advance of a council meeting; and *that* fact, combined with the disappointing engagement with the white men, had caused his mind to swirl with discomforting anticipation. Still, their losses, while greater than anticipated, had not been unacceptable . . . and they'd killed one white man, wounded three, and taken one woman captive; and she now pleased many warriors and worked hard, though she sometimes had to be beaten. We will keep her, he thought, until the warriors tire of her, then kill her and return her body to the whites to taunt and terrify them . . . or perhaps we'll kill her while they watch, then quickly escape into the forest.

He stopped in front of the great chief's lodge, scratched on the hide that covered the entry. One of Wahunsunacock's wives opened the flap, nodded toward the chief, who sat by the fire, staring into the flames. The Panther walked to the fire. "Great Chief, you summoned Kills-Like-the-Panther."

Wahunsunacock looked up, nodded, pointed to the other side of the fire. When the Panther had seated himself cross legged, Wahunsunacock handed him a white pipe with several shark's teeth embedded in the side. "Let us smoke, my friend."

Though the paramount chief's easy manner tempted the Panther to relax his stiff tension, he could not do so, retained his anxious, cautious edge. He nodded, received the pipe, took several deep draws; nodded again, handed it back to Wahunsunacock; waited respectfully for him to speak.

Wahunsunacock seemed in no hurry, took three lengthy draws, blew a large, lazy cloud of smoke over the nearly smokeless fire, then watched it float lazily upward toward the smoke hole. Finally, after a lengthy, reflective silence that heightened the Panther's discomfort, he set the pipe aside, looked stoically at the Panther. "As you know, before the sun sets tonight, a council of not only *our* people but of *all the tribes* of the chiefdom, except the Chesapeakes, will meet here to plan the destruction of the white men."

The Panther nodded.

Wahunsunacock again studied the fire with an indiscernible expression until finally, he looked back at the Panther, his thoughts and mouth apparently united. "What lessons did Kills-Like-the-Panther learn from his fight with these people?"

The Panther had planned to address this over-ripe question, though like all good leaders, he'd planned to state the lessons of the last fight as part of the strategy for the next. So Wahunsunacock's surprising bluntness dismayed him, further aggravated his concerns; for the great chief never asked a question without an important reason behind it and a serious, unspoken message within. And the Panther read *this* message as Wahunsunacock's displeasure at the outcome of the fight. "Great Chief, we found them better prepared than before and"—it pained him to say it—"better warriors than we expected to meet." He watched for a reaction, saw none. "They used not only their big sticks that bark but also very long bows . . . longer than our own, and their arrows came rapidly and accurately from greater range than ours." His stomach churned with embarrassment then burned with anger, lust for revenge. "As you know, we lost two warriors killed and two wounded. This was because Kills-Like-the-Panther failed to anticipate the white men fighting this way, but we have now learned what they are capable of. When we next fight them, we will remember these lessons and engage them with enough force to overwhelm and rub them out without excessive losses."

Wahunsunacock nodded, spoke in a subdued tone. "No warrior wins every fight, my friend, and all *great* warriors suffer defeats, and these defeats make them wiser and better leaders. Kills-Like-the-Panther is one of these great warriors and leaders, and he has learned well from that which did not go as planned." He paused, stared into the Panther's dark eyes. "How will he use these lessons in the final attack?"

The Panther said, "Great Leader, we must first watch the effects of hunger on the white men's behavior. We must wait for them to argue with one another, challenge their leaders." He paused, anticipated Wahunsunacock's next question. "We will watch them from the forest and from the Chesapeake village."

Wahunsunacock again gazed thoughtfully into the fire. "Will not the white men notice us among the Chesapeakes? And will not the Chesapeakes themselves be suspicious?"

"Any white men who see us will not know us from the Chesapeakes, and so, will not be suspicious, and the Chesapeakes are used to seeing us among them for trade and to collect tribute, and will not be alarmed." He started to tell the chief that he himself would sometimes watch the white men but thought better of it, knew the wise leader would counsel against it. Yet he knew, in spite of such counsel and the inherent risk of recognition, he would not be able to resist the temptation to glimpse the beautiful, young, dark-haired girl with eyes like the sky, convinced himself that he could watch her for days without her seeing or recognizing him. Still, he admitted as he unconsciously touched her knife scar in his side, there *was* that chance. But is not life built upon chance?

"And what of the warriors from the far north?"

"We are told they have no wish to be our enemies and that they return to their own people during the planting moon, which starts in a few days." He saw from Wahunsunacock's expression that he was less dismissive of these warriors, so he spoke quickly to preempt another question. "We also know that the white men again cut trees to close the seven gaps in their fort. If they do this before we attack, we will lose many more warriors. While it is important to let them grow weak from hunger and fight among themselves, it is *more* important that we attack before they close these gaps . . . and that time may be closer than we now expect."

Wahunsunacock sucked on his pipe, got no smoke, inspected the bowl. "Poor pipe. Won't stay lit." He picked up a small burning branch, held it on the bowl, and took several deep draws. "And what sort of attack does Kills-Like-the-Panther plan?"

The Panther looked stoically at Wahunsunacock. "We will approach the fort in darkness from four directions while all but the sentries sleep, though their sentries often sleep while they're on guard. We will carry eight concealed live embers; and when we near the edge of the forest, we will shield them with deerskins while we quickly make small fires and light arrows, which we will immediately shoot into their lodges to begin the attack. All of their lodges are grass and will burn quickly, perhaps trapping some inside. The whites will panic and be unable to mount a defense as we quickly enter the fort and begin killing them . . . all of them . . . except perhaps some women, who we can capture, bring here, and use for a time . . . if such is the wish of Wahunsunacock and the council."

Wahunsunacock nodded. "We will use these women then burn them so no trace of white people remains."

The Panther nodded, thought again of the dark-haired one; he knew he would never tire of her, would have to find a way keep her alive . . . at least until more white men came.

"And the Chesapeakes?"

"With warriors from seventeen tribes of the chiefdom, we will have as many as four hundred warriors . . . enough to surround and attack both villages at the same time. But we will tell only the Nansemond and Warraskoyack, the Chesapeakes' neighbors, that we plan to attack the Chesapeakes and rub them out. They will attack the Chesapeakes *with* us and later divide their hunting and farming grounds between them . . . so we must take care that the Chesapeakes not learn of our council meeting tonight." He watched Wahunsunacock's face for a glimpse of his thoughts, saw none.

Wahunsunacock nodded, studied the fire for a moment, then looked at the Panther. "Kills-Like-the-Panther makes a good plan. Let it be done as he says . . . before the planting moon has passed."

* * *

Emily, in her doeskin dress, knelt with Shines as they scraped the last bit of flesh from the two deer hides staked out in front of Shines' lodge. They'd seldom spoken but had occasionally glanced at one another—Emily's face saturated with fermenting anxiety and Shines' with painful empathy. Emily had repeatedly blocked thoughts of Isna's approaching departure; but each time, they quickly reappeared, saddened her to the point of tears. She knew he had to lead his men back to the Lakota, knew with equal certainty, she could not prevent it even if she were selfish enough to try, so she grudgingly accepted both realities though they pressed her heart like a tightening thumbscrew. 'Tis a cruel yet inescapable truth, she reasoned, that Isna, the man I love with every grain of my being, will leave, and no less cruel and inescapable that I am to have a child by an evil man I hate yet must rely on for whatever future awaits me—a man I must, today or tomorrow, again lie with and surrender my body to. So would it not be nobler, and less painful to both Isna and me, if I confronted reality and parted with him now before he tries to kill Tayler and loses his life on my behalf? I could not bear such . . . forsooth, I would kill myself. And regardless of what I do, my condition will soon be evident to all; and I'll be branded an adulterous whore, shunned, without friends, banished from the colony . . . in spite of what Tayler wants. Where will I go? What will I do? How will my child and I live? Oh, God, how will I care for my child?

She stopped scraping, sat up, stared into oblivion. Will it be a boy or a girl . . . like me or like Tayler? Who will it look like? She shook her head, forced the thoughts from her mind, resumed scraping, again thought of Isna's departure. She then visualized herself in Isna's arms two days before, a hair's width from abandoning restraint, wished now she'd yielded to her heart, knew her surrender would have melted Isna's iron will like butter in a hot cook pan. Damned inescapable morality . . . Mother's doing . . . Isna's, too . . . and how can I ignore God's commandments then ask for his help?

She felt Shines' eyes upon her, forced a tepid smile while her mind wrestled with the thought of ending her relationship with Isna that very afternoon. But, dear Lord, how?

Shines suddenly smiled, looked up at something behind Emily.

Emily turned, saw Isna looking down at her with his wry smile. She sprang to her feet, lunged to his arms, leaned her face against his chest, closed her eyes, and whispered, "Isna, my love . . . please, never leave me . . . never." Her resolve to end their relationship evaporated like steam from a boiling kettle. Desire flooded her mind; she decided she was incapable of anything but total, abiding love for him, no matter what pain was imposed by his leaving, determined to revel in his presence for as long as it lasted, ignore her life's daunting tribulations.

* * *

Lieutenant Waters' boundaries did not apply to the Chesapeakes and Lakota, so Emily decided she was Lakota when she was with Isna. Thus, the two again sat by the stream at her special place; and though she felt vulnerable to the Powhatans, she decided that dying with Isna at their hands was preferable to watching him walk away forever. She smiled coyly as she reached into the canvas bag on the ground beside her, stole a quick glance at Isna, then suddenly turned her back toward him to block his view as he peered around to see what she was doing. "Perhaps Isna will be patient and not try to see what he is not yet meant to see."

Isna recoiled, frowned, looked away with an insulted scowl.

Emily removed something from the bag, quickly held it to her chest, shielding it with her hands. "Isna may now look." She turned toward him, smiled, handed him a shiny metal hatchet with an eighteen-inch-long wooden handle and a nine-inch head, one end of which was a four-inch-wide cutting edge, and the other, a three-inch spike. Her eyes sparkled as Isna looked at her, slowly slid the hatchet from her hand.

He gripped the handle in his right hand, made several thrusting motions in different directions, rubbed the thumb of his left hand across the cutting edge, nodded, smiled. "Light . . . good balance . . . sharp. Isna has never seen such an axe. What rock is it made of?"

"It is called iron. We build all our weapons with it. 'Tis more difficult to break and much lighter than stone. We call it a hatchet, but the Chesapeakes and the other peoples here call it a tamahaac."

He nodded, smiled. "It is a good gift. Isna thanks Emily. He will kill many enemies with it . . . perhaps even Tayler."

A wisp of alarm blew across Emily's face. She opened her mouth to admonish him, sighed instead, shook her head with a futile look, then smiled. "Here." She reached into her bag, pulled out a knife with an eight-inch blade and wooden handle, the blade and part of the handle encased in a buckskin sheath decorated with red, yellow, and blue designs. "This is for Isna's other hand . . . when he fights Lakota enemies."

He took the knife, pulled it from the sheath, made slicing and thrusting motions, again tested the balance and edge, then slid it back into the sheath. "Emily gives Isna another good gift. He again thanks Emily." He studied the artwork on the sheath. "Good colors. Did Emily make the sheath?"

She beamed. "Yes. Shines showed Emily how to sew it and make the colors from berries and animal fat. Here, look at this." She rolled over so Isna could see her back, pointed at a similar sheath and knife tucked in her belt at the small of her back.

Isna smiled as she rolled back toward him. "As Lakota women do— out of the way for work but quick to find when needed." He studied her eyes for a lengthy moment, gradually trading his smile for a somber, reflective look. "But Emily is not like a Lakota woman."

She gasped; her eyes widened with shock then misted; her lower lip curled downward in a pout. "But Isna said Emily possesses all the virtues of a Lakota woman." She unconsciously rubbed her eyes.

Isna reached out, touched her cheek, softly brushed the tears from beneath her eyes. "Isna spoke poorly. Emily possesses *all four* Lakota virtues . . . and she is *better* than *any* Lakota woman. It is in good ways that she is not like a Lakota woman."

Emily raised a suspicious eyebrow, pressed her lips together, then relaxed into a cautious half smile. "What does Isna mean?"

He smiled. "Emily looks into Isna's eyes. Lakota women do not look into the eyes of a man they are not related to . . . and sometimes not even into their husband's eyes."

Her smile deepened.

"Lakota women do not give gifts to a warrior until they are married. Nor do they speak to him, other than secretly with their eyes."

Deeper smile.

"And Lakota women *always* do as their husbands command." He shook his head. "Isna thinks Emily will not be like this."

Wide, beaming smile. "Isna is right. Emily is a Lakota woman in *spirit*, but the rest of her is English. 'Twould be impossible for Emily to be otherwise."

"Isna understands this . . . he loves Emily as she is . . . he does not ask her to change."

They smiled softly, silently at one another for half a minute before Emily abruptly turned, pulled yet another item from the bag—a grainy, gray stone about four-inches square and an inch thick—handed it to him. "This is for Isna to sharpen his tamahaac and knife . . . so they do as he commands, quickly and cleanly." She abruptly turned away, dabbed sudden tears, sniffled. "Each of these things Emily gives Isna so he will remember her . . . as she will remember *him* with her doeskin dress . . . when he returns to his people."

Isna studied her with concerned eyes; slowly extended his hand, touched her cheek; slid the hand down her neck to her shoulder, pulled her to his side. "Isna's leaving troubles Emily."

She snuggled close, reached her arm around his waist, nodded slowly with closed eyes.

"It troubles Isna, as well, for we are past the *Moon-of-Popping-Trees* and have begun the Lakota *Moon-of-Sore-Eyes* that brings bright, shiny snow that blinds the eyes—the moon the people here call the planting moon." He eased her back, touched her eyelids, gently raised them, and stared into her sad eyes. "Certain Lakota talk of returning to the people in this moon . . . for it will take nearly *two* moons to reach them; and by then it will be the end of the *Moon-of-Tender-Grass*, and time for hunting, fishing . . . and for fighting Lakota enemies. All warriors are needed for these things . . . but still, Isna is uncertain."

Emily looked up at him. "Why is Isna uncertain? He must do what is right for his people."

"Like all human beings, Isna's spirit is his truth-bearer—the one who tells him what *to* do, but never what *not* to do. So Isna alone must decide what to do after his truth-bearer has spoken." He looked silently at the forest then back at Emily. "Isna's vision showed him what would happen in his life; part of it he understood and has fulfilled; but other parts remain mysteries and have *not* been fulfilled and *cannot* be fulfilled if Isna, who owns the spirit of Grizzly, is not with the little white fawn; for in the vision and in Emily's dream, Grizzly and the little white fawn are together before all else happens. So Isna's uncertainty is how his vision can be fulfilled if he leaves the little white fawn and returns to his people, as he must." He shook his head, breathed deeply, searched her eyes, then suddenly smiled. "But while this leaving confuses Isna, he knows he yet has many years to understand and fulfil his vision— and Emily's dream—for Isna knows he will live to be an old man and count many coup before he dies."

Emily again raised an eyebrow. "How can Isna know this?"

"Because Striped Face has told him."

"Striped Face?"

"Striped Face . . . though he stands close to the ground and is not large, he is the most ferocious four-legged, next to Grizzly. He possesses great strength and knowledge of things to come; and if a man kills a Striped Face, lays him on his back, cuts him open, carefully removes his insides without spilling his blood, lets the blood thicken, then looks inside, he will see an image of himself. If the image is of a *young* man, the warrior will die young; but if the image is that of an *old* man, the warrior will live to be very old. Isna did this as a young boy, and he saw the face of an old man. This is how Isna knows."

Emily grinned. "We have many such beliefs. We call them superstitions; sometimes they are right, and sometimes they are wrong."

Isna didn't smile. "Isna has never known Striped Face to be wrong; thus, he knows he will count many coup, kill many enemies, and live to be an old man with a walking cane in his hand. So he also knows he has much time to be with Emily and understand and fulfil the spirit vision." A thread of doubt suddenly wove its way into his expression. "But since Isna, who owns the spirit of Grizzly, must *now* return to the Lakota, how can he be with Emily, the first little white fawn in the vision . . . to honor and protect her for all her life . . . unless . . . unless he returns to her *here*?

For if Grizzly and the *first* little white fawn are *not* together, how can the later brown and white fawns—their children—appear and follow them for a time before they go off on their own? And without that, how can all the fawns vanish, except for the one brown fawn that turns into the old woman with the two black stones around her neck and Isna's vision pipe in her hands? And without the old woman, how can the *new* little white fawn appear beside her; so the old woman can place her hand on its head and a moment later vanish, along with the pipe and two black stones? And then, unless the old woman vanishes, how can the *last* little white fawn be left alone, grow into a mother blacktail who has her own little white fawn, who then has Isna's pipe and the two black stones that suddenly appear around *her* neck? She cannot." He sighed, shook his head. "But Wakan Tanka and Isna's truth-bearer have told him *only* that he must return to the Lakota . . . and that the vision will one day be fulfilled—not how or when. Isna's confusion is that he cannot see how *both* can happen, unless he returns *here* to Emily . . . but Wakan Tanka and Isna's truth-bearer have not yet told him to do this . . . which means, in time, they must tell him to do so . . . or to do something else." He shrugged his shoulders. "Perhaps they themselves do not yet know what to tell Isna and so, will wait until they do."

Emily's face bloomed with hope. "Does Isna say he could stay with his people for a time then return here to be with Emily?"

"It is *possible* . . . for Isna *wants* to be with Emily more than his words can speak."

Her cautious smile brightened to outright delight. "Emily loves Isna the same, wants with all her heart to fulfil the vision with him; she prays to Wakan Tanka that it be so."

He deliberated for a moment before his lips curved into a broad smile. "Lakota men live in the family circle of their wives, so why should this not be true for Isna and Emily?"

Emily's shoulders tingled; she smiled, flung her arms around his neck, kissed him long and hard. "Oh, Isna, yes, please do this. Emily would be with Isna forever. It *can* be so."

His eyes slowly contracted; his smile faded. "To do this, Isna would have to leave the Lakota forever . . . become like a white man." He stared at the forest. "Isna is a Lakota warrior . . . *unlike* a white man. He is not certain what a white man is . . . or that he can learn to be one. And what would Emily's people say?"

"Isna will be with Emily, and . . . and her people will accept Isna." She suddenly frowned, realized they'd *never* accept someone *they* considered a Savage marrying an English girl. And what would Mother think? Could any of them understand . . . or accept a Lakota in the colony . . . much less as my husband? She felt warm tears fill her eyes, trickle down her cheeks, then visualized Isna leaving, never to return. But she suddenly recalled that they treated Manteo well in England . . . treated him as an English gentleman . . . and Shines . . . everyone treats her well. So why not Isna? A sudden surge of hope pulsed through her veins. Perchance it *could* work. But *marriage* would be a far different matter, and . . . she noticed him watching her with an amused smile and admiring eyes. "What is it?"

"Emily and Isna need not decide *now* how they will fulfil Isna's vision and Emily's dream; but they must do so soon . . . and Isna must learn what a white man is, so he can decide if he wants to be one . . . Emily must help him understand this."

She stared into his eyes, felt her excitement subside to reality. How can he become an Englishman? He and his people are so different from Manteo and his, so . . . so Lakota, so deeply warlike . . . how could it be? And how could I ever ask him to give up what he is . . . to become something he will surely despise? And what of Tayler . . . and the baby . . . and . . . dearest Lord, what an endless nightmare my life has become. She unconsciously shook her head. 'Twould not be fair to him, and 'twould be completely selfish of me. Tears flooded her eyes. "Isna, I cannot ask you to be a white man . . . an Englishman." She shook her head; pressed her body against his, squeezed him with all her strength; fell into deep sobs, trembled.

Isna held her tight, closed his eyes, laid his head on hers, then whispered, "Isna will do this for Emily."

She looked up at him with tormented, teary eyes, shook her head. "No, Isna, I . . . I cannot let you give up everything you are and love. You will hate it."

He pulled her close, softly rubbed the back of her neck, kissed her hair. "Isna will do this for Emily."

"No, Isna, 'twould not be right, and . . . and . . . there is something Emily must tell Isna." She paused, summoned her strength, leaned back, looked into his eyes. "When the white man, Tayler, took Emily's body, he made her with child, and—"

"Isna knows this," he spoke flatly.

She blinked, gaped at him with disbelieving eyes. "How . . . how can Isna know this?"

"Isna knows. He has known from the beginning . . . and it matters not."

Tears again flooded her eyes. "But . . . but . . . oh, Isna." She pulled him close. "Emily loves Isna with all her heart."

"As Isna loves Emily . . . and will love her child."

"Isna, Isna, my love, we *must* find a way. I cannot be without you."

"Emily and Isna will be together . . . they *will* find a way. Their truth-bearers and Wakan Tanka will show them that way." He eased her slightly back, stared into her eyes, moved his lips slowly toward hers until they touched in soft, gentle passion.

* * *

They had sat a long while facing each other, hand in hand, searching their own and each other's minds for answers, when Isna finally spoke. "Isna will stay with his people for three moons before starting back to Emily at the beginning of the *Moon-of-Ripening.* The return trip will be quicker because of paddling *downstream* on the Mother-of-All-Rivers rather than *upstream*; so Isna *could* reach Emily in the *Moon-of-Colored-Leaves,* before the cold moons begin. The slowest part of the trip will be paddling up the large river that flows into the Mother-of-All-Rivers from the north and east." His face suddenly brightened.

"But if Isna does not carry furs of Tatanka, he will not *need* to paddle a canoe up the big north-and-east river; he can instead follow a straight path from the Mother-of-All-Rivers to, and then over, the mountains." He looked away, smiled as if he'd suddenly recaptured a lost thought, again faced her. "Isna now tells Emily that it was at a place far up this large north-and-east river that the Lakota once lived. From there they often traveled to a big lake four days' walk to the north—a lake with water that could be drunk and which was too wide to see across, but much smaller than the Mother-of-All-*Lakes* near where the Lakota now live . . . which is not far from where the Mother-of-All-*Rivers* is born." He smiled again. "The grandfathers say that it was at this smaller lake, in those old years, that Ptesanwin brought the sacred pipe to the Lakota. They also tell that in those times Tatanka roamed on this side of the Mother-of-All-Rivers, all the way to the mountains to the east, and became the center of life for the Lakota and other peoples."

"Why did the Lakota leave this place?"

"Too many strong enemies." He looked remote, lost in thought, then suddenly smiled. "The grandfathers also say it was at this same smaller lake that the Lakota first saw white men"—he paused, thought for a moment, then flashed ten fingers three times—"nearly that many grandfathers ago."

"White men . . . then? Isna . . . that's . . . that's thirty genera-tions . . . 600 years. What . . . what white men could have been here then? Do the grandfathers tell what these men looked like?"

"Yes. They were strong men with much fair hair on their heads and faces; and some wore hard hats like your warriors, but different . . . more round. And they carried big axes . . . much bigger than Isna's . . . and big knives like some of your warriors carry, but wider and shorter. The grandfathers still have some of these knives and axes, which seem to be made from the same stone as Isna's knife and hatchet . . . but a brown and red dust now lives on them."

Emily's eyes were wide with awe, her lips agape. "Rust." She pondered for a moment. "Does Isna know where these warriors came from?"

He shook his head. "Isna knows only that they first came from some-where across the large water that cannot be drunk, to the east . . . the same water as here." He swung his hand from north to south. "They came in big canoes, each with a tall, fierce wolf's head with big teeth, on the front. And each canoe had a big skin the color of snow on a tall pole in its center and many long paddles on the sides. It is said they first camped for a long time on a big island in the large water, many days north of our lake; but one day they brought their big canoes up a large river south of their island, pulling behind them smaller canoes that looked like the big ones. They left the big canoes at a place with white, churning water and carried the smaller canoes over the ground until they again found deep water and paddled further up the river to a large lake. The wind then blew them across the lake, where they continued up the river to a great waterfall; there they again had to carry their canoes on the ground until they could re-enter the river. They paddled upriver to a second big lake—the Lakota's lake—where they met the Lakota and remained with them for many seasons . . . made children with them . . . which is why, today, some Lakota, like Isna, have lighter skin and noses and cheeks more like white men than Lakota."

Emily's eyes swelled with astonishment; her mind churned. "Manteo told me these people visited the Lakota, but . . . but . . . Isna, why did they come?"

"It is said they came to see what lay beyond the horizon, for they were people of the water and thought they could take their canoes to new lands filled with things they sought. And that is all Isna knows of them . . . except that some of them continued across our lake and paddled up more rivers and across more lakes, including the Mother-of-All-Lakes, which the Lakota *now* live beside. The Lakota know this because after many seasons, these men returned to the ones who stayed with the Lakota, and took them back to their island to the north . . . in the bad water." He smiled. "They told us the bad water goes from the bottom of the world to the top."

Emily stared through him, her mind churning with wild thoughts. My dreams . . . after the massacre . . . and other times . . . Vikings talking about where to go, what to explore . . . an island where they'd settled. Dear Lord, it must have been them, but . . . yes, I remember. The dreams were real, as if I were there watching the men . . . and I remember it all as clearly as my name. And one of them—his name started with a *T*, sounded like *Trihh*-something—talked about . . . no, *thought* about . . . a girl . . . a girl in England . . . a girl he loved, wanted to return to someday . . . a girl who bore his child. But how can this be? How could I dream such things . . . see his mind . . . remember it all? Impossible. "Isna, if these people were who Emily thinks they were, they were called Vikings, and they discovered this land far earlier than anyone knows or suspects. And . . . and . . . their blood flows not only in you but also in *my* people; for they raided us for many years . . . and some settled with us . . . and . . . and Emily dreams of them . . . dreams as real as life, as if she were there with them, seeing everything happen as it truly did. Isna, I . . ."

* * *

Though she slept, Allie's body trembled. An unconscious smile creased her lips.

* * *

"Isna has heard of such dreamers among his people. They are always women . . . women with powerful gifts, perhaps like Emily . . . all four gifts of the circle of life, and—"

A distant bell clanged three times from the direction of the colony. "Isna. 'Tis the call to meeting. Something's happened. I must go quickly. It could be—" The crack of a discharging pistol ripped through the air, again from the direction of the colony. "Something bad's happened . . . perhaps an attack, perhaps . . . I must go now, quickly." She stood, kissed him, then turned, lifted her dress above her ankles, started toward the forest.

- 503 -

"Wait. Isna goes with Emily to the edge of the forest." He quickly slid his tamahaac and knife into his waistband, flung his quiver over his shoulder, and tossed the whetstone into Emily's canvas bag. Gripping his bow with his left hand, he took *her* hand with his right, led her into the trees at a jog. When they reached the clearing around the palisades, they stopped, quickly kissed. Emily jogged off toward the group of soldiers and civilians gathered in a cluster near the trees on the far side of the clearing. She saw more people running out through the gaps in the palisades, heard women wailing, men shouting. They all looked at something on the ground.

As Emily approached the crowd, she saw a pair of soldiers emerge from the forest. The people silenced except for muffled wails, spread apart, made a path to whatever they were looking at. One soldier said, "No one there, Sir. They're gone."

Lieutenant Waters said, "Very well. Sergeant Myllet, post a guard of six men along the perimeter. Smith and Gibbes, form a detail to . . . to properly care for these folk." He glanced at the ground beside him, shook his head. "Everyone else, please disperse. We will inform you when the burials will occur. Please disperse now and return to the village for your own safety."

Emily saw Elyoner and Ananias several yards into the crowd. Elyoner, Virginia in her arms, leaned and cried on Ananias' shoulder. Emily raised her hand to get their attention, twisted her way through the crowd, which was beginning to disperse toward the palisades.

Elyoner saw her. "Em, Em . . . don't go over there. 'Tis awful. Come here, I shall tell you what happened."

Emily walked slowly past the Dares in a daze of irresistible curiosity, fixed her eyes on the spot everyone had been staring at.

Ananias yelled, "Emily, do not look, do not go there!"

Emily continued until, between two men in front of her, she saw a man's legs on the ground. Two steps later, the two men turned to talk to each other, revealed the torso of a prostrate man lying still on the ground. Two more steps revealed his bloody head, its right side blown completely away, his eyeballs dangling, intact, from their sockets. She whispered to a man beside her, "Who is it?"

Without looking at her, the man whispered, "John Chapman. He's blown his brains out with his pistol."

Emily covered her mouth with her hand. "Dear Lord. Why?"

"That basket over there beside him."

"What is in it?"

"Mistress, you do not wish to know."

"Aye, I do. Please tell me."

The man sighed. " 'Tis Mistress Chapman—her ashes and bone fragments, her scalp, a piece of her dress, her wedding ring, and . . . and her genitals."

"Dear Lord." She dry heaved twice.

"One of the guards saw two Savages come from the forest, leave the basket, then run away. I don't know what happened next, but someone rang the gathering bell, and people came to this spot; Master Chapman was one of the first." The man choked, coughed twice. "When he saw what was there, he immediately pulled his pistol and shot himself in the head before anyone could stop him. A mess . . . poor folk . . . must have been horrible . . . what they did to her. Bastards. We must teach them a lesson."

Emily didn't hear, stared into the forest for a moment, then turned, walked back to the Dares, who awaited her in silence. Elyoner and Emily immediately embraced, wept.

Waters said, "Please, good people, return to the palisades. My men and a few ladies will prepare for the burials. We'll ring the bell when 'tis time. Now please disperse."

The remaining crowd began trickling toward the palisades. Elyoner stared at Emily, shook her head. "Em, 'tis awful, but I'm going to help with the burials. Would you take Virginia to our house and stay with her until . . ."

"Of course." She took Virginia, cradled her in her arms. "Come, baby, let us go." She looked at Elyoner then Ananias, shook her head, looked back at Elyoner. "Ellie, I pray your father returns soon." She turned, walked toward the palisades.

At the door of the Dares' cottage, Emily leaned Virginia over her right shoulder so she could open the door with her left hand. As she reached for the handle, someone touched her left shoulder. "Oh!" She spun around, looked into Tayler's cold, expressionless eyes. "Why . . . why did you do that? You . . . you frightened me." She eased Virginia from her shoulder to her arms.

"Sorry, Milady." Tayler smirked, stared down at Virginia for a moment. "A lovely child, for certain." He reached out, touched the baby's cheek.

"Get your hands off her." She tried to rotate Virginia away from him.

He pressed his body against her, squeezed her and Virginia against the door, caressed Virginia's cheek several times.

"Such soft skin." He held his eyes on Virginia, who started to squirm. "I've missed you, Emily . . . for you have not come to me as you promised." Keeping his fingers on Virginia's cheek, he laid his thumb on her other cheek then fondled both.

"I said, take your hands off her!" Again she tried to twist Virginia from his touch, but again he pressed her against the door. "Stop it! I've been ill, as you well know."

He continued caressing Virginia. "I don't believe you." He slid his hand down to Virginia's neck, began to caress her there. Virginia sputtered, began to squirm.

A bolt of desperate fear shot through Emily; a chill raced down her neck and shoulders. " 'Tis true, nonetheless. Now leave her alone."

"You know, Milady, if I cannot have you as my mistress, I shall have you the way I did the first time." He rubbed Virginia's neck more aggressively. She squirmed, cranked louder.

Emily's mind tumbled in confusion. What to do? Trapped. She started to tell him about their baby, decided it would change nothing. Oh, Isna, I love you so. "Let her go, Hugh! Can you not see she doesn't like it?" She raised her voice. "Stop it, or I shall scream!"

"Scream and I'll snap her little neck like a twig." He tightened his hand around Virginia's neck, squeezed. Her face began to turn blue; she thrashed, gasped for air, started convulsing.

"Hugh! Stop it! Let go of her!" She tried again to twist away, couldn't. "Stop! Stop!" Her breathing raced, heart pounded; she gasped, "I'll come . . . tonight. Now let her go!"

He relaxed his grip, stared into Emily's eyes for a moment. "Come two hours after the sun reaches the treetops. Do not be seen, and do not knock. I shall await you." Virginia gulped air, began to cry. Tayler bent over, plucked a twig off the ground, held it three inches from Emily's eyes, then snapped it in two. "Like her little neck if you fail me."

"I shall not . . . but I tell you now, you scum, though you may take my body for the rest of my life, you will never, *never* take my soul, and . . . and I shall kill you when I have the chance."

He looked sternly into her eyes. "Say what you will, Lady; but forget not that if you do, my friends will kill both the girl and your Savage friend, who, for some inexplicable reason, you appear to love." He turned, limped away toward his cottage.

Emily watched him until he disappeared behind the next cottage, then glanced down at Virginia. Stop shaking, Em. She looked up at the sun, gauged its time to the treetops. Perchance three hours, no more.

***

Waters stared silently at Cuthbert White for an extended moment, felt the awkward, expectant tension that hung in the room like a sudden fog. "We know 'tis true." He glanced at Roger Baylye and Ananias Dare. "Newton's crime against you deserved the most severe punishment . . . by the bye, how are your wounds?"

"Healing."

"Good. So continuing, it seemed prudent to *not* exact his punishment now but rather, use Newton's fear of execution to gain information regarding a situation I only *alluded* to in the past but will now provide you the details of." He drifted his eyes to each of the other loyal Assistants—Thomas Hewet, Christopher Cooper, Roger Prat, John Stilman, John Brooke, John Bright. "That *situation* is a conspiracy to undermine and destroy the colony; and 'tis in play at this very moment." He paused, gauged their expressions, wondered if any were part of the conspiracy. "We discovered that Master Newton is one of the conspirators. You can determine from a quick observation of absent Assistants, who some of the others are." Anxious glances and murmurs rippled through the room. Baylye and Ananias looked at one another then at Waters. "We also know of several *additional* conspirators, including Hugh Tayler, the leader, as well as the basic elements of their plot, but we hope to learn more from Newton in exchange for a possible pardon from Governor White upon his return"—he looked at White—"which we realize does not right, or atone for, the wrong he committed against you, Master White. However, if Newton fails to provide us useful information, he'll immediately find himself kicking air at the end of a rope." He again studied their faces. "I must also caution you to discuss this with no one; for you could unwittingly be talking to a conspirator, which would alert them to our knowledge of the plot. So please keep your silence and limit your discussion to only those in this room."

More murmurs.

Thomas Hewet raised his hand. "Lieutenant, can you not tell us more of the conspiracy . . . so we can better assist you in—"

The bell on Baylye's door tingled, announcing visitors.

Baylye said, "Who is it?"

"Thomas Stevens and John Sampson."

Baylye glanced at the others, held an index finger to his lips. "Come in."

Stevens and Sampson entered, noted the others present, then glanced knowingly at one another. Stevens looked at Baylye, said sarcastically, "Are we late? It appears the meeting has already begun."

Baylye said, "No, you're not late. The others arrived early, and we were merely chatting about other matters."

Stevens fixed a long, dubious gaze on Baylye, then said, "Very well, Governor." He looked at the other Assistants then back at Baylye. "Governor, John Sampson and I have talked to many in the colony about the Chapman incident, and all agree with us that something should be done immediately to punish the Powhatans. We therefore demand you dispatch Lieutenant Waters and his men, augmented by capable civilians, on a punitive raid against them. We're weary of sitting here waiting to be attacked. We must attack *them* instead and severely punish them for what they did to Mistress Chapman . . . and for what their deeds prompted *Master* Chapman to do to himself."

Baylye glanced at Waters, who immediately stepped toward Stevens. "Master Stevens, while your intentions appear noble, I fear the same unfortunate facts that precluded our pursuit of Mistress Chapman now preclude any thought of a punitive raid against a force as strong as the Powhatans."

Sampson said, "We expected that response, Waters, because we know you to be a coward, and—"

Waters advanced to within a foot of Sampson, glared into his eyes. "If you believe such, then I shall afford you the opportunity to prove it by facing me on the green, with the weapon of your choice . . . after the safety of the colony is assured. Until then, you'll have to settle for dreams and illusions of your military prowess and my lack thereof."

Sampson swallowed hard, scowled, swallowed again; he lowered his gaze to the floor, stepped back from Waters.

Waters glanced around the room, shook his head. "Gentlemen, I share your emotions regarding the Chapmans; but our military capability has, if anything, diminished since Mistress Chapman was taken, due to our increasing starvation and its consequences—physical weakness and degraded discipline. Still, if we had a hundred soldiers, I would consider such an undertaking; but we *do not*, and I therefore *will* not. Until Governor White's return with more troops, we've no choice but to remain here, be vigilant, and strengthen the palisades; for make no mistake, the Powhatans' increasingly bold advances clearly herald their intention to attack us in overwhelming force . . . perchance far sooner than we imagine . . . and perchance before Governor White returns." A sudden, grim silence descended over the room, as in a funeral parlor when people view the deceased.

* * *

One of the five soldiers treading cautiously behind Taverner through the forest said, "Christ the Almighty, Taverner, do you have any idea where you're going? I don't like being this far from the palisades; and if we haven't found anyone to kill by now, we probably never will."

Taverner said, "Shut up, Butler. Keep your voice down. Want 'em to hear us?"

Another soldier suddenly tapped Taverner on the shoulder, held a finger to his mouth, then pointed his hand and eyes ahead and slightly to the right.

Taverner held up his hand to halt the others, looked where the man pointed, and twisted his lips into a wicked smile. On the far edge of an unusually large clearing about forty yards across were three Savage women. All three were about seventeen or eighteen, bare topped, clad only in wrap-around hide aprons. Unaware of the soldiers, they knelt alongside a stream, their backs to the men, filling water bags, giggling and chatting with one another.

The soldier who'd alerted Taverner whispered, "Can't hear us . . . stream's too loud. Think they be Powhatans?"

"Nay. Can't be . . . too close to the colony." He looked at the man, smiled. "Who cares what they be? They be women and got cunts, and we ain't had a woman since we left England."

The other man returned the smile, slapped Taverner on the shoulder. "What do we do?"

"You be right. They won't hear us 'til we're close." He motioned the others into a tight huddle, whispered, "Spread out, walk slow and quiet-like 'til we're too close for 'em to get away. Then we'll rush 'em, take 'em down, and have our pleasure. What say you?"

The others nodded.

"Good. Everyone have a kerchief in your hand to gag 'em with. Can't have 'em makin' no noise." He smiled. "Look damn good, don't they . . . even though they be Savages." He motioned the men to spread out, move slowly, cautiously. When all were in place, he stepped from the trees, started quietly toward the girls, then signaled the others to do the same.

When they were ten yards away, a soldier stepped on a dead branch. It snapped loudly, brought the six to an immediate standstill, drew angry glares from the other five. As they resumed their stealthy march, one of the girls raised her head, looked right and left, stood, looked again, then peered back over her shoulder. She spied the six men, screamed, jostled her friends; they ran for the trees on the far side of the stream.

The soldiers immediately rushed forward. Four tackled the two closest girls, held hands over their mouths while they gagged and bound them. The other two men raced after the third woman, who'd nearly reached the trees. She screamed once before they tackled her, bound and gagged her, dragged her back to the others. All three cried, trembled. Taverner pulled a short rope from his belt, surveyed the girls, walked to one, looked at the soldier who held her. "We'll all have a turn with all three of them, Farre. But I be first."

Taverner wrapped the rope around her wrists, pulled her toward a nearby tree, smiled as he approached to within a foot of her; unwrapped her apron, dropped it to the ground, studied the patch of hair between her legs; then pushed her to the ground, handed the rope to Farre. He quickly undid his belt, dropped his pants to his knees, showing the girl his rigid prick, which she gawked at with horrified eyes. As he waddled up to her, he glanced at the other men, smiled. "I wager they all be virgins, men. So let's get started and enjoy our bounty. Don't get a chance like this every day." He knelt, crawled on top of the girl, forced his legs between hers, laid his prick in place, then thrust it forcefully inside her. She moaned as her maidenhead broke, and he began a rhythmic in-and-out motion that quickly accelerated to rapid, frenzied thrusts which lasted but twenty seconds before Taverner sighed, collapsed on top of the girl for several seconds, then rolled to the ground beside her.

He lay still on the ground moaning for a moment, rolled to his knees, stood, pulled his pants up to his waist.

Taverner looked down at the girl, watched her cry for a moment, then looked at Farre. "Your turn. Here, I'll hold the rope." He grasped the rope, traded places with Farre. As Farre dropped his pants, Taverner looked for the other men, found them twenty feet away and apart. One thrust wildly into his girl from behind, and the other from the front, while the third and fourth men held the terrified girls in place.

After each man had spent himself twice, Taverner said, "Come, men. We'd best not linger here in case these lasses be missed."

As he tightened his belt, Butler said, "What do we do with them, Taverner?"

"Naught but one thing we *can* do, you fool." Taverner walked over to the girl he'd raped first, stood over her as she cried quietly with her eyes closed. He pulled his dagger from his belt, knelt beside her, slit her throat, then cut off a breast as blood gurgled from her neck. He looked at the breast, thrust it into the bag at his waist. "A little remembrance, eh, boys?"

Butler puked. "Damn you, Taverner. How can you do that?" He looked down at the girl who lay whimpering beside him.

Taverner said, "To hell with you, man. We can't just leave 'em be." He walked over to Butler, knelt, quickly slit the girl's throat. "Want her tits?"

Butler puked again, stood, walked away as Taverner cut off one of her breasts, held it up. "Anyone want one?" When no one claimed it, he tossed it over his shoulder, then stood, looked at the third girl, who was already dead, saw that the man who'd killed her had her bloody scalp cut halfway off. "Hurry it up, Tydway!"

Tydway said, "Calm yourself, Taverner. I ain't goin' nowhere 'til she's got the same as what they done to the Chapman woman."

When Tydway had cut the scalp free of the girl's head and held it up for all to see, Taverner said, "Come. Let's hide 'em in the trees."

After they'd dragged the bodies into the trees and piled a foot of leaves on top of them, the soldiers regrouped in the clearing, retrieved their matchlocks, and trotted into the forest toward the colony.

***

Tears streamed down Emily's cheeks as she folded her mother's crinkled letter, laid it on the table beside her. She wiped her eyes then watched the last grain of sand fall through the neck of her hourglass. She glanced at the fire, focused for a moment on the yellow flames lapping at the nearly consumed log. *So wrong that I should have to do this . . . so wrong to give myself to a man out of wedlock . . . a married man, an evil man, a man without conscience. So many times I've agonized over this . . . so many times I've accepted my fate . . . but in truth, I* cannot *accept it. And so I agonize again and again.* She stood, walked to the table, flipped the hourglass upside down, watched the grains of sand begin to trickle through the neck. *One hour . . . one short hour before my next great sin . . . before he again enters my body.* She shivered for a second, crossed her arms around her chest. *Need some wood.* She walked slowly to the woodpile, picked up a pair of medium-sized logs, and laid them on the flames; she thought how quickly they ignited. *Fast . . . like the changes in my life since England—one minute, happiness and hope, and the next, neither.* She shook her head. *Nothing I can do about it.* She glanced at her father's empty bed then stared into the fire. *Pray, Lord, don't let it take long. I cannot bear it.*

She felt her abdomen. *Can't feel much, but*—"Oooh! A little pain there." *Perhaps I should tell Tayler . . . he'll know soon anyway.* She studied the crackling flames. *Perchance I've been wrong; perhaps knowing will change him in some good way.* She slapped herself gently on the cheek, snorted cynically. *Don't be foolish, Emily. Nothing will change Hugh Tayler. He's evil to the core.* She peeked at the hourglass again. *Going fast. Wonder what it will feel like this time . . . scarcely remember the last.* She shivered again, laid her face in her hands, wept softly, replayed the rape: her utter surprise, terror, despair, anger, involuntary pleasure, embarrassment. She composed herself. No good, Em. Won't change anything. She glanced at the hourglass. Too fast. Never been naked with a man . . . never seen a man naked either . . . probably frighten me. She wiped a new tear from each eye. I suppose I should undress here to make it go quicker . . . just wear my smock with a cape over it. She started to unbuckle her belt, hesitated, laid her hands across her lap, shook her head. No . . . not yet. No hurry. I wonder if he'll undress me . . . or expect me to undress myself . . . and what of him? Oh, God . . . Mother . . . Father, save me from this. How I've let you down. She touched her mother's letter in her apron pocket; felt, as always, for her missing black locket. George, thank the Lord you cannot see me now . . . but what if you can? Lord, give me strength. My Isna, how I betray you. How can I do this to you . . . you, so loving and true? But how can we ever be together if Tayler is alive? She again covered her face with her hands but only for an instant. "No! Stop torturing yourself, Em. The die is cast; you must live with it; so harden yourself, do what you must." Her hands began to quiver.

How can I sin so greatly and willfully? But do I not perform a higher good in protecting Virginia and Isna from harm? Yes . . . I do . . . but I betray my family and my love in so doing. My Lord, please show me a way to escape this evil. She spied a small stick on the floor, immediately thought of Tayler snapping the twig an inch from her eyes, shuddered. I can never escape him if he's alive. No; nor can Isna be with me. He'll kill, or try to kill, Tayler, and then Tayler's men will kill *him* . . . and that will be the end of it. And my baby and I will never live in peace. She stared into the blue flames at the heart of the fire, let her mind drift. Why do I not do as Emme and Ellie propose . . . end his miserable life now, risk the consequences, take the chance, find another way to support my child . . . Isna said he'd . . . she glanced at the hourglass. Nearly time . . . fifteen minutes. She looked back at the fire. Can I kill a man? The flames suddenly flickered back and forth like fingers waving sideways as if to say *no*. But what if I *do* kill him . . . and I'm condemned, hanged, or jailed . . . what becomes of my child? She shook her head. Dare not take such a risk. Killing him was never practical—too immoral, too difficult, especially for me alone—and Tayler's men might still kill Virginia and Isna, even if he's dead . . . so where am I? She stared thoughtlessly at the fire for half a minute. "You, Mistress Colman, have no satisfactory choices. You must either submit to Tayler, kill him, or . . . or kill yourself and your child. She shook her head. Would that I'd hung myself in the forest after the rape. She stared at the fire for a long while then glanced at the hourglass, saw that the last grains had fallen; she felt as if a noose had tightened firmly, harshly around her neck, felt a sudden wave of nausea sour her stomach. She shuddered, took a deep breath, stood, put three logs on the fire, picked up her cape. Fie! Meant to undress . . . no worry, he'll do it quickly enough. She tossed the cape over her shoulders, opened the door, looked around to make sure no one was near, then stepped outside, her heart fluttering like one of the little birds whose wings seem to hum.

* * *

The Panther's wife picked up a deerskin to lie on and a second to cover herself and the baby. She poked her head outside the lodge, saw no one nearby, waddled quickly out the door and into the forest. She'd selected her birthing spot months before—a well-hidden thicket of brush with a thick carpet of leaves. She'd hoped that when her time came, the snow would be gone and leaves budded on the bushes for better concealment. Her wish had been granted, but her anxiety had been heightened by the arrival of Nansemond runners only hours before to tell her husband and Wahunsunacock that the white men had raped, murdered, and mutilated three Nansemond women, not far from the Nansemond village.

The pains had become much closer; and though her water hadn't broken, she knew from what her mother and sister had told her, that her time was near. She smiled even as she doubled over with a stabbing shot of pain, thought how proud and happy her husband would be if she delivered him a son; for though he was too good a man to say so, she knew in her heart he wanted a son to replace the ones killed by the white men. She recovered from the contraction, stood erect, proceeded on her way.

After several more contractions, she arrived at the spot, worked her way into the thicket, felt her water break. She quickly spread one deer hide on the bed of leaves, steadied herself with a branch as she knelt, leaned forward on her forearms, then rolled down onto her back. She immediately decided it was too chilly to lie uncovered, so she pulled the second deerskin over her and braced for the next contraction. When it had passed, she raised her knees, pulled her deerskin apron above her thighs, began to push. Won't be long, she thought as an image of the Panther, a proud smile on his face, appeared in her mind, hovered there like a bird in a strong headwind.

*　*　*

Emily stopped in front of Tayler's door, willed her pounding heart to quiet, but it refused. She took two deep breaths. Lord, give me the strength to endure. Isna . . . Mother . . . Father, pray for me. I love you, Isna. She heard people approaching, quickly opened the door, stepped inside.

Tayler stood by the fire, clad only in his linen smock, which hung almost to his knees. The two stared awkwardly at one another for a moment as Emily pushed the door closed behind her, flipped her hood down, allowing her long, black hair to fall freely over the front and back of her shoulders, cover the side of her cheeks, highlight her deep, blue, unblinking eyes, which had a wild, threatening look like a dangerous predator deciding to strike.

Beguiled for a moment, Tayler finally blinked, slowly, haltingly parted his lips to speak. "Good evening, Mistress. Let me help you with your cloak." He stepped toward her.

Emily unconsciously leaned back against the door, silently watched his approach. Her heart again pounded; she stepped slightly forward as he removed the cape, hung it on a wood hook by the door.

He gently took her right hand with his left, led her slowly, almost ceremoniously, toward the fire. "Come . . . let us be near the warmth." When beside it, he stopped, faced her, took her other hand, stared into her eyes, which glistened hauntingly in the dim firelight. "I've missed you, Emily Colman . . . more than you can ever know." His voice quavered. "And I've thought again and again about what I would say to you at this moment."

Emily closed her eyes.

"And I tell you three things. First, I deeply regret what happened in the forest that day; second, you are the most stunningly beautiful woman, inside and out, I have ever known, and I love you with all my heart; and third, with every ounce of my being, I want this night to be the most memorable and passionate of your young life." He moved closer, laid his hands on her shoulders, kissed her slowly, softly.

She held her eyes closed, lips sealed, wondered if he could hear the wild, throbbing drumbeat of her heart.

"I know you hate me and have good reason to do so; but I hope, tonight, to replace those thoughts with new, amorous ones of the Hugh Tayler who will love and cherish you for all of our lives together." He slid his hands down her sides to her tiny waist, brushed her breasts on the way, kissed her again on the lips, then on the cheek and neck.

Eyes still closed, Emily tensed her body; her breathing quickened with his.

He kissed the other side of her neck, slid his right hand slowly down her side to the firm cheeks of her behind, caressed them, pressed his body against her front.

She felt his stiff cock then a sudden, involuntary rush to her head, a surge of fear. Her mind flooded with images of him on top of her, ramming his prick in and out in ever-quickening rhythm. She trembled like a frightened fawn. Dear Lord, help me. I do not want this. Mother, Isna, please . . .

Eyelids still pressed together, she felt him ease back, unbutton her shirt to the waist, untie the string of her smock, lay both back over her shoulders; felt the warm air of the fire swirl around her bare breasts; waited apprehensively for what would come next.

He began to kiss and lightly massage her breasts, whispered haltingly, "Beautiful . . . so perfect . . . so firm." He teased her nipples with his tongue, caressed her side and behind with his hands.

She felt her nipples stiffen, her breath quicken. Mother, dear God, make me hate this. She began to pant.

He continued to manipulate her nipples with his tongue while he pulled her skirt and smock up to her waist, slipped his hand beneath them, then began to smoothly feather the tender flesh of her thigh and behind. "I love you, Emily Colman . . . and I need you."

Her breasts heaved as his lips and tongue alternated between her nipples. She panted harder. How can I do this? Hate him. Lord, make him stop.

Through his smock, he pressed his cock against her, moved it in a slow circular motion against her crotch. A minute later, he eased himself to the side, slid his right hand between her legs, eased it up her soft thighs to the top, caressed her there.

Emily's mind enlivened with remembrance: his touch, his forcing himself between her legs, his first thrust inside her; the rupture of her maidenhead, the pounding of his body against hers; her pleasure, her hate, her climax, her despair. She felt the rising dampness between her legs; her chest, back, and forehead beaded with sweat. Her body rose and fell in sync with his hand until suddenly she felt the same urging she'd felt in the forest—that wild, desperate yearning for some mysterious fulfillment, a release from her burgeoning tension. Dear God, don't let it happen again. As she neared the precipice, Tayler suddenly removed his hand, untied his smock, dropped it to the floor; he touched her bare shoulders, pulled her gently toward his bed, then stopped, started to unbuckle her belt.

As his hand tugged on the belt, an unforeseen rage suddenly erupted in Emily's mind like an exploding powder keg. *Damn* the consequences! She reached behind her back, felt beneath her laid-back shirt and smock, yanked her knife from its sheath, and thrust it into his left side. It hit the bottom rib, deflected downward and vertical, penetrated only two inches instead of eight. She tried to force it deeper, but he jerked sideways, screamed in pain; he pushed both hands violently into her stomach, grabbed his bleeding side. "Damn you, witch! You've wounded me."

Emily stumbled several steps backward, gasped for breath, held the knife blade toward him. "Stay away from me, you bastard!"

He stepped toward her.

She waved the knife at him. "I said stay away!"

He stopped, leaned over, picked up his smock, pressed it against his wound. "You bitch! You'll pay for this!"

As she backed toward the door, Emily grabbed her cloak with her left hand. She flipped her shirt and smock up over her shoulders, flung the door open, rushed outside; twirling the cloak around her, she ran for the Dares' cottage. *Dear God, what have I done?* She burst into tears. *I've killed Virginia and Isna. Don't let them die, Lord. Please! 'Tis my fault, my selfish fault . . . foolish temper. Punish me!* She glanced behind as she neared the cottage, then stopped at the door, pounded frantically.

CHAPTER 14

Waters sat by the fire in his cottage, eyed his three sergeants with a somber look. "So that's where we stand with the Assistants. As far as Newton, I expect information from him on the morrow." He smiled. "But if he fails me, we'll pay him a late-night visit with a rope." He paused for the three to snicker, add their assent. "That said, the primary reason we're here tonight is so I may confirm what you already know." He sighed deeply. "I do not wish to sound defeatist, but I fear greatly for this colony's survival. Clearly, the Powhatans are a dangerous threat—strong and determined—and they've demonstrated their intention to effect our demise. Indeed, I expect them to attack soon . . . in the night . . . with overwhelming force." He shook his head. "I must confess . . . each night I awake and wonder if this will be the night. Forsooth, I fear that unless Governor White reaches us within a fortnight, we've little hope . . . not to mention the fact that we're slowly starving to death." He looked at the fire, murmured, "I'm loathe to say it, men; but if there were somewhere to escape to and the means to do it, I'd order an immediate evacuation of this place and go there with great haste . . . but there is no such place. So we shall remain here and do our duty."

The three sergeants nodded slowly, glanced solemnly at one another.

Waters looked back at them. "But perchance more imminent—and ultimately more dangerous than the Powhatans—is the threat from within." He frowned, shook his head. "Tayler and his conspiracy." He again paused. "While *that* threat is direct and serious in itself, it also aggravates the Powhatan threat, and my meaning will be clear in a moment. For now let us hope Newton provides information we can act upon to thwart these traitors." He paused, took a sip of water. "What worries me is that even if Newton spills his guts with valuable, damning information, unless we've enough loyal forces to prosecute the conspirators, it will matter not. So let us now identify each civilian and soldier we know is a conspirator."

They quickly identified five soldiers besides Taverner: Tydway, Butler, Farre, Dutton, and Allen, and five civilians besides Tayler: Willes, Stevens, Sampson, Newton, and Gramme. They also identified two additional soldiers and one additional civilian as *possible* conspirators. Waters then said, "That's more than a trifling proportion of our total strength, which returns me to the statement I said I'd clarify a moment ago. Whether the conspirators are hanged, jailed, or alive and free is immaterial, for we cannot depend on their help in defending the colony under *any* circumstance, and that is equivalent to the lot of them dying in the opening volley of the attack. Therefore . . . somehow . . . we must convince them to fight *with* us and settle other matters later; for 'tis certain the Powhatans will not care who fought and who didn't, once they've overrun us. They'll torture and kill everyone"—he stared briefly, resolutely into each man's eyes as he spoke—"but no matter what happens . . . how bad or hopeless the situation becomes . . . we four must do our duty and lead by example . . . until we breathe our last." He paused, again glanced from man to man, nodded once at each. "I know for certain you three will stay the course."

The three spoke simultaneously. "Aye, sir."

"Very well. By the bye, we will immediately execute any soldier who refuses to fight, whether before or during the fight . . . without discussion or trial. We've no room for leniency in this regard. Understood?"

The three again replied in unison, "Aye, sir."

"Good. Now, in order that you know what we face . . ." He coughed, smiled, shook his head. "Excuse the smile, but there's naught else one can do about this situation. I've heard the Powhatans can muster over four hundred warriors, not counting the Chesapeakes. So we, with less than sixty fighters—most of them untrained, and most unskilled—are outnumbered between seven and fourteen to one." He again shook his head, held his sheepish smile. "Encouraging, eh?"

The sergeants chuckled, smirked at one another and at Waters. Myllet shrugged. "Only seven or fourteen to one? Come now, Sir, that be a Sunday parade for Her Majesty's troopers. We thrive on the impossible. Bring 'em on." The others shouted *ayes* and *huzzahs*.

Waters smiled. "You're right, Michael, yet 'twould be better if the palisades were complete. Since they are not, next best is for us to find ways to compensate for that deficiency. So as a start, we mobilize and train every untrained civilian in some form of weaponry—matchlock, sword, bow, pike, pistol, spear . . . even slingshot; and we preposition powder and shot at each barricade, so we're not faced with shortages or delays during the fight. We also preposition water buckets, deer bladders and stomachs, and anything else that will hold water, at the barricades to cool our barrels if they overheat, at the cottages in case the Savages use fire arrows, and for drinking water in the event of a siege. We also keep candles lit, so we can quickly ignite our gun matches when the fight begins. And we enlist the women to make bandages . . . *now* . . . before the fight . . . and instruct them in the care of wounded. That brings me to the most distressing part of this . . . and that is what becomes of the women if we are overrun." He again studied each man, noted Gibbes' suddenly fearful look. " 'Tis with great difficulty that I say what I shall now say. Every man must know that when only a few men or the last of the ammunition remains, those few must immediately, and mercifully, dispatch our women and children in whatever manner they can . . . before they're taken by the Savages and suffer Mistress Chapman's fate." He paused, watched revulsion creep over each man's face like the shadow of an approaching storm cloud. "Have any of you heard of Masada?"

Smith said, "No, sir." The other two shook their heads.

" 'Twas a Jewish fortress atop a tall, sheer mountain, fortified in 73 AD by about a thousand fanatical Jews called the Sciarii. The Sciarii held off a Roman army of fifteen thousand for many weeks before the Romans finally built a very high ramp, which allowed them to reach the fortress walls on the mountaintop. They then fired the gate and waited for it to burn through. But on the night before it did so, the Sciarii decided to take their own lives, by suicide and killing one another, to preclude the Romans torturing and enslaving the men and children, and ravishing the women. 'Tis believed they used a simple slice of the knife across the throat to do the deed—like we do to kill a pig or cow for butchering. 'Tis quick and painless, and I think we should consider it the preferred method of dispatch . . . should such a grim moment overtake us." He waited for responses; but all three stared blankly through him, mouths agape. Finally, he sighed, said, "Since according to the Church, suicide and murder are grave sins, each person must choose for himself to either do *this* . . . or suffer whatever the Powhatans deliver upon us. And unfortunately, we must make this horrible decision soon . . . so we can be at peace with ourselves . . . and so all who may have to accomplish the task know what to do and who to do it to. There will be no time for decisions when the moment arrives."

The inescapable, hideous wisdom of his words reflected silently, odiously on all four faces. Gibbes faced the fire, stared into it, lips agape. The others looked hollowly at the floor and one another. Finally, Waters said, "Gentlemen, distasteful though they be, we must make these preparations with haste. Therefore, on the morrow I would like each of you to present me your thoughts on bolstering the barricades. Barring more creative inspirations, angled, sharp poles, pointing outward from the barricades across the palisade gaps, would make it more difficult for the Savages to scale the barricades. We could also dig wide pits *behind* the barricades, like Robert the Bruce and the Scots did at the battle of Bannockburn in 1314 to help defeat the vastly superior army of *our* King Edward the second. We obviously don't have metal caltrops to place in the pits; but we can drive sharpened, vertical stakes into the bottoms to impale any Savages who fall in." He took a deep breath. "But before we do anything else, we must convince our disbelieving populace of the dire need to undertake these preparations." He paused. "I expect considerable denial of the threat, and denial may translate into outright resistance to the proposed measures. Yet we've no choice in this, men . . . and we must begin now."

An onerous feeling like hot, humid, pregnant air moments before a summer cloudburst, infiltrated the room. After a long silence, Smith said, "Sir, what of Governor White?"

Waters pressed his lips together, contemplated his response. "Perchance he'll arrive in the next several days, but these preparations will stand us in fair stead even then . . . until we complete the palisades." He studied the floor for a moment, again squeezed his lips together. "There's another, rather unthinkable possibility I have not mentioned . . . because it just occurred to me . . . and that is the possibility that some event at sea, or in England, precludes Governor White's return." He took a deep breath, smiled feebly. "Bloody hell, men, we don't even know if Governor White *reached* England in the first place . . . or that he'll find our carvings at Roanoke and go to Croatan Island . . . or that our people at Croatan are still alive to tell him where we are." He shook his head. "Too damned many uncertainties and unknowns . . . and as if we've not enough bad news, I also expect the Powhatans to force the Chesapeakes to fight against us." He smiled philosophically. "But these are worst-case possibilities, some of which, hopefully, will not transpire. Yet if they do, 'tis a fact that some or all of us in this room will fall." He again surveyed their faces. "And if so, command will pass according to seniority. If I am killed or unable to command, Michael Myllet will assume command . . . then Thomas Smith, then Johnny Gibbes. Understood?"

All three nodded.

"Now the last thing I want to say . . . and I want to say it now, before whatever happens, happens . . . you three are the finest non-commissioned officers I've encountered in my admittedly short army career. I cannot imagine any with greater professional commitment and dedication to duty, and I want you to know that it has been a great honor to serve with you . . . all three of you. Thank you . . . and may our association not end here, now, in this land, but continue for many years to come." He blinked repeatedly, fought the urge to rub his misty eyes.

Myllet said, "Thank you, Sir. I've nurtured many a green lieutenant and supported many a senior officer, but never one with the God-given judgment and maturity you've shown in this command. God willing, we'll survive this; and if we do, I've no doubt you'll one day be a senior leader in Her Majesty's army. It has been an unequaled honor to support you, Lieutenant."

Smith said, "I, as well, Sir. Same thoughts."

"And I," said Gibbes. "You gave me an opportunity I might never otherwise have had; and I am most grateful for that, Sir." He saluted.

Waters returned the salute, started to speak, quavered, coughed twice, blinked. "Thank you, men." The four then stared awkwardly at one another for several moments before Waters smiled. "So . . . let us assume for a moment that Governor White returns on the morrow with more troops and planters, and we all survive the coming weeks; what are you three going to do with yourselves? Stay here? Return to England? What will you do without Savages and conspirators trying to kill you?"

The three gawked sheepishly at one another for a moment before Myllet pointed at Gibbes, who replied with a nod. "Well, Sir, I like the army, so Emme and I thought we'd return to England on the governor's ship, so I can see what other assignments are available. But if none capture my fancy, and I have a choice, we may return here and be part of the permanent settlement. Emme likes this new world . . . and Mistress Dare and Mistress Colman . . . very much and would like to stay; so returning is a very strong possibility, if the army agrees." He nodded at Smith.

Smith cleared his throat, looked at the floor. "Before she died in childbirth, my wife and I had two sons. But with the army and being gone most of the time, I couldn't raise them, so I gave them to my sister. They're now nearly grown, and I plan to talk to them about coming back here with me on a later voyage. Neither is interested in the army; but both have good journeyman skills, which should be useful as the colony grows. And our garrison here will always need experienced sergeants, so . . ."

Waters nodded. "And you, Michael?"

"Well, Sir, as you know, I've a wife and three grown children back home; but I cannot say I know them well, for soldiering has had me out of the country most of their lives." He smiled a broad smile. "I'd be lying if I said I didn't love the army more than anything in this world. 'Tis in me blood, and always will be, and I dearly enjoy and respect most of the fine men I've had the honor to serve with. But I suppose I shall return to England when we're relieved, and go see my family . . . get to know them again." He glanced at Gibbes. "Then, like Johnny, I shall see what assignments are out there; and if none of 'em capture me fancy, and I can persuade the assignors, I'll return here with the rest of you varlets." He smiled at Smith and Gibbes, punched both on the arm. "I always miss the danger and excitement of battle when I'm home. So I reckon I'm trapped into soldiering for as long they'll have me." He paused, looked at Waters. "What about you, Sir?"

Waters smiled serenely, looked vacantly past the men as if his mind were suddenly elsewhere. "There is a pretty young maiden in England . . . waiting for Lieutenant William Waters to return and marry her. He misses her dearly and would loathe being separated from her again. So though she does not yet know it, Lieutenant Waters may *also* volunteer to return here, as part of a permanent garrison." His smile suddenly deepened; his eyes lost their vacancy, focused on the three. "In time, I see a bright future for anyone with the courage to make a place for themselves here; and I would like to be part of that, while enjoying the equal pleasure of remaining an officer in the army." He smirked. "Of course, you realize the army may have altogether different plans for *all* of us . . . may even tell us our reward for exemplary performance is to remain *here* and school the new troops in New World battle tactics and strategy."

The sergeants groaned, grimaced, shook their heads, then slowly lapsed into silence. A moment later, all four stared reflectively at the fire, oblivious to the shadows and flickering firelight that danced hauntingly, forebodingly on their ruddy faces.

Waters wondered about the others—who would survive, what would they really do, what were they thinking at that moment? Were they digesting his grim expectations, thinking of home, the loves in their lives? No matter . . . to each his own thoughts. He stared into the blue of the flames. *I miss you, Rebecca Roberts. And I pray God one day returns me to your loving arms.*

* * *

Emily knelt sobbing at Elyoner's feet, grasped her skirt with a desperate grip. "I'm so sorry, Ellie . . . so ashamed . . . I was a coward . . . selfish." She looked up at Elyoner's face. "He strangled her, Ellie . . . while I held her in my arms . . . choked her until she turned red . . . would have killed her if I hadn't said *yes*." She again buried her face in Elyoner's skirt, wailed. "But . . . but I lost my courage . . . even as he undressed me . . . and . . . and now we're all at great risk . . . oh, Ellie, I should have done as he wanted. I know he'll come now and do what he said. Please forgive me . . . I'm so sorry. My Virginia . . . my Isna . . . I cannot bear it . . . my fault . . . all my fault."

Elyoner glanced distraughtly at Virginia, asleep in her crib, then at the loaded pistol lying on the table. Tears ran down her cheeks. She touched Emily's chin, gently pulled her up. "Em, please stand. You've *nothing* to apologize for, *nothing* to be ashamed of. 'Tis *not* your doing . . . only that foul, wretched, runagate is at fault . . . he alone. God, forgive me, but prithee deliver a pox upon him!"

Emily stood slowly, laid her head on Elyoner's chest, held her close, shuddered as she sobbed.

Elyoner stroked the back of her head and neck. "You poor, brave lass . . . all this time . . . this terrible burden . . . *all* alone . . . kept it to yourself, gave yourself . . . to save Virginia. God's blood! It enrages me! I knew he compelled you in some evil manner, but . . . but never did I suspect *this* . . . deserves to be drawn and quartered . . . filthy scum." She squeezed Emily close. "Em . . . you're such a noble lass! Cry . . . let it loose . . . then we shall—"

The door opened. Ananias stepped inside. "What ho? Ellie, what's happened? Should . . . should I leave?"

"No. Sit! We must talk."

While Emily whimpered in her arms, Elyoner told Ananias of Tayler's threat, that he'd strangled Virginia until Emily agreed to go to him, that Emily had been unable to go through with it, stabbed him in the side, escaped to their cottage. "So we must decide what to do; for Virginia, Em, and Isna are now all at grave risk . . . perchance you and I, as well . . . and this mad man runs free to do as he pleases."

"Lord in heaven!" Ananias looked at the fire, shook his head. "This is horrible . . . but . . . but the man's also a scoundrel in other ways you do not yet know of, my love."

"His conspiracy with Walsingham?"

Ananias blanched. "How . . . how do you know of that?"

Elyoner smiled. "I deduced it from what you've said . . . and from what Father told me. So what do we do?"

After a lengthy discussion of possibilities, during which Emily gradually composed herself, Ananias said, "Ladies, this is more complex than it appears. To begin with, until John returns, the colony's authority—Roger Baylye, the Assistants, and Lieutenant Waters—is gravely diminished by defections of soldiers and civilians to Tayler's conspiracy. And sadly, an event such as the hasty, premature arrest of Hugh Tayler could spark an outright mutiny, and—"

Elyoner glared at him, turned red in the face. "What do you mean *hasty* and *premature*? By the saints, what is *premature* about rape and extortion of venereal favors by threat of murder . . . murder of *your own child*?"

Ananias frowned, looked at the floor, swallowed hard. "Nothing, my dear. But what *could* be premature, with our fragile circumstances, is an *accusation* of rape that has not yet been committed . . . you know how rape trials go, and how difficult it is to—"

Emily burst into tears, buried her face in her hands.

Elyoner leaned her furious face an inch from Ananias'. "Ananias Dare, are you *totally* insensitive? By the Lord Jesus Christ himself"—she crossed herself, swiped blindly at the tears rolling down her cheeks—"how can you say that?"

"Lord help me! I'm only trying to be logical, Ellie. We cannot simply make an accusation and expect—"

Emily whispered, "Ananias"—she rubbed the tears from her eyes, sniffled twice, faced him—" 'twas not the first time."

Ananias stared at her, mouth agape, eyes glazed.

She then spoke casually, as if talking about the morning meal. "He raped me in the forest weeks ago . . . forced me to submit by threatening to kill Virginia if I did not . . . and I now carry his child . . . and he insists I be his mistress . . . and . . . and as Ellie said, this afternoon he choked Virginia while I held her in my arms. He'll stop at nothing to have his way with me . . . yet I *cannot* submit again . . . but I know not what to do . . . or what will become of me and my child. I'm so sorry, Ananias . . . Ellie . . . so ashamed." She again buried her face in her hands, sobbed. "All my fault."

Elyoner embraced her, glared at Ananias through her own tears. "Are you happy now? Look what you've done!"

Ananias pleaded, "Ellie, I . . . I . . ."

"Don't say *anything*! Just go sit somewhere while we cry . . . put your mind on what we should do. Poor lass." She stroked Emily's neck.

Ananias frowned, walked solemnly to the fire, sat on his stool; he leaned forward, elbows on his thighs, chin resting on his clasped hands, stared into the glowing coals.

After ten minutes, Elyoner said, "We're ready."

Ananias didn't move or speak.

"Ananias! We're ready. Come sit."

He gave a start, looked over his shoulder at Elyoner. "Oh! Sorry. Deep in thought." He stood, walked to the two, sat beside them, then looked at Emily, who forced a tentative smile.

"First, Emily, I'm deeply sorry this has befallen so kind, innocent, and wonderful a person as you." He shook his head. "We will see this varlet hang. The only question is *when*"—he looked at Elyoner then back at Emily—"for I fear our situation dictates that it will *not* be now."

He took a deep breath. "If you'll bear with me, I'll explain my logic. I'm certainly not a legal expert, but I *am* observant."

Elyoner and Emily held each other close, focused on Ananias while he reiterated the tenuous position the colony's leadership was in, as well as the challenges of prosecuting rape and extortion cases, under *any* circumstances. He then suggested dangers to informing more than Governor Baylye and Lieutenant Waters of events; particularly dangers to Emily, Virginia, and Isna. "So, what I'm saying, albeit not what any of us wish to hear, is that with our weakened authority, it may be safer to keep this to ourselves—ourselves being the three of us, Baylye, and Waters—until John returns with more soldiers; and meanwhile, vigilantly guard against Tayler and his men doing anything to threaten Em, Virginia, or Isna. I think, because of Emily's wounding him, Tayler may tread softly for a time, particularly if he believes his transgressions remain undisclosed . . . and mayhap he'll do so long enough for John to return, crush the conspiracy, and hold him accountable for his crimes. On the other hand, I fear that if he suspects that anyone besides Emily knows of his misdeeds, he'll be tempted to follow through on his threat as a matter of principle and credibility—even if it be through his proxies *after* his arrest. So"—he hesitated, eyed Emily cautiously—"I believe we should immediately inform Baylye and Waters of the rape and the extortion, so we have their added protection; but we must exact their promise not to prosecute Tayler until John returns." He shook his head. "Surely, he'll arrive within the week, so we should not have too long a time to engage in our deception." He looked at both with a pleading look. "Forsooth, I believe this to be the *safest* course . . . though 'tis most unpalatable. And Emily, you should also tell Isna what has happened and what we plan to do. He and his men may need to defend themselves, though I seem to recall hearing that they plan to return to their people in a matter of days. Is this so?"

Emily and Elyoner stared silently, glumly at one another as Emily's eyes filled with tears. She looked at Ananias, sniffled. "Yes, Ananias, that is correct. And I agree, your proposal *is* the safest course; but soon, the entire colony will know my condition, and I know not what I shall do or where I shall turn, and—"

Elyoner hugged her, said, "Emily, when the truth is told, no one will condemn you, for all the colony knows your moral strength and gentle kindness . . . and the opposite of Hugh Tayler . . . and . . . and Father will know how to help you. So fear not, my dear, dear friend." She shook her head. "You've suffered so much for Virginia's sake . . . and were it in my power, I would hand Tayler over to the Powhatans and instruct them to treat him as they did James Lassie, but slower."

Ananias took a breath, blinked twice. "Then we are agreed. I shall inform Baylye and Waters and exact their promise of silent vigilance. And, Emily, you will inform Isna?"

Emily nodded, rubbed her eyes.

Elyoner took Emily's hands in hers. "Em, you are staying here with us tonight . . . and moving in with us permanently tomorrow!"

Ananias said, "Indeed you are, Emily Colman." He waved his index finger back and forth in front of her face. "Do not protest!" He looked at Elyoner. "Ellie, I want you to carry your dagger and your father's pistol at all times . . . with the match lit. 'Tis good fortune he taught you to shoot. But since I am without such skill, I shall carry two daggers and a sword. And, Em, you must continue to carry your knife and *your* pistol. Thomas told me you're an excellent marksman, so you, too, should keep your match lit, and do not hesitate to shoot a scoundrel if need be . . . no matter *who* it is. Oh, and let us place your *father's* pistol here beneath your bed when you've brought it from your cottage."

Elyoner and Emily nodded grimly, then all three stared thoughtfully at one another until Emily finally spoke. "One of us must be at Virginia's side every moment . . . day and night . . . pistol in hand. We must *never* leave her alone. Hugh Tayler is insane and knows not right from wrong, but he's clever and deceptive . . . loves me truly and deeply . . . believes he needs me . . . and that only I can save him from himself. Therefore, he will let *nothing* stand in the way of his having me. So I beg you, please be vigilant with this precious young gift." She glanced at Virginia then back at the Elyoner and Ananias. "I shall find Isna in the morning and tell him what's happened."

Ananias said, "Does . . . does he know about . . ."

"Yes . . . and neither the rape nor the pregnancy has changed his feelings. He . . . he loves me . . . and I, him . . . and he wants to kill Tayler." Her eyes again filled with tears. "But . . . but as you say, he will soon return to his people, for he has no choice in the matter . . . and . . . and he will then be safe." She closed her eyes. *Oh, my Isna, how can I ever live without you?*

***

The sun was seconds from clearing the tree line. Waters said, "Here, Newton, help me with this log."

"Aye." Newton glanced around, saw Willes and Sampson surreptitiously eying him as they alternately pushed and pulled opposite ends of a six-foot saw, cutting another length of log from the downed tree at the edge of the clearing. He shrugged, raised his eyebrows, then turned back to Waters, bent down, lifted his end of the ten-foot log. "Whoa! Heavy!"

" 'Tis indeed. Ready to go?"

"Aye."

The two hoisted their ends of the log, wrapped their arms around it, staggered slowly toward the palisades. When they were halfway across the clearing, beyond earshot of the others, Waters whispered, "Speak softly . . . don't look at me and don't move your lips."

Newton fixed his eyes on the ground in front of his feet, whispered through his teeth, "Tayler and the others are stealing food from the Chesapeakes. Threatened to kill them if they don't cooperate or if they tell anyone."

Waters looked dead ahead, said softly, "What else?"

"Taverner . . . he . . . he . . ."

"What man? Hurry! Say it!"

"He and five other soldiers . . ."

"Wait!" Emme Merrimoth and another woman, both carrying water buckets, approached on their way across the clearing to the loggers. "Good day, Mistress Merrimoth, Mistress Glane."

Emme said, "You look as if you could use some help with that log, Lieutenant. May we?"

Waters smiled. "Thank you, but no. I think we'll manage."

"Very well. See you at yonder tree."

After a few steps, Waters whispered, "What happened?"

"They came upon three Savage women."

"Where?"

" 'Bout four miles from here."

" 'Twould be the Nansemonds . . . allies of the Powhatans. What did they do?"

"They . . . they . . ."

"Out with it, man!"

"They raped them . . . then . . . then killed 'em, and . . . and cut 'em up a bit, if you know what I mean."

My God, Waters thought. As if they didn't already hate us enough. This is disastrous. Should have put that mutinous dog away when we had the chance. Good Lord, what now?

"Tayler says Walsingham's ship is due as early as four days from now, no later than seven . . . even allowing time to go to Roanoke and Croatan. Plans to make his move soon. Says . . . says John White will *never* return . . . Walsingham will see to it."

"That's drivel. He's no inkling of that. If anything, the opposite is true, and Raleigh and White have trumped Walsingham. So watch yourself, Newton. Don't be thinking you're free." God in heaven, let it be so. And I wonder what Tayler's *move* will be. "Is that all? Be quick!" They were forty feet from a gap in the palisades, where three men waited to help set the log in place.

"By God, Lieutenant, you'd damn well better keep your word to me, or I be dead. That Colman lass . . . and her Savage . . . they be in grave danger . . . shouldn't be in the forest alone . . . 'cause—"

"Ho, Lieutenant!" William Lucas said. "Let us help you with that beast." He and the other two men stepped out from the palisades.

Waters said, "Thank you, men. Could you put it in place without me? Got an urgent matter to attend to. Many thanks." He handed his end of the log to Lucas, immediately climbed over the small pile of logs in the palisades gap, then sprinted for the Dares' cottage.

* * *

Elyoner held her pistol behind her back, opened the door a crack, peeked outside. "Lieutenant Waters, please come in." She opened the door.

Waters spoke rapidly. "No, Mistress, no time. Your husband told me what's amiss. Do you know where Mistress Colman is? Must find her immediately. She's in grave danger."

"My God. What—"

"Please, Mistress. Do you know where she is?"

"She went to the Chesapeake village early this morning to find Isna . . . said they'd be in the forest all morning."

"Do you know where?"

"No . . . I do not, but—"

He grimaced. "I'm going to form a detail and search for them immediately. Perhaps you could take your child and find your husband or Governor Baylye and inform them of this."

"Certainly, I . . . Lieutenant, please, please find them, quickly . . . I beseech you."

* * *

Emily and Isna sat side by side in the forest. Tears ran down her cheeks as she finished telling him about her encounter with Tayler and her discussion with Ananias and Elyoner. After a moment of quiet, his stern look softened to his wry smile. "Emily's heart beats strongly with bravery, the greatest of all Lakota virtues."

Emily brushed the tears from her eyes. "But Emily acted selfishly . . . foolishly. She has endangered those she loves . . . to save herself."

"No, my little white fawn, Emily did what was *right* for those she loves, for now they know of the danger that stalks them and can prepare to defeat it . . . is this not so? And will not Isna always be prepared to fight Tayler and his men? And will not the parents of the little one now be prepared to help you protect their child? And will not this evil man who hates himself and is a coward now wonder if his enemies wait for him and will try to kill *him*?"

"Yes . . . but, Isna, Tayler's men are as evil as he is and will now hate Emily and Isna more than before . . . and be more careful in their treachery . . . and perhaps, if Ananias is correct, try to fulfill their threats."

"Isna is not afraid. He will find these cowards who have twisted, knotted hearts and kill them, so Emily and her people can be free of them, for they will hurt your people and others if they remain alive."

Emily paled, shook her head as a vexed look clouded her eyes. "Isna, these men will not fight with honor, but from the shadows and behind." She sighed. "Ananias speaks wisely when he says we must wait for John White to return with more good men. Will Isna not heed his words?" Forsooth, he is so like a Viking: fears nothing, courts risk and violence, revels in danger, tempts death beyond all reason . . . for honor. Dear Lord, how can I love such a man . . . and how can I live with the constant, gnawing fear of his death?

"Isna *will* heed Ananias' words . . . for a time . . . because Emily asks this; but if John White does not come before Isna returns to the Lakota, Isna must kill Tayler, for he cannot leave Emily here while Tayler lives."

Emily sighed, stared at him, wondered when he would leave; she prayed for John White to return, arrest Tayler that very day. In less than two seconds, she visualized her transformation from a carefree girl in love with life to a debauched, pregnant, frightened woman, desperately in love with a man she couldn't bear to be without, but from whom she would soon part . . . a young woman with no future but that of unwed mother and whore to the man who raped her. And, she thought, even if Isna kills Tayler and escapes the wrath of his men, it won't help, for no one will accept his having killed a white man . . . even a wretch like Tayler . . . nor will they accept our being together in the colony. But if Governor White returns and prosecutes Tayler, then . . . mayhap . . . we will have a chance to be together. "When will Isna leave?"

He looked at her stoically. "Ten days . . . perhaps a few more. The Lakota are restless to return to the people . . . yet the thought of leaving Emily pains Isna's heart like the cut of a sharp arrow." A twinge of sadness crept slowly across his face.

Emily looked away, rubbed her eyes, then looked back at Isna. "Will Isna return to Emily?" She rubbed her eyes again, thought, I know his answer.

"Isna *will* return . . . he *must* be with Emily . . . but he does not know if he can become like a white man. They seem ignorant of the meaning of life and care only for themselves . . . not the good of the people. This is different from the Lakota, who shun or even kill people such as these, and it would be difficult for Isna to live like them."

"Isna, all white men are not like these evil ones. Many *are* good men and care for the people as the Lakota do—Lieutenant Waters, Ananias, John White, Roger Baylye, others—but Isna has not met these men, so he cannot know this."

He nodded. "Isna understands this; and so he tells Emily that even if he does not wish to become a white man, he *will* return to her . . . perhaps stay with the Chesapeakes . . . or the Monacans, in the mountains . . . and perhaps come to know some *good* white men, and then think more of becoming one of them."

Emily's face bloomed; she laid her hands on his. "Oh, yes, Isna. Yes." She took his hands in hers, looked pleadingly then sadly into his eyes. "If Isna stays with the Chesapeakes or Monacans, he will bring hides of Tatanka, and it will take him longer to return."

With a suddenly contemplative look, he said, "Yes. But three more important things chew on Isna's heart. The first is the killing of Tayler by Isna. If, as Emily believes, the white men will then hate Isna, he will not be able to remain here. Second, if Isna does *not* kill him before he leaves, Tayler will force himself on Emily . . . again and again. And last, unless your chief returns soon with many more men of strong heart, the Powhatans will overwhelm your village, kill all the men, and use the woman as wives for a time . . . before they kill *them*, as well."

Emily stared numbly at the forest, mused his words, grasped for the logic to refute them; she finally acknowledged their inescapable truth, yielded her mind to sprouting seeds of depression. She looked solemnly into his eyes. "Isna's words are true . . . what will we do?"

"Isna does not yet know. He asks Wakan Tanka and his truth bearer to show him the pathway ahead; they have not yet answered him, but Isna believes they will do so soon. No matter what happens . . . as long as he still breathes . . . Isna *will* return to Emily, *wherever* she is." He paused, touched her cheek. "Does Emily believe her people's leader will return soon?"

With suddenly misty eyes, Emily said, "No. She knows not why, but she does not."

He held her hands while reluctant tears crept down her cheeks, fell onto her chest; he hardened his look, stared silently at her for a long moment, then said, "It is difficult to know what to do . . . but Emily and Isna must soon decide."

Emily nodded, blinked at her tears. " 'Tis so. And Emily will also pray to God to show *her* the way." The two stared thoughtfully at one another until Emily suddenly forced a smile. "Will Isna now tell Emily about the dreamers among the Lakota?"

Isna nodded, smiled, then rolled onto his knees, turned to the north, sat back on his heels. Emily positioned herself beside him in a similar pose. He scraped a bare spot on the ground, drew the circle with a stick, marked the north, south, east, and west points on the circumference, then scratched the two lines that joined the north and south points, east and west points. "Isna said Emily was born a person of the north and east, with wisdom and enlightenment; he now believes she was also born a person of the south, with innocence and trust. But as Isna has also said, in Emily's short life, she has also touched the west and acquired a strong gift of introspection . . . her dreams tell Isna this is so, for no one can dream such dreams as Emily, and certain Lakota dreamers, without a strong looks-within gift of introspection that finds the dreams in her soul and mind . . . or without a deep, natural inno-cence that accepts the dreams and trusts them to show themselves with purity and truth. So Isna now tells Emily that he was wrong when he drew her position within the circle of life. Emily's true position within the circle"—he quickly drew a very small circle around the mark at the center of the large circle, placed a mark on it midway between the north and east lines—"is very close to the center and Wakan Tanka." He smiled, took her hand in his. "She approaches being a truly whole human being with all four gifts—her wisdom and enlightenment allow her to understand and respect many things, like Lakota ways and be-liefs; and her heart of innocence and introspection, which is filled with purity and truth, allows her to dream as no human being can dream, except for a few who possess the same gifts. And it is these gifts, and Emily's quiet way of possessing them, that draw Isna to her and cause him to love her above all things in the world." He paused, glanced at the circle then back at Emily. "Isna now tells Emily that all Lakota dreamers are women, and all have strong gifts of introspection and innocence, but none also possess the gifts of wisdom and enlightenment as Emily does. So Isna again tells Emily she is very close to Wakan Tanka."

"No, Isna. Emily cannot be close to Wakan Tanka. She was cruel to her father. She sometimes spoke angrily to her mother . . . and dis-obeyed her parents, and"—she bowed her head—"and she did wrong with Tayler."

"Emily did *no* wrong with Tayler. Tayler did wrong with Emily . . . against Emily's will. And all children sometimes speak badly to their parents and disobey them. This is the way of the human being, and these things teach us to use the free will given to us by Wakan Tanka. It is not a wrong." He turned back to the circle. "There are more things Isna will now tell Emily about the circle of life." He pointed at the north mark on the circle. "There is a color and spirit animal for each direction. The north's color is white, like the little white fawn with her wisdom, and its spirit animal is the wise Tatanka. The east's color is yellow, and its spirit animal is the far-seeing eagle. For the south, the color is red; and the spirit animal is the innocent, trusting, but short-sighted mouse. And for the west, the color is black, and the spirit animal, the bear; this is why Isna, who carries the spirit of Grizzly, wears black paint in battle. He also wears white, for his gift of wisdom." He paused, pointed at the center of the two circles. "But most important is the center, where all four gifts exist with equal strength . . . Wakan Tanka . . . the source of all that is good; the color there is green, and the spirit animal, the butterfly."

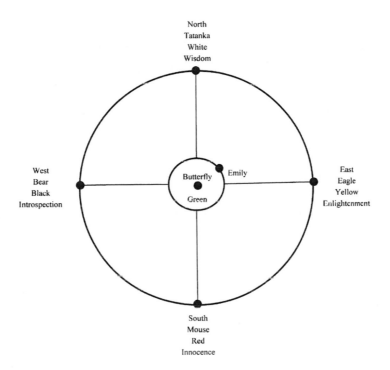

Emily gasped, trembled; chills raced through her body. "Saints in heaven, the butterfly is . . . is the center . . . Wakan Tanka?"

"Yes."

"Isna, I . . . I . . . look at this." She flipped her long hair downward over her face, exposed the back of her neck, then pointed to a small, purple, butterfly-shaped birthmark an inch below her hairline. "It itches when I dream of the Vikings and . . . and I feel like I'm there with them, feel their thoughts and feelings, their emotions, everything, as if I were a spirit they cannot see."

* * *

Allie cried out in her sleep. She trembled and panted; her heart raced.

* * *

Emily looked up, flipped her hair behind her shoulders, noticed his wry smile, doubting look. "Isna thinks Emily jokes."

He interlocked his thumbs and extended his fingers to imitate a butterfly, flitted it around her face, brushed her cheeks. After a few dives and zooms, it flew up to Emily's nose, pinched it.

"Fie!"

It then flitted under her chin, tickled her neck.

Emily giggled. "Don't! I'm ticklish!" She tried to catch his hands with her chin, but the butterfly was too quick, pulled back, flitted around for a second, then dove under her hair and tickled her behind her left ear.

She giggled louder, rolled away into a pile of leaves; but the butterfly pursued, attacked again. Emily rolled to her back, threw a handful of leaves in Isna's face.

He fell still on the ground beside her; but as she approached to tickle *him*, he opened his eyes, grabbed her wrists.

"You rascal! Let go of me! Let go!" She squealed, twisted, wrestled to free herself.

Their eyes met; the wrestling ceased. Isna eased his grip, pulled her gently on top of him; their lips drifted together; but as their tongues touched, he suddenly tensed, pulled away. "Did Emily hear that?"

She slid off him onto her knees, shook her head. "What was it?"

"A cry . . . a man's cry . . . fear or pain . . . from near Emily's special place." He sprang to his feet, pulled her to her feet. "Isna will go there and look." He snatched his weapons from the ground, started into the forest; slid his hatchet and stone war club inside his waist band; flung his quiver onto his back, nocked an arrow.

"Emily will go with Isna."

"No, Emily should return to the village."

"People in the village will have heard the cry and be on their way there. Emily will go with Isna. She has her knife and pistol."

"The village is too far away for anyone to hear so faint a cry." He shook his head, looked at her with a frustrated look. "Isna forgets . . . Emily is still an English girl and does not obey a warrior's commands." He sighed. "Come! Stay close."

The two trotted into the forest toward Emily's special place, less than a quarter mile away.

***

Ten yards from her special place and still concealed by the forest, Isna stopped, looked back at Emily, twenty yards behind, signed her to slow her pace, be stealthy. When she reached him, he took her hand, led her slowly, quietly to the edge of the clearing, where he motioned her to kneel beside him behind a thick, newly budded bush. Their first glance at the clearing revealed a man's body—a soldier's body—lying in the leaves about twenty yards away, his helmet on the ground beside him, and his head, which faced them, bloody and smashed in on the left side.

Emily gasped, held her eyes on the man, grabbed Isna's arm with a desperate grip, whispered, " 'Tis Johnny Gibbes . . . my friend. I must help him." She started to stand.

Isna grabbed her arm, pulled her back to her knees. "No. Do not move. There are white men here . . . Isna feels them, smells them, smells the fire on their big sticks that bark."

"Isna, I must go to him. He may yet be alive." She stood, walked slowly into the clearing toward Gibbes.

Isna whispered urgently, "Emily, come back!" She continued toward Gibbes. "Stubborn English girl!" He stood, moved soundlessly behind a tree, then drew his bow, stepped cautiously behind her, his arrow point moving right and left with his eyes as he scanned the tree line around the clearing.

When Emily reached Johnny Gibbes, she thought, *Isna's right, others here, no birdsongs, quiet . . . like the massacre.* She knelt, touched Johnny's cheek, leaned her ear close to his nose and mouth for a moment, then nudged his eyelids closed. Tears filled her eyes, rolled down her cheeks; a wave of nausea rose from her stomach to her throat. *Like George Howe*, she thought as she cupped her hand over her mouth. *Johnny, my dear friend . . . and Emme . . . my poor Emme.* She—

Hugh Tayler emerged from the forest; Thomas Butler and John Farre followed. Farre and Butler stopped, aimed their matchlocks at Isna, fifteen yards behind Emily. Tayler, pistol in hand, approached Emily from the front.

Emily looked at Isna, yelled in Lakota, "Run, Isna!"

Isna smiled, held his aim on Tayler.

Tayler said, "Good day, Emily." He touched his side where she'd wounded him.

"Curse you, Hugh Tayler. You've murdered Johnny Gibbes, and by heaven I shall watch you hang for it." She again looked at Isna. "Go, Isna! They mean to kill you." Isna stood firm, held his aim.

Tayler sneered, glanced at Isna. "Will you, now! Indeed! You and your Savage look rather outgunned at the moment." He looked back at Emily. "In truth, Mistress, this is a fortunate day; for though we'd planned to deal with you and your Savage, we've received the added bounty of Sergeant Gibbes following us here and revealing himself at a most opportune moment . . . for us. *Two birds with one stone*, as the saying goes. Now, as I've several times promised, I shall afford you the opportunity to watch your Savage die. Then you and I will finish what we started last night." He stopped two feet in front of her. "Give me your knife and pistol."

Emily didn't move.

"Now!"

"Take them yourself."

He slapped her face with the back of his hand; grabbed her shoulders, spun her around to face Isna; slid his right forearm, pistol in hand, across her throat; pulled her tight against him while he removed her knife, tossed it to the ground, did the same with her pistol.

Emily pleaded hoarsely, "Isna, please go!"

Isna started walking slowly, measuredly toward Tayler and Emily, his drawn bow fixed immovably on Tayler's head, eight inches above Emily's.

Tayler yelled, "Farre, quickly, kill him with Gibbes' pistol, then put it in Gibbes' hand and lay the Savage's body near him. Butler, if Farre misses, shoot him with Mistress Colman's pistol. Be quick!" He slid his left arm across Emily's chest, pinned her arms against her body, then pressed the side of his pistol against her right arm, just below the shoulder. "Now, Mistress Colman, watch your Savage die."

"Isna!"

Farre raised Gibbes' pistol, cocked the hammer, aimed, but Isna's arrow ripped through his throat before he could pull the trigger. Isna ran toward Butler, dropped his bow, grabbed his hatchet with his left hand, his war club with the right. Butler aimed Emily's pistol, pulled the trigger; but as the match ignited the powder, Isna dropped to the ground, waited for the ball to whoosh over his head, then sprang to his feet, rushed Butler. Butler's helmet fell off as he leaned to pick up his matchlock. He'd barely touched it when the two-pound rock on the end of Isna's war club shattered his skull like a glass jug. "Hiyaaa!"

As he turned to Tayler and Emily, Isna juggled his weapons to opposite hands, glared menacingly into Tayler's eyes; he started slowly, resolutely toward him, his hatchet cocked in throwing position over his head. In Lakota, he told Tayler to release her; but Tayler held her tight, stepped slowly backward.

"Emily, tell him to stop," Tayler instructed.

"Burn in hell!"

Tayler aimed the pistol at Isna, pulled the trigger. Emily heard the hammer, twisted to the right, pushed with all her strength to break Tayler's aim; Isna hurled his hatchet at Tayler's exposed left shoulder.

The pistol fired high into the air as the hatchet thudded deep into Tayler's shoulder bone. He screamed, shoved Emily to the ground, dropped to his knees; tugged on the hatchet handle, couldn't free it; reached for his dagger as Isna kicked him to the ground, raised his war club to smash his head. "Hiyaaa!"

Waters shouted, "Stop!"

Isna held the blow. He looked at Waters, lowered his club, nodded, then walked to Emily, who lay on the ground, knelt beside her. "Is Emily hurt?"

She trembled, moaned faintly, "No."

Isna stood, grasped her hand, helped her to her feet. She threw her arms around him, pulled him close, laid her head on his chest. "Isna, it . . . it was so fast . . . I . . . I've never seen anything so fast . . . so deadly . . . oh, Isna. Hold me."

"My little fawn."

One of the soldiers with Waters said, "Shall we bind the Savage, Sir?"

Waters said, "Why? You saw what happened."

"Yes, sir, but . . . but he killed two of our men, and nearly killed Tayler."

"Sad to say, those two needed killing. Attend to Sergeant Gibbes while I get the straight of what else happened."

"Aye, sir, but he's a Savage. We can't let him—"

"Did you not hear me, Private?"

"Yes, sir." He hustled toward Gibbes with two other soldiers.

Waters walked to Tayler, who lay on the ground moaning. He had removed the hatchet but writhed in pain as he tried to stop the bleeding. Waters looked at a nearby soldier. "You there, come help Master Tayler stop bleeding."

Ananias Dare and Roger Baylye arrived with more soldiers and Emme Merrimoth, who screamed when she saw Johnny Gibbes, rushed to his side. She knelt beside him, cradled his head, wailed wildly, "My Johnny, my Johnny!"

Emily knelt beside her, embraced her, rocked her back and forth. "Emme, Emme, I'm so sorry. Cry, Emme, cry."

Tayler quit moaning, said, "That Savage killed Gibbes. I saw him do it. Hit him with that club . . . same one he killed Butler with. We all saw him, tried to stop him."

Emily yelled, "That's a lie, Hugh Tayler!" She looked at Waters. "Isna heard Johnny scream; and we ran here, found him where he is now. Then Tayler and his men came out of the forest. Tayler grabbed me, and the two soldiers tried to kill Isna . . . then Tayler tried. The first shot was from that one over there." She pointed at Farre. "The second, from Tayler. The other man never got his shot off."

Tayler growled, "That's a lie, Lieutenant. We saw him kill Gibbes, and you *must* hang him!" Several soldiers murmured *aye*s of agreement.

Emme stopped crying, wiped her eyes, looked at Waters. "Lieutenant Waters, Johnny and I were walking in the clearing outside the palisades when we saw Tayler and those two slip out the front gate and into the forest. Johnny said something didn't look right, said he was going to follow them and see what they were up to. I wanted to go with him, but he told me to go back inside the palisades."

Emily walked over to Isna, translated Emme's words.

Waters said, "Thank you, Mistress Merrimoth." He shook his head, looked distraught. "I'm very sorry about Johnny, Mistress. He was a fine young man, an exceptional soldier with a bright future, and . . . and . . . I shall miss him greatly." He turned away, brushed his sleeve across his eyes. "And I shall personally ensure his killer hangs." He glared at Tayler.

Tayler shouted, "Damn you, Waters! I told you the Savage did this! He's killed three of your men and wounded me. Why in hell aren't you arresting him?"

Baylye and Ananias watched silently.

Waters looked at Isna. "Because he's committed no crime. I saw you hold Mistress Colman as a shield and try to shoot him."

Isna looked at Emily. "Perhaps Emily will tell her warrior chief that Isna will show him something."

Emily nodded, turned to Waters. "Lieutenant Waters, Isna would like to show you something."

"Aye. What is it?"

Emily nodded at Isna, who beckoned Waters to follow as he and Emily walked toward the edge of the forest. With Baylye and Ananias also in tow, Isna walked directly to a spot on the perimeter of the clearing twenty yards away, turned to Emily, pointed at boot tracks in the damp ground. "Tell them that this is where they talked. See the white man prints—three pairs here and one pair facing the other three?" Emily translated as he spoke.

A few feet away, Isna pointed to a roughed-up area with many deeper tracks. "Here, where the prints are deeper, is where they held him, wrestled with him, and killed him. And that flat place in the leaves, with blood on it, is where he fell." Isna then followed a clear pathway through the leaves, from where Johnny had fallen to the edge of the clearing, stopped; stood on one leg, lifted a foot; touched his heel, pointed ten feet into the clearing, where there were no leaves and the trail became two parallel furrows, each the width of a boot heel. He next pointed at two sets of complete boot prints, one pair on each side of two shallow, two-inch-wide, furrows leading back toward the forest. "This is the path they made when they dragged him into the clearing to lay their trap for us." He pointed at the furrows. "These tracks between the soldier footprints are from his heels."

Waters said, "How did they kill him?"

After Emily translated, Isna led them back to where the men had scuffled, pointed to an eight-inch-diameter hole in the ground. "With a rock . . . taken from here." He walked several feet deeper into the forest, searched the area carefully for a moment; suddenly stopped, leaned over; picked up an eight-inch rock, pointed at the blood splatted on one side; walked back to the hole, laid the rock perfectly in place.

Waters nodded, smiled at Isna, turned to Emily. "Mistress Colman, please thank your Sav . . . your friend . . . Eeesh . . ."

Emily smiled. "Eee-shnah . . . yes, I shall, Lieutenant."

While Emily spoke to Isna, Waters, Ananias, and Baylye walked a short distance from the others, conferred in whispers for a moment, then returned to the murder scene. Waters walked up to Tayler. "Hugh Tayler, I arrest you for the murder of Sergeant Johnny Gibbes. Since we've no jail or stocks, I place you under guarded house arrest. You are not permitted to leave for any purpose . . . not even nature's necessities. You may use a close stool and empty it yourself, once a day, under double guard. We will wait two weeks for John White to return and try you; but if he has not returned by then, you will be executed under martial rule." Sooner, he thought, if Walsingham's ship arrives first. He looked at the soldiers, pointed at two. "You and you, bind him and lead him to his quarters. Do not allow him to leave for any purpose. Sergeant Myllet will see to your relief in several hours."

"Aye, sir," the two spoke in unison.

"The rest of you men carry Sergeant Gibbes to the village in a manner befitting a fallen hero. Then retrieve the other two."

"Aye, sir."

Waters turned to Emily, smiled. "Mistress Colman, please tell Isna I hope I never have to fight him."

* * *

As Emily and Isna approached the Chesapeake village, Emily said, "Isna and Emily, and baby Virginia, are in great danger. Tayler is guarded, but he still has influence with his men. Emily believes they will try to kill us."

Isna stopped, laid gentle hands on her shoulders. "Isna welcomes this. Perhaps they are braver than their leader, and their scalps will be worth hanging on Isna's pole." He paused, looked somberly at the forest then into Emily's eyes. "Isna must tell Emily something he has not told her about the Powhatans."

Emily's look tightened; fear infiltrated her eyes.

"Two years ago the Powhatans killed thirteen white men who escaped the Roanokes and came here in a big canoe. These men stole food from the Nansemonds, who are neighbors of the Chesapeakes and members of the Powhatan chiefdom. They also killed two Powhatans with their big sticks that bark. The Powhatans and Nansemonds then overwhelmed them and killed or captured all of them. They tested the strength of those they captured, and found them weak. Emily must know that these people have no fear of white men." He paused again. "Isna has also seen Powhatans among the Chesapeakes . . . watching your village, measuring your strength. These are the reasons Isna believes the Powhatans will soon attack . . . perhaps Emily will tell her young warrior chief."

Emily blanched, nodded, stared silently into his eyes. *Endless danger, endless fear . . . whatever will become of us? Saints above, please speed John White to us.*

* * *

After she and Isna parted, Emily walked hastily toward the colony. When she was nearly to the palisades, an eerie, unnerving feeling riddled her senses—a familiar feeling of being watched. Instinctive fear flooded her mind, chilled her body. She shuddered, took a few more steps, fought the urge to stop, search for the source. *Dear God, I'm terrified, but why? What is it?* She stopped, looked at the tree line to the right. Nothing. Anxiety pounded in her heart as she slowly turned to the left, studied the tree line twenty yards away. She gasped; her eyes bloomed wide; her jaw dropped; her body shivered with terror. *His eyes . . . seething . . . boring into my soul . . . fear, horror . . . the massacre . . . dear God, the massacre . . . his hate . . . clubbing me . . . killing me. Cannot look at him.* She lowered her gaze, felt her senses numb, panted, trembled, felt a deep chill race through her body as she stared at her precious black locket hanging from his neck.

The Panther smirked, faded slowly into the shadowy forest.

Mother . . . dear God . . . help me.

* * *

Another cramp doubled Emily onto her bed. What's happening to me? Hurts so. "Ahhh! Mother, help me. Please make it stop." She rolled to her back, pulled up her smock, felt the wetness between her legs, looked at her hand. My God, I'm bleeding . . . badly . . . rags . . . need rags. Panicked, afraid, she rolled off the bed to her knees, screamed as another cramp stabbed her like a dull knife. "Someone help me!" She crawled toward her chest, doubled over with another cramp, threw back the lid; fumbled for her period rags, pulled them from the trunk; started to crawl to the bed, flattened onto the floor with another cramp. "Ooooooh." She rolled to her back, pulled up her bloody smock, stuffed the rags firmly between her legs, and squeezed them together. Another cramp. "Ahhh!"

Someone knocked on the door.

Emily moaned weakly, "Who is it?"

"Emme . . . I wanted to visit with you . . . Emily you sound awful; I'm coming in." Emme burst through door. "God's blood, Emily, what's wrong?!"

"Aaaah! Cramps . . . like a period . . . but worse." She panted, writhed. "Help me, Emme. I'm bleeding . . . gushing . . . don't know . . . don't know what . . . what it is. Faint . . . can't think . . . can't . . . talk. More . . . more rags . . . need more rags." Emily's head slowly relaxed onto the floor, eyes closed, body limp.

Emme knelt beside her, gently smacked her cheek. "Emily, Emily . . . awaken. Do not do this; you cannot die! Noooo!" She stood, rushed to the door. "Ellie, must get Ellie." She ran outside, raced toward the Dares' cottage.

CHAPTER 15

Tryggvi, Hefnir, and Bjarni, followed by about fifty other Vikings, walked through shallow water and onto the shore of a huge lake. As a large group of Indians approached them, Tryggvi and Bjarni lifted their axes and swords to the ready. From the corner of his mouth, Tryggvi whispered, "More Skraelings, Bjarni. Perhaps these will like you better than the others did."

"Go poke yourself, Tryggvi; they've never seen such a warrior and lover as Bjarni the Impregnator."

Tryggvi smirked. "I see you still have delusions from that hit on the head, and—"

***

Emme and Elyoner sat beside Emily as she lay on her bed in a clean white smock.

Groggily, Emily said, "I have to find Isna."

Elyoner said, "No, Em, you're not going anywhere. You've lost a huge amount of blood, and you'll probably fall on your pretty face as soon as you stand."

"Saints above, Ellie, you are such a fiddly old nag sometimes. I'm fine. I must see Isna, tell him what's happened. Have either of you seen him about?"

Both shook their heads. Emme said, "No, but we agree, he must be told what's happened because . . . because . . . it's changed things so greatly."

Emily sat up. "What do you mean?"

Emme and Elyoner eyed one another. Elyoner nodded, looked at Emily. "Em, you've . . . you've lost your baby. That's why you bled so much." She again glanced at Emme then back at Emily. "We've buried the remains with your father and covered the spot with leaves to avoid suspicion . . . we'll go there with you . . . when you're ready."

Emily stared blankly at her lap. "My baby . . . gone?"

"Aye, Em."

"As quickly as it came." She looked at Emme then Elyoner; tears filled her eyes; she blubbered, "How can God do such a thing to an unborn child? How?"

Elyoner said, "God works in ways we can't always understand, Em. He closes one door and opens another. And *your* closed door is the loss of a child you would have loved, but your *opened* door is freedom from Tayler."

Emily looked at her for a moment then lay back on the bed, rolled to her stomach, sobbed.

* * *

Waters and Myllet walked cautiously through the forest with four soldiers behind them. Waters carried a pistol in his right hand, a sabre in his left. Myllet had pistols in both hands, and the four soldiers carried matchlocks at the ready.

Waters stopped, whispered to the front soldier, Private Warner, "Where are they? How much farther?"

"Not more than two hundred yards, Sir . . . over there . . . past that thicket." He pointed his barrel at a thick bunch of bushes about thirty yards away.

"Very well. Proceed." Something doesn't feel right, he thought. Perhaps the strangeness of Warner's breathless message that Smith wanted him and Myllet to come quickly to his aid, perhaps the unsettling quiet of the forest, perhaps my imagination. Doesn't matter . . . something's not right . . . and I don't trust this friend of Taverner guiding us to this place . . . glad I brought the other three. Odd that Smith would call for Michael and me by name instead of simply asking for help if his situation is dire.

Twenty yards past the thicket, Waters stopped again, leaned toward Myllet, whispered, "Michael, I don't like it."

"Nor I, Sir. Hair's on edge over something."

"Michael Myllet, where's your armor?"

Myllet smiled. "You grabbed me on the way back from the privy, Sir, and—"

Phffft! Phffft! One arrow tore into Myllet's chest, the other into his stomach. He staggered two steps backward, fell motionless onto his back.

Waters yelled, "Cover, men! Take cover!" He leaped behind a tree. Something behind me. He looked back over his right shoulder, gazed down the bore of Warner's matchlock, heard the click of the serpentine clamp as it dropped the match onto the flash pan, saw the puff of smoke from the priming powder. He ducked and turned as the main charge ignited, but he was too slow; the ball ripped through the top of his right shoulder, slammed him against the tree. "Aah! Get that man!" He saw the other three soldiers tackle Warner to the ground, then glanced at Myllet. "God damn it, Michael! They've killed you. The sons of bitches."

He peered around the right side of the tree, saw Private Taverner and two archers—Tydway and Mylton, a civilian—all three without armor—emerge from cover, charge toward him. He leaned his pistol against the right side of the tree, aimed at Tydway, squeezed the trigger. The recoil sent a sharp jab of pain through his wounded shoulder. "Ow! Fie! Now what?" He saw Tydway fall to the ground as he pulled back behind the tree. *Phffft-thud!* An arrow stuck in the tree where his face had been an instant before.

He again peered around the tree, saw Taverner fifteen yards away, aiming his matchlock at the tree, and Mylton nocking an arrow. He leaned a foot out from the tree, tempted Taverner to shoot, no luck. He looked behind, saw the three soldiers struggling with Warner. On my own. No time to reload. He dropped the pistol, took the sabre in his right hand. Here goes. He charged around the left side of the tree, raced toward Taverner and Mylton at a dead run, zigzagging every few steps. He saw the smoke from Taverner's gun, heard the ball whoosh by his ear. Almost there. He zigzagged again, saw Mylton trying to track him with his bow. Five more yards, sabre ready, Taverner pulling dagger. "Ah!" Arrow in the leg; keep going, swing at Taverner, head falling off; back slice at Mylton, death cut across stomach—the Master would be proud—Mylton down, screaming, guts hanging out, mercy slash to head. Done!

Waters stood panting over the two dead men, eyed his bloody leg and shoulder, then glanced back at the three men holding Warner, their mouths agape in awe. He snapped the point of the arrow off, grimaced as he yanked the shaft from his thigh. He hobbled to Myllet, knelt beside him, touched his cheek. "Goodbye, my dear, dear friend. God be with you." He lingered a moment, said a prayer, then stood, wiped tears from his eyes, walked to the men holding Warner. "Stand him up, hold him fast."

They pulled Warner to his feet; a soldier gripped each arm while the third held a tuft of his hair with his left hand, a dagger at his throat with the right.

"Private Warner, under martial rule and the commander's wartime authority, I condemn you to die at this moment for mutiny and attempted murder. Release him."

"Sir . . . please . . . they made me do it . . . Taverner and . . . and—" He gagged as Waters' sword pierced his stomach, pushed through his innards to his spine. His body convulsed; blood and a gurgling sound oozed from his mouth. Waters thrust again, then a third time.

As the three soldiers lowered Warner's body to the grass, Waters thrust his sabre into the ground, dropped to his knees, gripped the hilt with both hands to steady himself. Dizzy. "Get help, men."

***

Emily sat cross-legged beside Isna on the stream bank at her special place, stared broodingly at the purling water as it rippled lazily around and over the rocks in the streambed. She unconsciously rubbed her eyes, thought how comforting the sun's gentle warmth felt on her face, wished it could stay that way until the next winter. She thought of her lost child, closed her eyes, imagined what it would have looked like—first a boy, then a girl. She looked into the stream, again rubbed the dampness from her eyes; flicked a blade of grass into the current, watched it spin, duck underwater in an eddy, then bob back to the surface; whispered to herself in English, "At the mercy of the water . . . swept away . . . spun . . . pummeled by powerful forces . . . like me and my fate, yet . . . yet it remains afloat." She glanced blankly at the forest while she smiled, spoke to herself within the sanctum of her mind. *And I shall do the same.*

Isna watched her with curious eyes, leaned his head slightly to the right, finally spoke in a tender tone. "What troubles Emily?"

She held her eyes on the forest, ignored his question for a while, then erupted into tears, speaking angrily as she sobbed. "Does Isna not understand that while Emily's body is nearly healed, her mind is not? Does he not know that she has just lost her child, a part of her . . . dead . . . gone forever? Does he not understand that Emily will never hold or nurse it, or watch it grow? Does he not know that this loss tears at her heart like a hungry true-dog?" She faced him with pained eyes.

He stared at her thoughtfully then nodded, reached out and took her hand in his.

She leaned into his embrace, moaned softly, "Forgive Emily's anger. 'Tis just . . . just so unfair to the child . . . first it has life, then not . . . yet the child itself is completely helpless. At least *we* have the power to *try* and save ourselves, but a baby . . . a baby has nothing."

He caressed her cheek. "Isna understands. He has seen this sadness before . . . yet Emily's grief will strengthen her . . . and she will need this strength in the days ahead." He gently stroked her hair and the back of her neck. "Isna feels Emily's sadness."

"Emily knows this is so, but 'tis not only for the baby and Isna's leaving that she grieves . . . there is also a great fear that saddens Emily, a fear Isna does not yet know of." She looked up at him. "When Emily and Isna last parted . . . at the edge of the forest outside the palisades . . . she saw the Powhatan warrior who tried to carry her away and nearly killed her at the Roanoke massacre. He watched her, stared at her, told her with his eyes that he wants to take her." She sighed. "He also studied the palisades, which means the Powhatans plan to attack us . . . as Isna has said."

He nodded.

"And . . . and he wore Emily's black locket around his neck. He must have found it at the massacre place, and . . . and Emily will never hold it again . . . her only remembrance of her father and mother." She stared vacantly at the forest.

"Emily has their memories in her heart . . . these cannot be taken from her." He hesitated, watched her ponder his words. "What does this warrior look like?"

She looked instantly fearful. "I shall never forget his face. He had a curved nose, thin, angry features . . . a long scar beside a strip of black paint from his left eye to his chin . . . and a strip of red paint down the bare right side of his forehead, across his right eye, to his chin." She shuddered. "He had a wild, hateful look in his eyes . . . and he hit Emily with his club . . . again and again . . . as if—"

"Isna has met this warrior . . . he is the one Isna wounded in the forest the day the Powhatans told the Lakota to leave the deer they'd killed. He is a powerful warrior . . . unafraid, and a great leader of his people. He is called *Kills-Like-the-Panther*. . . he and Isna will meet again."

Emily paled; a pall of fear spread across her face. She slowly faced him, studied his eyes. "How can this be if Isna leaves?"

He turned away. "Isna knows not . . . but it *will* be so."

She bowed her head, looked at the stream, spoke with a trill in her voice. "The planting moon is nearly full. Isna will leave soon."

He watched her for a moment then laid his hand on hers. "When the Powhatans attack, they will kill all . . . the men immediately, and the women . . . later. No one will be spared." He paused. "Isna will not abandon Emily to such an end. Yet Isna is troubled because the other

Lakota will not abandon *him* . . . but will stay and fight with him . . . and we will all die here together. But Isna does not want the other Lakota to die for him. He wants them to return to the people and live . . . as he wants Emily to live. Yet Wakan Tanka has not shown him how *both* of these things can be . . . and this troubles Isna's heart."

Emily's mind swirled; thin tears covered her eyes like mist on a window pane; she visualized her mother and brother walking ashore with John White, finding the colony in ashes, rotting, dismembered bodies scattered about. *No, I cannot* let these Lakota die for me . . . but what *can* I do? No choices . . . no escape. She fiddled with the grass on the ground beside her. There is but one way we can all live, and that is to not be here whenever the attack comes . . . either because we're gone forever or gone for a while. She stared at the ground in front of her for a moment then looked quizzically at Isna. "Perhaps Isna will again tell Emily what is expected of a Lakota wife."

He gave her a twinge of a smile and a suspicious look. "A Lakota woman gathers firewood, brings water, dresses the game killed by her husband, cooks, makes clothes, cleans the lodge, bears children, and"—his smile deepened—"pleases her husband . . . and obeys him in all matters."

Her eyes sparkled impishly. "Most of these are also expectations of a good *English* wife . . . but an English wife may disagree with her husband and sometimes . . . perhaps . . . disobey him . . . but not often if she is clever." She watched his smiling eyes. "Could Emily go with Isna to the Lakota . . . for a time . . . then return here later . . . when John White has brought more people and soldiers? Would this not save all the Lakota, and Emily, from certain death?"

Isna's eyes glistened. "Isna has asked Wakan Tanka to put this thought in Emily's mind . . . for Isna himself could not ask her this." He looked suddenly serious. "Emily's gifts of wisdom and enlightenment allow her to see things as a Lakota . . . and Isna already sees her as Lakota . . . and so it will be with *all* the Lakota."

"Oh, Isna!" A flash of hope filled her eyes but quickly faded to disappointment. "Emily is foolish. She has spoken with her heart, not knowing if her mind will agree. She has never thought of leaving her people, her family and friends, her way of life . . . perhaps forever; and though she has many times dreamed of herself as Lakota, as Isna's wife, she does not know if the dreams can come true." She leaned into his arms, laid her cheek against his chest. "Isna must ask Wakan Tanka to show Emily the pathway he wants her to take."

* * *

The two soldiers guarding Tayler's cottage snapped to attention, held their matchlocks at *present arms* as Waters approached with a brisk but limpy step and a determined, angry look on his face. He nodded at the guards then extended his right hand to open the cottage door, winced at the sharp pain that shot down his arm from his wound. He banged the door open with his left hand, carefully drew his dagger with the right; stomped into the room directly to Tayler, who stood a few feet away; rudely grabbed the front of his shirt with his left hand, poked the dagger point firmly against his throat. "You filthy, low son-of-a-whore, you're done. You and your fucking henchmen have murdered two fine men who were worth a thousand of you; and if you so much as blink the wrong way, you're dead; and I'm the judge, jury, and executioner. Understand?" He pressed the dagger harder, formed a deep, red dimple around the point.

Tayler quivered, tilted his head back, glanced down at the dagger. "I . . . I don't know what you're talking about, Lieutenant. How the hell do you—"

"Fie on you, you scum!" He sliced a shallow, three-inch cut across the bottom of Tayler's chin.

"Aah! You bastard. I'll see you die for that."

"Dead men see nothing, Tayler. Remember what I said." He waved the dagger slowly, menacingly an inch in front of Tayler's eyes, then slid it into its sheath, turned, walked out the door.

Tayler picked up a kerchief with his quivering hand, held it against his throat, then removed it, looked at the line of blood across it. A wave of nausea, followed by an airy dizziness, suffused his body and mind. He sat down by the fire, again held the kerchief to his throat. Painful . . . but not like the shoulder where that damned Savage sunk his hatchet into the bone . . . low, filthy swine, all of them.

He stared into the fire for a moment. But is that not the tale of my entire life: always someone causing me trouble, disrupting my plans? He thought of his sad youth, his sadder, more-troubled adulthood. Perchance I *am* insane . . . or partially so. But can an insane person know they're insane? Perhaps, but . . . but still, I'm not the man I should be . . . something's always been out of kilter . . . ever since I found Mother . . . hanging there, swaying gently, so still, so . . . so dead . . . abandoned me, she did. Aye, and that's when all the trouble began, when everything went askew. He glanced at the bloody kerchief. Bleeding's stopped. Prick! He tossed the kerchief into the fire, watched it burst into flame. Aye, 'twas Mother's fault. He felt his eyes dampen, as they did whenever he thought of her. *She's* the reason I'm this way . . . why I've done so much wrong in my life . . . never been able to right myself. Always needed someone like her . . . but then she lost her mind . . . or so it seemed . . . Stepfather's fault. Yes, I've *always* needed someone like her . . . someone strong, like . . . like Emily Colman . . . to save me from myself. He rubbed tears from his eyes, imagined Emily smiling affectionately at him, embracing him, wildly kissing his lips.

My Emily, how I've wronged you . . . but oh, how you've wronged *me*, as well . . . wronged me because you cannot understand how much I need you . . . how much I love you . . . how only you can save me. Still, I love you, will *always* love you . . . no matter what, no matter how you feel about me . . . can never give you up, must make you understand, make you mine, have you with me for all time. My Emily . . . my dear, dear Emily . . . must have you again, know your body, feel your warmth, your essence, your ecstasy. I *must* have you . . . at *any* cost.

＊＊

Emily nursed Virginia, watched Elyoner spin wool, Emme stare vacantly into the fire. She glanced down at Virginia. So good to hold you again, little one . . . missed you so. She looked at the fire. You could be my own child, my own baby, drawing life from my body. But *that* baby will never be . . . gone forever . . . buried . . . soon to be one with the ground, and . . . and . . . and no! Do not think such thoughts, Emily Colman. Think of naught but the future. But alas . . . that, too, brings pain . . . possibilities few and frightful . . . except for being with Isna . . . yet even *that* brings anguish; for though I would die to be with him, I see *not* how it can be. She imagined her mother and brother kneeling at her father's grave, sobbing, pleading with God to help them find some trace of her. She saw her father staring at her with a mournful look, mouthing words she could not hear, then George smiling contentedly at her. She shook her head. Dear God, what should I do? Pray, help me do the right thing. Please, Lord. She abruptly shook her head. Stop thinking of *yourself*, Emily Colman!

She looked at Emme. My poor friend. So sad for you . . . must feel like *I* did when George and Father died. Oh, George, so much has happened since you were here. Hope you've not witnessed it all. An unwilled smile spread across her face. Always wondered if people in heaven can see what happens on earth. I pray you're there, George, but that you see naught but good . . . though there's been precious little of *that*. She again looked at Emme. Got to get you through this, Emme. I miss Johnny, as well . . . so kind to me . . . helpful . . . told me the truth . . . tried to save me from Tayler . . . and then . . . to die like that . . . murdered. Her look soured. May his killers burn in hell, and thank you, God, for letting Isna send them there . . . all but one . . . who will receive his due in time. She took a deep breath, shook her head. Sorry, Lord, 'tis sinful to pleasure in another's misfortune; but please help Emme . . . not been herself since Johnny died . . . but truly, what else could one expect? Must make her talk, pull her mind from it. She sighed, glanced at Elyoner, met her stare, then flicked her gaze briefly at Emme and back to Elyoner, who replied with a nod. Emily said, "Emme, have you seen Lieutenant Waters since we treated his wounds?"

Emme shook her head, held her gaze on the fire. "Nay, but I'm told he's recovered well."

"Well, he's *you* to thank for *that*. I was certainly no help."

"You'd your own troubles."

She visualized herself lying on her cottage floor bleeding to death, then felt a gust of fear as she saw the Panther glaring at her, her precious locket around his neck. "Well, if you'd not found me, I'd likely not be here with you now."

Elyoner said, "Em's right, Emme. *You* were the one responsible for Waters' recovery . . . *and* for discovering Em's plight before it was too late. A born nurse you are." She paused, watched Emme stare at the fire. "And when Father returns, we shall all watch Tayler hang from a tree . . . or be parted from his head with a broadaxe."

Emme said, "You still believe your father will return?"

"Why . . . why, of course I do . . . I . . . I *must* believe so . . . 'tis our only hope, and without such hope—"

"*I* don't believe it. I don't think he'll *ever* return . . . at least not in time to save us."

Elyoner's face flushed. "How can you think that, Emme?"

Emme looked at her without expression. "Because 'tis true . . . I do not say it to upset you . . . how can you possibly believe otherwise?"

Elyoner stared at her, began to tremble.

"Something's happened to change things, Ellie . . . something beyond your father's control . . . for we all know he would be here by now if he could. *Something* prevents his return. You must know this in your heart . . . as Johnny and I did weeks ago . . . shortly after we made plans to return to England . . . to have our baby there . . . but then we . . ." Her eyes misted.

Elyoner looked stunned, stood, rushed to Emme's side, knelt beside her, hugged her as both began to cry. "Oh, Emme, you're with child!"

Emme blubbered, "Yes, but . . . but now there will be no one to . . . to help me raise it . . . no father . . . no . . ."

Emily's eyes filled with tears. "Emme! 'Tis not so. Ellie and I will help you." She flung Virginia over her shoulder like a bag of salt, stepped quickly to Emme and Elyoner, and caressed Emme's hair and neck with her free hand. "Please, Emme, have faith. I'm *so* happy for you." She felt a pang of sadness in her heart, a brief twinge of jealousy. Shame upon you for such a thought, Emily Colman. "We'll help you, Emme . . . Ellie and I, your baby's two Virginia aunts. I promise you."

* * *

They hadn't planned it that way, but Waters, Baylye, and Ananias stood in front of the other loyalists, faced Sampson and Stevens, who stood alone. Waters said, "I don't give a damn if you were hungry. We're all desperately hungry, but what you did was against Governor Baylye's explicit orders to not take food from the Chesapeakes. My God, are you daft? Without their help, our situation is hopeless. How the hell could you think stealing food from them would help *anything*, beyond filling your own selfish guts for a while? Fie on you! You've now alienated the Chesapeakes to where they won't share even a collop with us."

Sampson said meekly, " 'Twasn't us, Waters."

Baylye shook his head. "You lie, Sampson! Even Gramme and Dutton named you two as the instigators when they were under the lash. We've no time for such treachery and foolishness."

Stevens snapped, "Go to hell, Baylye. You can't prove a thing."

Waters stepped to within a few inches of Stevens, snarled, "We don't need to; and if you fail to grasp my meaning, ask your leader."

Stevens and Sampson eyed one another uneasily, looked back at Waters.

Waters glared at them then abruptly walked to the door, opened it. "Bring them in, Sergeant."

Smith and fourteen other soldiers squeezed into the tiny room. Stale smoke and body heat fouled the air, bedecked each forehead with beads of sweat. Waters wiped his brow with his sleeve. "Leave that door open, so we don't suffocate." He took a deep breath, looked sternly at Gramme, Dutton, and two other soldiers, then scowled at Stevens and Sampson. "You four men in uniform . . . and you, Stevens and Sampson—and your cohorts who are not here—are known conspirators against this colony." He paused for a ripple of underbreath murmurs. "And conspiracy against the colony is conspiracy against the *Queen*"—his eyes contracted to tiny, dark dots—"and conspiracy against the Queen, for soldiers, is *mutiny*. And both conspiracy and mutiny are treason. *Treason*, men! A high crime punishable by death. Did Tayler explain *that* to you?" He again paused to exploit the heavy, tense silence that enveloped the room. "Whether he did or not, I will now tell you Hugh Tayler is a dead man—either by the Powhatans' hands, mine, or the executioner's." He placed his hand on his sword. "His actions from here on will determine which it will be. But no matter who delivers the blow, Tayler's dead, and all of you conspirators must understand how this affects you. So listen well. You shall not have another chance at reprieve."

Sampson and Stevens glanced at each other more uneasily than before. Several soldiers did the same, shuffled their feet, wiped sweat from their brows.

After glaring briefly at each man in turn, Waters said, "We're slowly starving to death; and if the hunting and fishing do not improve with spring, we will all die a slow death together. But we will all die *faster* if the Powhatans attack us soon . . . as I believe they will. And that death will be faster *still* if you and the other conspirators persist in foolish noncooperation." He paused, smiled with facetious concern. "Now you men are probably wondering about Walsingham's rescue ship . . . where it is . . . why 'tis not here." He surveyed their tight, strained faces, saw he'd touched a tender spot. "Quite overdue, is it not?" Another pause. "In truth, I myself harbor *doubt* that John White will return in time to save us from the Powhatans, but I am *absolutely certain* Walsingham's imaginary ship will *never* arrive. He's far too clever to risk *his* position and life by openly challenging the Queen when he can accomplish his goal by risking *yours*." More silence. "So where does that leave us?"

No one spoke; all stared anxiously at Waters.

"It leaves us where we were a moment ago—awaiting an imminent Powhatan attack, by a vastly superior force, against our *inferior* force of *insufficiently trained* defenders, with serious gaps in their palisades, and scarcely enough firepower to survive a night. Now consider *this* for a moment: what will you be thinking when hordes of screaming, painted Savages swarm through the palisades bent on killing you and your women and children?" He again eyed the conspirators. "What will you do? Will you stand by and watch the slaughter . . . and then explain to the Powhatans you're on their side . . . that the whole idea of a colony was a bad one . . . that you'll leave as soon as your rescue ship arrives . . . and that no other Englishmen will come here? Is that what you'll do? And do you think they'll believe you? Or even understand you?" Silence. "I think not." More silence. "But if we all fight together, then perchance—just perchance—we might hold out until John White actually *does* return." He paused, shrugged his shoulders. "But if he does *not* return"—he smiled—"then we shall all wing our way to heaven or hell in good military formation."

Nervous laughter rippled through the room.

"So, to each soldier who has violated his oath and conspired to mutiny, I promise a pardon . . . *if* you fight with us . . . and *if* we survive . . . and *if* you remain loyal. I also promise immediate *death* to any who *refuse* to fight when the time comes."

Baylye stepped forward, cleared his throat. "I have been silent today. Lieutenant Waters has spoken well, but I now promise the same to any civilian conspirators."

Waters nodded. "What say you, men?"

Sampson and Stevens glanced at one another, their comrades, then Waters, nodded grudgingly. Sampson said, " 'Twould appear we are now with you, Lieutenant."

Waters nodded. "Good. And I now expect you to confer with your cohorts who are *not* here, and relay *their* decisions to me."

Both nodded.

Waters then eyed each soldier in turn. "And you?"

"Aye, sir."

"And you?"

"Aye, sir."

After every man had pledged to fight, Waters again nodded, took a deep breath, smiled. "So now you're all probably wondering how in Dante's hell we're going to do this, eh?"

Nervous laughter.

Waters looked at Smith. "Sergeant Smith, your turn."

* * *

While the Dares slept, Emily probed the reassuring depths of the fire. She tensed as a spark crackled, rose toward the thatch roof. She started to stand, take a swipe at it with the damp rag the Dares used to swat rising sparks, but it died a foot above the fire. So she sat back on her stump, resumed her reflective stare into the coals. *You always enchant me,* she thought . . . *conjure my deepest thoughts to the forefront of my mind. So now, my dear spirit of fire, help me weigh and deliberate the choices before me . . . heighten my feelings, my emotions, my senses . . . and yes, my reason . . . so all may battle to govern my mind.* She then stared expectantly at the gracefully swaying flames, waited for them to obey her command, fill her mind with persuasions of decision.

Minutes later, she smiled as if a bright candle had been suddenly lit within her. *Since the moment I met him—though I did not know it—I've wanted nothing but to be forever with Isna. But if he stays here, he and his men will perish with me, and* that *I cannot allow. And even if the unlikely occurs, and John White returns in time to thwart the Powhatan attack, I cannot ask Isna to become a white man. 'Twould kill him, and he would still face the dilemma of leading his men home. So what would be accomplished? Nothing! Therefore, I cannot let him stay under any circumstance.*

On the other side, if I go with Isna and the Lakota, we might all *reach Lakota land and survive. I love the Lakota way of life, its spirituality, its respect for all things; but . . . but 'twould be so different from* my *life, from* English *life. I'd become a . . . I hate the word . . . a Savage: no potpies, no Christmas pudding, no Christmas at all, no house, no bed, no pots and pans, no beer, no privy, no books, no church—all so* different. But strangely . . . so very strangely . . . none of this concerns me compared to being with Isna. So I *can* go with him; I *want* to go with him; for above all, I love him to the depths of my soul and will do anything to be with him. His soul is one with mine.

She broke a branch in two, threw it on the fire. But truly, how can I desert the colony in time of great danger and need . . . my friends, my mother and brother . . . Father? She again visualized her mother and brother crying over her father's grave, begging God to help them find her, discover her fate.

But what if Mother and Brother never come . . . or if *no* other Englishmen come? What then? And is not leaving with Isna much like escaping a sinking vessel, where the lucky ones find something to float on . . . and others do not; and some survive, and others do not? But what of George, who could have saved himself but instead did as Christ instructs . . . laid down his life for others . . . *no greater love hath any man.*

She closed her eyes, thought of her visit to her father's grave the day before. She'd explained everything that had happened since his death: John White's failure to return, the colony's imminent demise, her deep love for Isna, her conviction that going with him was the only way to preclude his sacrificing himself and his men in a futile fight, and her desire to someday return to find her mother and brother. She'd then asked him for his guidance and blessing on whichever path she ultimately chose.

She laid another log on the fire, again studied its pulsing blue heart, saw Isna's face within. So afraid to be without you. But I cannot let you die here; yet, how can I abandon my people in time of need? Dear Lord, what must Emily Colman do? She thought of the Lakota circle of life, thought of Isna explaining Lakota virtues to her, then smiled. Emily Colman must *forever* be with Isna . . . but does *forever* end *here*, when the Powhatans attack . . . or does it last a lifetime . . . *somewhere else?*

＊

Emily and Isna wore strained, anxious looks as they walked toward Emily's special place; neither spoke. As they crossed one of the clearings short of their destination, Emily glanced upward, immediately smiled at the sight above her. What a sky. . . beautiful, fluffy little clouds drifting in perfect formation across that little sea of blue . . . like cattail blooms, they are . . . floating on a lazy stream . . . like that first morning at Roanoke when George and I walked down the path to the sound to retrieve luggage from the ship. Her smile broadened. How excited I was to be in the New World . . . finally free of that miserable ship . . . such innocence . . . such ignorance of the trials to come. But in spite of all that's happened since, *that* day was packed as tight as our ship's hold with discovery and excitement. Her smile slowly dimmed like a spent candle that fades, flickers, and finally expires. But *this* day, *this* moment, my heart and soul burn with fear and anguish . . . fear of the unknown . . . anguish over what, in a few moments, I will say to Isna . . . for I've changed my mind twenty times since last night, and at this very moment I know not what I shall say.

As they neared her special place, anxiety pummeled her senses; nausea churned in her stomach, rose relentlessly toward the bottom of her throat. As they seated themselves on the stream bank, Emily collected herself, sighed, faced Isna with bloodshot eyes. "Emily must tell Isna her mind. She—"

"Isna must first tell Emily something that may *change* what is in her mind."

She blinked, glanced at him with wide eyes, parted lips.

He pondered the stream for a moment then faced her with a somber look that frightened her. He laid his hand on hers. "My little white fawn . . . the Chesapeakes say that tonight the Powhatans attack your people with over four hundred warriors. They fear the Powhatans may attack them, as well, since they have been your friends."

Emily gasped, looked away, swallowed hard; her jaw dropped; she dug her fingers into the cool, damp soil. "Isna, we . . . we will not survive such an attack."

Isna watched her in stoic silence.

"Saints above. Why cannot Governor White return now, today? We'd at least have a chance." She looked back at Isna. "Isna, I know not what to do." She put her arm around his waist, snuggled against his side.

He placed his arm around her shoulder and pulled her close, caressed her cheek with his other hand, held his lips against her hair.

" 'Tis coming undone . . . everything." She sniffled twice, began to whimper softly. "We will all surely die." She paused then whispered, "Isna will leave today?"

He hesitated for a moment. "No. Isna and the Lakota will tie themselves to stakes in the ground beside Emily, remain beside her . . . fight and protect her until each dies a great warrior death."

Emily covered her mouth, gasped. "No, Isna! You *cannot* do this. I sha'n't let you. You cannot die for me in a lost fight."

He eased her slightly away, touched her chin, gently guided her eyes to his. "Many Powhatan women will cry and slash their arms to mourn the men we kill."

"No, Isna, the Lakota must leave now . . . before the attack!"

"Isna and the Lakota will stay." He looked into her eyes. "We are warriors; and there is no greater honor than to die in battle against a strong, fearless enemy."

"Isna, no!" Fie on this warrior thinking . . . like the damnable Vikings and their insane death wish, reckless disdain for danger. How can I love such a man?

"There is another choice . . . the *only* choice that can fulfill Isna's vision and Emily's dream . . . but only Emily can make this choice."

She moaned, laid her face in her hands. "Oh, Isna, I so fear this choice. I've thought of it all night and day and cannot decide . . . because I am afraid to leave my people . . . especially now . . . knowing they will all die." She looked at him. "I must stay and help them . . . even though the end is certain."

"How will you help your people?"

Frustration, grief, uncertainty—all shadowed her face like a broad-brimmed hat. "I . . . I will carry water, load the big sticks, help wounded ones . . . perhaps fight."

"These things will not save your people."

"No, they will not . . . but I must do them anyway, and—"

"Then Isna will be beside you."

Her eyes pleaded with him; she shook her head emphatically with every word. "Noooo, Isna. Nooo! You must go . . . free yourself of this place, its evil, its danger, save yourself . . . your men!"

"Isna will remain."

Tears flooded her eyes; she shook her head, stared at him with dull, anguished eyes, wordless, parted lips, heaving breast. "Emily has kept a secret from Isna. Emily . . . Emily no longer loves Isna. She no longer wants to be with him, or the Lakota. She loves another . . . the English soldier chief . . . Waters. She will marry him tonight. She has loved him for a moon but has not found the words to tell Isna. So Isna should return to his people . . . today." She stood, looked down at him. "It pains Emily to say these things, but . . . but her words are true." A gush of tears rolled down her cheeks, dripped off her chin onto her breast.

Isna stood, stared into her eyes.

She shrank from his gaze then threw her arms around him, kissed him slowly, longingly on the lips. "May Isna's journey be safe . . . and may Wakan Tanka walk with him." She stood trembling, entranced by his sorrowful eyes.

He stared at her for a long, awkward moment then whispered softly, "Isna will love Emily until his last breath is one with the wind."

She moaned, turned away, ran into the forest toward the village.

***

Tayler sat by the fire, his writing board and a piece of parchment on his knee, pen in hand.

> *My Dearest Emily,*
> *'Tis with a heart heavy with grief, humility, and shame that I share with you the following horrible burdens I have carried in my soul . . .*

* * *

Emily stumbled through the forest, frantic with grief, nearly blinded by tears. Suddenly, an eerie, overpowering instinct seized her mind, commanded her to stop, listen to its voice. She stared blindly ahead for a moment then slowly relaxed her arms to her sides, leaned her head slightly back, closed her eyes, as if to revel in a refreshing summer shower. She heard only silence; strained for a sound, again heard nothing; tried to quiet her rapid breathing, her pounding heart. "Who . . . who spoke to me?" No reply.

Suddenly, they appeared . . . behind her closed eyes . . . in her mind . . . as clearly as if they stood before her. They held hands, smiled at her—smiles that filled her with peace and serenity, as when she was a little girl; smiles that melted her, sent chills dancing lightly down her back. She calmed herself but startled when Thomas Colman said, "Emily, you *must* go with Isna. No two people can love each other more. God wants you to be together."

Emily began to sob, tremble. Her mother said, "Emily, my dear, dear Emily. Your father is right. There can be no stronger love than you and Isna share. You *must* go with him. Think not of me and your brother. We will meet again someday. Go to *Isna . . . now.* He loves you so."

Emily wailed, "Father! Mother!" She spun about, began to run back toward her special place. "Isna! Dear God, let him be there." She tripped, fell to the ground, sprang back to her feet, sprinted on, gasped for air. Chest burning, can't breathe, go faster, don't fall, keep going, hurry, Em. "Isna . . . Isna . . . please . . . please be there." She burst from the forest into the small clearing; stopped, looked at the stream where she and Isna had sat; fell to her knees, sat back on her heels; buried her face in her hands, wailed. "No . . . dear God, nooo. What have I done?" She shuddered, tried to rise, couldn't, crouched, grieved on the forest floor. "The village . . . yes, the village . . . must find him before he leaves." She leaned forward to stand. A hand touched her shoulder. "Ahh!" she rolled away from the touch, looked up into Isna's sorrowful eyes.

He knelt beside her, took her hands in his, eased her to her knees, then pulled her close, laid his head on hers. "Emily. Emily. Isna loves you . . . will always love you."

She sobbed, moaned, squeezed him with all her strength. "Oh, Isna . . . my love. Take me with you . . . tonight . . . every night. Please . . . never leave me. Never let me go. Love me. I am yours forever. Love me . . . take me . . . take me."

* * *

Elyoner and Emily sat stiffly at the table, faced each other in awkward silence.

"Emily, what's wrong?"

"When will Ananias return?"

"Any minute. Why? What worries you so?"

"I'll wait until he returns. You must *both* hear what I've to say."

"Well, mayhap you'll tell me what you learned of your locket and the Savage from the massacre?"

Emily stared at the tabletop with bland eyes, scratched at a loose knot with her fingernail, watched the first ant of spring crawl relentlessly toward the center of the table. "His name is Kills-Like-the-Panther . . . a clever, relentless hunter of animals and men . . . a fierce fighter . . . a great leader of his people. His people call him *the Panther*. He's the one Isna wounded that day in the forest . . . when he and the Powhatans tried to take Isna's deer."

"I remember. Sounded frightening then . . . more so now."

She spoke flatly. "He *is* . . . and his very look chills me to the core of my soul. He's the most dangerous and respected Powhatan warrior. I shall never hold my locket again."

"Could Isna take it from him?"

"Isna leaves tonight."

"Tonight? Oh, Em! No wonder you're distressed."

"Yes, Elyoner, but that's only part of it, and I'll say no more until Ananias returns."

"I think I hear him grumbling now."

Ananias opened the door, walked inside. "Good evening, ladies."

Elyoner said, "You look unhappy, Ananias."

"Simply depressed by the arrival of the bad news we've expected for a month."

"And that is?"

"Our food stores are nearly depleted . . . and the Chesapeakes refuse to give us more . . . a bit of an irony since Waters just convinced the very scoundrels who stole from the Chesapeakes and created the problem, to come back to our side to fight the Powhatans."

"Why is *that* irony?"

"Because now if the Powhatans don't kill us, slow starvation will . . . and our own people created the problem. Waters considers the former far more likely, but no one but Baylye and Dare believe him. And in truth, Dare is somewhat dubious about it; for he still harbors the deep faith that Mistress Dare's father will soon return to rescue us, and—"

"You're wrong, Ananias," Emily said.

Ananias recoiled, looked insulted. "What do you mean, Emily?"

"The Powhatans attack tonight."

Ananias and Elyoner stared numbly at her, groped blindly for each other's hands. Elyoner glanced at Virginia asleep in her crib.

Ananias said, "But, Emily, how do you—"

"Isna told me. The Chesapeakes told him. They're coming, Ananias . . . tonight . . . over four hundred warriors."

The Dares stared dumbstruck at each other. Elyoner paled; her eyes dulled, assumed a spacey stare.

Emily said, "There's more. Isna says they will kill all the men outright but will use the women and children for a time before also killing *them*, as well, for they want no sign of our presence to remain."

Elyoner laid her hands on her cheeks, shook her head, again looked desperately at Virginia. "No, Em. This cannot be true. But even if 'twas, they would never harm the children. Would they not take them and raise them as Savages?"

"No. As I said, they want no trace of us left behind . . . in case more English come. They want no one to know what happened to us or who did it."

"But . . . but why do they hate us so?"

"It began with the fifteen soldiers left behind at Roanoke by the earlier colony, but 'tis mostly because of the prophecy Manteo spoke of . . . the prophecy by one of their holy men, that says a people from the land of the Chesapeakes will destroy them. So they do not see us as individuals but rather as a faceless threat . . . much as we see them. But the reasons matter not. They attack tonight."

Elyoner wrung her hands, again stared at Virginia, began to cry. "My baby . . . my poor baby. Let them kill *me*, but not my baby. Please, God, forbid it."

Ananias stared at the fire, seemed oblivious to Elyoner. "A fool I am. Seen this coming for months . . . done nothing except drown myself in the illusion that it would never happen . . . that John would return to save us. And now death glowers hungrily at us, and we've no escape. What a fool! Even—"

"No, Ananias," Emily said. "There *is* an escape. Listen to me! Isna and I have often spoken of him returning here to be with me, and also of me going with him to the Lakota; for, as you know, I love him deeply and greatly admire the Lakota. But when he told me of the Powhatan attack, I insisted I would stay, no matter what, and do what I could to help . . . though all will certainly perish. But then Isna said he and his men would *also* stay and fight . . . to the death . . . beside me."

Elyoner's eyes filled with tears. "Oh, Em, he's so noble, but—"

"I told him I could not let him do that, but he again insisted. There was no changing his mind; so the only way I could prevent him from losing *his* life . . . and those of his men . . . on my behalf . . . was to go with him to the Lakota . . . become Lakota . . . be with him and his people . . . forever. And Ellie, Ananias—"

"Emily . . . noooo!"

"Yes, Ellie, that is what I shall do, for I love him far more than words can tell. And being with him for eternity, however long it lasts, is all I want from this life."

Elyoner swayed back and forth, gnawed on her fingernails, shook her head. "Oh, Em, you love each other so, but what an awful decision to have to make . . . leaving your people, your family, your civilization . . . forever. 'Tis so final . . . so . . ."

"There is no decision, Ellie. I *am* going with Isna. 'Tis the Dares I'm concerned about. Isna and I want you to come with us. 'Tis your, and Virginia's, only hope; for"—she looked away then back at Elyoner—"for after the attack, there will be no English civilization here to be part of. No *person*, no *thing* of England will remain."

"Oooh . . ." Elyoner dragged her desperate gaze from Emily to Ananias, to Virginia, then back to Ananias. "Ananias, 'tis falling apart . . . all falling apart." She reached out to him, pulled herself into his arms, laid her forehead on his shoulder, moaned.

Emily watched patiently, her face tight with empathy.

Finally Elyoner looked up at Ananias, rubbed her teary eyes, then looked at Emily. "Em, Isna's offer is gallant; but Father will certainly return . . . perchance even today, and—"

"He may return, Ellie, but not soon enough to save you or Ananias or Virginia . . . or anyone else; and if you're all dead when he arrives, what will have been gained? I beg you, Ellie, Ananias, come with us, for Virginia's sake. Isna will also take Lieutenant Waters, Roger Baylye, and Emme if they wish to come. You would not have to go all the way to Lakota land. You could settle somewhere closer, somewhere safe, perchance with the Monacans in the mountains to the west . . . come back here when your father returns. Please, see the wisdom of it. Come!"

Elyoner was frantic, becoming hysterical. "But, Em, how can I desert Father's colony . . . our friends . . . our English way of life? I cannot do it."

Ananias' face flushed; his voice quavered. "Emily, there . . . there is a moral issue here. 'Twould be wrong of us to invite only friends to escape. We'd act as judge and executioner . . . as God himself. 'Twould be wrong and sinful to do so."

Emily shook her head. "Ananias, this entire, miserable situation is *wrong*. Practically everything that has happened to *me* is wrong. And the slaughter of mostly good, honest people by angry Savages is *completely* wrong. So we must save ourselves and those we love." She paused, suffered their confusion, their anguish as they glanced sadly at Virginia, one another, then back at Virginia. "And we cannot take *more* people because the Panther wants me for his own and will look for me; and when he does not find me, he will know I've escaped. And—"

Ananias said, "Who is the Panther?"

"The Powhatan Savage who tried to take me and nearly killed me at the Roanoke massacre."

Ananias squeezed his lips together, nodded.

"And when he also does not find Isna, whom he's sworn to kill, he will know we've gone together and *will* pursue us . . . and will eventually catch us, and we will have to fight until all of them . . . or all of us . . . lie dead. But if we move fast, we *may* be able to choose the place of the fight to our advantage." She paused, let them mull her words. "Then . . . perhaps . . . we will have a chance. Wakan Tanka . . . God . . . promises no more. But if we are many, we will move too slowly . . . fail to reach good ground before the fight . . . and we will all die."

Elyoner stared at Virginia, pressed her hands together as if praying, moaned, swayed back and forth.

Ananias looked stunned, defeated, shook his head. "I know not what to do, Emily Colman. 'Tis such a desperately weighty decision . . . so . . . so final . . . so little time to—"

Elyoner wailed, "I cannot comprehend this . . . looking at each of you . . . at Virginia . . . myself . . . knowing we shall not see tomorrow . . . won't even be buried . . . but rather, torn apart like James Lassie and Alis Chapman . . . scattered about to rot. My baby." She covered her face with her hands, whimpered softly, then looked at Ananias. "Cannot Lieutenant Waters and his men defend us . . . at least long enough for Father to arrive?"

"No, my love. Waters has but a handful of soldiers; and the rest are untrained civilians, most of whom fail to appreciate the Powhatan threat . . . and will never believe that it descends upon us this very night. In truth, we've heard before that the Powhatans are coming, but they've never done so. So why believe it now? 'Tis foolish indeed, but 'tis how the doubters will see it. So I fear Emily is right. If Isna's information is correct, there are but two choices: remain and nobly perish, or flee and make a stand, with a *slight* chance of survival."

Emily said, "Well said, Ananias; and remember, you make your decision for Virginia, not yourselves." She paused, glanced at Virginia, took a deep breath, spoke softly, but imperatively. "Ellie . . . Ananias . . . you must decide *now*, for I leave to meet Isna in the forest an hour after midnight."

Elyoner started to speak; but Emily anticipated her question, interrupted. "We will not leave together. Isna and his men are not certain where the Chesapeakes stand; so they will go cautiously, wait and watch to ensure they are not followed." She stood, flipped her shawl over her shoulders. "I return in half an hour. You must then tell me your decision." She walked to Elyoner, kissed her cheek. "Please come, Ellie . . . for Virginia's sake." She walked to Virginia, kissed her, stared at her for a moment, then turned, walked out the door.

Outside she stopped, breathed deeply, glanced at the sky, then watched evening's shadows swallow the last faint rays of the setting sun.

***

Emily sat with Lieutenant Waters beside the fire in his cottage. She relayed Isna's warning of the Powhatan attack, her plan to leave to save Isna, her hope that the Dares would do the same to save Virginia, perhaps return later. She also told him she'd asked Emme Merrimoth to come; but Emme had declined, wanted to remain and die near Johnny with their unborn child. She'd also said she had an important pledge to fulfill for Johnny but would not say what it was. Emily's eyes filled with tears; she paused, composed herself, told Waters she also wanted him and Governor Baylye to come but understood their commitment to duty would likely preclude their doing so.

Waters listened quietly then surprised her by smiling. "Well, Mistress . . . Emily, if I may call you that . . . I thought my military career would be longer than this; but I guess one can never predict such things, can one? And alas, you are correct. I *am* bound by duty to defend the colony . . . to the end; and I *will* do my duty, as will Governor Baylye. But I will inform him of your kind offer." He looked away for a moment then gazed deeply, lingeringly into her striking blue eyes. "You know, Milady, that day back at Roanoke, in the beginning, when I said you were an angel . . . I was right. You *are* an angel. No more beautiful, brave, kind, unassuming, and wonderful woman has ever graced this earth; and were it not for my commitment to one Rebecca Roberts in England and my duty to the colony, I would follow you to the ends of the earth."

Emily blushed, tried to smile. "You're too kind, Lieutenant."

"Nay, Mistress. I speak the truth. But since fate has chosen to proceed in the manner it has, I ask a favor."

"Certainly."

"If you ever again see England, would you be so kind as to go to York and tell my parents, Squire Richard and Mary Waters, as well as Rebecca Roberts, what befell me, that I did my duty to Queen and country, and that I died bravely in battle?"

Emily couldn't speak, tasted the salty warmth of sudden tears flowing down her cheeks to her lips. Dear God, he speaks serenely of dying, accepts it without fear. Yet, could any soldier view death in battle otherwise? I think not; but still, to know your life will soon end, that naught but pain and horror await you with dreadful finality . . . and still do your duty. Is this not the essence of courage—the steadfast resolve to face whatever comes, with honor, bravery, and dedication, no matter what? Lieutenant William Waters . . . so young . . . such an immensely fine man . . . will soon be no more. She bit her lower lip. "I shall, Lieutenant. I promise you. But . . . but I must also tell you that your strength and courage compel me to remain here . . . with my countrymen . . . face fate with them. 'Tis only—"

Waters shook his head, touched her cheek. "Nay, Emily. Do not torment yourself. You've made the proper choice. I do not know these Lakota, but I've seen enough to know that your Isna is as fine a man as the best Englishman I've ever known . . . and most certainly as noble, courageous, and proficient a warrior as there is in this world. A soldier senses these things. And though you embark on a bold journey, I know he will give you the love and care you deserve."

She rubbed her eyes. "Forgive me. Cannot seem to rid myself of these constant tears. But thank you, Lieutenant, you are again too kind." She stared into his eyes for several seconds then suddenly reached out, touched his shoulders, pulled him close, kissed his cheek. "Goodbye, William Waters." She slowly stood, sniffled, turned toward the door.

Waters rose. "Emily, the palisades will be heavily guarded tonight. We will make preparations until the attack comes. You must depart quietly through the west gap. I will guard that section after midnight and will watch for you and the Dares. Say nothing. Simply slip through the gap, veer left, and make directly for the forest." He took her hands in his. "One more thing . . . a matter of grave importance. Tayler's men have sworn to join the fight against the Powhatans, for 'tis in their interest to do so. But I believe they remain loyal to *him* and will continue to do his bidding . . . now and if we survive. So tell no one of your plan and show no sign of your intentions, in case you are watched."

An unsettling chill raced through her body. She nodded. "I shall heed your warning. Thank you . . . William."

He stared into her eyes, leaned slowly forward, kissed her lips, smiled. "Godspeed, Emily Colman."

* * *

The Panther's wife lay beside her sleeping young son, softly caressed his cheek with a mother's gentle touch. "You are handsome, my brave little warrior . . . like your father. And you shall grow to be as great a warrior as he . . . perhaps greater . . . and you shall make him proud . . . he, the Panther, the greatest warrior of the Powhatan chiefdom . . . its strongest and wisest war leader . . . the right hand of the great Wahunsunacock . . . the one Wahunsunacock relies on in all matters. Yes, you shall grow to manhood knowing this is so . . . and that you are of his flesh and destined to be great like him. He will know your strength from the moment you shoot your first arrow from your little-boy bow . . . and he will know that greatness follows him in his own lodge." She leaned close, kissed his cheek, studied his sleeping face. "It shall be so. So rest well, my little one. Rest well, so you may greet your father when he returns from the great victory he leads tonight."

***

Emily walked toward the Dares' cottage, brushed at her tears every few steps. Why must such a man perish in a lost cause? She thought of the first days at Roanoke when Waters had been the bastion of decisive leadership, faced each new challenge with the quietude and decisiveness of a far older officer. It had been the same ever since . . . a born leader of men, she thought. She shook her head. A waste. Damn you, John White. Why have you abandoned us? She took a deep breath, again wiped her eyes. Forgive my curse, Lord. I know not what has prevented his return, and 'tis unfair to judge or curse him.

Two more steps drew Emme Merrimoth into her thoughts. She saw her sorrowful, despairing face, tears streaming down her cheeks, felt her tight embrace, her kiss on the cheek when they'd said goodbye. Emily moaned, dabbed tears of grief from her eyes. Why, Lord? Why must it be this way? Why can't we live in peace? Why? And Shines . . . cannot even say goodbye to her. Shared so much, learned so much from her . . . like a sister . . . always smiling and happy . . . always helping. But dare not see her, in case the Chesapeakes—

"Mistress Colman."

Emily stopped, turned, saw a soldier approaching with a torch in his hand. "Yes?"

"Mistress Colman, I am one of Hugh Tayler's guards. He asked me to deliver this urgent message to you. I know not what it says, but he asked me to bear your response to him immediately. I can only be away a moment." He handed her a sealed parchment, extended his torch toward her. "Here, Mistress, read beneath my torch. I shall look away." He fixed his gaze on the cottage to his left.

Emily took the letter, broke the seal, unfolded the parchment.

My Dearest Emily,

'Tis with a heart heavy with grief, humility, and shame that I share with you the following horrible burdens I have carried in my soul. My conduct since meeting you, the fairest creature on earth, has been of a nature contradictory to the deep, unquenchable love I feel for you—the love I have felt since the first moment I saw you. I have acted as an evil demon, a cur, a vile miscreant. I tell you now, this is not who I truly am, or wish to be; yet I confess, I have been so since the death of my mother when I was a child. Still, I have striven valiantly to raise myself up, become a man of noble character. But I have failed, sinned against the one I love above all things in this world, and I am therefore not worthy of life. You, Emily Colman, are the only one who can save me from myself, you alone. And I hereby beg you, on my knees, to come to me, sit with me, speak to me, allow me to express my deep regret for my actions, and help me right myself, purge my mind of the evil that haunts me. I beseech you, please come to me this night, allow me to show you the Hugh Tayler I long to be; for without you, I shall surely end my life in despair.

I shall await you four hours after the sun sets, and please take care to let no one see your approach. I shall bribe the guards to be gone when you arrive, so do not knock lest someone hear you. I anticipate the joy of your presence, in deep humility and atonement for my deeds.

With love,

Hugh

Emily crinkled the parchment, stuffed it into her apron pocket, took a deep breath, closed her eyes.

The soldier retracted his torch. "Do you have a reply, Mistress?"

Emily's heart and breathing raced. *What should I do? He's insane but truly needs me . . . perchance I can help him . . . and he truly has a right to know of our child . . . and its death. But, Emily, what are you thinking? He wants to take you again; 'tis but a ruse. Do not be a fool.* Her hands trembled. *But if I do* not *go, what then? Waters' caution* echoed through her mind. *Dear God, help me! I* cannot *do this.* She looked at the soldier, thankful he could not see her tears. "Tell him . . . tell him my answer is *no.*"

"Yes, Mistress. In that case, I am now obliged to give you this second letter." He handed her another letter, again extended the torch, looked away.

Emily took the parchment, started to open it. *Saints in heaven, what now?* Her trembling hands fumbled it to the ground.

The soldier retrieved it, handed it to her again. "Here, Mistress."

She nodded, took the letter, broke the seal, unfolded it, held it to the light.

> *My Dearest Emily,*
>
> *If you are reading this letter, you have refused my humble, heartfelt plea. Therefore, I must state that anything you may have heard about my men becoming loyal to the governor and Lieutenant Waters is untrue. I exert complete control over their actions; and your failure to honor my request will unleash immediate retribution beyond your imagination, against you and those you love. Know, as well, that any disclosure of the contents of either letter, to anyone, will only worsen that response. So come to me at the appointed hour or suffer the horrible, inescapable consequences of your decision. And last, bear no weapons when you come.*
>
> *I love you as always,*
> *Hugh*

She turned from the torchlight, brushed her eyes, felt a numbing shock seize her body and mind. Mother, Father . . . dear Lord, saints above . . . what am I to do?

"Do you have a reply, Mistress? I must return to my post."

He will surely take me again . . . but if I do not go, he will certainly deliver his promised retribution . . . and his men will watch me, discover our escape . . . and it will fail. Oh, God, what am I to do? Why must it always rest on me? She stared into the darkness, took a deep breath. "Tell Master Tayler my answer is . . . is *yes*."

"Yes, Mistress." He turned, walked hastily toward Tayler's cottage.

Emily stood stunned; tears soaked her cheeks. Again . . . again I must do this. My God, how can I? How can I submit to such a man, sin, betray my love? God, help me. She glanced at the sky, saw the full moon glowing low above the horizon, the same bright star beside it as on the night they'd left Roanoke. So long ago . . . so many happenings ago . . . will I ever find peace? Her heart felt squeezed into a thimble. George . . . Father . . . Isna . . . Mother. She glanced at the sky, saw a long, narrow peninsula of black clouds pointing at the moon like the finger of death, felt and smelled the thick moisture that heralds heavy fog. What ever will become of me?

She turned, walked the last few steps to the Dares' cottage; stopped, took a deep breath; rapped on the door, opened it, walked inside.

Elyoner and Ananias busily stuffed belongings into a rucksack, hesitated, looked up at Emily.

"You're coming!"

Elyoner smiled. The two rushed together, embraced.

"Ellie, Ellie, I'm so happy. Saints be praised, you're coming."

"Ladies! To work! We've a long walk ahead and much to prepare."

* * *

As Ananias and Elyoner readied Virginia for a brief sleep, Emily watched another ant crawl across the tabletop. It stopped, changed directions several times as if uncertain of its destination, then proceeded toward the edge. You're as confused as I, little creature. What shall I do? She flicked the ant with her finger. Giving myself is a sin . . . as is condemning others to die for my obstinate pride. Dearest Lord, I'm again with none but dreadful choices. Will you not help me?

Elyoner kissed Virginia then placed two small toys in a rucksack for her—one, the doll Shines had made.

Emily stood; her bloodshot eyes glistened in the firelight. "I've something to attend to. I shall return in a while."

Elyoner said, "But, Em, you must rest. We've so far to go."

"I know, but 'tis important. Now listen to me . . . carefully."

Elyoner and Ananias looked worriedly at one another then expectantly at Emily.

"Do not leave the cottage . . . keep your weapons at arm's reach." She eyed Virginia. "And do not leave *her* alone for *any* reason." She took a deep breath, glanced at the hourglass. "If I do not return by the departure hour, do not wait. Go as planned. Isna will take you." Tears trickled haltingly down her cheeks.

Elyoner started toward her, tears of confusion glistening in her eyes. She stopped, shook her head. "Emily! Pray tell, what are you telling us? What is wrong? What—"

"Do not ask! Do *exactly* as I say." She pulled Elyoner into her arms, closed her eyes, held her long and hard. When she finally eased away, she tried to smile, shook her head, turned, and rushed out the door.

"Emily . . . Emily . . . please . . ."

***

Emily walked toward Tayler's cottage in a thickening fog. Fifty feet away, she stopped; searched for guards, saw none; rushed up to the cottage, stopped at the door, heart pounding, checked behind. Mother, make me strong. Tears poured down her cheeks, fell from her chin. God, forgive me. She opened the door, stepped inside.

The room was dim; at first she saw no one. Suddenly she gasped, covered her mouth with her hands, stared at a man's body lying face down on the floor by the bed. Tayler's coat hid most of the head but not the blood pooled on the dirt beneath him. Her heart pulsed. Is it him? She stepped closer, leaned toward the body. A man's hand suddenly cupped tightly over her mouth, snatched her head back against his chest. She mumbled a muted cry.

A deep, husky voice said, "Tayler's dead! Leave, tell no one!" He maneuvered Emily to the door, held her mouth with one hand while he opened the door with the other, glanced outside, shoved her out the door. "Go, do not look back!" He quickly shut the door.

Emily ran toward the Dares' cottage. Her heart rippled like a drum roll; but suddenly a refreshing gust of relief blew through her mind, teased her with excitement. He's dead. I'm free! But who . . . why . . . what happened? I care not. Dear God, thank you, I'm free!

***

After a sad, lingering wave at Waters, Emily led the Dares through the west gap in the palisades. Like predators, they treaded stealthily through the lifting fog, crossed the clearing, and entered the forest. All three wore rucksacks on their backs. Elyoner carried Virginia, whose rucksack had leg holes cut in the bottom; Ananias and Emily carried personal belongings, equipment, powder and shot, and a small amount of dried venison and fish. Each carried a small bladder of water, a knife, and a pistol with an unlit match, at their waist. The fog slowed their progress at first; but after a quarter mile, the moon emerged from the clouds, illuminated the forest like a celestial torch, bestowing an eerie feel to the pockets of dense fog that lingered around trees and low spots. All three stepped carefully, constantly searched for danger. As she pushed a tree branch out of the way, Emily heard Virginia cry; she stopped, looked back, saw Elyoner on the ground.

"Help me, Ananias . . . a hole . . . stepped in a hole."

Ananias grasped Elyoner's hands, pulled her to her feet. "Are you hurt?"

"Nay. I'll be fine. Em, can you see to—"

Emily whispered to Virginia, caressed her cheeks. "Shhhhh, little one. Do not tell the Powhatans we're here. Quiet now . . . that's it. You shall be fine. Hush now. That's it. Are you ready, Ellie?"

"Aye, onward."

A quarter hour later, Emily calculated they were slightly behind schedule, needed to accelerate their pace. She glanced back over her shoulder to tell the Dares they had to go faster, instantly stopped. "Ellie, what's wrong?"

Elyoner stood twenty feet behind Emily and Ananias, stared spacily at the ground.

Ananias whispered, "Ellie, what is it?"

"I . . . I cannot do this, Ananias." Sobs muddled her words. "I . . . I cannot."

"Elyoner, you must. 'Tis Virginia's only hope."

"No, Ananias. I've thought on it all night . . . even now, here, in the forest. I cannot do it . . . cannot desert the colony . . . *Father's* colony. I'm so sorry. Forgive me."

"Elyoner!"

"No! I'm the governor's daughter. 'Tis my duty to stay . . . to the end . . . die if I must."

"Ellie, what are you saying? We cannot—"

"Ananias! Stop! Take Virginia, go with Emily." Moonlight sparkled on her moist cheeks; her voice crackled with emotion. "Go now . . . before I completely lose myself." She wriggled out of her pack, held Virginia in front of her, stared at her with mournful, tortured eyes, then shook her head. "Why must it end this way . . . my dear, dear baby. How I love you." She squeezed her to her breast.

Ananias studied her then whispered softly, acquiescently, "Elyoner, my love, I feared this would happen. You are such a noble soul." He took a deep breath, exhaled slowly. "I, of course, will remain with you." They stared solemnly at one another for a long moment, held hands, then together embraced Virginia.

Elyoner turned slowly to Emily, tears flowing from her eyes. "Em, you are my very best friend in this world. None but you would I trust

- 584 -

with my child . . . my dear baby!" She held Virginia tight against her breast, closed her eyes. "Ohhhhh, my child . . . my Virginia. How I love you." She opened her glassy eyes, looked into Emily's, slowly handed Virginia to her. "She's yours, Em. Protect her, love her, raise her as your own. And when she's old enough, tell her about us . . . perchance return here, show her where she was born . . . where we died."

Emily grasped Elyoner's arms, shook her head. "Noooo!"

"Do this for me, my dear, dear friend. Please, I beg you."

Emily stared at her, didn't move, didn't speak, then slowly reached out, took Virginia in her arms.

Elyoner said, "God be with you, Emily Colman . . . pray for us."

Emily searched for words, found none. Elyoner and Ananias quickly hugged her, kissed her cheeks, laid their hands briefly on Virginia's forehead, then turned, faded into the darkness, back toward the colony. Emily stood stunned, numb, devastated, stared at the empty darkness where they'd stood a moment before; she tasted salty tears, felt their warmth as they crept slowly down her cheeks. *Ellie, my friend, my sister . . . Ananias . . . dear Lord, why? How can this happen? I shall never see them again . . . nor will Virginia.*

She sighed, abruptly turned, cradled Virginia in her arms, jogged off toward the rendezvous with Isna. Nausea dizzied her mind, soured her stomach. She imagined Elyoner and Ananias being hacked to pieces by crazed Powhatans, heard their helpless screams as they reached for one another. *Dear God, let them die quickly . . . all of them . . . and please care for Shines, and . . . oh, Lord, what if the Powhatans consider the Chesapeakes our allies . . . part of the prophecy . . . attack them, as well? Saints above, please, no. Pray thee spare Shines.*

Fifty yards later, Emily heard brush crack behind her. She stopped, turned; glanced at Virginia, who miraculously slept; heard the sound again, this time closer, then again. *Saints above, what should I do?* She shifted Virginia gently to her left shoulder, held her with her left arm while she reached behind her back with her right hand, pulled her knife from its sheath. She heard another crack, heard her heart pounding. She tried to steady herself, slow her breathing, was ready to run, when a surprise pulse of hope surged through her heart. Praise heaven, they've changed their minds . . . they're coming! Her lips slowly curved into a smile. Thank you, Lord. Thank you. She sheathed her knife, shifted Virginia back to her arms, then started toward the sound as she smiled with anticipation. "Ellie, I'm over here. This way!"

Suddenly she stopped; her smile withered; she stepped slowly backward, felt her mind muddle with confusion, panic. Hugh Tayler stood a few feet before her. She turned to run.

Tayler lunged at her, reached out, grabbed a handful of hair, pulled her toward him. She stumbled blindly backward, nearly dropped Virginia. He gripped her shoulders, spun her around to face him, pulled her close, glared into her eyes.

She felt his breath in her face, trembled, panted; her mind swirled in chaos; terror paralyzed her body. She clutched Virginia to her breast with an iron grip.

"Emily, my love, I feared I'd never see you again . . . that I'd never again feel the warmth of your body against mine." He sighed.

"Let me go! I came to you as you asked. There was a body . . . a man grabbed me, and—"

" 'Twas I who grabbed you. I'd no choice. One of the guards refused my bribe, would not agree to let you in or leave us alone. We struggled . . . I killed him." He looked momentarily remorseful. "But we got his body through the palisades and concealed while everyone ran about preparing for this imaginary Powhatan attack." He smirked. "Fools. There will be no attack . . . and Lord Walsingham's ship will arrive any day, and I shall return to England under his protection . . . and *you* shall accompany me and be my wife."

Emily's jaw dropped; her eyes swelled in disbelief. Isna, find me, save me. "But . . . but how did you . . ."

"I suspected you'd leave with your Savage, so I watched the Dares' cottage from the shadows . . . then slipped through the palisades just behind you and them when Waters resumed his preparations for the attack . . . but before his replacement took over his watch. So here we are, Emily Colman . . . you and Hugh Tayler . . . alone"—he noticed

Virginia for the first time, scowled—"*almost* alone . . . in this dark forest . . . under a glorious full moon . . . a fitting place for me to tell you again how much I love you and that I can never allow you to leave my life . . . especially with a primitive Savage." He shook his head. "Truly, why would you want to be with a Savage, when I can give you everything you desire? I will—"

"Because I do not love you, Hugh Tayler . . . and I *dearly* love *him*."

He stared at her in silent disbelief then spoke softly, affectionately, as if her words had dissipated before reaching his ears. "You are my salvation, Emily Colman, my reason for living, and I again beg you to forgive my transgressions. But whether you do or not, you *shall* return to the colony and England with me and be my wife."

Fear sliced through Emily, she trembled, her voice cracked with fury and fear. "Hugh Tayler, the Powhatans *are* coming tonight, and no one will be left alive. And your fantasies of rescue are the aimless meanderings of an insane man . . . as is your expectation that I will go with you and yield to you."

Tayler looked briefly insulted then smiled. "Milady, you may be correct about my insanity, but it matters not. And if you also happen to be correct about the Powhatans, then I shall die a happy man for having spent my final moments in the warmth of your body."

Emily jammed the hard toe of her shoe into his shin, tried to turn and run. Tayler groaned but held her fast, dug his fingers into her shoulders. Pain shot down her arms; she twisted left and right, tried to break free. "Curse you, Tayler! Let go!"

He grasped her wrists, looked into her eyes with the same crazed look he'd had at the rape; his breathing quickened; he pried her hands from Virginia.

Emily screamed as the baby fell to her back on the ground, began to sputter then cry. "Virginia! Let me help her, you swine." She jerked, twisted wildly, but he held her fast. He pulled her away from Virginia, yanked her into an embrace, and pressed his lips against hers. As he held her with one arm, he pulled up her dress with the other, then glided his hand over her thigh, caressed her behind, slid his fingers between her legs.

"No! Damn you, Tayler. Let go!" Tears filled her eyes; she tried to squeeze her legs together, felt his fingers pushing higher between them. Her pulse and breathing quickened. She heard Virginia screaming. God, help me. Please! Isna, find me, let me—

She heard a sharp grunt behind Tayler. He moaned and lurched forward, pushed her to the ground on her back, then yanked his dagger from his belt, spun about with a blind slice at whoever was behind him.

Emily saw a knife in Tayler's back, saw Emme Merrimoth drop to her knees, blood gushing from her sliced throat. She fell forward onto her knees and hands, gurgled, "Run, Em." Her eyes rolled back in their sockets; she collapsed to her face, lay still on the ground.

"Emme!"

As Tayler staggered toward her, Emily sprang to her feet, gawked briefly at Emme, then leaped the two steps to Virginia, grabbed her rucksack on the run, sprinted away.

She'd made thirty yards when she suddenly stopped, wrapped her arms protectively around Virginia. She started to the right, stopped again, felt terror paralyze her senses, cloud her head. Her legs buckled; she trembled. Thirty feet to her front and left stood sixty or more Powhatan warriors.

The Panther, painted as at Roanoke, stepped slowly toward her, three warriors at his sides. He stopped in front of her, glared into her eyes while the moonlight gave a fearsome, ghostlike aura to his painted face.

Emily dropped to her knees, shielded Virginia, waited for his deathblow.

Tayler yelled, "Emily, I love you!" She glanced toward his voice, saw him rushing toward her, his sword above his head.

The Panther stepped past Emily into Tayler's path, a stone tamahaac in his right hand, a knife in his left. Tayler slashed at his head; but the Panther sidestepped, sliced his tamahaac deep into Tayler's forearm, yanked it free, then waited for his next move.

Tayler screamed, sank to his right knee; quickly stood again, faced the Panther; grabbed the sword with his left hand, raised it for another slash. But before it moved, the three warriors seized Tayler by the arms and head from behind. The one holding his head yanked Emme's knife from Tayler's back, quickly sliced a six-inch slit across his throat. Tayler's eyes bulged; he gasped for air, spewed blood from throat and mouth, tried to speak, gagged. The Panther watched him with contempt then thrust his knife into the left side of his belly, sliced it slowly sideways, rib to rib, then up the middle to the bottom of his chest.

Emily vomited as Tayler's guts spilled from his body, hung from his waist like a rumpled apron. The warriors let his body crumple to the ground then followed the Panther toward Emily.

Emily stood, held Virginia over her left shoulder, backed away, reached for her pistol with her trembling right hand. Fie! Didn't light the match. Dear Lord, help me.

The Panther and his men suddenly stopped, focused their eyes behind Emily.

Emily glanced over her shoulder, saw Isna and his three Lakota a few feet away, their bows drawn, aimed at the Panther. No one moved.

The Panther motioned with his tamahaac for Isna and his men to leave. Isna smiled, spoke in Lakota. The Panther looked at Emily, jerked his chin slightly upward, signaling her to translate Isna's words.

She fought to steady her tumbling mind, finally collected herself, signed, "He said, ' 'Tis a good day to die.'"

The Panther looked at Isna, smirked, stowed his weapons, signed, "Not this night . . . but when we next meet . . . soon." He turned, vanished, ghostlike, into the darkness with his men.

Emily took a deep breath, trembled, fixed her eyes on Isna.

He walked slowly to her, touched her cheek, pulled her and Virginia into his arms, held them close for a long moment, kissed her hair. "We must move swiftly, my little one."

Emily nodded, laid Virginia on the ground; removed her rucksack of supplies from her back, handed it to Isna; knelt, checked Virginia, caressed her cheek, then slipped Virginia's rucksack onto her back. "We're ready."

Isna nodded, turned, led Emily and the Lakota at a brisk pace to the west.

Twenty minutes later, they crossed a stream, stopped to sip the fresh water, top off their water bladders. Emily said, "Isna . . . there were so many of them . . . why did they let us go?"

"The Panther leads the attack against your people. It will come from three or four directions, and *he* will give the signal to begin. He could not risk the noise or delay of a fight . . . or his own death . . . which was certain if we fought."

She nodded. "How quickly will he pursue?"

"They will celebrate their victory . . . perhaps until midday. Then he will pursue, but with only a few of his best warriors."

"Why only a few?"

"Because we have hurt them before, and he knows we are dangerous enemies . . . and there will be far greater honor in killing us if they are few."

Emily stared at him, fear in her eyes, sighed. *I shall never understand this thinking.* "How soon will they catch us?"

"Perhaps when the sun rises on the second day . . . but before we reach the mountains, and the Monacans, who would protect us."

Emily thought for a moment. "We will move slower because of Emily and Virginia. Perhaps Emily should—"

"Emily and Virginia will come with us. We must go now." He nodded at his men, turned to leave as the throaty rumble of matchlocks echoed in the distance. All five looked east, saw two yellow glows above the treetops, heard the faint shrill of war cries mingle with screams of terror.

"They attack my people."

Isna nodded. "And the Chesapeakes. That is the second glow."

Emily stared at him. "Isna . . . I did not understand how this would feel . . . all my people . . . Ellie, Ananias, Waters . . . my friend Shines . . . all will be dead in a few minutes . . . their heads smashed, bodies full of arrows, torn apart, burned, tortured. Isna, they're all going to die . . . all of them. I must help them."

He shook his head. "Emily cannot help them. No one can help them."

Emily looked back toward the village.

Isna laid his hands on her shoulders. "Emily, we have much distance to cover in a short time. We will not leave an easy trail, but we must move quickly if we are to find good ground before we fight."

Emily again visualized Elyoner and Ananias being bludgeoned and hacked to death, their bodies mutilated, burned on a huge fire. She said a quick prayer then sighed, stared into Isna's eyes, and as if she'd turned the last page of a book, said, " 'Tis done . . . I am ready . . . my new life begins now." And as dawn's first glimmer teased the horizon, she followed Isna toward the mountains, and their fate.

CHAPTER 16

E mily lay wide-eyed on her left side beneath a deerskin robe, cuddled the sleeping Virginia to her chest as she fought valiantly to exorcise the disquieting uneasiness that pervaded her mind and soul. *What will the morrow bring, what will remain, if anything, of my life, my dreams, my future, after this inescapable encounter that will soon overtake us?* She closed her eyes. *But what is it that troubles me so? 'Tis not the thought of dying itself. Nay, I've confronted death too many times already to fear it.* She opened her eyes, smiled to herself. *Nay, Mistress Colman, 'tis your heart and its fear of the very real possibility of losing your life before you consummate your commitment, your marriage, to the man you love above all in the world.* She glanced at the black sky above her. *Would that my friend the moon would escape those evil black clouds that hide her light, and allow me to see his face, so I might know his mind, understand what course this first, and perhaps last, night with him will take.*

A moment later, the moon slid unexpectedly from behind the clouds; she saw Isna's intense, dark eyes drilling into hers with the same disquietude that haunted her entire being. Her heart suddenly quickened; chills danced nimbly down her neck and back. *I know what I must do.* She whispered, "Isna and Emily will perhaps die tomorrow."

"Yes, my little white fawn."

"And this night—their first together—may be their last."

"Yes."

She held her stare for a moment then gently eased away from Virginia, laid the fur over her, stood, stepped quietly to Isna's far side.

He rose, took her hands in his; their eyes again met, spoke an unmistakable message.

Emily whispered, "Perhaps Emily and Isna will—"

"Will Emily be Isna's wife?"

Her apprehension fled, she smiled. "Yes. Will Isna take Emily?"

He smiled back. "Yes."

"Who will marry Emily and Isna?"

"When two people agree to marry, and a proper ceremony is not possible, they may commit to each other and marry themselves . . . and have a ceremony when they are able." He eased her closer, moved his lips slowly toward hers until they touched with a gentle, loving softness that belied the torrid emotions about to ignite between them. He leaned back, smiled tenderly at her. "Emily is Isna's wife . . . forever."

Her heart pounded with anticipation; her chest heaved. She held her eyes on his, slowly reached to the top of her right shoulder, untied the three ties that bound her doeskin dress at the top. The right side of the dress dropped to her elbow, bared her right shoulder and breast. One by one, she unfastened the ties on the left; the dress fell to her ankles. Moonlight bathed her body, accentuated the rhythmic heaving of her full, erect breasts, the small patch of hair at the top of her legs. With glistening, damp lips, she stared beguilingly into his eyes, felt the warm dampness of expectation rise within her.

He slowly reached to his waist, untied his loincloth, let it fall to his feet. He stared at her for a moment then held her hands, guided her down to his deerskin robe, pulled another on top of them, began to explore and caress her body.

Emily trembled, felt steamy perspiration dampen her body, a wave of primitive passion like she'd felt at the harvest dance. She touched his cheeks, panted, kissed him wildly, teased his tongue with hers; felt his manhood throbbing against her, reached down, softly caressed it; felt his lips on her firm nipples, his fingers between her legs, softly touching, slowly searching their way inside her. She surrendered her soul; her hips moved rhythmically with his touch as her passion billowed like a towering thunderstorm; her senses exploded, yearned for the precipice, the release that would complete her gift of herself to the man she'd love forever.

* * *

A grizzly bear and a small white fawn walked together. Soon, scores of brown and white fawns appeared beside them, followed them for a while, but then dispersed in different directions until all vanished, except for one brown fawn that turned into an old woman with two black stones around her neck and a Lakota vision pipe in her hand. A new white fawn then appeared beside the old woman, and the old woman placed her hand on its head. Then, along with the two black stones and pipe, the old woman vanished, leaving only the little white fawn, who then grew into a blacktail doe with its own little white fawn. But an instant later, the two black stones and pipe appeared around the little white fawn's neck, and she immediately changed form.

* * *

Behind closed lids, Allie's eyes swept wildly from stop to stop: right, left, up, down. Then a new dream began.

* * *

The knot in Emily's stomach tightened with each ray of advancing dawn as she nursed Virginia in the slowly fading darkness. She wasn't sure which was worse—the knot or the constant, feathery fluttering that encircled it like a covey of birds trying to escape their cage. She took a deep breath, looked down at Virginia. *We will fight today, little one . . . would that I were a Viking shield-maiden, skilled and fearless in battle, rather than a young English girl who knows naught but how to shoot a pistol. Then, perchance, I could help you . . . and . . . and my husband.* She smiled. *My husband . . . my love . . . saints above! I am married . . . the wife of a Lakota warrior . . . for the rest of our lives. A* sudden gust of uneasiness blew through her mind. But will *the rest of our lives* be an hour . . . or, pray God, a full lifetime. She closed her eyes, savored the night's three passionate, unrestrained ascents with Isna, their three euphoric, exhausting arrivals at the zenith.

Virginia smacked her lips as she released Emily's breast, then smiled, cooed at her. Emily shook off her thoughts, forced a tepid smile, caressed Virginia's cheek. The smile vanished as she imagined Elyoner and Ananias, their faces smiling at her, then two Powhatans holding Ananias while others repeatedly raped Elyoner. She then saw both dead, dismembered, their charred remains smoldering in the dying embers of the village. She shook the images from her mind. And you, my new daughter, will you see another day? She looked toward Isna, who knelt beside Soft-Nose twenty feet away with his back toward her, watched him whisper, draw in the dirt with a stick, point at the two gaps at opposite ends of the large boulder formation that surrounded them. Plan well, my love . . . plan well.

She hadn't given much attention to their location the night before, had been too exhausted to notice *anything*, but now she realized the boulder formation was like a small fort. The boulders all stood six to eight feet high, encircled an oval-shaped clearing fifty feet *long* east to west and twenty-five feet *wide* north to south, and had no passable openings between the boulders except for narrow gaps at the east and west ends. A solitary boulder about four feet high and five feet wide sat fifteen feet inside the west gap, close to the north wall; while two larger boulders sat on either side of the east gap, also about fifteen feet inside the protected area. Thank you, my Lord, for perchance thinking of us when you made this place.

Isna stood, turned toward Emily. She gasped, covered her mouth with her hand. A three-inch-wide band of black paint, outlined top and bottom by a thin white line, crossed his face like a mask, from just above his eyebrows to the tops of his cheeks, and sideways to his hair, which hung freely down both sides of his head to his waist. Each cheek had two half-inch-wide, vertical, red stripes an inch apart, that extended from the bottom of the black-and-white band to his jaw. A fifth stripe ran from the bottom of his nose, across his lips, to the tip of his chin. "Isna frightens Emily. She has never—"

He held his finger to his lips, looked, listened in all directions, sniffed the cool morning air. "The enemy approaches. 'Tis a *good* day to die!"

Her eyes tightened with fearful intensity. "Isna—"

A shrill bird cry arose from deep in the forest to the east. Then another, and another.

Isna looked toward the sound, nodded twice.

"What is it?"

"Striped-Face." He strung his bow. "He has seen the enemy." He checked the cutting edge of his knife, re-sheathed it. "Four of them." He gripped his tamahaac, swung it over his shoulder twice, tested the edge, stowed it at his waist, then pulled three arrows from his quiver, laid them and his bow on the ground. He removed his white eagle-bone necklace, stashed it in his rucksack, replaced it with his string of grizzly-bear claws.

"Where is he? Will they not find him?"

"He hides to the east, the distance a man can walk while someone guts a deer; and yes, they *may* find him, but not if he is well hidden. The third screech meant they've passed him by and are now between us and him, coming toward us from the east. If he is alive, he will follow them and attack from behind when they attack us."

"But why is he out there?"

"So we are not surprised. True-Dog hides to the west for the same reason."

Emily glanced at the west gap in the rocks, shivered; she felt another ripple in her heart, glanced at her trembling hands. So afraid . . . too much time to think . . . so different from the massacre.

"We chose this place because it is high ground with good cover; the enemy must come uphill and will not see us until they enter the gaps and we shoot at them."

She nervously bit off a chunk of dried venison, began to chew, stared at Virginia. What will happen to her if Isna or I die? Or . . . or if both of us die . . . or if the Panther takes me and . . . no! Do not think about it, Em. We *must* prevail. But still, I wonder what it feels like to die . . . like the massacre, I suppose. But I felt nothing after I saw the white light, so . . . so perchance 'twill be quick and painless. But if the Panther takes me, and all the warriors use me . . . dear God, what then? She shook her head, shuddered. I know *what then.*

"Soft-Nose and Isna will guard the east gap since that is where our trail leads. We will try to kill two with our bows before they get through the gap; but when the others rush us, it will probably be hand to hand until the end." He nodded as if listening to himself. "Still, if Striped-Face and True-Dog surprise them from behind, we can win. But if there are more than the four Striped-Face saw . . ." He shook his head.

Emily looked skittishly into his eyes, nodded, then removed her flint and some tinder from the small pouch at her waist, pulled her knife from its sheath. She knelt, held the flint on the tinder, chipped it with the knife until a few sparks took hold; leaned close, blew gently until the sparks flamed and quickly lit her pistol match, then extinguished the tinder with two rapid pats of her hand; returned the flint and unburned tinder to her pouch, stowed her knife. She stood, faced Isna. "What would Isna have Emily do?"

He smiled, nodded. "Isna is proud that his wife will fight like a Lakota." He touched her cheek, stared into her eyes for a lingering moment. "The Powhatans will suspect we are here, perhaps surround us. So we must also defend the west gap. *Emily* must do this . . . alone . . . from over there." He pointed at the four-foot boulder inside the west gap. True-Dog is out there to help you, but they may find him and rub him out. So if Emily sees or hears *anything*, and the fight has not yet begun, she must call quietly to Isna . . . loudly if the fight *has* begun." His look hardened. "Call to Soft-Nose if Isna is dead."

"Isna! Do not—"

"Whatever happens, Emily must not leave her position or remove her eyes from the gap. It may be that only she protects the west end."

She nodded slowly, her face suddenly pale, forehead beaded with sweat like dew on a window pane; her pistol trembled in her hand. So afraid. But I must—

"Hide the baby over there." He pointed to a little nook where two boulders on the north side came together eight feet behind Emily's boulder. "Put her in the back and cover her so she'll be safe and still."

"Isna, will . . . will they hurt her?"

He didn't reply, stared stoically into her eyes. "Do not be afraid, my little fawn. It will be over quickly. Waiting is the difficult part . . . waiting and guessing at what may come." He held her cheeks, kissed her lips. "Prepare yourself and Virginia . . . they will be here soon."

Emily nodded, stared emptily into his eyes, wondered if they'd ever hold each other again. She then turned, walked briskly to Virginia, positioned her in the back of the nook, covered her with a deerskin, and placed a few rocks around her for protection. She leaned down, kissed her forehead, stared solemnly at her for a moment. Sleep, my little one; and when you wake, 'twill be over. She stood, walked to her boulder, knelt on her rolled-up deerskin; wrapped her clammy hands around the pistol, cocked it; stole a quick glance at Virginia then fixed her eyes intently on the west gap. Stop shaking, Emily Colman. Be strong. Keep your wits . . . do not look away, do not move . . . so scared, stomach afloat . . . it all ends here. Mother . . . Father . . . George . . . help me, give me strength . . . Wakan Tanka, be with us.

A half hour passed. The chatter of small animals and birds enlivened the forest with music; Emily strained to hear any dissonant sound. Once, she thought she heard cracking brush, voices, suspiciously loud, frenzied squirrel chatter, but saw nothing. Suddenly, like the phantom breeze that heralds an approaching storm, an eerie silence descended over the forest. They're here . . . leaves . . . dry leaves . . . a twig . . . yes, they're here . . . too quiet . . . like the massacre. God, I'm afraid. Stop shaking, Em. She tightened her shaky grip on the pistol, stared nervously at the gap. Do not miss, Em . . . you'll have but one shot. She reached behind her back, pulled her knife from its sheath, laid it on the ground beside her.

Virginia stirred, sputtered, began to crank, quickly erupted into a rage of angry screaming.

Emily clenched her teeth. Watch the gap, Em! Do not look away. Virginia, stop!

Virginia screamed louder.

Emily bit her lower lip, dug her fingernails into the pistol grip. The gap, Em, watch the gap . . . feel them . . . they're here . . . do not look away . . . heart ready to explode. She lifted the pistol, rested the barrel on top of the boulder.

The crying escalated to a wild tantrum.

Emily glanced quickly at the nook then back at the gap. Dear God, make her stop. Something's wrong, must go to her. No, Em, hold fast, hold fast! They're here, so close.

Virginia gagged, began to cough then choke.

Fie! Emily turned, dashed for the nook, knew she'd blundered. Something behind me, can't look; dear God, Powhatans in east gap, Isna and Soft-Nose shooting, two Powhatans down, Soft-Nose down, arrow in back, Isna nocking arrow. She spun about on the run, tripped, staggered backward as she saw the Panther enter the west gap, his bow drawn at Isna. "Isna!"

As Isna spun left toward Emily, the Panther's arrow sliced through his left bicep and pectoral muscle, slid off his sternum, then stopped, pinning his arm to his side. He immediately fell to his right, hit his head firmly against the boulder; he slid to the ground, rolled groggily left, fumbled for his tamahaac as the Panther raced toward him.

"Hiyaa!" The Panther swung his war club at Isna's head, but Isna rolled right an instant before impact; the club struck rock. The Panther quickly swung again before Isna could move; but the ball from Emily's pistol blasted through his brain, slammed his shattered skull into the blood-spattered rock above Isna. His body crumpled onto Isna's chest.

Emily trembled, felt faint, ready to vomit; she stared with a horrified look at the two bloody, motionless men on the ground before her, failed to see the fourth Powhatan warrior enter the west gap, aim his arrow at her back. As he released, True-Dog's arrow tore through his neck, jerked his aim to the left, where the arrow glanced off Emily's boulder and into Virginia's nook.

"Hiyaaa!" True-Dog victoriously pumped his bow in the air as he rushed to help Soft-Nose. Emily's pistol dropped to the ground. "Isna!" She leaned over the Panther, grabbed his left arm with both hands, frantically pulled him onto his back beside Isna. Isna lay still, eyes closed, his face and chest covered with blood and brains, his left arm still pinned to his side. She dropped to her knees, cradled his head, leaned over him, sobbed hysterically, "Isna, 'tis my fault, all my fault! Wake up! Please, I'm sorry! 'Tis all my fault!"

***

Soft-Nose slept on his back in a clump of tall grass, a wide strip of cloth wrapped around his chest, a smile on his face, as if enjoying a pleasing dream. True-Dog sat nearby inspecting objects he pulled from his rucksack. Ten feet away, Emily knelt beside a rushing stream, wrung water from a large rag she had torn from the only cloth dress she had brought from Chesapeake—her too-tall dress. Isna sat nearby, propped against a tree, his raw arm wound glistening in the sunlight from the moisture of Emily's cleansing and its gentle bleeding. But the wound looked free of infection, as did the five-inch, lateral arrow cut through the fleshy part of his chest. Virginia lay in the tall grass a few feet from Isna, giggled as she occupied herself with the doll Shines gave her.

As she again rinsed and wrung out the cloth, Emily's mind stuck on the images that had relentlessly haunted her the previous night. Though far beyond mental and physical exhaustion, she'd been unable to sleep, had stared for long periods at the brilliant moon and thin tapestry of stars sprinkled like grains of salt around it. Her mind had repeatedly wandered its way through the day's abhorrent images, lingered on each, as if a slow-turning page in a picture book. Most unsettling had been the image of the Panther's disfigured face, his eyeballs blown from their sockets. A piteous sight, she thought . . . nothing like the frenzied, terrifying face that glared at me at Roanoke. She trembled at the recollection, felt a chill shoot down her back. *I wonder if he had a wife and children. I took his life from him . . . perchance from a wife and children, as well . . . the life of someone doing what he thought was right for his people. Strange, indeed, that we human beings fight, each believing we are in the right. Yet . . . yet in the end, I'd no choice but to save Isna . . . and I cannot forget that the Panther led the attack that annihilated my people . . . and the Chesapeakes.* She sighed, thought of Elyoner, Ananias, Emme, Waters, Baylye, Shines—all dead, brutally slaughtered, mutilated without pity . . . *all* of them gone . . . so final, so complete. *And now I've no one to long for or feel saddened about leaving. 'Tis over . . . a new life begins . . . for I am now a* Lakota *woman.* She raised her head proudly. *Wife of a great warrior who will give me many children.* She thought of her mother, her locket, wondered if the Panther had carried it with him, then sighed, looked forlornly at the ground. *I shall never see it again . . . my sole remembrance of my family . . . England . . . my heritage.* She shook her head, smiled. *'Tis gone, Em. You know that . . . so move on.*

She finished wringing out the cloth, stood, walked to Isna, knelt beside him. "The swelling is down, and this slow bleeding should stop soon." She smiled, kissed his cheek. "Emily's husband is a quick healer." She folded the damp cloth, gently swabbed the outside of his bicep then the inside. "But this journey will be hard on Isna and Soft-Nose, and we will miss Striped-Face's strong arms on his paddle." She looked suddenly thoughtful. "Isna, we collected Striped-Face's jewelry and medicine bundle for his family, but we did not give him a proper Lakota burial. Why not?"

"It is good to leave our dead unburied in enemy territory . . . the bones of a brave enemy in their midst will forever remind them that four Lakota warriors . . . and a Lakota woman . . . killed *their greatest* warrior and his three best men. They will always fear us."

She nodded. "Emily understands."

"And my little white fawn will also understand that, though we will miss Striped-Face when we reach our canoes, we need not travel fast.

We can take five moons, if need be." He grimaced as the cloth touched his chest.

"Emily will be more gentle."

He smiled. "Emily is *very* gentle . . . but sometimes a wound does not listen to the mind when it tells the wound not to hurt."

She smiled for a moment then suddenly bloomed with excitement. "Oh! Emily forgot! She has not yet told Isna of the dream she had the night at the rocks."

He looked at her expectantly then smiled his wry smile, interlocked his thumbs, flitted his fingers like a butterfly, as he'd done in the forest at Chesapeake. "What did Emily dream?"

She giggled. " 'Twas not that sort of dream, and Emily does not yet understand its meaning." She inhaled deeply, as if preparing to tell a long story. "Emily again saw Isna's vision, but . . . but this time, something new happened to the last little white fawn."

Isna watched her intently.

"When the two black stones and Isna's vision pipe reappeared around her neck, she turned into a beautiful—"

True-Dog tossed a leather pouch on the ground beside Isna, another between Emily and Virginia, which landed close to Virginia. "That one is Emily's."

She nodded, concentrated on tearing two more strips of cloth from her dress, wondered fleetingly what was in the pouch. She then smeared a mixture of mud and moss over Isna's wounds, began to wrap a bandage around the top of his arm. "Isna and Soft-Nose will bleed when they paddle canoes."

"We are Lakota. We will do what we must. And when we reach the first river, we will float downstream for many days, which will be a time for healing. We will be ready when we reach the Mother-of-All-Rivers and need all our strength to paddle north against the current."

Emily listened, nodded as she tied the ends of the bandage, then sat back on her heels to inspect her work.

Virginia suddenly squealed with delight, flailed her arms excitedly.

Emily looked at her. "What are you doing, you little rascal?"

Virginia held the pouch True-Dog had tossed between her and Emily; she had methodically scattered its contents in the tall grass around her.

Isna said, "I see our new daughter does not like her gifts and gives them to the grass people."

Emily smiled, glanced at the pouch. "What is it?"

"It is a warrior bundle. Warriors put their jewelry in them before a fight, as I did with my eagle-bone necklace. True-Dog found them when he followed the Powhatans to the west gap. Yours belonged to the Panther. See his mark there?" He pointed at a red panther face on the side of the pouch.

Emily's mind spun wildly. My locket! She frantically snatched the bundle from Virginia, shook it upside down. Empty. She dropped forward onto her hands and knees, crawled slowly around Virginia, brushing leaves aside, searching under every blade of grass. It has to be here!

"What do you seek?"

"My locket! He had my mother's locket. *Must* have put it in the bundle before the fight. It *has* to be here. Oh, Isna, where is it?" She lowered her face to her hands, moaned softly.

Isna rolled onto his knees beside her, caressed her hair, then gently lifted her chin. "Perhaps the Panther did not bring Emily's locket with him." He touched her cheeks, gently lifted her head until she sat back on her heels, rubbed her teary eyes. When she looked at him, he moved his left hand from behind his back. It held a pink flower—the first flower of spring. He extended it slowly toward her face, gently dabbed her tears, kissed it, then held it to her lips.

Emily stared at him teary-eyed, took the flower, kissed it, then touched it to her cheek. She slowly nodded, smiled a contented smile, leaned forward as he again held her cheeks, pulled her into a soft, lingering kiss.

***

True-Dog jogged to his position as advance guard. He was several yards into the forest when Emily, her flower tucked in her hair, walked to the stream, knelt, and scooped a handful of water.

As she stood and turned toward Isna, something in the grass caught her attention. "Isna!" She dropped to her knees.

All three warriors gripped their weapons, faced her.

"Isna, Isna, I found it!" She stood, dangled her precious black locket from her hand. When she opened the trap door, she found the lock of her mother's hair inside, stared at it as tears filled her eyes and a procession of images of her father and mother drifted slowly through her mind like leaves floating on a lazy stream. She shut the locket door, held it to her cheek, closed her eyes. Mother, I love you . . . I *shall* see you again. Tears of joy streamed down Emily's cheeks as she smiled at Isna, stared into his eyes; she slowly removed her first flower of spring from her hair, held it and her locket to her heart.

He softly touched her cheeks, gazed into her glistening eyes, leaned forward, gently kissed her lips.

And while Allie's heart and soul willed them to stay, the enveloping mists of time slowly encircled them until they were gone.

CHAPTER 17

A lone on the front porch of the ranch house, Allie sipped coffee as she waited for her mother to join her. She watched the first timid flicker of the morning sun grow relentlessly from the timbered mountaintops in front of her across and above the blue-black tent of sky before her. She'd stared at the same view her entire life—all times of day and night, all seasons of the year—had never failed to feel her pulse quicken at the raw, naked beauty of it, thank God for the privilege of being there to witness it. She'd always reveled in the solitude of the mountains, imagined herself an Indian or a mountain man, subsumed the residual feelings of awe and exhilaration they'd left behind in the forests and meadows, their harmony with everything around them, their often arcane sense that God himself surrounded them. *Wakan Tanka* . . . always here . . . in every *thing* . . . in every *creature*. She'd always felt his presence, had never had a shadow of doubt he was there, marveled that any honest being could experience the grandeur, the immensity, the feeling of utter insignificance extant in the Rocky Mountains, without believing some higher power had set it all in motion, indeed, resided there unseen . . . or perhaps quite visibly if one simply looked.

Allie hadn't dreamed that night—at least nothing she remembered. So she awakened with a stubborn disappointment, a nagging sadness, like the aftermath of a deeply emotional book or movie, hanging in her mind. She repeatedly forced herself back to Emily, relived all that had happened to her from the beginning through the end of the dreams—the innocence, joy, excitement; fear, anxiety, trauma; despair, desperation, depression; courage, love, sacrifice; resilience, perseverance. Funny, she thought, now that it may be all over, I have an overwhelming feeling of disappointment, perhaps even withdrawal; but on the other hand, I feel happy, at peace with where Emily is and where I'm headed. But I wonder if the next dream will be the *bad one*, the debilitating, crushing one that destroys my life. A frigid chill shook her body as she thought about her dangerous encounter with the drug she'd abused under the rationalized justification of more frequent and lengthy dream sessions—a rationalization that could have taken her life. Addiction is addiction, no matter what form it takes, and I will *not* do *that* again. But how will I deal with dream addiction, and what will I do when someone I've come to love dies an untimely, perhaps horrible death? She sighed, pondered her life of dreams that lay ahead, decided that knowledge would be her only viable salvation.

She smiled, felt a sudden surge of excitement about dreaming again, then suddenly visualized Emily's final dream—of the last little white fawn—the dream that answered all the questions, put everything before it in perspective. Damn it! Can't believe I keep forgetting to tell Mom about it . . . most important part.

When her mother arrived, Allie relayed the events of her last dream, grew reflective when she described the attack on the villages and Emily and Isna's consummation of their marriage, then bubbled with excitement when she described the fight and Emily finding her locket.

Nancy smiled softly as she shook her head. "What an incredible story. You know, I think what they say about real life being more exciting than fiction is true. So, do you think you'll—"

"Oh! Excuse me, Mom, forgot something." She shook her head. "Can't believe I forgot to tell you this; it's the most important part of the entire experience. The last night, Emily and I dreamed Isna's spirit vision, and—" She pondered something for a moment. "I don't think I ever told you about the spirit vision, did I?"

Nancy shook her head.

She quickly described the vision. "And it always ended with the last little white fawn, with the vision pipe and two black stones around her neck, but Emily and Isna never understood what that meant." She looked at Nancy with a haunting smile and sparkling eyes that gave her a striking, almost-hypnotic aura. "But that last night, the little white fawn turned into—"

The phone rang. Nancy stepped briskly toward the door. "Be back in a minute, Hon. Might be the guys."

Ten minutes later, Nancy returned. "Sorry. Dad needed some info I had to look up. He should be back in a couple hours."

Allie nodded.

"So, Allie Girl, you seem in much better spirits than the last time I saw you. No limit to what a happy ending can do, eh?"

"No kidding. And I've been thinking real hard about that. What if it *hadn't* turned out the way it did? Could've been really ugly. I mean, I might've been a total wreck, and . . . and, you know, that could happen the next time I dream . . . if it turns out bad." She looked away for an instant then back at her mother. "Somehow, I've got to find out what's going on with the dreams—why they happen, how they happen. Just knowing the *why* of it could save my life someday. So guess what?"

"What?"

"Well, it so happens the university just hired a world-class dream scientist to be its Endowed Chair of Dream Science, with the express charter of putting the university on the world map of dream theory. His name is Dr. Steven Dressler, and he has beyond-impressive credentials: a PhD in psychology, PhD in combined genetics and molecular biology as they relate to genomics, not to mention lots of additional study and practical experience in neuroscience—in other words, all the right tools to be a game changer in dream science. And, Mom, I'm going to meet him, tell him about my dreams, and talk him into putting me on his research team as an assistant *and* test subject. Hopefully, I'll also be able to get him to be my PhD advisor."

"That's my girl. Always have a plan, always shoot for the stars. So how are you going to meet him?"

Allie smiled as she opened the folder on her lap, removed a sheet of paper, and handed it to her mother. "Here's how. He's giving an initial lecture at the *U* next week, and I'm going to be there and introduce myself when it's over. Now, skip the background stuff at the top and read the synopsis of his theory. I've already memorized it."

Nancy eyed Allie suspiciously, then began to read.

In the course of their lifetimes, all people accumulate and store information, feelings, and experiences in their memories. Some past and present dream theorists believe all of this information may be retained in an individual's personal memory, as well as in a collective memory that exists somewhere as yet undetermined. The personal memory is like an internal hard drive of an individual's feelings and experiences, but it also includes those of all of a person's ancestors. *The collective memory is also like a hard drive of information, but it contains the memories and experiences of all humanity from the beginning of time to now. It is believed that all of humanity's memories and experiences are placed on the collective memory hard drive by a process called formative causation and its instrument, morphic resonance. As an analogy, think of the collective memory as being like "the cloud"; and each person's personal memory, or hard drive, backs itself up (continuously and automatically) to that collective memory, enabling all of humanity's experiences and memories to reside there.*

Human beings access their personal memories to varying degrees; however, most don't know, beyond their own personal experiences, what their personal memories contain, much less how to retrieve specific information. The collective memory is the same, but more so, because of its huge size. Thus, a given individual needs some way—call it the gift of a special username and password—to access specific information in both the personal and collective memories. People who possess this gift, though they have existed throughout history, are so incredibly rare as to be virtually unheard of.

When we sleep, our minds usually cannot find a coherent recent experience to place in the night's dreams. So a phenomenon called activation synthesis energizes our minds to fashion dream content from random tidbits of information floating around in the brain, which is why dreams are usually bizarre and disjointed. However, for the very rare person who possesses the username-password gift for accessing both the personal and collective memories, activation synthesis plays little or no role. Once triggered by some special event, their gift repeatedly takes them—in a very real, movie-like, and serial manner—directly to a true piece of history lived by an ancestor, or themselves. This is thought to occur through the integration of the person's ancestral information (personal memory) with similar information for all the people the ancestor came in contact with (collective memory) in the course of a particular historical saga. Finally, theorists believe that this rare gift passes from generation to generation within the selected family's genes and DNA; but one or more generation-skipping, and/or dormancy mutations may limit the gift to females of the family and to only one manifestation every century or so.

"Oh my God! I'm tingling all over."

Allie's head nodded like a metronome. "Mom, he's talking about *me* . . . and *Ian* . . . and . . . and *Emily* . . . and Tryggvi's English girl. I couldn't believe it when I read it."

Nancy stepped over to Allie's chair, bent down, kissed her forehead. "Allie, I'm so happy for you. Thank God for *all* favors, but *especially* for this one. I can't begin to tell you how worried I've been about you since all this started. And you're right, knowing the why and how of it will make it much easier to handle." She smiled. "I feel better already. And I have no doubt that my Allie Girl will indeed meet the doctor and convince him she's the breakthrough test subject he's been looking for. After they stared silently at each other for a moment, Nancy touched Allie's shoulder, smiled. "So wait here a minute while I run inside and get something." She turned and headed for the door.

Two minutes later, Nancy returned with a small cardboard box in her arms, sat beside Allie, and plopped the box on the small table between them.

Allie glanced at the box, then looked at her mother. "Is that Ian's box?"

"Yup. Can't wait to see what's in it."

"Me neither. But first, let me tell you what I was going to say when you got that phone call. Remember when—"

"Oh yeah! Forgot about that . . . but how 'bout we go through the box first. I'm burning to know what's in it."

Allie nodded. "Okay, Mom, but don't let me forget to tell you about Emily's last dream."

"Got it." Nancy opened the lid of the box, extracted the letter that sat on top, examined it. "Ian wrote this, and it explains her name and where she came from." She handed the letter to Allie. "Not the neatest penmanship in the world."

"Oooh. Really old . . . hard to read."

"Yeah, it is. I don't know when she wrote it, but it had to be a long, long time ago . . . like probably when *my* mom was a little girl. Pretty fragile . . . in fact, now that we know we have it, we oughta make digital copies of it and preserve the original somehow."

"Good idea." Allie held the letter in front of her, traced her index finger from word to word. "Oh my God. Ian was Lakota? *Ee-hahn-blay Ween-yahn . . . Dream Woman . . . Ee-hahn . . . Ian.*" She looked at her mother. "So *that's* where it came from . . . *Dream Woman!*"

"Sure fits, doesn't it?"

A minute later, Allie looked up at her mother. "Mom, do you know what this tells us about the dreams . . . the Lakota heritage, the tie to Isna and Emily?"

"I do, Hon, and thinking about it makes me tingle all over . . . oh! My mom also stuck a note in here." She retrieved a yellowed piece of stationery, scanned it. "She says here that Ian claimed we have European blood from a thousand years ago . . . and again from four hundred years ago."

Allie's eyes were tight beads of concentration as she stared into empty space, her mind swirling, grasping. She spoke quietly to herself, as if oblivious to her mother. "A thousand years ago . . . Tryggvi, his dreaming English girl, Bjarni, Hefnir . . . Vikings . . . like Emily and I dreamed . . . here in North America . . . checked it out . . . a place called L'Anse aux Meadows, the entrance to the St. Lawrence River, Niagara Falls, Great Lakes, Ohio River Valley, the Lakota. Holy shit. *And* four hundred years ago, so . . . so she must have—" She looked at her mother. "Mom, she *must* have dreamed about Emily"—she shook her head— "and known she was our ancestor . . . and Tryggvi, too . . . and Isna. This is wild . . . and . . . and Ian being Lakota ties it all together." Her eyes bloomed with excitement; she again detached her mind, stared vacantly through her mother, recalled the internet passage she'd read about the Lakota. "Ohio Valley a thousand years ago . . . then the headwaters of the Mississippi . . . and 1770 to 1780 . . . Lakota crossed the Missouri onto the plains . . . Dakota, Nebraska, Montana. My God . . . a direct line from Emily and Isna . . . and even the Vikings. Boggles my mind!"

The two stared silently at one another until Nancy suddenly blinked, twitched as if jabbed by a pin. "Oh! There's more! Look at this." She reached into the box, removed a reddish stone Indian pipe that had a four-inch-long stem slightly over an inch in diameter, with a hole in one end for a wooden smoke tube through which the smoke would have been drawn. A three-inch-tall bowl rose from the other end of the stem and widened toward the top, where the tobacco was once stuffed in and lit. Decorative designs had been engraved into both sides of the stem; but the long, hollow, wooden smoke tube had long since been destroyed. "Obviously, it was Ian's, but the *what-and-where* of it I've no clue of . . . pretty cool, huh?"

Allie didn't reply. Her eyes looked ready to explode, her mind swirled to another dimension—to Isna telling Emily of his vision quest: how his pipe had been offered to each of the four directions, Mother Earth, and the sky, then filled with a pinch of kinnikinnick for each, sealed with animal fat, and after the vision quest, taken to the shaman to be smoked. She reverently took the pipe as if it were a fragile, sacred relic, held it six inches from her eyes, stared at it, lips agape, chest heaving. After thirty seconds, she spoke slowly, softly, her eyes still fixed on the pipe. "*I* know the *what-and-where* of it, Mom . . . this"—her eyes filled with tears; she shook her head slowly—"*this* is Isna's pipe . . . his *vision* pipe. I saw it in Emily's dreams." Her tears glistened as she smiled, looked into Nancy's eyes. "*Isna's* pipe, Mom . . . from four hundred years ago . . . the symbol of everything in his vision—his connection with Wakan Tanka; Grizzly, his spirit creature; his destiny; his wife-to-be, his descendants; everything . . . on down to now." She stared silently, thoughtfully at it, rubbed her fingers along the engraving in the sides, closed her eyes, held it to her cheek. Finally, she sighed, opened her eyes, rubbed them, looked at her mother. "Mom, do we have any pictures of Ian?"

Nancy smiled, reached into the box, pulled out a wrinkled, faded, black-and-white photograph, handed it to Allie. "How's this?"

Allie slowly took the picture, leaned close to it to distinguish the details. Her eyes suddenly blossomed with recognition, then tearful awe. "Mom, Mom! This . . . this is the old woman from Isna's vision . . . and Emily's dream. I saw her. It's *her*, Mom . . . *Ian*. Right out of the vision . . . the old woman with the pipe . . . *this* pipe here in *my* hand, in *her* hand"—she shook the pipe, pointed at the picture—"and these two black stones around her neck . . . hard to see them, but they were in the vision and dreams, just as in this picture." She again shook her head. "Mom, there ain't no doubt about it. The dreams are for real, and Ian knew it for sure . . . and now I know it for sure, and I'll tell you why."

"Okay, but what's this?" She held out a closed hand to Allie, opened it a few inches from her eyes.

"Ahh!" Allie jerked backward as if afraid then gawked at the black locket in the palm of Nancy's hand.

"Allie, what's wrong?"

Allie slowly extended her trembling hand, took the locket. "Mom . . . this . . . this is Emily's locket." She shuddered. "My God, my mind's exploding." She slowly took the locket, stared silently at it for a long moment, then whispered to herself, "I'm holding something she held . . . four hundred years ago . . . like Isna and the pipe." Her voice cracked. "Oh, Mom! Mom!" Her eyes again filled with happy tears. "Remember when she found it at the end of the last dream? It was her most precious keepsake. Her mother gave it to her father when he and Emily left England. Oh, Mom. I can't believe it! Here . . . in my hand. So, watch this."

Her mother leaned closer.

"It has a secret door, and there's a lock of Emily's mother's hair inside. Watch!" She squeezed the sides to make the stem pop out. Nothing happened. She tried again. Still nothing. She glanced anxiously at her mother then used both thumbs to squeeze three more times with increasing force. On the third squeeze, the stem reluctantly extended. Allie quickly twisted it a full counterclockwise turn, half a clockwise turn, then pushed in to open the trap door, but again nothing happened. "Damn it!" She tried twice more without success. "Come on!"

"Take it easy, Hon. Don't break it!"

She tapped the stem gently on the tabletop—once, twice, three times. On the fourth try, the lid popped open. Allie stared dumbstruck at the contents. "Oh, no!" She removed a tuft of dark hair. "It's the wrong hair. It should be brown." She examined the locket. "But look here, on the back." She pointed at two faded letters. "See . . . the second one's a *C* . . . for Colman. But I can't read the first one—too faded. But look, you can still see part of the five and seven from *1587*, but that's badly worn, too. Got to be her locket. But why's the hair wrong?"

Nancy reached into the box, retrieved another item. "Is this it?" She held out a second locket, identical to the first.

Allie's heart boomed as she took the second locket. It had no engraving, except for a partial *C* in the same place as the *C* on the first locket.

Nancy said, "This one's *much* more worn . . . touched a lot more."

Allie nodded as she fumbled with the stubborn trap door. "Oh my God. Stop shaking, hands!" She squeezed the sides with maximum force until the stem grudgingly extended. She then applied the proper twists, pushed in on the stem to open the trap door. When the lid failed to open, she tapped the stem on the tabletop as before. On the second try, it popped open. Allie stared blankly then gradually smiled at the lock of brown hair inside. "*This* is Emily's locket . . . her mother's hair. Oh my God. I'm holding it in my own hands . . . something *she* held . . . then the Panther . . . then Emily again . . . and God knows who else." She visualized Emily alone by the fire at Roanoke, reading her mother's letter, fondling her locket in her other hand, speaking to her as if she were suddenly beside her from across the sea. "But here it is . . . Emily's precious locket . . . in my hand . . . shaking like there's no tomorrow."

Nancy picked up the first locket, stared at it for a moment, looked at Allie. "So whose is this?"

Allie smiled. "This must be the locket Emily's father gave to her mother, also on the day he and Emily left England. Emily told George they exchanged identical lockets . . . and his hair was dark . . . but . . . but how"—she stared at her mother—"maybe her mother, or brother, or both, eventually made it to the New World . . . but . . . but how did Ian come to have it?"

"I think *I* can answer *that* question. Smidgeons of this stuff are starting to come back to me—from a *long* way back—and I kinda . . . *vaguely* . . . remember my mom saying Ian had always had one locket, but Great-Grandpa gave her another one the day they were married; and she about fainted because *she* knew where it came from . . . even though he *didn't* . . . but he *did* know it had been in his family, like forever."

Neither spoke as Allie reverently turned the lockets over and over in her hands, caressed them, thought of Emily, her father, their adventures, their disasters. Suddenly, she grabbed the old picture of Ian, held it close to her eyes, shifted her gaze back and forth between it and the lockets. "Mom! I've got it! Look here, see those black stones around Ian's neck?"

"Yeah."

"Well, black stones are what Emily and Isna . . . and I . . . *thought* they were when we saw them in Isna's vision and Emily's dreams. But guess what?"

"What?"

She smiled. "They just *look* like black stones because they're so small in the picture. They're actually these two black lockets." She held up the lockets. "Look here . . . see the little holes drilled in the edges for a necklace?"

"Oh my God!" Nancy shook her head. "You're right."

Allie held the lockets in the palm of her hand, pondered them with teary eyes, then picked up Isna's pipe and the picture of Ian. "It's all true, Mom . . . all of it . . . everything . . . every last bit of it . . . everything I dreamed . . . everything I saw and felt . . . real history . . . *our* history, and—"

Her mother touched her arm. "One last thing from the box, Hon." She looked into Allie's eyes, handed her another picture, which she immediately snatched, stared at.

"There's Ian with the lockets and pipe . . . but who's the little girl whose head she has her hand on?"

Nancy smiled. "That would be your own mother, Ms. O'Shay . . . me!"

Allie's mind spun; she shook with chills. "Mom . . . Isna's vision . . . the dreams . . . the old woman—Ian—with the stones and pipe. Remember? She had her hand on the head of a little white fawn. And then Ian and the stones and pipe vanished . . . and . . . and then the fawn grew into a . . . a"—her voice quavered; she choked on tears—"a *doe* and had a little white fawn of her own, the *last* little white fawn." Allie laid the lockets and pictures aside, held her mother's hand, stared tearily into her eyes. "Mom, *you're* the doe . . . and . . . and I'm *your* little white fawn—the *last* little white fawn in Isna's vision. And, Mom, that's exactly what Emily and I dreamed in her last dream—the one I tried to tell you about earlier . . . and again, a few minutes ago." She rubbed her teary eyes, blubbered through her sobs, "At the end of the dream, the last little white fawn changed form, and . . . and, Mom . . . she changed into *me*. Emily actually dreamed of *me*! And as soon as I string these lockets and the pipe onto a necklace, they'll be hanging around my neck . . . exactly as in the last scene of Isna's vision, when the pipe and lockets suddenly appear around the last little white fawn's neck . . . and finally, in Emily's last dream, around *my* neck . . . and the vision and dreams will then be fulfilled." Mother and daughter stared at one another, their eyes filled with tears as they fell into each other's arms.

A half hour later, Allie and Nancy sat together, held hands, stared silently into each other's eyes, glanced at the lockets, the pipe, the pictures, pondered all that had happened since the dreams began. Allie said, "Mom, I wonder how the lockets and pipe got to Ian and Great-Great-Grandpa . . . what happened to them over four hundred years of American history . . . where they've been . . . who's held them, cherished them. Mom . . . I've got to know."

Nancy studied her daughter with deep, knowing eyes. "Allie, Hon, I think you're going to find out."

* * *

Alone in her room, Allie looked down at the lockets and vision pipe dangling from her neck, imagined centuries of wild adventures that had brought them to her great-great-grandparents. Suddenly, an impulse commanded her to turn off the light. She did so, walked to the window, stared out at a black sky filled with so many stars the Milky Way looked like a solid sheet of white from horizon to horizon.

In the ten minutes Allie stared blindly at the stars, thinking of Emily and seeing her together with Isna, she missed four shooting stars, but noticed the first glow of the three-quarter moon as it peeked over the eastern horizon. She stood at the window for another half hour, watched the moon and its bright companion star rise slowly into the sky. As she held Emily's locket to her cheek, she closed her eyes, begged to see Emily again. "Emily, wherever you are, I love you . . . will always love you."

And then, as if in a dream, a misty scene appeared in her mind. Emily, in her doeskin dress, stepped slowly toward her from the mist, stopped, stared into her eyes with a warm, loving smile, extended her arm toward her as if handing her something, then slowly faded back into the mist.

Allie stood motionless, eyes closed. No, Em! Don't go! Pleeease don't go. Come back to me . . . please come back . . . let me see you again; I miss you so. Eyes still closed, she held both hands over the lockets and pipe at her heart, savored the vision of Emily; she then sadly opened her eyes, turned on the lamp, stepped toward the bed. But she immediately stopped, stared straight ahead through a gush of bittersweet tears when she saw why Emily had come. On her pillow, like a precious, pink gem glistening on a blanket of snow, lay Emily's first flower of spring.

EPILOGUE

The basic historical events presented in this story, up to the time of John White's departure, as well as what he found upon his return in 1590, are true, including Manteo's visits to England, the circumstances and details of the elder George Howe's death, the accidental attack on friendly Croatans, the Spanish visit to Roanoke, and the Powhatan prophecy of doom. It is also true that the Powhatans annihilated the Chesapeakes out of fear of the prophecy, though the exact date is unknown. All English character names were taken from the actual Roanoke manifest; but all connections between those names and the events of this story, other than as stated above, are fictional.

Dangerous Dreams incorporates elements of six prevalent theories regarding the Lost Colony: that some escaped to Croatan Island and assimilated with the Croatan Indians; that the entire colony fled to the Chesapeake Bay area, only to be annihilated by the Powhatans; that the colonists likely considered moving inland from Roanoke Island and could have done so; that the colony was destroyed by a hurricane; that Spanish forces found and destroyed the colony; and that there was a conspiracy to undermine the colony and foster its failure.

The Lakota, or Sioux, in fact lived in the Ohio Valley until approximately the arrival of Columbus in the New World in 1492, at which time they migrated northwest to the area near present day Mille Lac, Minnesota, near the western shore of Lake Superior and the headwaters of the Mississippi River. They remained there until they moved west to the Missouri River in the early 1730s, then finally crossed the Missouri and moved onto the Great Plains after obtaining the horse from the Cheyenne tribe in the latter part of the 1700s. It is equally well known that before the white man, tribes from all over North America, including the Great Lakes region, traveled and traded throughout the continent for items they valued but did not have where they lived.

Viking explorers discovered North America and made several attempts to settle there around AD 1000, and possibly earlier. Some hypothesize that because they settled near the mouth of the Saint Lawrence River at L'Anse Aux Meadows, Newfoundland, they could have explored the Great Lakes via portages and the rivers that join the lakes. Viking artifacts, some of arguable authenticity, have been discovered in Minnesota and Wisconsin, adding to the curiosity, if not the credibility, of these hypotheses.

The scientific theories presented in *Dangerous Dreams*—such as activation synthesis, morphic resonance, formative causation, and the individual and collective memories—are legitimate theories with credible advocates and varying degrees of validation. The author believes that the fact that mankind's body of proven knowledge regarding dreams—why and how they happen, where they come from, and what they mean—is so remarkably scant that until disproven, all such theories remain in the mix. Accordingly, *Dangerous Dreams* weaves a logical, creative tapestry of explanatory fact, theory, the author's personal experiences, and imagination into Allie O'Shay's dream characteristics. And while the author makes no assertions as to the validity of any theory, or Allie's gift, when one studies these theories, even at an elemental level, it is impossible not to imagine that someday some of them might be proven—in part or in whole. Detailed dream science/theory information from *Dangerous Dreams*, Version One, absent from Version Two, may be found on the author's website (http://www.mikerhynard.com/) on the *About the Book* page.

* * *

Emily Colman never returned to Virginia, nor did Virginia Dare. But both lived full, happy lives with the Lakota; and over the next four hundred years, Emily and Isna's descendants—the many brown and white fawns—spread across North America. And as for Allie O'Shay, it was not at all obvious how both of the Colmans' lockets came to be in her great-great-grandmother's possession. In fact, it took her a lifetime of dangerous dreams and adventures to discover the truth. And the truth was not at all what she at first supposed.

ABOUT THE AUTHOR

Mike Rhynard is a retired operational fighter pilot, combat veteran, developmental test pilot, and aerospace engineer and consultant. In addition, he's been involved in cattle ranching since age seven and has been an ardent student of American history throughout his life. During his professional careers, Mike authored numerous technical publications. And in *Dangerous Dreams*, he integrated that experience with experiences gained from combat, cattle ranching, primitive survival instructing, and his extraordinary dreams; a lifelong love of American history; and a deep admiration for Native American heritage and spirituality. He then enriched and enlivened the blend with a passionate desire to present the past in the exciting, personal, and often terrifying manner in which it surely occurred.

Mike lives on the family ranch in the Rocky Mountains, with his long-suffering, but still loving, wife and a bunch of hopelessly adoring animals.

Follow Mike Rhynard and *Dangerous Dreams* on his website (http://www.mikerhynard.com/), Twitter (http://www.twitter.com/MikeRhynardAuth), and Facebook (http://www.facebook.com/MikeRhynardAuthor); and if you enjoyed *Dangerous Dreams*, please post a review on Amazon, Goodreads, LibraryThing, or any other site you choose. A list of suggested book club questions (http://www.mikerhynard.com/sample-page/), as well as a blog (http://www.mikerhynard.com/contact-mike/), can also be found on the author's website.

BIBLIOGRAPHY

Alchin, Linda. "Elizabethan Era." Accessed January 10, 2014. http://www.elizabethan-era.org.uk.

Bantock, Granville, ed. "Green-Sleeves." In *One Hundred Songs of England*. Public Domain. Boston: Oliver Ditson, 1914.

———. "The Keeper." In *One Hundred Songs of England*. Public Domain. Boston: Oliver Ditson, 1914.

Brown, Joseph Epes. *The Sacred Pipe: Black Elk's Account of the Seven Rites of the Oglala Sioux*. Norman, OK: University of Oklahoma Press, 1953.

Egloff, Keith, and Deborah Woodward. *First People: The Early Indians of Virginia*. Charlottesville, VA: University of Virginia Press, 2006.

rdon, Suzanne L. "The Renaissance Faire Forget-Me-Knot." Accessed nuary 6, 2014. http://www.museangel.net/caille.html.

t, Richard. *Early English and French Voyages: Chiefly from uyt, 1534-1608*. Edited by Henry S. Burrage. New York: Charles r's Sons, 1906. Accessed March 26, 2013. https://books. om/books?id=_yhAAAAAYAAJ&pg=PA240&lpg=PA240 hard+hakluyt+roanoke&source=bl&ots=_668iTnozQ&si MmhNwZsmjeAkbD0ST4As&hl=en&ei=VRZpTdGFM 9CmAw&sa=X&oi=book_result&ct=result&resnum=3 CgQ6AEwAg#v=onepage&q=richard%20h&f=false

lee, Ed. "Pastime with Good Company." In "The Lyrics nry VIII – Primary Sources." Accessed April 6, 2014. hhistory.net/tudor/the-lyrics-of-king-henry-viii/.

The Sioux. Norman, OK: University of Oklahoma

Hill, Ruth Beebe. *Hanta Yo: An American Saga*. Garden City, NY: Doubleday & Company, 1979.

Laframboise, Sandra, and Karen Sherbina. "The Medicine Wheel." Accessed January 25, 2015. http://www.dancingtoeaglespiritsociety.org/medwheel.php.

"Lakota Language." Accessed January 23, 2014 http://members.chello.nl/~f.vandenhurk/language.htm.

Mails, Thomas E. *Peoples of the Plains*. Tulsa, OK: Council Oaks Books, 1997.

Miller, Lee. *Roanoke: Solving the Mystery of the Lost Colony*. New York: Penguin Books, 2002.

Paper, Jordan. *Offering Smoke: The Sacred Pipe and Native American Religion*. Moscow, ID: University of Idaho Press, 1988.

Picard, Liza. *Elizabeth's London: Everyday Life in Elizabethan London*. New York: St. Martin's Griffin, 2003.

Bernstein, Josh. *Roanoke: The Lost Colony DVD*. Directed by Brandan Goeckel and Brian Leckey. A&E Television Networks, 2006.

Rountree, Helen C. *The Powhatan Indians of Virginia: Their Traditional Culture*. Norman, OK: University of Oklahoma Press, 1989.

Storm, Hyemeyohsts. *Seven Arrows*. New York: Harper & Row, 197?

Terry, Michael Bad Hand. *Daily Life in a Plains Indian Village* New York: Clarion Books,1999.

Warner, John F. *Colonial American Home Life*. New York: Watts, 1993.

Windwalker, Barefoot. "Lakota Lexicon." Accessed Febru http://www.barefootsworld.net/lakotalexicon.html.

Wikipedia contributors, "Matchlock," *Wikipedia, The Free* https://en.wikipedia.org/w/index.php?title=Matchloc id=667615324 (accessed March 5, 2013).